THE RED WINTER

THE TAPESTRY · BOOK 5

THE RED WINTER

WRITTEN AND ILLUSTRATED BY

HENRY H. NEFF

HHN Publishing

For James.
Sol Invictus!

Contents

Prologue

The Witchpeaks are the tallest mountains in the world. At
one time they were called the Himalayas, an "abode of snow"
in ancient Sanskrit, but no longer. That name—like so much
else in the world—had changed when Astaroth came to power.
Although the mountains were still wreathed in snow, they were
now named for their chief inhabitants.

Most of the witches lived below the timberline, but their holy
places were nestled nearer to the summits. Some were little more
than primitive shrines, perched on storm-lashed ledges where the
witches prayed to their gods and wove the wild magic of their
kind. But the most sacred spaces were inside the mountains,

carven temples containing treasures that dated back to Neolithic man. These were known as the *ossuaries*, and their treasures were not gold or jewels, but human hair, skin, and bone.

Living men were not permitted in the ossuaries, but one was now ascending the summit of great Ymir, which housed the largest collection of remains. The witch watching him could tell he was not a native Sherpa or one of their own servants. He carried no pack or walking stick—he did not even use a rope or ax to anchor himself when the gales came howling as they always did at sunset. Why Ymir did not shake off this foolish pilgrim, she could not tell, but it would happen soon. And so the old witch sat comfortably by the brazier, chewed her betel, and waited for him to die.

It was late when he reached her. He stood panting at the edge of the firelight, his tangled hair crusted with ice and crowned by the twinkling stars. Spitting her quid into a cup, the witch grinned and revealed a mouthful of filed, red-stained teeth.

"I was rooting for you," she lied. "I have never seen one climb the mountain as you have done. Ymir must favor you. A pity I must turn you away."

The stranger did not reply. *He must not speak our tongue,* thought the witch, and wagged a bony finger. "You cannot enter," she croaked in English. "I am sorry, but you must leave." With a smile, she bowed and made a sign of peace.

"I must enter," rasped the stranger, speaking Nepalese and stamping the snow from his boots. Tiny icicles fell from his gray beard and black cloak to shatter on the ledge's flagstones. He was a tall, rangy man with a weathered face and eyes like iron rivets. His voice was deep and assured. This was no lost soul, no poppy-addled wanderer seeking death or wisdom.

The witch smiled a different sort of smile.

"Men do not enter here," she growled. "Begone or I'll summon ghosts to devour your flesh and scatter your bones on the wind!" With a jangle of bracelets, she shook her arms free of her furs to show this stranger the many runes tattooed upon her brown skin. Even a fool must see that she was no trifle and that ancient spirits owed her their allegiance.

"I have entered here before," the man replied. "And each time I have climbed the mountain to honor your traditions. But that is slow work and now I require haste, Dame Hakku."

The witch's fierce grin evaporated.

"H-how do you know my name?" she sputtered. "Who are you?"

"Bram."

The very word radiated power. Even as he spoke it, the witch froze as though time had stopped. She stared ahead unblinking, her body stiff as a corpse while the man bent to wrap her furs warmly about her. When this was done, he strode away beneath the archway.

Hours passed before he returned, emerging like Virgil's shade from the ossuaries' depths. Night was fading, the stars growing pale as the first hints of dawn shone in the eastern sky. Miles below, the earth was hidden beneath a sea of clouds that stretched away to the pink horizon.

Dame Hakku remained by the smoking braziers, hunched like a gargoyle. She longed to move, to flee, to alert her sisters to this desecration. But she knew that it was folly. The witch had known it as soon as the visitor uttered his name. True sorcerers were as scarce as comets and there had never been any to match this one.

He stooped before her now, clutching a pair of Canopic jars from the deepest vaults. The witch wanted to scream. But she merely stared into those hard eyes, transfixed like a bird by a serpent. The eyes softened.

"I will return them," he promised.

"When?" she croaked, dimly aware that her spell had been broken.

In answer, the sorcerer touched Hakku's forehead. Her memories of the evening trickled away like water squeezed from a sponge.

"When we meet again," he whispered. "For the very first time."

And with that he vanished.

~ 1 ~

A CROWNLESS KING

Some demons were older than Prusias, and some were wiser, but none could match his appreciation for the absurd. His robes were of Tyrian silk; his golden throne was studded with gems and the bones of conquered foes. His Majesty should have felt as regal as a god! And yet, here he sat, slumped and bored while his dressings were changed. The malakhim hovered like fussy mothers, peeling old bandages away, dabbing ointment on the wounds, and applying fresh linen with a surgeon's skill and nurse's care. Shooing the fiends away, Prusias leaned forward to gaze at a nearby mirror. With a frown, the demon studied his face, turning this way and that, like an actor at curtain call. The bandages were unfortunate, but his hair was black, his lips were red, his teeth were as white as snow. He winked at the reflection.

Still a handsome fellow.

From below there was a mild cough. Prusias flicked his attention to his imp. The creature stood on the dais's topmost step, an inquisitive expression on his little red face.

"Eh? What's the problem?"

"Nothing, milord," said the imp. "It's just . . . well, our visitors have hardly begun the May report and there are several matters that will require the King of Blys's input."

"Kings don't give input, Mr. Bonn. They give orders."

"My apologies, milord. I spoke poorly."

Silence was a vastly underutilized tool, reflected Prusias. He studied its effect as his blue, feline eyes drifted past his chamberlain to the Workshop delegation: eight humans with drab gray uniforms and a tendency to drone. *Babbling about how the watch is made when I just want to know the time.* The demon's gaze settled on an engineer with a long, aristocratic face. The man's fear poured forth in intoxicating waves.

"I've met you before," said Prusias, his voice a gruff, drowsy baritone. "Your specialty is genetics, is it not, Dr. Wyle?"

The poor fool nearly curtsied.

"And why has the Workshop sent me a geneticist?" Prusias wondered. "I need weapons of war, not perfect babies."

"Of course, Your Grace. But many of the weapons and machines have biological components and . . ."

Dr. Wyle fell silent as the king's expression darkened. Rising from his throne, Prusias leaned upon a golden cane and bulled down the dais steps. Even in this hobbled human form, the demon was an imposing figure, towering and broad with a plaited beard and twisting thickets of coarse black hair. As Prusias loomed above the scientists, Blys's Grand Inquisitor turned from her work and set down her instruments.

"The dreadnoughts had biological components," Prusias growled. "They had flesh and eyes and tiny imp brains tangled up in all that machinery. And do you know what Rowan did with my beautiful dreadnoughts?"

The man cleared his throat. "They turned them against you, Your Majesty."

"Correct, Dr. Wyle. Just when I was poised to conquer Rowan, your dreadnoughts trampled my army and forced me to make a humiliating retreat. 'Biological components' led to quite a reversal of fortune, Dr. Wyle—a reversal so dramatic that some of my braymas saw fit to rebel."

Taking the man by the shoulders, the King of Blys turned him about so he could get an unobstructed view of the far alcove. When the scientist glimpsed the Grand Inquisitor and the figures splayed behind her, he nearly fainted. Prusias steadied him as though they were bosom friends at the end of a carouse.

"One table's still empty," the demon whispered. "Look hard at that table and explain why the Workshop's still putting 'biological components' in my toys."

Gasping, the man struggled to find his voice. "W-with infinite respect, Your Majesty, Rowan did not exploit a biological weakness, but a spiritual one. Our analysts believe Rowan's sorcerer was able to possess the dreadnought imps because their spirits had been severed to enable the summoning capabilities. When these halves were reunited, the souls they formed were imperfect and vulnerable to a sorcerer of David Menlo's abilities."

"And why didn't you anticipate this?"

"Forgive me, but this is hardly our area of expertise. The Workshop merely engineered the weapon's mechanical and biological components. Your magicians were responsible for the imps. The mechanical and biological components performed perfectly. If Your Majesty wishes, I would be happy to explain their basic functions."

The demon glanced sharply at him. *Is this insect making game of me?* No . . . his fear was too ripe, too present. Still, Prusias drummed his fingers lightly on Dr. Wyle's shoulder.

"It isn't wise to patronize me."

The scientist began to hyperventilate. With a roll of his eyes, Prusias gestured for his imp.

"Mr. Bonn, have chairs and refreshments brought for our guests. They look tired and I fear I've been too hard on our poor geneticist. I should like to hear more from Dr. Wyle."

The malakhim brought all that was required, silent and anonymous in their black robes and obsidian masks. While the engineers briefed him on various projects, Prusias enjoyed Bordeaux from a cup that had once belonged to Napoleon. Glancing at its seal, the demon reminisced on the emperor and how he'd begged for aid at Austerlitz. *What would that crafty little Corsican make of my situation?* But alas, Prusias had him poisoned centuries ago. The man should have honored his debts. Wiping his beard, the King of Blys took up an orthographic drawing and studied it by candlelight.

"What the bloody hell is this supposed to be?"

"Your navy, Your Majesty," answered the recovering Dr. Wyle.

"I already have a navy."

"Of course," said the engineer delicately. "But your fleets were somewhat depleted with the attack on Rowan and you've—I mean *we've*—lost more ships recently off the Isle of Man."

"Don't speak of that. More are building."

"But that will take months," said Dr. Wyle. "Meanwhile

Rowan's forces are about to sail for these shores. Over three hundred ships and a sizable army."

"A 'sizable army,'" chuckled the king. "Let them come! I can spare ten soldiers for every one of theirs. No, they've had their stroke of luck. My own braymas pose a greater threat than little Rowan."

"Unfortunately, Rowan is actively building a coalition," said Dr. Hayden, the Workshop's intelligence liaison. "Their operatives are making inroads with braymas of dubious loyalty. While Rowan's strength is not limited to its armada, its fortunes depend upon it. If this fleet were destroyed or significantly weakened, no one will entertain Rowan's overtures. They would have to abandon this war. Your enemies would remain isolated and scattered."

Prusias glanced again at the drawing, studying the ungainly shapes and contours. "And how is *this* going to destroy Rowan's fleet? It looks puny."

"It's not," said Dr. Wyle. "This model is based on a modified Humboldt strain whose elements we used to great effect in the dreadnought. And, of course, other species are present."

Prusias squinted. "In some ways it resembles your gargoyles."

Dr. Wyle nodded. "It's the eyes. They're unmistakable."

Prusias tossed the drawing with the rest. "Rot its eyes. I'm concerned about its brain. What's controlling it? And don't tell me it's a bloody imp!"

"Never again, Your Majesty," Dr. Wyle assured him. "These utilize an artificial intelligence similar to the one we employ in the pinlegs and the gargoyles. Rowan cannot possess them because there is nothing to possess. But perhaps the king would like to see a demonstration."

Taking the small filmscreen, Prusias watched a clip of the creature overtaking and devouring a whale. He gave an approving grunt. "How many do you have?"

"Three prototypes at present," replied the geneticist. "However, should His Majesty provide the necessary resources, we can initiate mass production. Even accounting for cannibalism, the accelerant tanks can produce dozens before Rowan reaches the Strait."

Prusias chuckled. "What do you think, Mr. Bonn? Shall we loose these horrors upon our Rowan friends?"

The imp cleared his throat. "A second navy sounds most appealing, Your Majesty. It also sounds expensive. My king is already heavily committed. This evening's festivities alone shall cost—"

Prusias cut him short. "Why on earth did I ask you?" he grumbled. "Of course you'd fret over pennies. You never think big, Mr. Bonn—that's why you're still an imp."

Mr. Bonn weathered the gibe with a bow, as he always did. Prusias wondered why he bothered with him. Mr. Bonn was a peculiar imp, hated bloodshed and the arena games. Would rather read a book than attend his lord's parties. For god's sake—he couldn't even take another shape! There were no spiders or bats, mice or moths in Mr. Bonn's bag of tricks. The imp was rather pathetic, and yet, whenever the king was tempted to devour him or release him from service, he found that he could not. *You're too sentimental, Prusias. It will be your undoing.*

Still, it could not be denied that the Workshop's accelerant tanks were horrifically expensive. Nature could be bent and bullied, but not cheated. Speeding up the dreadnoughts' growth had required vast quantities of food and rare minerals, enough to make a sizable dent in the kingdom's stores and coffers. Blys would feel this new investment; she would feel it deep down in her gut. Many slaves would starve, but Prusias consoled himself that new wars brought new slaves. Snatching up the authorization papers, he affixed his seal in plum-colored wax.

"Make my monsters, Dr. Wyle. I expect great things. What else do you have?"

The Workshop had a great deal. Reams of figures and charts and gobbledygook that left the king eyeing the clock. An hour remained until his next meeting—the meeting that *really* mattered. Growing restless, he seized a round of sample ammunition and turned it over in his hands. The twit blathering about frictionless masonry, Dr. Carlisle, ceased his droning.

"Did you have a question, Your Grace?"

"This casing," Prusias observed. "It reminds me of my Hotchkiss gun at San Juan Hill."

The man blinked. "I didn't realize you'd fought in the Spanish-American War."

Prusias grinned. These days, few humans remembered anything before Astaroth acquired the Book of Thoth. Those who did always seemed stunned—even chagrined—by the fact that other beings had experienced much more of "their" history than they had. Prusias found these little epiphanies charming. Humans were like newborns in a nursery: They thought the world began when they opened their eyes and ceased to be when they closed them. He chuckled complacently.

"Oh, I've fought in almost all the wars, Dr. Carlisle. Humans have always called upon me for help with their little squabbles. I've pillaged with Cossacks, marched with Crusaders, and fanned the very flames of Dresden. Fought in more wars than I can recall, but I've fond memories of the Hotchkiss. Always liked its kick."

He rolled the casing across the table to Dr. Carlisle and pushed up from his chair. The engineers stood.

"You've done well," said Prusias, finishing the wine. "You'll be my special guests at the party this evening. I daresay you'll find it interesting. Mr. Bonn will see to your accommodations.

My tailors will see that you have something to wear. Lord knows we can't have you showing up in that."

The demon gestured at their bland gray suits with a disbelieving sigh. Once the technologists had departed, Mr. Bonn saw that his lord intended to do the same and cleared his throat in his habitual "Surely-Your-Majesty-is-forgetting . . ." manner that Prusias found so tiresome.

"My king, braymas from the eastern duchies are begging an audience to discuss Yuga. She is moving once again and devouring their lands and subjects."

"I know what Yuga is doing, Mr. Bonn," replied Prusias. *What else would Yuga be doing?* All she did was drift and feed. By now the demoness was the size of a moderate kingdom, a gargantuan black storm whose tendrils probed for prey like blind, hungry leeches.

"But my lord, she is—"

"Guarding my flank, Mr. Bonn. What enemy would dare approach from the north or east when she is near?"

"But, Your Majesty, if we do nothing, she could drift over the mountains. She could even threaten—"

"Let me worry about Yuga," snapped Prusias, ending the matter. "Look after our Workshop friends and make my apologies to the braymas. They're all invited to the party. They can pester me then. For now, I have another appointment."

The imp anxiously consulted his scroll.

"There's nothing on my schedule."

The king quickly checked his bandages. "I'm well aware of that, Mr. Bonn. Not all of my doings are on your accursed schedule. I'll see you in my chambers at eight. Lay out something modern."

"Surely His Majesty isn't going alone," said the imp anxiously. "We do not yet know the full extent of the conspiracy."

He glanced at the alcove where the Grand Inquisitor was reviving her subjects for their next round of questioning.

Prusias's laugh boomed in the vast hall. "I'm sure assassins would flee before you! But don't worry. I care not if my enemies come by land, sea, or shadow. There's nothing finer than a fight before a party, Mr. Bonn. It's a conversation starter."

Leaning on his cane, Prusias chuckled and made for the exit nearest the alcove. Nodding to the Grand Inquisitor, he paused to glance at Lord Razael, who seemed to be coming to. The earl's garments had been cut away and he blinked in hazy confusion at his exposed midsection. When the traitor's eyes finally fell upon his captors, they shot wide with awareness. Straining frantically, the oni fought and flailed against his magicked bindings. When this proved futile, he tried to speak but only strained the stitches of his Glasgow smile.

"Shhh," said Prusias, patting his arm. "Save your strength, Razael. I'm not hearing confessions today. If you're lucky, you can announce your guilt tomorrow. Or next week. There's really no hurry, so lie back and relax, old friend. I'll have a pudding sent from the feast."

As he departed, Prusias glanced back at the Grand Inquisitor, who was poised and trembling, her arms bent at peculiar angles like some gargantuan praying mantis. She was one of his prized assets—a faceless nightmare bred to terrify those who were not easily frightened. Whenever Prusias wanted Razael to talk, he would talk. Andras, Yva, Kazhyk, Grazznu . . . they would all talk, beg forgiveness, and pray for a quiet end to their existence.

It was a shame about Razael. Prusias had known him for many centuries and he was always good company, if a tad fawning. His greatest gift had not been his wealth or even his talents at verse; it had been knowing his limitations. Razael never objected when other, more powerful demons thrust him aside or fed at his trough. It was how he'd persevered for so long, trailing the lions like a hyena hoping for scraps. *You should have stayed patient, Razael. Injured lions can still bite. So can a Great Red Dragon.*

Razael and the others were not alone in thinking him finished. Sprinkled among the many rumors were some unpleasant facts: Prusias's invasion had been repelled and a child had shattered his crowns and made him flee across the sea. Some naturally took these incidents as a sign of the king's weakness. Others concluded that the girl—and therefore Rowan—was invincible.

But they were mistaken. Prusias was *not* weak, and Rowan, much less the child, was far from invincible. As he descended a series of dim stairwells, Prusias recalled when the girl appeared and the instant he'd recognized what she might be. The revelation had shocked him into vulnerability, but it would not occur again. In any case, Prusias was confident that she would not be joining the assault on his kingdom. She would remain behind—a defender, a protector of those who had not marched off to war. That was her way. That had always been the way of her kind.

Yes, the girl was strong, but not invincible. *Nothing* was invincible. Prusias had abandoned such notions when Astaroth was humbled on Walpurgisnacht. Prusias would not have believed such a thing was possible. He'd always respected strength, and Astaroth had been *strong*. It was Astaroth who toppled mankind's governments, claimed the Book of Thoth, and refashioned the world. And as Astaroth rose to preeminence, Prusias had served him and taken pride in his master's might and wisdom. Astaroth had called himself the "Great God," and Prusias had believed him—believed with a fervor that now shamed him. Since Walpurgisnacht, Astaroth had retreated into disgraced obscurity. But Prusias would not slink off; he would not fade away into irrelevance. He would regroup. He would win. And he would remember Astaroth's invaluable lesson: everything had its weakness—even the "Great God."

Demigods, too!

The room Prusias had chosen for the meeting was small and out of the way, an afterthought in such an immense palace. Servants rarely visited this hallway and they never entered the last room on the left. Curiosity could be fatal in Blys and its servants knew better than to wonder why a particular door would not open.

Prusias did not enter from the hallway, but from a secret passage that ran deep beneath the packed and raucous Arena. Slipping inside, he shut the door and settled into an armchair. The windowless, lead-lined room was as quiet as a tomb. But it was not inhospitable; it boasted a small library and a marble fireplace with a Caravaggio glistening above it. The painting was not one of the artist's better-known works—too scandalous—but Prusias had always enjoyed it. It had been commissioned by a prominent Medici and cherished at his private retreat. Prusias could not recall why the man had summoned him, only that he'd wept when parted from his painting.

A knock interrupted Prusias from these thoughts. Glancing at the door, he gave a lazy wave with his cane and the heavy bolt slid aside. Three hooded figures stood in the hallway. Prusias glowered at the smaller one in the center.

"I wasn't expecting you."

The handler gave a deep bow before peering cautiously within. "And I wasn't expecting a king, much less a king alone. I'd expected one of your lackeys."

"You are one of my lackeys. Get in and shut the door."

As they entered, the king studied the handler. This one was always changing; he was hardly recognizable from the last time Prusias had seen him. His skin was almost indigo and covered with runes from recent skinscrolling. The eyes had an impish glow and cast nervously about, never settling for long. Even his aura was inconstant, its contours wavering and uncertain. *Poor fool doesn't know what he is or isn't.*

"I asked to see them," said Prusias, indicating the two assassins who had entered with the handler. "Why are you here?"

The handler shrugged. "The Atropos understood you wished to negotiate a contract. These two don't enter names into the Grey Book. That is my privilege."

"At my command," Prusias growled.

"At the command of any with the means to hire us, Your Majesty. Wise Prusias may have revived our order, but the Fates play no favorites. To invoke their wrath, one must follow the protocols and make proper tribute. Does His Majesty have proper tribute?"

"I have something far more interesting."

"We're intrigued," said the handler. He sat cross-legged upon the rug, upright and attentive. The assassins remained where they stood, staring impassively at the king. Their expressions were not inquisitive or hostile—not even blank like those in the king's opium dens. They were absent and present, careless and calculating. Unlike the handler, the assassins had no auras. They might have been two black holes hovering before his Caravaggio. That they were unarmed seemed of little comfort; their combined presence triggered profound unease. Prusias had never been so close to both at once. He resolved never to do so again.

"I want them to murder someone," he stated simply.

"Naturally," replied the handler. "But they already have a target. The Fates require his death first."

"That job will soon be finished."

A fiendish light flickered in the handler's pale yellow eyes.

"This is news to me, Your Majesty." The handler turned to his companions. "Have you failed to report something?"

Glancing down, the handsome one shook his head. The assassin's contempt was so palpable that Prusias wondered how the handler dared to turn his back. He clearly enjoyed some sort of hold or protection, but Prusias would not have trusted such measures. There was a dangerous unpredictability to these two; one could never quite guess the full extent of their capabilities. It came with their lineage. *If you cage a tiger, best know how high he leaps.*

Prusias reached for a crystal decanter of whiskey. "Max McDaniels should already be dead," he rumbled. "These two caught him near Bholevna and that Agent you possessed did the same at Rowan. Even when we cut his throat, he escaped to fight another day."

"It is a difficult task," the handler conceded.

Prusias nosed his whiskey. "Without proper tools, it's an *impossible* task. I see that now. I've witnessed it on the battlefield. It's why Astaroth always held an interest in the lad."

"He is formidable, but he's still just a boy."

"He is a *god*," snapped Prusias, his anger flaring. "His line is older than Bram's, his blood purer than Menlo's. His sire conquered the damn Fomorians! Our attempts might have succeeded when he was younger, but not anymore. The Hound has come into his heritage. No mortal weapon will slay him."

The handler's smirk evaporated. "What does the king suggest?"

Easing back, Prusias took a slow sip of his whiskey. "The cleanest solution would be to trick him into violating his geis. Should the Hound break it, he'd be as mortal as a mayfly."

The handler sighed. "The Atropos have searched and scried,

but the Hound's geis is as secret as his truename. We don't believe he even knows what it is."

Prusias had expected this. "Then the job requires better tools. It requires a weapon capable of slaying immortals."

The handler raised an eyebrow. "I know of only one, Your Majesty. And our target carries it."

The king grimaced. "Not that wretched thing." Prusias had evaded the *gae bolga*'s true bite, but he had certainly felt its sting. In the heat of battle, he'd thought the blows trifling—mere scratches compared to others he'd suffered throughout the ages. But the wounds were accursed. Two years later, they still festered and seeped through dressings that were perpetually renewed. Prusias hated the blade as much as he hated the Hound. "There are other options," he said. "Precious few, but they do exist. And my servants have acquired one. . . ."

The smaller assassin cocked his head. It was the first flicker of interest he'd shown in the meeting. *You'd never suspect they were twins*, thought Prusias. *This one doesn't even look human*. Indeed, those dark eyes had a chillingly feral quality. They might have belonged to an animal, one of mankind's gaunt and starving forebears.

The handler glanced eagerly about the room. "Is the weapon here?"

"Of course not. I won't permit it near my person. But when we've finished, a carriage will take you to a temple beyond the city walls. It awaits you there. . . ."

His audience listened closely as Prusias explained the relic's uses and limitations. It was an ancient object, chipped and brittle from eons spent in Nile mud. A hard blow might shatter it; sunlight would unravel its unholy essence. But if kept in the dark, if used as intended . . .

The assassins understood. Whether the handler did was not

important, but at least he had the decency to bow. "Once a name has been entered into the Grey Book, that life is immediately forfeit," he intoned. "The Hound's existence is an affront to the Fates themselves. Atropos thanks you for your gift."

"It's not a gift," Prusias growled. "I have another job for these two."

"Who else has affronted the Fates?"

"*She* has," Prusias snarled. "Rowan's new Ascendant."

"The Grey Book requires a name, Your Majesty."

"Mina. Although I can think of others less pretty."

"Mina will do," said the handler. "Of course, a new contract will require new payment."

"The weapon is your payment."

The handler pursed his lips. "Forgive me, Your Majesty, but as you said yourself, the weapon is just a tool. It cannot hire ships, bribe informants, or make tribute to the Fates. Powerful enemies are an expensive indulgence. If the king doesn't wish to pay our order's fees, there are many others he can consult."

"I already have," Prusias grumbled. With a discontented grunt, he removed a heavy ring and tossed it to the handler. "A down payment. I still have a war to fight."

Hefting the ring, the handler appraised its magnificent stone. The ruby was wider than his thumbnail. "This will suffice. For now."

Prusias rose. "Then our business is concluded. Your carriage will be waiting."

"At the front gate, Your Majesty?"

"Servants' entrance."

It was nearly eight o'clock when Prusias arrived at his private chambers, a suite of rooms whose opulence trumped Versailles.

Mr. Bonn was already present, standing dutifully by an array of outfits he'd laid out upon the massive bed.

"Good evening, Your Majesty. I trust one of these will serve? Personally, I think your guests will find the turquoise dashing." The imp gestured to a bright blue jacket embroidered with gold lace.

Prusias frowned. "They'll think I'm a waiter." Setting down his cane, he stood and considered the alternatives. His frown deepened. "Really, Mr. Bonn, this will not do. I said *modern*. What's modern about all these waistcoats and buckles? Silk breeches? I'm surprised there isn't a powdered wig."

The imp nudged a round box beneath the bed.

Checking his temper, Prusias spoke in a profoundly measured voice. "Tonight's party is important, Mr. Bonn. It is the first official function since my recent setbacks. I cannot—*I will not*—make my entrance looking like someone's great-aunt. Do you understand me?"

"I believe so, Your Majesty."

Snatching up the offending garments, the imp hurried out, returning minutes later with a suit whose midnight hues seemed to shift and deepen as it caught the lamplight. Slipping on the jacket, Prusias looked in the mirror to admire its cut.

"Who made this?" he asked.

"Bartleby."

"Double his pay."

"I can't. Your Majesty had him executed."

"Pity," Prusias muttered, turning to assess the drape. "He had talent. But at least he was good enough to make this before he died. This is just what I had in mind, Mr. Bonn. It seems you're not entirely incompetent."

"I'm relieved to hear it."

Prusias glanced down at his minuscule servant. "Is something troubling you?" he inquired, half amused.

"Of course not," sniffed Mr. Bonn. "Why would I be troubled that I don't enjoy my lord's trust or confidence? That would be a sizable problem and I'm incapable of big thoughts. Apparently that's why I'm still an imp."

Prusias sighed and sorted through a mound of cuff links. "Am I to endure a snit every time I make a joke or exclude you from a meeting?"

"You never used to exclude me."

"I wasn't always a king," retorted Prusias, selecting some diamond studs. "Kings have grave responsibilities, particularly in wartime. To win an empire, one must do great and terrible things. If I exclude you from certain meetings, it's to spare you from matters I know you'd find upsetting. Don't be too insulted, eh? We're moving up in the world."

"*You're* moving up in the world," observed Mr. Bonn stiffly. "I remain an imp."

Prusias chuckled. "Is that what this is really about? Achieving *koukerros*? Why, Mr. Sikes is still an imp and he's served Astaroth far longer than you've served me."

"With respect, Mr. Sikes is neither here nor there. My master has made promises."

The king's smile faded. He turned back to the mirror. "You should be grateful I haven't granted you *koukerros*," he muttered. "You're too tenderhearted to become a *daemon* true. By remaining my imp, you remain under my protection. Don't undervalue that, Mr. Bonn."

"You may be right," conceded the imp. "But I should like to have the choice."

"And you shall, my fine fellow, you shall. But I won't weaken myself by granting *koukerros* during a war. It demands too much energy and I must harbor all I have."

Mr. Bonn nodded. "When the war is finished, then. I have your word."

"Once the war is finished," Prusias assured him. "Now, if you're done pestering me, perhaps I can get ready."

When he had smoothed the final bandage, Prusias walked out on his balcony to gaze upon his capital. He had never seen it look more beautiful, nestled in its ring of mountains, every district alive with lights and music. Smoke from thousands of fires was curling lazily into the night and its aroma was mingling with the jasmine and lilies of his gardens. Not all the fires were decorative or celebratory, however. The weavers' district was ablaze, thousands of residents rioting for better wages or food or whatever. *Look at those beautiful colors,* he thought, as incandescent flames swallowed a warehouse. Prusias inhaled, the burning scents whetting his appetite as his gaze traveled to the city's towers and battlements. Here and there, Workshop gargoyles interrupted their gleaming white perfection. As he watched, one of the creatures suddenly scuttled in a crablike motion to a new perch, where it settled and recalibrated its weapons. Its guns would soon be trained on the city slums, or its gates, or even the bridges that spanned the ancient Tiber far below.

Many carriages were on those bridges. From these heights, Prusias could only make out their lanterns—hundreds of tiny lights creeping along in single file as they entered or left his splendid capital. The possibilities they represented held the demon spellbound. Some carried friends, some carried foes, and one contained two fearsome assassins. Prusias wondered which of the carriages was theirs, or if they had already crossed the river and acquired that grisly artifact. The demon grinned.

Prepare yourself, Hound. They are coming for you.

~ 2 ~

SHROPE HOVEL

Scholars classified hags among the lower orders of semiexotic, semi-intelligent beings. Their abrasive natures, willingness to be displeased, and readiness to eat the offending party set them apart from polite society. Lurking on the fringes of towns and villages, they inhabited dank cottages or burrows where they might brood over slights real or perceived. Strangers were meals, cooperation rare, and commercial enterprise unknown.

Which is why the Shropes were such an unusual family. The closer one ventured to Shrope Hovel, the plainer it became that they were not merely the area's most prominent hags, but also the leading creatures of any size, type, or persuasion. Ample evidence could be found in the form of regular signposts advertising the hags' presence and services. The latest stood upon a knuckled hill, its copperplate a siren's song to the weary and stupid.

Ease your feet and fill your tum
Rest your sore and aching bum
We got soft beds and fragrant soaps
Seasoned travelers Stay at Shropes!

Shrope Country Inn & Day Spa ~ 5 km
~ Humans welcome—Cash only ~

A pair of travelers stopped to contemplate the sign. The smaller of the two was Max McDaniels, a strapping youth in his late teens with wavy black hair and an amused glint in his hazel eyes. Max read this latest aloud, sparing his companion the need to fish for his monocle. The Russian ogre listened patiently until the call for cash-bearing humans. With a snort, he shook his head and spoke in a deep rumble.

"Bellagrog has fallen into old ways. Bob hopes his Mum has not."

"They can't have any customers," said Max. "Who's dumb enough to stay at a hag-run inn?"

The ogre gave a noncommittal grunt and gestured for the canteen. Weeks of summer sailing had scorched Bob's fair skin, but his back was straight and his blue eyes were bright with anticipation. His long strides swallowed up miles of gray-green hills, little rivers, and quiet woodlands in the west of what had once been England. Sipping from the canteen, the ogre turned to await the rest of their party.

Most appeared within the minute: a man, a woman, and a sagging mule that wheezed as he clopped toward the summit.

"L-lemonade," cried the mule. "My kingdom for some lemonade!"

With a grimace, the woman tugged at the mule's bridle. Despite her youth—for she was not yet thirty—Hazel Cooper's ramrod posture, old-fashioned glasses, and short brown hair lent her an academic air. Almost anyone would have marked her for a teacher. A prim mouth and withering stare hinted further that this was not a teacher to provoke. The mule, however, was oblivious.

"Come now, Hazel," he chided in a patrician baritone. "You're a so-called Mystic. What say you conjure up a trough of lemonade and put this smee in proper order, eh? Hop to it, woman. Pip! Pip!"

The teacher pursed her lips. "If you're parched, turn into a camel, Toby."

The shape-changer scoffed. "A camel? Humbug! During my glorious career, I've taken many forms, but never the ignoble camel. It's hardly a guise worthy of me."

As a newlywed, Hazel Cooper should have been enjoying a blissful honeymoon. But she, along with many at Rowan, had sacrificed personal wants in order to aid the war effort. Had she known her sacrifice would require traveling with a pompous smee, she might have reconsidered.

"Rather arbitrary standards for a former dung beetle," she observed coolly.

"That was entirely different," Toby sniffed. "I only employed that disguise to steal the crown jewels of Bohemia. I had to smuggle them out, you see, and—"

"Enough."

The command was delivered in a quiet Cockney accent that brought the smee to an indignant pause. The speaker was Hazel's husband, a middle-aged man, lean as a greyhound and pale as a specter. His clothes were black, along with his boots and a brimless wool cap that framed a face so scarred and burned it resembled a molten mask.

And while looks can be deceiving, in this case they were not. When things went bump in the night, Rowan sent William Cooper to silence them. As Commander of the Red Branch, it was his duty. As a dangerous man, it was his calling.

"I'll remind you that I'm lugging almost all the baggage," Toby groused. "I could be something sleek and sexy like . . . like a cheetah! Instead, I persevere as a lowly mule. And why? Why, to stagger on weary legs in abject service of my fellows. Some might grumble. Some might clamor for recognition or gratitude, but not I. You'll never hear me complain of—*Oh thank God!*"

The smee had glimpsed the sign.

"I call first bath!" he roared. "You heard me. And first crack at the buffet, too! The very thought of potatoes and cheeses, fruit pies and sweets . . ."

The Shropes could not have wished for a more eager and clueless victim. While Toby pranced and tittered at the prospect of a bed and a bath, the others took turns with Max's spyglass, which provided a view of the valley, several farms, and a distant cluster of buildings and pavilions.

"Half an hour if we set a decent pace," said Cooper, returning the glass to Max. "Let's get moving before we get caught in that."

The Agent pointed to a band of dark clouds looming beyond the northern hills. Already, the wind was picking up. Before they continued, however, the ogre cleared his throat.

"If Bob may say a word. He knows you have important business elsewhere and that you did not have to take him to find his little Mum. Bob is grateful."

"Of course," said Hazel. "We wouldn't have it otherwise."

"*But,*" added the ogre emphatically, "you must let him handle his affairs. Bellagrog may be difficult. She may not agree to let Mum go. You must not interfere."

"You're not going to throttle her," said Cooper, looking seriously at him.

The ogre's hands were spotted with age yet gnarled and tough as old tree roots. Glancing at them, he chuckled. "No. Bob is gentleman."

Toby stomped a hoof impatiently. "Yes, yes, we'll stay out of your incomprehensible 'hag quest.' Now, stand aside and let me set the pace!"

The eager smee went trotting down the hill, their baggage bouncing atop his back as Bob and the rest hurried after. Max lingered at the hilltop to await the party's stragglers.

The first to arrive was Scathach, a lithe young woman with black braids, gray eyes, and a fearsome infantry spear that rested upon her shoulder. Giving Max an exasperated look, she nodded toward a patch of trembling undergrowth. Something suddenly bolted forth, a black blur that might have been a kitten as it bounded up the hill.

But kittens were not nearly so dense. They did not have spiny coats or oversized claws, and they did not devour meat and metal with equal voracity. The snorting blur was not a kitten but a juvenile lymrill. Juvenile in both age and demeanor, for Nox knew better than to scramble up her steward and sprawl across his shoulders as though he were her slave. Despite many lectures, bribes, and pleas, the lymrill refused to behave and Max's clothes were now heavily scored and patched.

"Your father was never this bad," Max hissed, shifting her surprising weight. His charge merely yawned and methodically cleaned her claws.

"She rooted out a stoat," said Scathach, coming up the hill. "Big one, too."

Max nodded; he could smell the blood. "Shrope Hovel's just a few miles ahead."

With a grin, Scathach slipped her hand within his. "I can hardly wait!"

Other than Bob, no one was enjoying the trip to Shrope Hovel more than Scathach. It had been nearly two thousand years since the warrior maiden had inhabited this world. She had forsaken eternal life to return, but she never appeared to doubt her decision. If anything, mortality seemed to infuse her with a greater appreciation for life and even its mundane little joys. She loved learning about new things—or even very old things if they'd escaped her attention once upon a time. Her latest interest was hags.

"And so they sniff you?" said Scathach, continuing their earlier discussion.

"Only if they're reformed," said Max. "Reformed hags memorize some scents as 'not for eating.' Once a hag has sniffed you properly, you're safe from her. At least in theory."

"And do they smell? I imagine hags would smell very, very badly."

"I can't believe you've never encountered any hags."

"There weren't any in my homeland, much less the Sidh."

Max smiled. "Wherever humans live, hags won't be far away. They're pretty wily. Bellagrog's clever as a fox."

"And she's the head Shrope," Scathach clarified. "Mum's older sister."

"Right," said Max. "She fled to Rowan when Astaroth came to power. Mum had been at Rowan for decades, but when her sister showed up, everything changed. Hags are strictly hierarchical and Bellagrog's bigger in every way. Mum got shoved off to the side. And that was before the haglings even came along . . ."

"Haglings?"

Max nodded gravely. "Bellagrog spawned them one night and by morning they were all over the kitchens. Bawling. Pooping. Attacking. We had to fit them with muzzles. I wonder how many are left."

"What do you mean?"

Max considered how best to explain. "Haglings have it kind of rough. By the time the Shropes went on trial, I don't think there were more than five or six."

Scathach looked unsettled. "What happened to the others?"

When Max patted his stomach, she gasped.

"Mum?"

"Oh no. She'd never dare gobble up her nieces. But Bellagrog . . ."

"Their own mother ate them?"

"They're not the only ones. Spiders do it. Hamsters, too, I think."

"Hamsters don't run country inns."

"Well," said Max, "I never said a hagling's life was easy. Anyway, some must survive. Otherwise there wouldn't be any hags. I'll bet Number Five's still kicking. She was a tank."

Shaking her head, Scathach gazed ahead at Bob. "Why does he care so much about hags?"

"He doesn't," said Max. "He cares about Mum. They were like an old married couple. Always bickering but devoted to each other. I always thought Bob kept Mum in line. But now I think he needed her as much as she needed him. Maybe more."

"So why did she leave?" asked Scathach. "Wasn't she innocent?"

"Not exactly," said Max. "Mum was just as guilty as Bellagrog of trying to cook that Workshop man. But in light of the circumstances and her testimony, the Director suspended her sentence. It was Bellagrog who ordered her to leave."

"Couldn't she just have refused?"

Max shook his head. "Hag Law," he explained. "Scholars think hags are mindless brutes, but they haven't spent much time with them. Hags have all kinds of rules and customs about vendettas, gatherings, and who gets to be the boss. Bellagrog declared Hag Law and ordered her sister aboard the ship she was boarding. That was that. Mum didn't even bring a suitcase."

"But if Mum has to obey Bellagrog, how can Bob get her back?"

Max shrugged. "I don't know. But he doesn't want us to interfere."

"If that's the case, maybe we should have left him to it," observed the ever-efficient Scathach. "This detour's cost us nearly a week."

"The Fomorian isn't going anywhere," said Max. "And Rowan's fleet won't land for a month. We have plenty of time."

"And you know what they say about making hay."

"That it's a very good thing?"

"To make it while the sun shines."

Max eyed the darkening sky and the pall settling over the landscape. "Well," he reasoned, "if that's true, we're out of luck. Come on."

Nox didn't even stir as they caught up with the others and hurried on to Shrope Hovel. The weather was growing wild, spurring the group from a brisk hike to an anxious trot.

"So much for summer," laughed Scathach, catching Hazel's hat as a freezing gust nearly whisked it away.

The strange weather was an inconvenience for travelers, but it was wreaking havoc on the workers about Shrope Hovel. Dozens were running to and fro, trying to reinforce pavilions, tie tarps over rosebushes, and rescue what appeared to be preparations for a party. Chinese lanterns tugged at their tethers while colorful streamers soared clear away, twisting and tumbling over barns, buildings, and a leaning curiosity that could only be Shrope Hovel. In all the excitement, it took a moment for Max to register two surprising facts: he had yet to see a hag, and all of the workers were human.

With a clap of thunder, the clouds burst, drenching one and all in torrents of icy rain. Abandoning their efforts, the workers ran for shelter as lightning laced the sky. Max and the others hurried after, kicking up gravel and weaving through a noisy phalanx of sheep, goats, and geese. They piled in after the workers, crowding into a dark barn that smelled of dung, hay, and wet clothes.

It was only when someone lit a lamp that the workers noticed strangers among them, much less a ten-foot ogre. There followed an earsplitting shriek, an ineffectual panic, and finally an expectant silence.

"Hello," said Bob, nodding politely. "We are looking for Shropes."

"You ain't gonna eat us, then?" cried an unseen voice from the crowd.

The ogre looked amused. "Bob is sorry to disappoint."

There was a ripple of nervous laughter and some of the workers stood on tiptoe or inched forward to get a closer look. They were a mixed group: men and women, young and old, with hard faces and many scars. They reminded Max of Rowan's refugees and those he had seen at Piter's Folly, a human settlement in the midst of demon lands. Each had undoubtedly survived many horrors, but to find humans working for hags struck Max as profoundly odd. Apparently Toby agreed.

"Are you being held against your will?" he demanded of a nearby boy. When the astounded child failed to answer the talking mule, the smee spoke as though to a simpleton. "Are the hags using you for food?"

"No," said a woman. "They use us for farming."

Toby gave a disbelieving snort. "Farming you for meat, no doubt. Well, never fear, good woman. Your savior has arrived."

"Whatcha saving us from?"

"Grim death in a hag's belly."

"They don't eat us, sir."

"Slavery, then."

"We ain't slaves. The Shropes pay good wages."

"Verbal abuse?"

"Well, I guess that's fair," she muttered, the others nodding in agreement.

Shushing Toby, Hazel apologized for startling them and inquired if rooms were available at the inn.

"Ain't none to be had," said a man. "Inn's all stuffed up with hags, three and four to a room. Must be eighty of 'em here for the Naming, though Mistress Bellagrog might have to cancel if this storm don't let up."

"Naming?" asked Hazel, raising her eyebrows.

"The haglings are getting proper names," explained the little boy.

"I see," said Hazel, glancing at her companions. "And is Bellagrog home?"

"She's went out for a carriage ride," said the man. "But the little one's about. I saw her tending her hives. There she is now!"

Turning, Max glimpsed a squat silhouette trudging toward Shrope Hovel. Squinting at the figure, Bob lumbered out into the storm.

"Mum!" he called, giving a shy, almost hesitant wave. Turning, the figure merely stared as though Bob were a mirage, an echo from another life. Then, with a sudden wail, she tottered forward and clung to the ogre's waist.

Even when Bob kneeled, Mum could not quite reach his shoulder. Instead she buried her face in his armpit and sobbed like a child rescued from a nightmare. For a time the two simply huddled in the rain, the ogre patting the hag's wilted topknot.

Toby turned to his companions. "Is she always this unstable?"

"Shhh!" they hissed.

At last, the hag wiped her nose on Bob's shirtsleeve and waddled with him, red-eyed and blinking, into the barn.

"Th-there's my Max," she simpered, patting his hand and giving him a look of deep affection. "And that uptight teacher I never cared for. Hazel-Boon-with-Peas-and-Gravy. Yes, yes, that was her name."

"Hazel *Cooper*," said the teacher. "William and I were married last month."

"A lid for every pot I guess," said Mum. She looked Cooper up and down, mildly disappointed. "Still a beanpole, eh? Most humans plump up by forty."

"Well, I want to plump up now!" declared Toby. "Are you going to feed us or not, hag?"

With a startled "Oi!" Mum spun to face the impatient mule. "What we got here?"

"A master spy, saboteur, bon vivant, and international—"

"Stew meat," finished Mum, pinching the mule's shoulder with a distracted air. Recovering herself, the hag brightened and gazed about. "Yes, yes, we'll feed you. We'll fatten you right up. The inn's bursting with relations but we'll squeeze you into the Hovel. Maybe Bob will even help his Mum make lunch. That's if the big oaf hasn't forgotten how to cook!"

The ogre's eyes twinkled. "Bob remembers."

"No, you don't! You could never manage without me!"

"Mum," said Max. "There's someone I'd like you to meet. This is Scathach."

Turning, the hag smiled and offered a curtsy. "Bea Shrope, love."

"May I call you Mum?" asked Scathach.

"Do, girl, *do*!" urged the hag, gliding closer. "Pity such an angel should carry such a sharp spear."

"Mum," said Max. "Please sniff her."

The hag's smile curdled. "This ain't Rowan."

"I know," said Max. "But I'd consider it a personal favor. And, as you've noticed, Scathach carries a very sharp spear. . . ."

With shrewish indignation, the hag plucked up Scathach's arm. She sniffed once, blinked rapidly, and sniffed again. "There's good stuff here," she muttered, pinching and kneading the flesh. "Rich flavors, smooth textures. A terrine, maybe . . . yes, a delicious, delectable terrine."

Scathach remained stoic. "Thank you."

"Done!" shrieked the hag, flinging the arm aside and wheeling on the watchful workers. "I'd get busy with those decorations," she said pointedly. "If Bellagrog returns to find things all ahoo . . ."

"But the storm," protested the foreman. "These winds!"

Mum shrugged even as a gale made the rafters moan. "My sis don't care 'bout no storm. She'll want everything perfect for the Naming. Lots of folk to impress."

Leaving the workers to their unenviable task, Mum led Max and the others on a soggy scamper to Shrope Hovel. Surveying it, Max could not decide what it reminded him of until he recalled the rhyme of the Old Woman Who Lived in a Shoe. Indeed the Hovel looked like a shoe, or rather a battered, leaning boot cobbled together of various materials and styles. There was Georgian brick, Tudor beams, medieval thatch, an unfinished

Gothic spire, and a broken Baroque column lying near the front door that served no apparent purpose other than to look fancy. Max guessed it was stolen.

Despite its peculiarities, the Hovel looked warm and inviting. This impression of eccentric coziness was confirmed when Mum led them through a slanted door into a parlor with comfy chairs, an aged hearth, and bric-a-brac scattered about the many shelves and cabinets. Many portraits of hags lined the walls: hags in white wimples, hags in Flemish hoods, and a mottled, glaring enormity that could only be the infamous Nan.

The Hovel's ceilings were lower than most human dwellings. Max and Cooper had to duck knotted beams while poor Bob had to crouch as best he could and shuffle behind as Mum led them on a tour through various rooms. She chattered all the while, sharing tidbits like an enthusiastic docent.

"That's where Bellagrog pulled my pants down in front of a faun I liked."

"I used to hide in this sideboard when Nan was hungry. It locks from inside."

"See that dent in the wall? Bellagrog used me like a battering ram."

"But why would she do that?" inquired Scathach, looking perturbed.

The hag tittered. "I called her 'grotesque.'"

"And why did you do that?" sighed Hazel.

Mum merely shrugged. "It was the biggest word I knew. I called everything 'grotesque' when I was a hagling. Used to make Nan laugh."

"Speaking of haglings," said Max. "Where are they?"

"Oh, they're off in some secret location," answered Mum. "Sea-kwest-erred, as Bel says. Haglings is always sea-kwest-erred before a Naming. I don't know where they are. More importantly, neither does Bel."

Ignoring their stares, the hag continued down a twisting corridor that finally opened upon the grand and spacious kitchen. Even Bob could rise to his full height, creaking up to survey its redbrick walls; wormwood cabinets; and array of stoves, cauldrons, and ice chests. Mum scurried about, lighting lamps, shutting windows, and heaving wood into the nearest stove. Smacking soot from her hands, she looked anxiously at Bob.

"Do you like it?"

"Very much," said the ogre, taking an apron from his pack. "Let's cook."

While the others relaxed around a table, Rowan's former chefs boiled water, laid out ingredients, heated skillets, and began to bicker in their old familiar way. Soon there were onions sizzling, biscuits rising, and other delicacies that brought the smee to a swoon. Relieved of his packs, Toby had shifted into a black bear whose keen nostrils quivered as he padded about, drooling over various dishes until Bob shooed him away.

Outside, it grew so dark it looked like night was settling. Heavy rain lashed the windows, but the kitchen was snug and its table laden with steaming crocks and simmering dishes. Mum was humming, her topknot bouncing as she scurried here and there for napkins and silverware. Max was feeding Nox a piece of bacon when the bear wedged himself in at the table.

"I called first," said Toby. "You were all witnesses."

"There's plenty," said Hazel. "Even you aren't that greedy."

"Don't underestimate me."

"Well, I'm so hungry I could eat a house," said Max, elbowing Toby over.

"And Nox could eat a mouse," added Scathach.

"And I could eat me an OGRE!"

This last pronouncement did not come from the table. It issued from the hallway and was delivered with a throaty chuckle that made Mum shriek and drop a serving dish. The bowl shattered on the tiles, scattering buttered peas. Every head turned to stare at the mountain now filling the doorway.

Bellagrog Shrope was home.

Mum's sister had grown since leaving Rowan. She had always been a sizable hag, but now she was positively titanic—over five feet and three hundred matriarchal pounds simmering in a rain-soaked bustle. Suspicious eyes skipped from face to face as the hag chewed the butt of a cigar. Removing a bergère hat, she tossed it deftly onto a little stand where it proceeded to drip on the tiles.

"Well," she growled. "Ain't this a surprise? Ol' Bob, Boon, Cooper, and Handsome Max sitting 'round my table comfy as slippers. A fair maiden and a black bear, too. I done stumbled into a nursery rhyme. Come on in, gals, and have a look."

Bellagrog made way for a trio of hags to push in from behind her. The shortest was the shape and color of a blueberry, the next was bony and wore thick glasses, while the third's heavy makeup was so smeared from the rain that her features remained a glucy mystery. Inhaling deeply, she tittered as Bellagrog introduced them.

"This bonny blue girl's Smidge, the skinny-mini's Specs, and the gigglin' hulk's Gurgle."

"Ooh, they smells delicious!" squealed Gurgle, revealing a row of brown jagged teeth. "Just the thing after a soaking. If ya doesn't mind, I'll have the lad. . . ."

"Oi!" bellowed Bellagrog, snatching the hag before she could lay a hand on Max. "They is *guests*. Unexpected guests, true, but guests all the same. Hag Law!"

"Hag Law," repeated the others sulkily.

"And anyway," continued Bellagrog, "have a look at his wrist, Gurgle. No, the other one, you twit. That mark there."

Clutching her shawl, Gurgle blinked uncomprehendingly at Max's tattoo.

"Red Branch," explained Bellagrog. "Take a bite and it's curtains for poor, dumb Gurgle. And there ain't just one at this table, but three," she added, pointing at Cooper and Scathach's tattoos. "Now fancy that. War in the kingdoms, winter winds in June, and three Red Branchies in me kitchen. Something wicked's afoot!" She whirled on her sister. "Why they here, Bea?"

"Th-they were in the neighborhood," stammered Mum, sweeping up the broken dish. "They just p-popped by."

"Bwahahahaha!" cackled Bellagrog. "If you buy that, you're thicker 'n Gurgle. You expect me to believe this lot just happened by on Naming Day? Leave that mess and roll some kegs to the inn. Pre-party's in full swing. I'll be wantin' a word with this crew, so don't hurry back. In fact, it's best you stay away."

At this Mum exploded in teary hysteria.

"They're *my* guests and this is *my* Hovel, too, and they came to see *me*!"

Bellagrog turned upon her sister like a planet rotating toward its moon. "And I'm Bellagrog Shrope," she growled. "First-spawned, grandest-named, and carver of the Yuletide goose. Do as you're told, Bea, or it's eyeballs for earrings. Hag Law!"

"Hag Law!" cried the others.

Mum wilted in her sister's shadow. "B-but I've waited so long to see my Bob!"

"Almost three years now," jeered Bellagrog. "'S-someday my Bob will come. S-someday m-my Bob will rescue me!'" The other hags cackled at the impression, but Bellagrog merely shook her head. "Get going, Bea, and let a gal think."

As Mum bolted out, Bellagrog shuffled over to the head chair occupied by Scathach. The hag jerked a thumb.

"Move it," she ordered. "And fetch some more chairs from the dining room while you're up. Everyone works at Shrope Hovel— Dang it, she don't need yer help!"

This last outburst was directed at Gurgle, who was quietly slipping out after Scathach. Bellagrog rubbed her temples wearily. "If you're gonna cook up my food, you might as well eat it. Dig in, already. Cold bacon's a sin."

"I couldn't agree more!" declared the black bear.

"And what the heck is you?" asked Bellagrog, scooting over so the hags and Scathach could squeeze around the table. It was too many people for Nox, who jumped off Max's lap and stalked out of the room.

"I'm a smee, madam," replied Toby, wisely bypassing his usual litany. "Toby the Smee."

"A smee!" exclaimed Specs, peering at him down her long nose.

"Why you giddy 'bout a smee?" asked Bellagrog, sliding some ham onto her plate. "Never heard of no such thing."

"Oh yes, we have, Bel!" crowed Specs. "We learned about 'em in the old rhymes." She tapped the measure with a spoon.

It ain't a yam
It ain't a grub
You ain't gonna find 'em in a shrub
A better bet's to look in your tub
For the smee he likes his leisure.
He can change his shape—quick as a blink!
He can change his voice—and even his stink!
But the tasty smee can't handle his drink
And that's the way to catch 'im.

As she completed the rhyme, the other hags turned toward Toby.

"Wine?" pressed Smidge.

"Ale?" offered Gurgle, brandishing a mug.

"Twaddle!" scoffed Bellagrog, pushing back from the table. "This big ol' bear wants a double whiskey from me private cupboard. Just the stuff on a nippy day."

"Hear hear!" cried the smee, his mouth full of bacon. "Ouch! Who kicked me?"

"Toby will have water," said Hazel pointedly. "Water that I will taste."

Bellagrog sat glowering while others filled Toby's glass. With a sigh she passed the fried potatoes and set about the ham. "Heard about your father," she said, glancing at Max. "Condolences, love. Scott McDaniels was good company and I didn't mind him sharing me kitchen. Humans ain't always my thing, but he was okay."

"Thank you," said Max, oddly moved by her gruff sincerity. "He liked you, too."

She shrugged off the compliment. "You get satisfaction? You get the one that murdered him?"

Max nodded. He had slain the demon Vyndra on Walpurgisnacht, but revenge brought little comfort—the man who had raised him was still dead and buried. Apparently Bellagrog saw it differently, for she smacked the table and jabbed a meaty finger at Gurgle.

"Hear that, girlie? He hunted down his daddy's killer and got his vengeance right and proper. Take one of his and he takes ten of yours. He's more hag than you!"

"It wasn't quite like that," said Max, but neither hag was listening.

"Don't talks to me about what makes a hag," Gurgle huffed at her hostess. "You gots humans by the score round here and you don't take a nibble. Some say you gone soft since you lived at Rowan."

"Who says?" roared Bellagrog. "Gimme names and they'll be fattening me sows."

Gurgle folded her arms. "Never mind who. Just answer one thing."

"Let's have it!"

"When's the last time you supped on man?"

A vein throbbed at Bellagrog's temple. "I got businesses to run," she growled. "Fields to sow, crops to reap, soaps to sell, an inn to manage. Heck, I'm the biggest, richest hag in the land and you got the brass to question me at table?"

"You still ain't answered the question," pointed out Smidge, waving a sausage.

Bellagrog glared at her. "Couldn't say when I last supped on man," she muttered. "But I know when I'll be having soused hag's face."

"But we're your guests!" squeaked Specs. "Hag Law!"

"Hag Law," chimed her mates.

Easing back, a simmering Bellagrog surveyed them. "Aye," she conceded. "Hag Law it is. But I'll say this, Gurgle. Your sister's been gathering Workshop dust for years while you putter about. So don't go lecturin' me on what makes a hag a hag. If Gertie was my wombmate, I'd have brought her home."

"Is Cousin Gertie your sister?" asked Max, turning to Gurgle. With a blushing nod, the hag inhaled an ear of corn.

"We came across Gertie in the Workshop museum," said Hazel to Scathach. "The engineers display different species. Apparently, Gertie had the misfortune of falling into their possession. I'm very sorry, Gurgle."

Cooing appreciatively, the hag patted Hazel's hand and tried to heave her across the table. Cooper promptly stabbed her knuckles with a fork, which caused the hag to shriek and release her prey.

"Sorry," she said. "I never sat down with humans before. Did you know you go with peas and gravy, love?"

"I've been told," said Hazel, massaging her wrist.

"Don't you worry 'bout Gertie," said Bellagrog. "Leave it to the Shropes to take care of what shoulda been done by her own. *No Named hag shall go unrescued or unavenged.* Hag Law!"

"Hag Law!" cried the others in a clash of tankards.

"And just how you gonna see to Gertie?" pressed Gurgle skeptically.

"You'll find out tonight," said Bellagrog. "Now I wants to know why we got so much company—and dangerous company, too."

"What's so dangerous about us?" asked Toby, licking his paws. "We come in peace."

The hag fixed him with a crocodile eye. "You know the price on Max's head? For word of him, Prusias would fill my pots with gold. Every assassin in Blys has it out for Max McDaniels. There's probably a bounty on your sorry rump."

"Me?" said Toby, taken aback. "Why should anyone have it out for me?"

"You're from *Rowan!*" hissed the hag. "Ain't no itty-bitty school of magic no more. When mean old Prusias came to gobble Rowan, he got more than he bargained for, didn't he? Bwahahaha! Can't say I didn't raise a mug when I heard the news, but that game ain't over. Blood money for Rowan folk's mighty high—more if they got lots of trinkets."

She pointed at Hazel's magechain, a necklace whose many glittering ornaments were a testament to her accomplishments in Mystics. Smidge could be heard quietly calculating the teacher's worth.

"So you'd sell us to your brayma," said Hazel coldly.

Bellagrog chuckled. "Don't know that there is a proper brayma round here. Some nosy bugger tried to tax our goods, but we learned him, didn't we?" The hags giggled. "Nah, you'd have to walk far and wide to find a true demon in these parts. The bigger ones—the *important* ones—want lands closer to Prusias. Us Shropes are in the boonies and that's the way we like it. Unless we got something they want, the demons will leave us alone. We don't signify."

Cooper tapped the table. "If you're in the boonies, where do you get your information?"

Bellagrog shrugged. "Here and there. Goblins are blabbermouths if you toss 'em some coppers. Heck, I could tell you how many ships Rowan's got heading for Blys."

Cooper's voice was dangerously quiet. "And how would you know that?"

Bellagrog abruptly scooted her chair away. "Careful round this one," she muttered to the hags. "Don't you be looking at me like that, William Cooper. It ain't my fault that Rowan don't know nothing about dryads."

"Of course we know about dryads," said Hazel. "Sylvan spirits that protect sacred groves. They take the form of beautiful maidens, inhabit the trees under their care, and were valued as ladies-in-waiting by mystic noblewomen. Dangerous if provoked, but fond of poetry, especially haikus and sonnets. Incidentally, they also make lovely scents. I got William a bottle for a wedding gift."

The hags roared with laughter.

"I'll bet you read all that in a book," chortled Bellagrog, dabbing her eyes. "True enough, I guess, but you're missing the point o' dryads. They're the great gossips of the world! Every hagling knows they can't keep secrets and that they whisper 'em on the breeze until another dryad takes it up. You think all that sighing in the trees is just the *wind*? Ever wonder why you never seen a hag tinkle by an oak?"

"I can't say that I have," said Hazel, unconcerned.

"Well, if you did, you might put a thing or two together," said Bellagrog. "We stay on the right side of dryads. It's Hag Law."

"Hag Law!"

When Max realized he'd unintentionally joined the chorus, he coughed and hastily wiped his mouth. "So what else have you heard about the war?"

Bellagrog spread her hands. "Not much else. Just Prusias's Workshop thingees went mad and that he fled when the Faeregine appeared and cracked his crowns. That's got everyone talking."

"What's the Faeregine?" asked Max. "It was Mina who drove Prusias away. She's just a little girl."

"Just a little girl," chortled Bellagrog, shaking her head. "You think some 'little girl' scared off a great brute like Prusias? Bunk! The Faeregine's come again."

Max glanced inquiringly at Scathach, whose time in the Sidh made her an expert on many strange topics. But she merely frowned and shook her head as though the term puzzled her, too. Hazel sat up even straighter. Old Magic was one of her primary areas of study.

"Faeregine," she repeated slowly. "Etymologically, that sounds like 'Faerie Queen' or ruler of the Fey. Am I correct?"

Bellagrog shrugged. "I got no clue what *ettee-mole-ogically* means, but no matter. Faeregine's the old name as we learned in our rhymes. Even Gurgle will remember that one."

With a reverent bow of their heads, the hags recited:

With every Age a Faeregine
Born of stars and summer dreams

Heaven's gift, a midnight flower
She blossoms at the darkest hour
Hags must listen, hags must heed
The wishes of great Faeregine.

"The middle part's peachy," Toby critiqued. "But the beginning doesn't quite rhyme and those last two lines—"

"Don't matter," growled Bellagrog. "Faeregine's come again, sure as Sunday."

"What do you think, Hazel?" asked Cooper.

His wife straightened her glasses. "Probably an old superstition. I've never come across the term in the Archives. If a Faeregine really appeared every age to save mankind, scholars would have written volumes."

"Maybe yer scholars wasn't listenin' to the dryads," Bellagrog needled. "And when did I ever say the Faeregine's job was to save *mankind*? Typical human to assume it's all about them. Heck, maybe the last Faeregine was busy rescuing other folk from man. No other creature's made such a mess of the world. And now you're off to make war again."

"We didn't start this war," said Hazel coldly.

"But you're gonna finish it, ain't ya?" laughed Bellagrog. "One little victory's got Rowan so puffed up she's sailing off to root old Prusias out of his palace. Lots harder to invade a land than defend one. Hope your Director knows that."

There was a quiet knock and they turned to see one of Bellagrog's workers clutching his hat in the doorway.

Bellagrog cocked her head. "Whatchoo want, Jakes?"

"Beg pardon," said the man. "But the decorations are blowing away as soon as we get 'em up. Even if the storm stops this minute, we're running out of time. Can the Naming be postponed? Even tomorrow would be—"

Bellagrog nearly choked. "And let my freeloadin' relatives stay another day? Not on your life! Anyway, Naming's happening tonight, rain or shine. Get the lutins to help."

"They're drunk."

Cursing softly, the hag lit another cigar and puffed in peevish silence before suddenly glancing at Hazel. "You can make twinkly lights and all that hocus-pocus nonsense, eh?"

"Certainly."

"Well, get outside, eh? Time's a-wasting and we need this place all gussied up for the Naming. Everybody works at Shrope Hovel!"

The teacher peered glumly at the rain-spattered windows. "Very well," she said. Wrapping herself in a heavy blue shawl, she slipped out the back door.

As the door clattered shut, Max turned to Bellagrog. "How are you holding up with the war?"

The hag smirked. "War's always been good for us Shropes. Been moving plenty of product. Next month we're adding a line of canned vittles." She pointed to a shelf lined with samples. "You come across anyone who wants work, you send 'em my way. I needs all the hands I can get. Three hots and a cot. Fair wages and a bonus for those that earns it." She half turned to Bob. "I'm so desperate, I might even hire an old fart like you!"

As the hags cackled, the ogre spooned some strawberries into a bowl. With a groan, Toby pushed back from the table.

"Why do I do that?" he moaned.

"What's the matter with you?" said Bellagrog.

The smee belched. "Dear me! My apologies, good hag, but it appears I've overindulged. Is there a place where I could lie down? It helps my digestion."

An unimpressed Bellagrog nodded toward the hallway.

"Parlor rug. But don't you go snoopin' or making a mess. And *you* stay put, Gurgle!" she added as the hag also made to excuse herself.

"Pristine's my middle name," said Toby, promptly belching again. "Just a few minutes off my feet and I'll be a new smee. I think it must have been the cream. . . ."

As the bear padded out, Bellagrog turned back to Bob. "So, whatchoo say, old timer? Wanna work for me? I'll even throw in a new apron."

The ogre smiled. "Bellagrog is very kind. But Bob has job at Rowan."

The hag nodded as though this was the answer she expected. She folded her brawny arms. "So whatchoo doin' out here?" she demanded. "Fess up or get out."

The ogre cleared some of the empty dishes. "Rowan needs allies," he said in a measured tone. "We talk with those who might join fight."

Bellagrog gave an incredulous laugh. "You askin' the Shropes to fight Prusias?"

"No," said Bob. "Rowan ask others to do that. But since we not far, I ask if we make little trip to visit Shropes on Midsummer. All haglings get names on Midsummer, no? Bob has always wanted to see Naming. And—he will not lie—he wanted to see his little Mum. Bob is old and it might be last time he can. But he wants no trouble. If Bellagrog wants, we go."

The hag turned to Max. "That true, love? You're in these parts seeking allies?"

Max nodded. "These parts" was open to broad interpretation. "The Director didn't send three members of the Red Branch just to visit Shrope Corner."

Bellagrog grunted. "I didn't think she did." With a low whistle, she swiveled back to study Bob with her shrewd, piggy eyes.

"You sure are a sorry sack o' something. So you tagged along to see your Bea. Whatchoo think she was gonna do? Run away with ya? Bwahahahaha! Ya don't understand hags at all. Bea will do what I say till she's pushing up daisies. But you be my guest tonight, Bob—for old time's sake. Enjoy the Naming, have a bite or three, and then get your wrinkly behind off my property."

The ogre bowed to show his appreciation.

A crash sounded from another room followed by a panicked shrieking.

"Murder! Mischief! Fire!"

<h2 style="text-align:center">~ 3 ~</h2>

QUEEN O' THE MOUND

The cry came from the front of the house and was followed by a crash. Popping up from the table, everyone hurried out of the kitchen. Max was the first out the door, ducking through the doorway to rush down the hall. From the parlor, he heard gruff curses, breaking china, and a furious hissing.

"Go away! What's happening? Help! HELP!" shrieked a bloodcurdling falsetto.

Dashing into the parlor, the group arrived upon a confused and hectic scene. Five gray-skinned haglings swarmed about the parlor looking ferocious despite their colorful pinafores. Trapped within their midst was Toby. Unfortunately, the smee was in his native shape and could do little more than wriggle around an antique coffee table that had been flipped over. Although a smee's natural state—mottled, limbless, and tapered—was universally repulsive, the haglings were keenly interested in getting their hands upon him. The only thing keeping them at bay was Nox. Crouching by the smee, she whipped about, quicker than a mongoose, to swipe her claws at any who ventured too close.

"Oi!" Bellagrog bellowed. "What's going on?"

"We caught a magic yam!" cried a hagling.

"A yam that smells like meat!" crowed another.

With a gasp, the smee twisted toward the speaker. "I'm not a yam!"

"Sounds like a dandy," quipped a third. "Give 'em a nip, Five."

Five was the largest of the haglings, a powerful, swaybacked brute with a turnip-shaped head, beetle-black eyes, and a stubbly jaw. Dressed in periwinkle, she sucked a cut on her hand.

"I ain't getting near that kitty again without my cleaver."

"Oh no," cried Bellagrog. "No one's cleaving anything in their good pinafores. Gurgle, Gertie, and Specs, see yourselves out. *Haglings, line up!*"

While Bellagrog's cousins grumbled and left out the back way, the haglings acted as if their mother had cast a spell. Dropping their chairs and makeshift cudgels, they arranged themselves by height against the parlor wall. When all were at attention, the smallest curtsied.

"Number Seven!" she piped, a toady runt in puffy pink sleeves.

"Number Two," called the next, plucking her purple tights.

"Number One," cried her neighbor, twirling a greasy pigtail.

"Number Four," hissed a saber-toothed monstrosity.

"Five," muttered the last, folding her massive arms.

"Bwahahahaha!" cackled Bellagrog. "Naming Day hasn't

come too soon for Five, now, has it?" As Bellagrog heaved the heavy table upright, Cooper plucked Toby up by one twisty end. In two bounds, Nox settled in Max's arms, her coat resuming its glossy sheen as the quills lay flat. Nursing their wounds, the haglings glared sulkily at the lymrill. When Bellagrog ceased her inspection of the damage, she wheeled upon her daughters.

"Who broke me Nan's table?" she demanded, pointing at a crack down the center. "Tell me true."

"I will when you tell us what these humans is doing here," said Five.

"They is guests," retorted Bellagrog. "And watch yer tone. This ain't yer Hovel."

"*Yet*," growled Five, returning her mother's stare. An uncomfortably tense silence ensued. Max feared the two might come to blows, when Five suddenly blinked and looked away.

"That smirk ain't ladylike," Bellagrog snapped at Seven, who was enjoying the showdown.

"So why is the humans here?" asked Four.

"That oaf of an ogre brought 'em," said Bellagrog, pointing at Bob, who was half crouched in the hallway. "Seems he missed your aunt Bea and he wants to see ya Named. Speaking o' which, no more roughhousing or nipping—you'll ruin your dresses and appetites."

Five jerked her thumb at Toby, who had curled like a salted slug. "What about him?"

"Off-limits," sighed Bellagrog. "He's a guest and we don't need no bad juju. It's practically snowing outside. One of ye can help me with my hair. The rest can share your plans with these boys and see if they gots any pointers." The hag gestured toward Max and Cooper.

"Why?" demanded Five.

"'Cause they've been in the Workshop, sassy mouth. And

Red Branchies know more about this sort o' thing than the likes of you."

"I remember him," hissed Four, peering at Max, her nostrils aquiver. "He's the one what fished that Workshop git from the kettle."

Five's piggish eyes narrowed. "Aye, that's him—the boy who ratted us out. What's he doing here?"

"Dunno," answered Bellagrog, "but don't go blaming Max for us setting sail. He played it straight and I can't ask no more. It's your auntie what sank us. So show 'em your plans and see if they don't have a tip or two."

"Is *that* staying?" asked Two, looking anxiously at Nox.

"Nox won't hurt you," said Max, stroking the lymrill's glossy black quills. "She was just protecting Toby."

"Is Toby the yam?" inquired One.

"I AM NOT A YAM!" roared Toby, indignation trumping trauma. "I am a smee who was unjustly ambushed. You're lucky I'm a pacifist."

"But why aren't you still a bear?" asked Max.

"Oh," said Toby, growing sheepish. "Eating too much can cause us to revert to the 'form divine.' That's why I left the kitchen. Surely you've heard of Balthazar's Accident. Every smeegrub knows that unhappy tale."

"Nobody wants to hear about Balthazar's Accident," said Cooper, setting him upon a chair. Sitting down on the floor, he beckoned to the haglings. "Let's see your plans, ladies."

Max and Scathach sat beside him as the haglings crowded around, elbowing and jostling. Five unfolded a large sheet and smoothed it flat upon the table. Stroking Nox's ruff, Max surveyed a variety of maps, intricate diagrams, and dense blocks of small, neat writing. Cooper looked equal parts impressed and amused.

"So, what's the mission?" he asked.

"Operation Gertie," said Five proudly. "We're busting her out o' the Workshop."

"Right," said Cooper, drumming his fingers as though considering how best to dissuade the eager, young, and foolish. His pale eyes flicked back to the map. "You know the Workshop's almost seven hundred miles away?"

"'Course we do!" said Four.

"Across the Channel and over dangerous country?"

"We likes danger," sniggered One.

Cooper nodded. "And you know its museum is underground? Miles and miles underground?"

Two gave her sisters an incredulous look. "This fella thinks we just spawned!"

The Agent weathered five beady stares. "Let's cut to it, then. How are you going to infiltrate the Workshop, find ol' Gertie, and get her out?"

Max was stunned by the sophistication of the haglings' plans. Every stage was planned in meticulous detail and leveraged an impressive network of relationships. The Shropes had contacts with many merchants and shippers, some of whom did a thriving trade with goblins across the Channel. Some of these contacts worked for the Workshop and had access to various outposts and depots, including some near Verilius, the demon city that had once been Frankfurt.

"This here is right over a train depot," said Five, pointing to a building on her map. "Workshop's got miles and miles o' tracks and tubes underground. Most connect to mines and ports, but they've even got a fancy train to ferry bigwigs between the Workshop and Prusias's city. Anyway, the Spindlefingers—they're a goblin clan—are the ones that do most of the maintenance 'cause they can climb into wee places and don't mind the heat. They're gonna let us in that building and smuggle us into the Workshop proper."

"What's in it for them?" asked Cooper.

"Formula Thirteen," answered Seven. "That soap cuts right through grease and machine oil. Spindlefingers love it."

"We're giving 'em a year's supply to smuggle us in," said Five. "They looks away when we goes in and looks away when we comes out with Gertie. Easy as pie."

"Where'd you get all this info?" asked Cooper, his eyes fixed on the railway connecting the Workshop and Prusias's capital.

"Pompy Frogmaw," replied the haglings in unison.

"Who's he?" asked Cooper.

Five shrugged. "A goblin who's always trying to steal chickens. Last time we caught him, we whipped his fanny purple. He howled and said we'd catch it hot, 'cause Pompy knew 'important folk.' Said his cousins was tight with the Workshop and they'd give Pompy all kinds o' weapons to teach us a lesson. Well, when I stopped laughing, I gots to thinking. Maybe Pompy *did* have cousins that had something to do with the Workshop. So, we untied 'im, slapped a balm on his fanny, and gave 'im a crate o' soaps to share with these cousins. He showed up three months later with a big order from the Spindlefingers. Turns out they were batty for Formula Thirteen. That's how we started gettin' their business and some information besides—all on account o' little Pompy Frogmaw."

"He's coming to the Naming," said Two. "Bringing his cousin, too. They's picking up the Formula Thirteen and giving us a lift down to the Channel."

"This cousin," pressed Cooper. "He's a Spindlefinger? He works on the Workshop trains?"

"Aye," said Five. "He's a mechanic in the main depot, least Pompy says. We ain't met him yet, but 'is name's Ozerk."

The Agent looked hard at Five. "I want to meet Ozerk."

When the haglings had mentioned a railway linking the Workshop and the Blyssian capital, Max knew Cooper would be on it. The Agent was traveling with them for the time being, but his ultimate mission had nothing to do with Mum or even the Fomorian. Although Cooper was the Red Branch commander, the title was largely ceremonial. The man had no more interest in supervising people than his colleagues had in being supervised. The twelve members of the Red Branch were notoriously independent and each developed their own methods and specialties. Max and Scathach were its finest warriors, Natasha Kiraly its swiftest tracker, and Ben Polk its most merciless assassin. But William Cooper was unequivocally its finest overall Agent. His mission would be of prime importance.

Max suspected it involved infiltrating the enemy's capital, but he could not be certain. Despite his frequent attempts to wheedle information, Cooper would divulge nothing. The little Max knew he'd overheard two weeks ago aboard the *Ormenheid*. Late that moonless night, Hazel had taken her husband astern and voiced her concerns in an urgent hiss. The sea had been reasonably calm, allowing Max to make out the occasional snippet.

"*—not fully recovered . . .*"

"*—can send someone else. Natasha's capable—*"

"*—suicide mission!*"

At this last pronouncement, Cooper simply embraced her and gazed a long time at the sea. Max had not heard anything about his mission since, but there was little doubt that Cooper regarded this Workshop train—and a secret way aboard it—as having real value. The only issue now was to make sure they were dressed properly for the Naming.

Bellagrog had Number Seven lead them up to the attic, where they could store their things and change for the party.

The stairways twisted up three stories, leading them past many portraits and dim hallways. The Hovel was old but meticulously maintained. The banisters had an oiled gleam, as did the dark floors and moldings. Every aspect of the creaking house—even its smells—smacked of tradition in a way that was both oppressive and comforting. One could almost hear the footsteps of past generations, of hags great and small that had called it home.

Max peered out between the attic window's curtains. It took a moment for the scene to fully register. The sky was brightening from the passing storm, but the landscape had changed. Every roof and chimney, every leaf, hill, and paddock was sheathed in a thin coating of ice. The effect was so surreal and spellbinding that it was hard to differentiate between Hazel's faerie lights and the returning sunlight winking on the ancient hornbeams. There was no snow, or even frost—simply a dazzling, gleaming carapace that covered the rolling scenery.

"Look at that," said Max. "There's actually ice."

The others came over, peering out the window. Below, Bellagrog's employees were working frenetically to sweep up debris, restake tents, and plant what looked like a maypole atop an enormous mound of dirt.

Cooper grunted, squinting up at the sky, which had a peculiar, reddish cast. "That isn't normal. This is some kind of witchcraft."

Scathach opened the window to peer out. "Who would be doing this?" she wondered. "Who even could?"

"Don't know," said Cooper, tossing his pack onto an old card table. "But it's not going to make our jobs easier. Depending on the information I get from this Ozerk, I might need to peel off and start my mission tonight. Are you two all right seeking the Fomorian on your own?"

"Yes," said Max. "But what about Hazel, Toby, and Bob?"

"Bob is staying until he can leave with Mum," said the ogre firmly.

"Then you might be waiting a long time, mate," said Cooper. "If that's your decision, you're on your own. No hard feelings."

"No hard feelings," Bob agreed.

"What about me?" asked Toby, still in his native shape and lounging on a trunk. "I'm not staying here with a bunch of hags. Apparently, I'm ambrosia!"

"You and Hazel will come with me," said Cooper. "Once we're across the Channel, we've got safe houses you can use until the army lands."

"Or they could catch up with Sarah and Lucia," Max suggested. "I'm sure they'd be welcome in Enlyll."

Max's friends, Sarah Amankwe and Lucia Cavallo, had journeyed with them across the ocean until *Ormenheid* set them down on an isolated stretch of Blys's coast. A faun had been waiting at the rendezvous, a former Rowan charge that had agreed to guide the girls through the backcountry to their destination. If all had gone well, the two would be halfway to Enlyll, Connor Lynch's sun-soaked barony in what used to be the French Riviera.

Connor was not merely a former classmate; he was now a minor *brayma* in Prusias's kingdom, having surrendered a soul in exchange for lands and title. In a letter to Lucia the previous winter, Baron Lynch had encoded a message implying that Rowan should seek out the Elder vyes, as they might be valuable allies. While Ms. Richter could not spare any Agents to pursue such a cryptic lead, she had approved Sarah and Lucia's proposal to visit Enlyll and investigate.

"That decision can wait until we're across the Channel," said Cooper. "In the meantime, let's figure out what we're doing during the Naming. I'll want to speak with this Ozerk alone. Bob, what's your plan with Mum?"

From his pack, the ogre produced a small iron box. "Bob will see if Bellagrog likes gold better than bullying."

"Be careful," said Cooper. "Bellagrog's liable to get your gold and you're liable to get nothing at all."

"Bob will be careful," said the ogre quietly.

Hazel hurried into the attic, blowing on her hands. The shivering teacher was practically blue. "Have you ever seen such a Midsummer?" she asked incredulously. "I nearly froze out there, but I daresay the decorations came together nicely. Dear Lord! Now, what to wear, what to wear . . ."

"What do you mean 'what to wear'?" asked Cooper.

His wife was now searching through her things. "The Naming," she replied. "Surely you don't think we're going to attend wearing what's on our backs. We have to get ready."

"I look fine," said Cooper, glancing down at his dusty, muddied clothes.

"You most certainly do not," said Hazel briskly. "We've been sailing up rivers, tromping all over the countryside, and we're not going to attend a ceremony—even a hag ceremony—without cleaning up. You can wear that scent I bought you. You haven't even cracked the seal and it was very expensive." Her husband looked semi-mortified as she fetched a crystal bottle of amber liquid from his pack.

"A Hag Naming," said Scathach, now rummaging through her own clothes. "I didn't pack anything like a dress, but maybe I could improvise something." She glanced at Max. "What should one wear to a hag Naming party?"

Max arched an eyebrow. "Armor?"

By late afternoon, much of the ice had melted away and hags began emerging from the inn. They trickled forth in startling numbers and diversity: green hags, blue hags, frizzy heads and bald. Down the gravel paths they came, a procession of waddling tanks, hobbling crones, and lanky horrors that moved with a heron's undulating steps. Some wore dresses, others wore robes or even smocks, but all carried handbags.

But hags were not the only guests. From the surrounding woods and lanes, other creatures were arriving: elegant fauns and willowy dryads, cackling lutins, and tiny moss maidens that traveled in downy green clusters on the backs of their badgers. The goblins arrived last, cracking their whips and hallooing as their ponies and wagons came clattering up the gravel drive.

There was no receiving line or official welcome, no opening ceremonies or remarks. The party simply began and gained momentum as more guests arrived.

While the haglings had yet to make an appearance, Bellagrog was in fine form. She ambled about, shaking hands and clapping backs. Even when Max couldn't see the hag, her unmistakable cackle could be heard above the din of music and games, laughter and singing.

The only attendee who didn't seem to be enjoying herself was Mum. The little hag sat alone at a trestle table, sipping from a mug and eyeing the other revelers.

"How's the ale?" asked Max, sitting next to her.

"All right, I guess," came the glum reply.

"Have you tried the mince pies?" asked Scathach gamely.

"Which ones?" asked the hag with mild interest.

"I don't know. They had a shiny blue wrapper."

"Charna Schrupe's," sighed Mum. "Steer clear of those, dearie. Charna runs a mortuary."

Scathach went pale.

Bob came to join them, pulling over a barrel to sit on, as his legs would never fit beneath the table. The ogre was dressed in gray wool trousers, a gingham dress shirt, and his best suspenders.

One hand held a mug of steaming cider while the other cradled his moneybox.

"Tell me about Rowan," sniffled Mum, looking plaintively at him. "Tell me about my cupboard and my pots. Tell me about—"

"Here you are!" chortled a voice behind them. Max turned to see Bellagrog accompanied by a hunched, viridian hag wreathed in fox furs and wearing a purple kerchief about her tapered head. "Max, I want ya to meet Looker Magda. Magda's right famous among hags." Bellagrog lowered her voice. *"She's got the Gift."*

"The Gift?" said Max.

Looker Magda peered at him through a pair of cracked opera glasses. "I see things," she purred.

"Look at his mark!" exclaimed Bellagrog, pointing at Max's tattoo. "It's him! The Hound of Rowan come to bless my babies' Naming."

"I don't need to see his mark," replied Looker Magda dismissively. "I knew the Hound would be here. Why else would I have come?"

"For free food and drink, that's why," huffed Bellagrog.

Looker Magda ignored this. Her attention remained fixed on Max as she raised a bangled arm and pointed. "Behold a conqueror!" she intoned. "A king. A tyrant. Kithslayer. Kinslayer. Your own Furies come for you!"

"Nice to meet you, too," said Max flatly.

"Oi!" cried Bellagrog, snapping her fingers before Looker Magda's unblinking eyes. "I didn't bring you over here to insult 'im."

"Don't blame the messenger," sniffed the seer.

"If you see so bloody much, why don't you tell me who's gonna win the Greengully Stakes?" demanded Bellagrog.

"A horse."

"Buzz off," grumbled Bellagrog, sitting across the table from

Bob. Draining her mug, she set it on the tray of a passing faun with a stern directive to bring another. Drumming her fingers on the table, she looked at the sky and then around at her company. "More rain's a coming. Where's Scarecrow and Boon?"

"In the Hovel," said Mum, hooking her thumb. "I said they could use the kitchen for their meeting with Pompy and Ozerk. It's quieter in there."

Her sister's face darkened. "Did ya now? Since when does *you* give people leave to use *my* kitchen?"

Flushing, Mum stared at the table. "It's my house, too," she said meekly.

Snatching a fresh tankard from the faun, her sister thumped it on the table. "No, it ain't," she said pointedly. "You is an assistant beekeeper who's lucky she's got a roof over her lumpy little head. Don't forget that."

Bob leaned forward to rest his knotted hands on the table. "Perhaps Bob can do Bellagrog favor and take lumpy little head off her hands."

"How's that?" said Bellagrog.

"Bob wants Mum to come home," said the ogre evenly.

"She *is* home, ya toothless gimp. What's in that cider?"

"Bob must disagree. Rowan is Mum's home."

"Stuff and nonsense! Bea's a Shrope and this here's Shrope Hovel."

"Rowan is where she is happiest."

Bellagrog scoffed incredulously. "Happiness? What does happiness have to do with family? Oi! Ya think I'm gonna let some brute—and a *foreign* brute, too—waltz off with my only livin' sis 'cause she's mopey? Your brain's gone to mush."

"Bob will pay."

Bellagrog waved him away as though he were a bothersome

fly. "Get outta here. A hag o' my standing don't want no stinky hides or knucklebones or whatever a dumb ogre thinks is money."

Bob set his moneybox on the table.

A gleam kindled in Bellagrog's crocodile eyes as she sized the ogre up. "C'mon now," she chuckled. "Rowan pays you diddly. Don't yank a hag's haunch."

Opening the heavy clasps, the ogre emptied the box onto the table. The pile was mostly silver with a handful of large gold coins and semiprecious stones scattered throughout. The sight of this not-inconsiderable wealth drew many onlookers.

"What's goin' on, Bel?" asked a tipsy Gurgle.

But Bellagrog had turned beet red and was shaking with laughter. "Bwahahahaha!" she cried, trying to catch her breath. "This kooky ogre's tryin' to buy my sister! Look at that haul! You'd think Bea was the most valuable hag in the world!"

"She is," said Bob, ignoring the growing hoots and jeers.

Mum was utterly stunned. Her eyes darted from Bob to the money to her sister and back again. "That's your life savings," she whispered. "You'd give all that up . . . for me?"

"Yes," said the ogre, closing his hand over hers. "You are Bob's little Mum and it is time you came home."

"Take it, Bel!" shouted someone.

"That's ten times what wee Bea's worth!" called another.

"Try fifty!" Bellagrog chortled, wiping the tears from her eyes. "Bless yer heart, Bob. You sure did save your pennies. Whew! I ain't laughed so hard since Bea tumbled down a well trying to guess how deep it was."

Bob pushed the glinting pile toward her. "We have deal?"

Reaching into it, Bellagrog plucked a shiny gold coin and sniffed it as though that alone would tell her its authenticity. With a sigh, she tossed it back onto the pile. "Ain't nothing worse than temptation," she chuckled. "Bea's right worthless, but I can't sell my sister like she's a bushel o' cabbage. Wouldn't be right." The head Shrope wagged a finger at Mum. "See what you cost me, you ninnyhead? Don't think I won't remind ya the next time you wants to sleep in!"

It was too much for Mum. With an ungodly shriek, she leaped up from the table and bolted through the revelers. Max went after her, dodging through hags and goblins, fauns and satyrs.

Slipping through the crowd, he made his way down the wooded hill where Mum had fled. Behind him, drums had started to boom. Glancing back, he glimpsed the haglings marching single file from the barn in their starched pinafores. Among the watchful crowd, umbrellas were sprouting like toadstools as an icy drizzle began to fall. The drums played on.

It was not difficult to find Mum. The turf was wet, her footsteps deep, and broken branches pointed the way like semaphores. She had not gone far into the woods—just far enough to collapse by an icy stream bordered by some willows. Max hurried to her side.

"Mum," he said, looping an arm around her.

"I'm so tired of everyone laughing at me! I j-just can't take it anymore. Even the haglings treat me like dirt." The hag sobbed and sobbed, clinging to him like a barnacle as he tried to soothe her. From up the hill, trumpets sounded.

"The Naming," Mum wailed. "I'm missing the Naming!"

"It doesn't matter," said Max firmly.

"But it does," she sobbed. "They're my nieces! I carried 'em on me back and it's their Naming day!"

Cymbals crashed in the distance.

"Bel's named the first!" Mum cried. "It'll be Seven—she's the runt. Help me up!"

Max heaved the compact but improbably dense hag to her

feet. Wiping her nose, she clung to Max's arm as they trudged their way back up the hill.

Cheers and applause followed more cymbal crashes.

"Just two left," wheezed Mum, waddling faster. "I have to see Five get named. She'll be running the Hovel someday. Come on!"

Grunting and cursing, Mum forged ahead through the drizzle. As they climbed, Max heard Bellagrog's powerful voice carry on the chilly breeze.

"In another litter, Number Four mighta been top hag. Strong as an ox, a whiz at soaps, and she's got the deepest bite in the county. Just have a look at those choppers—show 'em, girlie!"

There was polite applause.

"But she ain't top hag and so she can't have a name longer n' six letters. That's Hag Law."

"Hag Law!" cried the many hags in attendance.

"Now," continued Bellagrog, "we already got Blip, Beet, and Boody. No more *B*s. I'm sick of 'em. Number Four's starting a new letter. And so, in honor of her choppers, I'm proud to present Clamp Shrope. Once she's got ya, she ain't lettin' go!"

Cymbals crashed. Mum collapsed into the wet grass.

"I can't," she gasped. "All their names are longer," she moaned. "Even Seven's. They're all longer than mine!"

"It doesn't matter," said Max. "You're Bea Shrope, the most valuable hag in the world. Students love you. Ogres quest for you. You are wanted on two continents. No other hag can claim these things."

"It isn't true. It isn't true! Keep going!"

Max strained his imaginative powers. "You are . . . a creative dresser. You inhabit a cupboard with grace and style. Your roasts are exceedingly tender."

The hag gripped his arm. "The secret's not to baste! It lets out all the heat!"

"I had no idea."

With a delighted squeal, Mum rolled onto her belly and pushed herself up. The pair reached the hilltop just as Number Five joined her sisters on the painted stage.

Five dwarfed the rest, outweighing Clamp by a good fifty pounds. The drizzle had flattened her hair into a dark, dripping mess, but there was no mistaking the wild, eager delight on her gray face as she surveyed the crowd. Bellagrog cleared her throat.

"Number Five. What's a gal to say? Every few generations, a hag comes along that raises the bar. She's tougher, meaner, and wilier than the rest. She sniffs out all yer traps and even lays a few of her own."

The crowd laughed, but Number Five looked oddly emotional. Even Bellagrog swiped an eye with a hankie.

"The Shropes are a proud lot," she said hoarsely. "I've worked hard to feather our nest and protect what's ours. Ain't always been easy. A gal worries it'll all go to pieces once she's gone. A gal wants to pass things down to one of her own—one who'll look after things with a firm and steady hand. Number Five's that hag. I love her. I hate her. I couldn't do without her. I give you Callastrophe Shrope!"

As the crowd applauded, there were several gasps and excited conversations. Mum counted rapidly on her fingers and gaped up at Max. "Bel gave her two more letters than what she's got herself!"

"Is that rare?" asked Max, draping a spare tablecloth over her.

"Never heard of it," said Mum. "One letter, yes, but not *two*!"

Bellagrog quieted the crowd.

"With great names come great expectations," she said. "Today, my haglings become hags and begin their coming-of-age quest." The hag gestured toward the drive and several large goblin wagons loaded with Shrope Soaps crates. "*No Named hag shall go unrescued or unavenged. Hag Law!*"

"HAG LAW!" thundered the crowd.

"That's right," said Bellagrog. "If my girls come back, they'll have Cousin Gertie in tow. Dead or alive, she'll be back where she belongs."

"Hear hear!" cried Gurgle.

"There's my girls," said Bellagrog. "Blip, Beet, Boody, Clamp, and Callastrophe. And to bless their names and this gathering, we got one more piece of business . . ."

"Queen o' the Mound! Queen o' the Mound!" chanted the hags.

"That's right!" crowed Bellagrog. "By tradition, Queen o' the Mound caps off a Naming. And we gots quite a mound to test whoever gives it a go!" She gestured toward the two-story mound of muddy dirt and rocks crowned by the many-ribboned maypole. "So, without further ado, let the contestants get ready!"

"What is this?" asked Max, spying several of the brawnier hags stripping down to long underwear.

"Queen o' the Mound," said Mum, as though it was self-evident. "Anyone who can hold on to the pole for five minutes gets the title and whatever she wants from the hostess."

"Does it get pretty rough?" asked Max, spying a contestant slipping a pair of brass knuckles over her stubby fingers. Other hags were ambling about, scratching their bellies and sizing up the other contestants.

"Beastly!" said Mum. "I never had the guts to enter one. There's all kinds of dirty play—biting, scratching, gouging, sawing."

Skirting the crowd, they made their way back to their table to find Hazel and Cooper sitting along with a pair of goblins that could only have been Pompy Frogmaw and Ozerk. But it was not the goblins that made Max gape.

It was Bob.

While the crowds cheered and jeered those hags that were positioning themselves around the mound, Bob sat on the barrel in a white undershirt and gray trousers, methodically folding the dress shirt he had removed. Bob was ancient and his skin hung loose on a lanky frame, but an elderly ten-foot ogre is still a ten-foot ogre. Even in his undershirt.

"Bob!" Mum hissed. "What are you doing?"

He pulled his suspenders back over his bony shoulders. "Playing game."

"But you can't!" said Mum. "It's called *Queen* o' the Mound!"

The ogre shrugged. "Game is for guests, no?"

"Yes," said Mum, considering. "Only hags ever enter but there isn't a rule that says others can't."

The ogre pulled one arm over his head to stretch. "Then Bob plays, too."

When nearby revelers realized what Bob intended to do, an excited buzz swept over the crowd.

"The ogre's gonna enter!" cried a ruddy-cheeked satyr.

This brought laughter and a fair number of jeers, for it seemed ogres were not terribly popular in these parts. As Bob made his way toward the mound, the crowds parted nervously.

"Boo!"

"A pox on ogres!"

"Go back where ye belong!"

"Spit and roast 'im! Boil and toast 'im!"

This last outcry was quickly taken up and repeated as a sort of cheer. Bob did not acknowledge it. He did not acknowledge the lutins that aped his plodding gait or the bits of tomato, pies, and cheese that now pelted him. The ogre simply walked on, the crowd closing behind him as he marched toward a scowling Bellagrog.

"Whatchoo doin', you dumb brute?" she demanded. "Put your shirt back on! We ain't boghags!"

Bob rolled his neck in slow circles. "After game."

"Queen o' the Mound ain't for ogres!" declared Bellagrog.

He continued plodding toward her. "It is for guests," he rumbled. "Bob is guest. You said so in front of these three." He gestured toward a stupefied Smidge, Specs, and Gurgle.

"Ya did say it, Bel," said Smidge. "And any guest at a Naming can play Queen o' the Mound. It's Hag Law."

"HAG LAW!"

This was shouted—with gleeful enthusiasm—by nearly every hag in attendance. The only exceptions were Bellagrog, her daughters, and fifteen mortified contestants.

When Bob reached the mound and took his spot around its perimeter, Max saw that the contestants on either side barely reached his waist. Lean as he was, the ogre outweighed any three hags together. One of them (Tortugla, according to a breathless Mum) backed away from the mound and shimmied back into her party frock.

"Boo!" jeered Bellagrog. "For shame, Torty! That's disgraceful!"

"You take my spot!"

But Bellagrog did not appear to have any intention of doing so. Instead, she narrowed her eyes at Bob. "Any hag what draws blood on this ogre gets a gold sovereign. Any hag what knocks him cold gets ten gold sovereigns."

"What if we kill 'im dead?" asked a one-eyed contestant, not even bothering to hide the hammer in her fist. "What's that worth?"

"No deaths," said the hostess firmly. "It's bad luck at a Naming."

"I can't watch!" hissed Mum, clamping a hand over her eyes and squeezing Max with the other. "Tell me what happens!"

"On your marks!" bellowed Bellagrog as the contestants eyed the maypole. "Get set . . . Go!"

Instantly, Bob seized the hags on either side of him by the ankle, whipping them off their feet as if they'd stepped onto snares. Even as the others tried to gang up on him, he swung the two hags like wriggling, flailing bludgeons. In an ogre's powerful hands, they made marvelous weapons. Bob even settled into a kind of rhythm, swinging one and then the other like overstuffed laundry bags that knocked his attackers aside like tenpins.

"What's happening?" hissed Mum, hopping from foot to foot. "Tell me what's happening!"

Max tried his best to relay the action, but things were happening very quickly.

"Bob's got two hags by the ankles and he's swinging them . . . Ooh! A hit! Two are down . . . one's getting back up. Another hit! There goes a tooth. No, I think that was an earring."

"What kind?" asked Mum.

"I don't know. Pearl?"

"That's Teelu," squealed Mum. "She loves pearls!"

"Three more hags are down," reported Max. "Bob's climbing the mound. Looks like one of his clubs is woozy. Oh! He faked left, dropped her, and got himself a new one. NICE WORK, BOB!"

"Where is he?" asked Mum anxiously. "Did he make it to the top?"

"Almost," said Max. "But some hags are clinging to him. One's biting his shin. Bob dropped his club and . . . Oh, what a throw! She's in the paddock."

"Which hag?"

"No clue. They're covered in mud."

"I hope it was Lolo," said Mum hopefully. "She acts so mighty and she's only got one more letter than I do! Now what's happening?"

"It's winding down," said Max. "He's just up there with his clubs catching his breath. The others won't climb up. Jeez, some are in bad shape. Bob plays rough. Now his clubs are begging to be let down. Oh. BOO! One tried to stab him after asking quarter."

"That'll be Hizzalu," said Mum. "She's always been stabby. She get him?"

"Nope. He tossed her in the paddock, too. Bob could throw the hammer . . ."

"He's fighting for me!" exclaimed Mum, jumping up and down. "My Bob is fighting for me!"

"And winning," said Max. "I think it's all over. No one's going to knock him off of there."

Removing her hand, Mum gazed up at Bob, who stood atop the mound, leaning against the maypole in the cold drizzle. His breath came in fogging gasps and he looked spent, but no hag was within fifteen feet of him. They lay sprawled in muddy heaps about the mound's base, coughing and sputtering, moving slowly as though a cyclone had just blown through the Naming.

The revelers counted down the minutes, clapping, laughing, hooting, and jeering. Max heard several insist this was the best Naming they'd ever attended—they'd be telling their grand-spawn about this. When time was up, the party roared "Queen o' the Mound!" and bowed to Bob.

The ogre returned the bow before descending the mound. His attention was fixed on Bellagrog.

"Queen o' the Mound will claim his prize."

"You ain't gettin' nothing!" snapped Bellagrog.

Bob wagged a finger. "It is Hag Law."

"HAG LAW!" cried the crowd.

Bellagrog spun about, taking stock of her grinning, delighted relations. Her eyes darted here and there, searching for an out, an escape from this highly public trap. With a murderous look, she gave a bloodcurdling howl.

"You want my sister, Bob?" Bellagrog cried. "Take her! TAKE HER! She's a worthless runt. Three letters to her name and it's three too many! She deserves to live with a toothless oaf!"

Mum was clutching Max's hand so tightly it had turned purple. Bob didn't acknowledge the insults. He merely climbed down the mound and took Mum's hand from Max. As Bellagrog witnessed this, the finality of what was occurring seemed to register. Her rage seemed to burn away in the cold drizzle, replaced by a blank, melancholy stare.

"Is this what you want, Bea?" she croaked. "My girls is all heading off. You leaving me, too?"

Mum was crying. Releasing Bob's hand, she waddled toward her sister and the two sobbed against one another while the stunned crowd looked on. At length, Bellagrog peered into Mum's face.

"Is this really what you want?"

Mum gave a teary nod. "Rowan's my home. I miss my cupboard."

"But . . . what if I never see you again?" whimpered Bellagrog.

Mum wiped away her sister's tears. "If I'm a free hag, that means I'm free to visit."

Bellagrog blinked as though consensual visits were an unfamiliar concept. "I . . . I guess that's true. Would you do that? Would you visit us?"

"If you're nice."

"What if I can't be?"

"It'll be a short visit."

Bellagrog nodded and slung a muscled arm around her sister. Clearing her throat, her voice reassumed its gruff authority. "I, Bellagrog Shrope, declare Bob the Ogre Queen o' the Mound and hereby renounce all claims on Bea Shrope. My sis is free to do what she likes, even if it means livin' in a stinky cupboard with a stupid ogre. A hag keeps her word. Hag Law."

"Hag Law!" cried the partygoers.

"Aye," said Bellagrog, cocking a suspicious eye at Bob as he walked toward her with his moneybox. He pressed the heavy box into her hand.

"To hire new beekeeper," he said.

Bellagrog was stunned. "I . . . I can keep the money anyway?"

The ogre nodded.

"Your sister is most valuable hag in the world."

Mum nearly swooned before burrowing into Bob, mud and all. He patted her topknot, but his attention remained on Bellagrog.

"Our business is concluded?"

"Aye," Bellagrog grumbled. "But you had this planned and don't pretend you didn't! You knew about Naming Days. You knew about Queen o' the Mound."

The ogre spread his hands. "Dryads gossip, no?"

Bellagrog glared up at him. "When did cooks get so stinkin' clever?"

A gnarled hand came to rest on her shoulder. "Before Bob was cook, Bob was ogre."

"Hooray!" exclaimed a pompous baritone. "Top-notch! Shall we get back to feasting? Strike up the band! Pass the brandy!"

Every head turned and stared at the speaker, a tartan-wimpled hag whose toothy grin began to waver. Bellagrog narrowed her eyes.

"Who is you?" she demanded. "I don't recognize ya."

"Er, I'm Bulbossa," replied the speaker, her voice resuming a haglike pitch. "Your cousin from the Orkneys."

"There ain't no Shropes in the Orkneys."

"We're MacShrupes."

"You ain't no hag," growled Bellagrog. "You're that bloody smee."

"A smee?" croaked Toby's neighbor, pinching his arm.

"A SMEE!" cried a dozen eager hags.

They converged like piranhas, tossing fauns and lutins aside in their eagerness to tackle the shape-changing delicacy. With a shriek, Toby bolted for the Hovel, holding up his petticoats until he regained his senses and changed shape. In a blink, Bulbossa disappeared and a tawny barn owl soared over the Hovel's roof, hooting and screeching.

"Give it up, ye silly things," roared Bellagrog, collaring a drooling aunt. "You'll never catch 'im. And he's right! It's time we got back to celebrating. *Full kegs make a dull party.* Hag Law!"

"HAG LAW!" cried the rest.

A fiddle struck up "Bless My Bonny Haglings" and the party resumed with a whoop and a clash of tankards. Bellagrog's daughters were hoisted off their feet and passed about their older relations, who tossed them high and clapped their hands before catching them at last. Shaking Bob's hand, Max struggled to find the right words.

"You are . . . quite an ogre."

Bob inclined his craggy head. "It has been good day."

"The best day!" exclaimed Mum. "I'm free! When do we set sail? When do we return to Rowan?"

"Someday," said Bob. "But Rowan's army sails for Blys. Armies need cooks. We go there, Mum. Ms. Richter needs us."

"She needs *me*," insisted Mum. "She misses my coffee and cakes and little ways. My cupboard can wait. To the front!"

"Oi!" said Bellagrog, bellying in. "Who's going to the front?"

"I am!" Mum declared patriotically.

"Well," growled Bellagrog, "you're a free hag, Bea. You can do whatcha like. But you're still a Shrope."

"What's that supposed to mean?" snapped Mum. "Of course I am!"

"Armies need vittles," observed Bellagrog coolly. "*Canned* vittles if ya catches my drift . . ."

Mum blinked. "I could bring our samples," she breathed. "I'll show 'em to Richter myself. The Director's putty in my hands!"

Bellagrog looped an arm about Mum's shoulder. "You're catching on fine. Let's talk this through, eh? With proper coaching, you could be a saleshag. . . ."

As the two hags wandered off, Scathach took Max's hand. "Did you have any idea what he was planning?" she asked.

"Not a clue."

"You're a deep old file, Bob," said Cooper. He clapped the ogre's back as he and Hazel joined the group. "Well played."

The ogre inclined his head.

"How was your meeting with the goblins?" asked Scathach.

"Profitable," said Hazel. "Ozerk certainly knows a good deal about the Workshop and their doings with Prusias."

"And?" pressed Max.

"Change of plans," said Cooper. "I need to head out. I can bring Hazel and the others with me but it would mean you and Scathach would have to seek the Fomorian on your own. Can you do that?"

Max glanced at Scathach. "Of course."

"Good," said Cooper. "That makes things easier. Meanwhile, I've got to get a message to Richter. The Spindlefinger said Prusias may have some new weapon in the works."

"More dreadnoughts?" said Max.

Hazel sipped her wine. "We don't know. It's hard to imagine he'd rely on dreadnoughts again, but who knows? It could be some variation."

Max nodded. "When are you heading out?"

"Tomorrow morning," replied Cooper. "The Spindlefingers have a cog waiting at the Channel. They'll smuggle us as far as Verilius."

A raucous cheer went up behind Max. He turned to see a flushed and muddy satyr shaking hands and doffing a tweed cap. The fellow was evidently popular, for others hurried over to greet him and press a mug into his grateful hands.

"Where ya been, Podge?" cried Smidge. "You missed the Naming!"

Drinking deep, the satyr wiped foam from his whiskers. "Sorry, love, but I had to wind about some. There's funny folk on the road. Dangerous folk. I'm lucky I made it here!"

A strange uneasiness came over Max. He tapped the satyr on the shoulder. "Who's on the road?"

The satyr turned, glanced up at Max, and nearly fainted. His ale spilled as he staggered back into several hags.

"Wh-whatchoo want?" he cried. "Why you following me?"

"Take it easy," said Max. "I've never seen you before in my life."

"Then who was that on the road, eh?" demanded the satyr.

The question was like a needle in Max's spine. He opened his mouth, but nothing came out. Cooper crouched to Podge's height.

"You saw someone like him on the road?" he asked.

The satyr could only squeak. Cooper snapped his fingers.

"Answer me. You saw someone like him? Someone like this boy?"

"No," Podge gasped. "Not like him. It *was* him."

Cooper looked grim. "How long ago?"

"I dunno," said the satyr. "Two hours. Maybe three."

"What is wrong, *malyenki*?" asked Bob.

"My clones are alive," said Max quietly. "They're alive and they're close."

Cooper shook his head, his eyes scanning the nearby tents and buildings. "They're not close. They're here."

~ 4 ~

DEVILS YOU KNOW

Cooper remained eerily calm. Taking a sip of ale, the Agent spoke in a casual, conversational tone. "Max and Scathach, get in the Hovel and fetch *Ormenheid*. Don't act like anything's amiss. I'll meet you by the basement stairs. Are you armed?"

"Always," said Scathach.

Cooper nodded. "Good. They might be in the Hovel."

Max's fingers twitched. Shock was swiftly giving way to anger. "I'm not running. I can end this right now. I want to."

The Agent set his mug on a waiter's tray. "You stay, this party might turn right ugly. Collateral damage, hostages, you name it."

Scathach tugged at Max's elbow. "Cooper's right. We have to draw them away."

The two wove through the revelers. Max tried to appear calm, but his hands were shaking. The Atropos had not merely marked him for death; they had hired his clones to do the deed. The last time Max had seen the pair, David Menlo had buried them beneath half a ruined castle. Apparently, it had not been enough.

Were they both here?

He couldn't be certain. Only one of the clones could be mistaken for Max's twin; the other looked barely human. As they neared the Hovel, he registered every face, every conversation, every shadow for any hint of their presence.

Stepping in front of Max, Scathach entered the Hovel first. A blade slipped from her sleeve into her hand as she took three swift steps into the kitchen, poked her head into the dining room, and scanned the downstairs hallway. Shutting the door behind them, Max followed her swiftly up the staircase.

In the attic, Nox was still dozing on Max's bedroll. She mewled irritably as Max plucked her up by the ruff.

"Not now," he muttered, setting her atop the clothes in his pack. The lymrill must have sensed their anxiety, for she lay flat without protest. From beneath her, Max fished the *Ormenheid*, an enchanted ship no bigger than a matchbox. Tossing it in his pack, he set to buckling a leather baldric from which hung a singular and terrifying weapon.

The *gae bolga*'s hilt was cool to the touch, but that didn't mean it didn't sense the tension, too. At the moment, the weapon was a short sword—a dark blade some eighteen inches long with whorls like Damascus steel. But it could also serve as a spear— Max's preferred weapon when he went into battle. The *gae bolga* didn't care which form it took so long as there was blood to spill.

The weapon was an extension of the Morrígan, a terrifying entity that prowled and feasted at the world's battlefields. Even Max was frightened of the weapon's power. The blade could cut, pierce, cleave, or slay anything—even gods.

The *gae bolga* had failed him only once. On that occasion, it had grown heavy and cold, as though reluctant to harm the enemies he'd been fighting.

Those very enemies were outside.

Or inside.

"Where's your armor?" asked Scathach, taking up her spear.

Max tapped his chest, where a corselet of nanomail was concealed beneath his clothes. He was rarely without it, or his enchanted ring that would burn whenever demons were near. Shouldering their packs, the two made their way downstairs.

Cooper and Hazel were waiting by the cellar door with Bellagrog.

"Hurry!" hissed the hag. Unlocking the cellar, she pressed the ring of keys into Max's hands. "Cooper says there's trouble and you needs a way out quick. We gots two. One pops you out a spell down the road. The other leads west, into the woods."

"West," said Max. "We want the river."

The hag pointed at a bronze barrel key. "That's the one. You'll need it this side and the other. Door's in the root cellar. Back wall behind the potatoes."

"How long's the tunnel?" asked Scathach.

"Quarter mile. Maybe more."

Max looked at Cooper. "What are you going to do?"

Before he even finished the question, the Agent's appearance rippled and changed into a mirror image of Max. Cooper was an unparalleled phantasmal—an expert at illusions. The false Max gave a wry smile. "I'm gonna give 'em a tour of the countryside."

"They have that magic compass," Max reminded him. "The

one you used to find me when I was in Prusias's dungeons. The needle always points toward me. They'll know they're following the wrong person."

Cooper disagreed. "Who uses a compass once they spot what they're looking for? With luck, you'll be far away when they finally figure it out. If there's trouble, we'll send up a flare. Godspeed."

Hazel embraced Max and Scathach. "Send a message to Richter once you're safely away. She'll get a message to us."

"Enough dawdling," huffed Bellagrog, urging Max and Scathach down the cellar steps. "You've brought me a heap o' headaches, Max McDaniels. But I always thought well of you. Your daddy, too."

Max kissed the hag's cold wet cheek. "Thank you, Bellagrog."

With a teary snort, the hag shooed him away. "Be off with ya. And if trouble comes, give it a kick from the Shropes!"

Down they went into the dark cellar, their boots scraping on the worn brick steps. Flicking his fingers, Max conjured a glowsphere that bobbed just ahead, illuminating stacked barrels and cheeses, cured meats, and jam jars. In the back was a small room piled high with carrots, beets, and potatoes.

Max shoveled the potatoes behind him, revealing a square iron door set into the thick stone. Using Bellagrog's key, Max pulled the door open and peered after the glowsphere as it drifted down the tunnel. "It's going to be tight."

The two crawled swiftly, shuffling ahead on knees and elbows. In some places they could crouch; in others they had to squeeze past tree roots that had broken through the surrounding brick. Max's face was slick with sweat. Within his pack, Nox mewled.

"Almost there," he grunted.

They wound left for some ways before the glowsphere revealed a straightaway. Here, the tunnel widened and began to slope upward. Max could see chests and barrels—emergency supplies—stacked on either end of another iron door. He hurried toward it.

"Wait," hissed Scathach as Max fit the key into the lock. "If they didn't follow Cooper, they could be outside. Let me go first."

Shaking his head, Max drew the *gae bolga*. It hummed as it left the scabbard, its handle warm as blood. Unlocking the door, Max pushed. The ancient hinges groaned as they gave way, spilling pebbles and mud into the tunnel.

Gripping the blade, Max stepped out from a hillside into a dark glade. The woods were almost silent. This was odd. While they'd gone some distance, the party at Shrope Hovel had been in full swing. Surely they should hear some distant music or laughter. But they did not. The festivities at Shrope Hovel had evidently stopped.

The air was clear and shockingly cold. Drizzle had given way to tiny snowflakes that twirled and floated like ash from a forest fire. Indeed, the sky looked as though a great fire were raging somewhere far off. The sun should have set long ago, but the night remained a dull, lifeless red.

Emerging from the tunnel, Scathach took one glance at the sky and made a sign against evil. "The Devil walks abroad."

Max locked the tunnel door. "Devils we know. Come on. The river shouldn't be far."

The sky's unusual, furnace-like glow was unsettling but it also lit their path. The pair ran, swift as deer, through the woods. Their footfalls made no sound; no birds cried out at their passing. They were two shadows racing against the wind.

They'd run almost fifteen minutes when Max saw the river. It was half a mile ahead, a glittering snake winding through the dark hills. Behind them, a bloodcurdling howl tore through the woods.

Max turned to see a fountain of screaming red flares rise above the forest canopy. At this distance, they looked like celebratory fireworks. But they were not.

"That's Cooper," Max panted. "They're coming."

Scathach tugged his arm and the pair kept running. Down the wooded slope they went, leaping over bushes and rocks that funneled them down to the last open stretch of country before they reached the woods that lined the river.

Nox yelped as Max took the final leap over the misty riverbank. He landed with a splash in the shallows, surefooted on the stones and silt. The river was not the biggest *Ormenheid* had sailed, but it would do—the longboat had a shallow draft and could skim along in just a few feet of water. Max tossed the tiny ship out onto the river.

"*Skīna, Ormenheid.*"

The magic ship did not drift with the lazy current but remained precisely where Max had thrown it. Like a tiny serpent, *Ormenheid* wriggled and flailed, lengthening and growing at a prodigious rate. Rising proudly from the water, the ship's hull stretched sixty feet from its tapered tail to its dragon-headed prow. Max and Scathach waded out to it, slipping between the oars extending from its sides.

Tossing his pack aboard, Max pulled himself over the side even as the sail was unfurling from the ship's single mast. Scathach was already on deck, a gray silhouette among the mists rising from the warm river into the wintry air.

As Max set Nox upon the deck, a tiny golden light zoomed from the woods. Looping around his head, the zephyss hovered by Max's ear like a bothersome mosquito. A voice was coming from it—Hazel's breathless, panicked voice.

"*Run, Max. They have some weapon just for you. We'll try to hold them off, but you have to run!*"

As Max went to draw the *gae bolga*, Scathach seized his wrist. "No," she pleaded. "Listen to her."

"I'm not going to let them die trying to save me."

"The Atropos don't want them," Scathach hissed. "They want *you*!"

Max seethed. *"Leita Ellan Vannin,"* he snarled, setting the ship's course for the Isle of Man. As the ship eased forward, Scathach released his wrist.

"Rowan's needs come before your pride."

He nodded, but glared at the shrouded shore and the hunched, twisting willows that lined its muddy bank.

Cries shattered the silence as birds took sudden flight from the trees, flapping and cawing into the night. Something was tearing through the woods, snapping branches as it neared the river.

One of the Workshop clones emerged, dark and huge. One hand gripped a saw-bladed spear; the other held a small compass. Gazing up from its needle, the clone's eyes fell first upon the *Ormenheid* and then upon Max. He trotted along the riverbank, keeping pace as the ship gained speed.

"Was that your friend back there?" he called. "He was good! Not a whimper when Omega caught him."

Max said nothing. A grin spread across the clone's handsome features. He beckoned. "Come ashore, brother. I won't make you suffer. I'll even console the girl—"

A blur slammed into the clone's back, knocking him off the bank. He fell into the river, entangled with something ferocious. Cooper's pale, bloodied face emerged from the water. The Agent's body was wrapped tightly about the clone, one arm clamped about the assassin's throat while the other strained to drive his kris home.

But the clone recovered. Seizing Cooper's wrist, he held the

Agent's blade at bay. Cooper gasped and strained with effort, but his opponent was much too strong. There was a hideous *crack* as Cooper's wrist snapped. Instantly, the clone seized Cooper's other arm and flipped the smaller man over his shoulder. The pair toppled, their struggles churning the water to red foam.

"Max!" Scathach shouted.

He turned just in time to see another dark figure burst from the forest and leap from the riverbank some fifty yards away. It landed near *Ormenheid*'s prow in a tangle of black hair and skeletal limbs only to pop onto its feet more nimbly than a cat.

The assassin bounded toward Max on twos and fours like an animal. Its eyes were dead black pools, its lips bared in a broken, jagged smile.

Scathach intercepted him, her spear slashing across the assassin's face even as her form faded to smoke and shadow. With a snarl, the clone parried the attack with one long knife and spun about in an attempt to bury the other in her back. But Scathach was quicker, slipping inside his reach to sweep his legs out from under him.

Instantly, the clone was back on its feet, its blades twirling and slashing as it sought to break Scathach's defense. But in this game, it was overmatched. Again and again, she parried or redirected his blows, driving the clone back in a furious counterattack.

Her spear struck home with a clap of thunder. The clone slammed against the masthead, clutching its ribs and the broken remnants of a knife. With a howl, it sprang onto the mast, climbing with spiderlike ease.

"He's mine," said Scathach. "Help Cooper."

Max had already leaped over the gunwale.

He ran swiftly on the river's surface, a feat Scathach had taught him in the Sidh. Once again, the *gae bolga* seemed reluctant to battle the clones. The blade weighed heavy and cold in his hand, an unwieldy length of dead metal. But willing or not, its edge was still sharp.

Somehow, Cooper had broken free of the clone's grasp. A dome now surrounded the Agent, a shield of swirling, rushing water that turned aside the clone's spear as he slashed and hammered against it. Cursing with rage, the clone forced his hand through the churning barrier and grasped at the hazy figure within.

Checkmate, thought Max.

Cooper popped up behind the clone even as it realized the hazy figure was an illusion. In a blur, the Agent drove his kris's point toward the assassin's throat.

The clone moved so fast it seemed that time skipped a beat. Cooper's blade never struck home. Catching his opponent's other wrist, the clone snapped it like a dry twig. With a howl, he seized the Agent by the throat and lifted him off his feet.

The water shield disappeared, sinking back into the river as Cooper's body went limp. The clone was throttling him like a terrier might shake a rat. Max would never reach him in time.

"NO!"

As the cry sounded, invisible hands yanked Cooper out of the assassin's grasp. The cry had not come from Max, but from Hazel.

The teacher stood on the riverbank, muddied and sobbing with rage. Behind her, whole trees were uprooting, their trunks twisting and cracking as they surged up and out of the soil. As her husband's body floated toward the bank, her face twisted in a scream.

"Ignis!"

The writhing willows erupted in bright flames. Descending the riverbank, they strode into the river, marching toward her husband's assailant like a platoon of massive infantry.

The clone barely saw Max coming.

Only his reactions saved him. The clone turned at the last instant, his spear redirecting Max's blow just enough to save his head. Even so, the *gae bolga* sliced clean through its shaft to cleave the face behind it.

The clone had not even gasped before Max struck him again with the *gae bolga*'s pommel. The impact shattered the clone's nose and sent him reeling backward. Seizing his breastplate, Max held him up and swiftly reversed his weapon for the kill.

But the *gae bolga* refused.

Time and again, its point shied from the clone as though a magnetic repulsion existed between them. Its intended victim laughed, his voice thick with blood.

"It knows its own!"

The clone's hand clamped upon Max's throat like a vise. As he squeezed, there was an explosion of pain followed by numbness. For a moment, Max merely blinked at the river's surface. The water was trembling, dancing with firelight as the trees drew closer. Squeezing harder, the assassin forced his head up so that Max had no choice but to stare into that bloody, leering face. The clone leaned close.

"Atropos a–kultir veytahlyss!"

Atropos cuts your life's thread.

A frantic rage overcame Max. Grabbing the clone's hand, he pried it off his throat and forced it back. The two were at a stalemate, locked in a furious struggle as each sought to overpower the other. Meanwhile the earth was shaking. The trees were almost upon them, hissing and crackling as their burning limbs stretched forth.

Blood was pounding in Max's ears. He knew the trees were close. He knew they might crush him as well as the clone. But he couldn't let go. The clone was weakening—he could feel it. He had to finish.

Something cut through the drumming in his ears. A shout—a scream! *Hazel? Who?*

"MAX!"

The voice was Scathach's.

He turned just as the other clone slammed into him. The impact knocked Max off his feet. River water choked his lungs as the second clone wrapped himself about Max like an octopus. Its teeth sank into Max's neck, worrying the flesh like a rabid animal while a hand yanked up Max's corselet. Twisting away, Max regained his footing and broke the water's surface just in time to glimpse the knife.

It wasn't iron or steel, but a wedge of chipped and sharpened stone. Something ancient. Something evil.

When the blade pierced his side, the universe seemed to shatter.

~ 5 ~

THE BOY WHO
CAME TO RODRUBÂN

Ormenheid sailed west. Its oars skimmed little rivers until they merged with wider waters that would lead it to the sea. Scathach sat near the mast, huddled in a storm cloak on the icy deck.

Beside her, Max lay bound and restrained within a cocoon of blankets. Nox lay beside him, her coppery eyes trained upon her steward. Now and again, she'd mewl and nuzzle his pale face, anxious for a response that did not come.

Scathach was grateful Max was sleeping. She was grateful

he still existed. She would never forget what had happened a few hours ago. It was seared into her memory.

When the clone tumbled over *Ormenheid*'s side, Scathach thought she had finished him. Valuable seconds had passed until she spied a ripple beneath the water, a ripple streaking toward Max. She had shouted—screamed!—but Max had been battling the other clone. Only at the last second did he seem to hear her. And by then it was too late.

The instant the assassin struck, there had been an explosion—an eruption of light and heat and sound. The river had boiled. Hazel's trees had disintegrated. The *Ormenheid* had been hundreds of yards away, but even it nearly capsized from the shock wave. Only Max remained in its wake, his body floating in the hissing water, his hand still clutching the *gae bolga*.

There had been no sign of Hazel or Cooper, or even the clones. Turning *Ormenheid* around, Scathach went to retrieve her love, almost numb with guilt and grief. Max was not moving. The wound at his neck was relatively minor, but the gash across his stomach was like a jagged smile gushing blood like a spring. She nearly despaired until she saw Lugh's brooch.

It was clasped to his baldric, a disk of carven ivory that looked red in the bloody, steaming water. If the brooch remained, so did Max's spirit. Her love was still alive, still present in this world.

He had screamed when she pulled him into the boat. Screamed as though every nerve was afire. He did not seem to see or know her. Blinded with pain, he scratched and scrabbled at his stomach like a wild animal. He had only made his injury worse, tearing the wound as though he hoped to dig it out, to expel its very presence.

"Morkün i-tolvatha!"

Die and be damned. The words came from the western shore,

faint and distant. But there was no mistaking the note of triumph in that voice. At least one of the assassins had survived.

When Max heard the words, he went berserk. He fought Scathach in an effort to rise and pursue the speaker. She had to restrain him, bind him with one of Rowan's passive fetters so she could tend to his wound. With a single, convulsive gasp, he'd lost consciousness.

She had stitched the wound as he slept. The cut was ugly, but not particularly deep—no vitals had been pierced. But it would not stop bleeding. Time and again she staunched the wound only to see red rivulets creep out from between the stitches and dribble down his side. Max was deathly pale, his body burning up with fever.

Scathach boiled water. Into it, she sprinkled dried leaves and herbs—agrimony and adder's tongue, figwort and foxgrove—that swirled together, sending up trickles of steam that brought the lymrill sniffing at the kettle.

The Sidh maiden was not a witch or a healer, but she knew some of the old rhymes and riddles that the wise chanted when wounds were grave and time was scarce. These she spoke, along with other, more personal pleas, to any old gods or spirits that might be listening.

Boiling down her brew, she separated its contents into a brackish tea and sticky paste. She tipped the former down Max's throat and smeared the latter on his injury before wrapping it with linen strips she'd torn from a shirt.

For the moment, she'd done what she could do. She was weary, but there would be no rest—not until she found the Fomorian. Even if Max were not in such a state, Scathach would have found it hard to sleep beneath such a sky.

Above, the heavens had turned a strange and violent crimson that seemed to aspirate with a dull pulse. The heavy clouds reminded her of dead cattle, their bodies swollen and bloated to the point of bursting. The sky looked poised to drown them in ash and fire, but it was only snow that floated down—crisp little flakes that eddied whimsically about before settling upon the ship and its occupants. Snow on Midsummer? Something had knocked the world off its moorings. Pursing her lips, she reached for another blanket and prayed the ship knew where it was going.

She gazed at Max. His face was no longer anguished, but blank and peaceful. In the firelight, he looked so young—as though years of toil had fallen away and he was once again the boy who came to Rodrubân. She would never forget that morning. It had changed her life forever . . .

When the youth appeared and demanded the right to cross Rodrubân's bridge, it was Scathach's job to judge if he was worthy. When the bridge nearly flung him into the abyss, she assumed he would turn back as so many had before him. When the boy had the audacity to try again, she cracked the span like a whip to cast the upstart down. But the youth had bounded clear and landed before the castle gates. When those gates were opened, when she beheld that face and Cúchulain's broken spear, she knew their fates were linked. And she had not been happy.

She'd barely glanced at Max as she led him from the courtyard through the ruddy glow of Hearth Hall, past the fountains of Summervyne until they came to Lugh's throne room. When she opened its golden doors to find the god actually present, she'd managed to hide her shock.

The audience had been brief. The High King appraised the boy, acknowledged him as his son, and dismissed him. His instructions to Scathach were simple.

"Break him."

Once they'd left the throne room, Scathach almost screamed. Long ago, when Lugh had granted her eternal life in the Sidh, he had taken

Scathach's shadow as a symbol of the mortal world she had left behind. Now he'd given her a new one in the form of a beardless boy to dog her steps and try her patience. She'd dreaded her task. For one, it had been ages since she'd had a pupil. For another, Scathach had not cared for the temperamental Cúchulain. This boy might have been his twin. And to crown all, the season was Yule, a time for hunting and feasting and merriment—not for babysitting a lad from overland and underland and all the lands between.

But she had no choice in the matter. Resigned to her fate, Scathach decided to test the boy's humility. A pupil who would not work, who bristled at orders, or demanded constant praise was a pupil who could not learn. The boy's possessions were taken from him. He was given rags for clothing, a stable for sleeping, and ordered to rise before dawn and complete whatever chores the shield maidens saw fit to assign.

On any given day, the boy might fetch water, muck filth, or hitch carts until the crickets sent him trudging back to his pallet. He never spoke, and it soon became something of a game among the shield maidens to see who could pry a word from their silent charge. Taking the form of a stable hand or townswoman, they might stop to inquire why a highborn should suffer such treatment. Was the youth not a noble prince? Where was his pride? Who could stomach such insults and call himself a warrior, much less a hero? The boy was a joke, a wayward fool, the laughingstock of all the Sidh. . . .

No matter the taunt or gibe, the boy would not look up or answer. And thus the weeks passed until late one evening when Scathach returned from a hunt to find all six of the shield maidens waiting in her quarters.

"I thought it was Ula's turn to report," she remarked, addressing a red-haired girl. But it was Ethlinn, the eldest, who rose and cleared her throat.

"The boy broke the standing stone."

Scathach stared. The standing stone was an ancient pinnacle of rock that jutted like a spire from a knoll beyond the eastern gardens. It was said Lugh himself had placed the stone to mark his lands when the Tuatha Dé Danaan had settled in the Sidh. It was a sacred landmark, the center of Lugh's kingdom.

"How did this come to be?" Scathach asked quietly.

"I meant no harm, my lady," blurted Ula. "I set him to building bonfires for Beltaine once he'd finished his other chores. Later, I returned to tease him as we've all done a hundred times before. He's never answered or even offered a glance, but when I called him 'the Bastard of Rodrubân' . . ."

"Yes?"

Glancing nervously at her comrades, the girl exhaled and shut her eyes.

"He struck the standing stone and broke it. With his hand."

"He chipped it, you mean."

"No, my lady. Broke it. When he struck the stone, it screamed like a banshee and cracked in two. The top tumbled down the hill and is lying in the gardens."

Scathach kept her composure. "Well," she concluded, "if he can break it, he can mend it. He'll begin tomorrow."

Early the following morning, she rose to personally supervise his labors. The dawn was wet and gray when the boy emerged from the stable sporting a grotesquely swollen hand. He offered no explanation or apologies, but merely followed her to the gardens where the broken slab was lying amid the flattened lilies. When told to restore it to its proper place, the boy left and returned with a team of horses.

Scathach tutted. "You would make others right your wrong?"

Holding the reins, the boy glowered for a moment before leading the horses back to their stable. Marching back, he crouched low and seized the stone from beneath. With a grunt, he began rocking the slab back and forth, straining to raise it upright. It rose slowly, wobbling and shaking until it towered over him. Squinting at the hilltop, he gave it a push so that it toppled forward. The ground shuddered beneath it. Once it settled, he crouched and repeated the onerous task of raising it.

As the sun rose and the day grew hot, the boy became a bruised and bloody mess. Dirt and sweat smeared his brow and flies swarmed in biting clouds, but he was still no closer to his goal. No matter how he attempted it, he could not flip or roll the stone more than halfway up the hill before it went crashing back down.

Scathach studied his reactions carefully. The boy never cursed or shouted, but merely watched, gasping and panting, whenever the stone tumbled back into the garden. And when the dust settled, he'd swat away the flies and stumble back down to seize the stone and try again. He was nothing if not tenacious.

On the third day, the shield maidens joined Scathach and together they watched the boy struggle and fail at his task. By the fifth day, crowds began to gather: some to cheer, others to jeer, and most to wager when the boy would collapse and the stone would have its vengeance.

By the ninth day, the battered boy was almost unrecognizable. At dawn, the crowds had already gathered, their chatter ceasing as the youth crouched to grapple with the bloodstained stone. With gritted teeth, he heaved it upright and the contest began anew. As the sun rose, the boy sputtered and stumbled, digging his heels time and again into the churned and trampled soil.

Some spectators had had their fill. As the day progressed, faces darkened and the muttering began. When the crowd finally cried out in protest, Scathach smiled.

"Do you want to kill him?"

"Plain murder is what it is!"

"For shame! A brave heart deserves better!"

Among her shield maidens, it was Ethlinn who finally confronted her captain. "I will not be party to this any longer. Cease this folly or let me help him!"

Scathach met her lieutenant's angry gaze. "When have I said you could not?"

Thrusting her spear in the ground, Ethlinn had hurried to the boy's side. Nes had followed, along with Ariana, Berrach, Eavan, and even Ula. Many townsfolk joined them, digging their fingers beneath the heavy stone.

Slowly but surely, they rolled the standing stone back to the hill's summit. Once it was restored, the crowd cheered and turned to congratulate the boy, who had slumped at its base. But it seemed his strength or his wits had deserted him, for he stared straight ahead as though his mind was elsewhere. Dismissing the crowd and her shield maidens, Scathach knelt by him.

"Look at me."

The boy glared up, his eyes brimming with defiance.

"You've earned better clothes and quarters," said Scathach.

"They carried the stone, not me. I failed."

Scathach shook her head. "No. You inspired others to help you complete a task you could not manage alone. And you've learned it's easier to break a thing than to mend it. You've the makings of a leader. Tomorrow, we'll see if you have the makings of a warrior."

The boy was already in the training yard, looking anxious and wary when Scathach and the shield maidens arrived the next morning. When told he was to spar with Ula, he had flatly refused.

"I don't fight girls."

Oh, how they had laughed! And when little Ula promptly disarmed him and spanked him with his own sword, they had positively howled! Purged of his misgivings, the furious boy snatched back his weapon and the yard soon rang with their efforts. Ula humbled him time and again, but it was evident to all that the youth possessed speed. Unfortunately, he did not possess any subtlety, footwork, or technique. He was painfully raw—almost every move a predictable, furious attack that left him vulnerable to innumerable counters. There was no patience or flow. No elegance.

But even Scathach had to admit there was vast potential. For one, their pupil was frightfully quick and strong. And there was no quit in him. If he could accept instruction, there was vast potential indeed.

As the weeks passed, it became clear that the boy possessed more than mere potential. By the new moon, Ula could no longer best him. Within two months, even Ethlinn had difficulty penetrating his defense or staving off the sudden, unpredictable counterattacks. The boy absorbed lessons like a sponge, mastering new feats and techniques with freakish intuition. More importantly, he exhibited a trait required of any champion—an almost manic refusal to lose. When pushed to his limits, he always responded, tapping deeper reservoirs of energy and will. And when he grew angry? Dear Lord! Not even Cúchulain possessed such a finishing strike. The boy was his father's son.

And he could no longer be called a boy. As spring became summer, he grew like barley in the fields. His bearing became that of a young man, a true champion of the Sidh. The shield maidens had certainly noticed and it came as no surprise when several requested Scathach's permission to bring him to one of the many feasts—not as a servant, but as her personal guest. Scathach sent each away disappointed.

"He is our pupil, nothing more."

But even she found herself looking for him during the Samhain celebration. He had not joined the feasting in Hearth Hall or sat listening to songs of the faerie folk in Summervyne. Curious, Scathach had at last climbed the many steps to his new lodgings.

The door was open. Peering within, she found him sitting at a small table and drumming his fingers while he studied several drawings. The drumming stopped.

"Have you come to test me?"

"No," she said. "I came to see why you were absent from the feast.

Ula and Berrach were concerned," she'd added, reddening at the lie. "What is that you're doing?"

"Nothing," he'd said, wiping charcoal from his hands. "Drawing."

"May I see?"

He'd shrugged and moved aside as she entered and came over to the table. The images flickered in the guttering candlelight: a bristly otter-like creature, a tall clock tower, a toothless ogre, and a man and woman sitting together before an evergreen strung with ornaments.

"I didn't know you were an artist, Max."

"I didn't know I had a name other than 'boy.'"

Scathach ignored the barb. "You've earned back your name," she replied. She gestured at the drawings. "Who are they?"

He did not respond at once, but seemed to be weighing whether it was wise—or even safe—to share anything about himself. It was odd how wounding his hesitation had been. Scathach found herself wanting him to trust her, even to like her. Such feelings were new and deeply unsettling.

At last, he relented. Sweeping his hand over the images, he explained that the creature was his lymrill, the clock a school land-mark, and the ogre a school chef.

"Aren't you afraid he'll eat the students?" asked Scathach.

"No. But we do worry about the hags."

Max had smiled as he said this, the very first since his arrival at Rodrubân. It appeared slowly, like the sun peeping out from behind a cloud. And, like the sun, its effect was transformative. It fairly com-pelled a smile in return. Grinning in spite of herself, Scathach cleared her throat and turned her attention back to the drawings.

"And who are these two?" she asked, pointing at the man and woman.

Max's smile faded. "My parents. Or at least I thought they were. I guess she's still my mother."

Scathach heard the edge in his voice. "Why are you angry with her?"

Max stared at the drawing. "She let me live a lie," he murmured. "She should have told me the truth—told me who my real father was. She never should have left. If she'd stayed, maybe none of this would have ever happened."

"You are the child of Lugh Lamfhada," Scathach reminded him. "It was never your lot to live a quiet life. You must become what you will be—a prince of the Sidh and a champion for the mortals of your birth world. From what I hear, champions are needed."

Taking the drawing, Scathach studied it closer by the candlelight. "Your parents have good faces, Max. Kind faces. Tell me about them, and your world. It's a place I left long ago . . ."

From that evening a friendship developed. Scathach found Max's account of modern life intriguing and enjoyed his newfound willingness to smile, laugh, and even share his sorrows or misgivings. She had never met anyone quite like him. He was so different from Cúchulain and other heroes she had trained. He was proud, of course, but not masterful or domineering. He learned quickly, worked hard, and was even polite to the servants—a fact that amazed Ula, who delighted in terrorizing them.

"Our pupil is having an effect on us," Ethlinn had remarked one day when she and Scathach returned from riding. She pointed to where Ula was loudly pardoning a stable boy for bringing the incorrect saddle.

"I suppose he is," said Scathach.

Ethlinn gave a sideways glance. "On some more than others."

Scathach tugged briskly on the reins. "What is that supposed to mean?"

The shield maiden bowed. "Forgive me, but my lady has never bothered to dine with a pupil or sit with one so long and late in Summervyne. There is talk."

"Your talk, doubtless."

"Aye," Ethlinn conceded. "And others. We all have eyes, Scathach. Our pupil is handsome and strong and the finest fighter we have trained. And he is a prince . . ."

"You forget yourself, Ethlinn."

"Haven't we all?"

Scathach had not replied, but dismounted and marched inside the castle gates and up to the battlements where Max was practicing with Ariana. The two were working on bruud gine—a technique for breaking an opponent's weapon. It was a tricky feat requiring exquisite anticipation, timing, and control. Success meant a disarmed foe; failure left one vulnerable and possibly injured from the attempt. Judging from the glinting shards that littered the battlement, Max was having success.

"Oh, how the smiths will curse him," laughed Ariana, fetching another sword from a stand. "Ten blades he has shattered in as many tries."

"Perhaps you're making it too easy," said Scathach.

She ordered a more challenging test by way of a private signal. Nodding, Ariana raised her sword and saluted to Max, who did likewise. Almost immediately, Ariana gave the champion's shout—the sian caurad—whose force buckled the boy's knees and cracked the stone merlons behind him. Leaping at her stunned adversary, Ariana swept her sword at Max's exposed neck in a vicious stroke called the táithbéim.

But he was too quick. Almost instantly, Max recovered from the sian caurad, spun beneath the táithbéim, and whirled about to bring his weapon down upon Ariana's outstretched sword. There was a discordant clang and her blade promptly broke into eight pieces. Dropping the useless hilt, the shield maiden turned to her captain as though to say, What did I tell you?

Max was looking far too pleased. Gazing past him, Scathach's attention fell upon two hawks circling one another above the distant hills. When one dove, the other followed, their screeches faint upon the wind. As Scathach watched them, Ethlinn's accusations echoed in her ears. Tearing her attention away from the hawks, Scathach strode to the weapons stand and chose a slender sword. Scuffing her boot to test the battlement's footing, she motioned Ariana aside.

Max's smile faded. Throughout his stay at Rodrubân, they had never faced one another. Scathach oversaw his training and demonstrated new techniques, but she left sparring and practice to the shield maidens. Until he could outduel them, there was little point in matching his skill with hers. But apparently, the time had come. Meeting his eyes, she raised her blade in a warrior's salute.

"When your blade shatters, be sure to yield."

Max had not replied. He simply touched his blade to his forehead and advanced.

The lesson lasted less than three seconds.

Scathach used the first exchange to gauge his speed—far swifter than even Ethlinn's. The second pass was to let him think he'd spotted a potential weakness. The third was a feint to gain position, the fourth a telegraphed repetition of the previous opening. Like a hungry trout, Max seized the bait and brought his sword whistling at the very spot where Scathach's blade should have been.

But it was not.

At the last possible instant, Scathach spun away, leaving Max's sword to spark harmlessly against the merlon. Before he could recover, her weapon flicked like a serpent's tongue to strike his blade two inches above its crossguard.

A true master of bruud gine relied on harmony rather than brute force. To an untrained observer, Scathach's attack might have resembled a playful tap rather than an exquisite combination of angle, speed, and placement. With almost casual grace, her blow shattered the sword as though it were made of glass. With a painful yelp, Max dropped the hilt and shook the sting from his hand.

"How did you—"

"Yield."

Max had almost laughed. "But my sword's in a thousand—"

Flicking her wrist, Scathach slashed him from chin to cheek. The wound was not deep, but a thin line of blood appeared and began to drip steadily upon the flagstones. Ariana gasped.

Max did not. He had not even flinched or recoiled, but simply stared at Scathach with a look of disbelief. By degrees, his expression hardened into a mask that betrayed no emotion, no glimpse of the Max whose company she had come to enjoy.

"I yield."

Nodding curtly, Scathach turned and tossed her sword to her shield maiden. "I think we have more to teach him, Ariana. If nothing else, he can learn to follow instructions. Come with me while he sweeps up this mess."

Ariana hurried after Scathach as she strode quickly from the battlements and down the broad steps to the central courtyard. When they were out of earshot, the girl spoke up.

"He's our lord's son! What have you done, Scathach?"

"Our lord's will."

"But to slash the prince's face!"

"He'll have worse shaving."

From that day forward, a gulf existed between Max and Scathach, as she knew it must. They no longer ate with one another or talked and laughed in Summervyne. Nevertheless, he remained her student and they trained together from dawn until dusk until he'd mastered every feat she knew. And when she found that she could no longer best him, Scathach sought an audience with Lugh.

The High King's hall had been empty that evening, its windows thrown open to the rain that drummed on its timbered roof. It was the grandest chamber in Rodrubân and on some occasions it seemed all of gold and flowered vines that twined like filigree. But tonight it was cold and dark, for no fires had been lit and its throne had seemed a tomb upon its dais, ancient and forgotten. Despite the empty throne, Scathach remained, for Lugh would know she was present and might appear if it pleased him to do so. His whims and whereabouts had always been fickle, but they were becoming even harder to predict. Years might pass between glimpses of the sun god. Some feared that he, like others among his kind, was growing weary of existence and preferred to sleep or wander in another form.

An enormous tapestry hung above the stone hearth, and Scathach raised her lantern to gaze at it. It depicted the Second Battle of Muigh Tureadh, the decisive contest between the gods and the giants. On that day, Lugh Lamfhada had led the Tuatha Dé Danaan to victory and slain Balor, his own grandfather who was king among the Fomorians. It was always easy to spot the sun god among the tapestry's embattled figures, for he was at its center and the threads radiating from his person seemed to shimmer. Even as she studied it, those threads grew brighter until she realized that the hall itself had filled with a golden light. A voice spoke.

"How does my son progress?"

She turned to find Lugh standing behind her, looking as strong and youthful as he had at Muigh Tureadh. But unlike his image in the tapestry, the god was not armed or dressed for battle. Instead, he wore robes of green linen and a silver belt and his countenance was gentle. Scathach kneeled.

"He progresses well. I have nothing left to teach him."

Lugh gazed thoughtfully at her. "Is he worthy of us, Scathach?"

"He is a true warrior, my lord. I have never taught finer."

"That was not my question."

She cleared her throat. "I believe he may become worthy. He is still young. Only time will reveal if he has strength and wisdom enough for what my lord wishes."

"You presume to know my wishes?"

"Of course not," said Scathach quickly. "Forgive me."

But Lugh looked amused rather than angry. "You were ever wise, Scathach. I do not doubt your guess. And seeing your sorrow, I do not doubt mine."

"My lord?"

"It is time you and the lad were parted," said Lugh, but not unkindly. "It is time for him to leave us and resume the errand that brought him to the Sidh. At dawn, others will come for him and you must say farewell. Give him this before he goes."

Handing her an ivory brooch, the god explained its purpose and sent her away.

Having gathered Max's things, Scathach climbed the many steps to his tower. The hour was late, but a light still shone beneath the door. She had not knocked, but simply stood and listened to the rain while trying to make sense of her emotions. There had been many and some were new opponents she had yet to master. She would not do so tonight, but she had to drive them back until her duties were fulfilled. Once the rain had stopped, she knocked and entered and said goodbye.

When Scathach's mind returned to the present, she found that Max was awake. His eyes were glassy slits, staring up through snow-dotted lashes.

"The sky," he croaked.

"Aye," she said, glancing up. "A crimson sky and snow in June. A sailor's delight."

A spasm of pain flickered on his face. His hands moved slowly beneath the blankets, searching for the wound. The passive fetter prevented him from reaching it.

"You were wounded," she explained. "With what, I don't know, but I had to restrain you. You must let it heal."

Max's voice was so hoarse and weak it nearly broke her heart. "It's not healing."

"Of course it is," she said sternly. "Watched pots never boil. Fussed wounds never heal. Leave it be."

He nodded. "What about Cooper?"

She'd been dreading the question. Now that it came, she gave a helpless shrug. "I don't know. There was an explosion. We must hope that they escaped it."

Max said nothing for some time while Scathach heated the remains of his tea. He grimaced as she coaxed it down his throat.

"Do you think it's snowing at Rowan?" he asked, staring up at the vast, alien sky.

Scathach wiped his chin. "I think it's snowing everywhere."

"Does it snow in the Sidh?" he wondered faintly. "I never saw any."

"Yes," she replied. "Even Lugh's reach does not extend everywhere and the Sidh has many kingdoms. It snows in the high places and when the Wild Hunt roams abroad. There is snow, yes, but never in summertime. These skies are evil. Would that Lugh were here to chase them away."

"Tell me about him."

His words were barely more than a whisper but their plaintive note was clear.

"You should rest," Scathach urged.

"No," said Max. "I know nothing about him apart from stories and legends. You know him. What he's like?"

She spread her hands in a helpless gesture. "Lugh is a god. You want me to describe him in human terms, but I don't know how. And I've spent little time in his presence."

"But you were his warden."

Scathach shook her head. "Even gods can grow weary and fade. Some of the Tuatha Dé Danaan have disappeared. Even those who remain are often asleep within their hills and palaces. Nuada Silverhand was slain; the Dagda has not stirred for an age. Goibhniu's forge is cold. Lugh is younger than they and very great, but he slumbers and dreams more often than he did. Only the Morrígan never sleeps. She is always moving, always hunting."

Max glanced at the *gae bolga* in its scabbard gilded with wolves and ravens. Scathach knew the Morrígan was a part of the weapon, that her essence was woven into its being. The goddess had always lusted after heroes—they were the sparks that kindled wars. Blood and death were her delight and she cared not whose. Scathach could never trust such an accursed blade. From Max's expression, it appeared he did not trust it either.

"Have you ever seen the Morrígan?" he asked quietly.

"No," said Scathach. "And I have no wish to. All the Sidh fear her."

"Does my father?"

"I don't think Lugh Lamfhada fears anything."

Max looked pained. "There must be something you can tell me. I know nothing about him."

Scathach watched snowflakes settle and melt on Nox's blue-black coat. She was no philosopher or poet. When the words finally came, they were halting and elusive.

"Lugh Lamfhada is noble and loving, a giver of life, savior of the fallen, a bringer of hope and harvests. And Lugh Lamfhada is proud and pitiless, a slayer of kin, the scorching sun that withers the farmer's crops. He is a summer storm upon the plain, beautiful and terrifying."

"A paradox."

"That's what gods are."

Max's ragged breath quickened. "Maybe he would help us," he gasped. "The Tuatha Dé Danaan aided our people before. Their magic built Rowan when Solas was destroyed. We're seeking the Fomorian when we should be seeking my father . . ."

"Never invite a god into this world."

"But—"

"*Never.*"

"Why?" demanded Max. "Lugh. The others. They could tip the balance. They could destroy Astaroth and Prusias and all the rest!"

Her patient was getting agitated. Taking a cloth, Scathach dipped it in a pail of cold water and pressed it to his burning forehead. Her voice was gentle, but firm.

"A god's nature is to shape and rule and master. Shall we defeat Astaroth only to see Lugh or the Dagda or—heavens forbid—the Morrígan take his place?"

When Max did not reply, Scathach leaned close.

"Do you know what happens when a god's at play in the mortal world?" she said softly.

"What?"

"Summer snow."

Max tried to smile, but could not. What little energy he had was spent. Closing his eyes, he breathed deep and gave a long, shuddering exhale. When his breathing steadied, Scathach kissed him and sang a song her mother had two thousand years ago.

The sky's red gloom smothered the dawn. The clouds had settled lower overnight and were now a sagging canopy that pressed down upon the world. A flock of puzzled geese went honking south, their calls fading like phantoms in the mist. *Ormenheid*'s oars plied on, the ship skimming upon seas as smooth as scuppered cream. Rising, Scathach saw that they'd left the land behind. There were no more riverbanks, no hints of land peeking from the horizon. The Isle of Man was somewhere ahead.

Max was still asleep. He'd grown paler throughout the night, and while Scathach didn't wish to wake him, his breathing worried her. It came in harsh, uneven gasps. Periodically, his body seized up, as though every nerve had been jolted.

Removing Nox from her resting place beneath his chin, she peeled back the outer blankets to examine his dressings.

What she found shocked her.

The inner blankets and bindings were drenched with blood. It had spread over his midsection and run upon the deck, cooling to a sticky pool in the cold. Unsheathing her dagger, Scathach quickly cut away the dressings to reveal the wound beneath.

The stitches and ointment were gone, as though they'd simply vanished or burned away. The exposed wound was still bleeding, its edges ugly and raw. Cursing, Scathach snatched up her needle and thread and set the kettle boiling.

Working quickly, she flushed the wound with hot water and a fresh mixture of herbs. Dabbing it dry, she passed her needle through his skin, sewing the wound tight as Max moaned in a fever dream. Before she could even finish the final stitch, the threads dissolved and blood began to seep and trickle through.

Her mind raced. The passive fetter was enchanted. Perhaps it would serve where common thread would not. Slicing the cord's end, Scathach unraveled several fine, silvery fibers. Threading her needle, she stitched the wound a third time, muttering a prayer with every pass. Once the gash was closed, she watched and waited.

The stitches held.

Nox started as she thumped the deck with joy. Crushing the last leaf of agrimony, she packed it over the wound and covered it with a clean piece of linen. The drowsy lymrill waddled over to settle in her lap.

From Max's pack, Scathach retrieved an iron ingot. Nox took it almost delicately, purring with satisfaction as the metal slid down her throat. Hugging the creature close, Scathach stroked the lustrous black quills of her ruff.

"The Fomorian will help," she whispered. "He's Max's kinsman and he's not far away. He'll save our Max."

Their Max did not awaken the rest of that day. He lay utterly still, his face cadaverous while the two held vigil. He'd lost no more blood, but his breathing was so shallow, Scathach could not keep her eyes off his brooch.

She heard the birds long before she saw the island.

The calls sounded over the ocean, thousands of cries and shrieks that sounded vaguely, horribly human as they carried out over the calm seas. Taking Nox, Scathach walked forward to *Ormenheid*'s prow where they saw gray seals rising and falling on the cold swells, staring curiously at the longship and its occupants.

A huge, ghostly shape emerged from the gloom. It was one of Prusias's war galleons, a gargantuan vessel that had been driven upon a jagged reef. What must have been a horrific collision had flipped the vessel on its side so that the foaming seas coursed like a river through its shattered hull. Perched upon its splintered masts were hundreds of skuas and gulls that silently watched the *Ormenheid* slip past.

As they neared the island, they encountered more shipwrecked vessels: carracks and cogs, clippers and lorchas scattered across the isle's coastline. Some, like the galleon, had apparently run aground while others were no more than charred hulks burned down to the waterline.

The spectacle grew more grisly as *Ormenheid* entered a cove where it could land. Piled corpses lined the beach like sandbags, the remains of vyes and ogres, ettins and demons. Birds and crabs had already stripped most of the edible flesh so that much of what remained was just armor and bone, hair and sinew.

Did the Fomorian do all this?

She'd hardly formed the question in her mind when her gaze drifted to a pillar that had been driven into the pebbled sand like a barrow marker. Five demons were nailed to the stone's summit, their grotesque bodies untouched by the birds and left twisting twenty feet above the beach. Each wore Prusias's colors and marks of rank upon their breastplates. They also wore expressions of fixed, almost frenzied terror. Beneath their feet, ancient Ogham runes had been chiseled deep into the pillar's pale stone.

They are gone. I remain.

Frightened as she was, there was no time to lose. As *Ormenheid* slid up onto the beach, Scathach gathered what would be needed. Laying Max upon the cold wet sand, she grabbed their packs and shrank *Ormenheid* down to its miniature size.

Scavenging limbs from fallen trees, Scathach made a hasty travois to transport Max. As she lashed the poles together, she tried to recall everything Max had shared about his previous dealings with the Fomorian. The warnings had been straightforward and severe: *Do not stare. Do not run. Do not lie.* Checking Max's dressings, she strapped him to the travois and dragged him up the sandy dunes.

She walked for hours, scaling hills and windswept ridges that peered down at the broad valleys. The landscape's colors were muted, summer flowers shriveled and gray from winter's ambush. There were few birds and almost no tracks in the snow. The only sounds were the scuff of her boots and the crash of distant surf. Despite the appalling massacre at the beach, the isle felt lonely and abandoned.

Again at nightfall, the sky retained its grim red cast. Scathach trudged on, late into the evening, until they reached a series of ancient hills dotted with weathered cairns. Weary and frustrated, she set down their packs.

"HELLO!" she shouted into the twilight.

Nothing answered but the wind. While Nox prowled about for prey, Scathach made camp and gathered enough material for a bonfire. Once lit, the bracken hissed and sputtered, sending smoke billowing up into the night.

"That's it," said Scathach, snapping a dead sapling and tossing it on the pile. "We want you seen for miles. You're going to catch us a Giant."

From out in the darkness there came a hiss, the sound of animals fighting, and a high-pitched squeal. Moments later, Nox waddled into the firelight, dragging a weasel in her powerful jaws. Settling down by Max, the lymrill set upon her supper. Scathach's stomach growled.

She'd eaten nothing since the Naming feast. Rummaging in her pack, she found a small wedge of cheese and half a sausage wrapped in waxed paper. Leaning back against their gear, she ate her supper and shook off sleep to keep the fire blazing. Wintry gales came screaming through the cairns as they nestled in the hilltop's lee.

As the hours passed, Scathach found herself listening to the trees, to the rhythmic, brittle clicking of their branches. They seemed to be calling to her, murmuring a song, as the comforting smells of turf and wood smoke lulled her mind down into a pleasant haze. She could almost hear the words, their sounds and syllables echoing softly in her ears.

> *Idle on the hill*
> *Rest upon a heath*
> *Lie upon a summit*
> *Its stones an ancient wreath*

Barley in the field
Honey in the comb
All is warmth and comfort
All is hearth and home
Lay down thy weary head
Let others lift thy load
Resume another day
Thy journey on the Road

You're dozing off, she thought irritably. *Stamp out the drowse.* But before she could rise, she relaxed. Sleep had been scarce and there might be none tomorrow. Max seemed at rest and the night was so peaceful. Gazing out at the landscape, she now saw hundreds of tiny lights winking in the gloaming like little blue and green fireflies. They were dancing, weaving through the air like little fishes swimming in a lagoon. And as they approached, the wind and the trees began their song anew. The words lapped at her soul and soon Scathach found herself wishing she might sprout roots and brambles and cling to this charming hillside forever.

At last, one of the soft blue lights settled on her knee. Blinking sleepily at its radiance, she glimpsed a tiny figure at its center. Scathach tried to speak but could offer only the faintest smile before her head bowed low. She barely felt the bindings as they twined about her wrists and ankles. When Scathach tried to move, she found she could not. But what did it matter so long as the singing continued? With a sigh, she lay back and let her eyelids flutter shut.

~ 6 ~

MYSTERIOUS MR. MENLO

Far to the south, David Menlo was lying languidly in a hammock slung aboard a war galleon, the flagship of Rowan's fleet. The ship had once belonged to Prusias but was captured during the demon's siege. Now it sailed toward Blys to wage war upon its former owner.

It was an enormous vessel whose size and opulence afforded luxuries that were not commonly found upon a man-of-war. Every officer had their own cabin and David's was a gleaming space of teak and brass with three round windows framing sky and sea. He enjoyed the view and the warmth radiating from a pot-bellied stove, but his chief delight was a small cooler stowed within a bench beneath the windows. This housed his coffee beans, a jug of milk, two mild cheeses, and a loaf of bread. With such a wealth of provisions, he need not leave his cabin for another day or two. That was treasure indeed, for what David wanted more than anything was a bit of privacy.

After all, he despised crowds and the warship was teeming with sailors, soldiers, passengers, and livestock. And it had never been David's choice or intention to accompany the main force to Blys. His original plan had been to remain at Rowan where he could continue Mina's instruction, assist the Archmage, and support the war effort from afar. But Ms. Richter had requested his presence aboard the flagship and she was the Director. While he had been known to flout orders with polite indifference, he was reluctant to do so during wartime. Not only would it undermine the Director's authority, but he also knew his presence would bolster the fleet's morale. There was the unpleasant fact that his skills might be needed. As someone who had sunk many ships, he knew just how vulnerable they could be.

The convoy comprised over three hundred vessels and one hundred thousand troops, not to mention siege equipment, supplies, and other necessities of war. It would never do to lose them. And while there were many skilled Mystics and aeromancers sprinkled through the fleet, there was only one David Menlo.

For all his formidable reputation, David was not an imposing figure. At first glance, strangers knew that Max McDaniels was *somebody*—his presence and physicality commanded instant attention. He was like a lion padding into a drawing room. But David required more careful study. At seventeen, he was barely five feet, skinnier than children half his age, and so pale that some assumed he'd wandered off from a hospital bed.

When strangers noticed his right hand—or, more precisely, its unsettling absence—their uneasiness multiplied. Where the hand should have been was only a stump of puckered skin that he often scratched, as though the wound itched or he needed to confirm his loss. Astaroth had taken it from David years earlier. Caressing David's hand, the Demon had spoken in a soothing voice before deciding to take it as punishment. With a sudden snap, Astaroth's smiling jaws had clamped upon his wrist. David recalled an appalling pressure, a searing pain, and then . . . nothing. His hand had been severed, devoured before he could even register what had happened.

David still had nightmares about the incident. He had nightmares about many things, but he never shared them with anyone. He was by nature a private person, but the war had intensified the trait to almost comic secrecy. He often kept his whereabouts unknown, communicated in unbreakable ciphers, and was apt to lie—ably and cheerfully—about any number of subjects. These might include social niceties (David didn't really care about others' new outfits or haircuts) but often extended to more important topics such as his family history and the true extent of his prodigious abilities. A superlative card player, David Menlo kept his cards hidden and an ace in reserve.

And while David liked to keep secrets, he *loved* to uncover them. This was hardly unusual among Mystics; a stubborn curiosity was necessary to studies of the arcane. But David's interest in secrets went well beyond scholarly diligence. It bordered on obsession. And his current obsession was not Prusias, or even Astaroth. It was Mina.

No one had spent more time with Mina since her arrival at Rowan. David designed her curriculum, supervised her lessons, and he—along with his mother and grandfather—served as the girl's de facto family. And yet, despite this intimacy, Mina was a puzzle that David had not been able to solve. She remained an utter mystery.

During their first meeting, he had hardly noticed her. She was merely one of many orphans living under Max's protection at a farmhouse in Blys. When David learned Prusias had imprisoned Max, he spirited the entire household to Rowan before the demon's servants could harm them. At first glance, he observed nothing unusual about her—she was just another frightened child hiding in a musty cellar.

David had smuggled the orphans to Rowan using one of his many tunnels—wormholes he'd created to connect his bedroom to various locations around the world. As teleportation often triggers a powerful nausea, most of the children became ill when they suddenly vanished from Blys only to reappear on a rumpled sleigh bed thousands of miles away. While David tried to calm the confused and sick, he had noticed that the youngest child—an unassuming dark-eyed wisp—was studying the bed itself.

Unlike her retching or wailing companions, the girl had not appeared sick or frightened. Instead, she looked *interested*—intrigued by the bed and the surrounding observatory. Touching her fingertips lightly to the headboard, she gazed up at the dome's twinkling constellations and gave a tiny, knowing smile.

She knows how to work the tunnel!

A second later, David dismissed the notion as absurd. There was no way the girl could have perceived the tunnel's opening, much less divined its password. But still . . . David knew that smile. He was often guilty of it himself. And just as he began to revisit the possibility, a very young and delighted whisper sounded in his head.

"Your magic is beautiful."

Two days passed before David had a chance to visit privately with her. His preparations for Walpurgisnacht were reaching their climax and he was intensely busy, but felt compelled to seek the child out. He'd already been expelled from Rowan for insubordination, but he still felt an attachment to the school. His own curiosity aside, Ms. Richter needed to know if there was a Potential—or something much more—among this little band of refugees. The girl was obviously sensitive to magic and skilled at veiling her own, but until that afternoon, David had no conception of her power and strangeness.

He had taken her for a walk in the Sanctuary along the edge of a wood that bordered a broad stretch of sand dunes. The two conversed telepathically, but David noticed that the girl continued to cloak her aura.

"What is your name?"

"Mina."

"That's a name you let others call you. What do you call yourself?" The girl merely curled her small hand around his.

"The patterns of your magic," she remarked. *"They are alive. They are original. You make them by seeing and feeling and knowing. You have much to teach me."*

David had stopped and gazed down at her, trying to decide if what he felt was elation or fear. No Mystic would have spoken like she had. Their language betrayed more rigid concepts, proven principles and formulae. This girl's grasp of magic seemed instinctive and artistic—almost like a sorcerer's. Until that afternoon, David had believed he was the only one. He decided to test her.

"Can you speak with animals?"

"If I like."

"Do they obey you?"

"If I wish."

"Show me."

"No."

"Why not?"

Mina had frowned. *"You didn't like it when Max and Connor said the Solas spell on these dunes. It made you angry."*

David abruptly released her hand. The incident had occurred during his first year at Rowan. Unless Max had told her the story, there was no way she could have known such a thing.

"Can you read my mind?"

"Not unless I'm touching you."

"Never do that again."

"I'm sorry. I couldn't resist learning what you are."

"And have you?"

She nodded. *"Your heritage is very—"*

"Secret!" snapped David. *"No one must know."*

"I'll tell no one," she promised. *"Did they know what you were in the Sidh?"*

Again, David tried to hide his shock. It was clear that Mina's glimpse of his line went farther than Elias Bram. The thought of another person—another sorcerer!—being privy to such knowledge made him feel profoundly vulnerable. He had experienced an unsettling impulse to destroy the girl on the spot. Thankfully, the feeling passed and he merely shook his head.

"I was a stranger there and I met none with your gift. Do you know what Max is?"

Mina's eyes shone. *"Wild Max is the great Sidh prince. When I needed a champion, he came."*

Her obvious affection for his friend had touched David. Even so, every statement she made implied something new and unsettling.

"Mina, did you call him to that farmhouse?"

The girl gave a shy, almost apologetic nod. *"I was too little to defend myself from that monster. I prayed for someone strong but I did not know who might answer."*

"I see," said David, masking his astonishment. *"Mina, I have

one more question and then I must go. It's unlikely I will return to Rowan or that we will meet again. But if I do return, I would like for you to become my student. Is that something that would interest you?"

The child had simply beamed.

Of course, David's Walpurgisnacht operation had been a brilliant success. He not only returned to Rowan, but he also did so with his long-imprisoned grandfather, the sorcerer Elias Bram. The Archmage was much more experienced and powerful than his grandson, but even he wasn't certain what to make of Mina.

That she was of the Old Magic was obvious, but there was an oddness to her that stymied classification. It was simple enough to trace Max's frightful power—he was a living demigod, the son of Lugh Lamfhada. The Old Magic in David's family was of a different flavor and vintage, but it, too, branched from the divine. But Mina's power . . . where did it come from?

David recalled Prusias's horror when she appeared upon the battlefield.

"What are you?" he had shrieked. "What are you called?"

But Mina had not answered. Instead, she had raised her tiny hand, shattered his seven crowns, and sent the demon fleeing back across the sea. At the time, David—like everyone else—had been startled by her sudden manifestation and stunned by what followed. With all the activity following the siege, it was some time before he could revisit the incredible sequence at length. Again and again, he returned to Prusias's questions: *What are you? What are you called?*

David believed Mina had allowed the demon a glimpse of her true self. And whatever that glimpse was, it had terrified a thousand-foot, seven-headed serpent. Following this extraordinary display, Rowan's council declared Mina the first Ascendant since Elias Bram. Each day hundreds of hopeful souls gathered at the base of Túr an Ghrian, hoping to see the wondrous child and her charge, the first true dragon in centuries. Since her arrival, Mina had accumulated many followers and titles, but David still did not know where she came from or what she called herself.

What was she?

He'd consulted numerous sources, hoping one might yield some insight. His assistant, a tireless domovoi named Jakob Quills, had packed the most promising tomes for his voyage. They were nearby, stacked between footlockers: Cuvier's register of mystical prodigies; Lady Blackwell's *Midgard Sparks: Old Magic among Humankind;* Francis Bacon's absurdly inaccurate theorems to approximate a being's spiritual energy . . . David's pale eyes wandered down the titles until it arrived at a cracked leather volume: *Children of the Dawn.* Feeling lazy, he rocked the hammock back and forth, hoping its sway would bring the book within reach. His fingertips had just brushed the spine when there was a knock upon the cabin door.

"Come in," he grunted, stretching in vain.

As the door opened, a curt "Good afternoon" was cut short by a horrified gasp. Glancing up, David saw a Highlands hare covering his eyes with a clipboard.

"Hello, Tweedy."

"Dear God, boy!" exclaimed the animal. "Where are your clothes?"

"Oh," said David, looking down. "I'd forgotten. It's very meditative to sit in a hammock naked. You should try it sometime."

The reply was delivered in a terse, disapproving brogue.

"I can assure the young gentleman that no member of the Highlands Burrfoots *ever* spent his afternoons lounging about a hammock contemplating his privates."

"I wasn't contemplating my privates," snapped David irritably. "I was thinking about something very important."

"Oh, I have no doubt," scoffed Tweedy, cleaning his spectacles. "But perhaps the gentleman will be so good as to abandon his 'meditations' and accompany me to the Director's cabin. And while he would undoubtedly prefer to parade his bare bottom en route, perhaps he will be so good as to dress like a decent, God-fearing sorcerer."

The hare waited while David, flushed and indignant, rummaged about for underclothes, a clean robe, and his cane. Their walk to the Director's cabin was punctuated by the hare's voluble reflections on the hierarchy of needs, Isaac Newton's celebrated chastity, and favorite quotations from the McGuffey Reader. Mercifully, these came to a halt when they reached the Director's door.

Ms. Richter's quarters were a series of connected, curving cabins along the stern's uppermost deck. Several people were sitting in the waiting room: two Mystics, an Agent from an elite cadre called the Bloodstone Circle, and a senior Workshop engineer who had defected to Rowan. Somewhere within, a somewhat exasperated-sounding Ms. Richter could be heard instructing a young assistant.

"Offer them drinks, Thalia," she sighed. "You should be able to handle scheduling hiccups on your own. I need to speak with David first. No, no, not one of those—the last was corked. Try one from the second row. . . ."

"Mr. Menlo has arrived, Director!" called Tweedy, standing on tiptoe.

"Send him back."

"Shall I accompany him?"

"Er, no thank you, Tweedy. Perhaps you could help Thalia serve the wine."

The hare drooped until an anxious-looking apprentice shuffled into the waiting room, staring fixedly at the bottle and glasses on her tray. As Tweedy leaped into action ("Handsomely, girl!"), David slipped past the apprentice, steadied himself against the ship's roll, and staggered ahead to the inner office.

He found Ms. Richter hunched over a bolted-down table that was covered with sheets of Florentine spypaper. Some of the parchments were dull and faded, others positively alive as words and drawings appeared mysteriously upon their surface. The authors were not ghosts, but living people who were transmitting messages from all over the world. At the Director's urging, David took a seat in one of the bolted chairs.

"Quite the weather we're having," she muttered, skimming one of the sheets.

David suppressed a sigh at the cliché. "The last sunset was very pretty."

Brushing away a silver strand of hair, the Director's bright, inquisitive eye met his own. "When was the last time you were on deck?"

"A day," David confessed somewhat sheepishly. "Maybe two?"

Securing the papers beneath several books, Ms. Richter stepped to one of the windows and pushed it open. A gust of frigid air came whipping into the cabin. Grimacing, David drew his robes about him as Ms. Richter yanked the window shut.

"A few more degrees and we'll be getting snow," she observed. "Midsummer flurries would be exceedingly strange at Rowan, much less this far south. This can't be natural."

"No," said David, coming over to inspect traces of frost about the window's edges. Releasing the latch, he pushed it open and let the cold air swirl about him. Closing his eyes, his mind drifted along with the wind until he could almost hear its vibrations, the subtle song of magic in its current. Gripping his cane, he murmured aloud, casting his voice into the wind as a fisherman might cast a lure into the waves.

"This is no mere spell," he said quietly.

"If it's not a spell, then what is it?" asked Ms. Richter.

David gazed out at the scarlet sky and the cold cobalt sea. "It's the Earth itself. She's slipping into winter. Her song is changing . . . the Book of Thoth is recomposing its score."

"Astaroth is doing this?"

He nodded.

"Why do you believe he would do such a thing?"

David pulled the window shut. "Maybe to remind us that he can."

"How severe could it get?"

"No idea. This could just be an early winter or another Ice Age."

Sitting at her desk, Ms. Richter rubbed her temples, glanced at a map of Prusias's capital, and sighed. "One thing at a time, Gabrielle," she muttered to herself. "Have you heard any news from your grandfather?"

"No." David did not enjoy lying to the Director, but prudence required it. The less that was said of Elias Bram's activities, the better. When it came to hunting Astaroth, David was his grandfather's only confidant, but even he only knew bits and pieces of the Archmage's doings.

Ms. Richter looked skeptical but resigned herself to his silence. "Do you think Mina is capable of counteracting this weather?" she asked.

"You're thinking of the crops," said David, knowing the Director's pragmatic mind would gravitate toward food shortages and a hundred other problems that would cascade from the unseasonal cold. She nodded.

"Unless Mina can hold this winter at bay, I'm going to order rationing."

"I would. Mina might be capable of controlling the weather for some vicinity but at tremendous cost. We left her behind to defend Rowan in our absence. I doubt she can do both. Order the rationing and see if existing crops can be harvested or replanted in the Sanctuary. It might not be affected."

"Can *that* counteract this weather?" she asked, glancing at his cane.

David turned it over, examining it. The artifact had once belonged to Prusias and bore the demon's famous love of wealth in its carved handle and bejeweled fittings. But its material value was infinitesimal compared to what was encased within: a page from the very Book of Thoth. Astaroth must have regretted his decision to favor his lieutenant with such gift. Prusias had not only rebelled, but also used the cane's power in ways contrary to his lord's wishes. Tapping it gently on the cabin floor, David gave a rueful smile.

"I'm afraid there's very little magic left in it. Prusias expended most of its power creating Gràvenmuir and preserving the Workshop's technologies. There's barely a flicker remaining."

Ms. Richter raised an eyebrow. "If the cane's magic enables the Workshop's technologies, would its demise nullify them?"

There was little doubt Blys's defenses would include many Workshop creations. One of the Director's priorities during the voyage was developing strategies to deal with any mechanized horrors they might encounter. Again, David shook his head.

"I don't think so," he replied. "I discussed that possibility with my grandfather and we arrived at the same conclusion. The cane has the power to create truenames but cannot remove or alter those that exist. Only the Book itself has that power. Besides, its page is nearly spent."

"I trust you'll use its remaining power wisely."

"I intend to," he said simply. "Is there anything else you'd like to discuss?"

"Oh, get comfortable, Menlo—you're not going anywhere for at least an hour." Calling Thalia in, the Director asked the apprentice to retrieve the Workshop engineer and reschedule the others. "I want you to sit in on my meeting with Dr. Bechel," she said to David. "He's had exposure to some of the technologies that may be used in Blys's defense. . . ."

For the next two hours, David sat quietly in the Director's cabin while Dr. Bechel detailed Workshop innovations such as frictionless walls and various munitions that made the sack of Blys seem wholly impossible. Even without advanced defenses, the siege of such a location represented an enormous undertaking. Ringed by mountains, the capital presented a single accessible face, rising in steep tiers that were guarded by mammoth walls and battlements. Each tier represented a new challenge, a distinct puzzle that must be solved before one could ascend to Prusias's palace.

Throughout these discussions, David's mind shifted into an abstracted state. He rarely juggled just one thing and was now tossing various problems about, considering them from different angles, weighing risks and rewards, probabilities and payoffs with fluid, almost superhuman ease. His greatest challenge was filtering. Without rigorous housekeeping, his brain could become cluttered, if not buried, by extraneous data. "Paralysis by analysis" some liked to joke, but David knew the dangers were very real. He had met many scholars whose inability to abandon "interesting tidbits" left them parsing minutiae while bigger issues glided past, unexamined.

Despite his extraordinary faculties and discipline, David Menlo was not a computer. He knew very well the human cost various operations might require. It was one thing to develop strategies and maneuver virtual chess pieces. It was quite another to recognize that the pawns and rooks represented real human beings, husbands and fathers, mothers and wives, sons and daughters. David had little patience with those who failed to grasp this and thus found Dr. Bechel's complacency irritating. Jotting down several notes, he flicked his gaze from the engineer and turned it upon the windows.

"David?"

He blinked to find the Director staring at him expectantly.

"Have you anything to add?" she asked.

"Very little," he replied, finishing his third coffee. "I disagree with some of Dr. Bechel's assumptions, which I've noted for you here. I also believe we'll need his expertise on hand if we can gain access to the control terminals in Phase Three. That operation's too complex to rely on relayed instructions in the midst of a battle."

The engineer blanched. "B-but that would require me to be physically present," he stammered. "I would be exposed to—"

"An eighty percent casualty rate," said David, coldly repeating the man's cavalier forecast from earlier. "But those were just your preliminary calculations. Now that you'll be taking part, I'm confident you'll identify ways to reduce that number."

He smiled pleasantly; Ms. Richter did not. Rising, the Director asked Dr. Bechel to remain for a private conversation while she escorted David out.

"Why must you terrify him?" she muttered once they were in the hallway.

"It's only sensible," David insisted. "He needs to be there."

"We'll be lucky if he doesn't jump overboard," she sighed, patting his arm. "Good night, Menlo."

Leaving the Director, David followed the long, low corridor

that led down to the galley in hope of scrounging supper. The way was warm and cramped, the air saturated with the smells of wood and pitch and close-packed humanity. Threading through clusters of soldiers, he joined a line of people waiting to be served onion soup from great copper pots. Once his bowl was filled, he took a hunk of brown bread, dropped it in the cradled soup, and retreated from the din.

On deck the night was almost crystalline, the stars present in dazzling abundance. They glittered in the cold air, obscured occasionally by the pitch of a mast or the billow of a sail. A trio of Mystics were sailing the galleon, one to call the wind, another to adjust its trim, and the last to steer their course. Their destination was growing ever closer. Within the week, the convoy would raise the former Rock of Gibraltar and slip through its strait into Prusias's kingdom.

All about the flagship, the fleet sailed in pristine formation. Witch-fires burned at every prow, three hundred bonfires whipping in the icy wind, illuminating figureheads of every description. Every available vessel had been conscripted into Rowan's armada, from Prusias's captured galleons to clippers, barques, sleek xebecs, and sturdy cogs. Each was crammed with men and matériel, each intent on taking the war to Prusias. It was an inspiring sight, as was the gathering on deck where many were singing along to a tune a soldier was playing on his fiddle.

They appeared blissfully alive—souls fresh from one victory and off to win another. While new recruits often shared a naïve, almost pitiable eagerness for combat, these were not new recruits. Every man, woman, and youth aboard had seen their share of battle. Instead, they seemed to be savoring the joy and camaraderie born of the notion that *they* were on the march; *they* were on the attack after years of living in stunned and helpless fear.

The wintry night seemed no more than a marvelous curiosity, an excuse to pass a flask and welcome its warmth in their bellies.

Sipping his supper, David took a turn about the deck and let the chill sharpen his mind for the sleepless night ahead. When he headed below, he went straight to his cabin where he paused to trace a design upon the door with his finger. Its symbols gleamed like moonlit silver before fading at the final glyph. The spell worked subtly; anyone who approached the door would recall urgent business elsewhere and leave. The ward was of David's own invention and he'd often used it when he craved uninterrupted study in the Archives.

He had not even cracked *Children of the Dawn* when there was a knock at his door. Had he traced the sigil incorrectly? Swinging out of his hammock, he marched to the door and flung it open.

Elias Bram stood outside.

~ 7 ~

LORD SALISBURY'S TALE

Sweeping past his grandson, Bram entered the cabin and stamped snow from his boots. David quickly shut the door.

"This is unexpected, Grandfather," said David. "Did anyone else see you?"

"Of course not," grunted the Archmage, tossing his cloak to dry by the little stove. "What have you to eat?"

David's beloved hoard of bread, cheese, and milk were gone in minutes. His grandfather seemed almost famished, as if he hadn't bothered to eat or sleep in days. His gray hair was a windswept mane and his cheeks were hollow with hunger, but his dark eyes crackled with intensity. The towering man might have been some half-crazed prophet. Wolfing down the second cheese, Bram took up one of the coffee sacks.

Anything but that.

"I'd be happy to make you some," David lied. Sniffing the sack, his grandfather merely tossed it down and plucked up Francis Bacon's book on theorems. Skimming the first few pages, the Archmage chuckled. David reddened.

"I know the theorems are wrong. I was just doing research."

"On what?" asked Bram. "And what could this pretender possibly have to teach you?"

"I'd rather not discuss it," David muttered. "You'll tell me it's a waste of time and ridicule my methods."

Bram tossed the heavy tome aside. "Nonsense. What are you researching?"

"Mina."

"You're wasting your time."

"And there we go . . . ," David sighed, boiling water to make the tea his grandfather would inevitably request.

"Would you rather I lie?" inquired the Archmage, picking a stray bit of cheese from his tangled beard. "Candor's a mark of respect. Coddling is for children."

Brushing the comment aside, David spoke in a measured voice. "Why is researching Mina a waste of time?"

"She has not yet chosen to reveal who or what she is. If I do not know, I doubt you'll find it in a book—particularly one by Francis Bacon. Incidentally, am I mentioned?"

"You have your own chapter."

"And?"

"Less than charitable," said David. "He declares you a public danger."

"I did break his instruments," Bram confessed. "The man was insufferable—holding court with his 'theories' and demanding the Solas elders hook me up to his contraptions. He was a charlatan. One can't measure what's forever changing. The Hound is proof of that."

"What do you mean?" asked David.

"His abilities defy prediction. They don't evolve—they erupt. Have you ever cast a spell on him?"

"Of course not," said David. "I combined our energies, but I've never bewitched him. He's my friend."

"I've tried," said the Archmage, unabashed. "Several times last year. He never noticed, I assure you, but the results were alarming."

"What happened?"

"*Nothing,*" whispered the Archmage. "Granted, they were minor magics, but they had no effect whatsoever."

"So what?" said David, irritated by his grandfather's ongoing suspicion of Max.

Bram glanced sharply at him. "You're far too bright for such a stupid remark. Mina adores him, but even she sees the risks."

David meditated a sharp retort, but thought better of it. "The same things have been said about you a thousand times over," he sighed. "They have been said about me. They will be said about Mina."

Bram shook his head. "The Hound is different."

"His name is Max."

"For now. Rulers often take new ones."

David met his grandfather's gaze. "He's not a king. He's not an emperor. He's not a tyrant or a conqueror. He's an Agent in the Red Branch—one who has risked his life time and again for me and for Rowan. I know him better than you do."

Bram's eyes glittered. "Do you know he nearly summoned Astaroth?"

David nearly dropped the kettle. "What are you talking about?"

"During Prusias's siege," his grandfather continued. "Right before you possessed the dreadnoughts. Astaroth very nearly materialized."

"How do you know this?"

"Because I was following Astaroth. We were both in Nether, both shadow walking. Even at a distance, I could sense his excitement when Max called upon him. The Demon wants your friend, David. He sees vast possibilities there."

"As a tool?"

"A vessel," Bram corrected. "When you rescued me, Astaroth was diminished. Although he has the Book of Thoth, it cannot mend his being or make him stronger. His origins are in another world, another universe, and thus beyond the Book's influence. But he can inhabit another's body—particularly if that person is foolish enough to summon him."

"I've summoned Astaroth," said David.

His grandfather gestured at his stump. "I'm well aware."

David poured hot water into a china cup. "It must be nice to have all the answers. Are you here to turn me against my friend or is there another point to this visit?"

Taking his tea, the Archmage stirred it thoughtfully. "You're more sentimental than I'd have guessed."

David stiffened. "Another shortcoming, I suppose."

Bram's voice softened. "No. You're loyal. I suppose that comes from having a friend like the Hound—like *Max*. You're not as lonely or angry as I was at your age."

"Didn't you have any friends?"

Bram laughed. "It's hard to make friends when you won't talk. I didn't speak until I was eight. Did you know that?"

"How would I?" said David wearily. "You never share

anything about yourself, Grandfather. I only know what's written in books or Solas's histories."

Bram grunted. "That's my fault. I've worked hard to hide my past, but I'm learning one can't escape it. It always finds a way to surface. That past is why I'm here tonight."

Reaching into a worn leather satchel, the Archmage retrieved a human skull and laid it on a footlocker.

"You've been in the ossuaries," observed David.

"Aye. But not tonight. The witches never robbed this tomb. They didn't know about him."

David studied the skull. It was relatively small and missing several teeth, but otherwise unremarkable. "Let me guess. Yorick?"

Bram smiled grimly. "A closer guess than you might imagine. This fellow enjoyed his Shakespeare, though he preferred *Othello* to *Hamlet*. You are looking at Robert Cecil, first Earl of Salisbury."

David recalled his history. "Adviser to Queen Elizabeth and King James."

"Yes," said Bram. "He was also my patron. Would you believe I'm still afraid of him?"

David had never seen the haunted, hunted look that now skulked in his grandfather's eyes. "I don't understand."

The Archmage studied his large, powerful hands. "My parents died in a fire when I was very young. I may have been at fault—I probably was. I had little control over my powers. We lived in Rotterdam and were very poor. When no relatives claimed me, a neighbor sold me to a ship, one of five bound for South America."

"How old were you?"

"Not yet six. The sailors were kind enough. They taught me how to knot and splice and other aspects of the trade. But I was a peculiar boy. I never spoke and rarely smiled. When the other ships became lost and scattered, we tried to make for the Japans. When bad luck continued, the crew took me for a Jonah."

"They didn't hurt you," said David uneasily.

"Not directly," Bram said. "They set me adrift in the East China Sea with a little food and water. My fate would be in God's hands."

David was appalled. "You were a child."

The Archmage shrugged. "It was nine days before my raft washed ashore near a fishing village. The people had never seen a European before. They thought I was a spirit—a *kodama* or *kawako*—who'd arrived in answer to their prayers."

The cabin was growing dark. David refilled his grandfather's tea and lit another lantern that he hung from a hook in the ceiling. "What prayers were those?" he asked.

"Deliverance," answered Bram. "Men from the village had cut trees in a sacred forest. Soon after, a creature took up residence in their temple. The villagers believed the gods had sent it to punish them."

"What was it?"

The Archmage gave a knowing smile. "A ki-rin."

David stared. *"YaYa?"*

"She was not yet known by that name," said Bram. "The people called her *Arashi*—"storm" in their language—for she'd destroyed half the temple. Assuming I'd been sent to drive it away, the villagers brought me to its steps."

"Were you frightened?"

Bram grunted. "Enchanted. I'd never seen a more magnificent creature. She rippled like black silk, bigger and more elegant than any animal I'd ever seen. It never occurred to me that she might trample or devour me. I walked right toward her."

"What did she do?"

"Made straight for me," recounted Bram. "It was quite a sight—a ten-foot ki-rin brandishing her horn and shooting steam from her nostrils. The villagers fled. But when she reached me, Arashi sprawled at my feet like a kitten. We had an understanding."

David laughed. "The villagers must have thought you were a god."

The Archmage raised his eyebrows. "Quite the opposite. One of them ran and informed the local lord, the *daimyo*, of what had happened. The daimyo feared I was a powerful oni, for what else could have cowed a ki-rin? He sent me on to Osaka where Tokugawa Ieyasu had imprisoned my former shipmates. The future shogun was an interesting man. He would not harm me, but neither would he permit me to remain in Japan. He ordered the Portuguese missionaries to send me home on one of their ships. The missionaries were displeased—they thought my feat was a mark of the Devil—but Tokugawa was too important a man to defy."

David mused on this. Tokugawa's helmet was one of the artifacts Rowan used to honor students who exemplified particular virtues. He'd had no idea the connection had anything to do with his grandfather.

"Did Arashi go with you?" he asked.

"No," said Bram. "She flew off like a thunderbolt shortly after we met. We wouldn't see each other for years. I was stowed aboard a Portuguese ship and began the long journey back."

"Straight on to Lisbon."

Bram chuckled. "Alas, no. The Portuguese were at war with the Dutch and English. Our ship was attacked and taken. It was a terrible slaughter—the first real bloodshed I had seen. The privateers had a witch aboard their vessel, a weather worker. She sensed something unusual about me and claimed me as her share of the prize."

"A prize," repeated David, saddened by the very notion. "You were handed about like a parcel of goods."

"Aye," said Bram. "But my whole life had been one long drift upon strange currents—it was what I knew. As it happened, the witch worked for the East India Company. She brought me back to London, where she lived with her husband."

"Were you treated well?"

"Wonderfully. They'd lost their only child to illness and had a mind to raise me as their own. Her husband was a playwright—not very successful, but happy in his work. Some of my fondest memories occurred in that little house. It was where I first found the courage to speak."

"What did you say?"

Bram's eyes twinkled. "*The meter is wrong.* The playwright was reading a new verse aloud and I saw fit to chime in. You see? I've always been a critic."

David stifled a laugh. "Did he appreciate it as much as I do?"

"More. He gave me an apple and promised a surprise later in the week."

"What was it?"

"A trip to the theater. Shakespeare's latest play was being performed at King James's court in Whitehall. The playwright's wife secured an invitation through her connections at the Company. We were to spend the night in style—a celebration of our first year as a family." Finishing his tea, the Archmage placed the cup back on its saucer. "But the evening took a turn."

"What happened?"

Bram gave a pained smile. "Robert Cecil happened. He was considered the cleverest man in the kingdom. It was said Lord Cecil knew everything that happened in London—a human spider whose webs hummed with secrets. He was also a man of diverse interests, and when he appeared onstage in the role of Iago, the entire court applauded. At the time I was puzzled— the actor was just a small, rather humpbacked man. But later I understood. People were afraid of him."

Rising, Bram peered out a window at the dark sea and dull red skies.

"There was a reception after," he continued. "As you can imagine, I kept to its fringe. My guardians were nobodies, our presence suffered only as a concession to the Company. I didn't mind. The spectacle of Whitehall, of lords and ladies and actors, was quite enough for me. I had no idea what the looks and sniggers meant. But they all stopped when he approached."

Turning from the window, the Archmage stared at the skull upon the chest.

"I remember as though it were yesterday: the crowd parting, Lord Cecil beaming as he made his way toward us. 'Who is this boy?' he cried. 'Who is this wonderful boy who appreciates the theater?' I hardly mustered the courage to whisper my name. Lord Cecil was enchanted by my shyness and invited me to spend the winter at his estate in Hertfordshire. There were actors and artists in residence—I could learn the trade from the very best while escaping the dirt and dreariness of London. *Wouldn't my parents like that?*"

Bram shook his head as he repeated the phrase. "He might as well have drawn a blade. My guardians stammered regrets and apologies, but their excuses were batted aside with laughs and smiles. I was being abducted in plain view."

"That's awful," David murmured. "Couldn't you say or do anything?"

Bram shrugged. "I was numb. And as you said yourself, I'd

been handed about like a parcel of goods my entire life. This was just another ship, another raft, another current. I left that night."

"And your guardians . . . they just let you go?"

The Archmage picked up the skull, turning it over in his hands as though it were a peddler's curio. "They couldn't have done anything. Robert Cecil was fast becoming the most powerful man in England. He was going to get his way. For their trouble, my guardians could have gold or the gallows. They chose gold. I don't blame them."

"So he took you to the country," David said, a thousand horrific scenarios unfolding in his imagination.

"I know what you're thinking," Bram said. "He never laid a hand on me. No, he was interested in becoming my teacher in the mystic arts. He had a far keener perception of magical energy than Robert Cecil's cousin."

David blinked. "Who was Robert Cecil's cousin?"

Setting down the skull, the Archmage picked up the very book he'd been ridiculing earlier. "A fellow named Sir Francis Bacon."

"You're joking."

"Small world."

David was far less amazed by this coincidence than the series of revelations concerning his grandfather's childhood. His mind was processing rapidly, as it always did. If the witches scoured the world to gather the remains of those who used magic, why weren't Robert Cecil's remains in their ossuaries? It was unlikely that they'd have overlooked such a high-profile person. The other possibility was that Robert Cecil had no magical gifts—none of the spark that made human beings witches, Mystics, or *mehrùn*, as the demons called them.

"How could Robert Cecil be your teacher if he wasn't magical?" David asked.

Bram inclined his head at David's deductive powers. "I do enjoy watching your mind work. As you surmised, Robert Cecil was not, in fact, my first teacher. That title belongs to Astaroth."

David's mouth went dry. "*Astaroth* was your first teacher?"

"He was. I didn't know that at the time, of course. I had no idea Lord Cecil was possessed, much less possessed by a being so powerful and insidious."

"When did you find out?"

"The following year," said Bram. "I must confess my time at Theobalds House was not unpleasant. The house was a palace, its gardens and grounds fit for the royal family. I was given access to books, to tutors. Busy as he was, my patron found time to personally instruct me in Mystics. I never had a finer teacher. Not even at Solas."

"You never suspected *anything* was amiss?"

"Don't mistake me," said Bram. "It was a very strange household. Visitors came at all hours—troupes of actors and mummers, dignitaries and scholars. Not all came by the front door. More than once I saw shadows or heard whispers whose origins eluded me. I was not allowed outside on certain evenings and parts of the estate were absolutely forbidden. Everything had a reasonable explanation, of course, and I didn't ask too many questions. As a boy who had lost many homes, I had no wish to lose another. Particularly one where I lived so well and had a teacher who assured me that I was special and had vast potential. I was complicit in my own deception. Not for the last time, alas."

The ship's bell rang out and boots padded by the cabin door as the crew and officers of the first watch went to their stations. The seas were growing rougher. The witch-fires of vessels in their wake were bobbing with the flagship's pitch. Beneath the hanging lantern, the Archmage resembled one of his own statues, a brooding collection of planes and shadow.

"But I could not always deceive myself," Bram muttered. "Late one night, a feeling of dread overcame me. I awoke, gasping and gazing about the dark room to find Lord Cecil present. He was in the corner, sitting in a chair and staring at me with an expression that chilled me to the marrow. I addressed him, but he did not answer. Whatever was looking at me was not Robert Cecil. I was too frightened to call out for the servants, so there I sat, huddled and mute, wishing I was dreaming and realizing that I wasn't. At dawn, his lordship suddenly blinked and left the room."

"He wasn't merely sleepwalking?" David asked.

"Oh no. Robert Cecil wasn't present until that moment. Something else had been watching me, something utterly alien. I believe that was my first real glimpse of Astaroth—of what he truly is beneath his layers of grinning flesh and pleasantries. I knew then I could not stay."

"Did you leave right away?"

"Shortly thereafter," said Bram. "The Gunpowder Plot had just taken place. Catholic conspirators had nearly blown up King James and parliament. The country was in an uproar and Lord Salisbury—for Robert Cecil had been given yet another title— was busy advising the frightened king and consolidating his power. Some whispered that Lord Salisbury had orchestrated the plot himself for just that purpose. In any case, King James became a frequent guest at Theobalds. He was there the night of the storm."

The Archmage began pacing.

"I was abed when it began. Such a storm! I'd never experienced anything like it in England. The entire palace shook from its fury. The windows in my room were rattling in their panes. When one shattered, I ran out to find a servant. But the house seemed deserted. I wandered about, at last coming to the wing where King James was staying. His guards were asleep in the hallway. The king's door was open. A light was flickering and dancing within. I couldn't help myself. I stepped past the sleeping guards and peered inside."

"What did you see?"

"King James," said Bram. "Unconscious, wreathed in witch-fire, and hovering high in the air. Lord Salisbury was beneath him, his arms outstretched as he chanted in a tongue unknown to me. My patron was not alone—his mummers lined the walls. I'd not been watching a minute when one of them turned and saw someone spying through the door. Even as it came toward me, someone seized my arm."

"Who?"

"One of the servants. A maid named Francis Cobb. She was a plain woman; one hardly noticed when she was about. I noticed her then, however, for she tossed me right over her shoulder and fled straight out of the palace. When we reached the high gates, she sprang over them like a deer and ran all the way to London."

"That was quite a maid."

The Archmage winked. "A Red Branch maid. We were soaked when we reached a house in the Strand. Miss Cobb wasted no time. She was taking me away, taking me to a place where I would be safe from people like Lord Salisbury. A place where there were others like me. We left before dawn and slipped down the Thames in a little boat bound for Ireland."

"She took you to Solas," breathed David.

Bram's eyes shone. "I wish you could have seen it. There was nothing to rival Solas when its veil was lifted and one beheld its cliffs and spires. When we finally reached the great gates, I found something waiting for me there, running wild on the gusts and green turf. A ki-rin I had known."

David gazed at his grandfather, almost embarrassed by his wariness. "Why are you telling me all this now? You've never mentioned any of this before."

Sitting, the Archmage took David's hand and held it between his own. He practically simmered with intensity. "The past is the key to our salvation. It is the key to defeating Astaroth, for understanding what he is and what he intends to do. To unearth his past, I must unearth my own, painful as that might be. I am not invincible, David. Should I fall, you may have to continue in my footsteps. You cannot do so if I keep secrets from you."

David looked into that hard, forbidding face. "How can I help?"

The Archmage nodded toward the skull. "By questioning Robert Cecil. It cannot be me. Our history might interfere."

"What do you want to know?"

"Why he originally summoned Astaroth. When Astaroth took possession of him. When Astaroth left. No detail is unimportant. You'll have to call upon his shade—I doubt there's a soul to summon."

David nodded. He had assumed as much. If Lord Salisbury had struck a bargain with Astaroth, the price had almost certainly been his soul. Those who died without their souls could still be recalled from their remains, but what answered was merely an echo, a wisp of spiritual static sponged from their bones. Shades could only share what they had known in life—and only if they were willing since the summoner had limited means to induce their cooperation.

While David did not normally use magic for mundane tasks, he did so now. With a wave of his hand, he pushed books and furniture aside to clear a space upon the floor while Bram sat down on a locker in the corner.

Pacing slowly about the room, David traced a circle in the air. A golden circle some five feet in diameter appeared on the cabin floor. Closing his eyes, he began to hum, his finger now drawing symbols of power: the rune of air, the sign of seekers, the mark of balance, the gray crossroads. They appeared at various locations within the circle, glowing glyphs that gave the room a greenish cast. Only one requirement remained.

Taking the skull, David placed it in the circle's center. There it sat, almost daring him to ask a question. Bram sat motionless in the shadows while David paced about the circle's perimeter, gazing at the skull and speaking in a quiet voice.

"I call upon the shade of Robert Cecil, Earl of Salisbury, adviser to Tudors and Stuarts, and dead these many years. I require service for your sins. Answer and find forgiveness. Answer and find peace."

The voice that answered was so faint and wavering, it might have been a breath of air. David nearly cursed the revelers on deck—their fiddling and laughter made it impossible to hear. From the corner, his grandfather made a subtle gesture with his hand. Instantly, the room was silent as a vault.

"Who calls me?" sighed the faint voice.

"My name is David Menlo. Four hundred years have passed since you perished from the earth. I need your help."

"Why should I help you?"

"To atone for your sins," replied David. "I know what you did, Robert Cecil. I know who you summoned."

"You know nothing."

David had little patience for these games. He paced about the circle, gazing imperiously at the skull and the faint halo of dust blowing and swirling about its crown. "I know you are Robert Cecil. I know that you summoned a spirit named Astaroth using an inscription you undoubtedly found in the Book of Abramelin. I know that you entered into a bargain with him, that he possessed you, made your house a nest of evil, and bewitched King James. You betrayed humanity, Lord Salisbury—now is your chance to aid it."

A long pause followed. There was a flicker within the circle, a subtle rippling in the air as a dim shape crouched over the skull. *"I did it for my country. I knew not how things might go astray. The Demon tricked me!"*

"You are not alone," said David in a more sympathetic tone. "He has deceived many before and since. Tell me what you did, Lord Salisbury. Tell me everything. Together, perhaps we can mend it. When did you summon Astaroth?"

"The year of the Armada," whispered the voice. *"The greatest fleet in history was going to invade. But its ships were turned away. I saved England."*

"I'd always heard it was Drake," remarked David.

Within the circle, there was almost a hiss. *"Drake was a common pirate. The Armada was destroyed by storms. Storms that I summoned."*

"Storms that *Astaroth* summoned," said David pointedly.

"They were my doing. I paid for them, body and soul."

"As you wish," said David indifferently. "Who taught you how to summon Astaroth? Unless I am mistaken, you are no Mystic."

"My cousin studied such matters," the shade whispered. *"He used to talk of arcane rites and forbidden books—a German manuscript containing Egyptian secrets. There were spirits one could call, he insisted. Spirits that would do whatever you wished if you followed the rites and paid their price. When the Armada set sail, he told me what to do."*

As the interview progressed, David imagined his grandfather must be disappointed. The nobleman's deal with Astaroth was rather standard. In exchange for destroying the Spanish Armada, Astaroth required his immortal soul. This provided little insight. Even more grating was the fact that Salisbury had no memory of the periods when Astaroth possessed him. He did not even recall acting in *Othello,* much less bewitching King James.

Still, David coaxed the shade's meager information with skill and patience. It was tedious work. Even as a shade, Cecil's vanity found ways to surface and it often tried to steer the conversation toward burnishing his legacy. David didn't have the heart to tell him that few living humans even remembered England, much less its long-dead ministers.

Plunging ahead, David nudged the interview toward its conclusion. "When was your last interaction with Astaroth?"

"Soon after the Gunpowder Plot," answered the shade. *"His imp told me my services would no longer be required. We would meet again at my death."*

David raised an eyebrow. "Mr. Sikes told you this? Not Astaroth himself?"

"Not Sikes—the other one. That's when I knew I was out of favor."

David stopped midstride. Bram leaned forward, an eager gleam in his dark eyes.

"What other one?" David pressed. "Another *imp*?"

The shade gave a fluid, languorous turn about the skull. *"Yaro,"* it answered. *"'Rhymes with sorrow.' That was his little joke. I preferred dealing with Sikes."*

A flash of lightning interrupted David's next question. Glancing out the cabin windows, he saw a second bolt lance down from the sky to strike the seas beside a trailing galleon. An instant later, the massive ship began to roll, twisting up and out of the water as though it were a breaching whale. Bram shot to his feet.

David was so stunned he could merely state the obvious.

"We're under attack."

BOOM!

The flagship ground to a shuddering halt, its timbers groaning as the ship pitched forward. David slammed into the bulkhead, striking his head as the cabin windows shattered.

~ 8 ~

FLOTSAM AND JETSAM

The small talk surrounding Prusias became even smaller. As the minutes ticked past, polite inquiries about a neighbor's lands and subjects dwindled to awkward observations about the weather, the condition of the roads, and the pitiable drabness of the Workshop humans.

The King of Blys glared at the fool next to him, a lord from Vrusk whose lands contained mountains of iron ore. It was the only reason the fop was suffered to live, much less attend the viewing. Glancing about the impromptu command center, Prusias wondered if this gathering had been wise.

Mr. Bonn had been against it from the start. The imp, as

usual, had taken great pains to enumerate all that could go wrong: offending the uninvited, the unthinkable prospect of defeat, and, of course, technical difficulties.

Technical difficulties. The king glowered at the Workshop engineers, futzing with their equipment, skittering with expressions of mounting anxiety.

"What do you make of this cold spell, Your Majesty?" inquired the ironmonger. "A contrivance of your enemies?"

Conversations hushed as Prusias turned to face his questioner. The smile died on the baron's face, a mushroom dripping butter from the end of his tiny fork.

The king smiled pleasantly. *You will never return to Vrusk, my friend.* Aloud, he said, "Which enemies would you be referring to?"

"R-Rowan," stammered the demon. "Of course I meant Rowan. Your lordship has no other enemies."

"If his lordship has no other enemies, why is his beautiful city burning?" inquired Lady Praav, a countess from Acheral. She gestured pleasantly to one of the windows where torrents of distant smoke were pluming into the night.

"A routine demonstration in the ghetto," Prusias growled. "Some smoke, but hardly fire. What can one say? Vyes are animals."

He laughed at the joke, but Lady Praav retained the pinched, disapproving expression that reminded him why he despised her. She was no demon, more of an immortal schoolmarm.

"Are we in danger?" she asked politely.

"Of course not," Prusias replied. "The vyes live within the lowest district, and Workshop gargoyles have already been dispatched. Any troublemakers shall be dealt with."

At the far end of the long table, an immensely powerful warlord blew a smoke ring from his amber pipe. The rakshasa gestured lazily at the flustered engineers, his eyes three emerald slits within his tigerish face. "I hope the gargoyles weren't built by these gentlemen," he purred. "You should let me bring my legions within the city, Prusias. They're more reliable than your toys."

The threat was obvious to everyone in the room—even the dullest imps, courtiers, and concubines. Other than Queen Lilith, Lord Grael was the closest thing Prusias had to a true rival. Unfortunately, he was far too valuable to eliminate at this stage of the war. If Prusias lost Grael's support, half the braymas in Malakos and Azur might revolt. Still, he could not let such an obvious taunt go unanswered. Prusias raised his glass.

"Very generous, Lord Grael. Fortunately, I have Lord Braiden's legions at my disposal. But rest assured I won't forget your offer."

With a knowing smirk, the rakshasa raised his glass. Lord Braiden was the unfortunate demon Prusias had chosen to make an example of at his party. Hundreds of guests had witnessed their king savagely batter and decapitate a powerful rival with his bare hands in the grand ballroom. Prusias had not even wiped the blood from his breathless, grinning face when he declared Braiden's lands forfeit and all his legions and servants property of the king. The message had spread among braymas like wildfire: *This could be you.*

Still, Prusias could not ignore the obvious. While the party had been a rousing success, tonight was turning into a disaster. As the servants poured more wine, Prusias surveyed his other guests: a score of vital braymas, several witches, a representative from the lesser demons who had settled the former Americas, his worthless advisers . . . His eyes settled on a human woman, auburn-haired and striking. She was seated at one of the side tables next to a kitsune who played the sweetest belyaël in Blys.

Unlike most humans, the woman seemed at ease among daemona. She couldn't be from the Workshop—this woman actually had grace and style. Turning, Prusias motioned for Mr. Bonn.

"Who is she?" he whispered in the imp's ear. "The woman seated next to Marahkül."

"Madam Petra, my lord. She was very influential among the human settlements before Rowan took her hostage."

"The smuggler from Piter's Folly?"

The imp nodded. "Yes, my lord. Apparently, she did not take part in Rowan's defense and felt uncomfortable remaining. She was permitted to leave."

Prusias's face darkened. "How do we know she's not a spy?"

"She blames Rowan for her husband's death, she prospered at Piter's Folly, she is being watched, and we have insurance."

"What insurance?"

"Her daughter," sighed Mr. Bonn. "Young Katarina is now our special guest and has been housed with the Workshop children."

The king grunted his approval. "Special guests" were hostages, an almost meaningless asset when dealing with other demons, but marvelous currency with humans. They became very compliant when their loved ones were threatened. The demon's eyes wandered hungrily over her figure to pause at a coppery gleam about her lovely neck. Prusias had a remarkably keen eye for luxury and could appraise most items at a glance. The smuggler's torque was not fashioned of copper or red gold; it was made from one of the rarest materials on earth—the quills of a lymrill. Prusias was exceedingly curious how it had fallen into the woman's possession. A greedy flame kindled in the demon's eye. The smuggler and her torque—he coveted them both.

"Invite her to dinner this week," he muttered. "In the meantime, find out what the bloody holdup is. If we can't view the attack, I want to know. I'm tired of sitting here grinning like a fool."

The imp bowed and walked briskly away to where Dr. Wyle was conferring anxiously with his colleagues. When Mr. Bonn had his word, the engineer nodded and mopped a face shining with perspiration. Beckoning to one of his associates, a young man monitoring a silver case adorned with dials and glass tubes, Dr. Wyle walked swiftly over. The malakhim stood aside to permit them approach. The engineer and his young assistant bowed.

"Your Majesty," said Dr. Wyle. "Please allow me to explain the difficulties."

Prusias cocked his head. There were so many powerful demons in the room that their auras overlapped into a nebulous haze. But now that Prusias could see Dr. Wyle's colleague up close, he noticed something very peculiar.

"I would very much like to hear your explanations, Dr. Wyle. Let's begin with why a Workshop engineer is *mehrùn*."

The geneticist blinked. "Pardon?"

Prusias pointed at the young man clutching his little gadget. "*Mehrùn*," he repeated. "Your colleague is a magical human. Were you aware of this?"

"I . . . I suppose he must be," stammered Dr. Wyle. "It didn't occur to me to mention—"

Prusias cut the man off and fixed his eyes on the *mehrùn*.

"Who are you?" he asked gruffly.

The young man had broad shoulders, short blond hair, and an earnest air. Prusias could smell fear, but the *mehrùn* kept his composure as he bowed. "Jason Barrett, Your Majesty. I serve in the Workshop's—"

"Dr. Barrett is not a regular part of my team," put in Dr. Wyle anxiously. "He's just a technician we borrowed to—"

The engineer fell silent as Prusias held up his hand. "Dr.

Wyle, if you interrupt, you will dine on your own tongue. Continue, Dr. Barrett."

"As I was saying, Your Majesty, I serve in the Workshop's communications division. Dr. Wyle asked me here to assist with the broadcast."

"So, you're to blame for all of this . . ." The demon simmered, gesturing at the blank screens lining the far wall.

"With all due respect, the Earth's atmosphere is to blame," replied the engineer. "There's been a sizable shift in its magnetic field that's interfering with our equipment. We're trying to adjust our instruments to compensate."

Prusias waved off the technical gibberish. "Will there be a show?" he asked pointedly.

"Yes, Your Majesty."

"Would you stake your life on it?"

"I believe I just did."

Prusias had to chuckle. Despite his present irritation, he liked this young engineer—he possessed a bit of dash so woefully absent from the average Workshop drone. "Were you aware that you are *mehrùn*, Dr. Barrett?"

"Of course, Your Majesty. I graduated from Rowan."

Prusias digested this slowly. "Did you, now?"

"Yes, Your Majesty. Five years ago. Top of my class."

"Good for you, lad. And how does a Rowan graduate come to be at the Workshop, pray tell?"

"They offered an internship and I accepted. This was back before the troubles began."

Prusias laughed and gazed about the magnificent room. "What troubles, Dr. Barrett? We seem to be doing rather well."

"Troubles for Rowan," the young man clarified. "Troubles for common humanity."

"Common humanity," Prusias repeated. "I like that phrase.

You're certainly not common humanity, Dr. Barrett—a Workshop engineer who hails from Rowan. Are you a spy?"

The question was asked with a casual air, but there was nothing casual about its underlying gravity. The demon studied the human closely, his senses attuned for the innumerable tells that betrayed all but the cleverest liars.

"No, Your Majesty. I'm not a spy. I enjoyed my time at Rowan, but I'm a member of the Workshop now. A member anxious to give Your Majesty his show."

Prusias nodded. He would have Dr. Barrett watched, of course, but he had passed his initial test. There had been none of the telltale signs of falsehood—not even an intensification of the fear that pulsed with every beat of that strong heart.

"How much longer will you need, Dr. Barrett?" said Prusias. "As you can see, my guests are growing restless."

The technician gestured at his silver case, whose tubes were giving off a faint, phosphorescent light. "Five minutes, Your Majesty. I believe we're getting close."

"Excellent," said Prusias. He turned to Dr. Wyle. "Do you have the time?"

The puzzled engineer retrieved an antique pocket watch from his coat. Taking it from him, Prusias rose from his seat and rapped his knife gently against a glass.

"Lords and ladies," he announced. "My honored guests. Please accept my apologies for the delay in presenting this evening's entertainment. I've been assured it is due to the Earth's 'magnetic field' and not the Workshop's incompetence."

This elicited some welcome laughter. Prusias scanned his audience, his eyes drifting to the smuggler, who was listening attentively. *What a delightful-looking woman.* He gave a smile just for her.

"I've also been assured," the king continued, "that the problem can be remedied and our show will begin shortly. Like you, however, I grow impatient for entertainment. And thus, while Dr. Wyle explains what you will be seeing, we will give this young man five minutes to fix his little problem. Should he fail, you may do whatever you like with him and the rest of his Workshop associates. Whether the show goes on or not, you shall be entertained."

Lord Grael sat up with interest, as did a number of other braymas. While Dr. Wyle began sweating like cheese, the technician turned his attention to his contraption, studying the tubes and adjusting its dials with admirable calm. Glancing at the pocket watch, Prusias waited for the slender hand to reach the twelve.

"Their time begins . . . *now*."

Heads turned toward Dr. Barrett as he spent several minutes adjusting various dials by infinitesimal gradations. Now and again, the glass tubes flared with phosphorescent light and the many screens flickered. But an instant later, the tubes dimmed and the screens went dark.

"Frequencies are all over the place," the technician grumbled. "We need a better antenna."

"How much time does he have, Your Majesty?" inquired Dr. Wyle anxiously.

"Ninety seconds," replied Prusias.

Sweat was streaming down Dr. Wyle's face as he gazed about at the demons, his ashen colleagues, and the blank displays. Meanwhile, Dr. Barrett set down his receiver and stared at it, as though it were a particularly challenging puzzle. Spittle flew from Dr. Wyle's lips.

"What are you doing?" he cried. "Pick it up! Keep adjusting it!"

Dr. Barrett ignored him, choosing instead to gaze about the magnificent room, at its many fixtures and ornaments. Prusias looked on with interest as the technician strode suddenly toward Madam Petra.

"What is that?" Dr. Barrett asked, pointing toward her torque.

"My necklace," she said coolly.

"No," he said impatiently. "What's it made from?"

"A lymrill's quills." She turned to allow her fellow guests a glimpse of the wondrous metal.

"Can I have it?" asked Dr. Barrett.

"Certainly not."

"Just for a moment," he pressed. "Please."

With a glance at her host, Madam Petra slipped the coppery torque off her slender neck and let it dangle round her finger.

"Ten seconds," said Prusias, locking eyes with the smuggler.

Snatching the torque from her hand, Dr. Barrett raced back to the receiver. Prusias glanced back at the pocket watch.

"Five . . . four . . . three . . ."

Dr. Barrett touched the torque to the receiver. Its tubes blazed like bottled flares, causing the wall of Workshop screens to flash on. Their images, although moving swiftly, were crystal clear.

"Bravo!" cried Prusias, clapping his great hands. "And they say necessity is the mother of invention. Ha! It's desperation. Well done, Dr. Barrett."

Rising from the table, Lord Grael approached the screens, pipe smoke trailing from the corners of his mouth. "What are we looking at, Prusias?"

"The assault on Rowan's fleet."

The rakshasa squinted, trying to make sense of the chaotic images. It looked as though hundreds of individual cameras were racing along ship decks, up masts, over bodies, while great waves crashed over the side, washing over the lens or sending the little cameraman on spinning, careening journeys into the gunwales.

"When did this happen?" asked Grael, his expression grave and contemplative.

Prusias laughed. "It's happening right now, Lord Grael! We are witnessing the assault as it occurs. Dr. Barrett, is it possible to focus on one or two images? This many is too difficult to follow. A view of activity aboard the flagship would be ideal. Dr. Wyle, if you would explain what we're seeing."

Sliding a panel out from the receiver's base, Dr. Barrett adjusted several controls. The frenzy of images upon the screens were quickly reduced, consolidating down to a few dozen and then finally to two. Prusias watched Dr. Barrett's face closely as the young man looked up from his controls to monitor what was happening on the screens. There was no emotion upon his face, no indication that these were his former friends, classmates, and teachers under attack. Dr. Barrett was just a competent technician doing his job. He might have been training his camera on butterflies.

Good, thought Prusias. *I'd hate to get rid of him unnecessarily. Unlike Dr. Wyle, this one doesn't buckle under a bit of pressure.*

A single, very dark panoramic scene appeared on the screens. A recovered Dr. Wyle cleared his throat.

"Ladies and gentlemen, as you know, Rowan launched a sizable force several weeks ago. To intercept them, we have engineered a highly predatory organism whose natural capabilities have been enhanced with a mechanized exoskeleton and even skinscrolling. With His Majesty's support and blessing, we have produced a shoal of sixty creatures in a highly accelerated time frame."

"How big is that creature?" asked Lord Grael, staring at a squidlike tentacle that whipped across the screen.

"Almost as long as a Hadesian galleon," replied the engineer. "Two to three hundred feet, depending on the individual specimen. Our estimates suggest they will sink even the largest warships in less than twenty minutes."

Lord Grael's smirk vanished in gratifying fashion. *That's right, friend,* thought Prusias. *Once they're finished with Rowan, these monsters will be lurking off your coast and strangling your trade. And when you can't pay my levies, I'll offer your lands to your own braymas in exchange for your head. You won't last a week.*

Dr. Wyle scrolled to another image, a split screen of two repellent, insectlike creatures. "While the kraken is designed predominately as a ship destroyer, it's also a troop carrier. Each specimen is capable of depositing forty-eight pinlegs and twelve scorps upon any ship it's attacking. The pinlegs create havoc and relay information back to command while the larger scorps engage enemy personnel. Both have been programmed to recognize and prioritize high-value targets. While a crew fends off the scorps and pinlegs, the kraken destroys their ship. Dr. Barrett, if you would optimize the output spectrum . . ."

Another adjustment and night turned into day, revealing an ocean teeming with ships and monsters. The formation of the Rowan fleet was like an arrowhead. The krakens looked like pale, bloated squids with round luminescent eyes and chitinous plates armoring portions of their heads and tentacles. The creatures had struck the larger ships in the vanguard where a furious battle was being waged. From the aerial view, it had an almost serene majesty with heavy seas churning into foam while sails flapped and fluttered away like party streamers. Here and there, gargantuan tentacles flailed up from the sea to crash upon decks or wrap themselves about the hulls and masts.

Naturally, Rowan was responding. Bolts of lightning shivered and forked down from the sky, striking the whitecaps and krakens as they surged beneath the surface. Wherever the lightning struck, great puffs of steam rose like geysers.

Satisfaction ripened in Dr. Wyle's voice. "This is playing out like our simulations. As you can see, Rowan's Mystics are utilizing electricity. While this is a sensible response, it is also doomed to failure since the krakens possess hyper-regenerative abilities. Unless catastrophic damage is inflicted in a very short period of time, the beasts will repair their injuries. Rowan would have more success if they focused on one at a time, but of course they don't know that."

This pronouncement was followed by a dry, rasping laugh.

Cold fish, this one, reflected Prusias. With humans, cruelty and cowardice were often found together.

One of the braymas thumped his table as a frigate suddenly broke in half. The sea was already littered with wreckage. Prusias focused on one of the largest galleons—*his* galleon—as a second kraken fastened on to it. The gargantuan vessel had almost tipped onto its side, masts and spars snapping as the monsters tightened their hold.

A massive flash of lightning rippled across the screen. An instant later, the screen ghosted completely, bathing the room in a phosphorescent glow.

"Switch to another feed, Dr. Barrett," said Dr. Wyle calmly. "Nothing to worry about, ladies and gentlemen. Some lightning just got too close to that particular pinlegs. Ah, there we are . . ."

The aerial feed resumed as another pinlegs swept over the scene. Great clouds of steam billowed past its lens, revealing the galleon as it began to right itself like a bobbing cork. The krakens were sinking back into the sea, their tentacles sliding limp and lifeless off the decks.

A cold knot formed in Prusias's stomach. "Who's on that ship?"

For the moment, however, Dr. Wyle was speechless.

The king wheeled upon Dr. Barrett. *"Who's on that damn*

ship?" The technician quickly adjusted his controls, switching the feed to one from a pinlegs upon its deck. The creature was racing along, weaving between fallen bodies and wreckage as it scuttled toward some objective. Sound flooded the viewing room, a cacophony of cries, groaning timbers, and the rapid *tink-tink-tink* of the creature's many legs. It passed under a slower scorp that was apparently rushing at same target.

Dr. Wyle found his voice. "Someone important. All the pinlegs and scorps are heading for them, so it must be a top-priority target. The Director, possibly, or—"

"Menlo," Prusias growled, lumbering forward to glare at the figure onscreen.

The young sorcerer's pale face grew larger, crisper as the pinlegs scuttled toward him. He was bleeding profusely and leaning against the splintered base of a mast, but the boy seemed to have his wits about him.

Was he standing over someone?

When Prusias glimpsed the fallen person's face, he almost shouted. He restrained himself, however. The glimpse was brief, the face obscured, and the pinlegs was moving swiftly, its lens trembling as it zoomed in on its target. Several other pinlegs and scorps were even closer, all converging upon David Menlo.

Scowling, Menlo raised his hand. Instantly, the pinlegs and scorps jolted backward, as though they'd struck an invisible wall. For a second, the screen showed only sky as the pinlegs was flipped onto its back. It righted itself in a flurry of kicking legs and snapping feelers, but soon it was flipped again, now flying backward in a dizzying, alternating jumble of ship and sky. A sharp crackle of static and the feed went dead.

"Switch to another," ordered Prusias, his eyes locked on the screen.

"Those on deck are out of commission," reported Dr. Barrett. "I'll switch back to an aerial view."

Instantly, the screen illuminated, relaying a flyby over the flagship's deck. David Menlo remained where he'd been, but every pinlegs and scorps had been blasted a hundred feet away where they lay in tangled, smoking heaps of legs, body segments, and stingers.

The onscreen image began to shake violently.

"What's happening?" asked Lady Praav. "Is that an earthquake?"

"The camera's airborne," Lord Grael muttered. "Why would an earthquake make it shake?"

Prusias turned toward Dr. Barrett. "Why is it doing that?"

The technician frowned at his receiver. The light within its tubes was pulsing wildly, creating little arcs of electricity that danced against the glass. "It's some sort of atmospheric disturbance," he reported. "I'll switch to a higher altitude."

The new feed showed a broader view of the sea—a sea that appeared to be hissing and boiling as steam billowed off its surface. Beyond the flagship, another galleon sheared in half, a kraken wrenching the stern away in an explosion of splintered timbers. Prusias cackled.

But again, the picture started trembling, jostling and shaking violently as though a train were rumbling past.

"Can't you fix that?" snapped Prusias. The technologists were ruining his show.

"I'm trying, Your Majesty," said Dr. Barrett. "It's just . . ." The technician trailed off, his mouth agape as he stared at the screen. Several people gasped as all muffled conversations ceased. Prusias turned back to the screen.

Ships were rising into the air. Dozens of carracks, frigates, even Hadesian galleons were being lifted slowly out of the sea as though by invisible cranes. Water streamed down their broken hulls, running over the krakens that clung to them. In the midst of this impossible scene, hovered a tiny, solitary figure.

Bram.

As Dr. Barrett zoomed in, Prusias's fears were confirmed. He saw the man all too clearly, his arms outstretched, his hair whipping wildly about. The sorcerer looked like a rabid wolf, his eyes blank and white, his face twisted into a strained and snarled grimace.

Gods, what a foe!

The picture flickered and dimmed suddenly, as though its energy was drawn away, absorbed by the sorcerer. Bram was glowing now, his body crackling with heat and light. Prusias glanced at the technician's machine. Its tubes were almost dark. He gazed back at the screen, resigned to what was about to happen.

When Bram screamed, great bolts of energy shot from his hands, striking the nearest krakens and instantly arcing to the others to form a buckling, incandescent latticework. Krakens split apart, their exoskeletons melting as they dropped from the hovering ships like huge, shriveled spiders. The display was growing brighter. From the corner of his eye, Bram saw the technician set down the receiver and back away.

The tubes exploded in a spray of tiny glass shards as the receiver skittered off the table. Every screen went black. Madam Petra's torque clattered onto the inlaid floor, where it rolled in a slow, wobbling arc before toppling over.

No one spoke. All eyes followed the king as he paced slowly past their tables and bent down to pick up the smoking torque. There was a hiss as the metal touched his flesh, but the demon paid it no mind. He was too busy processing, soaking in what he had just seen. He set the torque down on the smuggler's dessert plate.

"Thank you for letting us borrow this," he muttered absently.

The woman nodded, her fear mingling wonderfully with her perfume. Returning to his table, Prusias called for wine. A servant hurried over to fill his glass.

I'm surrounded by insects, mused Prusias, noting that the servant's hands were trembling. With an inward sigh, he glanced up at his guests and raised his glass.

"A toast! To your entertainment and my victory."

Wary looks were exchanged as the braymas and other guests raised their glasses and took a sip. Only Lord Grael abstained. Leaning back in his chair, the rakshasa puffed on his pipe with an insolent smile.

"What victory is that, friend Prusias?" he called.

Wiping wine from his mouth, Prusias fixed the demon with a penetrating stare. "Were you not attending, Grael? My victory is all but assured."

With a savage laugh, the rakshasa thumped the table so that its dishes clattered. "I'm just an old warrior, Prusias," he confessed amiably. "I have not your taste for politics and cleverness. Only a warped mind, a *human* mind, could prize victory from what I just saw."

"That's your problem, Grael," replied Prusias. "Your imagination has a very short leash. You see a battle that's been lost; I see a war that's been won. Let Rowan crow about their 'triumph' at sea. They've lost dozens of ships, thousands of people, and— unless I'm very much mistaken—they've also lost their Director."

"How do you know that?" inquired Lady Praav.

"She was at David Menlo's feet," replied Prusias, sniffing his wine. "I only had a glimpse, but I don't believe I'm mistaken. No, I'd wager Gabrielle Richter has seen her last sunset."

The demon glanced at Dr. Barrett, curious if the news would have any effect on the Rowan graduate. But it had not. The technician looked as impassive as his colleagues. *You spoke true, my boy. You do belong to the Workshop.*

"Their Director doesn't matter," spat Grael. "What matters is Bram. You said he wouldn't fight Rowan's battles."

"I was as surprised as any to see him," said Prusias. "The man didn't lift a finger to defend Rowan when we besieged them. Why should he do so now?" The demon shrugged. "I don't know why he aided them, Grael, but I'm pleased he did. Magic has its price, you know—even for one such as he. That display we just witnessed was very impressive. And very costly. It will take months, perhaps years, for Bram to recover fully. Rowan just fired its biggest weapon before their army even landed!"

Lord Grael sat perfectly rigid, almost pinned by Prusias's stare.

"Someone pour my friend some wine," said Prusias, grinning savagely at his rival. "He neglected to toast my victory."

The wine was poured and set before Lord Grael, who eyed it as though it were hemlock. Nevertheless, the demon stood and raised the glass high.

"To Prusias and his victory! Your brayma salutes you."

Draining the glass, the proud rakshasa smashed it on the floor and stormed from the chamber. Most of his guests looked horrified, but Prusias merely chuckled.

That's just how I like you, Grael—humbled and angry. God help the first enemies I set you upon!

~ 9 ~

AN OKLAHOMA GIRL

David winced as the moomenhoven's needle passed through his skin. The cut was above his right eye and superficial, albeit bloody. Mystics were being rationed for true emergencies—injuries that could not be treated with needle and thread.

He had expended a great deal of energy destroying those two creatures that attacked the flagship, not to mention the pinlegs and those larger, scorpion-like horrors. Despite the many questions crowding his mind, he had to overcome an urge to lie down and rest.

To take his mind off the pain and his exhaustion, he focused on the hanging lantern that illuminated this dark corner. Its swinging was almost hypnotic, as was the sound of seawater sloshing through the galleon. Plucking at his wrist stump, he listened to someone calling a cadence for those working the pumps.

This ship won't sink, he thought. *Battered and flooded, but still seaworthy.* He wished his certainty extended to other vessels in their fleet. *Naiad* was certainly destroyed—he had seen her shorn in half, her bowsprit swallowed by a wave. He'd heard others say the same of *Andromeda, Norn, Seastar,* and *Bellerophon.* There would be others, of course, and innumerable casualties.

Loss was a funny thing. There was a David Menlo who cared too little, who regarded others' needs and feelings with profound indifference. And there was a David who cared too much, who processed life and loss with a poignancy that threatened to overwhelm him. Balancing the two required tremendous focus, which is why he'd chosen this quiet corner for his treatment. He needed time to think, to regain control.

Splash. Splash, splash.

David did not bother to open his eyes. As the moomenhoven finished the final stitch, he heard a familiar brogue.

"Is the young gentleman recovering?"

"I'm fine, Tweedy," said David. "How are you?"

"Uninjured," said the hare hoarsely. "Thank you for saving us, Mr. Menlo."

"That was my grandfather."

"They say you dealt with the two that attacked this ship."

"I suppose I did. You're welcome, Tweedy. Any sign of my grandfather?"

"Not since he vanished."

A curious silence followed. Tweedy never wasted an opportunity to fill a conversational vacuum, to declaim on matters great and small. David opened his eyes.

Tweedy was crying.

The gruff little hare slumped against a bulkhead, sobbing silently as he hugged his clipboard against his gray-brown belly. Easing off the table, David knelt in the water and stroked the animal's long, trembling ears.

"What's wrong, Tweedy?" he asked.

"I . . . I apologize," he stammered.

"Shhh," said David. "What's wrong? Why did you come to find me?"

Wiping a paw across his eyes, the hare straightened and assumed a formal manner. "Mr. Menlo, your presence is required in the Director's cabin. Are you fit to walk?"

"Yes. I think so."

Thanking the moomenhoven, David followed the hare through the bowels of the vast ship. Mystics, carpenters, and domovoi were hard at work, pumping seawater and repairing the damaged hull. He avoided eye contact, only nodding as people paused from their work to thank him for what he'd done on deck.

What had he done?

His duty, no more. Pretending it was heroism always made him uncomfortable. He was no more heroic than anyone else who'd done his or her part. His magic was just more powerful. That didn't make him a hero; it simply made him gifted.

But gifted or not, he was tired. Bone weary. His chest ached; the scar above his heart burned. It always did when he channeled so much destructive energy. His outlay was a pittance compared to Bram's, but he'd scraped his coffers dry. What David needed was sleep. He prayed his audience with the Director would be brief.

She'd been unconscious when he found her, injured either by a broken spar or one of the larger creatures he'd seen incinerated in her vicinity. Given the chaos on deck, he hadn't had time to inspect her closely. In that split second he'd seen her breathing.

Her only visible wound was a jagged, foot-long splinter that had pierced her upper arm. Given this, his focus and energies had naturally shifted to repelling the attack. Only when it was over did David realize someone had taken Ms. Richter below.

Triple the usual number of guards was stationed outside her cabin door. Among them, David recognized several members of the Bloodstone Circle, a cadre of Agents second only to the Red Branch. *These ones aren't assigned to this ship*, thought David. *They must have come over from the* Typhon. *But why? Right now there are a million better uses for them than standing outside a door—even the Director's.*

The guards stood aside as David entered for the second time that evening. Ndidi Awolowo, Ms. Richter's chief adviser, stood in the waiting room engaged in quiet conversation with two Mystics and a wizened dvergar. The dvergar and Miss Awolowo were a study in contrasts. The former was short and squat with mottled gray skin and eyes like small white pebbles; the latter was tall and regal in colorful robes, an ageless Nigerian beauty with skin like polished horn. Her large, dark eyes fell upon David as he entered. She offered a grandmother's smile, both happy and sad.

"There you are," she said. "Thank you, Tweedy. That will be all."

"I could stay," volunteered the hare.

Miss Awolowo shook her head. "I'm sorry but there is a protocol to follow."

With a dutiful bow, the hare withdrew and David was left in the waiting room with Miss Awolowo, the dvergar, and the Mystics. When Miss Awolowo took his hand, David's unease intensified. *What was going on? Where was Ms. Richter?*

The others followed as she led David into the cabin that served as Ms. Richter's office. There, he saw Joseph Vincenti, Rowan's retired Instructor of Devices, and Armand Black, Captain of the

Bloodstone Circle. Both men were grave as they eyed the table where the Director lay.

Two moomenhovens were attending to Ms. Richter, their practiced hands anointing her strong but tranquil face with camphor oil. A pastor was sitting in one of the unbroken chairs. He looked wearier than David felt as he perused his Bible, thumbing from page to page in search of a reading. Why was he doing that?

The realization struck David like a silent thunderbolt.

Ms. Richter was dead.

Miss Awolowo was somber but composed. "There will be time to grieve later," she said. She set a box upon the desk, its top embossed with the Rowan seal. Taking a key from around her neck, Miss Awolowo opened it and removed a large envelope sealed with wax and twined with silvery, glowing cobwebs. She turned to the dvergar.

"Aurvangr, would you verify that it is intact?"

This the dvergar did, inspecting the seal with a jeweler's lens and murmuring words in Old Norse. Pronouncing it sound, he returned the envelope to Miss Awolowo, who promptly opened it with a silver knife. She slid several papers out, found the one she was looking for, and invited the Mystics to inspect it.

"Would you please attest that this was written by Gabrielle Richter?"

Each of the Mystics held the paper in turn, their fingers dancing lightly over its surface as though they were reading Braille.

"It is authentic," they confirmed.

"Thank you," said Miss Awolowo, taking it from her. "Do Armand Black and Joseph Vincenti concur that the protocols have been followed?"

"We do," replied the men in unison.

"Very well," said Miss Awolowo, holding the sheet up to the

lantern. "These are the succession wishes of Gabrielle Richter, twenty-fourth Director of Rowan."

The parchment gave off a golden glow. Tears filled David's eyes as Ms. Richter's voice filled the cabin.

"I, Gabrielle Dorothy Richter, being of sound mind and body, do hereby name my replacement should death or incapacity prevent me from fulfilling my duties. This is the Director's privilege in times of war. While the appointment is temporary, my successor shall assume all powers, privileges, and responsibilities of my office until the Council can agree upon a permanent replacement. In the event of my death or incapacity, Rowan's acting Director shall be . . ."

David shut his eyes. *No. Someone else. Anyone else.*

". . . David Menlo."

All strength seemed to leave his body. Clutching a nearby table, he slid into a broken chair. Gazing up, he found that all eyes were upon him. The Mystics and dvergar were impassive, Vincenti was nodding, but Armand Black merely turned to Miss Awolowo.

"Not Bram?" he asked.

"Apparently not," replied Miss Awolowo. "You heard Gabrielle as well as I."

Armand Black voiced his objections as though David weren't in the room. "He can't be Director. He's still a boy!"

Miss Awolowo held up a warning finger. "There is nothing in our laws to deny David Menlo's legitimacy as acting Director. His age is irrelevant. The choice is Gabrielle's and that choice is clear."

Armand looked to David in appeal. "Surely you see the foolishness in this. Rowan is at war! Our losses in this attack are bad enough—we can't compound them by naming a teenager Director. This has nothing to do with your capabilities, Mr. Menlo. It has everything to do with how this would be perceived by enemies and potential allies. Ndidi, you would be far more suitable as acting Director."

Miss Awolowo shook her head. "This is Gabrielle's choice and hers alone. You can voice your objections at a later date. The sole purpose of this gathering is to enact Gabrielle's wishes and invest David with the rights and responsibilities of Director."

The woman's calm, absolute authority made a profound impression. With a bow, Armand apologized. Clearing his throat, David spoke up.

"You're right," he said, addressing Agent Black. "I shouldn't be Director." He turned to Miss Awolowo. "Is it possible to decline the appointment? I don't think I'm the person for his job."

"That is certainly your privilege," she replied. "But I would like a word before you make any decisions. May I have that word?"

"Of course."

The others filed out, even the moomenhovens who arranged Ms. Richter's hair and coverlet before scurrying out. When the door closed, David placed a silence charm upon it—no sound would escape the cabin.

"How did this happen?" he exclaimed, gesturing in disbelief at Ms. Richter's body. His grief was surging to the surface, commandeering any and all emotions. "I saw her on deck! She was unconscious, but nothing like . . . this!"

"Poison," said Miss Awolowo. "She was wounded by one of those Workshop creatures while her attention was on the monsters attacking the ship. A stinger pierced her arm. The toxin worked swiftly. I don't believe she suffered."

David reeled. "It wasn't a splinter," he muttered.

"Come again?"

"I saw a splinter," David explained. "Stuck in her arm. But it was a stinger. I . . . I just left it there."

"You were busy saving this ship," said Miss Awolowo pointedly. "You did exactly as Gabrielle would have wanted you to do. You are not responsible for her death."

David said nothing. The assessment was kind, but he was not so certain he agreed. The reality, the weight of his predicament, came pressing down upon him. He struggled for breath, for the words to form and lead him out of this trap.

"Miss Awolowo, I *can't* be Director."

"Gabrielle disagrees."

"She's mistaken."

"I disagree."

David gave a helpless sort of laugh. "How can I be Director, Miss Awolowo? I was expelled from Rowan!"

She shrugged. "And deservedly so. You weren't attending your classes and disobeyed a slew of orders. Never was there a more deserving candidate for expulsion. What of it?"

"I'm unqualified."

The woman placed a hand on his shoulder. "David, no incoming Director is qualified when they assume the office. Each must grow into the role."

As David considered this, a question nagged at him. "How did you know?"

"Know what?"

"That she intended to name me," he said.

"She told me," replied Miss Awolowo simply. "I've always been Gabrielle's confidante, you know. She was younger than I, but she became my closest friend, even my mentor. She had you pegged as a future Director when you were a First Year."

"You're joking."

"Not at all. I even remember the day. It was when she realized you were stealing grimoires from the Archives. She debated whether to punish you and ultimately decided against it. Gabrielle had a keen sense of when to rein someone in and felt that you needed latitude to explore. 'Mark my words,' she'd say. 'If that boy doesn't blow himself up, he'll be the best Director Rowan's ever had.' She adored you."

David's cheeks flushed hot with shame. "I used to think she was stupid," he said quietly. "The year I was expelled—when Gràvenmuir was built. I disagreed with almost everything she did or said. I decided to fight the war alone, do everything alone. It was only last year that I finally started to understand how complicated her job really was. It's not easy being Director."

"No," said Miss Awolowo. "It's not. The demands are great, the problems challenging. You cannot please everyone and will fail if you try. But Gabrielle had a wonderful system for simplifying problems. Do you know what she'd do?"

"What?"

"She'd make herself a milkshake and walk through the orchards. And on that walk, she'd ask herself a simple question: 'What would an Oklahoma girl do?'"

"I didn't know she was from Oklahoma," David murmured, studying Ms. Richter's face. Even in death, it looked assured.

"Gabrielle was from a tiny town," said Miss Awolowo. "Even smaller than my village in Nigeria. Her grandmother was Cherokee, but the rest of her people had been Sooners. She joked she'd always be a frontier gal—a lost little tumbleweed that blew all the way to Rowan. She never forgot her roots. Whenever Rowan's problems threatened to overwhelm her, she took comfort from that question: *What would an Oklahoma girl do?* As Director, the problems she faced were more complex than those she'd faced as a child, but she tackled them the same way—with courage, integrity, and humor. That question kept her grounded amid all the noise and chaos. The milkshakes helped, too."

David tried to smile. "I've never thought of myself as a leader," he said. "What if I can't be like her?"

Miss Awolowo tutted gently. "You mustn't try to be. She was Gabrielle Richter. You are David Menlo. You're different people. It's only natural that you will lead in different ways." The old recruiter gave him a shrewd look. "There are many kinds of leaders. Too often we confuse a forceful personality with leadership. This is a mistake. Those with different talents and styles can reach the same mountaintop; they just take different paths to get there."

David gazed up at her, mindful that his heart was no longer fluttering like a caged and frantic bird. There was nothing magical about the effect she was having on him. The calm she induced was simply an extension of her poise and compassion.

"You make me feel better," he muttered.

Miss Awolowo winked. "Why do you think Gabrielle kept me around all these years? There are times when every Director needs to vent their frustrations to someone who will simply listen and not judge them. I was that person for Gabrielle. I can be that person for you."

David nodded, his insides twisting at a final confession. "There may be other reasons I shouldn't be Director. Reasons having to do with . . . my heritage."

Miss Awolowo raised her eyebrows. "David, you do not need to tell me anything you do not wish to. But it may comfort you to know that Gabrielle suspected what I believe is troubling you."

"I'm not talking about my grandfather."

"Neither am I," replied Miss Awolowo. "Don't forget that I recruited you, David. Your powers fairly screamed 'Old Magic.' As you can imagine, many people were interested in your background. Given your mother's challenges, speculation centered on your father, but there is no mention of a Mr. Menlo."

"No," said David. "There wouldn't be."

"The only things we turned up were records of your heart transplants and the fact that your mother changed her name from Brahms to Menlo."

"I did that," said David. "When she was growing up, no one called her Emer. They just said 'she's Bram's' like she was branded cattle. Some clerk even recorded that as her official name. It was insulting. When I was seven, I broke about a dozen laws and changed it."

"Why did you choose Menlo?"

David shrugged. "I liked Thomas Edison. He was the 'Wizard of Menlo Park' and I thought that was pretty cool. I guess we're lucky I didn't choose 'Spider-Man.'"

Miss Awolowo smiled. "How could you know what people called your mother when she was young?" she asked. "Emer was born hundreds of years ago. Did she tell you this herself?"

David nodded. "In her way."

"What way is that?"

"My mother's brain is damaged, but she never forgets anything. Sometimes she'll recite things she's heard, whole conversations verbatim. That's how I learned what my father was." David gazed imploringly at the woman. "I can't be Director, Miss Awolowo. I can serve Rowan but I can't lead it. My kind isn't fit."

Miss Awolowo frowned. "If I ever hear you say something like that again, I will become angry. 'Not fit.' What nonsense! If you really believe you're destined for evil, why resist? Why make the choices that you have?"

David was numb. The fact that he was even having this conversation was mind-boggling. He'd never had this conversation—not even with his grandfather. Bram knew, of course, but they talked around it. Miss Awolowo beckoned at him.

"Say what you are," she urged.

That word. David had read it, and researched it, but he'd never actually spoken it. He unlocked it from its prison and led it forth, allowing it to squeeze past his lips.

"A cambion," he whispered.

Cambion. He'd actually said it! The truth was out in the world, even if it was confined to this cabin. David Menlo was a cambion, the offspring of human and demon. And now Miss Awolowo knew. She might have suspected, but now she *knew.* The fact that he couldn't take it back was strangely liberating. David blinked, amazed by emotions he was experiencing.

Miss Awolowo shrugged. "So you're a cambion. Am I supposed to recoil?"

"If you like."

"I'll pass," she said. "With all due respect, however, I must take issue with your definition. A cambion is not what you are."

"Then what am I?" asked David.

"You are your choices," she replied. "And those choices say that David Menlo is kind, a good friend, a loving son, a wonderful mentor for Mina, a tireless worker, and Rowan's savior many times over. He *happens* to be blond, a powerful sorcerer, and a cambion. But these are mere facts—they tell us nothing about David Menlo's character or what he has chosen to be. Our choices in life define us far more than entries on a birth certificate. You are being asked to make a choice now. You must choose whether to accept Gabrielle's faith and trust in you."

"Lots of people won't want me to be Director."

"I've lived a long time," Miss Awolowo sighed. "I have yet to see a leader who enjoyed universal approval. If those are conditions you require, David, you'll be disappointed. Even worse, you might not take risks and become the leader you could be. You assume being a cambion is a handicap, but it bolstered Gabrielle's belief that you were the person for the job."

David almost choked. "She chose me *because* I was a cambion?"

"No," said Miss Awolowo firmly. "She chose you for the qualities I've already mentioned. However, I think she thought it might help. The world we're living in has changed. Even if we're victorious, even if we topple Prusias, things will never go back to how they were. Those who have reawakened or entered this world are not leaving. If there's to be lasting peace, humans, demons, and other beings must find ways to coexist. A cambion might be the bridge that's needed."

"How did Ms. Richter know I was a cambion?"

"She had suspected from your First Year, but her suspicions were confirmed the night we expelled you."

David recalled that evening, the knock on his door and the brief interview with Ms. Richter and Miss Awolowo. He had been in the midst of his experiments, which were highly toxic to demons.

"Blood petals," he muttered. "How did you know they were dangerous to me?"

"I didn't," said Miss Awolowo. "It was Gabrielle who noticed the strange red flowers, your gloves, and the sheen of ointment protecting your skin. And then, of course, there was your declining health. She palmed a petal when you weren't looking. Her analysis revealed properties extremely toxic to demons but harmless to everything else. Blood petals don't even make humans sneeze, but you appeared to be having a mild reaction. You're not the first cambion who has tried to hide his nature, David. You were just the best at it."

David was astonished. Everything Miss Awolowo said was true. He had saturated his skin with protective salves and slowly built up a tolerance, but experimenting with the petals had still taken a fearsome toll. This conversation was still difficult to process.

Ms. Richter knew I was a cambion and didn't care! Miss Awolowo knows I'm a cambion and doesn't care! He had spent his entire life hiding the fact. His ceaseless efforts to mask his aura had stunted his growth and even weakened his body to the point his heart had given out. In his mind, his extreme measures had been worth it. He was spared the stigma of being half demon, of being despised by both races. And while demons were stronger than humans in many ways, they had their own vulnerabilities. If others learned David was cambion, there was the possibility he could be summoned—even against his will if the party learned his truename.

While the price was high, his efforts had worked—not even demons could tell David was a cambion. Only Mina had known right away. *And she hadn't cared either!*

David's entire world was turning upside down. The idea that he might no longer have to hide this aspect of himself was simply staggering.

"Should I tell my friends?" he wondered aloud, thinking of Cynthia Gilley and Max. They were the two people closest to him. What would they think?

Miss Awolowo shrugged. "That is up to you. But I doubt it will bother the people who are dearest to you. They love you for who you are—not your family tree. Does your grandfather know?"

"He knows what my father was."

"And does he accept you?"

David nodded. He walked over to Ms. Richter's body and took her hand. She had given him the greatest gift he had ever known—the gift of acceptance. He looked deeply in the Director's tranquil face. *I'm going to make you proud.*

Tucking Ms. Richter's hand under the coverlet, David turned to Miss Awolowo.

"I'll do it."

Ndidi Awolowo didn't need to be told twice. With a curt nod, she opened the door and called the others back in. Ten minutes later, David swore his oath and Rowan had a new Director.

Over the next few hours, the moomenhovens removed Ms. Richter's body to continue the burial preparations while Mr. Vincenti and others took the lead on tallying and repairing damage from the attack. Meanwhile, Miss Awolowo gave David a crash course on being Director.

Cases of papers, files, reports, and official correspondence were piled before him. The amount of information was staggering: updates on Rowan's crops, food stores, civil defense, academic reports, personnel, Sanctuary matters, official correspondence . . . The categories, much less their contents, seemed endless. Fortunately, Miss Awolowo was on hand to make sense of it all. While she gave a brief overview of these and other subjects, she assured him that administrators could tend to these affairs. However, there were matters that required the Director's immediate attention.

These top-secret files were stored in an inlaid chest without a keyhole or clasp. It would yield only to the Director's touch. Removing the documents, David scanned their contents while other areas of his brain organized the data, analyzed its implications, and constructed patterns. Not even Bram could match David's capacity to absorb and analyze information. Even so, it was challenging to digest so many revelations and secrets in one sitting.

Some files revealed secret locations and passages at Rowan;

others listed suspected traitors, detailed backchannel communications with prominent braymas . . . David learned that Ms. Richter had been corresponding with Queen Lilith, the ruler of Zenuvia, for over a year. A year! There were scrolls from the witch clans and communiqués from Dr. Rasmussen, former chief of the Frankfurt Workshop. David's pale, colorless eyes flipped through a dossier concerning Elder vyes that left him speechless. Closing the folder, he rubbed his eyes and stared idly at his cup of lukewarm coffee.

"Jakob?" he called.

Jakob Quills, David's research assistant, came bustling in with a steaming pot of coffee. The domovoi touched a bristly knuckle to his skullcap.

"I need you to organize this using our system," said David wearily. "The documents are encrypted, but I've labeled corners. When's the service?"

"Tomorrow morning, sir," replied Jakob, setting down the pot. "Miss Awolowo's preparing the eulogy. Rest of the fleet's been informed."

David nodded. "What are our losses?"

"Thirty-one ships, over eleven thousand souls, sir. We've sent boats to search for any survivors. Doesn't look good."

"Has Mina been told?"

"Miss Awolowo plans to inform her once she's finished."

"I'll do it," said David. "Would you get me her spypaper? Max's, too, while you're at it. The Red Branch dossier's the one by that lantern. Just bring the whole thing."

The proper files were found and set upon David's desk, and the domovoi departed. Rubbing the sleep from his eyes, David glanced out the windows. It was easy enough to mend broken glass, but this weather was another matter. The panes had nearly frosted over, allowing only a hint of the ruddy red sky beyond.

It's only getting worse. We need to make landfall.

The hovering quill acted as David's scribe. It dipped its nib in the glossy ink and set about the spypaper like a hummingbird.

Dear Mina,

We were attacked near the Straits. Richter is gone and I am now Director. Winter is settling early and I fear it will be very bad. Rowan must ration everything. If you see my grandfather, tell me immediately. He might not be well.

Sol Invictus,
David

The ink soaked into the parchment, transmitting the message to little Mina in Túr an Ghrian. He wondered how she was doing. By the time Rowan had set sail, her charge Ember had already grown to the size of a moderate python. *How fast did dragons grow?* He'd have Jakob track down whatever information the Archives had. Meanwhile, he needed to reach out to Max.

How would Max respond to news of Ms. Richter's death? Like David, Max had also fallen in and out of the Director's favor. But they had been close—particularly in the weeks leading up to Prusias's siege. Still, Max was in the Red Branch. He'd seen death aplenty. Best to simply tell him.

David opened Max's file, found the square of spypaper, and laid the Director's decrypting glass upon it.

No recent messages.

That was odd. Anyone leading a DarkMatter operation was required to report every forty-eight hours. Frowning slightly, David reached for Cooper's folder. The Agent's latest message was not written in his hand, but Hazel's.

Gabrielle,

Urgent: Workshop clones tracked Max to Shrope Hovel. We attempted diversion but were unsuccessful. The clones boasted they have a weapon that can kill him. Max was wounded. There was an explosion and we were knocked unconscious. I do not know if Max or Scathach survived.

William and I are injured but proceeding across the Channel with Toby. William's arms are broken, but I am mending them. He intends to complete his mission and has acquired a contact to help him do so. I will await further instructions from you.

Sol Invictus,
Hazel

David's weariness vanished. He called sharply for Jakob, who bustled into the cabin looking startled.

"Yes?"

"I have to do something," said David. "I am not to be disturbed unless the fleet comes under attack."

"But what if Miss Awolowo—"

David cut him off. "Not unless we're under direct attack, Jakob. Understood? Place guards at the door."

The domovoi bowed. "Yes, Director."

When Jakob withdrew, David locked the door with a gesture. Another wave sent the furniture, boxes, cases, and papers to the corners, leaving an open space in the cabin's center. As David stared at it, his pulse began to quicken.

While only the most prudish scholars considered shadow walking "black magic," all agreed it was dangerous. The feat involved sending one's soul on a journey into Nether, the hazy borderlands between the world of the living and the dead. While shadow walking, one's soul could travel vast distances in a short time. But there were daunting risks.

For one, the place was a disorienting landscape in which it was easy to get lost or lose sight of the path that led back to one's body. And one was not alone. There were other travelers in that vaporous murk, other spirits that glided past on errands of their own or had become lost eons past and gone mad in their fruitless wandering. And finally, Astaroth was known to shadow walk—it was how he often spoke with others without putting his physical form at risk. If David encountered the Demon in that realm, things might turn very grim indeed.

David had not shadow walked since Walpurgisnacht. He had done so often enough in the months leading up to that fateful night, but never since. The act took a toll on his constitution and the experience always frightened him. Once he'd become severely disoriented and wandered for hours before regaining his bearings. More than once he'd glimpsed some monstrous silhouette drifting past in the gloom. He wasn't certain which was more terrifying: eternal solitude or nightmarish company.

But he was shadow walking tonight.

Rowan's Director needed to know if two Red Branch agents were alive. David Menlo needed to know if his friends needed his help. It was his fault the Atropos possessed a compass that enabled them to track Max.

Gathering himself, David inscribed a magic circle and drew the ancient symbols that would enable his spirit to leave his body and slip into the Nether. When all was ready, he knelt within the circle, closed his eyes, and traced the seven letters of his truename.

~ 10 ~

NETHER

Wise visitors to Nether followed the same rules as schoolchildren: don't stray, don't dawdle, and don't talk to strangers. David followed these rules religiously, but he never felt at ease in Nether. Everything about the realm was *off*. One's surroundings and landmarks might have been familiar—for Nether overlapped the living world—but everything looked as if it were viewed through a pane of warped, smoky glass. There were no colors. Everything appeared in shades of gray—from charcoal skies to gunmetal seas to veils of pale mist that drifted in a perpetual sigh across the realm.

In Nether, one's senses often behaved in bizarre and

unpredictable ways. The earth might tremble from a silent thunderclap while whispers might carry for miles. There were times one felt agreeably weightless and others when every step required Herculean effort. For visitors, the only predictable sensation was cold.

Nether's cold was unlike anything found in the living world. It had a clinging, viscous quality that felt as though one were wading through a pool of spectral oil. Nothing seemed to dampen or guard against it. Whenever David shadow walked, each step was a draining reminder that he was an outsider.

Peculiar as it was, there were compelling reasons to visit. Some believed Nether harbored ancient and powerful artifacts. Others sought counsel or wisdom from its permanent residents. David's reasons were more practical—Nether could serve as a shortcut, a means to travel far more swiftly than one could in the physical world. While shadow walking wasn't instantaneous like teleportation, a skilled shadow walker might cover a mile with every dreamlike step. While in the Nether, David could not touch things in the living world, but he could manifest enough for others to see him as a ghostlike figure. In this form, he could converse with them or even possess the bodies of soulless creatures to perform basic tasks.

Of course, such visits had risks. Most immediate was the danger to one's physical being. Back aboard the flagship, David's body was sitting in a trance, utterly helpless and vulnerable.

David had not only left his body behind, but he also left behind much of his power. Just as light and sound behaved differently in this realm, so, too, did mystic energies. Within Nether, magic either failed or yielded unexpected, potentially dangerous results. But David never stayed to experiment, for that could lead to shadow walking's greatest peril—the danger of becoming lost.

For Nether was something of a spiritual tar pit, a plane

brimming with lost souls and spirits that had stumbled in and never found their way out. One could hear them wailing in the mists, glimpse them groping through the twilit landscapes as they tried to find their way back to bodies that may have wasted away centuries ago. Unless they could possess another living body, they would be lost in Nether forever. Each was a cautionary tale to complete one's task and get out.

That was certainly David's intention. Once he gained a sense of direction from the fleet's orientation, he set off. The earth almost seemed to rotate beneath him as his spirit strode north over the gray sea. Above, the sky was a surreal, roiling canvas of mist and cloud. There were no stars. In Nether, one never glimpsed the sun, stars, or moon—its heavens were always overcast, a perpetual gray twilight without time or season.

In the middle of the ocean, one encountered fewer spirits than one might on land or near old cities. Prusias's capital was built on the ruins of ancient Rome. In Nether, that area was practically overrun with spirits—they crowded the lanes and hillsides, crying out to living passersby like hungry beggars in a marketplace. But here at sea, Nether was eerily quiet. There were some lost souls on the ocean, but they were rare—distant wisps that soon faded from view.

In ten minutes, David had traveled a vast distance. He still had almost a thousand miles to go, but each step brought him a mile closer. He shivered with cold, but he was calmer than he expected—his mind was humming along in a state of controlled urgency. In ten or fifteen minutes he'd reach the Isle of Man and be able to help his friends.

And then David saw the light.

It came from behind, sweeping over him like a lighthouse beam. David turned and gasped.

A storm was pursuing him.

It was not a storm of rain or thunder, but something akin to a living eclipse, a writhing darkness wreathed in a nimbus of pale lightning. It raced toward him over the waves, gliding swiftly above the swells. Its size became apparent as it closed.

Was it Yuga?

The mere thought of that hurricane-sized demon sent David reeling in blind, almost frantic terror across the sea. Even as he fled, David knew it was folly. His pursuer was far too swift, his options far too few. In such a landscape, David was like a wounded rabbit limping across the plain. There was nowhere to run, nowhere to hide. It was only a matter of time before it drew the attention of something bigger, something swifter. Something hungry.

The storm enveloped him, huge and overpowering. It crushed down upon him even as it lifted him up, spinning him about in a deafening roar. He was sent skittering across the waves like a skipped stone. Plucked up, he was whipped to and fro and sent tumbling again over the seas. David screamed, his voice echoing into the great gray twilight.

Something screamed back.

It screamed back with his voice. It screamed with other voices. More joined it, by twos and threes, tens and twenties, so that soon Nether itself seemed to be screaming in an unearthly, dissonant chorus. Again, terrifying forces plucked him up and shook him like a cat might shake a kitten.

It's toying with me.

He was yanked upward, his spirit whipping about a funnel of churning, pluming darkness. David had never felt so tiny, so powerless. The idea of resistance, of fighting back seemed so pre-posterous that he simply shut down.

Please.

Instantly, the screaming stopped. Its echo faded as David's

spirit was set down gently upon the sea. Stunned, he floated above the gray swells in the midst of a swirling funnel. Slowly, the funnel collapsed upon itself, sinking into a boiling, frothing island of black pustules. Here and there huge tendrils formed, snaking out from the seething mass to hover before David as faces formed within them.

"What would you like me to be?"

"What would you like?"

"Would you like to be me?"

"What would you like?"

The faces were male and female, young and old, angelic and fiendish. There were dozens of faces, hundreds of faces, smiling and intertwining, casually devouring one another only to be reborn a moment later. Again and again the questions were repeated. David shut his eyes and curled into a ball.

The voices diminished. One by one, they fell away, mingling into one another and combining to form a single honeyed tenor.

"What would you like me to be?"

David opened his eyes and beheld Astaroth.

The chimerical stew was gone. The being that hovered before David was slender and androgynous. Long, shining black hair framed an alabaster face that was fixed in a prim, solicitous smile. His robes were white and he shone with an inner radiance.

"Do you prefer this?" inquired Astaroth, gesturing at his current form. "If not, I can go back. I can always go back."

"I prefer it," croaked David.

"Do you really?" pressed Astaroth playfully. "Your actions say otherwise. But I'm glad you ventured into the Nether. You've saved me the trouble of hunting for you elsewhere. Did my lesson take?"

"What lesson?"

Astaroth tutted. "I should have thought it was fairly evident.

It shames me to be so crude, but nothing else seems to get through. Here is the lesson, David Menlo: I can destroy you the instant I choose. I can destroy Rowan the instant I choose. Prusias. Lilith. Any and all."

"So, why don't you?"

Astaroth leaned close, his eyes crinkled slits. "Because you're children!" he laughed. "I've come to understand that. Children! I must discipline you with love and patience. Look at you! Even now, nations wage war while the earth freezes beneath their feet. Must I starve the world? Set Rowan adrift? Raise mountains to topple false idols? When will my foolish little children mind their loving parent?"

As David listened, a profound horror overcame him. There was no correlation between the Demon's words, his smile, and the dead black eyes.

"May I speak?" he asked softly.

"Of course," replied Astaroth. "What would you like to say?"

"I don't know what you are," David ventured. "I don't know how old you are or even where you come from. But I do know you will never get what you want. You want desperately to be our Creator, but you're not our Creator. You will never be our Creator."

"But I have the Book of Thoth."

"You do," David acknowledged. "And so you must know that it's just a tool. A gardener's tool, but it did not create the garden. Tell me. Who created Thoth? Who created Nether and Fey and the Sidh? Who created Oblivion?"

Astaroth's smile grew dangerous, but David pressed on. "Lesser gods may rule these places, but they did not create them. You pretend we are your children, Astaroth, but you know that's not true. You can force us to bend the knee, you can obliterate us, but to what purpose? It won't make you God."

Astaroth stared at him with blank, ravenous eyes. "And what is God? Tell me that, David Menlo."

All David could do was offer a helpless shrug. "I don't know."

"Does it frighten you not to know?"

"It would frighten me more to think that God was something I could possibly define or understand."

Astaroth nodded, but his mind seemed a million miles away. And then his mouth twitched. The ensuing smile was so mechanical, so alien and contrived that David had to master every instinct to flee.

"I want to stand before this God," said Astaroth softly. "I want to know him, serve him, devour him. Is this possible, David Menlo?"

"I don't know."

Astaroth did not speak for some time. The Demon merely stared ahead, his eyes dead black windows into some other world, some other universe. David hovered before him, unable to run but wilting from Nether's debilitating cold. Despite his mixed blood and Bram's heritage, David was mortal. A mortal's spirit could not be parted long from its body. His wits were fading as his spirit began to drown in Nether's cold. He could no longer mask his aura.

With a blink, Astaroth seemed to notice him once again. "You've shed your cloak," he muttered absently. "I see you clearly now. How Bram must have seethed at his daughter's shame. Are you ashamed of what you are, David Menlo?"

"No. Not anymore."

Astaroth nodded and touched his own face, gingerly handling its edges as though it were a fragile mask. He cocked his head, studying David as though he were a butterfly twitching in a poisoned jar. "You're dying. Dying here in Nether. Should I let you die, David?"

"No," David gasped. "I have to live."

Gliding forward, Astaroth cupped David's face in his trembling hands. The grin grew manic as tears flowed freely down the Demon's luminescent face.

He's coming unhinged.

"'I have to live,'" Astaroth repeated softly. "That is the most beautiful thing I've heard this age. I *want* you to live, David Menlo! I want you whole when I draw your God out of hiding. *I want you whole when your God is devoured!*"

Astaroth kissed David's forehead. Searing heat flooded into David's body, driving off Nether's cold as if he'd taken a tot of hot brandy.

"Go," whispered Astaroth, pointing north. "Complete your errand and save the Hound. After all, we mustn't let her have him!"

Releasing David, Astaroth strode away east across the Nether sea. In three strides, the Demon disappeared from view.

David turned and ran.

He continued on, fueled by panic and the fire Astaroth had kindled within him. His head was buzzing as a prickling sensation spread throughout his body. It radiated out from his head and heart, inching along until it made his hands and fingers twitch.

His hands.

David stopped and stared. In Nether, his form was spectral and translucent, but there was no mistaking what he now waved before his own face. Astaroth had restored his hand. There was no more stump, but a ghostly hand with a pale scar about the wrist where the two had been rejoined.

When David waved it, it responded. When he wiggled its fingers, they did just as he asked. He experienced an onslaught of conflicting thoughts and emotions. Joy. Disbelief. Suspicion. Gratitude. Among the many, gratitude was the most puzzling.

Should David be grateful that Astaroth returned what he'd taken so violently? Had his hand been restored to his physical body or did it exist only in Nether?

What a strange day. In the space of a few hours, he'd been transformed from a sorcerer with one hand into a Director with two. What would his grandfather say about all this? What would his grandfather say about this strange interview with Astaroth? What did the Demon mean about drawing God out of hiding and seeing him devoured? What did Astaroth mean when he said they mustn't let "her" have Max? *Who was "her"?*

What would an Oklahoma girl do?

David almost laughed as the question entered, unbidden, in his mind. He supposed an Oklahoma girl would finish what she'd started. Much had changed, but Max and Scathach's peril had not. Clearing his mind, David pressed on.

He went first to Shrope Hovel, gliding silently over the countryside and the hags' leaning house to find it dark and quiet. David entered the Hovel, slipping through a window where the hags had neglected to place protections. He walked silently through the house, glimpsing Bob sleeping in the attic and Bellagrog writing at her desk in the drawing room. Mum was in the root cellar, cutting vegetables and squeezing them into tins. She shivered as David drifted through her, sensing the secret passage that lay behind a mountain of potatoes.

David glided swiftly down the secret passage. They'd undoubtedly made for a river, intending to take *Ormenheid* to the Isle of Man and seek the giant. Had they reached him?

A step later, he emerged from the secret tunnel. Another two steps and he reached the river and surveyed the devastation. What trees remained had been blown over, twisted from the ground and stripped of their bark and branches. From above, the scene looked like scorched toothpicks had been scattered about a central point. It was a wonder anyone had survived.

There were other spirits about, of course. They glided to and fro across the shadowed landscape. David ignored them, his spirit carrying over the trees to follow the rivers until they fed into the Irish Sea.

David had never shadow walked to the Isle of Man or managed to view it through his observatory dome at Rowan. The Fomorian's isle was hidden from prying eyes. As David approached, he saw the reason why.

The island was veiled with a twinkling, dewy mist. It would not have been visible in the living world, but in Nether the curtain shimmered and undulated, encircling the isle like an earthbound aurora. Even if Max or Scathach tried to send a message, David doubted it would get through. The Fomorian's magic was exceedingly strong—far stronger than David's, much less scraps of Florentine spypaper. The giant tolerated no intruders, no spies, no magic but his own.

Passing within the glimmering veil, David walked along the isle's coastline. He witnessed firsthand the ruin of Prusias's ships and the bodies scattered along the foamy shoreline. He found the pillar and the demons hanging like grisly ornaments. The devastation wrought by the Fomorian was simply incredible.

Of the Fomorian himself, there was no sign. Gliding inland, David's spirit swept over the snowy hills, silver rivers, and broad black forests. The isle was as shadowed and quiet as a tomb.

What was that?

Below, he spied a glimmer. It winked in and out of sight, flashing like moonlight on a spiderweb. It ran like a slender seam across the face of a hill crowned with cairn stones. A faerie mound, if ever there was one. If Max and Scathach had been on this island, the faeries would know. David descended, his eyes fixed on the dark hillside and its elusive shimmer.

He proceeded cautiously, for one could never guess how faerie folk might behave. Most, such as dewdrop faeries, were harmless beings wholly concerned with their own quiet ways. But other faeries were fiercely proud, hostile to humans and any others who might encroach upon their territory. Individually, only the greatest faeries posed a real threat to trained Mystics, but with sufficient numbers even the least could work powerful enchantments. David did not know if faerie magic could extend into Nether; he only knew that his did not.

Mortals—even those who were shadow walking—could not enter a faerie mound unless they were welcomed. While shadow walking, he could not even knock. There was music coming from within the hill, faint but unmistakable. David gazed about, hopeful that other faeries might be approaching. There were none, only a night bird skimming low in search of supper.

David was on it in an instant. His spirit entered the animal, commandeered its simple brain, and wheeled back in a swift arc to the faerie mound. Flying along the seam, he found a small opening, no larger than an egg. Taking a pebble in his beak, he thrust it through the narrow opening. It fell and clinked against something far below. David took up another, pushing it through with his sharp beak and churring in the bird's voice. More pebbles, more clinks below until finally David heard something break. The music stopped.

A face appeared at the narrow slit, narrow and tapered. It spoke in the language of Fey, the words tumbling one after the other in a melodic burr.

"A nightjar wishes to warm himself," the faerie called.

"He broke my dish," cried another. "Send him off!"

"You've angered my host," said the faerie from the corner of her mouth. "You must be off, but I will leave a cake among the cairns."

"Invite me in," said the nightjar. "I must speak with you."

The faerie gasped, stared, and flitted out of sight. Seconds later, a great gash of white light appeared in the hillside. David hopped back as faeries emerged like angry hornets from a hive.

Some were, in fact, no larger than hornets or baby mice, but others were tall and regal, their silver hair crowned with holly and thistle. David was startled by their diversity. Judging by their many kinds of dress, some hailed from Eastern Europe or even Asia. David had never heard of faeries from distant lands convening with one another. Those that lived in Rowan's Sanctuary generally stuck with their own kind. One jabbed at the nightjar with a slender spear.

"What is this bird that speaks?"

David's spirit stepped forth from the nightjar to stand upon the hillside. Free once more, the bird gave a cry and skimmed off into the night. Several of the smaller faeries backed away or dived down into the hill. But the larger ones held firm, eyeing David's ghostlike spirit with cold apprehension. The tallest stepped forward.

"What do you want, demon?"

The word stung like a blow. David sighed inwardly. He had forgotten his true aura was visible. If he was going to live openly, he would have to get used to such reactions.

He bowed. "Only half a demon, lady."

"Demons are not welcome here," she said. "Or perhaps you did you not see our lord's message on the beach?"

"Is your lord the Fomorian?" asked David. "I am seeking him."

"Are you here to surrender?" she sneered. "He does not want your lands, demon. Fly back to Prusias."

"I don't serve Prusias," said David coldly. "I am here to find my friends. They were seeking the Fomorian. One is his kinsman and is rumored to be hurt. Have you seen them?"

An undercurrent of whispers swept across the faeries, but the lady frowned. "Our lord has no kinsmen and your kind has no friends. You are a liar, demon. Be off before we sing you into a stone."

David scowled and raised a finger in warning. "The next time you call me a liar, you may regret it, Phaëllia. For now that I have seen you and heard your speech, I know who you are. And I know the words to bend, bind, or break you. Do not test me."

The faerie backed away. "Who are you?"

"David Menlo."

Several faeries gasped. A tiny dewdrop faerie, just a little winged bulb, darted forward to loop about David.

"He's her teacher!" she cried to the others. "I've heard her say his name!"

"Whose teacher?" said Phaëllia, frowning.

"The Faeregine!" sputtered the tiny faerie.

Phaëllia stiffened and looked David up and down. "That's impossible. He is daemona. The Faeregine would never . . ."

"Who is the Faeregine?" David interrupted testily.

"You call her Mina," sang the excitable dewdrop. "Mina Faeregine she shall be called, sister, daughter, mother to all!"

Faeregine, thought David. *Well, that's something new and interesting. I wonder if Jakob has ever heard the term.* He glanced at Phaëllia. "Mina—the Faeregine as you call her—is indeed my student when I'm at Rowan. But Rowan is at war and we have no time for lessons. And I have no time or wish to argue with you. Did a young man and woman visit this isle? They are dear to Rowan and all who fight against Prusias. He is the Fomorian's kinsman."

Phaëllia looked increasingly nervous. The faerie masked her emotions well, but David had a gift for reading faces. *You know exactly where they are. You've hidden them from the Fomorian and now you're terrified you made a mistake. Let's heap on a little more fear . . .*

"He is not merely the Fomorian's kinsman," David continued. "He is the son of Lugh Lamfhada, the Hound of Rowan, and the Faeregine's savior when she faced danger in Blys. If you have made an error, now is your chance to fix it."

"Tell him, Phaëllia!" hissed a doe-eyed sprite.

"Is he alive?" asked David, mustering all the calm he could.

"He is," sniffed Phaëllia. "Barely. The lad is accursed. He will die soon."

"What of his companion?" asked David.

Phaëllia gave an indifferent shrug. "She sleeps. They both sleep, down under the hill. She had the audacity to camp by the cairns—"

David silenced her with a glance. "Does the Fomorian know they're here?"

Phaëllia drew herself up. "My lord charged me with defending his isle while he recovers, not to bother him with trespassers."

David turned to the dewdrop faerie. "What is your name, beautiful lady?"

"Valla," she squeaked, bowing low in a hum of tiny wings.

"Valla," said David gently. "Please find your lord and tell him the Little Sorcerer begs an audience with the son of Elathan. Tell him that his kinsman is gravely wounded and that Phaëllia is holding him captive on this isle."

"But Phaëllia will punish me!"

David shook his head. "Phaëllia is about to have far graver concerns. Please hurry, Valla. Time is short."

As Valla flitted toward the open hillside, Phaëllia held up a hand. "Stop! I will fetch our lord myself. Bring this Nether wight underhill and take him to his friends."

At the faeries' invitation, David slipped within the hill, traveling down, down into the shimmering caverns beneath. It was a shame, he reflected, to visit such a place while in the Nether. Ivy twined along the walls and floor, running along tables where the faeries dined on milk and saffron from iridescent seashells. Following Valla, he glided into a grotto where the incoming sea tumbled and sprawled over limestone falls to fill dark pools where faeries bathed and admired their reflections.

Above the pools, set into alcoves, lay Max and Scathach. Their arms were crossed atop their chests, clutching their weapons. They might have been marble statues of a young king and queen from another age. Gliding closer, David saw that Nox was there, too, clinging to Max's side in an enchanted sleep. David wanted to touch them, to feel their warmth, and assure himself that they were still alive. But he could not. David's eyes fell upon the blood trickling down the alcove's side to pool upon the floor. Max was dying before his eyes.

Boom!

The cavern shook. Within Nether, the sound was deafening—a hollow, concussive jolt. It must have been much the same in the living world, for the bathing faeries looked up in alarm.

Boom!

The second jolt sent them fleeing from the pools. Flicking water from their wings, they zoomed off in glowing sorties, disappearing into little side tunnels or up into hollowed roots that poked here and there from the cavern ceiling. Instinctively, David backed away from the sound, his eyes watching the largest tunnel—a monstrous opening some thirty or forty feet in diameter.

Boom!

An entire wall gave way, crashing into the glittering cavern in a rush of sound and seawater. Something gargantuan forced its way in, crumbling stalactites as it crouched beneath a crumbling arch. A great horned head loomed into view, animal and human, wild and wonderful, its beard dripping brine upon the stone.

~ 11 ~

BLOOD MAGIC

Max knew he was in the Fomorian's caverns before he opened his eyes. There were the sounds, of course, the acoustics of vast spaces and dripping water, and the hypnotic drumming of surf. One could almost hear the lichen growing, sense tree roots twining through soil, and feel the air brushing one's cheek as a pixie or faerie went skimming past. And there were the smells: sea and stone, wet moss, burning beeswax, and an animal smell like a flock of sheep that's been led out of the rain. These details told Max quite a bit, but all he really needed was the giant himself.

The Fomorian had his own peculiar gravity, an aura that seemed to warp the air about him. He was like a mountain on a prairie—he didn't have to move or make a sound, but his presence diverted the waters, parted the sky, and quietly shaped the lives of those within its shadow. The Fomorian did not merely dominate a landscape; he defined it.

A voice spoke, deep as a canyon. The words it spoke were Old Irish, their syllables a pleasing tumble of sound.

"He wakes. We must decide, for she is close and longs to take him. Can you look at me, Hound?"

Max opened his eyes to find that he was on a slab of stone in the midst of a huge cavern the color of old sea glass. Its walls danced with light reflected from hundreds of candles and the faeries that flitted here and there from little alcoves and perches. Above loomed the giant.

The Fomorian had changed since Max had seen him. He looked tired and worn. Streaks of gray shot through his plaited hair and beard while dried blood flecked his ramlike muzzle. Many wounds laced his broad face and throat. Where there had once been five eyes, there were now four. The fifth was just a scorched and empty crater.

"You're hurt," Max croaked, his voice barely audible.

"Aye," the Fomorian said. "I'm hurt. You're hurt. The world's grown perilous. You're near to crossing over, kinsman. Do you want to live?"

The giant posed the question with no drama or urgency. He might have been asking if Max preferred sugar in his tea.

"Yes."

"Think before you answer," the Fomorian urged. "I see a hard road should you stay. Death might be kinder. You can slip away now, surrounded by friends. There is no shame in dying from this wound. The blade that made it has slain a god before."

Max strained to sit up, but was far too weak. "I want to live," he breathed. "Help me. I know you can."

The Fomorian sat quietly, as though weighing options and their consequences. "Blood magic is strongest," he said. "But it has its price. You saw this when the lymrill gave its life to reforge your blade. Other sacrifices must be made."

"Then we will make them," said a voice.

Max turned his head to see Scathach rise from a stone bench nearby. She stood before the Fomorian, frightened but defiant. The giant gazed at her gravely.

"Will you, now?" he asked. "You are mortal, lady. Are you willing to share the little life you have? You will never get it back."

"I won't hoard my years just to bury those I love."

"Scathach," said Max quietly. "I don't want your life."

"It's mine to give. Rowan will never win this war without you."

"Rowan needs you too," Max reminded her.

"And it shall have me," she said proudly. "I'm not going anywhere."

The giant's largest eye, a yellow orb with a goat's square pupil, flicked back to Max. "Even if sacrifices are made, that wound will never heal. Together, we may close it, but it will always yearn to bleed. We are cheating Death of her prize."

Scathach pressed her hand upon the stone slab near Max's side. Her palm came up red. "We're wasting time."

Max's arm was numb, but he managed to reach out and curl his fingers around hers. His flesh was so pale he hardly recognized his body as his own.

"I can't take your life," he said quietly.

Scathach pressed his hand to her lips. "You're not," she insisted. "Just a few years of old age and you're welcome to them." She gazed at Max a moment, her eyes brimming with tears, before turning to the giant. "What do you need from me?"

The Fomorian beckoned to a squat, long-fingered faerie with

a birdlike face. It brought a stone bowl, a silver knife, and some soft leather pouches. Setting the bowl upon the slab, the Giant abruptly seized Scathach by the wrist. She barely flinched as the knife opened her forearm and a river of red ran streaming into the bowl. As the giant squeezed, faeries began to gather close, drawn to mortal blood—a maiden's blood—and the magic it could make.

The Fomorian chanted, the words coming with a slow, deliberate rhythm. Max listened, his mind slipping back into a fog.

> *A draught of years*
> *Of love and life*
> *To stem a tide of woe*
> *Iron, water, storm, and strife*
> *Blood spilled by a hallowed knife*
> *We cheat the Hunt, the Hound it seeks*
> *His wounds we knit, his flesh we keep . . .*

As he chanted, the Fomorian's speech became less distinct, his words condensing into a low hum that made the stone vibrate. More faeries arrived from the tunnels and pools. Their glow filled the cavern, but all Max could focus on was the Fomorian, who was slipping into a trance. He stared through Max, huge and wild, a weathered monument to some forgotten god. When the Fomorian drew the knife across his palm, he gave a primal howl that shook the caverns.

Max was vaguely aware that faeries were now coming forward, yielding their slender hands to the knife's sharp bite. Their blood mingled with Scathach's, red and silver, mortal and Fey.

At last, Max fell asleep. His consciousness settled like a grain of sand within an oyster, destined to produce something strange and perhaps even wonderful. His ensuing dreams were extraordinarily vivid.

The first involved David. Max saw his friend walking beneath a gray twilight, making for a forest whose trees bobbed and rocked like ship masts. Beyond them, Max could see Blys, Prusias's capital rising in gleaming tiers within its armored mountains. The city was smoking, its halls ablaze with light as mechanical creatures squatted and shuffled on the battlements. The city's walls were overflowing, its citizens and soldiers streaming over bridges to settle in sprawling camps upon the snowy fields.

Snow. It was everywhere. Max saw it in Blys. He'd seen it whipping through David's floating forest. He saw it as far south as Zenuvia, driving gales of ice that bombarded Lilith's palaces. Far below, a goblin cog cracked on in a desperate race to reach a harbor. Tiny figures scrambled about on deck, taking down sails as a gargantuan wave—a true widow maker—broadsided the vessel. The ship was driven under the water in a cresting mountain of foam.

The winter's reach extended to Rowan. Max saw the school clearly, Túr an Ghrian rising like a shining white obelisk beneath a bloodred sky. It towered above the cliffs and Old College, its summit lost in a swirl of dark clouds and snow. In his dream, Max heard Old Tom's chimes ringing across the campus. There were still students at Rowan, young apprentices that would be matched to charges, configure bedrooms, and begin their studies of Mystics. Against a backdrop of war and snow, Max found this comforting.

He had never seen Old College so empty. Only a few apprentices hurried along beneath the streetlamps, clutching books or scrolls. To Max's eyes they were babies, round little puddings too young to join the war effort. *I must have looked the same.*

If the students looked young, Rowan's remaining teachers

looked ancient. A few were gathered atop Maggie's steps, clutching their robes and cases as they gazed up at the raw and windy sky. They might have been a group of Oxford dons debating whether to fetch umbrellas before their evening stroll. How did the Director ever lure this group out of their retirement? With carrot and stick as she always did. Gabrielle Richter was a master.

Max decided he'd have a peek in her office. He walked down Rowan's paths, passing wilted flowers, the marble fountain whose waters gave off an eerie mist, obscuring its cherubs and hippocampi. Despite the cold, the Manse looked cheerful enough. There it waited, solid and familiar, its ivy crisp with frost as smoke trickled from its chimneys.

Inside, a pair of First Years copied each other's homework in a sitting room off the foyer. They didn't notice Max, didn't look up as he turned down the narrow hallway that led to the Director's office.

As Max strode along, he took notice of the portraits lining the wall. He'd always found them mildly absurd. One would think important people sat around enduring mild indigestion. He stopped to appraise Ms. Richter's.

It was just as unfortunate. A tastefully dull oil painting in a gilded frame whose subject sat at a desk with a sober, introspective expression. The portrait revealed nothing of the Director he knew. Max had never seen Ms. Richter sit that way much less wear such an insipid expression. No, she was frank and firm—occasionally intimidating—but she knew just when to soften a moment with a bit of levity. Max missed her. In some ways, Gabrielle Richter was the closest thing he had to a mother since his own had passed out of his life.

He slipped within her office, taking in its paneled walls, the maps, the elegant French doors that looked out upon the gardens. All the furniture was draped with canvas as though everything were being moved or put into storage. Desk, chairs, settee—everything was covered up but for a steaming coffeepot upon the desk. *That isn't right,* thought Max. Where would anxious students be reprimanded for breaking curfew? Where would captured vyes sit while Mum threatened to eat them? A mistake had been made. Max would have to speak with someone.

He went out the French doors, crossing the patio and the orchard. Mourners stood by one of the sacred trees, gazing at a large apple made of gold. Max sympathized but did not stop. War was hard; more golden apples would decorate this orchard before it was finished. He couldn't mourn everyone.

Max made his way to the Sanctuary, proceeding through its hedge gate to walk beneath an arched canopy of interlacing tree branches. Peering ahead, he was delighted to see that the Sanctuary was, as yet, untouched by winter. Its meadows were green and gold, its sky a pale blue with just a hint of cloud drifting over the mountains.

Emerging from the tunnel, Max saw the Warming Lodge, a low, timbered building overlooking a tranquil lagoon. Nolan would know what was happening with Richter's office. Max made a beeline for its porch, his fingers brushing the tall grasses. Arriving at the porch, Max found Nolan's fiddle lying on a rocking chair, but no sign of the man himself. The lodge's door was locked. Max knocked.

Something most unsettling opened the door. A second glance revealed it to be Gregory Wyatt Nolan. He was dead, of course—had died during Prusias's siege—but even death couldn't keep the man from looking after Rowan's charges. There was nothing hostile about his aspect, but the corpse couldn't speak. It had no tongue and what little flesh remained on its bones was riddled with maggots. Max guessed that the shorn ribs had been his death wound, but the skull was also fractured.

What are those?

Max stared at Nolan's teeth, for the man's skull seemed to have extras—two entire rows of jagged, predatory incisors set into grooves above and below the normal allotment.

"Have you seen Ms. Richter?" he asked. "Someone's packing up her office."

Nolan's corpse stood aside and pointed within. Max squeezed past him, entering the Warming Lodge where sunlight filtered lazily through the rafter windows. Entering the main room, he walked down the long aisle, passing stalls and terrariums populated by a menagerie of magical creatures. Max didn't see Ms. Richter, but he did spot a familiar dark mound resting by the haystacks at the aisle's end. He couldn't blame YaYa. She'd earned the right to nap as often as she wished.

"Don't wake her!" hissed a voice.

Max turned to see Scott McDaniels in one of the neighboring stalls. He was dressed in his burial suit. Unlike Nolan, he had not decayed. The man looked just the way Max remembered him and so tantalizingly real that Max almost went to him. But he restrained himself. Scott McDaniels was dead, just as Nolan was dead. He was no more real than the sunken goblin ship or those apprentices cheating on their homework. Max ignored him.

"Don't!" Mr. McDaniels cried. "It's not what you think!"

Max waved off his concerns. "It's only YaYa," he muttered, but his smile faded as he came closer. The ki-rin resembled a gargantuan black lioness with a broken horn atop her head. There was no gloss to this animal's coat, and its fur was not black, but dark gray. The creature stirred as Max approached. A heavy head swiveled toward him.

It was the wolfhound.

Max had been dreaming of it since he was twelve. The monster was larger than a cart horse, with paws the size of dinner plates. As it rose, a bloodcurdling growl sounded in its throat. Max turned to leave.

But the clones had entered the Warming Lodge. They walked casually toward him down the aisle. The big one bore his spear and radiated an air of smug triumph. The gaunt, feral one radiated only death. Max stared at the weapon in the wild one's hand. It looked to be no more than a chipped wedge of flint or ebony, but what pain it had caused! Max had never experienced anything like it. The blade didn't merely cut flesh; it frayed something far deeper—one's tether to eternity.

The clones broke into a trot. Max reached for the *gae bolga,* but it wasn't there. Warm air tickled his neck. The wolfhound's growl became a rough, throaty challenge.

"What are you about? Answer quick or I'll gobble you up!"

Max turned just as the animal attacked. He caught it by the jaws, its teeth puncturing his flesh as he forced them away from his face. Staggering beneath its weight, Max was driven back toward the clones. The wolfhound's breath was a furnace blast as it snapped and clawed, straining ever for his throat.

The clones were close. Max could hear their footfalls, the clink of armor. Dropping his shoulder, Max turned and hurled the wolfhound into the clones.

It howled as their weapons pierced its sides. Max backed away, watching spellbound as the clones fell upon the animal, stabbing deep into its writhing body. The Warming Lodge's residents fell into a bleating, crying panic. Kicking the wolfhound over, the bigger clone raised his spear for the kill.

But the feral one held up his hand. His companion stopped, lowering his weapon reluctantly. Leering through a tangle of hair and broken teeth, the assassin approached Max and offered him the stone knife.

Max closed his fingers about its worn handle. He liked this

blade. It was brittle and probably useless against armor, but it was *hungry*. And, unlike the *gae bolga*, this weapon wasn't fickle. It craved Max's blood, the wolfhound's, even that of the clones. It had craved blood ever since Set scattered Osiris all over Egypt.

Hefting the knife, Max looked down to where the monster sprawled on the floor.

The wolfhound was gone.

It was Scathach who lay there, Scathach crumpled in a gasping heap while her life trickled away through her torn gray cloak.

Max screamed.

"Hush!" Scathach whispered, wrapping her arms about him and rocking him against her. "You're just dreaming."

Gasping, Max let his weight fall against her. For a long minute he just lay against her, his hands traveling over her back and shoulders, searching for the wounds he'd seen her suffer.

"Was it Failinis?" she asked gently. Max had told her about his recurring nightmares and it was her opinion that the wolfhound was Failinis, the very beast that sat before Lugh's throne.

"It was the wolfhound," Max panted. He didn't want monsters to have names.

Sitting up, he held Scathach's face in his hands. She smiled at him, looking beautiful if careworn.

"You look better," she said. "The Fomorian's magic has worked. I've been so worried."

Max glanced down. He wasn't wearing his own clothes, but a white linen robe. And he was no longer on the stone slab, but a down bed whose frame was made of twisted driftwood. He looked about the room, a small cavern of pale stone whose floor was strewn with rushes. Water was dripping outside. Through the walls, Max heard the faint crash of surf.

"How long have I been asleep?" he asked.

Scathach pushed the damp hair out of his eyes. "Three

weeks," she said. "Maybe longer. I lost track. It's easy to lose track here."

"Where's the Fomorian?"

"Resting. He gave a great deal of himself to save you. It was many days before your wound would knit."

Max opened his robe to see his side wrapped with a green silk bandage stitched with runes. Scathach stopped him from peeking beneath it.

"Meet your new best friend," she said. "You must never take it off. The Fomorian says it will prevent the wound from opening."

Nodding, Max eased off the bed and tried to stand. His legs trembled like a newborn foal's. Clutching Scathach's shoulder, he steadied himself.

"Your strength will return," she assured him. "You haven't been up for over a month. It's natural to be shaky."

"A month? You said three weeks!"

"Three weeks since the giant began to heal you," she explained. "It's been over a month since you were wounded. Once we arrived here, the faeries sang me to sleep and held us captive. We're lucky David found us. We might have slept forever."

Max frowned, trying to make sense of what Scathach was saying. "Wait," he said. "*David* rescued us? How is that possible? He's with Ms. Richter and the fleet. They must be two thousand miles from here!"

Taking his hand, Scathach led him back to the bed. "I think you should sit for a moment," she said. "David has visited several times to check on you. He comes to us from Nether. I've had news from him. Important news."

Max knew that expression. He had seen it many times before—on Scott McDaniels, policemen, mourners. To see it now on Scathach set every nerve on edge.

"Just tell me."

"The fleet was intercepted. Prusias launched an attack using Workshop creatures. Bram destroyed them, but we suffered casualties. The Director was one."

"Ms. Richter's hurt?"

"She's dead."

Max could only nod and close his eyes. A moment later, he rose, steadied himself, and walked slowly about the room. "How?" he asked.

"I don't know."

Another nod.

"Who's Director?"

"David."

Max stopped pacing. If there was anything that could be salvaged from such a tragedy, this might be it. Some person, some brilliant and courageous person had the good sense to name David Menlo Director. David would doubt himself—he always doubted himself when thrust into the spotlight—but Max had more faith in David's abilities than anyone else's.

"Thank God."

"There is some other good news," said Scathach, trying to cheer him. "Cooper and Hazel are alive. David said Cooper's going to be okay and is intent on his mission. Apparently, he's even roped Toby into it."

"Toby? Those two can't work together. Cooper will murder him."

"That's what I thought, too, but then I imagine a smee might be very useful when infiltrating the Workshop and Prusias's city."

"David told you what Cooper's mission was?"

"He did," she replied. "He's Director now. David knows everything about every DarkMatter operation. He even assigns the new ones."

"I report to him," said Max, somewhat amazed. "I report to my roommate. He'll never let me live it down."

"We both report to your roommate," she pointed out. "And you should know he's given us a new assignment. We're to set out as soon as you're able."

"We already have a mission," said Max. "We have to enlist the Fomorian."

"That's not going to happen."

"Why? He'd be an incredibly powerful ally."

"Oh, I have no doubt of that," said Scathach. "You should see the beaches. They're littered with ships and demons. Prusias picked the wrong island to invade."

"Exactly," said Max. "That's why we need him."

"The Fomorian will fight to defend his island, but he won't leave it."

"Have you asked him?"

"I have."

"And what did he say?"

Scathach shrugged. "That his place is here. Many faerie folk have taken refuge with him. They live under his protection."

Max frowned. "Faeries. They take us prisoner and now they're the reason the Fomorian won't help us? Whose side are they on?"

"Their own," Scathach replied. "To be fair, some have been trying to make amends. Some are proud and aloof but I can't fault their generosity. They sacrificed a great deal of their blood and magic to aid you."

"Sacrificed," said Max, musing on the word. "And what about you? What did you have to sacrifice?"

Scathach looked away and gazed at the bandage wrapped about her forearm. "I don't really know. A bit of strength, maybe. A bit of magic. Perhaps some years. I am changed, but I couldn't say how."

"I wish you hadn't."

Her eyes met his. "Wouldn't you do the same for me?"

"I'd do anything for you. You know that."

Taking his hands, she pulled him toward her. "I do know that," she whispered. "Which is why my decision was no decision at all."

The ensuing kiss was rudely interrupted by an excited lymrill. Streaking into the room, Nox bounded onto a bedpost and then onto her steward's shoulders. Max staggered beneath her weight and toppled back onto the bed.

"Jeez, you've gotten heavy!" he exclaimed, tipping her onto his pillow. "What are they feeding you?"

"Gold," said Scathach disapprovingly. "The faeries have plenty and like to bribe her with it. Nox has always been a diva, but now she's a spoiled diva. Yesterday, she hissed when I tried to give her iron."

"Nox," said Max sternly. "Iron is good for you. Gold will make you soft."

The lymrill did not seem to mind this prospect. With a cheeky mewl, she rubbed her back against the pillow and spread her claws to admire their golden tinge. Max poked her tummy, his fingers navigating the prickly quills to feel for extra padding. There was none. Nox was as solid as a tank—an even denser tank than she had been.

"She must weigh over a hundred pounds," he marveled. "Nick never weighed this much and she's not even half his size."

"Not for long," said Scathach, sitting and stroking the lymrill's ruff. "They've also been feeding her from their table. The faeries say she'll be the size of a lion."

"Why are they being so nice to her?"

"Because she's your charge," Scathach said. "Evidently, nothing's too good for a friend of the Faeregine."

Faeregine. Max put aside his anxiety over a lion-sized lymrill to try and place the word. He'd definitely heard it before.

"That's what the hags called Mina," he recalled. "The faeries call her that, too?"

Scathach disentangled Nox's claws from her bracelet. "Yes, they do. They practically worship Mina. They talk about her like she's a god."

"Mina's human," said Max decisively. He was unsure how he knew, but he was almost certain. "She's not faerie."

"The faeries agree," said Scathach. "They say whenever the Faeregine is reborn, it becomes whatever is threatened most. They say she's returned this time as a human child."

"What does the Fomorian say?"

"He doesn't say much about her. He's more interested in David."

"He and David have a funny history. Did he tell you about it?"

"Not exactly," said Scathach. "But the last time David visited, the Fomorian stared at him and said something like 'Sorcerers are all the same. They steal your secrets and keep their own.' He was really angry."

Max frowned. "What did he mean by that? What secret was David keeping?"

"I don't know. David tried to speak privately with him, but the Fomorian refused. What secret did David steal?"

"The Fomorian's name," Max replied. "Or really, the fact that he doesn't have one. When we first came here, the giant said he'd help us if David could guess his name. But if David guessed wrong, the giant would take his head."

"How did David figure it out?"

Max couldn't help but grin at his memory of the occasion. "By *looking* at him! It was the craziest thing, Scathach. David just stared at the giant for hours like he was some sort of riddle. At dawn, he sat up and recited the Fomorian's entire family tree. He's the son of Elathan. Apparently Elathan was so ashamed of his child's appearance he refused to give him a name."

"Why doesn't the giant just give himself a name?"

"He needs a truename," Max clarified. "The Fomorian can't fully live or die without one. He just continues to exist, age after age. David promised to give him one."

"That's so sad."

"It is. I'm sorry to hear the Fomorian's angry with David. I really thought those two understood each other. I wonder what David's secret is." Max hesitated. "I saw him when I was dreaming. He had two hands."

Scathach raised an eyebrow. "You saw that in a dream?"

"And I saw Blys," Max continued. "There were things on the walls and thousands of people streaming out of the city. And winter—winter's everywhere, Scathach. Even in Zenuvia and at Rowan."

Max stopped. The rest of his dream came flooding back. His visit to Ms. Richter's office; had the covered furniture been telling him Ms. Richter was dead? And the coffeepot! Had that been some sign or symbol that David was the new Director? The mourners in the orchard . . . had that been *real*? Max's mind raced ahead to his visit to the Warming Lodge: Nolan's corpse, the man's inexplicable teeth, and that awful scene with the clones attacking the wolfhound. But that hadn't been the wolfhound. It had been Scathach.

"What's wrong?" she asked.

"I . . . I don't know," said Max, sitting back down. "My dream. The wolfhound."

"You always dream of Failinis," she said soothingly. "Did he ask you his question?"

Max nodded.

"And did you answer?"

"No. I've never answered."

"Well," she said, "I suspect when you do, he'll stop bothering you. Dreams are strange things. You must have overheard me asking David about his hand."

"What are you talking about?" asked Max uneasily.

Scathach laughed. "How else would you know he got it back?"

Max grew dizzy. Leaning forward, he stared at the stone floor. "I think I'm going to be sick."

"Do you want some water?"

"No, I . . ."

Doubling over, Max vomited on the floor, his stomach heaving up great gouts of dark red blood and silver faerie essence. It splashed on the cavern floor, running off to pool at its lowest point. Max was shivering as sweat beaded and ran off his body. His wound ached; he yearned to tear off the sash and examine it. Retching, he vomited again. Scathach fetched a towel from a table.

"The giant said this might happen," she said, cleaning him up. "It's the faerie blood. Humans can't tolerate it."

"I'm not human," Max muttered, wincing from the pain in his side. "I . . . I think it's done something to me. Awakened something."

"Do you want water?" she asked.

He shook his head. The nausea was fading, but he felt very weak. "I need air," he said. "Fresh air."

"We're free to wander the caverns."

"No," Max gasped, his head spinning. "Outside. I have to get outside. I can't be down here anymore. I need to go outside."

"The Fomorian said to stay here. He said it could be dangerous outside."

"Since when have you been afraid of danger? I'm not looking to slay a dragon. I just need fresh air. I feel like I'm drowning down here."

While Scathach fetched Max's clothes, he mopped up his mess. He didn't recall drinking the giant's draught or anything beyond the initial few verses of his chant. Had the draught changed him? His dream was certainly unlike any he'd had before—was it prescience? No. He wasn't seeing the future; he was seeing recent events or the present as it happened around the world. That was something else entirely. He wished David were there.

When Scathach returned with Max's things, she was armed for battle.

"I just want a sniff of air," said Max.

"And the Fomorian said it might be dangerous," she reminded him. "We can go, but we'll go prepared. Take this, will you? I don't want to touch it."

The *gae bolga* lay sheathed atop Max's clothes. He took it, along with a short rod of roughened steel Rowan's dvergar had made for him. When Max touched the rod to the sword's pommel, it promptly swallowed the hilt up to its guard. Once firmly attached, the rod lengthened so that the *gae bolga* was transformed from a short sword into a long spear. Max thumped it on the floor.

"There," he said. "A weapon and a walking stick. My legs are still a little iffy."

Scathach looked modestly away as he dressed. His travel clothes had been cleaned, his black tunic mended. His boots had been resoled and his shirt of nanomail gleamed like molten silver. He slipped it on, aware that Scathach would insist. Pulling on the rest of his clothes, he left the ivory brooch for last.

He held the brooch in his hands a moment, thinking about

his dream. Scathach said Lugh had made it for Max, that it had a very special purpose.

"This is for when I die," he said, studying its Celtic sun.

"A grim way to think of it," said Scathach. "It's meant to bring you home when your time here is finished."

"What would have happened if the Fomorian hadn't healed me?"

Scathach shrugged. "I only know the brooch's purpose. Lugh didn't explain how it works or what's supposed to happen. Only that it was for you and would bring you home to the Sidh when your mortal days had ended."

"The Sidh isn't my home."

Scathach wrapped a heavy shawl about her shoulders. "Do you remember where you were born?" she asked thoughtfully.

"Of course not. I don't even remember my first house. We moved when I was three."

"And you're only eighteen," she observed. "You think of Rowan as your home now, but will you in two thousand years? Will you even remember it?"

Max said nothing.

"You're becoming an immortal," she reminded him. "An eighteen-year-old god. In many ways, that means you're still an infant. You don't yet know what home is."

"Well, how old are you?"

"I'll never tell," she replied coyly. "Now that I'm mortal, I get to reset the clock. I can't look more than twenty, can I?"

"You're still an older woman," said Max. "Some might call you a cradle robber."

Scathach was aghast. "That's a terrible thing to say!"

"You just said I was an infant."

For a moment, Scathach simply stared. Then she chuckled.

An evil, utterly unnerving giggle as she helped Max on with his cloak.

"What are you laughing about?" he asked tentatively.

"Nothing. I just thought of how I'm going to get my revenge. Don't worry. It won't happen soon. You'll have plenty of time to forget it's coming."

"I was kidding, you know."

She batted her eyelashes. "Oh, I know."

"You're not a cradle robber. There's no need to get revenge or anything."

"Why should you worry?" she asked innocently. "You're an immortal. And it's not like you're a deep sleeper. Oh wait—you are!"

Again with that awful laugh!

"I'll set Nox on guard," Max warned.

"Good luck with that. She'll be off gorging with the faeries."

Nox bounded after the pair as they left the room. The small cavern opened onto a larger one, a great hollowed space of gray-green stone with several pools of bubbling hot springs. Three naiads were sharing one, soaking their sleek bodies and appraising Max with more than mild interest.

"Don't you look fine, up and about," said one.

"Thank you," said Max.

"Why not come for a swim?" suggested another, hopping out to sit on its edge and dangle her legs in the water.

"We're going for a walk," huffed Scathach. "Put some clothes on."

The naiad gave Scathach a dreamy, condescending smile. "I wasn't talking to you." Her gaze drifted back to Max. "Don't waste your time with mortals, my prince. Their lives are short and their beauty fades. She'll only break your heart."

Max decided not to say anything until they'd left the cavern and traversed several more. Scathach was walking quickly, her knuckles white upon her spear.

Other than the naiads, they saw no faeries and no trace of the Fomorian. The final cavern they entered was the largest yet, a natural amphitheater of polished stone containing a still pool of dark water. Below the pool's surface Max could see huge, ghostly images flitting beneath—broken ships and shattered skulls and ravens in vast, unsettling numbers.

"This is the giant's scrying pool," said Scathach. She gestured ahead to a torch-lit opening on the far side of the water. "Those stairs lead to the surface."

They skirted the pool, keeping to its narrow ledge. Now and again, Max would glance at the images, but they were too close, too abstract to decipher. Passing under the archway, they climbed a series of rough steps that wound up toward daylight.

"I'm surprised there's anything human-sized in here," said Max.

"The Fomorian's not always a giant," said Scathach. "After he healed you, he grew much smaller. He was scarcely taller than Bob when he went off to rest. In the Sidh, they always said Fomorians were powerful sorcerers. He can probably be whatever size he likes."

"I guess that's true," said Max. "On my first visit, he carried Cooper, David, and me in his hands like we were beetles. He must have been bigger than a dreadnought."

"Let's hope he isn't that big if he catches us. He warned us to stay inside."

"He warned you," said Max, peering out the narrow opening at some gray, windswept dunes. "I didn't hear a thing. Besides, I'm a sick, delirious patient who needs fresh air. We won't be gone long."

Nox bounded ahead while the two walked along a ridgeline

that overlooked the sea. The sky was reddish and heavy with clouds, but here and there the sun poked through like lances of golden light. It looked to be late afternoon.

Despite a bit of sun, the temperature was far colder than he remembered it being at Shrope Hovel. It wasn't merely chilly, but a stinging, teeth-chattering cold that fairly begged one to stay indoors. When they did set sail, they'd need warmer gear. *Ormenheid* could do many things, but she couldn't change the weather.

Still, the cold air and a brisk walk were having their intended effect. They woke him up, driving off the drowse so that Max was finally thinking clearly after his injury and weeks of sleep. He revisited his dream and earlier conversations. What had the Fomorian said when Max awoke?

"We must decide, for she is close and longs to take him."

What had he been talking about? Who was 'she'?

He glanced up. Scathach had stopped and was pointing with her spear at the beach below. Coming beside her, Max gazed down at a broad stretch of icy sand.

"The Fomorian's handiwork," she muttered.

While scavengers had done their work, the carnage was still evident. Max stared at the wall of piled corpses, the shattered ships, and the bodies swinging from the pillar like criminals at a crossroads. An army had shattered on this beach, broken like a wave upon a rock.

"We need him," Max concluded. "He has to come to Blys."

"He won't," said Scathach, staring out at the horizon. "I've already asked. I even begged and that's not something I do very often."

"He's my kinsman. Maybe I'll have better luck."

Scathach lifted her chin and squinted as the sun's red rim

dipped beneath the clouds. "I forgot. Of course he'll listen to you. You're both immortals."

Max gave her a sideways glance. "Is this about that naiad?"

Scathach turned and gave her shadow a downcast glance. "She's not wrong, you know. It's foolish to fall in love with mortals. You should be with your own kind."

"You are my own kind. You've lived in the Sidh. You know it better than I do."

"I'm cast out," she said softly. "There's no ivory brooch for me. When my time is up, I go into the ground."

"Don't say that."

She shrugged. "It's the truth. I don't regret my decision—I'd do it again. But there will be times it makes me sad. You have to give me that."

"Fine. But no more talking to naiads."

A grudging smile appeared. "I've never liked them," she confessed. "Not even in the Sidh." With a sigh, she turned and continued along the ridge.

They walked in silence, Scathach brooding while Max puzzled over his dream and what the faeries' or Fomorian's blood might have done to him. Were these strange dreams a temporary phenomenon or was he doomed to see hints of what was happening in the wider world? Max didn't think he'd like that. Peter Varga experienced visions and they seemed to take a haunting toll.

The cold deepened as the sun set. Max's toes were numb and his lashes speckled with snow, but he was in no hurry to return to the giant's caverns. Marvelous as they were, they seemed cut off from the world. Out there, beyond the darkening horizon, Rowan's fleet would be making landfall near Blys. A month, maybe two, and the siege would begin.

Something caught Max's eye.

A raven was ahead, calling shrilly as it soared high upon the wind. Others answered its cry, flapping out from the leaning pines by the hundreds. They scattered, some screeching past while others wheeled and dove behind a gray, sparse hill. As they disappeared, it sounded like even more ravens cried out in greeting or challenge.

"Something's going on over there," said Max. "Let's have a look."

Scathach glanced doubtfully at the red twilight settling over the isle. "It's getting dark. We should get back."

But Max had to see what the fuss was about. Ravens were attracted to carrion. If there were this many, then a feast must have been present. More of Prusias's soldiers? Perhaps. If so, they had made it much farther inland than their comrades. And why would they come here? There was nothing but hills and a few streams.

"Max," said Scathach. "I think we should head back. Something isn't right."

"Head back, then," he said. "I want to see."

He trudged ahead, leaning on the *gae bolga* as more ravens settled on the trees and hilltop. Nox was walking alongside him now, a mouse dangling from her jaws. She stopped as something padded over the summit.

It was a wolf—a leering, emaciated wolf whose ribs could be counted through its mangy coat. Baring its teeth in a territorial snarl, it turned around and disappeared down the hillside.

"Max!" called Scathach.

He ignored her. There was something on the other side of this hill and he had to see it. The ravens grew louder. Several hopped about the hilltop; others flew back up into the sky to wheel like vultures over a carcass. The *gae bolga* was growing warm, even hot to the touch. Its blade was trembling, pulling Max forward like a divining rod.

The hairs on Max's neck rose one by one. His arms felt like cold lead. So did his legs. His blood was ice, every heartbeat a piercing agony. Only a tiny corner of his mind could process that Scathach was now beside him. She was trying to reach for his hand, but she kept missing. Her fingers merely grazed his wrist.

The Old Magic was kindling within him. It roared up in challenge to whatever was beyond that hill. But it had no outlet. His wound had left him far too weak to respond, to channel that flood of energy. It raged within him, a caged inferno.

More wolves peered over the hill, crippled and sick, panting and growling. One held a rotting arm between its jaws like a dog might carry a bone. When enough had gathered, they stole down the hill like shadowy nightmares. Surrounding Max and Scathach, they escorted them toward the hilltop like a snarling honor guard.

Max railed silently at his foolishness. The Fomorian had warned them and he had chosen not to listen. But was that even true? Had he chosen to ignore the warning or had something chosen for him? He tried to shut his eyes.

Don't look at her, he told himself. *If you don't look, she won't have any power over you! Don't look!*

He might have wished for a spaceship. His eyes refused to close. They remained stubbornly open, fixed upon the scene unfolding before him. Their gaze traveled over starving wolves and mangled corpses and a sea of squawking ravens to settle on a spare, shrouded figure washing clothes in a stream.

It was the Morrígan.

~ 12 ~

A Lady in Black

The ravens croaked and squawked, cocking their heads at Max as he walked down the slope to the streambed.

The hillside, and indeed all the valley, was choked with bodies: demons and vyes, ettins, ogres, and humans all in various states of decomposition. Some looked freshly killed, others were just sun-bleached bones, but all were fair game for the ravens and wolves. The Morrígan's attendants gorged themselves, picking at corpses like it was a grisly buffet.

The Morrígan had yet to acknowledge them. As Max drew closer, he saw that her shroud was not of cloth but raven feathers. It hung loose and open, revealing a withered, naked body of dark gray flesh riddled with open wounds. Matted black hair hung limp about her face, spilling over her shoulders and back. Her arms were lean and strong, her fingers nimble as she rinsed and squeezed the tunics and banners of the fallen. Something moved beneath her shroud; a tiny hand reached out to clutch a tangle of the goddess's hair. Peering closely, Max saw not one, but two small infants suckling at her breasts.

"Do you know me?"

The Morrígan's voice was female, worn with age, and surprisingly quiet. Its restraint hinted at simmering rage, the prospect of sudden and appalling violence. She wrung bloody water from a ripped and tattered cloak. "Must I repeat myself?"

Max cleared his throat. "You are the Morrígan."

A finger wagged its disapproval. "Others may call me the Morrígan, but not you, Hound. I am your partner. Say it."

Max hesitated. The last thing he wanted was her putting words in his mouth.

"Say it," she repeated, laying the cloak on the bank and taking up a tunic.

"You are my partner."

She nodded, but her face remained hidden. "I am," she said. "For we have made a pact, you and I."

"What pact is that? I don't remember making any such thing with you."

"I give you my blade, you give me conquests—you give me blood and bodies and sustenance. Thus far, it has been feast or famine. I prefer to feast."

"I don't kill for killing's sake."

The Morrígan shook with silent laughter as she dipped the tunic again into the stream and scraped it with her taloned thumb.

"You will do whatever it is I require you to do," she said. "You will be whatever I require you to be. My partner. My justice. My lover. My slave. Do you understand?"

Max glowered. She was a goddess and her essence was in the *gae bolga*, but he would not be cowed. "I'm no one's slave."

This time her laugh was audible. Setting down the tunic, she pried one of the infants from her breast and held it over the stream. The baby was gray and wrinkled, a bawling newborn girl. Caressing a cheek, the Morrígan lowered the child into the stream and held her astonished face beneath the icy water.

"What are you doing?" Max cried.

"Beg me to stop."

Max looked at the baby, her hands slapping the water's surface.

"Stop!" he cried.

"Beg me."

"Please! I'm begging you. Please let her up!"

Chuckling, the Morrígan lifted the hysterical baby out of the water, thumped her twice upon the back, and set her back to suckling. The other infant hardly noticed. Max still had yet to see the goddess's face.

"Of course you're a slave," she said. "You're a slave to modern morality. You're a slave to the wishes of others. Bram, Menlo, Mina, Astaroth—they all use you, manipulate you, command you. I gave you a weapon to conquer the world, and here you are begging others to do the fighting. You could break Prusias tomorrow—shatter all resistance if you'd simply embrace what's already in you."

"It's your power—the *gae bolga*'s power. I don't want it and won't be a slave to it."

"You are mistaken," said the Morrígan. "The *gae bolga* only channels what's within you. That power is yours, not mine. It is time you shook off this mortal cloak and become what you are meant to be."

"And what is that?"

"King and conqueror," she intoned, dragging a bloody banner through the water. "Astaroth, Prusias, Rowan, Lilith, witches, the Workshop—there are too many factions. The world is crying out for strength. Not Astaroth's. He'll never understand the world he wishes to rule. It must be you. You have the strength."

"I don't have the wisdom. Or the desire. I don't wish to rule."

Shaking her head, the Morrígan wrung out the banner. "You think you're being noble," she observed with cold disapproval. "Billions will die—have died—because no one yet has had the strength or will to impose peace. You have that strength and you refuse to use it. Is that nobility or cowardice?"

It was Max's turn to laugh. "The Morrígan wants peace?"

For the first time, he beheld the Morrígan's face. She raised her head slowly, her hands brushing back her black, blood-crusted tangles so that he could look directly upon her. Her skin was dark, her nose as hooked and sharp as a raven's beak. The mouth was too broad, the bloodstained lips too thin. They were parted in a loose, hungry grimace that revealed worn and pointed teeth. If the Morrígan had eyes, they were set very deep. Those red-rimmed sockets might have been empty, but Max had no doubt she could see him.

"Are you mocking me?" she inquired coldly. "Should I turn my attention to your companions?"

Max glanced at Scathach and Nox. Both were rigid and staring ahead, but their gazes were blank and unseeing.

"The lass spent time in the Sidh, but she is mortal now," the Morrígan observed. "Shall I let her see me? Care to witness what my presence can do to mortals?"

The Morrígan was threatening to turn her aura into a weapon.

Max had never seen such a thing done, and had no wish to. He'd always thought of auras as an indicator of a magical being's strength or power. While animals were sensitive to auras—even those given off by normal people—few human beings could perceive them unless they encountered a very powerful one.

Max had encountered many powerful auras. By far the greatest had belonged to Lugh, the Fomorian, Astaroth, and now the Morrígan. Their auras were fundamentally different from those of lesser spirits and even greater demons. One could feel the power radiating from them, almost crackling at invisible frequencies. Max knew his aura was powerful as well—when the Old Magic burst forth, his enemies could not even look at him—but he had never thought of it as something that could be manipulated and controlled.

But perhaps he'd been wrong. The Morrígan was doing so now, keeping it at enough of a simmer to paralyze Scathach and Nox. What would happen if the Morrígan chose to unveil her presence entirely? Max did not want to imagine the consequences. It would be like staring at an eclipse.

"No," said Max. "Please don't."

"Your heart is too weak to be a god," she spat. "Invite me in and I will do what you cannot. Let me use your body, Hound. As partners, you can end this war and I can sate my hunger. What say you?"

Max shut his eyes. "No. I can't. I will give the *gae bolga* back to you. I don't want it if this is what it costs."

The Morrígan tutted. "My boy, my boy. I'm afraid that's impossible. Your blood is in the blade, too. We are one now, Max McDaniels, and I won't be ignored."

"The blade may be ours, but my body is my own."

The Morrígan considered this. "There is another way," she mused.

"What way is that?"

"Give me a son!" she hissed. "Give me a son and I will raise him. Give me a son and he will do what his father could not. Give me a son and I will bother you no more."

When Max remained silent, the Morrígan began to laugh.

"Don't let my appearance dissuade you. I can be whomever you like."

As she spoke, her nightmarish visage gave way and the Morrígan became Scathach. When Max hesitated, she gave a knowing leer.

"Perhaps your heart's confused."

With a sudden rippling, The Morrígan's appearance changed. Scathach's dark hair turned to auburn; a fair complexion became tan and freckled. She was Julie Teller, exactly as Max remembered her during his first week at Rowan.

"You never forget your first love, do you?" said Julie.

"I'm not giving you a son," said Max.

The Aussie girl leaned forward and flashed a devilish smile. "Perhaps you'd prefer someone more . . . experienced?"

Petra Kosa lounged naked on the bank, impossibly beautiful and alluring. "Come sit beside me," she cooed. "Just for a minute. If you don't like it, we can always stop. But I don't think you'll want to . . ."

Max could not pretend the sight of those curves and perfect skin was not enticing. He knew that it was an illusion, of course. He knew that he was being plied and manipulated. But it was not easy to ignore. Idle hands weren't the devil's playground; it was the gap between *can* and *should*.

Max shook his head, uncertain whether the gesture was meant for the Morrígan or himself. "I'm not fathering some monster for you to raise," he muttered. "And I'd never betray Scathach."

Petra Kosa's seductive form vanished, replaced by the

Morrígan's true guise. The goddess fixed her attention upon Scathach's blank face.

"Is this the problem?" she breathed. "Love for a mortal? Love for an outcast? That can be remedied."

The *gae bolga* moaned as Max unsheathed its blade and pointed it at the goddess. "Don't touch her. Don't even think it."

The Morrígan's eyes never left Scathach.

A shadow fell over them.

Ravens screamed and took to the air; wolves snarled and loped behind the goddess. Max turned to see the Fomorian standing atop the hill, a battle-ax slung over his shoulder. Several of the faeries were with him, sitting atop his curling horns or peering out from his snow-dusted pelts.

How something so large could move so silently was unnerving. In one stride the Fomorian descended the hill. Scooping up Scathach and Nox, he held them in his great hand and bowed to the Morrígan.

"Go in peace."

The goddess looked amused. "You cast a large shadow but do not pretend you command here. Bend your knee and pay homage."

"These are my lands. I bow to no one here. All of you must go."

The Morrígan smiled. "Say my names."

"The one that speaks is Macha," said the Giant. "At her breast are Badb and Nemain. You are one and the same, mother to each, sister to each, daughter to each. You are the Morrígan and I ask that you leave my isle."

The Morrígan made no attempt to rise. "Give me your name and I will go."

"I have no name."

The goddess leered. "I thought not. You're not lord of this

isle. You're not lord of anything. You're merely Elathan's shame. But let your ax fall, bastard. Show the Morrígan your power. She longs to see it."

The goddess's and the giant's auras were like two colliding storm fronts. The ravens were silent, the wolves whining and watchful as they slunk about their mistress. With a grunt, the giant slung his ax into a strap upon his back.

"You cannot harm me unless you're attacked," he said. "You cannot harm anyone here. Not directly. That is the price of your passage to this world. That is why you want my kinsman."

"Your kinsman?" the Morrígan laughed. "Little does he resemble you. The Hound is fair as any in the Sidh. Even proud Elathan would have claimed him."

"I know what I am and my roots are sunk deep," the giant growled. "This is my isle and you must go. You are not welcome here."

"Am I not?" said the Morrígan. The goddess gazed at a faerie that was clinging to one of the giant's horns. "What is your name, shining one?"

The faerie appeared petrified to be addressed directly by the Morrígan. Averting her eyes, she bowed low.

"Simara, my lady."

"You've more courtesy than your master," said the Morrígan. "You may accompany me back to the Sidh, my dear. All who dwell with Elathan's bastard may accompany me. I will leave this very hour. Those who spurn my invitation shall be denied the Sidh forever. Go and tell the rest."

With a flutter of wings, the faerie hovered hesitantly before the giant.

"Do what you must," said the Fomorian. "Paths to the Sidh are few. The Morrígan's offer will not come again. You are free to go. Many will wish to join you."

The faerie zoomed off, weaving through the falling snow like a dragonfly. Max scowled at the Morrígan.

"They're what he loves most," he said. "Why would you take them from him?"

The Morrígan was unmoved. Her dark eyes fixed upon him as she raised a finger in stern warning. "Worry about what you love most. Invite me in or give me a son. Which shall it be?"

"Neither."

Dipping her hands in the stream, the Morrígan washed them clean. "So be it. Youth will have its way. But tell me, Hound. Has anyone shared your geasa with you?"

"No."

"Ask the Fomorian to tell you. It is time you knew. But keep them close—don't even tell the girl. If your enemies learn your geasa, they will use them against you."

"Why are you telling me this?" Max asked quietly.

"Because one ill turn deserves another."

With a soundless laugh, the Morrígan rose to her feet. Clutching the infants, she walked straight into the nearest hill and disappeared. In her wake, a golden light peeped forth from the hillside. Where it shone, the soil slid away to reveal a man-sized tunnel leading deep within the earth. Into the tunnel flew the ravens, screeching and cawing. The wolves came next. Last went the faeries.

They appeared from everywhere to accept the Morrígan's invitation. A few stopped to bid the giant farewell but most were too anxious to depart for the Sidh while the portal remained open. The Fomorian watched their exodus in silence, his expression unreadable. He might have been carved of stone but for the occasional flick of his lamb's ears. When the tunnel dimmed and the gate faded, he turned and walked up the hill, crunching bodies and armor beneath his great hooves. When he noticed Max following, he scooped him up without breaking stride.

Max sat within the giant's cupped hands. Scathach and Nox were no longer frozen and spellbound, but sleeping peacefully. The Fomorian's hands were warm and dry, his skin thicker than elephant hide and covered with scars the size of kite shields. The wind whistled through gaps in his fingers. Max peered out to see a dim red sky. Below them, snow blew across the dark hilltops.

The giant did not go straight back, but went instead on a rambling walk around the isle's perimeter. He had grown so large he could pace its entire coastline in less than an hour. Hills and forest, beaches and cliffs slipped steadily past. The Fomorian might have been a mountain of mist as he walked the boundaries of his land. His footfalls made no sound. They seemed to drift past small villages and lonely farmsteads like fog off the Irish Sea.

Max was surprised to see there were humans living on the island. He supposed he shouldn't have been. There were humans living here before Astaroth came to power. The isle was probably one of the safest places for people in the aftermath—so long as they didn't anger the giant. Cities had faded, of course, along with most peoples' memories of life before Astaroth, but there still must have been millions of people scattered across the world, surviving as best they could in this new age. Mankind was nothing if not resilient.

There had been humans in Zenuvia, too. And Piter's Folly. Thousands of refugees arrived at Rowan every day—perhaps more since their victory over Prusias. Humans even lived in Blys's capital. In his own way, Prusias was very fond of humans, their passions and quirks, their talents and foibles. When Max had been his unwilling guest, he'd heard the King of Blys quip that he wished he'd been born human. The real joke was that he wasn't kidding. Not entirely.

There were times Max wished he'd been born human, too. He didn't want to be Lugh's son, to be an object of interest for gods and demons and everything in between. Life had been simpler before he'd known anything about magic or the Sidh or even Rowan. He wanted to go back, wanted to be that boy again. What would life have been like if he'd never boarded that fateful train to Chicago?

Fateful.

Was it fate? Did he have any say in how his life would unfold or was he simply marching along to the beat of an invisible drummer? Or was one's life a combination of both—an opportunity to exercise free will at pivotal, orchestrated moments?

What choices had he made tonight? He chose to leave the giant's caverns and wander the isle until they fell under the Morrígan's spell. Had that truly been a choice? The question weighed heavily, for the consequences of his meeting with the goddess seemed enormous.

He had made an enemy tonight, an immensely powerful enemy at a time when he could not afford one. It was one thing to bring the Morrígan's wrath upon himself, but Scathach and the Fomorian were now involved. The giant had lost a great deal this evening. What would Scathach lose? Should he have done what the Morrígan asked?

His mind went back to what Scathach had said aboard *Ormenheid*.

Never invite a god into this world.

To give in to the Morrígan would have been doing just that. Max suspected Scathach would have agreed with his stand. He just prayed she wouldn't be the one to pay for it.

It was late when they returned to the giant's home. The

caverns were dark and largely empty. There was no singing or feasting, not telltale glimmers of faerie light from the depths of tunnels or pools. A few of the dewdrop faeries remained, but the Fomorian's chief companions would be sea, stone, and tide.

Crouching, the Fomorian set them gently on the floor so Max could take Scathach and Nox to their room. Laying them on the bed, Max covered them in blankets and returned to the main cavern, where he found the Fomorian roasting oxen before a roaring fire. Max sat on a nearby boulder and watched him turn the spit.

"I'm sorry," said Max.

The Fomorian grunted. "They will be happier in the Sidh."

"I should have heeded your warning," Max admitted.

Four eyes swiveled to look at him. "You did heed my warning."

"You told Scathach we should stay in the caverns."

"Not that one," said the giant. "When we reforged your blade, I foretold that the goddess would tempt you—that she would try to make you a conqueror. Tonight, you did what few have the courage to do. You said no to the Morrígan."

"I'm afraid of the consequences."

"They may be difficult," the giant admitted. "The Morrígan does not bring joy or contentment. That is not her nature. Your choice will have consequences. Whether good or evil, none can say. You chose what you thought was right. That is all one can do."

Max said nothing but stared into the fire as though it might hold his fortune. Fat dripped onto the coals, hissing and crackling.

"Do you know my geis?" he asked the giant.

The Fomorian gave a reluctant nod. "Geasa," he corrected. "There are two."

"Would you tell them to me?"

"I will," he said thoughtfully. "It is your right to know them. But tell me first why you wish to know."

This puzzled Max. "Aren't I supposed to know my geasa? How can I be sure I'm obeying them if I don't know what they are?"

Max did not know much about geis or geasa other than they were magical prohibitions often placed on royalty or powerful beings at their birth. To break one's geis was taboo and could trigger serious consequences.

"You are still alive," the giant observed, pulling the ox off the spit. "If one breaks a geis, their days are numbered. But the Morrígan did not mention yours to keep you from breaking them. She knows a simple truth: those who know their geis are far more likely to break it."

"Why would that be?"

The Fomorian shrugged. "They come to believe it's their destiny. If I showed you a thousand doors and said you could enter all but one, which would you wish to open?"

"The one forbidden to me."

"Of course," said the giant. "Which is why it can be wiser *not* to learn one's geis. Those who do tend to linger at its door."

As the giant snapped and sucked the bones, Max wavered on whether he truly wanted to know what his geasa were. He decided to change the subject.

"Scathach said she told you why we came."

The Fomorian nodded, licking grease from his fingers.

"Would you come with us?" asked Max. "Would you come and fight for Rowan?"

Tossing the bones upon the fire, the giant shook his shaggy head. "To me, there is little difference between Prusias and Rowan. Both have come to my shores; both have hunted me. I care not who wins, only that I am left alone."

"I saw the beach," Max said. "Do you really think Prusias is going to leave you alone? If Rowan's defeated, Prusias will crush his remaining enemies. And when he does, he'll come back with enough force that you cannot resist him again."

"And what of Rowan?" asked the giant. "What will happen if Rowan wins and becomes a great power on earth? Do you think your scholars will let me be? No, they will seek to leech whatever wisdom and secrets I possess. As they have always done."

"I don't know what happened in the past," said Max. "But I believe things could be different. David speaks for Rowan now and he's your friend. I'm sure he'd honor whatever arrangements you wished."

The Fomorian gave a scornful laugh. "That one is a trickster. I have given the little sorcerer much thought since you first visited me. He was courteous and kind. He promised to give me a name but he never will. He is false. They are all false."

"I don't understand. What did he do to you?"

"He deceived me. Do you know his lineage?"

"He's Elias Bram's grandson."

"Aye," said the Fomorian. "He is. And that line is very great. Bram is descended from Fionn mac Cumhaill, one of Ireland's great heroes. Fionn was descended from Nuada Silverhand, who was king before Lugh."

Max gazed at the giant. "David also has kin among the Tuatha Dé Danaan?"

"He did once. But Nuada is no more. He died at Magh Tuireadh. Your line and David's intersect in many ways, but your blood is purer. Your sire is Lugh Lamfhada. Many generations separate the sorcerer from Nuada. Still, his mother hails from Fionn mac Cumhaill and Elias Bram. A proud heritage, or so I'd once believed."

"I still don't understand," said Max. "What is there to be ashamed of?"

The Fomorian's face darkened. "A father's blood will tell. The sorcerer deceived us both. He is a demon."

Max actually laughed. "David can't be a demon!" He held up his hand to show the giant a silver ring upon his finger, a gift from David when they learned the Atropos were using possession to control those close to Max. "This grows hot whenever a demon is close by. It's never even grown warm around David."

"That means nothing," said the giant. "If the sorcerer could veil his true nature from me, he can hide it from whatever spirit is bound within that trinket."

Max considered this, the blood petals, and a hundred other explanations and possibilities. Weighing all of this against the person he knew, Max came to a simple conclusion. "So what?"

"He is a *demon*," repeated the giant, emphasizing the word as if Max hadn't heard him.

"So his father was a demon. I guess that makes him a half-demon or whatever they're called. So what? David isn't evil."

"Blood will tell."

"Has your blood told?" Max asked. "Your father was cruel and shallow. He didn't even give you a name. He was a monster but you're not. You're not cruel or shallow. At least I don't think so. You chose to be something better. So has David."

"He hid what he is," muttered the giant darkly.

"I'm starting to see why."

The giant said nothing, but stared into the flames. Max sat for several minutes, meditating on these latest revelations and letting the fire's warmth sink into his bones. At length, he stood.

"Would you tell me my geasa?" he asked.

The Fomorian considered him gravely. "You still wish to know?"

"Yes."

The giant nodded. "Very well. These are the bonds that were placed upon you at your birth: *The Hound may not refuse a dying wish or knowingly slay his kindred.* If you break either geis, your life is forfeit. Do you understand?"

Max nodded, committing the words to memory. "I'm pursued by assassins that share my blood. Would they count as kindred?"

"If they share your blood."

Max frowned. "But I've already slain one. Why didn't that geis take effect?"

The Fomorian considered. "Did you know he was your kin when you struck the blow?"

Max recalled his battle with the clone in Prusias's Arena. He'd only known his armored, faceless opponent as Myrmidon. It was not until the match was finished that he learned whom he'd been fighting.

"No," he said. "I guess not. But the others . . . I know who they are. Are you saying that if I slay them, I also slay myself?"

The giant's response was not comforting. "A geis is often inconvenient," he said. "Perhaps your friends can deal with these foes."

Max wasn't certain he had any friends who could deal with the clones. Cooper already tried and was thoroughly overmatched. This could turn out to be a serious problem. But for now, he wanted to check on Scathach and Nox and get some rest.

"We'll leave tomorrow," he said. "Thank you for helping me."

The giant inclined his head. "Go in peace, Hound. I do not expect we will meet again."

"Maybe not," said Max. "But I want you to think about one thing before I go."

The Fomorian gazed down at him.

"You've lived a long time," said Max. "In all those years, how many people have understood you, offered you their friendship, and vowed to give you what you value most? Because that's what David Menlo did. Whether you choose to help him is up to you, but he deserves your respect."

The Fomorian said nothing. Max walked across the vast cavern, his eyes trained upon his long shadow. Stopping at the archway to Scathach's room, he turned back to bid the Fomorian farewell.

But the giant was gone. Only the fire remained, its smoke winding up and out a hole in the ceiling.

The next morning, Scathach had no recollection of their hike or meeting the Morrigan. Max did not tell her of it or of his conversation with the giant. They woke early, prodded Nox into reluctant motion, and breakfasted alone in the great cavern. There was no sign of the giant, but supplies had been left for them—barrels of fresh water, salted fish, smoked venison, and tart green apples. There were also warm sealskins and furs, for the weather was only getting colder.

As they checked their gear and coaxed Nox into trying a herring, Scathach shared their new objective. "We're to make for Enlyll."

Max made a face. "Enlyll's five hundred miles west of Prusias. Why doesn't David want us joining Rowan's army?"

"I think he wants us to recruit an army."

"Enlyll's just a little barony," said Max. "If it could supply many troops, Ms. Richter would have sent experienced Agents there, not Sarah and Lucia. Technically, Connor's one of Prusias's braymas but I can't imagine he has that much influence."

"How long has it been since you've seen him?"

"Almost three years. Connor left the same day Mum did."

"Well," said Scathach, "apparently Connor's made some new

friends. David said he'd send us all the details using spypaper. Once we sail beyond sight of the Fomorian's island, it should work again."

"Elder vyes," Max mused. "That's what he's sending us after. Two lived near the farmhouse where I first met Mina. Nix and Valya were kind, but they weren't soldiers. Not even remotely. Unless David knows something we don't, we might fail at two missions."

"David wouldn't send us to Enlyll if it wasn't important."

Anxious as Max was to join up with Rowan's main force, he had to agree. Still, he wasn't thrilled with this new assignment. He hadn't been chosen for the Red Branch because he was Rowan's best spy or diplomat. Max was a fighter and Blys, not Enlyll, was where the fighting would be. Rowan's fleet was probably just making landfall.

Still, Scathach was right. David weighed his options so carefully it was likely the operation's success depended on Max's and Scathach's direct involvement. He supposed they would know more once they had sailed beyond the Fomorian's influence and the spypaper could work once again.

While he'd prefer to rejoin Rowan's army, it would be good to see Sarah and Lucia and enjoy a reunion with Connor Lynch. Max had changed a great deal in the past three years. He imagined Connor must have, too.

By midmorning, they had activated *Ormenheid,* which rose and fell on the cold gray shallows. The wind was already blowing in frigid gales and Nox huddled beneath sealskins by the prow where she fixed her steward with a sour stare. The lymrill was trading gold coins and warm, leisurely days for an open boat on wintry seas. She was less than pleased.

When Max secured the last of the barrels, he thumped *Ormenheid*'s salt-crusted masthead. "Leita Enlyll," he murmured.

The enchanted ship pushed forward through water, its prow carving a path between two wrecked ships.

While Scathach lit a fire, Max gazed back at the isle, hoping for a final glimpse of the Fomorian. But there was no sign of the giant upon the bluffs or beach. There was only a small dark figure that watched them depart. She stood motionless on the cold sand while her ravens wheeled about the dull red sky. A lady in black.

~ 13 ~

A Lady in Red

As *Ormenheid* braved the Irish Sea, David Menlo sat in a pavilion off the coast of what had once been Italy.

He had not planned to land on the island of Sicily. Nor had he intended to take shelter on the former African coast the previous week. He'd originally planned to sail the fleet close to Blys—to Rome, as it was called on the old maps—but he was learning that weather outranked any general and could make a mockery of even the best-laid plans. If it did not improve, they would have to find some way across the strait and finish the journey on foot— over five hundred miles of hilly terrain in enemy territory.

And this weather showed no sign of improving. It was not

merely the cold—a cold that sheathed the ships in ice—but the wind and snow as well. The former came screaming at all hours and from all directions, bending and even snapping masts with the fury of a hurricane. While the snow was less ferocious, it was a constant, unyielding nuisance. Visibility was nonexistent, the entire world a billowing wall of white beneath a dull red pall of sky. Early August in the Mediterranean and they might have been in Antarctica.

At least the tent was warm, thought David. There were braziers and carpets and, while the roof sagged from the snow, it served to insulate it from the cold and wind. Reaching for his coffee, David glanced at a particular sheet of spypaper he kept close by. To his immense delight, ink spots blossomed on the page to form words written in a strong, familiar hand.

> *Aboard Ormenheid. Fomorian won't come. Bound for Enlyll. Send operation details when you can. Very sorry to hear about Ms. Richter, but happy they chose you to replace her. You'll do great. Don't get a big head.*
>
> *Max*
>
> *p.s. The Fomorian told me your "secret."*
> *If it's true, I don't care.*

The news about the Fomorian was disappointing but hardly a surprise. Smoothing the parchment, David erased its contents and prepared to compose a reply. As he dipped the pen, a voice sounded from behind him.

"Are you writing in your diary again?"

The amused English accent belonged to one Cynthia Gilley, David's girlfriend and former classmate. Setting down his pen, he turned to see her round, cheerful face looking deceptively innocent at the table where she was sorting mounds of reports and correspondence.

"I don't keep a diary," he insisted. "I keep a *journal*. The Director is required to. And I'm not writing in my journal but replying to Max. He and Scathach have set sail."

"To rendezvous with Sarah and Lucia?"

"That's classified. You're not even supposed to know what Sarah and Lucia are doing."

"But I do know what they're doing. Incidentally, they're having a lot of fun."

"Shhh!" said David, eyeing the tent's entrance. "Wait, how would you know they're having a lot of fun?"

Cynthia shrugged. "Lucia stole some spypaper before they left. We send each other notes."

David pursed his lips. "She shouldn't have done that. *You* shouldn't be doing that. Tell her to destroy it."

"When has anyone been able to tell Lucia anything?"

David paused. Cynthia had a point. Lucia Cavallo was notoriously strong-willed. Besides, he doubted real harm would come of it. From Sarah's official reports, it sounded as if the time they'd spent in Enlyll had been predominately social. They'd heard rumors of Elder vyes and potentially seen one leaving Connor's castle, but there hadn't been anything resembling an introduction, much less discussions. But if such talks could take place—if Ms. Richter's files had been accurate—what allies they might be!

While Lucia's notes to Cynthia were probably harmless, one couldn't be too careful. The last thing David needed was to be accused of lax security when so many were already critical of his appointment as Director. Some were skeptical that one so young could handle the office. Others found it highly suspicious that he had emerged from Prusias's attack with the Director's title and a mysteriously restored hand. Whispers had started and many made their way to him. *David Menlo had orchestrated the attack. David Menlo is in league with Prusias. David Menlo is in league with Astaroth!*

There would always be critics and conspiracy theorists, he reminded himself. Still, he needed to win people over and manage things intelligently. Now was certainly not the time to reveal he was a cambion. Such news might trigger an outright coup. The Fomorian's reaction to David's secret had been a painful, albeit valuable reminder that not everyone would be as accepting as Miss Awolowo, Max, and Cynthia. Someday, David would reveal his true lineage. But first he had a war to win.

"Tell Lucia to tear up the paper," he sighed. "I hope you haven't shared anything about the army's movements or situation."

"Oh no. We really just talk about Connor."

"Oh?" said David. "How are he and Lucia getting along?"

Connor Lynch's obsession with Lucia had been an open secret since their very first year at Rowan. In many ways, they were a perfect match: Lucia enjoyed dismissing her many suitors while Connor relished the chase.

"Mixed," Cynthia replied. "I think Lucia was expecting to find the same old Connor from Third Year. But he isn't anymore, is he? He's a young man, the ruler of a barony, and—if Lucia's to be believed—a bit of a playboy."

"Connor's always been kind of wild," David reflected. "He mooned a café when we were First Years. Most playboys probably start out mooning cafés."

Cynthia filed a stack of papers. "Well, he's moved on from mooning cafés. Now he hosts big parties and spends his days hunting. There are lots of humans on his lands and apparently quite a few girls. Pretty girls. Girls who are more than a little interested in 'his lordship.'"

"Maybe Lucia doesn't like having competition."

"Maybe," said Cynthia, pulling her red hair back in a ponytail. "But Connor certainly led her on in that letter, didn't he? He made it sound like he's been pining away for her—and *only* her. Maybe the letter was just to sneak us a message about the Elder vyes. He didn't mention he'd found other shoulders to cry on."

"Is he dating these other girls?"

"Define 'dating,'" said Cynthia dryly.

As a shy and introverted newcomer to these topics, David was quietly amazed by Connor's life. Dating multiple girls? Did people do such things? *Could* people do such things? While it was tempting to let his imagination wander, David realized he was on dangerous ground. He affected a look of polite indifference.

"Sounds complicated."

"Ha!" Cynthia laughed. "You can say that twice. Lucia says if she gets another dirty look from one of Connor's admirers, she'll curse the lot into swine. Him too."

David frowned. "Sarah hasn't mentioned any of this in her reports."

"Sarah's too busy snogging with Markus."

David put down his pen, inwardly amazed. Sarah Amankwe was a Nigerian classmate whose intelligence, athleticism, and reliability had her on track to be a top Agent. While he knew Lucia would be distracted with Connor, David assumed Sarah would be spending every minute trying to make contact with Elder vyes. Apparently, he'd been wrong. "Who's Markus?"

"One of the captains in Connor's trading fleet," said Cynthia. "But it sounds to me like he spends more time raiding than trading."

"Sounds like he's a pirate."

"Oh, I don't know. I think she's just having fun. They're two girls off on an adventure. Right now they're all excited to attend a médim Connor is hosting in a few weeks. Sounds a little scary to me."

"I'm sure they'll be fine," he assured her. "Especially if Connor's hosting. There are strict rules around médim that govern what's permitted and what's not. Violence involving anything except certain rituals is strictly forbidden. It'll be more like attending a ball where the guests are mostly spirits."

"Well, now I'm a little jealous," said Cynthia. "They'll get to wear fancy dresses and dance with pirates and braymas and spirits. Lucia will wear green, you know. She looks amazing in green. I kind of hate her when she wears green . . ."

"Me too," said David, only half listening. He was staring at his spypaper, considering whether to insist that Max and Scathach should travel overland. *Ormenheid* was a wondrous vessel—an artifact of the true Old Magic—but even she might not be a match for this weather. The image of that small, open craft navigating thirty-foot seas made David queasy. He sent a brief message to that effect, promising more details on their mission but recommending that they seek shelter and travel by land if the weather did not relent.

It was certainly not relenting where he was. Each day, David walked out to stare at the stretch of water separating their impromptu settlement from the mainland. It was not far, a mere afternoon sail in pleasant weather. But the unnatural fury of those seas and wind was shocking. It was everything the aeromancers and Mystics could do to shield the coves where the ships were moored. Rowan had one more stretch of water to cross before they could make landfall and march on Blys. But to protect the fleet during its final dash across this murderous strait would be beyond the aeromancers' powers. It would be beyond his powers, too. The Archmage might be able to manage it, but he had vanished since destroying Prusias's monsters. David presumed his grandfather was recovering at Rowan or some other refuge, but his status and whereabouts remained a mystery. No, Elias Bram could not bail them out of this. David reflected on Lord Salisbury's tale of the Spanish Armada and how it was weather, not Sir Francis Drake, that ultimately proved its doom.

David cursed.

Cynthia looked up from her papers. It was not like David to voice his frustrations, much less with vulgarity. She said nothing, but watched silently as he rose to contemplate a large map of Blys.

"We're still far from Prusias's city," he mused. "If this weather doesn't ease up, we may have to march five hundred miles up the peninsula. With this weather, we'd be lucky to make two or three miles a day. Very lucky. What's the latest on food?"

Cynthia consulted a logbook. "According to the original estimate, we have almost a year's worth on hand, but we're going through it faster than they'd projected. The weather's making people sick and some of the livestock have died."

"How much livestock?"

Cynthia found the latest report from the grooms, hands, and swineherds. Her eyes traveled swiftly down the list.

"Fifty-seven cows, nineteen bulls, one hundred and three sheep, three hundred and forty-one chickens, forty-seven goats . . ."

"Is that cumulative?" asked David, aghast.

"This week."

David drummed his fingers on the map while the wind screamed outside. "Napoleon said an army travels on its stomach. We can't sit here while our supplies dwindle away. This weather will have ruined any crops planted between here and Blys. We could exhaust our stores before we get within sight of Prusias's city."

"We do have a lifeline," Cynthia reminded him. She gestured at a large traveling chest sitting by several boxes.

Despite its humble and even battered appearance, the trunk was David's most prized creation. While Bram and Mina could teleport, David could not. And while David had created wormholes between his bedroom in Rowan's Manse and locations around the world, those locations were fixed. The trunk represented his first successful attempt to create a moving wormhole—a portable conduit that connected his bedroom to wherever the trunk happened to be. It was the only reason Cynthia was in this pavilion and not at Rowan, where she had remained to tutor apprentices.

"We could bring food through it," Cynthia suggested. "We might even bring smaller livestock. The Sanctuary hasn't been affected by this weather. Crops are growing and—"

She stopped as an Agent from the Bloodstone Circle, an elite cadre of bodyguards, rang a small chime and entered the tent. The man stared at Cynthia.

"I wasn't aware the Director had company," he said.

"Agent James, this is Cynthia Gilley, my particular friend," said David. "You may be seeing her from time to time."

"Sir, it's imperative that we screen everyone for your safety."

David gave a noncommittal grunt and asked what he could do for Agent James. The man glanced uneasily at Cynthia as if the information was highly confidential.

"A visitor has arrived," he said significantly.

David raised his eyebrows. "A royal visitor?"

"Yes, Director."

David sat up and assessed his appearance in a mirror. There was only one person this could be. "Give me five minutes," he said. "Is the visitor corporeal?"

"No, sir. Shadow walking."

David nodded, his mind racing. He glanced about the tent, wishing that it looked more like a command center and less like the office of an overworked teenager. Demons were painfully hierarchical; it was important to make a good impression.

"Five minutes, and you are not to mention this visitor to anyone, Agent James."

"The Bloodstone Circle takes confidentiality very seriously," said the man stiffly. "We even take vows. Perhaps the Director was unaware."

"Sorry," said David. "I don't mean to doubt you, but this meeting is a little delicate. More than a little delicate. Five minutes and please send the visitor in."

With a bow, the Agent departed. David swiftly escorted Cynthia to the trunk.

"You have to go," he said, opening its heavy lid. "I'm sorry to kick you out, but this meeting is extremely important."

"Who is it?" hissed Cynthia, stepping inside the trunk but peering at the tent's entrance.

"I can't say. I'm sorry, but I can't. If things go well, you'll find out soon enough."

"All right, all right," she grumbled. As Cynthia was much taller than David, she bent down to kiss him. "Good luck. Write me!"

She disappeared into the trunk as though descending a flight of steep wooden steps. When David closed and locked it, a sliver of golden light peeped through the keyhole. Cynthia would already be back at Rowan, sitting on David's sleigh bed and battling the nausea that usually followed teleportation.

With an absent wave of his hand, David straightened up the tent—covering maps and papers, rearranging furniture, and dimming several lamps in deference to a guest who might prefer darkness. Dipping his hands in a basin, David quickly washed his face, smoothed his hair, and glanced at himself in the mirror.

You'll be fine.

A second later, Agent James announced his visitor.

"Queen Lilith, ruler of Zenuvia."

The demoness glided in, a translucent ghostlike lady in a long gown of deep red silk. She was one of the oldest demons on Earth with roots that went back farther than Babylon. Rumors and myth clung to her like cobwebs. Some insisted she had been the wife of Adam. Others claimed she was a fallen goddess, a mother of demons and vampires that dined on lost or naughty children. David paid little heed to such rumors—the older a spirit was, the more their name was intertwined with history and legends, real or imagined. In any case, the rumors associated with Lilith had little bearing on this meeting. For David's purposes, she was simply an important chess piece—a ruler who had once served Astaroth, had no wish to serve Prusias, and controlled most of what had been Asia.

Even while in Nether, the Queen of Zenuvia exuded a regal and formidable presence. She was far taller than David and exquisitely beautiful. Her face had a languorous, ageless quality with large, almond eyes and lips that were as dark as wine against an olive complexion. Her black hair twined and curled like garden creepers, tumbling down from a slender golden tiara marked with her sigil—a crescent moon entwined with a sprig of hemlock. She stopped to stare at David, her gaze lingering on his restored right hand. David bowed deeply.

"Greetings, Queen Lilith," he said. "Thank you for accepting my invitation."

She gave an almost imperceptible nod of acknowledgment. Her voice was soft and measured, its accent Middle Eastern. "I have not seen you since Walpurgisnacht. You are changed, David Menlo."

"I am," he said. "So is the world."

"You are whole," she observed wryly. "Only Astaroth could have restored your hand to you. You have seen him, then."

David nodded. There was no point denying it.

"Where is he?" she asked, a malicious gleam in her dark eyes.

"I don't know. I encountered him unexpectedly in Nether. If anything, the Demon is unpredictable."

The queen's lip curled. "That one is no true demon. He fooled us."

"He's fooled everyone."

Lilith nodded and walked slowly about the pavilion. "So, what is it Rowan wishes to offer me?"

"An alliance against Prusias, naturally."

A smile played about the corners of Lilith's mouth. "Rowan wishes to make pacts with *daemona*? The world has changed indeed."

"War makes strange bedfellows."

"That it does," she replied. "But my lands are not at war."

"Not yet," said David. "But if Rowan is defeated, it's only a matter of time before Prusias turns his attention to Zenuvia."

Lilith shrugged. "Zenuvia is far and Zenuvia is strong. And the more Prusias comes to rely upon the Workshop, the more he disgusts his own braymas. If he declares war on my kingdom, many of his followers will abandon him. Prusias does not worry me."

"If Prusias does not worry you, why have you come?"

The demoness studied David as though he were a noteworthy painting. "Curiosity. Not many mortals could fool Astaroth. And I knew your grandfather of old. He summoned me once upon a time. I wished to see what his kin was like—particularly as he now speaks for Rowan. And I have missed seeing the Old Magic among humans. They were always the most interesting."

"And I thought only Prusias was interested in humans."

"Don't be absurd," said Lilith, resuming her perusal of the pavilion. "Most daemona are interested in humans. After all, mankind can summon us. It is the price we pay for lingering in this world. Humans may only be mortal, but they hold great power over us. If goldfish could summon you, would you be interested in them?"

David ignored the barb. "What if you could have a lasting peace with humans? No more summoning. No more war. You have your realm and humans have theirs."

"I already have my realm."

"For now."

"Is that a threat, David Menlo?" she asked coolly.

"No," said David firmly. "Rowan wants a sustainable peace. But peace will be impossible while Prusias rules Blys. If he's defeated, we have an opportunity to negotiate new rules to govern the relationship between humans, daemona, and other beings."

The demoness looked bored. "Rowan already signed a treaty with Astaroth. A treaty Rowan violated."

"That was entirely my doing," said David plainly. "That treaty's provisions were intended solely to isolate and humiliate Rowan. What I'm talking about is different. The agreement I envision is to lay the foundation for a new age. It's to be a partnership among equals."

Now Lilith looked amused. "But you're not our equals. We're immortal; you are not. Even the greatest *mehrùn* die within a few centuries. Humans will never again rule this world as they once did."

David nodded. "I'm aware of that. But the pendulum is not going to swing as far as you might believe. Don't underestimate mankind. While it's true that humans live and die, they also evolve and adapt. We've entered a new age, one in which Old Magic has reawakened. There will be more *mehrùn* than ever before, and they will be more powerful than those that exist today."

"Perhaps we should hunt all *mehrùn* down before they become a threat."

"Over half are born to nonmagical parents," said David. "Killing *mehrùn* won't stamp out magic among humans."

"All humans, then. We can simply exterminate you."

David shrugged. "Then there will be war. But let's be honest. If that's what demons wanted and it was easy to accomplish, it would have been done. Astaroth thought he was invincible and was exposed before his entire court. Prusias thought Rowan was ripe for conquest and learned a painful lesson. Humans are stronger than daemona likes to pretend."

"That may be true," said Lilith. "But mankind's greatest army is huddled on a frozen shore. I have doubts you will even reach Prusias much less defeat him. If I support Rowan, I will anger many demons only to join the side most likely to lose. An alliance with Prusias would make more sense."

"And what would that gain you?" asked David. "You know perfectly well Prusias will turn upon you when it's convenient. In the meantime, he'll make outlandish promises. I'm sure he already has. I'll even venture a guess . . . the Americas?"

Lilith said nothing.

"Of course he did," David chuckled. "The Americas have a thousand independent rulers that bow to no one. Prusias is more than happy to offer you a theoretical title to something he doesn't control. What he really wants is for you to stay out of his war and consolidate those territories on his behalf. Once you have, he'll secretly sponsor uprisings against you, force you to exhaust your resources suppressing them, and snap up everything once you're spread too thin. You'll have done his dirty work in the Americas and given him the keys to Zenuvia, too."

The queen frowned as though David's analysis echoed her own misgivings. Still, she remained unmoved.

"Neutrality also has its benefits," she observed. "One can see how things unfold while the value of one's allegiance increases. What will Rowan give Zenuvia for its aid at the decisive moment? What will Prusias? Yes, I think perhaps neutrality is best."

David looked hard at the demoness, her ghostly form shimmering in the dim pavilion. "You don't have to join with us, but can you promise Zenuvia won't sign a pact with Prusias?"

"No," said Lilith. "But I will say that I have not yet done so. I will wait and watch. If the time comes when an alliance with Rowan might serve my interests, you will hear from me. As a token of good faith, I leave you with something to ponder."

"And what is that?" asked David.

The queen bent to study an onyx rook on an antique chessboard. "Why has Yuga never attacked Prusias's capital? It's curious, is it not? Yuga is supposed to be a mindless terror, a monster that hungers for all life, but she's never approached the world's most populous city when it's practically on her doorstep."

The observation's implications floored David, who was privately furious for not making it himself. Why *hadn't* Yuga gravitated toward Prusias's capital? Was she truly mindless? Did Prusias have some means of controlling her?

"Interesting question," he confessed. "I don't suppose you know the answer?"

"If I did, I certainly wouldn't give it away," she replied. With a bow, the demoness glided toward the door. "Farewell, Director. If you don't freeze to death on this little island, perhaps we'll meet again."

Lilith departed, slipping through the tent. Would she go directly to Blys and bargain with Prusias? Probably. Lilith would always do what was best for Lilith. Still, her thoughts about Yuga were profoundly interesting. Would Prusias's imp help them? He had before—Mr. Bonn had warned David when Prusias intended to attack Mina and the other children at Max's farmhouse. David couldn't summon Mr. Bonn against his will, of course (an imp's bond to his master precluded outside interference), but perhaps they could get a message to him.

A tiny grasshopper landed on David's desk and began rubbing its forelegs together. David glanced at it, curious how it could survive in such cold. He brushed it off the paper so that it hopped onto a lamp and then onto the enchanted trunk. It peered inside the keyhole as though it sensed something unusual about it. David cocked his head.

"Hello, Grandfather. How long have you been listening?"

~ 14 ~

SERVANT OF THE
STARVING GODS

As the grasshopper expanded, antennae and extra legs receded until it no longer resembled an insect but a worn and grizzled Archmage. He sat on the trunk, his robes frayed at the hem, clutching a leather satchel.

"Greetings, David," he said. "Or do you prefer Director?"

"David is fine."

Rising to his considerable height, Bram gazed down at his grandson. "Very good. To answer your question, I've been listening for almost an hour. Inexcusably rude, but curiosity got the best of me. Incidentally, I approve of your lady friend and this ingenious trunk. I don't approve of that," he said, gesturing at David's hand. "What bargain did you make with Astaroth?"

"None," David replied. "I encountered him in Nether and he restored it to me. I didn't have much choice in the matter. Evidently, he wants me 'whole when he destroys God.'"

Bram's eyes kindled with interest. "Tell me everything."

David told his grandfather about his conversation with Astaroth while shadow walking. He detailed Astaroth's appearance and behavior, the Demon's assertion that his "children" needed to be punished, and finally his theory that Astaroth was going insane with the realization that he could never be God. He then turned to Max and Scathach, how he'd rescued them from the faeries and how the Fomorian had done his best to heal Max's terrible wound. Bram listened carefully but did not comment until David was finished. When he finally did, his words were sharp.

"You should relinquish the Director's title," he said pointedly. "I never imagined such titles or trappings interested you."

"I didn't ask for the job," said David coldly.

Bram continued as though he hadn't even heard his grandson. "Conversing with Astaroth. Negotiating with Lilith? How can you be so foolish? If anyone knew what you were . . ."

"Some do," David replied. "And you needn't look so shocked. That I'm cambion doesn't bother me anymore. I don't see why it should bother you."

"You're my blood," the Archmage growled. "Emer is my daughter . . . Of course it bothers me. Putting aside my feelings as a father, you cannot negotiate with demons. They are not trustworthy."

"I'm surprised by the squeamishness," said David calmly. "You've summoned more spirits than anyone. You know perfectly well that not all daemona are malicious. Some *are* trustworthy, even kind."

Bram gave a bitter laugh. "If you think Lilith is kind and trustworthy, you are sadly mistaken. She's over seven thousand years old and has been worshipped as a goddess. Adulation is what she craves, not some Utopia where humans and spirits share the world. She will interpret everything you said as weakness—both Rowan's and your own."

"She's free to do what she likes," said David. "I enjoy being underestimated. Even by my relatives. It usually plays out in my favor."

Bram laid a hand upon his grandson's shoulder. "I don't underestimate you. But you are young still and bear tremendous responsibilities. To negotiate with demons . . . mortals often regret such bargains."

"It's only politics," David reminded him. "I'm not selling my soul. As Director, I'm happy to speak with anyone—friend or foe—to advance our cause. I don't pretend that Lilith harbors any love for Rowan. But I also don't pretend that we can afford to ignore potential allies. Lilith could help tip the balance in this war. So could the Elder vyes. So could the Workshop or the witches. Rowan cannot win this war alone—particularly when we can't count upon you to aid in the fighting."

"I've already done too much," said Bram heavily. "Destroying those Workshop creatures weakened me. I've not spent so much energy since Solas fell. I can perform some minor magics, but it will be many months until I am myself again."

"Can you still teleport?" asked David, keenly aware that research into Astaroth's origins depended heavily on this rarest of abilities.

"Occasionally," Bram replied, pouring himself the remains

from David's coffeepot. "Usually when I'm touching Mina's dragon."

"Ember strengthens your magic?"

Bram nodded. "When one's near him—if he allows one near him—you can feel the Old Magic. It saturates the air. Ember's no mere wyrm, but a true dragon. A stormdrake I think, for the elements seem to obey him. There is no snow on Túr an Ghrian when he is there and the flowers bloom when he slithers through its gardens."

"How big is he now?"

Bram considered. "Two hundred feet. Maybe more. Within a year or two, he'll measure thrice that. The oldest dragons stretched across entire river valleys and slumbered for centuries between feedings. Someday, I suspect, Ember will be such a one, but not for many years."

"Is he a danger to Rowan?" asked David seriously.

"Not so long as Mina is nearby. In any case, Ember has no interest in humans as food. Unless he was provoked, I think there's little danger."

"If he can control the weather, maybe he can help us," David mused. "Do you think he would?"

"You'd have to ask Mina," said Bram. "The dragon won't obey anyone else. She's using Ember to help control the Sanctuary's weather and ensure a harvest. And it doesn't hurt to have a dragon at Rowan when its armed strength is elsewhere. If you use Ember for the siege of Blys, Rowan might become vulnerable."

I don't need Ember for the sack of Blys, thought David. *I just need him to escort the fleet as closely as possible.* He glanced at his trunk. *Could we teleport Ember here?* He'd never fit in the trunk, of course. *Perhaps we could make him smaller.* David was an exceedingly gifted alchemist. He could brew a potion to change the size of most creatures, but he suspected dragons were impervious to conventional magic. There was much written about true dragons such as Typhon, Tiamat, and Yamata no Orochi, but few scholarly works about their biology or powers. Those who tried to study them were generally eaten or incinerated. David imagined that true dragons had much in common with humans like himself—the Old Magic within them made their capabilities wildly diverse and unpredictable. Still, a trip to Rowan would be in order.

"Fair points," David conceded. "I'll take it up with Mina. But first I want to know why you're here. Hopefully it wasn't just to spy on me."

"No," said Bram. "It was to ask for your help. I have been trying to locate Yaro."

"The other imp who served Astaroth. The imp Lord Salisbury mentioned."

David had not forgotten their interview with Lord Salisbury before Prusias's attack on the fleet. The news that Astaroth had once used an imp other than Mr. Sikes was a significant finding.

"Aye," said Bram. "Mr. Sikes is untouchable, but Astaroth released Yaro from bondage and I doubt very much he was granted *koukerros*. Yaro may know little of Astaroth's true past, but he is an important piece of the puzzle. Without a fuller picture of Astaroth's origins, it will be very difficult to discover his truename or the means to destroy him."

"How are you going to find Yaro?"

"With this," said Bram. From his pocket, the Archmage produced a ring of brass and iron with a faded hexagram on its face. David recognized it at once.

"The Seal of Solomon," he breathed. "It's been lost for two thousand years. How did you get it?"

"Many rumors about this ring are false," Bram replied. "It has been accounted for up until it came into my possession almost four hundred years ago. Djinn summoned by this ring laid the foundations of Túr an Ghrian at Solas. Since those days, the seal has been passed secretly to the Archmage whenever a new one was named. I cast it away when Solas fell lest Astaroth come to possess it. It has not been easy to find, but I have recovered it at last."

"What does it do exactly? The legends are vague."

"Its powers are many," Bram answered. "Those who wear it will find they can perceive spirits, understand them, and even command those of lesser stature. If a sorcerer wears the ring, however, its true potency is realized. While wearing the Seal of Solomon, you will be able to summon and master all but the greatest spirits without bothering with inscriptions and truenames."

"That's rather useful," said David.

"Indeed," said his grandfather. "But like any powerful item, it has its dangers. Demons and spirits hate the Seal and the one who wears it. And the ring's power is a temptation unto itself. King Solomon was uncommonly wise and possessed considerable restraint. He never abused the ring. I do not have his gifts, however. For me, the ring proved too enticing."

"How did you use it?"

"Very poorly," Bram muttered. "Not at first, of course. At first, I used it sparingly and only to serve the public good when I'd exhausted other means. But soon I found myself using it in other ways—to serve my vanity, to assert my superiority, and to acquire things that did not belong to me. In short, I used it for evil."

David looked hard at Bram. "Did you use it to win Brigit's hand?"

While his grandfather's courting of Brigit was a popular legend, David had heard a darker version. In that tale, Elias Bram had not been a dashing suitor defying death for the woman he loved. Instead, he had been an arrogant, selfish man who could not stomach that his friend, Marley Augur, had found love before he did. Allegedly, Bram had threatened the woman's father into naming a price for her hand—a price only he could meet.

David's question brought a flicker of pain to Bram's face. "Aye," he confessed. "Solomon's Seal helped me complete the tasks set by Brigit's father as conditions to wed her. It is the great shame of my life. I betrayed my closest friend and forced a woman who did not love me into marriage. You heard the tale from Astaroth I suppose."

David nodded. "He told Max. Max told me. Did Brigit ever grow to love you?"

His grandfather said nothing for some time. When at last he spoke, his voice was clear but measured.

"I believe so. Your grandmother was not one to hide her true feelings. She despised me when we were married—would not even look at me much less share my bed. But I was patient. Over time, I think she came to believe that it was her purpose to make me a better man and steward of the powers I'd been given. Our marriage had poisoned roots, but it found a way to grow and even blossom in its own peculiar way. Without her, there's no telling what I might have become. She saved me."

"I guess legends aren't always true."

"No," said Bram. "It's always dangerous to meet one's heroes. We want them to be perfect, but of course they're riddled with flaws—larger flaws, for they're cast from larger molds. It took me decades to acknowledge my limitations and fallibility. You are much farther along that path than I am. Despite my criticisms earlier, I have great faith in your judgment. If I didn't, I would not do this."

Bram handed his grandson the Seal of Solomon. The ring was surprisingly heavy and warm as David hefted it. He feared it would be too big, but once he slipped the ring over his finger, it contracted to a comfortable and pleasing fit. A tingling warmth traveled up his hand and arm and spread throughout his body.

"I like this ring," he remarked.

"Good. I would like you to summon Yaro with it," said Bram. "Astaroth knows I am weakened, David. He is hunting me. Twice now, I've barely escaped him and dare not travel through Nether until I am recovered. In the meantime, I must conserve and rebuild my energies. Even at Túr an Ghrian—even under Mina and Ember's protection—I am in danger. The ring is useful for my quest, but I do not trust myself to use it. I know from experience its powers are too great a temptation. And thus I pass it along to a worthier keeper and ask you to call upon Yaro. I do not have the strength to do so without the ring and it is important that you hear whatever information Yaro may have. My quest may ultimately fall to you. We must stop Astaroth before he does something far more drastic than this unholy winter."

"I understand," said David. "I'll try to contact Yaro. Do you want to stay or would it be safer for you to return to Rowan? You can use the trunk."

"No, I want to hear Yaro for myself. I will observe in a different form."

"Will that weaken you further?"

Bram chuckled. "I've changed shape so often it requires very little of me. It's more of an instinct than spellwork."

"Very well," said David. "Does the ring require me to do anything specific? Any special words or incantations?"

"Merely concentrate on the spirit you wish and say its name. The ring will do the rest."

With a soft exhale, Bram changed into a gray spider smaller than a fingernail. It crawled up the trunk and slipped within the keyhole, turning about so that tiny eyes peered out from within its shadow. Stepping to the tent's entrance, David set a ward upon it that would prevent anyone from entering.

Once all was ready, he settled into a comfortable chair, ran his finger over the face of Solomon's ring, and focused his mind on his objective.

"Yaro," he said softly. "The Seal of Solomon commands your presence."

A tall slab of worn and weathered stone materialized several feet away. It wobbled a moment before falling ponderously over and chipping a corner. Rising from his chair, David stared down at it.

It was an ancient headstone whose faded inscription was topped by a sightless green man disgorging leaves and fruit from its fearful grimace. While David could make out a few words in Latin, the letters were shallow and worn, so it was difficult to make out much else. From its lichen-mottled mouth issued a dry, creaking voice.

"Yaro is here."

"Yaro who once served Astaroth," David confirmed, inwardly amazed by the ring's power.

"Astaroth and Taluman, Bankou and Phyrael, Malah and Allu. They are one and the same. I served him longest and in all his names and forms."

"And yet here you are," David observed. "Bound in a head-stone. Did Astaroth confine you here?"

"It was Sikes. Mad and jealous Sikes. Curse him for eternity!"

"I want to know everything from the beginning," said David. "When and how did you come to serve the spirit now known as Astaroth?"

"It began in Jericho," Yaro answered. "At the time I served a human, a trifling magician. In the marketplace, he purchased a scroll from a hooded stranger—a foreigner by his speech—who spoke of a mighty spirit that could be called if one knew the proper words. I warned my master of the dangers, but he would not listen. He yearned for power. He called upon the spirit that very night."

"And Astaroth came?"

"Allu," hissed the green man. "He was Allu then. He wore the same robes the foreigner had been wearing, but when the hood was drawn back, there was no proper face. There was only a mouth. When my master beheld what he'd called, when he saw it step beyond the useless inscriptions, he fell to the floor and covered his eyes. I could only watch as Allu consumed my master and then his slaves, one by one."

"How did you survive?"

"Allu wanted an interpreter. He needed someone to teach him the ways of men and daemona, for he was still a stranger here and wont to make mistakes in his speech or habits."

"And you agreed?"

"I had never been in the presence of such power. I could only obey."

"So what is he, Yaro?" asked David. "Where does he come from?"

"From Outside," intoned the green man. "It comes from beyond the stars, beyond the veil, beyond Nether and the Void. It is not alive or dead, male or female, young or old. Its masters slide over us and under us and through us, but they lie beyond infinity."

David's pulse quickened. "Astaroth's *masters?*"

"Yes," Yaro hissed. "Old gods. Starving Gods that ruled a dying universe. That is all that Allu told me. He shared more with that treacherous mortal Sikes."

David looked sharply at the blank, haunting eyes of the green man.

"What do you mean, Sikes is mortal? He's an imp."

"No," intoned the headstone. "Sikes was mortal once, a son of Egypt himself."

"Egypt himself," David repeated. "You mean Sikes was the son of a pharaoh?"

"Yes. He was Neheb then—youngest son of Nectanebo II, last of the Egyptian pharaohs."

"How did he become an imp?"

"The only way a mortal can."

"Murder?" said David.

"As you say. I am forbidden to speak of his crimes. But Neheb can tell you. Neheb can tell you of the Starving Gods and their servant's truename. It was Neheb Astaroth loved. It was Neheb whom he trusted. Neheb holds the answers you seek."

"Sikes, you mean," said David.

"Neheb."

"They're one and the same."

"Those who commit crimes against the gods cannot escape their punishments," whispered Yaro. "Sikes may live free, but Neheb lies with the damned. And there, there may he rot until the Judgment!"

As these last words were shrieked, the green man's face split asunder and the headstone split down its center. The smell of brimstone filled the air, burning David's nose as he crouched and examined the broken pieces. There was no trace of Yaro and no answer when David tried calling him again. The imp simply was no more.

"He's gone," said David, turning to the trunk.

The spider was already crawling from the keyhole to the floor. In a blur of metamorphosis, it became the Archmage. Crouching next to David, he plucked up half the green man's face.

"Very peculiar," said Bram. "I've never seen anything like that before. It seems that Yaro triggered a powerful curse."

"A geis?" asked David.

"Geasa don't work instantaneously," said Bram. "Very strange. It's all very strange. It fairly reeks of a trap."

David nodded. "If Astaroth wants to hide his origins, why would he allow Yaro to live?"

Bram frowned and studied the piece of fractured stone as he handled it. "It's hard to say. Yaro served Astaroth for thousands of years. He might have been spared out of gratitude or to fulfill a promise. But of course Yaro might have been left alive for a more nefarious purpose. Astaroth is cunning. It's not inconceivable that he would use Yaro to set a trap for anyone who was prying into his origins."

"So, you're confident this Neheb really existed and that he became Mr. Sikes?"

"Yes," said Bram. "Spirits called by Solomon's Seal cannot lie to its bearer. They are bound to truth—or what they accept as truth. Yaro believed that Astaroth hails from another universe, that he served these 'Starving Gods,' and that Neheb knows important information. Of that I'm certain."

David frowned. "I don't like it one bit. Yaro introduced this Neheb, suggested he knew Astaroth's truename, hinted where we might find him, and promptly vanished. That's a baited hook."

"Aye," said Bram. "But it's bait we may have to take. We can't afford to ignore such information. I will verify what I can, of course—the existence of this Neheb and so forth—but if Astaroth set this trap, the ruse will withstand scrutiny."

"How could Neheb and Sikes be in different places if they're the same person?" asked David.

"Sikes must be fashioned from Neheb's body and spirit," said

Bram. "A portion of Neheb's remains—perhaps even a portion of his spirit—could be elsewhere."

"And do you have any idea where that might be?" asked David. "This place where he might lie until the Judgment."

"The pharaohs are famous for their tombs," said Bram, "but if Neheb and his family were exiled from Egypt, we won't find him in the pyramids. Yaro also said he was 'damned' for a crime against the gods. Murdering a royal parent or sibling would qualify and would further explain how he became an imp. I doubt he's buried anywhere near his family."

"Do you think Neheb used magic?" asked David.

"You're thinking of the witches," Bram observed.

David nodded. "If the witches collect the remains of those who have used magic, Neheb might be in their ossuaries."

Bram began pacing. "I think it very likely that Neheb knew some magic. Either Neheb summoned Astaroth or he became acquainted with him in some other way. It's possible Astaroth served his father as an adviser or court magician. Regardless, I think only a student of the arcane could spark Astaroth's interest, much less become his most loyal servant."

"Maybe we can find someone who knows what became of him," said David. "I've never been in the ossuaries. Do they have a place that's set aside for the damned?"

"If they do, I've never seen it. And I've spent a great deal of time in them."

David stretched and rubbed a bleary eye. With the fleet's difficulties and incessant meetings, he'd not slept ten hours in the past week. Coffee could only do so much and he still needed to brief Max and Scathach, check on various missions, and investigate why Yuga never encroached on Prusias's city. The amount of work was simply extraordinary. He knew he needed to do a better job of delegating, but that was easier said than done. Bram patted his grandson's shoulder.

"Heavy is the head that wears the crown, eh?"

David shrugged and suppressed a yawn.

"I'll leave you to your business," said Bram. "Thank you for helping me, David. And thank you for taking Solomon's Seal—I feel better knowing that it's in your possession. Focus on your army and the task before you. I'll return to Rowan and see what else I can learn of Neheb and where we might find him. Shall I ask Mina to send Ember to you?"

"No," said David. "I'll try summoning spirits first. If they can't ferry the fleet across, we'll see if Ember can help. Until then, I'd rather he remain at Rowan—especially if you're going to be there."

"I'm grateful," said Bram. "The more time I spend in Ember's presence, the sooner my strength will recover. I fear I'll need every ounce."

"Say hello to Mina for me."

"I will," replied Bram, cupping David's cheek before glancing down at the broken pieces of headstone. "Sorry about the mess."

David sighed. "What's one more?"

He opened the trunk and stood aside as Bram stepped within. With a grunt of professional approval, the Archmage descended the steps that would take him to the wormhole. When David shut the lid and turned his key, there was a pulse of light and the Archmage was gone.

Stretching again, David sniffed and glanced up at a portion of the tent where the roof was sagging. The snow was relentless. Stirring a brazier's coals, he let its warmth sink into his bones while he studied Solomon's Seal by the firelight. How would demons react when they learned a cambion possessed and used the very ring they hated?

Donning a heavy cloak, David exited the tent. Agent James stood outside, his beard crusted with snow as he warmed his hands by a brazier and chatted with another member of the Bloodstone Circle. When the pair saw the Director, they stood at attention.

"At ease," said David absently. He gazed about at the seemingly endless tents staked upon the beaches and along the cliffs. There were thousands of them, rippling in the gales that blew off the dark gray sea. It was the sea that interested David, that treacherous strait separating Rowan from the Italian peninsula and the final march toward Prusias.

The Agents trailed him as he walked down to the shore, shielding his eyes from stinging needles of ice. Other than sentries, David saw few people. Most were huddled in their tents, waiting for the order to continue on. David trudged past tents and a makeshift cattle pen, inhaling the smells of livestock and cooking fires.

Solomon's ring grew warm as David stood at the water's edge. He sensed naiads nearby, along with sea faeries, water demons, and elementals. Each would serve—even the old marid that lived far beneath the churning depths. They would check the wind and calm the seas and see the fleet to its final shore. David turned to Agent James.

"We sail tomorrow."

~ 15 ~

THE CONSPIRATORS' BALL

Harine was one of the wealthier regions in Prusias's kingdom. Comprising most of what had once been France, it nestled between Lebrím to the west and Blys to the east. Enlyll was a small but prosperous barony situated on Harine's southern coast, an area greatly favored by the rich long before Astaroth came to power. At the moment, however, its beautiful beaches were gray, the grapevines were frozen, and the harbors were empty.

Under normal circumstances, the road to Baron Lynch's estate would have been broad enough for two carriages to pass one another. But a heavy snowfall had complicated matters. The long drive had been shoveled, but the snow still rose in steep banks on either side, threatening to bury the tall lamps whose staggered brilliance served to brighten an otherwise dark and dreary evening.

Given the snow and the fact that many carriages were already parked along the drive, Baron Lynch's bundled and harried servants were forced to direct traffic and clear lanes for those who were coming or going. Max and Scathach were among the latecomers.

It had been over six weeks since they'd set out from the Isle of Man. Ten days had been spent aboard *Ormenheid* as the longboat battled the elements. Valiant as she was, the boat had been caked in ice and her sail was in tatters when they finally despaired of reaching Enlyll by sea and ordered her into the Bay of Biscay. Although *Ormenheid* had been leaking and battered, Max knew she would also repair herself—even as she sat in his pocket.

The journey overland had been slow but far less harrowing. On the first leg, they'd had a guide—the very same faun that had escorted Sarah and Lucia to Enlyll. While Fenluc was amiable and intimately acquainted with the region, his routes through the backcountry necessitated long, cold treks through deep snow and thick brambles. Without David's latest orders, they might still be slogging through the hilly Harinean forests.

The message had come ten days ago, shortly after Rowan's forces made successful landfall on Blys's mainland.

September 5

Dear Max,

An opportunity has arisen. It might be dangerous, but I believe the risks are worth it. Our forces have landed and seized Kathvha, a duchy along the King's Highway some three hundred miles south of Blys. When we occupied the town, Peter Varga came across a piece of propaganda—a flier boasting that "Max McDaniels, the notorious Hound of Rowan, has been slain by King Prusias's handpicked assassins." Naturally, Peter saw the possibilities and brought it to my attention.

Connor Lynch is hosting a médim later this month. Sarah and Lucia have procured a guest list and it includes a number of braymas and dignitaries who could be very valuable. While I know you had intended to visit Enlyll in secret, a public appearance by the "deceased" Hound of Rowan could be very valuable. Prusias will look either incompetent or untrustworthy: either serves our purpose. Your attendance would also send a clear message that Rowan has arrived as a world power. After all, our forces are now advancing on Prusias even as our representatives openly attend a médim within his borders. I think such a gesture could help make inroads with potential allies.

Whether or not to attend is up to you and Scathach. Regardless, your primary objective remains the same: to open a dialogue with the Elder vyes and bring them over to our side. Classified reports suggest their abilities and numbers may be considerably greater than I'd assumed. If your observations support this, you're authorized to negotiate everything I mentioned in the last letter. Candor will be key—don't gloss over our history with them.

Should you decide to make a public appearance, it's critical you make a strong impression. Spare no expense when it comes to your dress or transport—you will be functioning as our official ambassadors. Rowan has secret accounts you can draw upon at Thaler's or Gilderbach's. Branches of each bank can be found in Almuir, the largest city you will pass en route to Enlyll. You should be able to buy

*whatever clothes and transportation you require. Bribes go a
long way in Almuir and its residents couldn't care less about
Prusias's war. Don't pinch pennies.*

Sol Invictus,
David

p.s. Cynthia insists I say hello from her. Hello.

Max and Scathach both agreed with David's recommendation. Leaving the snowy hills and forests behind, they had made for Almuir. They spent less than a day in that bustling city but still managed to spend an extraordinary amount of Rowan's money. When they departed Almuir, they did so in a royal blue carriage pulled by a team of spirited chestnuts that champed and snorted in the wintry air.

"Stop doing that," Scathach muttered as they waited yet again for their carriage to be waved ahead.

Max glanced sharply at her. "Doing what?"

"Fretting about your shoes."

"How did you know that?" he asked, amazed.

"You keep looking to make sure you haven't scuffed them."

Max glanced at them—boots of supple black calfskin polished to a subtle and uniform gleam. "I can't help it," he confessed. "They cost a month's wages."

"This carriage cost ten years' wages," she pointed out, running a manicured hand over its leather and polished sandalwood. "You have to forget it. If you look self-conscious, it will spoil the whole effect. Pretend you're back at Rodrubân."

Max grunted. "You want me to muck out stables?"

Scathach playfully kicked his perfect boot. "No. Pretend you're attending one of the festivals. You were dressed up at those and didn't seem self-conscious."

"No one was watching me."

"That's what you think," said Scathach, smiling. "Forget about the clothes and the carriage and all of that. They'll do their job and we'll do ours."

"And what's our job again?" he quipped, licking his thumb and trying to wipe away the scuff her shoes had left.

Scathach checked her makeup in an obscenely expensive folding mirror. "To be *that* couple."

"The couple everyone despises?"

Leaning across the seat, she kissed him. "The couple everyone's talking about."

Borrowing her mirror, Max glanced at his new haircut and the thin white scar on his cheek. Scathach promptly snatched it away.

"No looking in mirrors," she declared.

"Why not?" said Max. "You do."

Scathach shrugged and slipped the case back in her clutch. "I'm a woman. There's nothing worse than a man aware of his own good looks. Cynthia told me it's one of the reasons she fell for David. He's not self-conscious in the least."

"David's worn bathrobes to class."

"And now he's the Director," Scathach muttered, peering out the window to see if the traffic jam was relenting. "There must be three hundred carriages. Probably twice as many guests, and most owe their allegiance to Prusias. I know médim have rules prohibiting bloodshed, but we can't let our guard down."

Max glanced at the *gae bolga*. The short sword was safely in its sheath, lying on the seat next to a dozing Nox. While violence was prohibited at médim, guests would still be armed. For many demons, their weapons were marks of rank and would be displayed in prominent fashion. While it was tempting to do the same, Max and Scathach had decided a more subtle statement would be better. The *gae bolga* would hang at Max's side, attached to the baldric he wore beneath his tapered red justacorps. Max chose the color as a subtle reminder to those at the médim that he was Bragha Rùn—the "Red Death," as so many had cheered on his way to victory in Prusias's Arena. The long coat would permit a teasing glimpse of the legendary blade, but no more. Underneath his shirt and waistcoat, he wore his nanomail and the Fomorian's sash. The wound's dull ache was constant, but thus far the giant's spell had kept it from opening.

"These days everyone looks like an enemy," said Max. "The *gae bolga* can fit under my coat, but what are you going to do? You can't walk around with that at a party." He gestured to Scathach's nicked and oiled spear.

"No," Scathach sighed. "I suppose she'll have to sit this one out. Spears and pearls don't really go together. But never fear." From her pack, she produced a slender poignard whose gray sheath was inlaid with a Celtic sun in mother-of-pearl. "A gift from the shield maidens when I was made captain."

She smiled, but Max caught a glimmer of sadness as she fastened the dagger to a strap about her calf. He couldn't blame her. When Scathach left the Sidh, she'd surrendered more than immortality—she'd given up her home and friends. Some wounds could not be mended, not entirely.

The carriage made a sudden lurch as the road opened up. When they'd gone another forty or fifty yards, they rounded a copse of snow-speckled trees and climbed the final rise to Connor's manor.

Max leaned over Nox to see Connor's house coming into view now, a castle in the Renaissance style that stood atop a promontory commanding a view of the inlet far below. Its doors were flung open and its windows blazed with light so that its gables and towers shone pale and golden against the dirty red sky. Pavilions dotted lawns milling with figures human and otherwise. When they reached the circular drive, a human footman in a light blue coat opened the carriage door and bowed.

"Welcome to Enlyll, Your Excellencies," he said in French. "With whom do I have the pleasure to speak?"

"Scathach and Max McDaniels of Rowan."

The prim footman blinked and switched to heavily accented English.

"Honored," he said. "We had word that you would be joining us. My name is Anton. Lord Lynch is looking forward to seeing you. While I am sorry to report the rituals have already taken place, the festivities will continue until dawn. Will you be staying with us?"

"We will," said Max.

"Very good," said the footman. "We'll have your things brought to your room. You're to stay in the same wing as Mademoiselles Lucia and Sarah. I understand you all know each other."

"We do."

Anton gestured for a pair of boys to remove the luggage from the carriage. "You are most welcome here, of course, but the situation is a trifle delicate. Do you wish to be announced or would you prefer a less conspicuous entrance?"

"An announcement," said Max. "Can the lymrill wander or should she remain in our room?"

Anton shrugged. "Whatever she prefers," he said. "The baron prefers a casual household. There are very few rules here."

Despite her freedom, Nox preferred to remain with Max and Scathach and followed the pair as Anton led them around a marble fountain toward a flight of broad steps that led to the front doors. Max's warning ring burned so hot that he removed it and slipped it in his coat pocket. There was little point in being told demons were near when a dozen were in plain view, loitering outside by the fountain where they sipped wine and exhaled tobacco smoke in great curling plumes. One of them—a tall, owl-eyed demon with deep blue skin and an ibex's curling horns—gestured carelessly with one of his six arms as he conversed with a fox-faced kitsune. The arm was grotesquely fractured, the bone pressing visibly against the skin.

"Did he compete in the *amann*?" asked Scathach, referring to the "arts of blood," a traditional médim contest.

"That he did," said Anton. "It was held yesterday. I'm sorry you missed it. Count Rhugal made a valiant showing."

"Who won?" asked Max.

Anton lowered his voice. "Lord Grael."

Max looked sharply at Anton. Grael was a very powerful demon who ruled one of Blys's ten grand duchies. What would Grael be doing here? His domain was Malakos, not Harine. It was unusual that so powerful a demon would bother attending a médim hosted by a minor brayma in a rival's territory. Anton gave them a discreet but significant look as he escorted them up the steps.

"We've had some unexpected . . ."

Anton did not finish this sentence, however, for as they entered the marbled foyer, a number of heads—human and otherwise—turned to appraise the new arrivals. Clearing his throat, Anton struck a small chime on a nearby stand.

"Ladies and gentlemen, Monsieur Max McDaniels and Mademoiselle Scathach of Rowan."

Silence. At least it was silent in the foyer. From the ballroom, Max could hear music and laughter, but those guests standing about the foyer's floor or lingering on its double staircase merely stared in open, unfeigned astonishment. As Max and Scathach bowed, an imp darted out of the room, nearly colliding with someone who was coming to see the new arrivals.

"There he is!" cried Connor Lynch, brushing the imp aside. "Max McDaniels—it's been too bloody long!"

That it had. Max could not help but break into a broad grin as Connor came toward them, spreading his arms wide and splashing red wine over the rim of his goblet. He almost staggered into Max, crushing him in a brotherly embrace and nearly spilling his drink on Scathach's dress.

"My God," he laughed. "It's been what—almost three years?"

Connor's Dublin accent had thickened since leaving Rowan and indeed so had he. His chest was broader, his cheerful face rounder, and even his chestnut hair had expanded into a wild, Dionysian crown of tangled curls. His bright blue eyes were somewhat glassy with drink, but still possessed their old mischievous glint.

"Isn't he supposed to be dead?" Connor laughed, turning to the other guests.

"Well," said Max, "don't believe everything you hear."

"Rowan is at war with our king!" barked a brash, one-eyed oni from the lower steps. "Why do they find welcome here?"

Connor merely laughed and turned his back on the demon. "I'm not welcoming *Rowan*. I'm greeting an old friend. And if you're such a loyal subject, Gnoshi, why are your soldiers still at home?"

Guests chuckled as the oni glowered. Connor turned his attention to Scathach.

"Connor Lynch," he said, bowing to kiss her hand.

"Scathach," she replied.

"A lady of consequence, I see," muttered Connor, noting the Red Branch tattoo on her wrist. "Would you give your host the honor of a dance?"

Max rolled his eyes. "That didn't take long."

Connor flashed a rogue's grin. "I don't see a ring, brother.

And I'll be dead and buried before I pass up a chance to dance with a girl this pretty."

"One dance," Scathach agreed.

"Or two!" Connor cackled, pulling her through the crowd.

Lucia is going to murder him, thought Max, following after with Nox padding at his side. Following their stay with the Fomorian, the lymrill had undergone a growth spurt and was now the size of a large house cat, a house cat that fancied herself a tigress, for as Nox waddled forward, she thrust out her powerful chest and returned every stare with an air of defiance.

Most eyes, however, were on Max. Their attitudes and reactions were almost as varied as the races in attendance. Some were hostile, but many were simply shocked, curious, or even awed. There were whispers and anxious glances. Aside from believing him dead, many people here had probably seen him fight in Prusias's Arena, or even at Rowan. When Max's blood was up—when the Old Magic drummed in his ears—he became something else, something divine and indomitable. It seemed many were having a hard time reconciling the terrifying tales of Rowan's berserker with the youth now making his way through their midst.

A pasty, corpulent demon wearing a long bejeweled coat and an embroidered fez intercepted Max before he could get through the archway leading to the ballroom.

"The Hound of Rowan," he gushed. "We've never been introduced, but I had the pleasure of watching Bragha Rùn in Prusias's Arena. What a performer! You made me piles of money until the grylmhoch. There, I'm afraid I had to bet against you."

"I would have bet against me, too," said Max pleasantly. "You're Coros, I believe."

The demon's toadlike face flushed with pleasure at being recognized. In fact, the only reason Max knew him was because Toby had impersonated the merchant years before when they'd snuck past Mad'raast, a gargantuan demon that once guarded the Strait of Gibraltar.

"I am indeed," the demon simpered. "Is this your first médim?"

"No. I attended one at Gràvenmuir before Bram cast it into the sea."

"All this violence," groaned Coros, shaking his head ruefully. "I long for the day when things have settled down. The war is ruining me!"

"I'm sorry to hear it," said Max, not believing a word. In addition to being Blys's largest trader of silks and spices, Coros was allegedly its biggest smuggler and owned hundreds of human slaves. He had no wish to converse with such a revolting character, but he knew others were listening. "With luck, the war will be over soon."

"I hear Rowan's forces have landed on the mainland," said Coros.

"That's the rumor," said Max, accepting a glass of wine from a servant.

"Curious that you're not with its army," observed the merchant, his tone an invitation for Max to supply the missing details.

"Is it?" said Max. "I thought the surprise was that I'm not dead. This is the second time Prusias has started that ugly rumor."

Coros and several others chuckled. The merchant's piggish eyes fell upon Nox.

"What a magnificent creature," he cooed. "Is that a lymrill?"

"It is."

"Remarkable," exclaimed the demon. "Do you know have any idea what that animal would fetch on the open market?"

"I'm glad I don't," said Max genially. "I'd be tempted to sell her whenever she eats my shoes. It's a pleasure to meet you,

Coros, but please excuse me a moment. I'm neglecting my date and our host is not."

More smiles from the watchful onlookers. Hopefully, word of their arrival was spreading.

"Honored," said Coros, raising his glass. "To peace."

Max raised his glass to Coros and those around him. Guests parted as he and Nox continued on, passing under a sculpted arch to enter a great hall that was serving as the main ballroom. The space was enormous, a study in pink marble whose columns supported not only a frescoed ceiling, but also ornate balustrades where guests could retreat from the din and survey the festivities below. Gazing up, Max scanned the revelers and found a pair of familiar faces: Sarah and Lucia.

The girls were pointing to a slender staircase behind a low stage where musicians—humans, satyrs, and kitsune—were playing a galliard. Nox followed at Max's heels as he climbed the staircase, greeted a speechless brayma, and joined the girls in their little balcony.

Sarah Amankwe was the Sixth Years' most promising Agent-to-be while Lucia Cavallo was an incredibly gifted Mystic who was highly adept at Firecraft. Tonight, the pair looked like fashion models. A strapless black gown complemented Sarah's athletic figure and gleaming brown skin while Lucia wore a dress of pearlescent green that went perfectly with her olive complexion and dark brown eyes. While Sarah's hair was close-cropped, Lucia wore her black tresses in a French braid that showcased her singularly lovely face.

"You two look beautiful," said Max, embracing each of them while Nox rattled her quills in greeting.

"When David told us you were coming, I couldn't believe it!" exclaimed Sarah, giving him a sisterly once-over. "Everyone was saying you were . . ."

"Dead," said Lucia matter-of-factly. "But you are not. You look good, but too skinny. I blame Toby."

The Italian beauty frowned. She had never cared for the smee. It was something of a minor miracle she had not flung him overboard when they sailed across the ocean together. Max laughed.

"Why do you blame him?"

"He ate everything on that boat," she snapped. "Three times I caught him stealing Kettlemouth's sardines!"

"Where is Kettlemouth?" asked Max. Lucia was rarely without her charge, an enormous red bullfrog whose unpredictable singing could trigger amorous feelings.

"In our room," Lucia sniffed. "Wrapped in furs by a fire. This weather is no good for my baby."

Sarah rolled her eyes. "We couldn't chance him singing," she explained. "Maybe Nox would like to keep him company."

Apparently this sounded agreeable to Nox, for the lymrill rattled her quills again and gazed up at her steward expectantly. Nox and Kettlemouth had gotten along famously on their voyage—the lymrill enjoyed napping beneath the frog's dewlap.

"Where's your room?" Max asked.

"In the south wing," said Sarah. "I'm sure Eloise will be happy to take her."

Even as Sarah spoke the name, a plain-faced servant girl of twelve or thirteen came forward from where she'd been standing unobtrusively by a column. Upon her uniform was the Enlyll emblem, a blue chevron adorned with three white seashells.

"Eloise has been spoiling us since we got here," said Sarah.

The little maid reddened and gave a slight curtsy.

"Eloise, this is our friend Max McDaniels," said Lucia, speaking French. "He's cute, no? But the real beauty is Nox.

Would you take her to our room, please? She and Kettlemouth are old friends."

"Tout de suite," said Eloise, stooping as though to lift Nox. Upon glimpsing the lymrill's claws, she paused and spoke in halting English. "The creature . . . is friendly?"

"Very friendly," Max assured her in his own version of French. "But don't pick her up—she's too heavy. Just wave one of these and she'll follow you to the moon."

From his pocket he produced a handful of thin iron plates and handed them to the young maid. "Nox," he said. "This is Eloise. She's going to take you to see Kettlemouth. I'll find you later."

With a snort, the inky black lymrill trotted after the grinning Eloise as she led him down the arched, lamp-lit corridor.

"I need to be down there," said Max, gazing down at the ballroom floor where Scathach had finished dancing with Connor and was now conversing with a trio of kitsune wearing red silk robes. He needed to be seen and make as many contacts as possible. "Come with me."

"You go, Sarah," said Lucia, furrowing her brow. "I'm staying where I can watch everything that scoundrel is doing."

Sarah shot a glance at Max. "Someone isn't very happy with Connor."

"Look at him!" hissed Lucia, her knuckles whitening on the balustrade. "He can hardly stand up. And those girls—giggling like hyenas at everything he says!"

Max spotted Connor by a pair of glass doors that evidently led out to some gardens. The Lord of Enlyll was gesticulating wildly as he regaled a group of pretty young women with a story that had them spellbound. With an offhand gesture, he delivered what was apparently the punch line, for they all burst into peals of laughter. Connor, looking pleased, called for more wine. Lucia merely looked murderous.

"Come on," urged Sarah. "You can't spend the entire médim this way. He has to entertain his guests!"

"Ha!" scoffed Lucia. "'Entertaining his guests.' That's all he does! And always the pretty ones. Look at that girl he's talking to. She used a trowel for that makeup."

Sarah threw an arm around her friend. "Putting that girl down won't make you feel better. Connor's being a jerk. Boys—sorry, Max—can be jerks! But you're Lucia Cavallo and you're on an adventure! Don't let Connor spoil it. Let's go have fun."

Lucia lifted her chin, revealing a hint of her old, formidable self. Dabbing her eyes, she took a long, slow breath. "Of course, you are right. I promise to be better . . ."

She paused as Connor led the young lady out onto the floor. Max heard Lucia mutter something as she made a subtle gesture with her hand. Below, Connor's partner sneezed in a violent spasm that covered his appalled face in phlegm.

"Starting *now*," said Lucia, her eyes twinkling as one of Connor's servants rushed in with a handkerchief.

"Lucia!" hissed Sarah.

"I feel better," said Lucia serenely. "Let's go down, shall we?"

As they made for the stairs, Sarah filled Max in on the médim.

"Things really began two nights ago," she said. "That's when most of the guests arrived and they held the *alennya*. The braymas and more important merchants spend the days in private conferences or going off in little hunting parties."

"What are they doing?" asked Max, pausing at the top step.

Lucia's eyes flashed. "Conspiring about what they'll do—or won't do—to support Prusias in the war."

"Have you been able to attend any of these meetings?" asked Max hopefully.

"Of course not," said Sarah. "There are people here who'd like nothing better than to turn us over to Prusias. But we've gotten some information."

"How?" asked Max.

"Eloise," replied Lucia. "I dote on that girl. She doesn't attend the meetings but other servants do. She's been very good at getting information out of them."

"And?"

"There's lots of dissension," answered Sarah. "The human braymas want to side with Rowan because they think it's only a matter of time before the king turns upon them. But since Prusias has their souls as collateral, they're frightened to do anything too openly."

"What about the demon braymas?" asked Max.

"Mixed," replied Sarah. "Some are loyal, but almost none approve of his relationship with the Workshop—they worry its technologies will be used against them. Some have threatened to abandon Prusias unless he destroys the Workshop."

"Prusias will never agree to that," said Max, descending the stairs.

"Most share your view," said Lucia, "which is why many are waiting to answer his call to arms as long as they can. No one thinks Rowan can defeat Prusias, but some hope we might weaken him so they can topple him after we've failed."

"Which braymas feel this way?" said Max.

Sarah waited for a tipsy couple to pass them. "Most of the braymas from Raikos and Bryllbatha," she whispered. "Yuga forced them to flee their lands and they're demanding that Prusias give them new ones. And there are some here who used to serve Rashaverak. Prusias promised to spare Rashaverak's life once he surrendered, but no one's seen him since. Most think he's either dead or being tortured in Prusias's dungeons. Rashaverak's braymas aren't very happy about that."

"Have you told David this?" asked Max.

"Of course," said Lucia.

Max paused by the stairwell.

"Any luck making contact with Elder vyes?" he asked.

"We'll fill you in later," said Sarah as they reached the ballroom floor.

"Just tell me if any are here," said Max.

Lucia nodded and glanced significantly at a slender, middle-aged woman in a beaded orange gown. The woman stood not five paces from where Scathach was now conversing with a massive brayma wearing steel-riveted plate.

"What's her name?" he murmured.

"Lady Nico," Lucia whispered. "We don't know for certain, but—"

She stopped as several laughing guests emerged from the stairs behind them.

The hall was growing even more crowded as guests returned from hunts and news of Rowan's Hound got about. Most conspicuous among these was a group of armored oni. As Max joined Scathach, he noticed Connor bowing before them and making gestures of explanation. Whatever he was saying, it did not appear to appease them. The largest, a boarlike hulk, thrust Connor aside and strode toward Max. The crowd parted rapidly as he advanced. Max turned as the demon loomed above him.

"You're not welcome here," the demon growled, his breath tinged with sulfur. The air about the oni shimmered with heat, as though it were about to ignite. Other than Scathach, nearby humans looked spellbound by the angry spirit's aura.

"You're not my host," Max observed calmly. A number of

onlookers gasped as the oni unsheathed a sword whose serrated blade must have been six inches wide. Connor ran over, his face growing pale as he spoke rapidly in the demon's language.

"Véda! Véda, Rikku Brayma! Juthir nùl molo médim!"

The oni whirled on Connor. *"Nùl piro elu-daemona, homna!"*

Connor flushed with anger. "I am mehrùn," he said firmly. "And I am your host, Lord Rikku. You will address me properly and obey the rules of médim."

"You are mehrùn," the oni acknowledged grudgingly, "but you've no right to speak our tongue. And this one," he said, pointing his sword at Max. "This filth is the enemy of my king—of *your* king. You should mount his head on a spike!"

Connor stubbornly shook his head. "This is Bragha Rùn. Prusias himself declared him Champion of Blys. Of course he is welcome here. Even if he was not, violence is forbidden at médim."

The demon spat on the floor. "This is no médim!" he roared. "No human may host médim! I spit on this farce. I spit on you. And I spit on the Hound!"

Whirling, Rikku swept his blade at Max's head. Max's reactions were supernaturally swift. Dropping his wineglass, he swept the *gae bolga* up in a blur that shattered his attacker's blade and decapitated him.

The Morrígan's blade gave a triumphant, piercing scream as Lord Rikku's headless body crashed to the marble floor. The rest of the hall was utterly silent as guests and servants gaped in tense, mute horror. Max stared past Connor at Rikku's companions, the other braymas grouped by a large marble pillar. They looked grim but did not appear to have any intention of attacking. The *gae bolga* went silent as Max sheathed it.

Max bowed to Connor. "I beg pardon for breaking the médim's customs. Would you like me to leave?"

"No," said Connor, recovering his wits. "We all saw it was Lord Rikku who violated tradition." He raised his voice so all could hear. "To Bragha Rùn!"

"Bragha Rùn!" roared most of the hall, raising their glasses in salute.

Max's heart was beating swiftly, but his hand was steady as he borrowed Scathach's glass and raised it in acknowledgment. He sipped the wine—a spicy red—and reveled inwardly at his good fortune. Lord Rikku could not have done them a greater favor. Not only was Max McDaniels alive, but he also had publicly and blamelessly dispatched a powerful brayma. The point would not be lost on Rowan's enemies—or potential allies. By dawn, news of the evening's excitement would have reached every corner of the kingdom.

"Well, come on!" cried Connor, after draining his glass. "There's still good wine to be drunk. Let's hear something lively!"

The musicians struck up a spirited reel as Rikku's imps rushed in to retrieve both parts of their former master. While Connor went to ask one of his admirers to dance, Max felt Scathach's warm hand close about his.

"That was a perfect *bruud gine*," she observed complacently. "I'm craving a dance, but I don't think now is the time." She nodded at the growing throng of guests eager to make his acquaintance.

Max was not surprised. Demons placed tremendous store in displays of skill, strength, and bravado. Even those who despised Rowan would honor what they'd just witnessed.

Releasing his hand, Scathach left his side to greet Sarah and Lucia. The two looked badly shaken by the sudden outburst of violence. Max could not worry about that, however. He turned to find that Coros had pushed to the fore of those wishing to speak with him.

"I abhor bloodshed," lied the merchant, adjusting his fez. "But I've never seen such speed, such mastery with a sword! I was a fool to wager on the grylmhoch! What an honor to have made your acquaintance."

"Thank you," said Max. "Perhaps you'll be kind enough to introduce those with whom I haven't had the pleasure."

"Of course," said Coros, pivoting on a golden slipper. "It's my delight to introduce the Lord and Lady Gris of Livalia, a marvelous estate outside Almuir . . ."

The crowd turned into a sort of receiving line, with Coros embracing his role as social lubricant. The merchant knew everybody, and he often peppered his introductions with anecdotes and details that helped Max remember names and faces, and assign their potential value. While he hoped some might join Rowan's side, if he could convince others to simply stay out of the war, so much the better.

As the evening wore on, the names and faces began to blur. There was Baron Tarkan, the Countess of Bryndle, the notorious Widow of Verdival, assorted merchants, a shipmaker named Tinto, and a slew of other dignitaries. Most were demons, but several were human. One elderly gentleman Max even recognized as a former resident of Rowan—a retired teacher who chose to accept the offer of land and titles that Prusias had made to mehrùn.

These people were wealthy, of course, and lived on lush estates replete with art and servants, but few wielded real power in their persons or the forces at their command. And thus there was a decided change in atmosphere when Lord Grael entered the hall.

Max saw him at once—a twelve-foot rakshasa with a tiger-like face, three green eyes, and an eland's corkscrew horns. Blood hissed as it dripped from the demon's broad muzzle and fell onto his breastplate. Either the duke had just returned from hunting or something much more sinister had transpired. When their eyes met, the Duke of Malakos strode casually toward Max, wiping his face with a towel handed up by a white imp, just one of a dozen attendants. The demon's aura was astoundingly powerful.

Guests scattered from the demon's path like startled quail. Max had just been introduced to Lady Nico, the woman Lucia said might be an Elder vye. At Grael's approach, she politely excused herself even as Scathach came to stand by Max's side. Connor hurried over, so drunk by now that he nearly crashed into one of Grael's imps. He twisted aside at the last second and merely fell at the duke's feet.

Lucia darted in to help him, muttering angrily in Italian as she pulled him to his feet. For a moment, Connor managed to focus on her fuming, heartbroken face before he craned his neck up at Lord Grael. His words were barely intelligible.

"No vilenss," he slurred. "No vilenss at maydeem . . ."

Instead of becoming angry, Lord Grael seemed bemused as he shifted his gaze from Max to his host. The demon's voice was a patrician baritone, both courteous and dismissive. "Please instruct us on the rule of médim, Baron Lynch. You articulate them so clearly."

"No. Vilens!" repeated Connor emphatically.

"Violence, did you say?" said Grael. "Of course not. Médim doesn't end until dawn. I wouldn't think of violating *our* traditions. Please introduce me to your guests."

Connor leaned heavily on Lucia. "This is Max McDaniels and—wait, what was the lady's name?"

"Scathach," said Max stiffly.

Grael bowed to her. "Charmed," he purred. "Lord Lynch was undoubtedly safe at home and in his cups during the Siege of Rowan. But I recognize you. You answered Gunnir's challenge on the battlefield and rode out to meet him. I honor you, Lady Scathach. Gunnir was a fine archer but no swordsman."

"Are you a fine swordsman, milord?" she asked politely. The difference in their sizes was unsettling. Scathach barely came to the demon's waist.

Grael gave a deprecating smile and patted the pommel of a brutal-looking greatsword. "I dabble. Perhaps someday we'll meet on the field, eh? Your spear against my sword."

"I look forward to it," said Scathach.

"Splendid," said Grael, lighting a pipe and taking a long, luxuriant pull. As he exhaled, his emerald, luminescent eyes flicked down at Max. "Well, I see Prusias was mistaken. The king has been crowing of your death."

Max met the demon's gaze. It was impossible not to be impressed by Grael. Aside from his size, the demon exuded an aura of power and command that simply compelled lesser beings to fall in line. Max understood why some thought he was a threat to unseat Prusias. A being like Grael would only respect someone as arrogant and assured as he was.

Max decided to increase his own aura and experienced a pleasing sense of control when it responded just as he wished. His display was very brief, like an invisible solar flare. His friends would not perceive it, but the demon most certainly would. And, if Grael was as intelligent as Max suspected, the little glimpse of Max's true nature would give him pause.

"Prusias is always crowing of my death," said Max pleasantly. "But here I am."

Grael cocked his head with a knowing smile. "Aye," he said. "Here you are. I've longed to meet you, Hound. Vyndra was a very old friend, as were others you've slain."

"You must be very lonely."

Smoke shot out the rakshasa's nostrils. "Oh, I manage. Alas,

I cannot blame you for their deaths. This is war, after all. And Vyndra murdered your father—or rather the poor fellow pretending to be." The demon chuckled. "No, this evening gives me great pleasure. To think I'd find you in this backwater!" The demon laughed and inclined his great head. "Enjoy the médim, Hound, and don't forget that it ends at dawn. One would hate for anything to happen to you."

The room almost gave a collective sigh of relief as the duke left to converse with the oni that had been Rikku's companions. While tensions had eased, some guests still looked unsettled—as though Grael's mere presence at the médim was a cause for concern. Max glanced over as Lady Nico reappeared at their side.

"Well," she said, "your arrival has certainly made the evening more exciting. I fear Lord Grael has a point. When the médim ends, things could get even more interesting. How long do you intend to stay in Enlyll?"

"We're in no rush," said Max. "Baron Lynch is an old friend and we enjoy meeting his new ones. I haven't even had a chance to go hunting."

"Are you an avid hunter?" inquired Lady Nico.

"For food," said Max. "Not much for sport."

"Well, fox hunting is all the rage here," Lady Nico sighed. "It's a bore and even more excruciating to watch overdressed fools galloping up and down the countryside blowing their silly horns. No style or subtlety—nothing like falconry."

"I've never tried it," said Max.

"Oh, it's far more interesting," said Lady Nico, tucking a strand of black hair behind her ear. Everything about her manner and clothing suggested she had a refined upbringing, but she wasn't stiff or overly formal. While some would say her nose was too long and her green eyes rather small and far apart, the woman's self-confidence gave her tremendous charisma. "The relationship between falconer and falcon is one of mutual respect rather than one trying to dominate the other. I imagine you and your lymrill enjoy a similar bond."

"No," said Max. "Our relationship is completely defined by dominance. I'm practically her slave."

Lady Nico smiled. "She seemed happy enough to follow you across the hall. Do you ever take her hunting? I would like to see a lymrill hunt."

"She hunts on her own," said Max. "And unless I'm craving worms, rats, or metals, I don't think I'd care for what she finds."

A young servant approached Lady Nico and curtsied. "I beg pardon, my lady, but you asked to be told when it was approaching two o'clock."

"Thank you, Marisela," said Lady Nico, before turning to Max and Scathach. "I do apologize, but I must say good night. My home is several hours away, and I have important business tomorrow. Given this snow and the roads . . ." She rolled her eyes. "It was a pleasure meeting you both. Perhaps we'll go hunting someday."

As she turned to go, Connor staggered over.

"Don't say yer leaving!" he cried, mopping sweat from his brow. He fumbled at Marisela's sleeve. "Tell yer coachman Lady Nico's stayin' the night. Run along."

Lady Nico gestured for Marisela to remain where she was. "Alas, I must bring my evening to a close. Perhaps you should do the same, Lord Lynch. After all, dawn is but a few hours off and you must be fit to bid your guests adieu."

Connor sulked like a petulant child. "I'm not going to bed. It's my bloody party."

"Then perhaps some hot tea," suggested Lady Nico. "Not everyone finds your current state or behavior very becoming." She nodded toward Lucia, whose teary eyes were boring holes in his back. Connor turned to face her.

"What's got you in a twist?" he demanded.

It was a slap heard 'round the world.

Connor recoiled, wincing as Lucia's scarlet handprint surfaced on his ruddy face. Throughout the hall, there were a few hoots but most looked on with embarrassed disapproval. Without another word, Lady Nico swept from the hall.

Connor seemed oblivious to the highly public scene that was unfolding. Rubbing his cheek, he gave Lucia a painfully artificial laugh. "Pretty good!" he exclaimed. "Better 'n tea, anyway. That slap done made me thirsty. Where's Royce?"

A slender, reserved-looking youth in Enlyll regalia seemed to appear out of thin air to fill Connor's goblet. The Lord of Enlyll drank deep, wine dribbling down his chin to run down the front of his embroidered shirt. As he tipped the goblet back, he lost his balance and thudded onto his backside. The great hall was nearly silent, the only sounds those of the winter winds howling outside.

"You are not who I thought you were!" Lucia cried, her tears flowing freely as she clutched her wrap and walked swiftly out of the hall. Sarah hurried after her, leaving the side of a young man with whom she'd been dancing earlier.

Max was disgusted. He scowled down at Connor, who seemed more intent on salvaging his wine than any shred of dignity.

"Get up," Max hissed, extending his hand.

"I'm okay," Connor mumbled, reaching for the goblet before it rolled away.

"Get up!" Max snapped, grabbing a fistful of Connor's sleeve. With a curse, the Irish boy slapped his hand away and half rose as if he intended to strike Max. But the baron slipped, falling hard onto his hip and kicking out at the goblet in his frustration.

As several girls and servants went to assist his "lordship,"

Max glanced at Scathach. "Come on," he said quietly. "Let's see how Lucia's doing."

The two walked swiftly from the hall. Max struggled to balance his conflicting emotions. He wanted to throttle Connor, to dunk him in water until he stopped making a fool of himself. But Max was heartbroken, too. It was unspeakably painful to see Connor reduced to such a state. Max had looked forward to this reunion for years only to find that his old friend no longer really existed. Wealth and leisure had not been good for Connor Lynch.

Several guests tried to say good night, but Max merely nodded and swept past them. Lord Grael stood by the hall's entrance, a wry smirk on his imposing face as he raised his glass to them. Max ignored him and asked a valet to take them to their room.

As Max and Scathach climbed a curving staircase, they passed many revelers and caught sight of more out on the grounds where lamps burned like ghostly sentinels among the snowy gardens. From below, music was playing once again, but its superficial gaiety only served to sour Max's mood. Thus far, their mission to Enlyll felt like a professional success and a personal failure. Had they failed Connor somehow?

Scathach knew what he was thinking. "We can't live others' lives for them," she said. "We can try to help them, but their lives are their own."

"I know," Max said. "But it still hurts. I feel bad for Lucia. And I'm sorry you didn't get to meet the Connor I remember."

"Don't lose hope," said Scathach. "I'm sure Lucia hasn't."

If Lucia hadn't lost hope, she was doing a marvelous job of hiding it. When Sarah answered their knock, they overheard seething torrents of Italian.

"Come in," said Sarah graciously. "Look out for flying footwear."

Even as she spoke, a pair of glittering pumps soared across the elegant chamber to join a heap of other shoes. Turning, Scathach thanked the maid, who hurried away as Lucia let fly with more obscenities and a pair of stylish boots. Slipping inside, Max and Scathach closed the door and locked it behind them.

Lucia stood barefoot by a canopy bed piled high with clothes and furs and expensive-looking luggage. Upon the bed's pillows lounged Kettlemouth and Nox. The former was wearing a flannel nightcap and losing his perpetual battle with consciousness while Nox seemed to be having the time of her life. Not only was the lymrill sitting on a pillow (something Max would not allow), but also Lucia had given her a mound of stockings to chew—silk stockings! This she did with great enthusiasm, giving mewls of solidarity whenever Lucia launched a shoe.

"What are you doing?" asked Max delicately.

"Packing!" shouted Lucia, flinging a fur stole into a suitcase.

"That's quite a wardrobe," said Scathach. "You didn't bring all that from Rowan."

"Oh no," said Sarah, leading them to several chairs by a comfortable fire. "Connor's been very generous since we arrived. He's given us clothes, shoes, furs . . ."

"Everything but respect!" raged Lucia, launching the last of her shoes before padding over to slump against the marble mantel. Her lip quivered, and she gazed at them with an expression Max had never seen on her before. She looked pitiably young and lost.

"I just want to go home," she sobbed, looking at them in hopeful, earnest appeal. "I never should have come here. I feel so stupid."

Before anyone could reply, there was a soft knock at the door.

"Who is it?" called Sarah.

"Eloise," replied a small voice.

Max got up and opened the door to find the maid standing on the threshold with four mugs, a steaming carafe, and a plate of cookies on a silver tray. The girl curtsied. "Pardon," she said. "I thought my mistress might like some *chocolat*?"

Lucia waved her into the room and blew her nose as Eloise set the tray upon an ottoman and filled the mugs with cocoa. Sliding a sugar cookie onto a plate, she brought it and a mug to Lucia.

"Thank you," Lucia sniffled, throwing her arms around the maid. Eloise looked a little startled but touched by the gesture.

"It is nothing," she said modestly. "You and Mademoiselle Sarah have been very kind to me. Good guests," she said, offering a shy smile.

"I want to give you something," said Lucia. "I'm leaving tomorrow and never coming back. Take what you like," she said, sweeping her arm at the mounds of expensive clothes. "Take everything."

The young maid considered the pile a moment with a shrewd eye. "You know what I really like?" she said, turning back to Lucia. "I like to see the butterfly again."

"Really?" Lucia sniffled. "But that's nothing."

"Not to me," said the girl, bringing the others their hot chocolate. "It reminds me of summer."

Lucia glanced at the mullioned windows, all spidered with frost. "Very well," she said. "The butterfly you shall have. Eloise's butterfly."

With a word, she extinguished the room's lamps so that the fire was the only source of light. The flames obeyed Lucia's coaxing hands like a living thing, sinuous and mesmerizing as they snaked out of the hearth to form twining symmetries. Eloise stared as the flames became a shimmering butterfly. As the butterfly grew, its trembling wings blossomed with colors in a shifting, prismatic display that made Eloise gasp. Larger and larger it grew, its translucent wings nearly touching the walls as it hovered above them. It floated there a few moments, impossibly beautiful, before unraveling like a spool of fiery thread and returning to the hearth.

"That is magic," sighed Eloise, her face aglow as she searched the ceiling for any glimmering traces. "Thank you. Does my lady truly mean to leave us so soon?"

"I don't know," said Lucia glumly, sipping her hot chocolate. "I want to leave this minute but we'll need to make proper arrangements."

The maid curtsied. "Just ring for me if you need anything."

"You should go to bed," said Sarah. "It's so late."

The maid gave a rueful smile. "Médim does not end until dawn. Until then, it is work, work, work."

"If you see the baron, give him a kick for me," muttered Lucia.

"As you wish," said Eloise gravely. "Thank you for the butterfly."

Taking the empty carafe, the maid departed, leaving the four to discuss Lucia's righteous anger as well as Lady Nico and other interesting—and potentially valuable—people they'd met that evening. Sarah, a fine warrior herself, could not get over the suddenness of Max and Rikku's encounter.

"It was over so fast," she marveled. "I was looking right at you but didn't even see you strike him." She turned to Scathach. "Did you teach him how to do that?"

"I taught him the technique," Scathach replied. "But you can't teach that kind of speed or instincts. Max was born with those."

"It impressed Lady Nico," said Lucia. "I was watching her."

"I want to know what you've learned about the Elder vyes," said Max. "What made you suspect she might be one? She doesn't exhibit any sign of being a vye in human form—no sneezing, no reddened eyes."

"She can do magic," replied Lucia simply. "There have always been rumors that Elder vyes have their own schools."

"How do you know she can do magic?" asked Scathach.

"Connor dragged me out on a hunt, but I lagged behind when he started flirting with one of those village trollops. When the hunt galloped past the woods, I saw her slip out of them holding the fox."

"And?" said Scathach.

"She set the fox loose, changed into a falcon, and flew away."

"Maybe she's a witch," said Max.

"She has no skinscrolling," Sarah reflected. "At least not that we can see. And her estate is supposed to be one of the wealthiest in Harine. Witches live with their clans in the wild. Lady Nico learned real magic somewhere and it wasn't at Rowan."

"What did Connor say?" asked Max. "I assume you asked him about her."

Lucia scowled. "He wouldn't say anything. Not anything worthwhile. The idiot writes me love letters and tells us to 'seek the Elders' and then ignores me and refuses to talk about them."

A clear restatement of her grievances threatened to rekindle her former fury. Before those flames could catch, however, Scathach changed the subject. "It's a shame she left so soon. What do you know about those kitsune—those three in the flowery robes? They didn't seem to have much love for Prusias."

This sparked a broader discussion of the braymas, merchants, and other guests they had met throughout the evening. They needed to update David, and Max wanted to give him more than a generic list of names but a prioritized assessment of those who might be helpful.

"Grael muddies things," said Max wearily. "Some of the

guests seem nervous that he's here. They're probably afraid he's reporting everything back to Prusias."

Sarah looked anxious. "Do you think he intends to attack you once the médim is over?"

"Possibly," said Max. "But I doubt it would happen right at dawn. If Grael intends to attack, he'll wait for a less obvious opportunity."

There was another, almost apologetic knock at the door.

"It's almost five o'clock," moaned Sarah. "Who could that be?"

"If it's Connor, slam the door," said Lucia firmly.

This time Scathach got up to answer. "Who is it?" she asked.

"Pardon," came the familiar voice. "It is Eloise."

As Scathach opened the door, Max saw the maid looking somewhat pale. On a small tray, she bore a small envelope sealed with scarlet wax.

"What is that?" asked Lucia. "A note from Connor?"

"Forgive me," said Eloise, stepping into the room. "But I was instructed to deliver it to the gentleman and await his reply."

She brought the envelope to Max. Its seal was a thorn-twined rune.

"This is from Grael," he said.

"Don't touch it," snapped Scathach. "It might be poisoned."

"Poison's a violation of médim," said Max. "Besides, no demon of Grael's status would use it—especially not on something with his seal. There's no glory in killing with poison."

"There's plenty of glory in killing the Hound of Rowan," said Scathach. "And we don't know this letter came from Grael. It just has his seal."

"Who gave this to you?" said Max to Eloise.

"The duke's secretary," replied the girl. "The white imp."

Max could hardly forget him—he'd never seen an albino imp

before. Taking a napkin from the cookie tray, he picked up the envelope and opened it using Scathach's poignard. Sliding the paper out, he flipped it open and scanned its contents. They were admirably brief:

I command many legions.
This war can end by Yule.
A private word, if you please.
Safe conduct is assured.
Discretion is required.

Max showed it to Scathach, who raised her eyebrows.

"What is it?" asked Sarah.

"Grael wants to see me. In private."

"You're not actually thinking of going?" exclaimed Lucia.

"Of course I'm going," said Max. "Grael's rumored to want Prusias's throne. I have to hear what he's proposing."

"But you're not going alone," said Scathach pointedly.

"We'll all go," Sarah volunteered bravely.

"No," said Scathach. "You two stay here. If we're not back in an hour, get out of the castle." She looked at Eloise. "Are there secret ways out of here?"

Eloise shrugged. "All castles have secret ways."

"Promise me you'll get them out if something goes wrong," said Scathach.

"*Oui,*" said Eloise earnestly. "I promise, mademoiselle."

"We're going with you," Sarah insisted.

"You're not," declared Scathach flatly. "It's a nice gesture, but that's an order."

Sarah looked incredulous. "Are you pulling *rank*?"

"Absolutely."

"What gives you the right?" demanded Lucia.

Scathach pointed impatiently at her Red Branch tattoo.

"Please don't argue," said Max. "Sarah and Lucia, pack your stuff. Forget all the gifts and just take what you need. If the meeting with Grael turns ugly, you'll need to get out of here."

"Give me five minutes," said Scathach, taking their room key and disappearing next door. Not three minutes had passed when she returned wearing her dark mail shirt and well-worn traveling clothes.

"I kind of liked that dress," said Max ruefully.

"You'll see it again," said Scathach, leaning her spear against a table while she laced her boots. "But I'd rather be able to move than look pretty. Are you ready?"

It was a long walk to Lord Grael's chambers, for the duke had been given a suite of rooms at the opposite end of the castle. To avoid watchful eyes or even a potential ambush, Eloise took Max and Scathach by an indirect route involving a secret passage and two narrow flights of servants' stairs. With dawn rapidly approaching, the castle had grown quieter. From the great hall, Max could hear only the faint music of a belyaël as its owner played the lengthy, hauntingly beautiful piece that traditionally brought a médim to its close. When the music ended, so would any and all protections the gathering afforded its participants.

The belyaël was still playing, however, when they arrived at the private wing where Grael was staying. At the entry to its hallway, they encountered the white imp Max had seen in the ballroom. The duke's secretary glared at Eloise.

"It took you long enough!" he hissed. "The médim is almost over and Lord Grael did not wish for its conclusion to alarm his visitors."

"My most humble apologies," said Eloise meekly. "I thought it best to take slower ways with fewer eyes."

"No matter," snapped the imp. "Take them in and be quick!"

Max stopped the girl before she could walk ahead. "You can leave, Eloise," he said. If there was an ambush waiting, Max didn't want her walking into it. "Don't wait for us. We can find our way back."

Max and Scathach continued past several rooms until they reached a pair of grand double doors at the end. They stood ever so slightly ajar. As Max reached to knock, the music in the great hall abruptly ceased.

With a kick of her boot, Scathach nudged both doors inward.

It took Max a moment to register the scene before him.

Lord Grael leaned back in a chair, his countenance frozen in a terrifying rictus as he stared blindly up at a chandelier. At first glance, Max thought the demon was dead, but he recalled that rakshasa turned to fiery smoke when they perished. Whatever was wrong with Grael, it probably had something to do with the translucent, pulsing organism affixed to his throat.

Behind the demon stood Lady Nico. To her right was Connor Lynch, looking as grim and sober as a judge.

The rest of the room's occupants were vyes.

~ 16 ~

THE RASZNA

"Come in, Max," said Connor calmly. "We haven't much time."

Max heard a gasp from behind them. Turning back to the hallway, he saw Lord Grael's secretary crumpled on the floor. Eloise was crouching over him, checking for a pulse as she slipped a slim knife back into her apron. Her eyes met Max's: young, frank, and purposeful. This little maid was no stranger to violence. Max turned back to Connor.

"Sarah and Lucia . . ."

"They're safe," said Lady Nico. "They ingested a sleeping draught and have been taken out of the castle along with your charges."

"What's going on?" Scathach demanded.

"A revolution," replied Lady Nico. "Please come in. A rakshasa's death is rather dramatic and it would be best if the door was closed."

Max and Scathach entered, eyeing a group of dark, wolfish vyes that were cleaning their weapons by the bodies of Grael's bodyguards and servants. Eloise followed, dragging Lord Grael's secretary into the room and closing the door. The imp was still alive but would not be for much longer. From a wheeled trunk, the girl retrieved another pulsing, grapefruit-sized organism and set it upon the imp's chest. Anemone-like tendrils sprouted from its glistening surface to probe the imp's face. Hooking itself to the imp's soft throat, the organism pulled itself up and over its chin as more tendrils sprouted to tunnel into the base of its subject's skull. The imp's body shuddered as though it received an electric jolt and the organism began to expand and contract like a luminescent bellows. Max was utterly repulsed.

"What is that?" he asked.

"A vampiric mnemonculus," answered Lady Nico. "It's leeching the imp's memories, just as the other is stealing Lord Grael's. No easy task to paralyze a demon of his stature."

"So, he's alive?" said Scathach, peering at the rakshasa.

"For now," said Lady Nico coolly.

Max and Scathach entered, shutting the door behind them as the mnemonculi continued to perform their grisly duties. Vyes were straightening up the room and dragging Grael's guards through a secret passage in the chamber's far corner. The vyes were similar to others Max had seen but these were taller and had finer features than the norm. The ones that seemed to be in charge wore silver armbands, which might have indicated their rank. Max's eyes returned to the mnemonculus at Grael's throat. It was pulsing more rapidly.

"It's almost finished," Lady Nico observed. "Get Pascal."

From a gilded box, a vye plucked a familiar, yamlike shape. It wriggled angrily and doubled back to seemingly (for it had no visible eyes) glare at its handler.

"*Imbécile!*" it roared in French. "I was sleeping. Put me back at once!"

The vye was unmoved. "You sleep enough. Time to work."

The disgruntled creature was smaller than Toby and a slimy chartreuse rather than Toby's mottled brown, but there was no mistaking the bulbous midsection, tapered ends, or pompous manner. The vye held the wriggling smee over Lord Grael.

"Okay, okay," it grumbled impatiently. "I have him down."

The vye tossed the smee high into the air. As it flipped end over end, the smee's ignoble shape transformed into that of the regal and imposing rakshasa. With an acrobatic landing, Lord Grael's doppelganger crouched over the original, peering closely at his motionless face. Max could not get over the smee's transformation—even Grael's finery and armor had been replicated to the last detail. For the time being, however, the smee's voice remained unchanged.

"He's coming to," sniffed Pascal.

Lady Nico turned to Connor. "Are you prepared to do this? There can be no going back."

The Irish boy nodded.

"Connor," said Max. "What are you doing?"

But his friend didn't answer as Lady Nico motioned to one of the vyes who brought forth a short bronze sword, not unlike a gladius. The blade was stained with age, its metal etched with ancient writing. Taking the handle, Connor hefted the weapon and glanced down at Lord Grael. He nodded to one of the vyes, who promptly took a firm grip of the pulsing mnemonculus. Raising the sword, Connor took a slow, deep breath.

"Now."

With a squeal, the mnemonculus was snatched away. In one swift stroke, Connor beheaded the Duke of Malakos. There was a flash of light, a searing wave of heat, and the powerful demon melted away in a noxious, tumbling cascade of smoke and ash. When the smoke cleared, Max saw Connor's sweat-begrimed face staring at the rakshasa's empty armor. His hands were trembling.

"Well struck," said Lady Nico, taking the sword and embracing him. Several other vyes followed suit. The last mussed Connor's hair and the baron grinned in spite of himself.

"We're in it now," he muttered.

"What is all this?" Max demanded. "Was that letter from Grael or from you?"

"Grael," said Lady Nico, handing the bronze sword to an attendant. "I am sorry you couldn't have your chat, but we couldn't allow the demon's schemes to interfere with our own. We have our own uses for Grael and they don't involve an alliance with Rowan."

"So you know what he wrote," said Scathach.

"Word for word," said Lady Nico. "We can see everything that happens in this room. Why do you think it was given to him?"

"Connor—" said Max warningly.

His friend turned to him. "You have to trust me. We're not working against Rowan. We've got the same enemy. Grael's more valuable like this."

Max glanced at Scathach, whose expression made her attitude clear.

Do you trust him?

Lady Nico turned to the other vyes. "Get Luis. Once he and Pascal are settled, we must be off."

Luis, a purplish smee, was brought forth in the same

wriggling and grumpy manner as Pascal. It was apparently his job to mimic Lord Grael's secretary, for moments later, an albino imp stood before them wearing the identical gaudy couture as his now-deceased counterpart. To Max's immense disgust, both smees began ingesting the squealing mnemonculi.

"This is going to take a while," Pascal remarked, his voice now a perfect replica of the duke's baritone. "Grael is thousands of years old. Lots of memories to absorb."

"You don't need to know everything right away," said Connor. "Just enough to fool other guests into believing you're him. Let Luis do the talking at first. The imp will have fewer memories. You know what to do?"

Lord Grael and his secretary looked insulted.

"We have been working on this for months," retorted the imp. "We know the plan better than you do."

"Good luck," said Connor. "Max and Scathach, please come with us. There'll soon be—"

"Fire!" cried a voice elsewhere in the castle. The call was quickly taken up, followed by a distant stampede of running feet.

"That's our cue," said Connor.

Eloise darted into the secret passage, trailed by several vyes and Lady Nico. Connor came over to Max and Scathach. Somehow, the Irish boy looked both weary and exhilarated.

"Come on," he urged. "I know you've got questions, but you've got to trust me."

"Where are Sarah and Lucia?"

"At the other end of this passage," Connor assured him. "I promise."

Even if Connor had changed, he couldn't imagine him letting harm befall Lucia or Sarah. And unless Eloise was a remarkable actress, her affection for his friends was real. While Max didn't enjoy dashing off into the unknown, they had to seize this chance. Their mission was to make contact with the Elder vyes and win them over to Rowan's side. This was certainly the opportunity—even if it came of crashing their operation.

Max nodded at Connor, who looked relieved as he led them toward the secret passage. Its entrance had been cleverly disguised within an ornamental buttress in the room's corner. Slipping past the vyes awaiting Nico by its entrance, they followed Connor into the cold, dark tunnel.

Despite torches burning at regular intervals, the passage was still very dim and uncomfortably narrow so that Max jostled against the damp walls. Even less comfortable was the fact that there were vyes ahead of them, vyes behind them, and very little room to turn around.

"So," Max whispered, "all of that was an act. You're not really a debauched playboy but a cold-blooded assassin?"

Connor glanced back with a devilish grin. "I'd like to think I'm both."

Max thought he heard Scathach groan.

The passage soon joined a larger tunnel that was better lit as it extended in a gentle curve to the north or northeast. Here, the group broke into a trot that went on for several hundred yards until they arrived at a ladder that extended up toward a rusted trapdoor. Eloise climbed the ladder first and knocked urgently with the flat of her small hand.

The door opened to reveal a vulpine-looking vye who reached down to pull the girl up as the others clambered after. Max climbed swiftly up the rungs, emerging into a musty cellar lit by a single oil lamp. Several vyes awaited them there. One handed Connor a cloak.

"This is my gamekeeper's lodge," panted Connor, taking the cloak and putting it on. "We have horses outside and a long ride ahead of us. Your things are already in the sleds. Wear these and pull the hoods low."

Two vyes handed Max and Scathach cloaks similar to Connor's. As Scathach pulled hers about her, she seemed to blend in with a stack of barrels and jam jars behind her. Connor grinned.

"Pretty neat, eh? Better than standard camouflage."

When all had their cloaks, the group filed upstairs—a score of vyes with silver armbands, Lady Nico, Eloise, Connor, Scathach, and Max. Max was almost certain the silver-armband vyes were an honor guard for Lady Nico, who must be a person of considerable importance. Out the cozy lodge they went into the frigid morning where the sun, a glowing sliver of red-orange, was peeking over the forest's rim.

Mounts were outside, powerful horses clad in the same material as the party's cloaks so that they were superbly camouflaged against the morning. Eight were hitched to covered sleds, but the others stood free, ears twitching as they grazed on nettles.

Eloise waded through the deep snow to pull back a sleigh's blanket. Beneath it, Lucia, Sarah, Nox, and Kettlemouth were in a drugged but peaceful slumber.

"I had to give them a sleeping draught," said the girl apologetically. "I had no time to explain, and Mistress Lucia was so angry. I didn't think they would come."

Max nodded. He was not happy, but he understood why she had taken the precaution. As he checked on his friends, he noted that the horses and sleds were resting easily on the snow's icy crust while those on foot had to trudge through the deep powder.

"It's the horseshoes," Connor explained as a mounted vye led three bay stallions over to a tree stump. "Your mount won't leave tracks for anyone to follow. Here, you ride Hob."

Using the tree stump as a stool, Max gripped the pommel of Hob's saddle and pulled himself up. From behind them, there were distant cries. Max turned his horse around to see dark smoke rising above the treetops.

"Not to worry," said Connor, mounting his own horse and taking up the reins. "The fire at the castle is mostly show—just enough to create a little confusion, clog the road, and make me look like a victim."

"So where are we going?" asked Scathach.

"Lady Nico's lands," said Connor. "We can talk there. I know you've got lots of questions." With a rueful glance at his burning home, he followed Lady Nico as she spurred her mount into the woods.

They rode for hours, blending with the landscape and leaving no trail as Lady Nico led them over hills, through forests, and across icy streams. It was an exhilarating ride, if frigid. Snow was falling again and the flakes stung Max's eyes as Hob forged ahead.

The long ride gave Max time to process what had just transpired. Lady Nico said a revolution was underway. A revolt by Harinean nobles against Prusias? Were Elder vyes the only ones involved? How did they intend to use Lord Grael's doppelganger? Would the smees return to Prusias as assassins? As spies? And why had they required Connor to slay the rakshasa? Was that merely to prove his loyalty to the revolution or was there a deeper significance?

Max had a million questions and wished dearly that he could spend an hour with Connor to get candid answers. Would Connor provide them? *We're not working against Rowan,* he had said. Connor identified with Lady Nico and the vyes—not with Rowan. Regardless of where Connor's allegiance lay, Max's objective was clear: to win the Elder vyes over to their cause.

Even if Connor could serve as a bridge or mediator, the mission would be difficult. They had failed to convince the Fomorian to join the war and he was Max's own kindred. Rowan had fought and hunted vyes for centuries—there was a lot of history there, almost all of it bad. His own misgivings would have been far greater if he had not become friends with two Elder vyes during his stay at the farmhouse in Blys. Nix and Valya's kindness had shattered most of Max's assumptions about their kind. Rowan wanted to move beyond the past and reach an accord. Would the vyes?

David had given them vast latitude to reach an agreement, but Max was no statesman. At Rowan, Alistair Wesley used to insist that negotiation was both art and a science. The art derived from the negotiator's experience and intuition; the science stemmed from data—from knowing as much as possible about the other party's needs, resources, and urgency. As a negotiator, Max had almost no experience and very little data. He hoped he was up to the challenge.

Lady Nico's lands lay thirty miles from Enlyll. Whether it was due to the magicked horseshoes or simply superb conditioning, their mounts maintained a tireless pace and they stopped only briefly to water at a stream and allow Max to check on his sleeping friends.

The sun was hanging like a dull red ornament behind a veil of gray clouds when they reached the high, thorny hedge that bordered Lady Nico's lands. Iron gates swung inward at their approach, admitting them into a scenic expanse of snowy fields and old stone buildings where workers were stacking hay and tending to livestock. In the distance stood Lady Nico's castle—a Gothic masterpiece encircled by a broad moat that reflected the reddish sky. Max spied something gliding in lazy circles about the tallest tower.

While its silhouette was batlike, its size was not. At a distance, the creature appeared to be no smaller than the tower's entire roof. It circled once more before accelerating straight up like a glider catching a sudden draft. Rising high above the tower spire, it slowly crested and promptly disappeared in a dive beyond the castle.

Was that a dragon?

Max glanced at Scathach. She was standing tall in the stirrups, her eyes fixed on the tower. Clearly, she had seen it, too. The creature did not reappear, however, as they covered the final stretch and crossed the moat's long causeway. Servants were waiting as they passed through the gatehouse and arrived at an inner courtyard. Swinging off her horse, Lady Nico walked over to Max and Scathach.

"Welcome to Wyrmwood," she said, removing her gloves. "You must excuse me for the time being. As I said, there is a revolution under way. Lord Lynch and Eloise will see that you and your friends are comfortable. I should not be long."

Ten minutes later, they were sitting in a comfortable library while servants brought roasted chicken, cheeses, and warm breads that crackled when Max tore off a piece. Using a dropper, the little maid placed amber liquid on Sarah's and Lucia's tongues. Instantly, the girls stirred. With a yawn, Lucia sat up and looked about.

"Where are we?" she murmured, blinking at the portraits and bookcases that lined the unfamiliar room. Her eyes fell upon Connor by the fireplace. "You!"

Connor winced but nevertheless braved Lucia's glare to sit on the edge of the long sofa. "We're at Wyrmwood, Lady Nico's estate," he said evenly. "I owe you many explanations and am praying you'll hear me out."

"Do you know why we came to Enlyll?" said Max.

"I thought it was to see me," said Connor.

"I'm not joking," said Max. "You asked us to trust you and we did. Now I want answers. Do you know why we're here?"

"Yes," said Connor plainly. "Rowan wants an alliance with the Elder vyes."

"Then why haven't you introduced us to them?" asked an outraged Lucia. "Sarah and I have asked often enough!"

"I'm sorry," said Connor, "but Rowan's Agents have killed an awful lot of vyes over the years. There are some trust issues there. But believe me when I say you've met a few Elder vyes already. Why do you think Eloise was assigned to you? They wanted to get a sense of who you really were—what better way than to see how you treat a servant? The fact that you and Sarah were so kind to Eloise is a big reason they decided to bring you here."

"How do you know all this?" asked Max. "How did you get so close with vyes?"

"I think everything will make more sense if I start at the beginning," said Connor.

Lucia narrowed her eyes. "Talk."

Taking a sip of tea, Connor cleared his throat and looked at his friends. "When I left Rowan, I only wanted revenge against Alex Muñoz. I was willing to sacrifice anything to make that happen—even my soul. Since Rowan was conquered, I thought I'd have a better chance if I struck out on my own."

Lucia was listening intently. As Connor spoke, Max was struck by the contrast between this young man and the drunken fool from last night's médim.

"Honor's a funny thing," Connor continued. "When I settled in Blys, most of the people on my lands had nothing. Many lost their families when Astaroth came to power. They were confused—they couldn't remember much of their past or even the world as it used to be. My own little crusade began to feel petty. I might only have been a minor baron, but my lands were good and I was able to get some things done."

"What have you done?" asked Max.

"Protected my people," Connor replied proudly. "Twelve thousand humans live in Enlyll. Not one's been murdered or mistreated by demonkind since I got established. When demons come to Enlyll, they know to behave."

"And how do you force demons to behave?" asked Scathach.

"Trade, natural charm, and powerful friends."

"Friends like Elder vyes?" asked Max.

Connor nodded. "They call themselves the Raszna," he said. "When I met Lady Nico, I had no idea what she was. Prusias had invited some Harinean nobles to attend his Arena games. We sat in the same box when Bragha Rùn fought his first match against a two-headed vye. Lady Nico seemed less than pleased."

"It upset her a vye was fighting in the games?" asked Lucia.

"No. It upset her that Straavh fought like a brute. She called him an embarrassment—as though his performance reflected poorly on her. Funny thing for a human to say."

"When did you find out what Lady Nico was?" Max asked.

"After the final match," Connor answered. "Bragha Rùn had slain Myrmidon and left the Arena. They paraded Myrmidon's body around and I thought it was Max. Others thought so, too, because a cheer went up that the Hound of Rowan was dead. Lady Nico's servants clapped with everyone else, but she told them to stop when she saw I was upset. When she asked if I'd known you, I said you'd been my closest friend. She then asked if you were as bloodthirsty as your reputation."

"What did you say?" asked Max.

Connor shrugged. "I said you were worse—that you dined with ogres, supped with hags, and chased lymrills all over Rowan's Sanctuary."

Even Lucia gave a reluctant chuckle.

"Nah," said Connor, waving off the joke. "I said you were my best mate and not to believe all the stories. She said she didn't—she'd heard a kind word or two about you from other quarters."

"Nix and Valya," Max mused. The aged couple had lived near Max's farmhouse in Blys and had become trusted friends.

Connor nodded. "They talked about you like you were their son. And someone else vouched for you."

"Who?"

"I'm not allowed to say," said Connor curtly. "What I can say is that Lady Nico became my mentor. Once she trusted me enough to share she was Raszna, she's helped me become a better ruler, continued my education in magic, and become the closest thing I have to family. When Prusias devoured King Aamon, Lady Nico knew he'd eventually turn on his own braymas and seize all power for himself. We started planning a revolution. That's when I sent Lucia that love letter urging her to 'seek the Elders.'"

The Italian's eyes flashed. She stabbed a finger at Connor. "If you were planning something, you should have told me!"

Connor gave her a pleading look. "I couldn't, Lucia. Some landless braymas arrived weeks ago and requested lodging leading up to the médim. My castle's been crawling with them and their servants for weeks. Some were undoubtedly spies for Prusias or one of the dukes. I had a role to play and couldn't afford to break character for anyone—not even you. It was my job to play the happy, helpless drunk. Your disgust actually helped sell it."

"I'm glad you could use me," snapped Lucia. "I hope it's paying off."

"It is as we speak," said Connor.

"How?" asked Sarah.

Connor's face took on a grim, set expression. "Not one

brayma that's loyal to Prusias will make it out of Enlyll. Even now, they're being ambushed."

"And 'Lord Grael'?" Max said.

"His imposter will return to Prusias with false information about the Harinean revolt before resuming command of his legions."

Max gave a low whistle. "You trust a smee to do all that?"

"Don't forget about the mnemonculi," said Connor. "The smee won't have Grael's abilities, of course, but he'll know everything the duke did."

Max whistled again and glanced at Scathach.

"We need to tell David," she said pointedly. "He needs to know an imposter is commanding some of Prusias's forces."

Lady Nico's voice sounded from the doorway. "That will have to wait," she said. "I apologize, but we've had to confiscate the spypaper in Agent McDaniels's pack."

Max turned on her. "What is this?" he demanded. "You have no right to—"

Lady Nico held up her hand. "Again, I do apologize. This is a delicate time for all concerned. Half my servants refuse to come near this library."

"Why?" asked Max.

His hostess laughed. "Because Max McDaniels is here! Do you have any conception of your reputation among vyes? We are in uncharted waters. Even I'm anxious. We are taking a risk and you must be patient. I've just been communicating with our leadership and they would like to meet you. If you are willing, I will take you to them. They are a few hours away."

"We're willing," said Max at once.

"There are conditions," Lady Nico cautioned.

"What are they?"

"You must surrender your weapons and agree to be bound."

"Absolutely not," said Max.

"Please understand," said Lady Nico diplomatically. "Rowan has traditionally been our enemy. My masters will not permit you and your companions to enter our realm armed."

Max considered a moment. "We'll go unarmed, but none of us will be bound. We're not prisoners." Unbuckling the *gae bolga* from his baldric, Max placed the short, heavy blade on a side table. "A pledge of our good faith."

Lady Nico motioned to Eloise, who went to take the weapon. Max held up a hand.

"Handle it by the scabbard. On your life, don't unsheathe it. Understood?"

The girl plucked up the awful weapon as instructed, using a handkerchief as a buffer. The blade moaned hungrily. Blanching, Eloise carried it swiftly to where an armored vye was waiting with a wooden case. The *gae bolga* went into it, followed shortly by Max's dagger, Scathach's poignard, Lucia's boot knife, and Sarah's longsword. Scathach's spear and Sarah's *naginata*, a pole-arm with a curving blade, were taken by another vye.

"Thank you," said Lady Nico. "No one will touch your weapons, I assure you. Now, if you would come with me."

Hefting a groggy Nox into his arms, Max followed the others as they filed after Lady Nico. Lucia shooed Connor away when he offered to carry Kettlemouth, who was dozing in his cushioned cage. As Sarah and Lucia joined Scathach toward the front, Connor fell in step with Max.

"She's pretty upset," Connor observed.

Max shot Connor a sideways glance. "Why would she be upset? You've only ignored her for weeks, flirted with other girls, drugged Kettlemouth, and kidnapped her."

"Nonsense," said Connor. "I hosted her in a glorious castle, exposed her to some amusing anecdotes, provided her charge

with some much-needed rest, and whisked her out of a dangerous situation."

Max gave an admiring grunt. "Nice spin."

Baron Lynch shrugged. "Facts are facts. A smart ruler pol-
ishes them up a bit."

"Well, Mr. Ruler, what's going to happen to Enlyll now that
it's rebelled?" asked Max, shifting Nox as they descended some
stairs.

Connor gave a wry grin. "Oh, Enlyll hasn't rebelled," he said
innocently. "Landless braymas attacked my poor barony following the médim. Unfortunately, many of the attending braymas
were killed in the fighting, my castle has been damaged, and
I was badly wounded. Lord Grael himself will confirm these
rumors while pointing the finger at several supposed loyalists.
The ruse isn't perfect, of course, but it doesn't need to be. With
Rowan's army closing on Blys and half of Harine in revolt, Prusias will be far too busy to bother with little Enlyll . . ."

"And if Prusias ultimately wins this war?"

Connor shrugged. "Then we're all up a creek."

He lowered his voice as they reached a small chapel. Oil
was burning upon an altar before a bronze statue of Romulus
and Remus suckling from a wolf. A pair of towering black vyes
clutching halberds stood guard on either side of a door that presumably led down to the castle's crypts. Their eyes were bright
yellow and had a feral, defiant glint as they settled upon Max.

"Don't stare," whispered Connor, leading Max up the nave.
"They'll perceive it as a challenge."

Passing between the fearsome guards, Lady Nico, Eloise,
Sarah, Lucia, Connor, Max, Scathach, and several other vyes
descended a steep flight of stairs that continued for a surprising
distance. Initially the walls were dressed stone, but they soon
became rough, bare rock. Torches guttered in their brackets as

warmer air blew up from below. The descent reminded Max of the seemingly endless stairs down into Rowan's Archives.

"How far down does this go?" asked Sarah.

"Pretty far," said Connor. "If it didn't, visitors might hear the—"

A raptor's screech, hoarse and raw, sounded from far below them. Lucia stopped dead. "What was that?" she hissed.

Lady Nico turned on the stair. "Wyverns," she said. "Wonderful creatures if properly handled. I don't believe you have any in Rowan's Sanctuary."

"No," said Sarah. "Not that I've ever seen."

"Was that a wyvern I saw circling the tower when we approached?" inquired Scathach.

"It was," said Lady Nico, continuing down the steps. "We've been breeding wyverns since the Middle Ages. The one you saw this morning was Phineas—he's the grand old man around here and has a few special privileges. He was born the same year as Louis the Fourteenth."

"Are they dangerous?" asked Lucia, glancing at the plump and juicy bullfrog in her arms.

"Not the ones at Wyrmwood," said Lady Nico. "And I have yet to see a wyvern eat a Nile Croaker. Sheep are more to their taste."

The steps ended at a twelve-foot door bound with iron and marked with a sigil of a spiny serpent on a blue field. Placing her hand upon the seal, Lady Nico spoke a word of command and turned the heavy, vaultlike handle. As the door opened, a strong animal smell permeated the air. Nox whined and fidgeted impatiently in Max's arms. He set her down on the stone floor where she proceeded to nose at the doorway, her quills bristling.

As Max walked through the door, he understood Nox's caution. The space they entered was an enormous cave where stalactites protruded from a ceiling some hundred feet above them. While lanterns were burning along a long wooden platform, clusters of luminescent fungi on the walls provided most of the ambient light, which revealed several large tunnels branching off the cavern. A screech echoed around them. Along the cavern's ceiling, Max saw a pair of dark wings twitch and unfold, as though their owner was stretching.

The wyvern was one of several that were hanging upside down among the stalactites. The drawings Max had seen in Rowan's compendiums often depicted wyverns as two-legged dragons, but these creatures resembled sleek bats far more than scaly reptiles. Upon the platform were several vyes wearing thick leather gloves and aprons. One blew several notes on a reedy whistle. Instantly, one of the wyverns dropped from the ceiling and plunged in a controlled, swooping glide to land on the platform and snatch a proffered sheep leg in its jaws.

Aside from its wings, the wyvern did not really resemble a dragon or a bat. Its dark gray coat was as smooth as a Weimaraner's and the head bore an unmistakable canine aspect despite its curving black beak. Its slit yellow eyes were far smaller than Max might have expected, but its large, hyena-like ears suggested that hearing was its primary sense in these dark, almost nocturnal environs. While its wingspan must have been thirty feet, the wyvern's body was no larger than that of a powerful horse that walked upright on two taloned feet and possessed a long, whiplike tail. The creature looked like it was born to fly, and fly very swiftly. A long leather saddle was attached to its back via a system of straps. From the number of stirrups, it appeared the creature could carry three riders.

"Max and Scathach will ride with me," said Lady Nico. "Sarah and Lucia can go with Eloise."

"I can take them," offered Connor.

Lady Nico raised an eyebrow. "You're still learning. Eloise is the better rider. You can go with Xerxes."

"I'm driving," insisted the vye, one of Lady Nico's guards.

"But I'm a baron!" Connor exclaimed.

Xerxes gave a gruff laugh. "In Enlyll you're a baron. Down here you're just a pup. A pup that needs to slow down on the turns if he wants to keep his royal head."

Connor scoffed. "I'm great at turns," he insisted, hurrying over to another wyvern as a handler called it down from the ceiling. The two jostled over who would claim the front seat and control the reins that connected to the creature's bridle. The vye triumphed and Connor was forced to climb, grumbling, into the seat behind him.

"Be sure to hold on tight," chided the vye, wrapping the reins about his fist while a handler lengthened the stirrups. Lucia snickered as a handler helped her and Kettlemouth up into the saddle of Eloise's mount.

Meanwhile, Scathach was already up on a wyvern's back. She settled into the saddle behind Lady Nico, who was showing her how to hook her boots properly into the stirrups. Draping Nox over one shoulder, Max climbed up behind Scathach and slid into the final spot. Although the wyvern leaned forward to keep the saddle relatively level, it was nevertheless awkward sitting astride it. The creature's inclination was to walk upright and occasionally its instincts would override training and the wyvern would begin to rise to a standing position. From what Max could tell, experienced riders took this in stride. Newcomers held on for dear life.

The lymrill was no longer sniffing the wyvern with curiosity but now examined the saddle's rigging as though she intended to make modifications. Max snatched her away from a strap she had begun to gnaw and propped her between his legs as though they were going to ride tandem down a slide. As a handler adjusted his stirrups, Max leaned forward to grip a pair of worn metal handles that protruded from the cantle of Scathach's seat.

"I hold on to these?" he asked the handler, trying to mask any trepidation.

"That's right," said the vye. "Grip with your knees and lean into the turns. You can fasten the lymrill in with that belt."

Spying the strap in question, Max pulled it across Nox's tummy and fastened its clip to a bolted ring. "Should I use my heels at all?"

"Not unless you want her to sting you," replied the vye, gesturing back at the wyvern's tail, which was curling up behind them like a scorpion's. At its tip was a glistening black spike the size of a walrus tusk.

"No heels," Max confirmed. He glanced over at Sarah, who was grinning broadly in the seat behind Lucia. She looked like she was ready to claim her own wyvern and soar off into a tunnel.

"Get comfortable," said Lady Nico, twisting in the saddle to look back at them. "It will be a long ride through the tunnels until we reach our destination."

"Where are we going?" asked Max. Evidently they would be staying underground. He wondered if they would be going to one of the secret schools that the Elder vyes were rumored to have. David had referred to one in his letters—a place called Arcanum—but urged Max and Scathach not to let the Elder vyes know Rowan had heard of it unless an agreement was reached.

Lady Nico gave a cryptic smile. "East."

Shaking the reins, Lady Nico barked a stern command to the wyvern, which wheeled about and sprinted down the platform, keeping very low and flat. Nox jostled and mewled with every step until the wyvern suddenly spread its wings and soared like a fighter jet leaving an aircraft carrier's deck. They were suddenly skimming thirty feet off the cavern floor when the wyvern banked and accelerated into the nearest tunnel.

The wyvern's speed was astonishing. Max could not even guess how fast they were going. The tunnel was a luminescent blur as they zoomed over colonies of fungi that resembled vast, neon archipelagos passing swiftly in their wake. Max hunched forward, staying low and keeping Nox warm as they crouched beneath the screaming currents of moist, rushing air. Occasionally, he'd turn back to see the other wyverns racing after them, drafting in each other's slipstream.

They stopped only once and it was an experience Max would not soon forget. From up ahead, the call of a horn could be heard above the rushing wind. It was soon followed by a series of bright flashes of light.

"Hold on!" cried Lady Nico. With a powerful flap of its wings, the wyvern veered upward and made for a large alcove that had been carved into the tunnel's roof at an angle to form a slanting observation deck. With a screech, the beast landed and turned around so that it could peer down at the tunnel below them. Seconds later, the other wyverns soared onto the ledge and turned about in similar fashion. Sarah was panting happily. Lucia's hair looked as though she'd spent the afternoon in a wind tunnel. Eloise hopped off their wyvern to tighten their stirrups.

"Why did we stop?" asked Scathach.

With a grimace, Lady Nico shook out a cramp in her hand. "A digger's coming," she said. "The big ones can fill up an entire tunnel, so we have to get out of the way."

Now that air wasn't whipping past Max's ears, he could hear the rumbling. The earth itself was shaking and several pebbles dislodged from the rock above to bounce down and off the ledge on which they were perched. Clutching Nox tightly, he stood in the stirrups to peer down, over the wyvern's folded wing. Far below, he saw the tunnel floor, its surface speckled with tiny glowing fungi.

The view disappeared as something filled the opening beneath them. At first, Max thought it was a rockslide, for there were chunks of stone and quartz embedded in what appeared to be a slow but smoothly flowing river of ochre debris. But as it flowed past, he perceived a hint of ringed sections and even mottled scars on what was clearly a living organism.

"Is that a *worm*?" he shouted, hoping to be heard over the now deafening rumble. Lady Nico nodded and indicated she would answer momentarily.

Max stared down, transfixed by the creature's gargantuan size. The tunnel was nearly twenty-five yards in diameter and this creature filled it to the brim. As it continued sliding past, he tried to hazard a guess at its length. Four hundred feet? Five hundred? A blue whale would look like a minnow next to such a monster.

At last the body began to taper and Max could see sections of the tunnel floor, now coated in a glistening layer of translucent slime. In the worm's wake came six Elder vyes mounted on mules and carrying flares, lanterns, and horns. The fact that they appeared so tiny only underscored just how gigantic the worm was. As the vyes rode past the ledge, one glanced up and gave a casual wave before sounding his horn.

"All's clear," said Lady Nico. "We shouldn't have to stop again."

"What kind of creature was that?" breathed Scathach.

"An Ymirian worm," answered Lady Nico. "That was a big one. They were discovered in Himalayan valleys ages ago. We've been using them for six hundred years. The adults can bore a mile through solid rock in a week and their secretions sustain the fungi. Very useful creatures."

"How do you control anything that big?" wondered Max.

"They're really quite docile," replied Lady Nico. "Our people guide them using special tuning forks. While they're practically blind, they're very sensitive to vibrations. They can cause unintentional damage, of course, but they rarely grow violent. How are you bearing up with the flight? It can take some getting used to."

"I want my own wyvern," declared Scathach.

Lady Nico laughed and urged their mount forward. "Make a good impression and you may get your wish."

The wyvern gave a cry as it leaped off the ledge and changed direction with a swift's acrobatic grace. The other wyverns followed suit and the group sped on.

For the next two hours, Max tried to ignore his cramping hands and legs and focus on the meetings ahead. Already it was evident that these Elder vyes were a far more established and capable group than he had assumed they would be. Nix and Valya had been wonderful, but they were just a kindly couple living in the country. Lady Nico and her followers seemed like an entirely different people, organized, capable, perhaps even ruthless. This network of tunnels was a marvel, much less the fact that he'd just seen them assassinate a powerful rakshasa before dispatching an imposter to take his place. Thus far, the Elder vyes had exceeded his expectations. Max hoped he could exceed theirs.

He was shaken out of his thoughts by a glimmering ahead of them. The tunnel was coming to an end and a far brighter light was shining from beyond its aperture. Max had to shield his dark-adjusted eyes as the wyvern raced toward it.

Through the opening they shot, swift as an arrow, to soar over an astonishing spectacle. The domed cavern was miles across and lit by bright clusters of fungi along its roof. Max was almost certain Old College would fit within it. From its walls, a dozen waterfalls gushed in misting cascades to feed several lakes and a broad river that wound across the entire cavern. Bridges spanned its narrowest points, elegant structures of pale stone that connected two halves of a sprawling city.

This has to be Arcanum, thought Max. According to David, Arcanum was the Elder vyes' largest city and greatest school of magic. No one from Rowan—or even Solas—had ever set foot within it.

Gazing down, Max saw that the city's buildings were constructed of the same local stone, a pale granite or marble that gleamed by the light of blue witch-fire lamps. Structures reminiscent of Roman temples radiated out along curving avenues from a cluster of larger towers and buildings at the cavern's center. Max noticed few straight lines among the architecture, but rather curves, bends, and spirals.

He dearly wished David could see what he was seeing. There was nothing in his letters to suggest anything of this scale or sophistication. As they descended, he clutched Nox close and leaned over to watch a group of rangy vyes herding a flock of small piebald sheep toward a hill crowned with flowering trees. How did trees live down here? He suspected it had something to do with the strange luminescent mushrooms nearby. Max desperately wanted to go down and explore.

But exploration would have to wait, for the wyvern was flying toward the city's center. Banking around the largest tower, it screeched and soared up to a large, buttressed observation deck that extended from the tower's face. Vyes were waiting there: rangy handlers wearing leather aprons and gloves and an entourage of very tall, very thin vyes wearing crimson robes. The robed vyes waited by an arched portico while the handlers saw to the wyverns and helped the inexperienced passengers down.

Setting Nox on flagstones, Max walked in a circle, getting his legs under him after such a journey. His legs were painfully stiff, his hands half clenched into claws from clutching the handles. Smoothing his coat, he plucked several quills from the fabric. With an eager mewl, the lymrill trotted toward a trough filled with mutton that the handlers were rolling out to the wyverns. Max had no idea if wyverns were territorial about their food, but he had no wish to find out. Hurrying after Nox, he scooped her back into his arms.

"Don't worry, my beauty," said Lady Nico, scratching Nox's chin as the others dismounted and began rubbing sore muscles. "We'll see that you're fed once your humans have been properly introduced."

She led the group toward the tower where the tall, robed vyes were waiting. Max could tell his friends were nervous, and indeed so was he. Interacting with so many vyes in their natural form would take some getting used to.

Fortunately, the vyes assembled before them were not particularly fearsome-looking. Instead, they were an older, scholarly-looking set with mottled fur and several hints of cataracts among the dark, intelligent eyes. The central figure was seated in a chair fitted with poles so that it could be carried. His great head was bowed with age and frailty. A female vye, younger than the others and wearing robes of gold rather than crimson leaned close to the seated vye's ear and spoke in a language unfamiliar to Max. The old vye nodded, gripped the armrests of his chair, and forced his trembling body up.

Nine feet tall he stood, but Max imagined he must have been ten feet or more in his prime. The vye's fur was a mottled gray, tipped with silver. Glassy orange eyes peered out from the vye's deep sockets, surveying each visitor before settling on Max. The vye's hoarse voice came in slow exhalations as he spoke in the same unfamiliar language Max had heard earlier. Bowing low, Lady Nico translated.

"This is Archon, our leader. All Raszna recognize his authority. He is pleased to welcome the famous Hound of Rowan to Arcanum. He is surprised at your youth but confesses that everyone looks young these days."

Max bowed at the waist, said that he was very pleased to meet Archon, and asked leave to introduce his companions. This he did, and in turn Archon introduced them to the other vyes, who were apparently professors of various disciplines at the school. The specialties were so different from those at Rowan: Geologia, Hydeshifting, Elixae, Masquing, Apocrypha . . . Max listened carefully, aware that Hazel Cooper would want to hear about every single one.

When introductions had been made, Archon asked to see Nox and Kettlemouth. Each suffered their introductions rather well. Nox even managed to flatten her quills into an agreeably smooth coat when the ancient vye reached out a trembling hand to stroke her. Archon turned to Connor last and spoke with measured gravity. Lady Nico translated.

"It has been a year since Archon saw Lord Lynch. Does he greet him as a brother or merely a friend?"

"A brother," said Connor.

Archon glanced at Lady Nico, who nodded and spoke rapidly. Max distinctly heard the word *Grael*. The vye grunted and gazed at Connor with unmistakable respect. Beckoning Connor forward, Archon embraced him, touched his forehead to Connor's, and muttered, "Ruva" before passing him along to his colleagues, who did the same. By the time they had finished, tears shone bright on Connor's cheeks. Sitting back in his chair, Archon spoke again to the visitors while Lady Nico translated.

"Archon invites you to refresh yourselves and dine with his

colleagues in Amber Hall. He asks for a private word with the Hound of Rowan. Is this acceptable?"

"It is not," said Scathach. "We agreed to lay down our arms, but Max is not going anywhere alone."

Lady Nico translated for Archon, whose response was curt.

"Committees solve nothing. One to one is best."

"I don't disagree," said Scathach. "Give me my spear and several hostages and he can go with you."

This seemed to amuse Archon, who gestured at his wizened colleagues to indicate she could have whomever among them she wished. Scathach shook her head.

"Lady Nico, Eloise, and the Lady Isu at your right."

Archon frowned as though Scathach's choice of hostages either surprised or displeased him. Indeed, Max wondered why she had chosen these particular hostages with such certainty. As disgruntled as Archon looked, Scathach did not appear to have any intention of changing her choice. Max knew she wasn't wrong to be insistent. At such a meeting, it was important to establish rules and mutual safeguards.

As much as Rowan needed the Elder vyes, they could not gloss over past history. There was a reason the Raszna lived deep underground. Rowan's predecessors had driven them there, and Max was not oblivious to the attention the Raszna paid to his and Scathach's tattoos. For them, the Red Branch symbol undoubtedly held a terrifying significance: *these are the enemy's best killers.*

And while Rowan's motivations for the meeting were clear, the Raszna's were less so. It was important to be cautious. If nothing else, the médim had shown that Elder vyes had their own agenda while Arcanum's existence spoke to a people who were incredibly patient, disciplined, and capable. Max doubted the Raszna did anything hastily.

"Why these hostages?" asked Lady Nico, translating Archon's gruff response.

"Because Lady Nico is your daughter, Eloise is your granddaughter, and Lady Isu is your favorite wife."

Lady Nico's prim smile vanished. She gestured to Archon before answering Scathach directly. "You have excellent intuition. May I ask how you knew?"

Scathach shrugged. "A parent's love is easy to see. And, forgive me, but Lady Isu is too young to be your mother and she was not introduced as a scholar. Our host either has more than one wife and chose to bring her, or his previous wives are no more. In either case, Lady Isu is his favorite."

Archon looked impatiently at Lady Nico. When she translated Scathach's explanation, he gave a barking laugh and muttered something with an offhand air.

"You remind him of his first wife," said Lady Nico.

"Is Scathach's proposal agreeable to you?" said Max, addressing Archon. With a resigned nod, the vye gestured for a cane.

"It is not agreeable, but it is acceptable," said Lady Nico.

One of the armored vyes that had traveled with them from Wyrmwood came forward with Scathach's spear. She took it and bowed politely as Eloise, Lady Nico, Archon's Lady Isu came to stand before her. Leaving Nox with Sarah, Max bid his friends farewell and followed Archon and one of the professors into the tower.

~ 17 ~

APOCRYPHA

Max descended broad stone steps that curved into a hallway and led to a carven door whose relief depicted seven scrolls. The professor, a stooped and languid vye with tawny fur and yellow eyes, produced a key and slipped it into the lock.

"I speak English," he informed Max in a soft voice. "My name is Volsu, the Apocrypha scholar. I will translate in Lady Nico's absence."

"What is Apocrypha?" Max asked.

Amusement flickered in the old vye's eyes. "Truths or blasphemy," he replied. "Apocrypha are contested lore and scriptures.

Some believe them and some do not. Arcanum is riddled with Apocrypha."

Archon spoke sharply and Volsu bowed.

"His lordship desires me to translate everything that is said."

"Understood," said Max. "What language is Archon speaking?"

Once he'd translated, the vye pushed open the heavy door. "Etruscan. Please come in."

He stood aside to admit Max into a long, narrow room with a high barrel ceiling. Its crimson walls were lined with mahogany bookcases densely packed with bound manuscripts and labeled cases full of scrolls and sheaves of parchment. The room's other furnishings consisted of a long table, a dozen chairs, and a candelabrum whose wicks kindled into pale gold flame at a word from Volsu.

Closing the door behind them, Volsu invited Max to make himself comfortable. Whenever the vye spoke, he made certain to translate for Archon, who lowered himself with some difficulty into a chair at the table's center and gestured for Max to sit opposite him. There was a knock and a young servant entered, bearing a large tray laden with fruit, bread, hummus, and skewers of cold lamb.

With an imperious grunt, Archon dismissed the servant and uncorked the bottle of pungent wine. He poured two glasses, one for Max and one for himself. Apparently Volsu was to do without. Archon raised his glass and spoke.

"My lord toasts your good health and commends your choice of a mate," Volsu translated. "She is formidable."

Max blinked. "Er, thank you. Lady Isu seems like a fine wife."

Archon inclined his head and sipped his wine. Setting down his glass, he appraised Max thoughtfully before speaking.

"What does Rowan want from the Raszna? I have heard rumors, but I want to hear from you," said Volsu.

He cuts right to it. David had recommended candor and thus far everything Max had seen of Archon seemed to support that approach.

"Rowan wants friendship."

Archon shook his head and wagged a chiding finger. "Rowan wants allies," said Volsu, interpreting. "Even if Prusias's braymas abandon him, the demon can muster many more troops than those now marching toward his gates. Rowan is far from home and vastly outnumbered."

"Not if the Raszna and Rowan fight together," said Max.

Archon touched his fingertips together and spoke in a solemn tone. "For over two thousand years, your order has tormented Luperca's sons and daughters," Volsu translated. "You forced us to abandon our homeland, drove us down into the darkness, and hunted those who remained above. And now Rowan desires our help?"

Max spread his hands. "I can't undo the past. I will freely admit that I used to believe all vyes were the enemy, monsters intent on destroying humankind. It wasn't until I met two Raszna that I began to learn otherwise."

Archon listened stoically. At Max's mention of Raszna, he shook his head.

"You refer to Nix and Valya," said Volsu. "We are aware of your interactions with them. They are not Raszna."

"I'm sorry," said Max, looking from one to the other. "I thought Raszna was your term for Elder vyes. Am I mistaken?"

Speaking to Volsu, Archon gestured at a tapestry upon the far wall whose aged and intricate needlework depicted a family tree with three main branches. The Apocrypha scholar nodded. "His lordship thinks it wise to clarify who and what we are.

Not all vyes are Elder and not all Elders are Raszna. Those who would be allies should know one another, should they not?"

Those who would be allies. That sounded promising. It was certainly better than the Fomorian's flat refusal. Max raised his glass. "I wholeheartedly agree."

Volsu stepped aside so that Max had a clear view of the tapestry. At its top were the familiar figures of the infants Romulus and Remus suckling from a wolf.

"All vyes descend from Luperca, the goddess who nourished Romulus and Remus. All vyes honor her, for it was her gift that gave us life and brought us into being. What you call Elder vyes are the descendants of Remus. They are the mehrùn among our kind and have inherited Luperca's wild magic."

"So Nix and Valya told me," said Max.

"Did they speak of the Raszna, Elohir, and Magyarün?"

"No."

"They are tribes," Volsu explained. "Factions that arose from a schism long ago. The Raszna focused on our communities, founding schools and developing our craft. The Elohir had no interest in such things. They were restless and nomadic, wanderers of the earth. Some settled among humans and lived their lives, but they became strangers to us and never studied at the great schools."

"Are Nix and Valya considered Elohir?" asked Max.

Volsu nodded. "Yes. We have some contact with the Elohir and may lend each other assistance, but they are not Raszna."

"And what of the Magyarün?"

When Max said the name, Archon's face twisted into something dangerous.

"The Magyarün are the cause of many woes," said Volsu, translating his lord's angry mutterings. "The Magyarün fell into darkness and preyed upon man. They are the ones responsible for infecting humans and creating the lesser vyes that have plagued mankind. Astaroth's servants used the Magyarün and these lesser vyes to enable his return. The fools thought they would inherit the earth, but the demons scorn them. Few are braymas in the new order. Most slink about the demon cities—addicts and beggars until they're called upon to fight for their new masters." Archon paused and tapped a sharp nail upon the table. "One might say the demons use them like Rowan would use us."

Max set down his glass and met the vye's piercing gaze. "We're not asking you to fight for us. We're asking you to fight *with* us. I will ride and fight with the Raszna myself."

Archon glanced sharply at Volsu and ordered the scholar to repeat what Max had said. This Volsu did, although he added some additional remarks that made Archon bristle.

"Have I said something to offend?" asked Max.

"No," said Volsu, rather coolly. "Our lordship is intrigued by your statement. He is under the impression it touches upon a particularly controversial prophecy within our Apocrypha."

"What prophecy?"

But Volsu was enduring another scolding from Archon. Apparently, the vye seemed to think his interpreter was overstepping his bounds. When Volsu spoke again, his tone was markedly more reserved.

"I am to apologize for interjecting my opinion. I am to make you aware that I have only a scholarly interest in Apocrypha, that I am a skeptic who does not personally believe in Galia's words. I am also to inform you that Archon is not a zealot nor the only Raszna to believe Rowan's Hound could be our *moschiach*."

"What is a *moschiach*?" asked Max.

"Messiah," came the flat reply.

Max said nothing. What did one say to something like that? He could almost feel the unblinking gazes of Archon and Volsu.

At length, Archon spoke and directed Volsu to retrieve a box from a high shelf. The scholar obliged his master but made a disapproving grimace when ordered to open it. Inside, Max saw a stack of letters written by the same hand. To Max's great surprise, many were on paper bearing Rowan's seal.

"My lord invites you to read them," muttered Volsu, his grimace tightening. He clasped his hands behind his back as though restraining himself from further comment. Max took the topmost sheet.

> The consensus at Rowan is that Old Magic is reawakening. My scouts discovered an ulu and a lymrill this past month—two species long thought to be extinct. They've already been matched to new students whose tests hint at vast potential. Their names are David Menlo and Max McDaniels. Each was nearly intercepted by the Magyarün before coming here. Other Potentials have been abducted. The Director is furious. Finding them has become her top priority. Rowan's Agents are on high alert for vyes. Those masquing at surface should go underground. The Red Branch is hunting.
>
> GWN

When Max read the initials, his mouth went dry.

"Gregory Wyatt Nolan," he breathed.

Archon sniffed, a twinge of sadness rippling across his proud features. Max reeled in disbelief.

"Nolan was a *vye?*"

"His birth name was Även," answered Volsu. "His grandmother was Archon's sister. All the Raszna mourned his death."

Max shook his head. It was inconceivable that Nolan was a

vye. Vyes could be detected—there were proven tests and tricks to identify them. Nolan had graduated from Rowan, had lived there all his life. How on earth had he been able to do so without being discovered? The idea that Nolan had been a vye shocked Max more than learning David Menlo was a cambion. After all, there had always been something mysterious and supernatural about David. But Nolan? Rowan's Head of Grounds had been at Rowan for decades. Every Rowan student, teacher, and charge regularly crossed his path. How could he possibly keep such a secret for so long? Could Nolan really have been a vye?

The dream!

Max's spine tingled as he recalled his recent nightmare. In the dream, Nolan's corpse had answered the Warming Lodge door—a corpse bearing a second set of canine teeth. He'd chalked up Nolan's strange appearance as one of those strange little details often found in dreams. But he had been wrong.

"I can't believe it," he muttered absently. "How could he escape detection?"

Volsu translated Max's question and Archon's response. "Passing as human is the first skill they master, for it is essential to survival. Även was uncommonly gifted—it's why he was chosen to infiltrate Rowan. He was ten when he left Arcanum and went to live with a foster family. Your recruiters found him a few years later and he passed their tests. When Även graduated from Rowan, he dedicated his life to better understanding its people and caring for the creatures in its Sanctuary. His dream was always to secure peace between our peoples."

Archon shook his head sadly.

"He loved Rowan."

Max felt profoundly conflicted. "He was a spy."

"An ugly word," translated Volsu. "Även was tasked with learning more about those who had been our enemy. We never asked him to undermine Rowan or act against any who lived there. Even if we had, Även would have refused. He believed in the Apocrypha's prophecy that a messiah from our enemies would lead us out of hiding. Även believed that messiah was you."

At Archon's command, Volsu took a letter and placed it before Max.

> The Hound should have died tonight. William Cooper cut his throat. The Red Branch's leader has been possessed and is now in service of the Atropos. I saw the Hound shortly after and the lad was unhurt—not a scratch. No mortal could have survived the wound he received. I cite this as further proof that he is, indeed, the moschiach foretold by the Prophet. We must invite him to Arcanum. Should Rowan survive the coming siege, I will endeavor to bring him myself. I believe he would come of his own accord. The Hound has a noble heart.

As Max read the letter, he found himself mourning Nolan all over again. He dearly missed the man's grin, his fiddle, and the relaxed, easy way he had with everyone, from YaYa to Ms. Richter to a frightened First Year. To Max's embarrassment, a tear ran down his cheek and dropped with a soft patter upon the letter.

"You cared for Även," said Volsu, relaying Archon's quiet observation.

Exhaling slowly, Max put the letter aside. "Of course I did. He was my friend."

Looking up, Max saw that Archon's expression had softened. Their eyes met and within the vye's somber gaze, Max perceived understanding and even sympathy. And in that moment, Max knew that Archon's misgivings had been put to rest. The vye might not trust Rowan, but he trusted Max—as Även had done.

Volsu, however, was growing agitated. When Archon desired him to divulge an Apocryphal passage containing the Prophet's words, the scholar demurred. While his first refusal was mild, the second saw him bare his teeth in a sudden snarl.

Archon shot to his feet.

Max would never have guessed the ancient vye could move so quickly. Archon loomed above the disobedient scholar, trembling with rage. Volsu's snarl vanished. With a throaty whine, he averted his eyes and stared at the floor.

"My lord asks your forgiveness," Volsu translated quietly. "It is unacceptable that you were made to witness such behavior. Volsu shall be punished, but first he shall produce Galia's prophecies and translate the passage concerning *moschiach*."

Like a whipped cur, the scholar slunk to a locked display and retrieved an ivory case with a glass top. Inside were seven tubes. Removing the seventh, Professor Volsu carefully slid its scroll free from its casing to reveal a parchment that had been torn and mended in several places. Scattered across its surface were small dark stains, as though it had been spattered with blood long ago. Pointing to a passage halfway down the scroll, Volsu began to translate the unfamiliar words and letters.

"Do not despair, for Salvation is coming. In a time of war, one of our ancient enemies shall deliver us, a youth whose light shall be a beacon to those who would live free. The moschiach shall unite us and lead us against a common foe. His sacrifice shall heal the world and bring about an age of peace."

At first, Max said nothing. Like most prophecies, it was open to many interpretations.

"When was that written?" he asked.

"The late twelfth century," replied Volsu. "Two hundred years after Solas drove us underground and Arcanum was founded. The prophet was a female named Galia. This was her final proclamation. Shortly thereafter, she was stoned to death in Amber Hall."

"Why was she killed?"

Volsu's eyes glittered. "Her people had been defeated, humiliated by an order determined to exterminate them. Insisting that the Raszna would someday embrace this enemy and follow him was not a popular notion." The vye glanced sideways at Archon. "Even today, many would reject such a proposal."

Archon waved off Volsu's warning as though such things were already well known to him. Max leaned forward. "I am not a scholar and I do not know what to make of prophets and apocrypha. But I know we have a common enemy. Surely it would be better to unite our efforts. We have the same objective."

"Volsu is correct," said Archon. "Not all believe in the Apocrypha. Not all will believe you are the *moschiach* or easily forget the past. They will demand more than kind words and an old prophecy."

And so the negotiation begins, thought Max. He was grateful Archon was a pragmatist. It was clear the old vye wanted an alliance but needed Max's help to craft a proposal his people could accept.

"I have been empowered to offer the following," said Max. "In exchange for the Raszna's allegiance, Rowan offers not only peace, but also a share of any lands we might acquire when Prusias is defeated."

As Volsu translated, Archon's face remained expressionless.

"But we recognize that trust must be earned over time," Max continued. "To this end, we propose an academic exchange. Raszna will have an opportunity to study at Rowan while our apprentices attend classes at Arcanum. The Director suspects we can learn much from one another and that our schools are the key to building familiarity and friendship."

This brought an approving grunt from Archon, who muttered something to Volsu. The Apocrypha scholar nodded and said something hastily in reply. *He's pushing for something,* thought Max.

"An exchange is a very good idea," said Volsu. "But our scholars would also require access to your Archives."

Max had expected this. In his instructions, David had predicted the Raszna would demand this privilege. Rowan's Archives made scholars drool even before Astaroth caused much of the world's technology and printed matter to fade from existence. It was the greatest repository of history and magical knowledge on Earth.

"That could be arranged," Max allowed. "David Menlo could be very helpful in this regard. The Director has a passion for magical research and is a considerable practitioner."

Archon chuckled as Volsu translated. "You have a gift for understatement. Även said the boy is a prodigy and Bram's own blood."

"He is," said Max. "And when this war is over, our Director intends to indulge his passion and found a new school, a university where the greatest minds can collaborate on deeper mysteries. Since the Middle Ages, magical education has focused on learning old tricks. David Menlo intends to discover new ones and would like the Raszna's help."

Volsu almost gasped. The opportunity to break new ground, to found a university, and collaborate with the likes of David Menlo went straight to the old scholar's heart. He eagerly relayed this final provision to Archon, who clasped his hands and furrowed his brow in thought.

"The world is changed," said Max. "Old enemies must put

aside their differences if they're to survive. Rowan isn't seeking a short-term alliance but a long-term partnership with the Raszna. I think our proposal reflects that."

Archon nodded and conversed quietly with Volsu before turning back to Max.

"Your new Director has made an offer that merits serious consideration. Guarantees would be necessary, of course, along with suitable hostages and a council to settle disputes, but there is enough here to bring before the people. There is a special gathering tonight. I would like you to attend as my guests."

"Thank you," said Max. "We would like that."

Archon held up a hand. "You may be challenged," he said sharply. "Raszna do not follow those weaker than themselves. While everyone knows the Hound of Rowan's reputation, in person he is very young and much smaller than some who will be present. War chiefs might be tempted to test you. If this happens, do not respond. Lady Nico or myself will intercede."

Max said he understood and Archon rose stiffly to escort him to the door. Outside, ten armored vyes were waiting to escort Max to Amber Hall. Each was armed with a saber and carried a heavy polearm.

"Are so many guards necessary?" said Max.

When Volsu translated, Archon gave a gruff laugh.

"They are," said Volsu. "Until you are safely returned to Lady Scathach, Archon's loved ones remain at her mercy. It is a long walk to Amber Hall. Archon prefers not to tempt fate."

"Are you coming with us?"

"No," reported Volsu. "My lord has much to consider and to prepare before this evening's gathering. He bids you farewell and leaves you to Lupo's talkative company."

Lupo arrived a few seconds later, a young page who was rather short and scrawny. His fur was reddish and foxlike, and his robes were brown and rather plain compared to the sumptuous crimsons worn by Archon and the Raszna professors. He was not a particularly impressive specimen, but he was friendly and eager to show off his city during the walk to Amber Hall.

"That's the Masquing wing," he said, pointing to an archway as they walked down a broad corridor. From within, Max could hear a teacher and the answering chorus of very young voices. "You can't move on in school until you master it."

"So every Raszna can appear as human," said Max.

"Of course."

"Do you have just one human shape or can you change it?"

"Just one shape," said Lupo. "There's human in us, you know. Masquing isn't like hydeshifting. We're not borrowing another creature's shape but putting on our other face. It's like turning your clothes inside out."

"Would you show me?"

The guards stopped as Lupo paused and furrowed his brow. With a shudder, his face suddenly rippled and he changed into a skinny boy of ten or eleven with reddish brown hair, a weak chin, and a forehead spotted with pimples. One of the guards muttered something to another in Etruscan. Lupo whirled on him.

"I'm not done growing!"

The boy transformed back into a vye, but not before Max saw his face flush red.

"Do you know Eloise?" asked Max, changing the subject as they continued.

"Of course. She's in the class ahead of me. Eloise is tops."

"Tops?"

"Tops in everything," said Lupo. "Masquing, fencing, elixae. You name it. If she'd been born male, she might have been Archon someday. See that statue? That's Tiberius—he's the Archon who tamed the first wyverns."

Lupo pointed up to an alcove where a black marble statue glared down at them.

"Very nice," said Max. "But is Archon a name or a title?"

"The master of Arcanum is always called Archon," said Lupo. "Even masters from the other schools have to call him that, though they don't like it much."

"How many schools are there?"

Before Lupo could answer, a guard interjected in a harsh flurry of Etruscan. Max's eager tour guide scowled.

"He says to watch my tongue," huffed Lupo. "That information is for Archon to share. I'm to remember that you're the enemy."

Max glanced at the guard who had spoken. The vye returned his gaze with a look of cold, unblinking suspicion.

"But Eloise," said Max, turning back to Lupo. "She can never be Archon? Even if she's 'tops'?"

Lupo laughed. "Of course she can't! Whoever heard of a female Archon? If females could be Archon, the Lady Nico might succeed her father—not Fenwulf."

"Who's Fenwulf?"

"He's the master of . . . one of the other schools. Everyone thinks he'll be next. He's not a fighter like our current Archon, but he's a brilliant elixist. He re-created the Lupercan Draught."

Again a guard snarled and Lupo ceased, albeit with a sulky glance. He stopped to direct Max's attention over a stone balcony, which looked down upon a paved avenue that wound along the river. The avenue was teeming with Raszna carrying picks and other mining tools.

"Shift change," explained Lupo. "My father's probably down there. He's been working like crazy since a gildhünd sniffed ormeisen off one of the new tunnels. He says the scent's centuries old and the ore's probably worthless, but you can't let something like that go."

Max was puzzled. "What's a gildhünd?"

Lupo squinted, scanning the miners until he spied in their midst a dozen lean hounds with pale, silvery coats. "There's a few. They're special dogs that are bred to sniff out veins of precious metal. If ore's close by, they'll find it. They give off different yips to let you know what they've found. They've even got a yip for ormeisen."

"What is ormeisen?" asked Max. "I've never heard of it."

The vye looked very pleased to know something his famous guest did not. "Dragon iron, of course. I thought everyone knew that."

Max let the comment slide. "What's so special about it?"

"It can kill spirits dead. Even the big ones other metals can't hurt."

"That sounds like Zenuvian iron," said Max, recalling the preposterously expensive substance he had acquired by bartering his torque with Madam Petra.

"Why do you call it that?" asked Lupo earnestly.

"Because it's mined in Zenuvia."

The vye laughed and promptly covered his mouth. "I'm sorry, but that's just an awfully stupid name. I mean, ormeisen isn't just found in Zenuvia."

"Okay," said Max, smiling tightly. "Why do you call it dragon iron?"

The vye offered a pitying look. He spoke slowly, as though to ensure maximum comprehension. "Because you only find it where a dragon was born."

Max suppressed an urge to flick his guide's nose and focused instead on this interesting tidbit. If Lupo was right and dragon iron lost potency over time, then the ore found in Zenuvia must have been located near a recent hatching. To Max's knowledge, the only true dragon that had been seen in the last millennium was curled about Mina's bedchamber. *Was Ember the source of Zenuvian iron?*

"Well, I see I've startled and amazed you," said Lupo happily. With an impatient growl, the guard captain plucked him up by his ruff. Dangling the young vye like a misbehaving kitten, the guard invited Max to continue on their way.

As they walked, Lupo went limp as a noodle and vowed savage retaliation when he "hit his growth spurt." Neither approach made much of an impression upon the stony captain.

"That's the Hydeshifting wing," murmured Lupo glumly, gesturing to an archway whose stonework was carved into the likeness of various beasts and birds. Apparently a class was letting out, for a score of young vyes in orange robes spilled into the hallway beyond the arch. Several females caught sight of Lupo and giggled.

"Put me down!" he hissed to the guard captain. "Please!"

The captain relented and Lupo quickly smoothed his ruff and robes. He glanced sidelong at Max. "I'm sorry if I was rude. I don't mean to be. My mother says I can get too 'familiar.' Whatever that means."

"It's okay," said Max. "But maybe we should get to Amber Hall."

"Right," said Lupo. "Would you mind if I just did one thing?"

"Of course not."

The young vye turned to the watching girls. "Hound of Rowan!" he called, pointing vigorously at Max. "The other pages were too scared."

Taking Max's elbow, Lupo strode boldly ahead. He might have been leading a dangerous criminal to his cell. Max sighed.

Indeed, Baron Lynch was the first person he saw as they entered Amber Hall. He was standing with Lucia and Sarah before a vast mural that seemed to tell the story of the Raszna's journey underground and the founding of Arcanum. Connor was pointing down to a section of floor beneath the mural that had been roped off, as though it was hallowed ground. Max's eyes drifted up to the mural and surrounding walls, for the entire room looked as though it had been thickly glazed with amber. Its surfaces were as smooth as glass and gleamed in sumptuous shades of honey and gold, pale yellow, and sienna. Its colors were alive, dancing and shifting by the light of a single, massive brazier at the hall's far end. Next to the brazier, a somber vye in black robes stood upon a dais next to a tall oil jug called a lekythos.

Scathach and her hostages sat at a long table playing a game that resembled chess but whose board had several tiers. Eloise was staring fixedly at the pieces on the lowest level, her tongue caught between her teeth as she rolled a captured bishop between her hands. Lady Nico and Lady Isu rose as Max and his escort marched toward them. Scathach, who had been trying to distract Eloise, pushed back from the table and hefted her spear. Her eyes fell upon the armed guards and her grin faded to a tight, hard line.

"I've brought him back," announced Lupo, stopping before them. "You can release the Lady—"

"Quiet," Scathach ordered. She looked keenly at Max. "Who was my youngest shield maiden?" she asked him.

"Ula."

"Who fashioned the brooch at your neck?"

"My father."

She nodded. "Are you wearing your favorite shirt?" she asked.

"I am."

"Good." With a fluid movement, she drew her poignard and stabbed his chest.

Eloise gasped, Lupo fainted, but Max merely braced himself. He felt a jolt of pain as the blade's lethal point was turned aside by the nanomail corselet he wore beneath his outer clothes.

"Well," said Scathach, examining the poignard's tip. "It seems you really are my Max. A smee can't replicate that—even if it has your memories."

Eloise clapped with delight and turned to Lady Nico. "Did you see that, *maman*?"

"Indeed," replied Lady Nico, taking her daughter's hand. "We have had a clever keeper. Now that her Max has returned, will she permit us to go free?"

"With pleasure," said Scathach, setting down her spear. "You've been very gracious hostages." She made a small bow to Eloise. "Thank you for teaching me arcadia. How close were you to taking both my towers?"

"Four moves," answered Eloise gravely. "Maybe three."

"We'll have to play again sometime."

Eloise said she would be very happy to and stared at Scathach with something approaching reverence. Twice her mother had to tell her to get her woozy schoolmate a glass of water. Once revived, Lupo was plucked up by the guards, who carried him and his water glass out of the hall. Lady Nico turned to Max.

"How was your meeting with Archon?"

"I'm sure he'll tell you the details," he replied, scratching Nox's chin as the lymrill sidled up to him.

Connor, Sarah, and Lucia came over to join them, also eager for news of Max's meeting. Max turned to Lady Nico.

"Is there someplace we can bathe and change?" he asked. "Archon has asked us to attend tonight's gathering. After horses and wyverns, I could use a change of clothes."

"Of course," said Lady Nico. "I keep an apartment here and you're welcome to use it. We'll have your clothes and packs brought to the room. Eloise can get you situated while I see Lady Isu back to my father's quarters."

Lady Nico's rooms were not far from Amber Hall, just a brief walk down several corridors and up a short flight of stairs to a pair of large double doors. Pressing her small hand against a stone, Eloise growled a harsh, guttural command that unlocked the doors. Max realized he had yet to see Eloise or her mother in their natural guise. It was easy to forget the two were vyes.

Inviting them in, Eloise led them through the apartment, through a bedroom, and into a bathroom that had a large tub and a pair of marble sinks beneath a polished mirror. Max saw that the sinks and tub had copper faucets as if . . .

"Does hot water come out of those?" asked Lucia eagerly.

"*Oui,*" said Eloise, smiling as she demonstrated. The two spoke in rapid French. Max was able to make out something to do with the waterfalls and hot springs.

"The girls clean up first!" Lucia declared, snatching up a towel and ushering Max and Connor out of the bathroom. Eloise accompanied them into the sitting area, said a few words to Connor, and bowed as she excused herself.

"We're to make ourselves at home," said Connor, setting a copper kettle to boil in a fireplace. From the bathroom, Max could hear Lucia exclaiming with delight as steam trickled out from beneath the door. Failing to wake Kettlemouth from a nap within his cage, Nox came to settle on Max's lap. Reaching in a pocket, Max found a remaining ingot and let her pluck it from his fingers.

"First chance I've gotten to see you alone," reflected Connor, opening a canister of tea leaves. "What do you think of Arcanum?"

"I'm still in shock," Max confessed. "About it. About you. What have you been doing, Connor? Archon said you're to be honored at tonight's gathering. What's that all about? Why did Archon call you 'ruva' when we were introduced to him?"

"It means 'brother,'" Connor explained. "I'm going to be made an honorary member of the Raszna."

Max stared at him. "How did that happen?"

"It's been moving in that direction for a while," Connor answered. "When Lady Nico and I became close, I eventually met other Raszna and started spending more time with them. Some of it was business—cooperating on trade, planning initiatives against Prusias—but most of it was social. I liked them and they liked me. They made me feel at home. When they asked if I wanted to join the tribe, I said yes and have been earning my stripes, so to speak."

"Was killing Lord Grael a requirement?"

Connor nodded, nosing about a few tins and finding one with several cookies. He tossed one to Max. "Not him specifically, but a 'great enemy' of the vyes. Grael did plenty to them in Malakos. No one else at the médim would have qualified, except you."

"Am I really a great enemy?"

"To some vyes, you're *the* enemy," laughed Connor. "I'm not sure if you know anything about Magyarün, but you're practically their bogeyman. The Raszna have heard all the stories."

"Archon told me about Nolan," said Max, watching Connor's face carefully. He wanted to see if Connor had known, if his friend had been sitting on this shocking piece of news. Connor finished his cookie and wiped the crumbs from his cloak.

"I'm glad," he said. "I wish I could have told you myself, but Även's a big secret. Only Archon's allowed to share something like that with an outsider. I only know because I'd heard Lady

Nico tell Eloise about Nolan when he died. When they realized I knew, they swore me to secrecy."

"Is Archon trustworthy?" asked Max. "I'm not asking as a representative of Rowan. I'm asking as a friend. Archon seems open to the idea of a Rowan-Raszna alliance, but if he was lying, this gathering could be dangerous for us."

"Archon is trustworthy," Connor assured him. "He's tough and has a short temper, but he wouldn't go back on his word. But there are others you'll want to be wary of. Did Archon mention the Apocrypha?"

"He did."

"Then you know there are some who see you as the *moschiach*. And there are others who find that idea crazy and would rather see you dead."

"Where does Fenwulf fall?" asked Max.

Connor wrinkled his nose. "How'd you hear about Fenwulf?"

"Lupo mentioned him," said Max. "He said he's likely to be the next Archon."

"Aye," said Connor, sitting down and scratching Nox's ears. "That's true. I haven't interacted much with Fenwulf since he's normally at Silverfalls, which is another school a long ways east of here. I probably shouldn't be telling you this, but the Harinean revolts are partially about Silverfalls."

"How so?"

"Yuga," said Connor. "I don't know if you've heard about her, but she's a demon the size of a freaking typhoon. She's been devouring the eastern duchies and is getting close to where Silverfalls is hidden. It doesn't matter that the school's hidden in the mountains. If Yuga senses life nearby, she can get to it—even if it's buried deep. Lots of goblin tribes have found out the hard way. Many braymas have lost their lands to Yuga. They're furious Prusias brought her into this world and don't think he'd have done it if he didn't have some way of controlling her. They think he's happy to let her gobble up his rivals while he pretends she's beyond his control. Prusias doesn't know much about the Raszna, but we've sent messages through these braymas and others trying to get him to do something about Yuga. Since he doesn't bother to respond, we're hoping the Harinean revolts will twist his arm a bit. To get Prusias's attention you have to show you can hurt him."

Max recalled his own narrow escape from the living, feasting storm. "Maybe you're right, but I've seen Yuga up close. I'm not certain anyone can control her."

"Well, Archon and Fenwulf mean to make Prusias try," said Connor. "But when it comes to Fenwulf and the Apocrypha, I don't think he's a believer. He wants the Galian memorial removed from Amber Hall. Thinks it causes some people to deify her."

"What memorial?"

"I was showing it to Lucia and Sarah when you came in," said Connor. "Part of the floor's roped off where a prophet was stoned to death. There are bloodstains and gouges that have never been cleaned. It's become a holy place for those who believe in the Apocrypha. Fenwulf and some others want it removed."

"Will he be here tonight?"

"Oh yes," said Connor. "Silverfalls has been evacuated. Its people have crowded in here. Fenwulf's been at Arcanum for a few months and I should be grateful. I can't really become a proper member of the Raszna without him."

"Why's that?" asked Max.

But Connor only flashed an enigmatic grin as a knock sounded at the door. He set down his kettle to answer it. Several of Lady Nico's guards entered, bringing their packs and belongings from the sledges. Among the items, Max saw Sarah's *naginata* and searched in vain for the *gae bolga*. He demanded to know why it hadn't been returned and was told to take it up with Archon. When the vyes had left, Max located his traveling coat only to find his spypaper was also missing.

"What are you looking for?" asked Connor, sipping his tea.

"A piece of old parchment."

"Florentine spypaper," said Connor knowingly. "The Raszna use it, too. Handy stuff."

"Well, I want mine," Max snapped. "David needs updates or he'll think we're in danger."

"You *are* in danger," Connor pointed out. "Not danger that you can't handle or I wouldn't have allowed them to bring you here. How is David?"

"Busy and probably worried."

"Is he gonna send Cooper after you?"

"Cooper's got his own assignment."

"In the thick of things, I'd expect. Can't believe he married Miss Boon! When Lucia told me, I nearly fell off my chair. Didn't think he was the marrying type. Her neither, come to think of it."

"People change," said Max, eager to shift the conversation back to the Raszna while he had Connor alone. "How many Raszna are there?"

"More than you might guess," said Connor. "There's five schools. Arcanum and Silverfalls are the biggest, but there are two more in Blys and one in what used to be Brazil."

"How many Raszna are in Blys?" asked Max. Raszna that lived overseas were too far to be helpful in a campaign against Prusias.

"A few hundred thousand?" said Connor. "Maybe half are military age."

Max whistled. If the Raszna joined Rowan, they would more than double the size of its army. "Are they good fighters?"

"There's an understatement," said Connor, having another cookie. "We didn't even have any war chiefs with us during the Grael operation. Those are some seriously big boys—even bigger than Grael."

"Really?" said Max, trying to picture a vye of that size. It was a little unsettling. "If the Raszna are so strong, why have they stayed in hiding?"

"You'd have to ask Archon that," replied Connor. "But with Astaroth's rise to power and all these wars, it hasn't been the best time to raise their profile. The Raszna aren't in a rush. They've made a good home here, but vyes are meant to live under the sun and stars. The Raszna won't stay underground forever."

"Do you think they'll be open to an alliance with Rowan?" asked Max.

Connor shrugged. "I couldn't say. The timing's good, common enemy and all that. And you're the right person for Rowan to send—*moschiach* and all. But there are some who hate Rowan. And if the people get the impression you're treating them as junior partners or inferiors, it'll never happen. Are you offering good terms?"

"I really think we are," said Max. "David put a lot of thought into them. Archon and Volsu seemed impressed."

"Well, that's a start. If you think Archon's for it, that's a good sign. His word carries a lot of weight. Even his critics respect him. Same with Lady Nico."

"Speaking of which," said Max. "Why aren't she and Eloise in vye form?"

"They rarely are. Raszna who spend a lot of their time among humans get used to wearing their human skin. It becomes more natural—so natural they don't give off any signs of being vyes."

As he finished, the bathroom door opened and Sarah emerged, trailing steam from her wooly white bathrobe. "Have they brought our—"

She left off as she spied their bags and belongings. Padding over, she grabbed the girls' packs and headed back toward the bathroom. "We'll be out in a few."

"Psst!" hissed Connor. "Lucia still mad at me?"

"Why should I tell you?" said Sarah coolly.

"Because I'm desperate."

"Well," she said, "if you're that desperate, I'll give you a hint. Lucia loves Kettlemouth and Kettlemouth loves to eat. Feed the frog, win the girl. His tin's in the red bag."

Sarah disappeared into the bathroom while Connor found the tin whose flowery design belied its slimy, foul-smelling contents. Nox sniffed with interest as Connor plucked up a limp, long-dead night crawler. Within his cage, Kettlemouth cracked a bleary eye.

Dangling the worm, Connor unlatched the cage to let its bulbous occupant squeeze out of the opening. With a *splat*, the crimson bullfrog hopped heavily onto the floor and followed Connor to a sofa, where he climbed onto the baron's lap, rolled onto his back, and proceeded to dine on worms, beetles, and horseflies in the manner to which he was accustomed. Connor moaned softly.

"This is bloody disgusting."

"I'll leave you to it," said Max as the girls came out of the bathroom. Easing Nox off his lap, he went to grab his pack. A bath would be excellent, and he was anxious to change his clothes. The Almuir finery was well and good, but he wanted to send a different message this evening. Military dress would be better. Rowan was asking the Raszna to go to war, not to a ball. When Max relayed this to the girls, Sarah and Scathach agreed readily enough, but Lucia protested.

"I want to look nice," she huffed, toweling her wet hair as she laid out several outfits.

"School robes or travel clothes," said Max. "We're Rowan ambassadors tonight."

"You and Scathach maybe," Lucia sniffed. "Sarah and I are just along for the ride."

"Nonsense," said Scathach. "You laid the groundwork."

Lucia rolled her eyes. "Please. The Raszna only revealed themselves when you and Max showed up. Our own mission was a failure."

"Au contraire," put in Connor, grimacing as he dangled another earthworm into the bullfrog's expectant mouth. "You did lay the groundwork. Eloise vouched for you in a big way. She's young but her mother's Lady Nico and her grandfather's Archon."

"Is that really true?" asked Lucia dubiously.

When Connor swore that it was, Lucia took out her Rowan robes, laid them over a chair, and removed her magechain from its velvet box. It glittered red in the room's lamplight, its rubies, fire opals, and red beryls a testament to her masteries. A magechain was part of the official Rowan uniform, but Max cleared his throat when she slid a gem-studded cuff over her wrist. Lucia headed him off.

"Not a word," she warned. "You wouldn't be here without me. And, after all, it's just a little sparkle from my Connor."

My Connor.

Max glanced over to see the Dublin youth's face break out into a happy grin. Fishing through Kettlemouth's tin, Connor plucked up a particularly juicy fly and placed it on the unfurling tongue.

Two hours later, the group's playful mood grew serious when

Eloise and Lady Nico returned, still in human form, with an armed guard to escort them to Amber Hall. Both the lady and her daughter were dressed in dark robes with amber trim.

Rowan's representatives presented a more soldierly appearance. Sarah wore her corselet of silver mail, while Max and Scathach dressed in the formal uniforms of the Red Branch: a gray tunic over black mail, along with black boots and breeches. Scathach had her poignard at her hip, but the *gae bolga* was missing from the box. When Max asked Lady Nico about this, she assured him it would be returned when he left Arcanum. Rather than argue, Max went unarmed. In any case, it would send a more confident message if he went without one. Besides, he intended to rely on his aura.

Max had to be careful, of course—his control was still imperfect—but Galia's prophecy had convinced him that his aura could be invaluable at winning the Raszna over. Archon had said the Raszna would only follow strength. If Max managed his aura properly, he might convince them they were not only following strength, but also following the *moschiach*. Even so, much would depend on Archon. How the Raszna leader positioned a Rowan alliance to believers and skeptics alike would be critical.

Amber Hall was packed when they arrived with Lady Nico. Its atmosphere was very different from the aged, scholarly reception that greeted them. The hall was hot, the air saturated with a wild, animal smell—a scent of sweat and blood and fur and musk. Conversations appeared intense and heated, sudden surges of movement and crowd flows indicating a simmering, escalating threat of violence. The Raszna seemed poised to riot.

Max had never seen vyes like these. As they paused at the threshold, his eyes fell upon some who stood twelve feet or more, nightmarish figures wearing gleaming armor of black scales. They looked like an entirely different species from the comically harmless Lupo. A few were so large they might have been mistaken for Egyptian statues of Anubis or Set. But these weren't statues; they were laughing, arguing, or howling as the mood (and drink) took them.

"Should we go in there?" whispered Lucia, looking pale.

"Don't get spooked," said Connor. "War chiefs are a rougher set than the professors. They always shake things up." He gestured toward a group of armored vyes standing near the roped-off, sacred spot of Galia's murder. "Just don't show fear, eh?"

"My God," hissed Sarah. "They're *huge*!"

Indeed they were. "Follow me," said Lady Nico, leading them along the hall's perimeter toward the burning brazier where Archon was seated at the foot of the dais. Among the nearby professors, Max saw Volsu and a tall, sleek black vye wearing pearly gray robes.

As they crossed the room, many eyes followed them. There were some in Amber Hall who had been waiting for this moment all their lives. Max carried himself with a calm, commanding arrogance that moved people out of his path. It didn't matter if anyone liked him; he needed the Raszna to respect him. He wanted his aura to be subtle—an impression of self-possessed authority and command. If he was successful, not even the wildest war chief would consider challenging him.

"*Moschiach*," gasped a voice to his left. Max turned to see an elderly female vye in crimson robes drop to her knees and bow her shaggy head. Several others followed her example, murmuring the sacred word and bowing as he passed.

It was an uncomfortable feeling. Max had seen people behave this way with Mina and it always made him uneasy. It was one thing to lead people; it was quite another to be seen as a religious figure or player in an ancient prophecy. Within the eyes of those who kneeled, Max perceived an unnerving array of emotions that ranged from love to fear to predatory hunger.

The hall grew quiet. Hundreds of eyes now followed Max, Scathach, Lucia, and Sarah as Lady Nico led them toward Archon. Connor left their group, falling back to stand with Lady Nico's guards. Max walked on, his attention upon a towering war chief who was pushing roughly through the crowd to head them off.

But when he looked directly upon Max, the fearsome vye hesitated. Having nearly reached them, he suddenly stopped as if uncertain what to do. Slowly, he lowered his great head and stood at respectful attention as they passed. Max heard Sarah exhale. The hall was nearly silent. The only sounds came from the brazier's flames.

As they reached the dais, Lady Isu helped Archon to his feet. The old vye looked solemn but pleased nonetheless to see them. He shook each of their hands in the human custom, unhurried and apparently unconcerned that the entire hall was watching in tense silence. Lady Nico introduced them to Professor Fenwulf, who was the black vye in the gray robes Max had seen with Volsu.

Fenwulf spoke perfect English with an Eastern European accent. Offering a civil bow, he asked why David Menlo was not present.

"He is with Rowan's army," Max explained.

"A shame," said the Raszna. "It is customary for leaders to treat with one another, no? Instead he sends his proxy. Not an auspicious beginning."

"He sent the *moschiach*!" hissed Fenwulf's neighbor.

Fenwulf gave his indignant colleague an amused glance. "Our people are scientists and scholars, students of the great mysteries. We can't make decisions based on the ramblings of an unbalanced woman who died a thousand years ago."

"The Apocrypha—" retorted the academic.

"—are delightful fairy tales," finished Fenwulf. "Not even Volsu believes them."

This statement threatened to trigger angry debates until Archon silenced them. Even Fenwulf ceased at Archon's command. He straightened and watched the Raszna leader as Lady Isu helped him up the dais steps. Clearing his throat, Archon's deep, hoarse voice filled Amber Hall. Speaking in an undertone, Lady Nico translated for the visitors.

"Tonight, we remember Även. My sister's grandson, our brother and friend. His bones lie at Rowan, but his spirit is free and hunts with Luperca in the afterlife. Tonight, I ask that you keep Även in your heart as I share with you matters of great importance. We must be wise, for decisions we make tonight will shape lives for many generations."

"*Moschiach!*" cried a harsh voice from the hall's far reaches. Several others took up the call, but Archon silenced them. Max gazed out at the crowd, composed. Focusing his mind, he let his aura intensify so that his presence was subtly—but undeniably—something more than human.

"*Moschiach,*" repeated Archon, glancing down at Max. "It is not so much a word as a hope—a dream that some have nurtured for a thousand years. Many here believe in Galia and pay tribute to where she was slain." He gestured to the roped area beneath the mural. "Our Även held Galia's words sacred. He believed the Hound of Rowan was the one she foretold—the enemy who would lead us out of hiding. And here he has come—here to Arcanum in the midst of war. Even Galia's critics must acknowledge this is a strange coincidence."

Fenwulf folded his arms, listening intently.

"The Hound knew nothing of our prophecies," Archon continued. "He has come to us as an emissary. As you know, Rowan marches in force upon Blys. They desire us to march with them, to join them in this war and end the reign of Prusias."

Archon held up his hand as many began to snarl and protest. "First, hear what they propose," he urged. When they were quiet, the Raszna leader shared David's proposals in a calm, authoritative voice.

Many vyes looked amazed. Even Fenwulf glanced sharply at Volsu, as though seeking confirmation that this was true. The Apocrypha scholar gave a subtle nod.

"I hold nothing back from you," declared Archon. "We cannot make this decision with half-truths or secrets between us. That is not the Raszna way. And so, I will confess that I am a believer in Galia's prophecy. I was not always, however. It was Även who made me see, Även who convinced me that Rowan did not have to be our enemy forever and that their Hound was honorable. I believe with all my heart that he is the *moschiach* of whom Galia spoke."

Archon gazed down upon Max as he said this. And Max knew the old vye was not lying, for his eyes and his voice betrayed currents of deep and powerful emotions. Reaching beneath his robe's collar, the vye removed a thick chain of interlocking silver hands. Leaning upon his cane, he raised it high above his head for all to see.

"A believer cannot lead us," he declared. "Faith alone cannot dictate the path we take. If we are to join with Rowan, Galia's skeptics must also believe it is the right course. Her skeptics must believe it is time to cast aside old grievances and embrace new possibilities. A skeptic should lead us. And thus, I bestow the title of Archon and my chain of office to the Master of Silverfalls."

Lady Nico nearly gasped. It was clear she had no idea her

father had intended to do this. Even Fenwulf looked stunned. He walked mechanically up the dais steps and bowed to receive the ponderous chain as Archon placed it around his neck.

Archon embraced his successor. "You are my brother and I have faith in you."

"Thank you, Archon."

The ancient vye smiled. "I am merely Üden once again. *You* are Archon. The chain is heavy. Wear it well."

Fenwulf's face lost every trace of its sardonic qualities. Max had to admire Üden's cunning. The Master of Silverfalls struck Max as the type to snipe from the sidelines and imply he would make a more suitable leader. When thrust in that position, however, such people often developed a greater respect for their predecessors and the burdens of leadership. This seemed to be the case with Fenwulf. He was obviously moved by Üden's gesture, but he also faced a pressing decision. The decision was not his alone, but the Archon's opinion carried considerable weight. Should he turn Rowan down and risk angering those who believed the *moschiach* stood before them? He turned to face the Raszna, his long fingers fidgeting with the chain.

"This is . . . unexpected. Üden has led our people for many years and we owe him a debt we cannot repay. Let us remember that it was Üden who strengthened Silverfalls, plumbed the Grottos, and sent his own kin to infiltrate our enemy. We have not had a finer Archon since Tiberius himself." He bowed deeply to Üden.

"But I am not Üden," he continued, his voice growing stronger. "I was the Master of Silverfalls and we do not have an Amber Hall. We do not have Galia's blood upon our floors or vow to keep these flames burning until the day of deliverance." He gestured to the brazier behind him. "Arcanum is the Raszna holy land and I was not raised amid its prophecies. I am but a pilgrim here."

Scathach frowned at these words, but Max remained impassive, aware that many eyes were watching their new Archon and himself.

"We are the Raszna!" shouted Fenwulf, spittle flying from his bared teeth. "We are strong without Rowan. Even now, the fires of rebellion burn across Harine. We did this! Our people have sunk ships, slain braymas, and sent a shiver of fear throughout Prusias's empire. We must honor Titus, Vechna, Pollox, and Anthül." He indicated four gargantuan war chiefs standing together. "They are heroes! We must honor the Lady Nico, for she has been at the heart of our operations on the surface. It was she who brought Enlyll's ruler into our fold."

To Max's surprise, the new Archon turned and gestured for Connor to join him on the dais. This Connor did, looking somewhat queasy but determined. The new Archon rested a hand on his shoulder.

"This human—this mehrùn who was once our enemy—has fought with us, bled with us, and risked all to aid our cause. Üden has named him *ruva*, our brother, and Baron Lynch has pledged his life to our people. Shall he be our brother in name only, or shall he be our brother in flesh, blood, and spirit? Shall we make him a true Raszna?"

"*Raszna!*" roared the hall's occupants.

From his robes, the Elder vyes' great elixist produced a vial of dark, murky liquid. Its stopper was a silver wolf's head and its glass was traced with glowing runes. The crowd howled as Fenwulf placed it into Connor's trembling hand.

"*Connor!*" cried Lucia. "What are you doing?"

The Dublin boy turned to her. "I'm crazy for you," he declared plainly. "I have been since our first day at Rowan. This won't change that."

Removing the stopper, Connor stared at the vial with mingled fear and excitement. Closing his eyes, he took a deep breath before gulping the potion down. After the final swallow, his body convulsed and the vial shattered in his hand. He doubled over, gasping, his hand bleeding freely upon the dais. When Lucia cried his name, Connor swiveled his head and seemed to stare through her with a face that was no longer fully human. His eyes were pale yellow and feral, their pupils mere pinpricks as his jaw protruded slightly and his ears lengthened into subtle points. Max watched, horrified and fascinated by the transformation. Was Connor really going to turn into a vye?

The answer was no—not completely. Seconds later, the transformation ceased and Connor straightened, sweating and shaking, to take stock of his new self. He had grown several inches, his hands had lengthened, and his eyes retained their wild cast, but he remained predominately human. Embracing him, Fenwulf mopped away the sweat that had beaded on his brow.

"You have begun your journey," he said. "In time, this form will look as we do, for Luperca's essence has entered you, as it did our ancestors long ago. The draught makes you a true Raszna, not a lesser vye such as those infected by the Magyarün. Connor Lynch is forever changed; he is not dead. He will always be your human shape. Try and you will see."

Nodding, Connor closed his eyes and diminished slightly. His features grew rounder and when he opened his eyes, he was the same old Connor they'd always known.

"Say something," urged Fenwulf gently. "You are Raszna now and have a right to be heard in this hall."

Max glanced at Lucia. She was crying, sobbing as Sarah comforted her. Both girls appeared in a state of disbelief. Clearing his throat, Connor wiped away his own tears and gazed out at the hushed and watchful crowd. He spoke in halting, uncertain Etruscan.

"Forgive my accent," he said. "And please forgive my mistakes. I know you will—you're family now and you can't get rid of me."

There was laughter in the hall and several vyes shouted, "Ruva!" Connor acknowledged them with a grateful smile.

"Brother," he repeated, taking a moment to exhale as the word's meaning and significance registered fully. "I like that. I feel like your brother—I've felt welcomed ever since Lady Nico brought me before you a year ago. I've never been one for destiny or prophecies, but I believe with all my heart that this was meant to happen."

Connor paused, struggling with his emotions. He turned and looked at Max. "*Moschiach*," he said. "I can't call him that. I can't even call him the Hound of Rowan. To me, he's always been Max McDaniels—the first and best friend I made at Rowan. And I can't speak to the Apocrypha or to Galia's prophecies. Only you and Archon can decide if the Raszna should join with Rowan. But I will say that Max McDaniels and David Menlo can be trusted. I'm dead certain of that, and so was Även. They will honor the peace they have promised."

Thanking them, Connor bowed and stepped aside.

"A new Raszna," Fenwulf reflected proudly. "It has been almost a hundred years since we named a human 'brother.' And this is the first time we have shared Luperca's essence with a former enemy. This is a day to mark with a white stone. But, as Üden said, the decision we face is one that will shape the lives of future generations. Üden has spoken for Rowan, but I think we must hear from them ourselves. Shall we invite the Hound to speak?"

"Yes!" howled the wild, fierce crowd. Several cries of *Moschiach* echoed in the vast hall. Turning, Fenwulf gestured for Max to join him upon the dais. Max did so, intensifying his aura even more as he climbed the steps. The more attention he paid to his aura, the more he found he could control it. It was like turning the knob of a finely made lamp. With each tiny adjustment, the flame would brighten or dim. While he could do it quickly if he chose, at the moment he increased by smooth, steady increments.

When he reached the top, he gazed out upon hundreds of anxious faces. Max took his time, surveying the audience in silence and letting them see him—truly see him for what he was. Max noticed that Sarah, Lucia, and Connor were gazing with the same expressions of frightened awe that marked the Raszna's faces. They were not looking upon their friend; they were staring at a god.

"There is no such thing as Fate," said Max, and his voice rang with irresistible authority. "Our choices shape our destinies, choices we make of our own free will. Rowan has already chosen. We have chosen to rise up openly against a tyrant who would conquer every people and every kingdom. We ask the Raszna to join us in this fight, to combine our forces against a common enemy and establish a new order—one in which Rowan and the Raszna are joined as equals."

He paused, his eyes sweeping the hall and his enraptured audience. The air was still and hot. Sweat ran in a slow, steady trickle down his back.

"Do not join with Rowan because you believe I am destined to deliver you. Join because *you* choose to have that power—the power to leave these halls and return to the world above. You have allies there. You have friends. Friends who will ride, fight, and die with you. I am but one of them."

His gaze settled upon the war chiefs, who stood at attention, their faces grim and fierce. Max knew the critical moment had come.

"Fate has no power," he declared. "The Atropos have written my name in their Grey Book. According to the Fates, I should be dead. But here I stand. Alive. Strong. Defiant. Will the Raszna stand with me?"

Their answer was deafening. Amber Hall shook with the Raszna's howls and its floor trembled with their stamping and the thud of great spears and halberds upon the ancient floor. There was a surge in the crowd, a parting as several war chiefs shouldered through the throng and took hold of the brazier's base. Its keeper backed away, knocking over the lekythos, which spilled its oil in a vast, spreading pool that ignited as the brazier crashed to the floor. The crowd surged away as sheets of flame roared up, nearly licking the amber ceiling. Leaping clear, the Raszna war chiefs joined their brothers and sisters in a wild, exultant dance.

"It seems our choice is made," said Fenwulf, backing away from the flames and turning toward Max.

"Are you with us, Archon?" Max asked.

Nodding, the vye embraced him, thumping his back as the hall's roars grew even louder. As Max disengaged, he looked again upon his friends. He was glad to see Connor and Lucia holding hands, but something in their expressions as they gazed at him triggered an unmistakable twinge of sorrow. He found the same change on Sarah's face and knew something might have changed forever. He was no longer Max McDaniels, their old classmate from Rowan. That Max was gone. They looked at him now as though he were something infinitely grander and even frightening. Sad as it was, Max could not dwell upon it. There was no sense denying who he was or what he was becoming. He took comfort in Scathach, who was also gazing at him, but with love and pride, not awe. She had been immortal in the Sidh and lived in the company of gods. Scathach would always understand him in a way that others could not.

Üden was coming up the steps, helped by Lady Isu and Lady Nico. The vye looked old and tired, but radiant—as though a great burden had been lifted from his broad shoulders. Giving Lady Isu his cane, he steadied himself before taking both Fenwulf and Max's hands in his own.

"I am proud of you," he said to Fenwulf, his daughter translating for Max's benefit. "You listened to the people."

Fenwulf bowed. "I am humbled by your faith in me."

With a grunt, Üden cupped Max's face with both hands. *"Moschiach,"* he said affectionately.

Max smiled. "I don't believe in that."

The old vye fixed him with a shrewd look. "I do."

Releasing him, Üden reached into his robes and brought forth the *gae bolga* and returned it to its proper owner. The short sword hummed as Max's fingers closed upon the warm handle. Max buckled the scabbard to his baldric, happy to have the weapon's reassuring weight at his side.

"I need my parchment," Max said. "David Menlo will want to know we've reached an agreement."

Fenwulf nodded. "I'll want to speak with your Director as soon as possible. It will take time to muster our forces and march upon Prusias. And we must discuss strategy. United, the Raszna and Rowan are formidable, but so is our common foe. Prusias controls the Workshop. His defenses are considerable."

"We have someone working on that," said Max.

"Who?"

"A professional."

~ 18 ~

THE PROFESSIONAL

Over the course of his career, William Cooper had been many things: a spy, thief, soldier, saboteur, inquisitor, rescuer, and assassin. Many jobs. Many hats. But all of them executed by a man who took his work very seriously. For William Cooper was a professional who did whatever was required to complete his mission. At the moment, that meant killing a man.

The engineer was no longer resisting. He stared at Cooper's reflection in the gleaming boiler, stared with blank astonishment at the pale stranger who had suddenly appeared, clamped a strong arm about his throat, and brought his life to a swift and silent conclusion. When the eyes went dim, Cooper gently lowered the man's body to the floor.

"Is it over?"

The voice was Hazel's. She was huddled in the corner, her eyes averted from the scene.

"It is."

Crouching, Cooper methodically stripped the man's watch and security badge. The engineer was in his twenties, very fit, and possessed the blue-eyed, Eurasian features that were a common by-product of the Workshop's eugenics programs. Removing a slim computer from the man's breast pocket, Cooper pressed the engineer's still-warm thumb against its biometric sensor. The dark screen illuminated.

"What are you doing?" Toby whispered from behind Hazel.

The smee had taken the form of a gray rat when the engineer entered the boiler room. The man's unexpected appearance had startled Hazel, who'd knocked over a wrench that had been propped against a wall. It had clattered to the floor, causing the engineer to draw a sidearm and hurry along the boilers toward the dark corner where they'd been resting. Four steps later, the engineer was dead.

Ignoring Toby's questions, Cooper studied the computer screen as he scrolled through a series of menus. He soon found what he was looking for—a detailed map of the Verilius Depot, an underground train station near what used to be Frankfurt, Germany. A tiny blinking dot appeared in a mechanicals room in the station's northwest quadrant.

There we are. His eyes darted to a tiny grid of updating data. He checked the engineer's watch and swiped past various screens to locate the latest train schedules.

Cooper was anxious to get moving again. They had already violated one of his basic rules by staying in one place for more than twenty-four hours. And now someone had happened by. Killing the engineer had not solved their problem; it was simply a stopgap as they sought a way into the Workshop.

Their problems had started with Max's clones. The assassins had left Cooper badly injured—two broken wrists and a concussion that had him seeing double for a week. He had recovered at Shrope Hovel where Hazel had set his bones, accelerated their healing with spellwork, and Mum and Bob had cooked for him in their old, familiar way. The impatient haglings had not waited for him to mend. They had set out the morning after the Naming, clopping off in their little wagons to rescue their aunt Gertie from the Workshop museums, where she was on display. They'd taken the Spindlefingers goblin with them, for it was his clan that maintained the Workshop's trains and could smuggle them inside the depot.

That was over two months ago. By now, the haglings would have succeeded or failed in their quest. The latter was more likely, but Cooper nurtured a sliver of hope that somewhere a confused and disheveled Gertie was on her way back to Shrope Hovel. He didn't dwell on it, however. He had his own operation to complete and he was well behind schedule. Every day Rowan's forces were getting a little closer to Blys. Unless Cooper was able to activate the Workshop asset and infiltrate Prusias's capital, Rowan would face a slew of advanced and mechanized defenses. If that happened, the odds of a successful siege dwindled considerably. He could not fail.

He'd always worked best and quickest alone. Now he had partners. Given his injuries, Hazel had utterly refused to leave him while Toby tagged along, reluctant to remain with the hags. While his wife and the smee had talents that made them useful, they nevertheless slowed him down. Partners demanded explanations; partners wanted a voice in decisions; partners needed sleep.

Sleep. Cooper had to admit he could use some. He hadn't been dozing for more than ten minutes when the engineer stumbled upon their hiding place. The last rest he'd taken was over three days ago before they'd snuck aboard the freight chutes that brought them down here. He wasn't in crisis yet—he could endure several more days before his capabilities would decline—but it was important to sleep when one could. And Hazel needed rest more than she ever had. He longed to send her back to Rowan.

But there was no turning back now. Not for any of them. Weeks of cautious, stealthy spycraft had gotten them from Shrope Hovel across the Channel and then another four hundred miles until they reached the outskirts of Verilius and the depot two miles beneath it. They were nearing his operation's first objective—activating an undercover asset that was stationed in the Workshop's headquarters some twenty miles away. The remaining distance should have been trivial, for the Spindlefinger had sworn there were trains that shuttled regularly between their location and the Workshop. But apparently the goblin's information was out of date.

Cooper had spent the last day and a half sneaking about the depot and getting familiar with its operations. From what he could tell, it was used almost exclusively to store and transport raw materials. The station rumbled as sleek trains carrying coal and iron, grain and chemicals came screeching into the cavernous facility for equipment checks, maintenance, and repairs by the Spindlefingers. These trains were not bound for the Workshop headquarters, but for manufacturing or processing facilities located throughout Prusias's kingdom. While there was a track connecting the Workshop to Prusias's capital, it no longer seemed to be in use. Cooper had watched its tunnel for over twenty-four hours without seeing any trains or even work crews that might have been making repairs. By all appearances, Track 11 was not in use.

The engineer's computer, however, would confirm it. Locating the train schedules, Cooper saw that Track 11 had been grayed out.

"All right," he muttered, turning to the others. "Here's the plan. We're going to move and move quickly. No trains are running through here to the Workshop. We'll have to go on foot."

Toby moaned.

Cooper cut off the smee's inevitable protest. "It's not that far, just twenty-three miles. The Workshop's deeper than this place, so it'll be downhill. The real issue is what we'll find when we reach the end. The tunnel could be sealed off."

"Is there an alternative?" asked Hazel, cleaning her glasses.

"We could sneak aboard a train bound for another destination and try to connect to the Workshop from there."

"That sounds better," said the rat. "Ride in comfort, I say."

"It would be on a cargo train," Cooper reminded him.

"Maybe someone's shipping pillows," mused the smee hopefully.

"What do you think we should do?" asked Hazel.

Cooper massaged his wrists, grimacing slightly at the pain. The bones had mended but were not fully healed. Discomfort was constant and could be excruciating when he exerted himself. He tamped the pain down to a place where it would not distract him.

"The tunnel would be quickest," he said. "If the grade isn't too steep, I can run that far in ninety minutes to scout if it's open. The return would be slower. Maybe six hours there and back."

"Be realistic. You haven't slept in days."

Cooper waved off Hazel's concern. "I'm fine. I'm more

worried about you. You can't run that kind of distance. Especially not in your condition."

Toby looked at her. "What condition is that, pray tell?"

With an almost shy smile, Hazel patted her stomach. "I'm pregnant. Just a few months, but there's no use keeping it a secret anymore."

The smee offered his hearty congratulations. "You know, I won't be insulted if you name him Toby. Just a thought. Although as I'm currently a rat, I'm partial to cheese names. 'Manchego' has a certain flair. . . ."

"Enough," said Cooper. "We have to move quickly—that engineer might be implanted with sensors that track his whereabouts. His computer certainly is. Toby, do you think you could fly down the tunnel as a bird and see what's at the far end?"

"I suppose," reflected the smee. "Although the ol' latissimus nub won't like it. What kind of bird?"

"Something small with endurance," Cooper answered. "You'll have to fly over forty miles there and back as fast as you possibly can."

"That might not be necessary," remarked Hazel. "Mystics can solve our problem."

"Not shadow walking," said Cooper flatly.

"No," said Hazel. "Nothing that risky. What I'm thinking of is a technique where my spirit leaves my body but remains in this world. The range isn't limitless, of course, but I might be able to send it far enough. In any case, it's worth a shot. I could be there and back in minutes while leaving Toby rested in case he has to carry me."

"What are the risks?" Cooper asked. Every drug had side effects; so did every spell. He used magic as sparingly as possible.

"It's rather tiring," Hazel conceded. "And my spirit would be out in the open, vulnerable. If something happened to it . . ."

"Yes?"

She shrugged. "I could die."

Cooper shook his head. "Absolutely not."

Hazel laid her hand over his. "Agent Cooper, it's a good risk. In five or ten minutes we can learn whether that tunnel can get us into the Workshop proper. It's only dangerous if there happens to be a malicious spirit lingering between here and there. The chances of that are slim. Agreed?"

He nodded. It was not his nature to quibble with facts or truth, even when his emotions were involved. "What do you need from me?"

"Keep watch on the door," she said. "A disruption while my spirit is outside my body could create problems."

He did as she said, scooping up Toby and padding quietly to the door. The room was located at the end of a corridor and its door had a grating set in its lower half so that he could sit and see if anyone was coming. Seven minutes had elapsed since the engineer had entered the room and met his end. He doubted anyone would miss him so soon. He glanced down at the palm-sized computer and its blinking location signal.

"When she's finished, you'll carry her," he muttered to Toby, more bluntly than he'd intended.

"Of course," replied the smee. "A mule will be just the thing for a steep grade."

"Good man."

The smee was about to reply when they both heard a sharp intake of breath. Looking down the row of boilers, Cooper saw Hazel sitting cross-legged before several inscriptions she'd drawn on the floor. Their glow illuminated not only her unseeing face, but also the contours of a wraithlike shape beside her. It shimmered like heat waves, a subtle rippling in the air, before it turned and strode through the wall.

Cooper tried to relax, but tension gripped his shoulders like talons. He had sincere faith in his wife's abilities. After all, Hazel Boon had been all the talk when she had been a student. *She had been considered Rowan's great Mystics prodigy until David Menlo arrived.* But it was agonizing to watch her sitting nearby, her mouth agape, eyes rolled back, her body twitching and shuddering. The Hazel he loved was gone; only her flesh remained in this hot, humming room.

The computer in his hand jolted with vibration. A message in German was flashing on its screen: *Need you back here—there's news from Blys. Leave the boiler. Spindles can fix.*

Cooper cursed silently. A digital keypad appeared on the tiny screen. He carefully typed out his response: *Five minutes. Almost finished.*

The next message came almost immediately: *Five minutes, but Anschutz says no more. You know how he gets.*

Anschutz might get more than he bargained for, thought Cooper grimly. Stealing over to the engineer's body, he quickly stripped it of its uniform. The man was shorter than Cooper, but their builds were roughly equivalent. Shoving his own clothes inside his pack, he gathered their things from the room's far corner and set them by the door. Digging through one of the pack's front pockets, he retrieved a leather flask with a silver topper.

"Really, William," chided Toby from where he was sitting by the door. "Drinking at a time like this? Well, a tot can't hurt, I suppose. Give it here, eh?"

"You don't want this," said Cooper, shaking the flask to stir up any contents.

"What's in it?"

"Ferrites."

Toby gasped. "Those treasure-destroying crawlies? Why do you have those?"

"Because they eat through metal."

"And flesh." The smee shivered. "And bone. And whatever else they can get. To think I've been loitering next to ferrites!"

While the smee continued to reflect on ferrites and their unsavory reputation, Cooper returned to scanning the train schedules. A shipment of machine oil was due to depart on Track 6 in fourteen minutes. The device vibrated as a message appeared.

Where are you? Anschutz is getting angry.

Cooper quickly typed a response. *I said five minutes. Tell him he can come and get his hands dirty.*

Are you serious?

Yes.

Your funeral.

Toby has been reading over his shoulder. His whiskers bristled. "Are you mad?" he exclaimed. "The supervisor is going to come down!"

"Only if we're lucky," said Cooper, glancing over at Hazel. She was breathing quickly, almost to the point of hyperventilating. Her eyes were vacant, but now and again, her face twisted into a painful grimace. Her spirit must be nearing its limits. A sharp cry escaped her lips.

Before Cooper could go to her, he heard someone coming down the corridor. One person, making swift and angry footfalls.

Herr Anschutz.

Toby scuttled out of sight behind a boiler as Cooper unsheathed his kris. Its blade undulated like a serpent, its weight and balance reassuringly familiar.

Anschutz never saw who or what ended his life. He stormed into the room, glared about for his subordinate, and stiffened as Cooper's blade made its swift, silent entry into the base of his skull. There was very little blood. It was like turning off a switch.

"What did we gain by that?" hissed Toby.

"Time," said Cooper, wiping the kris's point. "Anschutz is a bully. Nobody's going to pester him. Not when he's on the warpath."

Sheathing his knife, Cooper hurried over to check on Hazel. Her face had relaxed and her breathing was less ragged. He wanted to take her pulse, but he was wary of touching her. Physical contact could be dangerous to those in a trance.

The inscriptions flared suddenly as a shadowy form emerged from the wall and stepped back into Hazel's body. With a jolt, she blinked and her mismatched eyes rolled forward to focus on her husband's face.

"The tunnel's open," she gasped. "There are guards at the station's entrance to the Workshop, but few along the platforms. Dear Lord, I'm spent . . ."

She took a moment to catch her breath. Sweat was running freely down her forehead while her entire body trembled.

"That was difficult," she confessed. "The farther my spirit went, the more it wanted to come back. The pain is rather excruciating. I almost gave up."

Cooper kissed her dampened forehead. "But you didn't."

She noticed Anschutz's body by the door. "What? Who in the bloody hell is that?"

"A supervisor," said Cooper, scrolling through the train schedules. "This train should work. We've got five minutes to get them aboard."

"Who's boarding what train?" she asked, clearly puzzled.

There was no time to explain. After telling Toby to become something even smaller, he asked Hazel if she could fade. Fading was a type of illusion that required little energy and could be very useful under the right circumstances. It didn't work in bright light or if the caster needed to move quickly. And it was useless if someone had already spotted you. But for sneaking through the shadows, fading was just the thing.

"Of course I can fade," said Hazel indignantly. "Any Third Year can fade."

"Good," said Cooper, showing her the map on his device's screen. "I want you and Toby to sneak into Tunnel Eleven, go a hundred yards, and wait for me. Got it?"

She nodded. "What are you doing?"

He hooked a thumb at the bodies. "Buying time. With any luck, we'll be in the Workshop before anyone realizes there are intruders. Hurry now. If I'm not there in ten minutes, go on without me and make contact with the asset. I'll catch up if I can."

Toby was already waiting by the door, a tiny gray mouse no bigger than a toddler's thumb. Rising, Hazel erased the floor inscriptions and shouldered her pack. Giving Cooper a peck, she promptly faded from view. In the dim red light of the boiler room, she was practically translucent. A moment later, she slipped out the door with Toby running beside her.

Cooper checked the opening at the base of Anschutz's skull. Tearing a strip of cloth from the supervisor's shirt hem, he wrapped the wound so that it wouldn't leak. Arranging the bodies side by side, Cooper leaned one against each shoulder so he could lift them together. With a grunt, he stood, balancing them like two sacks of grain before slipping out the door.

He walked steadily, shifting his burdens slightly, his attention fixed on the corridor ahead and the vast, octagonal cavern beyond. There was no need to be quiet. The depot echoed with droning loudspeakers, idling engines, and the barking of goblins as Spindlefingers scurried about in greasy overalls.

It was mostly goblins on the depot floor, doing the work, driving the cargo loaders, and seeing to the massive trains idling on the tracks, their engines sending up clouds of vapor that obscured the distant roof. Along the far wall, past a yard of unused train cars, were the freight elevators they had ridden down from Verilius.

As he'd done when they entered the depot, Cooper disguised himself as a Spindlefinger. In his mind's eye, he was long-armed and potbellied with a broad back that bent beneath its load. He wasn't carrying bodies but two barrels of machine oil to add to a shipment scheduled to leave on Track 6.

When he was a Rowan student, William Cooper had been marked as a future Agent in only his Second Year. His athleticism, analytic capabilities, and temperament were ideally suited for the role. When graduation loomed, it was common knowledge that Cooper had received offers from every prominent field office, as well as the elite Vanguard. But almost no one knew about the offer he'd very nearly accepted. It had come from Annika Kraken, the new Head of Mystics, who had wanted to hire him as an Instructor of Advanced Illusion. Cooper was, she maintained, the most gifted phantasmal she'd ever taught.

He didn't take the job, of course. He elected to become a field Agent and would soon earn a place among the Red Branch. But Cooper never lost his talent or affinity for illusion. Indeed, it went hand and glove with his profession. Illusion was all about conviction. The best practitioners truly believed that whatever they were seeing, hearing, smelling, and experiencing was *real*—at least in some corner of their minds. Conviction strengthened the effect. In Cooper's mind, he was not a Rowan Agent hiding behind an illusory guise; he *was* a Spindlefinger goblin who was rushing to load two final casks of oil.

Upon seeing Cooper, the foreman grunted and pointed irritably at a flashing light above Tunnel 6. Hurrying up a mechanized platform, Cooper lowered the engineers and their computers into a cargo hold, propping them amid the crates and barrels. Once he had placed the devices in their owner's hands, he climbed back down the platform. As he descended, the foreman blew a whistle and waved to another goblin up by the engine. A horn sounded, lights on the train flashed, and its cars sealed shut. As the train rolled toward the tunnel, the attending Spindlefingers ran alongside, catching hold of side rails and shimmying down its length until they disappeared within a compartment beneath a central car. Spindlefingers traveled with their trains.

But not this Spindlefinger. Cooper trotted along for a few meters but stopped as he passed a stack of crates. Walking around them, he reversed course and made his unhurried way toward Track 11. Halfway there, he stopped to buckle his imaginary shoe on the platform between Tracks 8 and 9. As he did so, he casually splashed his flask of ferrites on the tracks and underside of the nearest engine. The tiny organisms were suspended in an oily liquid but would activate once they came in contact with the metal. Within a day or two, they would have eaten through sheet metal, rails, cables, pinions, and a host of other mechanical necessities. In a perfect world, trains would break down en route and disrupt vital shipments or supply lines. Rising, Cooper continued on his way. When he passed behind a mound of coal, he promptly faded and slipped unseen into Tunnel 11.

Hazel and Toby were right where he'd asked them to wait. Once he reached them, the smee changed into a sturdy mule and Cooper helped Hazel onto his back.

"What did you do?" she asked.

"I stowed the engineers on a train bound for Vrusk. Even if their computers are tracked, it'll be hours before anyone can confirm what happened to them. Hopefully that gives us a little time. And some ferrites might have found their way onto some trains and tracks."

"Sabotage!" cried the smee, with something like relish.

"A little here, a little there," said Cooper, before catching sight of Hazel's frown. "What's the matter?"

"I wish we hadn't had to kill those men," she said quietly.

"So do I," said Cooper. "But we're on a DarkMatter Operation that could save thousands of lives. I'm not wasting winks over those two. The Workshop built Prusias's dreadnoughts and pinlegs. Their creatures attacked Rowan and killed our friends. Their creatures killed Richter. They're not innocent civilians, Hazel."

She pursed her lips. "You're right. I know you are. I've just . . . never seen someone killed in cold blood before."

Cooper looked hard at both of his companions. "We're spies in enemy territory. If we're caught, we'll be interrogated and executed. If danger threatens, our first option is to hide. If we're discovered, I'll neutralize the threat. If I need your help, I expect you to give everything you have. Understood?"

Hazel and Toby nodded. Tightening the straps of his pack, Cooper turned and started a brisk pace.

The tunnel's grade was steep but perfectly consistent. Its rails hummed with electric current but were not dangerous to touch. The walls were bare, smooth rock with fluorescent lights every fifty meters. Every hundred meters, emergency alcoves were cut into the rock so workers could take shelter from approaching trains.

Cooper registered these facts and a hundred others as he jogged along. He no longer needed to think about such things; he just did them out of habit. His brain was constantly observing, processing data, and planning contingencies. The most challenging operations rarely went according to plan. The best Agents were able to assess, adapt, and improvise when circumstances changed. It was what separated the good from the great. Antonio de Lorca had been a genius at improvisation—a born guerilla who had passed his knowledge down to his protégé.

He focused on his first objective: to find and activate an undercover asset. This part of the plan had worried him from the onset. Years before, the asset in question had volunteered for psychnosis, an obscure discipline that many viewed with skepticism. In theory, the practice enabled one to implant an agenda within the subject's subconscious using a combination of mystics and psychological techniques. If successful, the effects were impossible to detect; the asset had no memory of the experience, bore no trace of enchantment, and would pass any lie detector. The asset did not become a robot or act suddenly out of character, but gravitated slowly toward beliefs and actions that aligned with the implanted instructions. The process was so subtle, so gradual that its critics questioned whether it actually worked.

Richter was a believer. We'll see if she was right.

They'd only been running twenty minutes when the tunnel started rumbling behind them. Workshop trains traveled very fast. There was an alcove ahead. He had to act quickly.

"Ignis!"

Yellow flames engulfed the tunnel behind them, racing up the walls to meet at the ceiling. Slamming his shoulder into Toby, Cooper steered the panicked smee toward a nearby safety alcove. From behind came the deafening blare of an emergency horn. Someone aboard the speeding train had seen the flames and was trying to brake, giving them a few precious seconds.

Snatching Hazel off Toby's back, Cooper pulled her into the alcove as the smee blinked back into a mouse. They pressed themselves flat as the train screeched past them in a great whoosh of hot wind. Its cars were three feet away, a blur of metal and lights that slowed to a groaning halt.

Down the tunnel, Cooper heard human voices, anxious and impatient. An engineer was shouting to the Spindlefingers in the goblins' own tongue.

"What's he saying?" Cooper whispered to Toby. As smees utilized many disguises, they spoke any number of languages.

"He wants the goblins to check for damage," squeaked the mouse.

Already, Cooper could hear the patter of small boots and the jingling of tools as Spindlefingers fanned out along and beneath the train. Tapping Hazel, Cooper mouthed the word *fade*.

The two blended out of sight just as a lanky goblin squeezed past the alcove, shining a flashlight along the train's undercarriage and muttering to himself. Cooper waited several seconds before poking his head out. To his left, the goblin was making his way down the cars. To his right, the train's lights were illuminating clouds of water vapor and silhouetting a distant goblin. He turned quickly to his companions.

"There's a compartment up ahead where the Spindlefingers ride. We could sneak aboard and take the train right into the Workshop station. Better cover."

Hazel looked anxious. "What about the goblins?"

"I'll handle it. Now or never."

Hazel and Toby nodded. Squeezing his pack against his chest, Cooper slid out into the narrow opening and led the others down the line of cars. The train was vibrating, hissing now and again as steam shot from exhaust valves.

Thirty feet later, he saw the Spindlefingers' compartment. It was built into the bottom of the central car, a virtual crawl space with a hard bench and several large tool cases. The compartment was empty.

Cooper pointed Hazel and Toby to the far end, crawling through the narrow opening and wishing for the millionth time he wasn't quite so tall. The space was cramped and stank of grease and goblin, but it would do. Once they had squeezed into the corner, Cooper stacked several toolboxes as a buffer between them and the goblins that would soon return.

"Keep still and quiet," he whispered. "They may not notice us."

Hazel faded as Toby became a beetle. Folding his legs up so that his knees touched his chin, Cooper went absolutely still and imagined he was the compartment's bulkhead.

The Spindlefingers returned in ones and twos, climbing nimbly into the compartment and sliding down its bench. A few sniffed once or twice and looked puzzled, but a horn blared and the floor hummed as though a surge of electric current had been restored. Two more Spindlefingers clambered aboard even as the train started to move. The stumbled into their fellows, triggering squeaks and snarls as they jostled for seats. One barked at the Spindlefinger nearest Cooper, gesturing that he should scoot farther down. The goblin shrugged, hooking a thumb at the heavy toolboxes and illusory wall. Cursing him, they slid the grating shut and squeezed in as best they could.

As the train accelerated, Cooper counted their blessings. Arriving via train was far preferable to emerging from a tunnel on foot. Illusions were less effective when viewed through a camera's cold, objective lens. And the Workshop's cameras were probably attuned to pick up heat signatures—signatures that might be rather conspicuous sneaking out of a decommissioned train tunnel. Trains meant busy crews and lots of noise and activity. Cooper had made do with far less.

It took less than seven minutes to complete the journey. While the tunnel lights zipped past, the Spindlefingers played a game with cards fashioned from copper disks. There were jeers and hoots and money trading hands. At one point, Cooper's neighbor actually elbowed him in his excitement. But Cooper didn't move and the elated goblin didn't notice anything amiss.

As the train slowed, the Spindlefingers packed away their game and stared straight ahead in anticipation of their arrival. Their dull, unblinking expressions reminded Cooper of commuters he used to pickpocket as a boy on the London Underground. That world seemed something from a dream.

The tunnel's rock gave way to fabricated walls and platforms of chrome and glass. The compartment brightened, causing the Spindlefingers to shield their small, reddish eyes in unison. Cooper didn't move; he simply concentrated on maintaining the illusion and looked for signage that might indicate their level or location.

He had visited the Workshop's headquarters on two occasions. The first was when he was relatively new to the Red Branch and snuck in with Antonio de Lorca to spy on the engineers' latest initiatives. The second was several years ago when he'd accompanied Max McDaniels and David Menlo on a quest to recover Bram's Key. Cooper's memory was excellent and he recalled everything he had seen on both visits—the Workshop's layout, research areas, dormitories, and transportation networks.

The main building was an inconceivably enormous pyramid set within an even larger cavern four miles underground. He had arrived by car on his last visit and there had been no visible train tracks leading into the gargantuan facility. Unless something had changed, they would be arriving at a sublevel somewhere beneath the main gates. Living quarters were located in the pyramid's upper levels, reached by pod tubes that could be accessed at frequent intervals throughout the facility.

When the train eased to a stop, the Spindlefingers clambered out, one after the other, and filed toward the back of the train.

"We wait ten seconds and go," Cooper whispered. "How do you feel, Hazel?"

"Rather exhilarated."

He glanced over to gauge her sarcasm. There was none. His wife was beaming.

"This cloak-and-dagger stuff's exciting," she observed. "I'll be in the Red Branch yet."

Cooper grinned. "Forget fading, then. Light's too bright anyway. Can you manage a nondescript engineer?"

She flexed her fingers. "I think so."

"And how about you, Toby?" asked Cooper.

The smee fired up at once. "Child's play!"

"Good. Follow my lead and let me do any talking."

Three Workshop engineers climbed out of the cramped compartment and walked forward through clouds of cool water vapor. The station was large and brightly lit with half a dozen tracks and platforms. A robotic feminine voice was speaking over a loudspeaker, welcoming the arrivals.

As Cooper climbed a stairwell onto the platform, he saw that passengers were this train's only cargo. And not just any passengers, but senior personnel and dignitaries from the capital. Among the engineers and diplomatic liaisons, Cooper counted ten imps, three kitsune, and an imperious rakshasa wearing golden robes and an expression of bored, smoldering disdain. This certainly explained the unscheduled train; rakshasa went wherever they liked whenever they chose. Judging by the anxious expressions on the Workshop guards' faces, this visit was a surprise.

Setting down his pack, Cooper pretended to search for something, anxious for the demons to go well ahead before they followed. While Toby's shape-shifting could fool most demons, Cooper's and Hazel's illusions would not. Demons could perceive auras. Spying two mehrùn would make a rakshasa very curious.

While the rakshasa posed a potential problem, he also served as a wonderful distraction. The demon's presence so terrified and overwhelmed the engineers that no one gave Cooper and his companions a second glance as they brought up the rear and left the platforms through the sliding doors.

They followed the group for fifty yards into a glassed atrium with artificial sunlight before Cooper led them off down another hallway. He walked confidently, pretending to be reading something on the imaginary device his illusion was holding while Toby and Hazel trailed behind him. A pair of junior engineers was waiting at a pod bank. Cooper halted beside them, nodded hello, and went back to consulting his imaginary computer. The engineers continued their quiet conversation.

A pod arrived within thirty seconds, a silvery egg-shaped vehicle that slid to a smooth, hovering stop within the tube. The junior engineers stepped aside so their superiors could enter first. Cooper brushed past them and occupied one of the molded seats that ringed the pod's interior. Hazel and Toby sat next to him as the two engineers filed in. They remained standing.

"Where are you going, sir?" asked the first in German.

"Dormitories," muttered Cooper, his accent flawless.

"Eh, which ones?"

"You tell me," said Cooper irritably, flicking his pretend computer screen. "I need Dr. Barrett. Jason Barrett. This damn thing isn't working." He flicked it again.

"Would you like me to look at it?" offered the engineer.

Cooper shook his head. "Just look up Dr. Barrett for me, eh? It's urgent that I speak with him."

The other engineer produced his computer at once and began searching. "It's a busy day for everyone, I see."

"Why?" asked Cooper. "What are you two doing?"

"Joining the search party," replied the first. "There's been a security breach."

Leaning forward, Cooper casually moved his hand toward the blade at his hip. "You're joking."

"Not at all, sir," replied the second. "Something's been stolen."

"What?"

The engineers exchanged embarrassed glances.

"A hag."

"Pardon?"

"A hag, sir. There was a specimen in the Exotics wing, and it was discovered missing this morning."

"When was it stolen?"

"We don't yet know," said the first. "The security camera was disabled and a hole was cut in the exhibit glass. The hag was taken and a note was left in her place."

"What did the note say?"

The engineers reddened. "Obscenities, sir. Misspelled obscenities. They don't bear repeating."

Cooper stifled a smile. "It must be a prank. Who on earth would steal a hag?"

"We don't know, sir, but Dr. Rasmussen's furious. He's taken a special interest in the case."

I'll bet he has, thought Cooper. Bellagrog, Mum, and the haglings had nearly devoured the Workshop's former leader to avenge their cousin's captivity. The idea that there might be hags nearby—stealthy, vengeful hags—must have terrified him.

"Well," said Cooper, "good luck with your search. Now, if you will tell me where I might find Dr. Barrett."

The second engineer tapped his screen. "SE-Sixteen, Apartment Four," he said. When his colleague input the destinations, the pod proceeded smoothly ahead. It went about two hundred yards before reaching a vertical tube and accelerating straight up, gliding serenely past a dozen floors until they were staring down at the vast, interior spaces of the main level where redwood trees stretched toward artificial sunlight that filtered down from a false ceiling hundreds of feet above. The last time Cooper had seen those trees, he was marching out the front gate where Astaroth, Marley Augur, and an armed host were waiting for them.

The trees disappeared as their pod glided up past several floors dedicated to research and laboratories. It came to a stop and the young engineers bid them good day and departed. When the doors closed, Toby exhaled.

"How can you stand it?" he asked, mopping his forehead.

"What?" asked Cooper.

"You're hiding in plain sight!"

"So are you."

The smee pinched his fleshy cheeks. "But this is actually me! You two are just sitting there, plain as day. You might as well write *spy* on your foreheads."

"You already know who we are," Hazel pointed out. "Your brain expects to see us and thus you do. Have a look at our reflections."

The smee glanced at their images, faint in the pod's smooth, curving glass: a middle-aged engineer and a younger one whose features were not dissimilar to the man Cooper had strangled. Mirrors strengthened illusions. A person who questioned an illusion in the flesh would almost always believe it in a mirror. Cooper had exploited this fact on many occasions. Once or twice it had saved his life.

"Well, I suppose I can unclench," sighed the smee. "And apparently the haglings have rescued the hapless Gertie. Good for them. I never thought they could pull it off, the beastly nippers. What's the plan when we reach this Dr. Barrett's room?"

Cooper rose as the pod slowed. "We knock. If he's not home, we hide and wait."

"And this fellow attended Rowan?"

"Valedictorian," said Hazel. "An excellent student."

Toby clucked his tongue triumphantly. "And now he's our spy!"

Cooper looked down at the smee. "Jason's under psychnosis. He doesn't think he's on our side anymore. Stay back until until the trigger phrase takes hold. I may need to subdue him."

The pod came to a halt, its doors opening as it hovered before an intersection of modern residential corridors. Leaving the pod, they entered a profoundly subdued environment whose neutral walls were smooth, the lighting recessed, the artwork tastefully bland. A piano sonata played from unseen speakers, but beneath the music, one could detect the Brownian buzz of energy coursing through the walls and floors. A woman's voice, calm and artificial, interrupted the music.

"This is a security alert. Unauthorized persons may be at large in the Workshop. The museum wing is closed until further notice. Report any suspicious activity to Central Command. Have a productive day."

Following posted signs, they made their way to SE16, which was a corridor in the pyramid's southeast quadrant. Soft music was playing once again as they passed a young engineer munching a piece of fruit and clutching a computer tablet as she trudged off to work the evening shift in some laboratory. She nodded hello, her features eerily similar to those of Hazel's illusion. The Workshop was a great believer in the economies of scale. When they liked something, they made it again and again. This extended to human beings.

Jason Barrett answered on the third knock. Apparently he had been asleep, for he stood shirtless in the doorway, looking tousled and somewhat annoyed. "What is it?" He yawned. "This is the first I've slept in two—"

Cooper leaned forward. "Three little kittens have lost their mittens."

Upon hearing the rhyme, Jason's face went slack. He opened his mouth as if to speak and promptly shut it again. He looked profoundly lost and disoriented. "Am I dreaming?" he wondered aloud.

"No. Invite us in and we'll explain."

The young man stood aside as they stepped in, gazing at Toby and Hazel as if they, too, were apparitions. When he closed the door, Cooper dispelled his illusion.

"You know who I am?"

Jason nodded slowly, his eyes traveling over Cooper's scarred, disfigured face. "Are you here to kill me?"

"Of course not," Hazel interjected, dropping her own disguise and becoming a familiar face. "It's excellent to see you, Jason Barrett. You're looking well."

"Miss Boon?"

"Mrs. Cooper," she corrected, smiling. She eyed the apartment and its stark kitchenette with pinched disapproval. "Do you have any tea?"

"Just coffee," said Jason, pointing absently at a machine.

"You're worse than Menlo," she sighed, breezing past him to investigate. "Will I need an advanced degree to operate this?"

"Just hit the green button," Jason murmured, his eyes falling on Toby. "Who are you?"

The smee's engineer puffed out his chest.

"His name's Toby," said Cooper, heading off the smee before he could recite various monikers and exploits. "Have a seat, Jason, and I'll explain."

The young man sat at a small dining table, staring at his

visitors as though still trying to process what was really happening. Placing his pack upon the table, Cooper sat across from him.

"When you graduated from Rowan, you volunteered for a process called psychnosis. Under its influence, you became a staunch Workshop convert capable of earning trust and advancement. All these years, you have been our man on the inside—you just didn't know it." From his pack, Cooper retrieved a slim metal box and slid it across the table.

"What's that?" asked Jason, looking anxiously at it.

"A package. From yourself."

Frowning, Jason picked up the box and turned it over in his hands. When he tried to open it, he found that it was locked. "I think it needs a key."

Cooper gestured at Dr. Barrett's neck. "You're wearing it."

The engineer's hand drifted up to a chain that had his parents' initials engraved on a small charm. Removing it, he examined its length before squinting at its unusual clasp. When he fit the clasp into the keyhole, the box's cover sprang open. Inside was an envelope. Breaking the seal, Jason removed a folded letter.

"This is my handwriting," he breathed, his eyes moving slowly down the page. Jason's eyes widened in what seemed like blossoming awareness. Rowan's top psychnosist—a scholar named Vivek—had told Cooper the subject's letter almost always ensured successful reorientation. It looked like Vivek may have been right.

Putting down the letter, Jason closed his eyes and massaged his temples. Hazel set down a coffee before him and took the neighboring seat. When Jason opened his eyes, a steady, determined gaze had replaced the look of foggy bewilderment.

"I remember," he said. "I remember everything."

"Good," said Cooper. "Because I need to know everything you do about Prusias's Workshop defenses."

"Okay," said Jason, drumming the table with his fingers. "Let me think of the best way to break it down.

Revived with coffee, Jason provided them with a concise overview. It was a sobering discussion. Even if Rowan's army could win its way to the city gates, Jason did not believe they could possibly break or force the gates open. The walls were no better, standing hundreds of feet high and constructed of something called folded masonry.

"Perhaps we could scale them," Toby suggested.

Jason shook his head. "Their surface is almost frictionless—far slicker and smoother than anything you've ever touched."

"Are all the walls made of that?" asked Cooper.

"No," said Jason. "Too expensive. Just the outer curtain. Even if you could somehow breach the walls or gates, five dreadnoughts are stationed within."

"Are the dreadnoughts still controlled by imps?" inquired Hazel hopefully.

"Not after David Menlo possessed the ones attacking Rowan. Prusias banned that approach. These dreadnoughts can't be summoned instantly to a location by a pinlegs but they can't be possessed either. They use artificial intelligence."

It was Cooper's turn to massage his temples. Until David had possessed the dreadnoughts, the colossal creatures had been poised to obliterate Rowan.

"Are more dreadnoughts stationed throughout the city?" he asked.

"No, they make too many people nervous. Once you get to the inner tiers, the only Workshop creatures you'll find are gargoyles. You'll find them throughout Blys."

"What on earth are gargoyles?" asked Hazel, frowning.

Pushing back from the table, Jason led them into a small office with a sleek workstation. Sitting down, he input a password and leaned forward into a retinal scanner before pulling up several images that made Toby recoil.

"What in the bloody hell is *that*?"

Cooper shared Toby's disgust. The creature resembled a muscular spider with many eyes, suction-padded feet, and a tusked and tentacled mouth. From the orthographic drawings, it looked to be some twenty feet tall with a multibarreled artillery turret on its back and a control capsule containing two human operators.

"It's highly mobile and has three different guns with different calibers and ranges. The smallest can fire a hundred rounds per second without overheating."

"How accurate are they?" asked Cooper.

"They don't miss. Once a target's chosen, the computations are instantaneous—distance, elevation, wind speed. Here's a demonstration. I'll warn you it isn't pretty."

Punching a key, Jason pulled up a film clip showing a gargoyle leaping onto a vertical test wall and running powerfully up its surface. Once atop the battlement, the hideous creature turned about just as three gazelles were simultaneously released from automated cages spaced well apart on a field. The frightened animals promptly bolted in three different directions. The gargoyle's guns moved in a blur of flashing muzzles. The gazelles simply vanished into red mist.

"Dear God," breathed Hazel.

Cooper stared at the screen. "How many of those does Prusias have?"

"Six hundred."

Toby let out a shriek. "Six *hundred*? Six hundred of those monstrosities shuffling about the city walls and mowing down everything in sight? We have to contact David and tell him to turn the army around!"

Jason glanced quizzically at Toby. "Are you an Agent?"

"Why do you ask?"

"I've never heard an Agent shriek before."

Toby scowled. "I am a smee, sir. A smee that will not be a party to needless slaughter. Cooper, I appeal to you—we must stop this madness. Rowan cannot possibly—"

Cooper held up his hand. He asked Jason to replay the clip in slow motion. This time he could actually see the guns independently aim and fire at the three targets from the back of the stationary gargoyle. The sequence was so swift he had missed it the first time. "No human did that," he muttered. "What are the operators for?"

"They steer the gargoyle using controls connected directly into the creature's brain," said Jason. "A computer fires the guns."

"How does the computer select its targets?"

Jason zoomed in on the gargoyle's compound eyes. "The computer's tied into the gargoyle's vision, which can pick up movement, heat signatures, you name it. Once the gargoyle's in attack mode, the guns will target anything in the kill zone that isn't an HVA."

"What's an HVA?" asked Hazel.

"Sorry," said Jason. "I give almost everything an acronym—helps me remember. HVA stands for 'high-value asset.' Prusias doesn't want important persons killed indiscriminately. He prefers them captured."

Cooper nodded, his mind working rapidly. "How does the gargoyle differentiate between acceptable targets and HVAs?"

"Facial recognition," replied Jason. "Surveillance photographs of HVAs have been registered in a database. The gargoyle only needs a glimpse to assess whether a target is one."

"What if the HVA's face is hidden?"

"Then it's classified as expendable. The computer makes the decision very quickly."

Hazel, arms folded, had been pacing the room, deep in thought. She stopped suddenly and stared again at the clip, which was playing on a loop. "What if it can't make a decision?"

"I don't understand," said Jason.

Her face shone with excitement. "What if the targets' features were changing?" she asked. "Shifting so quickly the gargoyle wasn't certain what it was looking at? What would it do?"

Leaning back in his chair, Jason studied the ceiling. "I don't know for sure," he confessed. "But I *think* it would keep trying until it could make a decision."

Cooper's heart rate quickened. "It won't fire until it makes a decision? Even if it never arrives at one?"

"No," said Jason slowly. "It shouldn't."

Cooper picked Hazel up, twirled her around, and kissed her. "You're brilliant. Do you know that?"

She flushed pink. "I've been told that once or twice, yes."

He kissed her again before setting her down, his mind racing with possibilities. The gargoyles' design flaw wouldn't ensure a successful siege course—far from it—but Hazel's insight offered a glimmer of hope.

"How would the Workshop respond if gargoyles failed to fire automatically?" he wondered. "Could they override the targeting system and tell it to forget about HVAs?"

"In theory," Jason mused. "But if the targeting system's stuck in a loop, new commands might not get through. It would require a reboot."

"How long would that take?"

"Ten, maybe fifteen minutes."

"Could the guns still be fired?"

"The drivers can always disable the targeting system and operate the guns manually, but that would prevent the computer from rebooting."

Cooper nodded. "So they'd have to choose between firing their weapons manually or waiting to reboot the targeting system."

"Correct."

"Do the drivers spend much time training with the guns?"

"Almost none. The targeting system's so much better, they rarely bother—"

Jason turned in alarm as a loud knock sounded at the apartment's door. Shutting down his workstation, he led them out, pointing at a hallway closet. Cooper left it for Hazel and Toby, while he followed Jason into the main room, grabbed his pack off the dining room table, and slipped within the closet by the door. Leaving it slightly ajar, he set down the pack and unsheathed his kris. The knocking grew almost frantic until Jason opened the door. Someone stormed right in.

"Why don't you answer my calls?" the visitor demanded.

Cooper didn't need to see the man to know he was middle-aged, half drunk, and bordering on a nervous breakdown.

"Calm yourself, Dr. Wyle," said Jason coolly. "I turned it off because I needed some rest. I haven't slept in two days."

The man laughed bitterly. "Sleep? We don't get to sleep! Haven't you heard the news?"

"About the missing museum hag?"

"Not that, you idiot! A special train's arrived from the capital with a rakshasa aboard. He's to escort a group of us back to Blys. Your presence has been 'requested.'"

Jason sounded stunned. "But I'm just a technician. I don't run anything."

Dr. Wyle chuckled. "That's what I told them, but they insisted. Apparently you made a favorable impression on His Majesty during his little viewing party."

Silence.

"What are you upset about?" Dr. Wyle sneered. "You've always been so eager for promotion. Well, here's your chance! Just don't disappoint our beloved king. If you do, we'll be hosing you off a wall."

"When are we supposed to depart?" asked Jason quietly.

A pause. "Sixty-seven minutes."

"I need a drink. Would you like one?"

"Dear God, yes."

"Whiskey?"

"A double. Neat."

Through the closet door's opening, Cooper saw Dr. Wyle sink heavily onto a couch. The man was not a eugenics experiment—few of the senior engineers were. Instead of exotic, blended perfection, he had a long, pale face with an aquiline nose and melancholy brown eyes. Dark hair was turning gray and his sunken cheeks suggested a recent and dramatic weight loss. He stared dazedly at the carpet, blinking only when Jason pressed a tumbler into his hand.

"Do you think we made a mistake?" he said, as though speaking to himself.

"What do you mean?" asked Jason, sitting in a nearby chair.

Dr. Wyle shrugged and sipped his drink. "Throwing our lot in with Prusias."

"Don't let anyone hear you say such things," said Jason sharply. "I'm going to forget I heard it."

"I'm not the only one," said Dr. Wyle. "Our enemies aren't as weak as we assumed. Harine's in outright revolt and Rowan's army's closing in."

"You don't honestly think they're a threat," said Jason, with a subtle note of disdain. Cooper was impressed; the young man was adjusting quickly and playing his role with some skill. Cooper doubted Dr. Wyle would notice that anything about Dr. Barrett was amiss. The Agent hoped that held true for others.

Dr. Wyle picked absently at a hangnail. "I don't know what to think. There are reports of vyes streaming out of the mountains to the north. Thousands of them. Tens of thousands!"

"Isn't that a good thing? Vyes serve Prusias."

"Not these kind. The vyes here seem to hate them. They call them 'Raszna.'"

"Things will work out."

A scornful laugh. "Will they? Two of our colleagues were just discovered dead in a cargo train. I'm telling you, Dr. Barrett, things are going bad. I think even Prusias is hedging his bets."

"What do you mean?"

Dr. Wyle grimaced. "I shouldn't say anything. I don't know for certain."

"Tell me."

The engineer took a slow, deep gulp and exhaled. "I overheard the rakshasa ask Dr. Tressel for the Workshop's architectural plans—Prusias's imp is interested in our vaults."

"So what?"

Dr. Wyle finished his drink and fixed Jason with a bloodshot eye. "I think the king wants a bunker. A fortified little nook where he can retreat if things go wrong."

"Then Dr. Tressel will build him one. She'll probably be promoted."

Dr. Wyle's smile was so hollow, so defeated and crazed it sent a chill down Cooper's spine. "Do you honestly think anyone who knows about the king's secret bunker will be allowed to live?"

"You're being paranoid, Dr. Wyle."

"And you're being naïve, Dr. Barrett. But I thank you for the drink." Setting the empty glass upon the table, he rose from the couch and made for the door. He paused three feet from where

Cooper was hiding. "Pack for a week. I'll meet you at the platform. Don't be late."

When the engineer departed, Jason closed the door and rested his head wearily against it. "Did you hear all that?" he murmured.

"Every word," said Cooper, stepping out.

Hazel and Toby entered from their hiding spot in the hallway closet. Turning away from the door, Jason gave his guests an almost helpless smile. He might have been walking to the gallows. "What should I do?"

Cooper clapped him on the shoulder. "Pack a bag, Dr. Barrett. We've got a train to catch."

~ 19 ~

A JOVIAN VIEW

It was a frigid morning in late January when King Prusias walked onto his balcony to survey his enemies. There they were, hordes of tiny toy soldiers carpeting the frozen hills below. Each camp was like a glittering city whose torches and banners flickered in the dull red dawn.

It was not the sight of Rowan banners that made him seethe. Or these upstart Raszna that had flowed down from the Alps these past months like snowmelt. No, these were simply enemies. Prusias could deal with enemies. It was betrayal that infuriated him, fawning liars and traitors that set his teeth to a slow grind. But he consoled himself with a promise. When this farce was complete, when his enemies were crushed, the king would focus his attention—unwavering, personal attention—on punishing those demons that had risen against him. Each turncoat upon that field would squirm and plead and weep for death. And Prusias would not give it to them.

"My lord?"

Smoothing his heavy black beard, the king glanced down at Mr. Bonn. The dutiful imp was standing at his side, his red skin turning almost blue with cold.

"My lord, you need to don your armor. Lord Grael and your captains will be arriving shortly."

At the mention of Grael, Prusias gave a grim smile. Today, Lord Grael would trample the king's enemies before perishing valiantly on the field of battle. Although Grael's victory was all but inevitable, his upcoming assassination was a delicate business that had required careful planning. There was no denying Grael was a brilliant general and that his troops obeyed him with fanatic, berserker loyalty. Of course, these admirable qualities made him too dangerous a rival. And thus, once he'd served his purpose—once he'd ground Rowan's little coalition to pulp— one of Grael's aides would dispatch his master and earn *koukerros*.

Prusias stared out at the armies camped across the river, far beyond the range of his gargoyles, catapults, and mortars. *Poor fools*, he thought. *You've spent weeks huddled there, waiting for more allies to show. How many graves have you dug for your frozen dead? After so much toil and sacrifice you won't even make it across the river to my gates. Pity. I'd have liked to see the gargoyles in action.*

With a grunt, Prusias left his balcony, following Mr. Bonn into the scented warmth of his bedchambers. The malakhim were waiting by the king's bed with fresh bandages and a gleaming corselet of black, overlapping scales. He suffered their ministrations, grimacing as they fit the heavy corselet over his massive head and chest before buckling the gold-hilted broadsword at his side. The armor and the sword were expensive props, a concession to Mr. Bonn, who suggested a king must show solidarity with his troops. Prusias found the notion absurd; he wouldn't be anywhere near the fighting. In any case, Prusias rarely used weapons in battle. The demon preferred his hands. Or teeth.

Glancing at his reflection, Prusias admired the darkly handsome features looking back at him: the leonine mane of black hair, the heavy brow, luminescent cat's eyes, the thick and plaited beard. The demon never understood why so many women today seemed to be attracted to pretty men as opposed to the masculine splendor in his mirror. Perhaps his look was outdated. He smoothed his bandages.

"There's been no sign of Bram, I take it."

"None," said Mr. Bonn. "Not for months. And our spies report that the child, Mina, remains at Rowan as you predicted she would."

Prusias nodded. "What of Lilith?"

"I cannot speak for her whereabouts, but her forces remain in Zenuvia."

Prusias chafed at the mere thought of Lilith's cunning and patience. "She's conspired somehow with Menlo," he growled. "I know she has."

"The queen readily admitted she'd met with him," Mr. Bonn reminded him. "And if Lilith wanted to betray you, why doesn't her banner fly with the others?"

"Because she's plotting something else!"

Mr. Bonn recoiled at the outburst, assuming the submissive posture he adopted whenever his master's temper flared. Prusias liked to see him this way, docile and terrified. Saliva pooled in the king's mouth. When the imp found his voice, it was barely a whisper.

"My lord, without her forces present, Lilith is no threat. But if your enemies concern you, there is always Yuga. You can send her against them if you choose."

Prusias almost laughed. "Bring Yuga near the city? Are you mad? She'd devour the entire capital."

"I was under the impression that Your Majesty can control her."

"Nothing controls Yuga."

"But the green stone—"

"Is merely a beacon," Prusias sighed. "Having the means to call Yuga does not make her my puppet, Mr. Bonn. And we don't need her to smash this rabble on our doorstep. Grael will be enough."

"Of course," said the imp delicately. "But if he is not . . ."

Prusias stood taller as one of the malakhim buckled a fur-lined cloak about his broad shoulders. He chuckled at his servant's misgivings. "If Grael should falter, we still have walls they cannot scale and a gate they cannot break. We have catapults and archers and do not forget our Workshop horrors, Mr. Bonn. Do you really believe a mob of humans and vyes can overcome dreadnoughts and gargoyles? Ha!"

"Of course not," said Mr. Bonn. "But it is wise to prepare for contingencies. We all need a plan B, as it were. And thus, if Your Majesty will indulge me, I've taken the liberty to acquire a . . ."

The imp hesitated.

"A *what*, Mr. Bonn? Spit it out."

"Er, a body double, Your Majesty."

Prusias was rarely speechless, but he stared now at Mr. Bonn. Was the imp joking?

"You see," Mr. Bonn explained, "if things go ill, we can whisk you off to safety while an imposter remains behind."

"I'm aware of what a body double is," the king simmered.

"What I do not know is why you believe the Great Red Dragon would need one. Do you think me feeble?"

"No!" squeaked the imp. "It's simply a precaution. As is the retreat I've had prepared."

"What retreat?"

"A bunker deep inside the Workshop, my king. There was an ancient vault that I've had repurposed and fortified on your behalf. Should our enemies enter the city, we can fall back while your double remains to inspire your troops."

"No enemy is entering my city."

"Of course not," said the imp hastily. "That would be unthinkable. But my king must acknowledge that unthinkable things have happened. They happened on Walpurgisnacht. They happened on the fields of Rowan. Prudence demands a plan B."

Prusias exploded. "Failure demands a plan B! I won't hear this talk much less entertain it. Mention this bunker or body double again, and I'll have you flayed. Is that clear, Mr. Bonn?"

"Yes, my lord."

Mastering his temper, Prusias exhaled, checked his bandages in the mirror, and noticed that one was already spotted with blood. Cursing softly, he gestured impatiently at one of the malakhim to replace it. It was time to meet Lord Grael, and he was loath to betray any weakness.

The conference with Grael and his officers was mercifully brief. In it, Grael shared his plan to divide his troops and smash the enemy's flanks. Lord Grael's legions comprised a hundred thousand riders. It was a smaller force than the army camped outside the capital, but the rakshasa was unconcerned and declined reinforcements from Prusias's own legions garrisoned within the city. The general reasoned that his troops—heavy cavalry, demons, and deathknights riding armored mounts—were going against starving humans and vyes, most of whom were on foot. While there were other demons among the enemy forces, turncoat braymas and such, their numbers totaled no more than ten or fifteen thousand. Grael's own legions were sufficient to overwhelm this enemy; he had no wish to trade speed for greater numbers. He also had no wish to share the glory. Indeed, the duke was so certain of a lopsided outcome, he wagered that traitor braymas would turn upon Rowan in a desperate bid to earn the king's forgiveness.

The king would *not* forgive them, of course, but Grael's confidence did lift his spirits. And Prusias was not ungrateful. He was even tempted to call off Lord Grael's assassination, but he let the impulse pass. In his heart, Prusias knew his rival had to be eliminated. If Lord Grael presented a threat before, it was nothing to what he would pose in the wake of today's victory.

Don't worry, Grael, we won't forget you. I might even build you a monument. Something in bronze.

The king's spirits were still buoyant when he and his entourage arrived at his sun terrace, a broad stone platform that offered sweeping views of his city and surrounding lands. While the morning was dark and horrifically cold, Prusias wanted to hear the roar of battle, to see the armies clashing on the field. He wanted a Jovian perspective.

He also wanted company.

The smuggler was not yet aware of his arrival. Madam Petra was waiting at his breakfast table, her attention fixed on a gargoyle, whose arachnoid body twitched and trembled on a nearby parapet. The smuggler's eyes wandered over its many legs and bulbous belly to fall upon the Workshop operator adjusting its controls. The man flashed an admiring smile—a smile that was met with cool disdain as Madam Petra looked away. Prusias had never beheld such a fetching profile.

The woman turned, her eyes falling upon the king where he stood with Mr. Bonn and a retinue of guards and servants in the shadowed archway. Rapping his cane on the flagstones, Prusias crossed the terrace and beamed at her. She rose at once, curtsying low and surrendering her hand for a kiss. Prusias lingered over her flesh's scent, its softness, before releasing it.

"How good of you to join me," he purred, pushing her chair in for her. "I trust the hour isn't too early?"

The woman searched the servants and guests as they continued to arrive on the terrace. "Where is Katarina? Mr. Bonn said my daughter—your *hostage*—would be joining us."

Prusias made a creditable show of surprise. "Did he, now? I don't know why he would make such promises. A battle's not a fitting spectacle for a girl Katarina's age. No, it's better she stay in the Workshop with her new friends and playmates."

"I was told she would be here," insisted Madam Petra stiffly.

Smoothing her luxuriant stole, Prusias leaned close to whisper in the smuggler's ear. "And I was told your door would be left unlocked. But alas, it would not yield. Perhaps tonight I'll have better luck."

With a chuckle, he sat across from her and peeked at the warm croissants as a servant set down a basket. Madam Petra turned away from him, casting her gaze upon the armies camped across the river, at the thousands of tents and pavilions dotting the frozen, snow-choked landscape.

"Is something going to happen, then?" she asked wearily. "They've been camped there for weeks. I'd assumed you were collecting rent."

"Not rent, my dear. Casualties. This accursed winter's destroyed everyone's harvests. There are food riots here in Blys, so you can imagine the state of things out there. Rowan's trek was frightfully slow. Don't forget they made landfall almost six months ago. It took them five months to march five hundred miles and set up their little camp. Five months of brutal cold, dwindling supplies, and constant harassment by my braymas along the King's Highway. While that miserable goblin clan brought them some supplies, it's not enough. They're eating their horses. Belts and shoes will be next. I don't know about you, but I wouldn't want to be camped by vyes when they get too hungry . . ."

"What are they waiting for?" said Madam Petra.

"Well, they're making a show of building siege engines and trying to cut off my trade," Prusias chuckled. "But I'd imagine they're hoping more allies will show—they've been promising the moon to any who will listen. Some minor braymas have gone over to their side, but no one important. But Lord Grael—you remember him, my pet—is going to sweep this rabble from my steps."

The smuggler sniffed. "I should have brought my opera glasses," she mused, squinting at the distant tents.

"No need," said Prusias, gesturing at a team of Workshop technicians who were emerging with screens and equipment. "You'll be able to see whatever you desire."

"If that's the case, why are we sitting here in the cold?"

Prusias laughed. "No technology can replicate the roar of a live battle. There's nothing like it. We'll hear the din all the way up here."

"You're very brave to get so close."

Prusias's smile faded. "Careful, my dear. You really must be more careful." His attention fell upon Dr. Barrett, the technician he had requested. "Good morning, Dr. Barrett. I trust we won't have any technical difficulties today."

"No, Your Majesty," replied the engineer, setting up a large screen by their table. "But if issues arise, perhaps the lady will once again lend us her jewelry."

The king's eyes fell upon Madam Petra's torque, that slender horseshoe of hammered, coppery lymra about her neck. It was more valuable than any jewel—than anything in his treasury—and Prusias knew perfectly well who it really belonged to. The king's hand drifted to the bandages upon his face, to the aching wounds they concealed.

"You've never shared how you came by such a remarkable object," he remarked.

"I made a bargain with its former owner," the smuggler replied.

"Are you afraid to say his name?" Prusias chided.

"Of course not," said Madam Petra coldly. "Max McDaniels."

Dr. Barrett glanced up from his work when the Hound's name was mentioned.

"Did you know him, too, Dr. Barrett?" inquired Prusias.

The engineer blinked. "I . . . yes, I suppose I did. I met him the year I graduated from Rowan. He was just a boy then, of course."

"Just a boy," Prusias chuckled. "Have you seen him lately?"

"No, Your Majesty. It's been several years."

"The boy's all grown up. Let's see if we can locate him, shall we?"

The king sat back as the engineer turned on the monitor, selected a camera from along the outer battlements, and panned across the distant armies. The camps really were a squalid sight, a veritable slum of steaming ditches, muddied snow, broken wagons, tents, and gaunt figures huddled about campfires for warmth. Rowan's people looked wretched while the Raszna appeared little better. Prusias had never seen such enormous vyes—some were larger than ogres—but they appeared considerably less fearsome slouched against their great wains, thrusting gobbets of frozen gray flesh at whatever was caged within. Grael was right: These enemies were more liable to beg than to fight. The turncoat braymas at least had some style—colorful silk banners, gleaming armor, and mounts that didn't look like they were going to keel over. But they were too few. One good charge and this pathetic "siege" would be over. One of the largest tents came into view, a grand pavilion flying Rowan's banner. Several people stood outside its opening.

Prusias smacked the table. "There he is! Zoom in and focus the damn thing."

The image steadied and sharpened as the central figure grew larger. There he was indeed: Max McDaniels, tall and grim, conversing with none other than David Menlo by the entrance to the Director's pavilion. The pair appeared oblivious that an attack was coming. Prusias's pulse quickened with excitement. The demon's blue, feral eyes drifted to the weapon in the Hound's hand. Prusias had felt its sting as a sword, but now it was attached to a spear shaft, its accursed blade still sheathed from view. Long seconds passed before he realized the technician was addressing him. Glancing up, Prusias cleared his throat. He found his mouth had gone dry.

"What?" he rasped.

"Would you like me to lock this camera on him?" repeated Dr. Barrett. "It will go where he does."

"Yes," said Prusias immediately. "Bring other screens, but keep this one on the Hound." The king turned abruptly to Mr. Bonn. "Fetch that snake from the Atropos. I want him here immediately."

The imp relayed the order to a page, who promptly wove a hurried path through the king's arriving guests as they stepped out onto the terrace. He nodded at Lady Praav, ignored her imp's greeting, and turned back to Madam Petra.

"So," he continued, "you were going to tell me how you acquired that torque. It must be quite the tale."

"Nothing so extraordinary," she replied. "He needed my help to bypass proper channels and acquire something he couldn't afford. I demanded the torque as collateral."

"And what did he acquire?"

"Iron," said the smuggler. "That iron from Zenuvia your kind finds so distasteful. The boy used it to equip his troops."

"Dragon iron," Prusias mused. The stuff was positively hateful. It bit far deeper than ordinary metals—could wound even a greater demon. When this war was over, he'd have every scrap collected and sunk to the ocean floor. Still, the stuff was not nearly as rare as the material of which the Hound's torque was made. Prusias suspected Madam Petra knew that very well. He decided to play a game.

"What would it take for you to part with it?" he asked.

She frowned. "It's not for sale."

"Come now," said Prusias. "A smuggler knows that everything is for sale. I have the souls to prove it. Thousands of them, my dear, each trapped in a jewel until its owner dies and the soul belongs to me." He leaned forward and grinned like a mischievous schoolboy. "The only question is price. Would you part with that torque for a thousand gold pieces?"

"Of course not."

"Ten thousand."

"You're wasting your time."

"I see," Prusias chuckled. "Let's try a different currency—one more relevant to mortals and mothers."

"What's that?" said the smuggler, forcing a tight smile.

"Time. Would you trade that torque for a day with your daughter?"

The smuggler's smile faded. "A day with Katarina?"

"Correct."

"Nonsense," she scoffed. "You'd have to return her to me and allow us to go free. We'd require lands, servants. The torque is worth that and more."

"But that's not what I'm offering," said Prusias, grinning sadistically. "I'm offering one day with your daughter. You've probably squandered hundreds, but I'm wagering that a day with Katarina has far more value than it used to. After all, this would be a day when you could hold her once again, stroke her hair, and tell her that you love her . . . no matter what might happen. That sounds like a very valuable day."

As Prusias watched a tear trickle down the smuggler's cheek, he realized these were his favorite moments with humans—those occasions when the fragile creatures were torn between want and need, love and greed. Emotions played upon the woman's exquisite features in subtle, intoxicating combinations. All her life, Madam Petra had chosen the pretty bauble. Would she do so again? Prusias watched intently as her emotions intensified. A decision was coming.

"He's here, Your Majesty."

Prusias turned to see Mr. Bonn with a rumpled, frightened Atropos representative. "Did we wake you up?" he inquired pleasantly.

"I must confess I was sleeping, Your Majesty."

"Are the quarters I've provided adequate?"

The handler swallowed. "They are, my king."

"Good. I'm glad you're comfortable. Tell me what you see on that screen."

The camera showed Max McDaniels walking through the

camp and stopping to converse with some armored vyes who hailed his arrival. Two even embraced him.

The handler cleared his throat and plucked nervously at his skinscrolled chin.

"That is Max McDaniels, Your Highness."

"Yes, indeed. The very target you've been hired to eliminate has been camped outside my walls for over a week. Is this news to you?"

"It is not, my king. We assumed he was dead because the compass we use to track him ceased working for several weeks. When it indicated he was alive and traveling, the clones interrupted another mission and resumed their pursuit. They were closing in on him near Enlyll when the revolts began and he disappeared. The next they saw him, he was leading an army of vyes out of the mountains. But rest assured, my king, the assassins are tracking him."

"Why would I need them to track him, you idiot? There he is!"

The handler held up his hands. "I understand that," he said cautiously. "But the target is surrounded by an army. If you wish the assassins to risk such a low-probability strike, we can certainly honor those demands. There's a chance they may succeed. However, it's far more likely they would be detected, encounter overwhelming opposition, and we would lose not only the clones but also the artifact Your Majesty entrusted to them. If that happens, they cannot perform the other task you have hired us to do."

Prusias smoldered. He was tempted to throttle the oily little snake, but the snake wasn't wrong. It would do no good to squander these assassins on a foolhardy attempt. The clones were far too valuable as was the stone knife they carried. They had caught the Hound before. They would do so again. He needed to be patient.

"Enjoy the show," Prusias muttered, dismissing him without a second thought. Looking past the handler, he saw that the terrace was now teeming with nobles eating, drinking, and gazing curiously at the many screens set up throughout. Dabbing a drop of blood from a bandage, Prusias glanced at Mr. Bonn's pocket watch and rose from his chair. Conversations ceased as all eyes fell upon the king.

"Ladies and gentlemen," he said. "Today is a special occasion. As you know, my enemies have gathered from near and far, traveled thousands of miles and endured countless hardships for the privilege of dying at my doorstep. How obliging of them." The king paused for laughter, forced though it was. "While their efforts are appreciated, you can see for yourselves that the poor wretches are suffering. Today, the legions of Lord Grael, our esteemed Duke of Malakos, shall put these upstarts and traitors out of their misery . . ."

Right on cue, a horn blew. Its call was faint, its origins distant, but there was no mistaking that sound. It had terrified quarry for thousands of years. It came from a rakshasa hunting horn.

As the horn faded, another took up the call. And another. And another. Hundreds of horns. Thousands of horns! Even at these heights the sound saturated the air, triggering a cascade of shattering icicles throughout the city.

Going to the railing, Prusias looked down to see windows and doors were being flung open as the king's startled subjects sought to see what was amiss. And from the city's lowest tier, the soot-grimed districts that housed his expendable workers, plumes of oily black smoke rose lazily into the red sky. The rabble would riot over anything—arena matches, opium prices, and food rations. Now they were rioting over sound. Prusias chuckled. Some would embrace any excuse to burn down their houses.

As amusing as Prusias found his ghettos, he was far more

eager to gauge Rowan's reaction to Grael's horns. He glanced at the viewing screen. The Hound had ceased his conversation and was staring at Prusias's city with a hard, contained expression. The lad's eyes darted here and there, as though trying to pinpoint the source of that terrifying call. His searching gaze found no enemies approaching. Lord Grael's legions had assembled in secret behind the capital, shielded by the surrounding mountains. When they came into view, it would be to cross the bridges and cover the final stretch—the open country where their mounts would acquire the murderous speed and momentum to overrun everything in their path. Even now, Prusias thought he sensed a slight tremor running through the terrace railing. It felt like a mild earthquake.

His enemies could feel it, too. Gazing out, Prusias saw that their camps were a frenzy of motion—tents ripped down, soldiers fetching their weapons, and Raszna leading great batlike creatures down the ramps from their wains. For all the activity and commotion, Prusias had to admit there was very little panic or chaos. Despite their wretched condition, his enemies were disciplined. Even now, he could see infantry formations taking shape, spears and pikes glinting in the thin hints of sunlight that penetrated the sagging clouds.

It really was marvelous to watch events unfold from such a vantage. Whenever Prusias was in the midst of a battle, his world was an explosion of light and sound, bloodlust and rage. From a distance, however, a battle was nothing of the sort. From these heights, the patterns and movements resembled something choreographed, a dance of opposing geometries. Prusias could not think of anything where the contrast between watching and doing was so profound and yet both were so enjoyable.

The atmosphere on the terrace was growing electric. Most of his guests abandoned their tables to crowd along the terrace railing to witness the moment when Grael's legions would gallop into view. Only Madam Petra remained sitting. She slouched low in her chair, arms folded across her lap, while she stared blankly ahead.

"You're going to miss the show, my dear."

She did not answer.

Prusias caught a snowflake on his tongue, gazed up, and saw that more were coming. Many more. *Let it come,* he thought. *And let her sulk!* Seizing a bottle of champagne, he tipped its contents into his mouth and welcomed the bubbles in his belly. He smacked the railing and glanced at Dr. Barrett's screen.

The Hound was mounted now. He rode upon a barded warhorse, cantering along the front lines of infantry, roaring encouragement to Rowan and Raszna alike. Prusias would not have needed a camera to locate him anymore; the Hound's aura was visible even from this distance—a shimmering radiance that surrounded his person and was growing brighter every second. The lad wore no helmet, carried no shield. His only armor was a light mail shirt. His only weapon was that awful spear. It was unsheathed now, and Prusias knew the blade would be wailing, keening for blood. Standing tall in his stirrups, the Hound raised it high, brandishing the weapon for all to see.

The effect it had was chilling.

Every soldier, every Raszna—even the rebelling braymas— raised their lances and swords high and screamed in answer. As Prusias beheld his enemies and the frenzy overtaking them, he realized Grael had been wrong. No one would be running away this day. These soldiers would fight.

A spasm of hatred passed through Prusias. His hatred of the Hound ran deeper than any he had nurtured throughout his long existence. The intensity puzzled even him. The two had history, of course, but he had history with others, including Bram. The

Hound had given him his wounds—a perpetual humiliation—but Prusias had despised him long before that. The demon suspected its true origins went back to the Arena where Bragha Rùn had won so many victories. How the crowds had adored, even worshipped, him . . .

Prusias almost laughed. Was he merely *jealous*? Jealous of the youth's grace and prowess? Could it really be that simple and petty? Perhaps it was. The king was a political animal, a master of leverage and manipulation who expanded his power through calculated risks—risks borne by others. Prusias glanced at Madam Petra's torque. The Hound had bartered a priceless treasure to save a few brief and worthless lives. And there he was, young and handsome, leading his own troops into battle, an Achilles at Troy. Wiping crumbs from his beard, the demon glowered at the screen and felt his hatred deepen.

"There they are!"

The cry had come from Lord Yrkün. Prusias looked out just in time to see Grael's legions burst into view. They came from the north and south, two separate columns of heavy cavalry. Each streamed around the mountains, racing at a furious gallop that made their banners snap in the wind. It was a magnificent spectacle, one that caused the entire city to cheer as Grael's legions thundered over the great bridges and spilled onto the opposite bank. Once on open ground, the horses ran even faster. Displaying exceptional skill, the cavalry changed formation at full gallop. The two columns scattered and then closed ranks to form murderous wedges—wedges designed to obliterate everything in their path. Prusias held his breath as the two formations began to close in a swift, steady convergence upon the enemy.

And yet . . . those enemies were not responding.

Prusias gripped the rail tightly. Something was wrong. A hundred thousand horsemen were bearing down upon them and they had yet to take a defensive posture, ride out to meet their opponents, or even flee. He glanced up at the screen. The Hound was sitting astride his horse, flanked by Rowan and Raszna captains. A formidable-looking group, but they were not leading a charge to meet Grael's legions. They were waiting for something . . .

Prusias hurried to another screen, swatting aside his guests until he found one that was trained on Grael. The rakshasa was leading the column on the left, leaning forward in his saddle with his lance leveled. He didn't seem to find anything amiss. Prusias gazed out at the battlefield. Grael's forces were within several hundred yards of their target, the wedges coming together like two great fists.

Dropping his lance, Lord Grael blew his horn.

Like a flock of birds changing course, Grael's wedge suddenly—inexplicably—veered sharply to the right.

Toward his own troops.

Prusias's guests' cries and shrieks coincided with a jolting crash as one column collided with the other. Steel crumpled, horses and riders flew high in the air as Grael's troops plowed a bloody furrow through their comrades.

As Prusias scanned the unfolding carnage, it became clear that this was no accident. The troops in Grael's column were attacking the others—spearing, hacking, and trampling in a determined, vicious assault. The victims were trying to regroup—Prusias saw Lord Rhugal making a valiant attempt to rally his men—but most were so disoriented they could muster but a pitiful defense as their attackers closed in about them. It was not a battle but a slaughter.

Swallowing his shock, Prusias wheeled to find Grael's secretary—that albino imp who had been such a willing conspirator against his master. He had seen the insect conversing earlier with Lady Praav. The king seized Mr. Bonn by the collar.

"Where's Grael's imp?" Prusias demanded.

"His secretary?"

"Yes, his secretary. Where is he?"

"H-he left five minutes ago, Your Majesty," stammered Mr. Bonn. "But he did make his apologies. He even left a note." He handed the king a letter.

Prusias tore open the little envelope.

> *Grael died months ago.*
> *An imposter is leading your cavalry.*
> *There may be others in your midst.*
> *Perhaps on that very terrace . . .*
>
> *Regards,*
> *David Menlo, Director*

p.s. Caligula's own guards murdered him on this very day in January. Coincidence? Or does Fate have a sense of humor?

Prusias crumpled the paper.

"Your Majesty, what's happening?" asked a panicked voice. Prusias turned to see Coros, that corpulent sneak with a finger in every pie.

"I'm not certain, friend Coros. Have a look and report back."

Seizing the merchant by his ermine collar, the king flung him twenty feet over the railing. Coros seemed to hover a moment, his stunned face staring at the king while he clutched and snatched at the empty air. Prusias watched him fall. A long, somersaulting plunge that ended abruptly on a spired dome.

Prusias ignored his guests, ignored their appalled expressions. Instead, he gazed out upon the battlefield. As he feared,

Rowan's forces were advancing upon what remained of Grael's legions, even as they continued to fight one another. The Hound was leading them, riding ahead of his captains and screaming like some savage from another age. A blinding brilliance burst forth from the lad as he struck Grael's legions like a thunderbolt. The king shut his eyes.

"Your Majesty."

The voice was Mr. Bonn's. Prusias gazed down. The imp was standing at his side, trembling but dutiful.

"My king, the situation in the worker districts is escalating."

It was true. The city's lowest level was ablaze as thousands of tiny figures surged through the twisting streets. Through the torrents of black smoke, Prusias could make out figures carrying makeshift ladders to try and scale the walls that separated them from the wealthier districts.

He was not going to panic. Searching among his guests, Prusias found Dr. Wyle trying to disappear behind a statue of Venus. He gestured for the man to approach.

"Dr. Wyle," he said calmly, "how many gargoyles are in commission?"

"Five hundred and eighty-nine, sir."

"Very good. We have a situation in the worker districts. I want every gargoyle not already on the outer walls deployed to snuff that disturbance. This riot is to end within thirty minutes. If that means I need to replace every single worker, so be it. And if our enemies venture within range, we'll show them what the gargoyles can do. Is that understood?"

"Yes, Your Majesty," said Dr. Wyle.

Recalling David Menlo's note, Prusias held up his hand. While the note was obviously intended to make him paranoid, he could not discount the fact that it might be true.

"Bring that one here."

Dr. Wyle beckoned at the twitching, mechanized monster on the nearby wall. Like an obedient spider, the gargoyle scuttled down from its perch on the neighboring parapet and made a disconcerting leap onto the terrace, landing heavily on its eight legs. The king's guests screamed, backing against a marble fountain. He couldn't entirely blame them. The monster's head resembled a cross between a spider and a squid with numerous luminous eyes the size of soup plates. A beaked mouth was flanked by two large fangs and fringed with tentacle-like feelers that writhed and probed the frigid air. Upon its bulbous back, two humans operated controls in a protected cockpit, their visored faces illuminated by the instrument panel. As the monster rose to its full height, there was a faint whirring of machinery as its guns recalibrated.

"What would you like it to do, Your Majesty?" asked Dr. Wyle nervously.

Prusias gestured absently at his guests. "Keep them where they are. If anyone moves, turn them into jelly."

"Shall I join them?" asked Madam Petra coldly.

"No, my dear," said Prusias, taking up the champagne bottle. "You will sit there and look pretty. Dr. Barrett will make the pictures work. And Dr. Wyle will communicate with my monsters. The excitement's just beginning." Sipping the champagne, he grimaced and tossed it over the railing. "Open another bottle, Mr. Bonn. That one's flat."

A fresh bottle was opened and the king seized it before Mr. Bonn could pour it into a flute. Ridiculous things, champagne flutes. Swigging deeply, Prusias gazed down at his city and watched as hundreds of gargoyles responded to his orders, hardly breaking stride as they left their posts along the higher battlements to scuttle across gardens, clamber over mansions, and leap down to snowy rooftops in a breakneck descent. Blys's citizens scattered as they came, ducking into shops or houses as the monsters shambled past toward the gates.

Beyond those gates, Rowan's forces had finished the last of Grael's legions. They were advancing now, forming ranks as they marched toward the bridges that spanned the river. The Hound was still leading them, no longer blinding but radiant as he rode ahead of a quarter million footmen, archers, and knights. High above the army, wheeling in the snowy skies, hundreds of Raszna were mounted upon wyverns. Prusias wondered at their purpose. They were far too high to attack. Surveillance possibly, but he assumed David Menlo would have more sophisticated means. He longed to send sorties of Stygian crows after them, but the creatures could not abide extreme cold and the brutal winter had decimated their ranks.

No matter. If the wyverns swooped too low, the gargoyles would blast them out of the sky. Gulping more champagne, Prusias watched as his enemies advanced steadily toward the bridges. Once his enemies stepped upon them, once they began to cross the snow-gorged Tiber, they would be within the gargoyles' range.

The Hound was getting wonderfully close. Prusias turned to Dr. Wyle. "Forget the rioters," he snapped. "I want the gargoyles focused on the bridges. The fools are about to cross."

Dr. Wyle relayed the order on his device. Prusias watched as the gargoyles altered course, leaving the burning slums and taking positions instead along the massive outer walls. Stationed by the gates, and nearly as tall as the wall itself, were the king's five remaining dreadnoughts. The creatures swayed like sleeping elephants, dormant until they might be needed.

The Hound was approaching the central bridge. He halted just before the broad span, resting his spear across his saddle to gaze up at the gargoyles poised upon the distant battlements.

At his signal, a platoon of soldiers came forward from Rowan's ranks. Prusias could not see their faces, for they wore heavy cowls and bowed their heads like a file of monks. Trotting past their captain, they stepped upon the bridge and raised their hoods in unison.

The soldiers had no faces.

No, that wasn't correct. The soldiers were wearing masks—blank masks akin to a fencer's except these seemed to flicker and blur with subtle distortions. Prusias thought he saw an image—the suggestion of a face, but it was gone too quickly to be certain. Another face—or a vague hint of one—suggested itself before vanishing. The masks weren't blank at all; they were simply changing too quickly for his eye to follow.

Prusias watched in stupefied silence as the soldiers reached the bridge's midpoint. Nearby, he heard Dr. Wyle whispering urgently into his device. The king turned slowly toward him.

"Dr. Wyle, are the gargoyles in position?"

"Yes, Your Majesty."

"And are those enemies within range?"

"Yes."

"Then explain why the gargoyles aren't firing."

"Th-that's what I'm trying to ascertain, Your Majesty," sputtered the engineer. "It seems the creatures—their targeting systems—are confused. They can't decide whether they should open fire."

"Of course they should open fire!"

The engineer tried to answer but hyperventilated. Gasping for breath, he urged Dr. Barrett to take over. Taking his colleague's device, the young man tried to meet the king's angry gaze.

"The gargoyles are programmed to fire at anything within range that isn't a high-value target. Right now, they can't decide whether those soldiers are fair game. The masks are confusing them. To bypass this issue, the drivers would have to operate the weapons manually."

"Then do that," Prusias snapped.

"That will mean slower, less accurate fire."

Prusias leaned close to the young man and whispered, "Dr. Barrett, if they're not shooting in five seconds, I'll swallow you whole!"

The engineer issued the command. Within three seconds, several gargoyles opened fire. A hail of bullets struck the bridge, wounding two of the masked soldiers while the rest scattered, leaping off the bridge to plunge toward the icy river.

The wyverns plunged at the first sign of fire. Hundreds came screeching out of the sky, diving at the gargoyles like vast birds of prey. The gargoyle operators tried to react, to retrain their guns upon their assailants, but few could do so in time. The collisions were tremendous. Wyverns struck the gargoyles at full speed with their splayed talons, knocking them clear off the wall or taking hold of their flesh and maiming them in a frenzy of talons, teeth, and stingers.

The wyverns had been carrying Raszna and some of these could now be seen upon the wall—huge vyes that fell upon downed gargoyles, obliterating the cockpits and their occupants with heavy blows from their halberds. There must have been a hundred running free now upon the outer wall, racing across the broad parapet to blockade stairways before the king's soldiers could arrive. Within the worker districts, there was an explosion and a roaring cheer as a fireball rose into the sky.

Events were occurring so quickly, Prusias strained to make sense of them. He willed himself to focus. His gargoyles were no more, enemies were on his walls, and a riot threatened to con-sume the most populous tier of his city. The riot, he realized, had been a planned event, orchestrated with the same care and cunning as the destruction of his cavalry and gargoyles. One by one, his defenses were being peeled away, excised with surgical precision. Blys was being dissected.

Still, all was not lost. The rioters were walled in, his gate was unbreakable, and he still had half a million troops to defend his city. His enemies had landed a punch or two, but he was still on his feet and there were many rounds to go. He turned to Mr. Bonn.

"Send General Braiden's troops out the postern gates to engage the enemy outside the walls. Deploy half my Imperial Guard to enclose the worker districts. The archers shall fire from the surrounding walls and towers; footmen will defend and reinforce the gates to Tier Two. This riot must be contained. I want Laetho's forces to reclaim the outer wall from those vyes. His people should be equal to the task."

The king turned to the engineers. "Do we still have any of those mortars we replaced?"

"Less than half," said a recovered Dr. Wyle. "Most were melted down for their metal—the gargoyles rendered them obsolete—but there are still several hundred in the armories."

"Have the ogres bring them to those batteries," he added, pointing to a series of squat fortifications built into mountains above the outer walls.

"That will take time, Your Majesty. They have to wheel them up the ramps."

"Then get started," growled the king.

While his subordinates relayed his orders, Prusias returned his attention to the bridges. He had not bothered rigging the bridges with explosives because he had wanted his enemies to venture within range of his gargoyles. He regretted that decision now. His enemies were now flowing over the spans like army ants. Until his forces regained control of the massive walls, there was little he could do but watch as Rowan's Mystics and siege engines converged upon the great gates.

The gates. Blys's scale was designed to awe its visitors, to convey a sense of its ruler's power. Nothing in the capital—not even the royal palace—reinforced this impression more than the great gates. They were set into the outer walls like sliding blast doors, forty feet thick, thirty stories tall, and sheathed with steel plating several feet thick. In addition to their gargantuan size, the gates utilized the same technology employed in the Humboldt krakens, compounds that absorbed energy with remarkable efficiency. The gates used them to a much greater degree. No one—not the Hound, Menlo, or even Bram—possessed the power to break them.

As he reflected on this, Prusias felt a flush of pleasure. He sipped his champagne, dimly conscious that the wind and snow were picking up. Let it! It would hamper his attackers far more than it hampered him. Alarms and horns were blaring throughout the city, but he didn't concern himself with these. They were simply noise. At the moment, he was more interested in patterns of energy and inertia, those subtle shifts of momentum that often defined a prolonged struggle.

And what he saw pleased him. Many wyverns were dead, their arrow-riddled bodies strewn across the parapets. Their Raszna handlers were still fighting but they were now outnumbered and were being driven back by Laetho's brutes. That little skirmish would soon be over. His gaze swept down to the worker districts.

While some enterprising rioters had managed to scale the walls, it was a futile gesture, for they had nowhere to go. Unless the mobs could somehow break out and storm Tier 2 en masse, the workers would remain penned in. In the meantime, their district was a raging inferno that would suffer a withering hail of arrows. Poor fools. Rowan's spies incited them to riot, had promised them a better life. And what would the humans, vyes, and goblins get? A fiery death trapped in their own slums.

Brilliant flashes shone from beyond the walls, illuminating the entire landscape. Glancing at the screen, Prusias saw the Hound looking on as hundreds of Rowan and Raszna spellcasters unleashed bolts of raw, iridescent energy at the gates. The air itself was catching fire, sparking and smoking, and the gates began to glow a dull, angry orange as the bolts struck the surface. But the Mystics could not sustain their efforts for more than several seconds, and whenever they halted to regroup and recover, they found they had made no lasting damage. The marvelous gates were good as new.

The king crowed as enemy siege engines rained their little pebbles on his walls. He laughed as the Mystics tried time and again to put a dent in his gates. Meanwhile, the workers were burning in their slums, taking shelter behind whatever they could as arrows rained upon them. The most desperate massed at the gates to Tier 2. It was almost moving to watch them hammer against them, surging back and forth in a futile effort to force them open. The gates were heavy steel, their locks controlled by Workshop computers. No mere mob—no matter how frenzied or numerous—would succeed in breaking them. They fell by tens and hundreds. The spectacle was like watching bees attempt to escape a blocked and burning hive.

Things were not yet so grim for the invaders outside his walls, but they soon would be. Braiden's legions were arriving from the king's garrisons built into the mountains, tight phalanxes of spear and swordsmen that outnumbered the attackers. Braiden's shock troops had already fallen upon Rowan's forces at the southern portion of the wall and were pushing them back, forcing them into range of—

Boom!

Even Prusias started at the first explosions—a concussive series of mortars lobbed from his batteries. The shells burst in phosphorescent flashes among his attackers, sending horses, ballistae, and bodies sprawling into broken piles. Glancing at one of Dr. Barrett's screens, Prusias spied the Hound and almost whooped aloud.

The Hound had been knocked from his horse. The dying mount lay on its side, while the lad tried to get up. He was bleeding, leaning upon his spear and gazing dazedly at the distant battlements. A woman ran to his side. She was young and surprisingly familiar. Where had he seen her? The memory came to Prusias in a flash—she was the lass who'd slain Gunnir at the siege of Rowan. She'd fought the assassins when they'd cornered the Hound. The girl was his guardian angel.

And that angel was helping him to his feet, wiping the dirt and blood from his face as the Hound regained his bearings. His aura was growing brighter, a brilliant halo of golden light. More mortars exploded, shattering Rowan and Raszna, Mystics and vyes alike. They were pulling back, away from the murderous hail of explosives and projectiles now raining from the outer walls as Laetho's forces retook them. Prusias cackled as a heavy stone tumbled five hundred feet to obliterate an enemy trebuchet. Gravity was a wonderful thing.

And so were Braiden's legions. They were sweeping in from the side now, driving Rowan's forces into the heaviest concentration of mortar fire. The fighting below was absolutely furious, a roar and clash that could be heard even above the chaos in the worker districts. In the screen, Prusias saw the Hound and the maiden rushing on foot to meet these new attackers. There was an explosion of light as the Hound struck, followed by a shock wave that leveled hundreds. Braiden's troops fell back and they were not the only ones. Even Rowan's forces were fleeing from the Hound. All but the maiden. A chill ran through Prusias. Outside his gates, a god of war was loose.

But that god was not here. He was out there—out in that deafening carnage where mortars were falling, Braiden's troops were regrouping. The gates would hold, the Hound would tire, and the king's enemies—broken and exhausted—would succumb to cold winds and hot steel. It was only a matter of time.

Time. Prusias gazed up. Whatever vague hint of sun there had been was already setting. How much time had passed? Eight hours? Ten? He'd hardly noticed—had barely bothered to breathe, much less eat in all this excitement. Prusias was famished, exhausted, exhilarated. He glanced down to see the smuggler, a huddled blue misery.

"We'll dine soon, my dear," he chuckled. "Inside where you'll be more comfortable. This will soon be finished . . ."

The demon trailed off as a roar sounded from the worker districts. Prusias had almost forgotten them, their fate a foregone conclusion. But something had changed. Rioters were surging at the gates, joined suddenly by thousands who had taken shelter behind burning buildings. Prusias wheeled on Dr. Wyle.

"Are those gates opening?"

Dr. Wyle was already consulting his computer tablet, his anxious face illuminated by its screen. Blinking rapidly, he tapped the screen. "There must be a mistake," he muttered.

"What mistake?"

"It seems someone's entered the code to open the gates separating the worker districts from the rest of the city."

"How is that possible?"

"I . . . I don't know," the engineer stammered. "The command can only be given from a secure location in the city. The person would have to be on-site."

"Show me!"

The Workshop man tapped hurriedly on his screen. Seconds later, he was staring at something that made him gasp. Prusias snatched the device from the man's hands and found himself looking at a camera feed from a control room terminal. Someone was looking back at him—a pale, scarred man wearing a black cap. Prusias knew that face, had seen the fellow grapple with Grahn at the Gràvenmuir médim. Upon seeing the astonished king, the man touched two fingers to his temple.

"The Red Branch sends its compliments."

Offscreen, Prusias could hear a woman's voice. "William, there's an awful lot of smoke in here. Don't you think we should be going? Toby's getting sick."

The man nodded. "Aye, love. A mob's coming this way and they'll be out for blood." With a wink at Prusias, the man shattered the camera with of the point of a blade. The screen went blank.

Thrusting the tablet back into Dr. Wyle's hands, Prusias hurried to the balcony. Far below, hundreds of thousands of workers—maddened with fire and fear—were pouring through the open gates into the districts of Tier 2. There were no gargoyles to stop them, only half his Imperial Guard—ten thousand troops—who thought they would be firing upon confined and helpless targets. As the mob engulfed them, they were swept away like sandcastles at high tide. A terrifying thought occurred to Prusias. Swallowing his fear, he turned to Dr. Wyle.

"That man can't open the main gate from there, can he? Only I have that authorization?"

"Correct, Your Majesty."

Prusias surveyed the escalating chaos. The worker districts

were contained in a section that took up roughly a third of the lowest tier. Help was nearby, if he was willing to break a few eggs. He was.

"I want the dreadnoughts to destroy that mob before they can reach Tier Three."

"My king," said Dr. Wyle. "The dreadnoughts are not designed for fine work. They'll obliterate everything in the lower districts—buildings and rioters alike."

"What of it?" snapped Prusias. "We can always rebuild. Once that mob is neutralized, this siege is finished. The invaders will die outside my gates."

But even as Dr. Wyle issued the command, Mr. Bonn tugged urgently at his master's elbow. The little imp could not speak. He merely pointed west—not at the great gates or the furious fighting outside them but far beyond. Beyond even the glinting ruins of Grael's legions. He pointed toward the distant sea.

A storm was coming, a storm far swifter than anything in Nature's arsenal. Even here, even with the din below, one could hear the rumble of thunder as the heavy, swirling front of thunderclouds swept toward his city.

Prusias could only stare as the storm assumed something like a physical shape. At first, its form could only be guessed at—an amorphous suggestion of a torso and limbs that advanced upon Blys like a colossus of roiling, billowing vapor. But with every gargantuan step, the figure solidified and its features became clearer. They were wild features, horned features—the features of an ancient and forgotten god. A god Prusias had failed to bribe or conquer, a god who had finally left his isle.

It was the Fomorian.

Leaning down, Prusias unceremoniously yanked the torque from Madam Petra's throat and turned to his speechless imp. "Mr. Bonn, I think it's time we discussed plan B."

~ 20 ~

DRAGON HUNTING

Just outside Blys's gates, Max and Scathach stood panting amid their fallen adversaries. Max's senses were returning, coming into focus as his battle fury dimmed. Many of the nearest enemies had fallen; the others were falling back, fleeing in apparent terror from something behind him. The earth was shaking, groaning with tremors that toppled wains, staggered the living, and bounced the dead like broken mannequins. Max turned as a vast shadow fell over the river and bridges. Its gloom stretched across the battlefield, climbing the massive walls as the Fomorian approached. And all who felt that shadow—every soldier and spirit—fled before it.

Max and Scathach were no exception.

They scattered with the rest, thousands parting in a mad dash to escape the giant's path before they were crushed. As he backed away, Max remembered the demons he'd seen on the giant's beaches, those lifeless husks who thought they'd invade his isle. He understood the terror stamped upon their frozen features.

The giant did not even appear to notice the tiny beings scattering before him, fleeing for the mountains or over the bridges. Hundreds of feet he stood, so huge that he could almost peer over the walls and seize the dreadnoughts that had just withdrawn from the gates. His form was nearly solid now, his legs trailing billows of mist and vapor as he strode across the river and closed upon the city gates. Arrows and bullets peppered his flesh, mortars burst before his eyes, but the Fomorian did not slow or falter. He merely advanced, his eyes white-rimmed with rage as he chanted ancient spells of earth and iron, blood and breaking.

Max did not know what had triggered the giant's appearance. Whether he had chosen to answer their plea, exact revenge against Prusias, or even to make up for the unkind words he'd said about David. Whatever the reason, the Fomorian was here and the game had changed.

Rearing back, the giant smashed his maul against the great gates as a man might take a sledgehammer to a door. The impact sent Max and Scathach flying, tumbling in a heap to rest by a fallen shedu. Scathach was yelling to him, but Max could not hear her. He could not hear anything but a dull, painful ringing. Glancing up, he saw that the gates were dented and smoking. Glowering, the Fomorian drew back his maul and prepared to strike another blow. Max covered his ears.

When the giant's hammer fell, great cracks and fissures appeared in the surrounding stonework. Again and again, the Fomorian struck the gates and walls, hammering them, punishing them, tearing away huge chunks of masonry with his bare hands. That the gates would fall was no longer in question; the Fomorian seemed more intent on reaching the dreadnoughts.

He would soon have that chance. Moments later, the gates and much of the surrounding wall gave way. They crashed inward, a section some fifty yards wide, as massive clouds of dust and grit mingled with the swirling snow.

Blys was breached.

With a roar, the giant charged through the gap, disappearing behind the veil of fire and smoke to overtake the dreadnoughts and drive them to the side, away from the gates. Max glimpsed a dreadnought's tentacle, saw the glint of the Fomorian's maul rise up and descend with terrifying force. It was like witnessing a battle from another age, an age where old gods and monsters clashed for supremacy. But Max could not stop to watch; Blys was breached and there was no time to lose. He had to rally every Rowan and Raszna soldier who had the strength and will to follow.

Gripping the *gae bolga,* he pushed himself up. Prusias's infantry were still in shock from the giant's appearance. Many were fleeing over bridges or retreating en masse toward the mountains from which they had emerged. Those that remained resumed their heated fighting with Rowan and Raszna along the outer wall. Max had to put an end to these skirmishes; they were mere distractions from the main chance.

Seizing the reins of a riderless horse, Max swung himself into the saddle and cantered up and down the battlefield, shouting at all within earshot to follow him. Scathach did the same, shouting at all within earshot to get inside the city. Max was shining once again, burning as bright as a fallen star. And those who beheld him did not doubt or question, quibble or pause—they found heart and strength and purpose. They rallied by the thousands, by the tens of thousands, to answer his call.

Through the breach, through the smoke and dust and fire they raced: humans and vyes, centaurs and Cheshirewulfs, aged Mystics and teenaged refugees. They poured into Blys, giving the embattled Fomorian and dreadnoughts a wide berth. Max and Scathach rode at the fore with several Raszna war chiefs. Beneath great stone arches they stampeded, sweeping past abandoned markets and bazaars, crossing the burning slums and ghettos as they made for the city's upper tiers and the districts reserved for Blys's elite. They needed to make a push for the palace.

There were no gargoyles to hinder them, no troop formations or organized defenses as they ascended the city. But the streets were littered with the bodies of Prusias's troops, dead workers, and the remains of shattered barricades. Max could see the mob ahead. Cooper had done his job; they had passed into Tiers 2 and 3 by the tens of thousands. Ahead was a sea of teeming, raging humans and vyes, pulling down statues and setting fire to anything that would burn in the vast square whose three gates sealed off the city's upper tiers reserved for nobility.

Coming to a halt, Max turned and told Scathach and the war chiefs to keep Rowan's forces and the Raszna back. The mob was in a destructive frenzy and liable to attack any group they saw. Max rode toward them alone.

Thousands turned as Max approached, his aura visible even to the humans. They gazed upon him as the Raszna had done, with a mixture of fear and awe that drove them into obedient silence. Men and women, vyes and goblins began to bow, to kneel and prostrate themselves on the frozen cobbles.

"Get up," Max shouted. "This is your day, and it's not finished. The fighting will be harder near the palace. Strike down any who resist. Give quarter to those who surrender."

"Why?" cried a teenaged girl, her face badly singed. "They'd never give it to us!"

"Which is why you're better than them," Max answered. "You're not animals. You're not slaves. You're not thieves or vandals. You're free people with hearts and souls and honor." He raised the *gae bolga* in a grim salute. "Sol Invictus."

Their roar shook the square. *"Sol Invictus!"*

The workers closed behind Max as he rode toward the central and largest gate. Cooper had hoped to get these open as well, but Max suspected the Workshop's people had by now shut down or incapacitated the control room he, Hazel, and Toby had infiltrated.

Now that Max was here, it would not matter. The doors were covered with gold leaf and elaborately engraved, but beneath this ornamentation was thick steel plating. The *gae bolga* sank through it without the slightest quiver or resistance. The blade might have been cutting foam. When he'd carved out the contours of an opening some twenty feet wide, Max moved aside so the workers could push against it. A cheer went up as the door crashed inward. Hundreds upon hundreds started rushing through, dashing through the gap to renew their long, laborious ascent toward the palace.

Max knew the way would not be easy. These districts were home to the king's nobles, to greater demons with wealth and status, private security and many servants. David had assured Max and the Raszna that he would take steps to minimize resistance once Rowan's forces reached the upper tiers, but he hadn't revealed what form this help would take. But Max knew better than to doubt his friend. If David said he had a plan, then a plan he had.

Max's plan was to create more openings. The one was a start, but it would take too long for everyone to funnel through it.

Speed was of the essence and thus Max guided his mount against the tide of streaming workers, pushing through them so he could carve openings through the other two gates. He had just finished the third when he heard a woman's voice, hoarse and panicked, yelling his name.

Madam Petra stood twenty feet behind him. Scathach had the smuggler gripped firmly by the hair, her poignard at her throat.

"Please!" cried Madam Petra, struggling in vain. "I must speak with you!"

The smuggler's appearance was almost absurd—rich clothes and furs muddied and tattered. She wore one diamond earring, but the other had been ripped from an ear that had bled onto her white stole. Her face was almost as pale as she stamped with a frantic desperation.

"Please!" she cried. "You must help me!"

Max looked past her as a shuddering crash sounded far below where the Fomorian was battling the dreadnoughts. All of Blys was a battleground. He didn't have time for a person who had profited when Rowan was attacked and who had abandoned it for a life of luxury among the demons. She'd made her bed. He gestured for Scathach to turn her loose. "Let her go. She can't hurt us."

Scathach disagreed. "She could be working with the Atropos. We know they're close."

While it was true a Raszna outrider had spied the clones eight days ago, Max could not worry about the Atropos in the midst of a battle. Still, Madam Petra's eyes had widened at hearing the name.

"I know about the Atropos!" she blurted. "I know where Prusias is! I . . . I can help you, but only if you help me!"

Only if you help me was practically the woman's mantra. Still,

Madam Petra did have a talent for acquiring useful information. Max moved away from the opened gate, away from the inrushing tide of workers and soldiers, so that he and Scathach could hear what the smuggler had to say. Scathach dragged the woman over, her blade still pressed to her neck.

"You have ten seconds," said Max. "Prusias first. Where is he?"

"I won't tell you," gasped Madam Petra. "Not unless you promise to help me."

Max shook his head. "Tell me what you know or go on your way. I'm not bargaining with you."

Tears shone in the smuggler's eyes. "B-but you must!"

"Five seconds."

Madam Petra bit her lip, her eyes darting here and there as her mind cast about for angles and opportunities. Max snapped his fingers beneath her nose.

"At Piter's Folly, you said you liked nothing better than a desperate seller," he reminded her. "You're the desperate seller, Petra, and you're running out of time. What do you know?"

"The Atropos are close!" she hissed. "The assassins have been tracking you since you were at Enlyll. I heard their representative talking with Prusias."

He shrugged. This wasn't news.

"What else? Where's Prusias?"

"*Not* in the palace."

"What's that supposed to mean?" said Max impatiently.

"*A* Prusias is in the great hall, but not *the* Prusias. I saw the king slip away with Mr. Bonn and some malakhim. An imposter is ordering the palace's defense."

"Where did he go?"

She gave a knowing smile. "Into his private elevator. An elevator that leads to the underground trains."

"He's fleeing to the Workshop?"

"Your guess is as good as mine."

Max fell silent, weighing Petra's information. He was dimly aware that fires were burning now in the city above them, wild infernos spitting gouts of black smoke into the crimson evening. Far below, Blys's lower districts were almost wholly obscured in a flickering fog of devastation. Everywhere was noise and confusion, torrents of Rowan and Raszna fighters streaming through the gates. A cry sounded behind them. Max turned to see a pair of leaping Cheshirewulfs drag a fleeing oni from his charger. The demon landed heavily on his back, the animals worrying at his throat.

What to do with Petra's information? The woman could be lying, of course. There was nothing she wouldn't say or do if it suited her. Still, unless Max was badly mistaken, her desperation was genuine. And if the king really had fled, they needed to hunt him down. Getting their hands on Prusias—whether dead or alive—was crucial to declaring victory. Max turned to Scathach.

"What do you think?"

"I think she's playing a game," said Scathach coolly. "She wants something and needs you to get it for her. Perhaps it's something to do with that bruise around her neck. Where's Max's torque, Madam Petra? Did someone 'borrow' it?"

The smuggler scowled. "Prusias took it—*stole* it like a common thief! I hope it chokes him. But that's not what I want. I just want my daughter. I want Katarina!"

"Where is she?" Max asked.

"The Workshop! Prusias keeps children hostage to ensure their parents' cooperation. Take me there! Our roads lie together!"

Max frowned. If he and Scathach made for the Workshop, they would leave the battle at a pivotal moment. Madam Petra was untrustworthy and had her own agenda. The entire scenario could be a trap, a wild-goose chase, or simply a mother's frantic scheme to enlist powerful allies. Even if Petra was speaking the truth, there was no guarantee Prusias would be at the Workshop. After all, the smuggler had only seen the king slip onto an elevator. The rest was speculation. He had to speak with David.

Two days earlier, David Menlo had given the Rowan and Raszna commanders small mirrors that could be used to communicate with his pavilion. They were to be used only in true emergencies, a point David had stressed repeatedly. While he would not be participating directly in the fighting, Rowan's Director would be *consumed*—his word—with his own initiatives. Unless the issue was of major strategic importance, David Menlo was not to be disturbed. Max thought this qualified.

Ducking into an empty doorway, Max produced the mirror, clicked open its clasp, and spoke the password. The mirror clouded, its surface swimming with a pearly vapors until Max found himself staring at Cynthia Gilley's round, blinking face.

"Max!" she exclaimed. "What do you need?" Cynthia's voice was anxious but hushed, as though she didn't want to disturb nearby proceedings.

"To speak with David."

"He's very busy. Is it urgent?"

"Yes."

Setting down the mirror, Cynthia disappeared from view. She'd left the mirror propped up, however, allowing a glimpse inside the pavilion. Max caught his breath.

The tent was filled with demons.

Squinting, Max held the mirror close. He couldn't make out any summoning circles, but the demons appeared to be imprisoned, trapped within shimmering columns of energy. Among them, Max recognized some from Prusias's inner court, including several influential braymas. This must have been what David meant by minimizing resistance in the upper tiers—he was summoning away its most powerful residents! Toward the back, he spied someone walking among them—a woman, very tall and trailing a red gown. She turned so that Max beheld her profile.

Lilith!

He had not seen the demoness during any of the siege planning. She must have held talks with David in secret. Now it appeared the Queen of Zenuvia was helping the Director to summon these enemies and keep them captive throughout the siege. Someone picked up the other mirror. The Director's pale, preoccupied face came into view. "Yes?"

Max relayed Madam Petra's information. He did not go into his fears or misgivings—David would already know the risks. The Director listened intently, his expression distant and thoughtful. Once Max was finished, David excused himself for several moments. When he returned, he was with Peter Varga, a member of the Red Branch whose spectral eye granted a hazy, sporadic prescience.

"Max," said David. "Your report echoes impressions that Agent Varga's been getting. It's worth pursuing. Where are you in the city?"

"Felljinn's Square, by the gates to Tier Four."

David nodded. "Go down to the third tier. In the northeast corner, you'll find stairs that lead down to the station. Cooper's already near that location. Look for him and Hazel on the platforms. Peter will meet you there. Your objective is to find and capture Prusias."

Max's disappointment must have been readily transparent. *"Capture,"* David repeated. "We need him alive, Max. I can't explain right now, but trust me."

"Understood."

"Sol Invictus."

Max replied in kind before returning to Scathach and Petra. Pocketing the mirror, he glanced down at the anxious smuggler.

"It's your lucky day, Petra. Don't fall behind."

They made for the third tier, winding down the broad avenues and switchbacks. Max dimmed his aura entirely as they hurried past burning buildings where Raszna and Rowan soldiers were busy rounding up or subduing those who had tried to hide or resist. These appeared to be in the minority; most of Blys's residents were either kneeling in surrender or busy fleeing by whatever exit or means they could. No one attacked or challenged the running trio, not even the ogres and ettins that were busily looting shops. From the worker districts below, there was a deafening roar. Peering down into the haze, Max saw a dreadnought toppling, its tentacles wrapped tightly about the Fomorian's neck. Max wanted to go to the giant, to help him battle the dreadnoughts, but that wouldn't get them any closer to Prusias.

"There it is!" Scathach cried. She pointed to a vast, columned portico built into the dark mountainside. Despite the smoke pouring from its entrance, dozens of people were rushing in. Most wore the gray uniforms of Workshop personnel.

To the station they ran, dashing up its broad steps and then into a hazy chaos of warm steam, acrid smoke, and a press of human and goblin bodies pushing and jostling in a mad race down to the trains. Some squeezed onto pod tubes while others raced down escalators and stairwells, stepping over or trampling those who had fallen.

Things were even more frenzied on the platforms. There were twelve tracks but only three trains, and these were already brimming with passengers desperate to be under way. Fistfights were breaking out as more and more people tried to squeeze and crowd aboard the trains, which connected the capital to the Workshop and to other major cities throughout the kingdom.

Max heard gunshots, saw one of the trains lurch in an abortive attempt to depart.

Amid all the chaos, Cooper was strangely conspicuous. The Agent slipped effortlessly through the crowd of engineers, expending little energy and no emotion. Catching sight of Max, he gestured toward the farthest platform, a platform whose tracks were empty. Max bulled a path down the steps. In characteristic fashion, Cooper didn't waste time on pleasantries.

"Any sign of Peter?" he asked, nodding to Scathach and sparing Petra only a passing glance as he continued to scan the stairways.

"No," said Max. "David just said he's on his way."

With a frown, Cooper glanced down at a Workshop device he held in a bandaged hand. There was another bandage about his neck, dark with clotted blood.

"You're hurt," said Max.

The man waved off his concern. "I'm fine, mate. Lucky shot. Missed the artery. Peter better hurry, though. Our train's ready."

"What train?"

Cooper hooked a thumb at the empty track behind them. "The one this mob can't see. We commandeered it before it could leave. Hazel and Toby are already aboard. She's got the conductor bewitched, and he's keeping the train hidden. Who's the spare?"

"This is Petra Kosa," said Max. "She's—"

"I know that name," Cooper muttered. He fixed the smuggler with an icy stare. "You're Prusias's concubine." There was no accusation in the Agent's tone. William Cooper had done enough terrible things in his life that he wasn't much interested in judgment. He was interested in facts. Madam Petra reddened.

"I'm no such thing!"

Cooper shook his head. "You're lying. Don't ever lie to me.

I'll know it before you do. You're His Majesty's concubine. You leading us into a trap?"

Tears pooled in the smuggler's eyes. "No traps," she said, looking away. "No schemes. I just want my daughter."

Cooper appeared unmoved. His attention flicked away from the smuggler as one of the trains departed. Steam shot from its exhaust valves and its horn blared as it accelerated smoothly down the tracks. Goblins and even some engineers clambered down the platform and ran after it, frantically trying to catch hold of something, anything before the train disappeared into a tunnel.

"There he is," said Cooper, nodding as Peter Varga's unmistakable face appeared at the top of the staircase. The Agent hobbled swiftly down the steps. People moved abruptly out of his path, as though thrust aside by invisible hands.

"I take it that's ours," Varga panted, nodding at the invisible train behind them. Max wondered if the Agent's ghostly, prescient eye could see through illusions.

Cooper nodded. "Hazel's already aboard. Come on."

As they hurried down the platform, the sleek, glossy white train seemed to materialize. Its illuminated blue windows revealed cars packed tight with Workshop personnel staring anxiously at the crowds mobbing the other trains. Many were agitated, shouting ahead at the driver, anxious to be away before their own train was swarmed.

Frightened eyes fell on Max and his companions as they boarded the last car. Cooper led the way, moving people aside as they pushed their way forward. No one checked him or protested. They were met with little more than sullen stares as they moved to the driver's compartment. Cooper smacked its metal door.

"It's me."

There was a sound of mechanized bolts unlocking. The door opened outward to reveal Hazel Cooper, standing aside so they could slip within the driver's cab. Max entered last. As he squeezed into the compartment, he noticed one unconscious engineer slumped against the wall while the driver was awake but clearly under a spell. The man sat upright, his hands resting on a throttle and a blinking instrument panel of chrome and glass as though awaiting instructions. While his posture was alert and attentive, the face Max saw reflected in the windshield was slack and vacant. The cab was cool and humming quietly, its interior bathed in blue light from the instrument panel. Reaching past Max, Cooper pulled the door shut.

"Let's go."

Leaning over the driver, Hazel spoke to him in a soothing voice. With an unblinking nod, the man pushed the throttle. The train began to move, gliding smoothly over magnetic rails. Looking through a side window, Max saw hordes of people racing after them. The illusion must have been dispelled when they started moving.

But the mob would not catch this train. It was accelerating safely and smoothly into a bright tunnel that would bring it to the Workshop. Beside Max, Madam Petra exhaled and shivered, wiping soot and sweat from her brow. Her auburn hair hung dank and limp about a beautiful face now lined with worry.

"What is *she* doing here?" demanded Toby from where he stood upon the co-driver's dashboard in a finch's guise. The bird eyed Madam Petra with sharp disapproval.

"Looking for Katarina," Max replied, sheathing the *gae bolga*'s blade and leaning the spear against a bulwark. "She's just along for the ride. She's got nothing to do with our mission."

"And, er, what is our mission?" inquired the smee. "I hope it involves a proper meal. I'm fairly famished. What's on the menu?"

"A Great Red Dragon," said Scathach, taking a drink from the canteen of water Cooper was passing around.

"Prusias?" The smee shivered. "Heavens!"

Cooper nodded. "Here's the plan. We've got six hundred miles or about two hours until we reach the Workshop. Rest up while you can. Once we're there, we've got one objective: to take Prusias alive."

"Why alive?" asked Scathach.

"I don't know," Cooper replied. "But the Director says it's crucial. Perhaps Peter can enlighten us. I'm guessing that's why he's here."

Agent Varga eased gingerly into the empty seat beside the driver. He'd only recently regained the ability to walk, much less scramble through a chaotic train terminal. Swearing softly in Hungarian, he massaged his knee.

"I don't know why David wants him alive. My task is to recover my soul. Mine and many others."

When Astaroth had given Prusias his kingdom, the latter offered lands and titles to mehrùn in exchange for their souls. A surprising number took the demon up on his offer—sacrificing the next life for land and luxury in this one. When a young Connor Lynch sought to take the demon up on his offer, Peter Varga substituted his own soul for Connor's.

"Does Prusias have many?" asked Scathach.

The prescient nodded. "My soul is but one of thousands in the demon's keeping. Each is locked within a jewel, imprisoned until its human dies and it can be devoured. Wherever Prusias has fled, these jewels will be close, for his kind values souls above all else—they fuel *koukerros*. The Director has tasked me with recovering them. He hopes my own stake in the matter will trigger visions of the demon's location."

"Anything so far?" asked Hazel.

Peter gave a wan smile. "I'm having visions, but not the one I desire."

"You can see the future?" asked Toby excitedly.

"At times."

The finch cocked his small head. "What are you seeing now?"

Varga shrugged. "If you must know, I've just seen my death."

Hopping closer, the smee spoke in a hushed, fascinated tone. "Do you die at the Workshop?"

"Toby!" exclaimed Hazel, shooing at him.

Varga only chuckled. The smee's frank curiosity seemed to amuse him. "Indeed, I do."

The smee was floored. "You know exactly when and where you'll die?" he asked, simultaneously appalled and delighted.

Varga shook his head and gazed ahead at the hypnotic blur of tunnel lights. "My visions suggest possibilities, no more. I've seen myself die countless times and in countless ways. One gets used to it. Tomorrow is promised to no one."

"So, how might you die?" pressed Toby eagerly.

Varga sighed. "In this vision, I'm crushed. In others I've drowned, burned in fires . . . even died from a horse's kick on my grandfather's farm."

Toby hopped even closer. "You know, a man with your talents could make a fortune in horse racing, roulette, cards . . . the possibilities are endless! But you'd need a partner. An amiable chap whose expertise spans turf and baize—"

Hazel pinched his beak shut. "What's our plan when we reach the Workshop?"

Cooper scratched his patchy blond stubble. "If Varga can't locate Prusias, we'll have to find him ourselves."

Max turned to Madam Petra. "What did you hear about his bunker?"

"Nothing much," the smuggler confessed. "Mr. Bonn only mentioned it this morning. He talked about a 'plan B' involving a bunker and a body double. He didn't say anything more specific."

Cooper glanced sharply at her. "You're sure the double stayed in Blys?"

"Positive," she replied. "I saw him barking orders at the Imperial Guard right after Prusias disappeared into an elevator."

The Agent nodded as though convinced she was telling the truth. "All right. Back to tracking down Prusias once we get to the Workshop."

"How big is it?" asked Scathach.

"Huge," replied Cooper wearily. "It's a pyramid, miles wide at the lowest sublevels. It'd take weeks to search it."

"We don't have weeks," said Hazel matter-of-factly. "If we don't know where he is, let's eliminate where he isn't. I think it's reasonable to assume a secret bunker won't be in a busy area. I imagine it would be rather small and tucked away."

Cooper nodded. "If we can access a control center, we could scan the Workshop using surveillance cameras."

"They won't have cameras near the bunker," said Varga.

"Agreed," said Cooper. "Areas blacked out to surveillance become a priority."

Toby gave an anxious shiver. "Let's say we actually find him. How are we supposed to take him, eh? I've seen Prusias when he changes form. He's enormous!"

"If the bunker's small, he won't be able to transform," said Scathach.

"I don't think Prusias would accept that," said Varga. "If he's cornered, he'll want to fight. And he's far more dangerous in his serpent form."

"It doesn't matter what form he takes," Petra whispered. "He's still the Great Red Dragon." She was studying her hands, the rings and bracelets that adorned them. "He can't be appeased. He'll take and corrupt and devour everything. It's what he does."

Her eyes darted to Max and the *gae bolga*. "You must kill him! Slay him with the only weapon he fears."

Cooper shook his head. "The Director wants him alive."

Petra looked down. "Then you will be devoured."

"She has a point," reflected Hazel. "Prusias is ancient. Very few weapons or spells will work against a spirit that powerful. How are we to subdue him?"

"Well, what did Mina do?" wondered Toby. "She handled him readily enough. Shook her little fist and sent him squealing over the sea."

"Mina cast him out," Hazel replied. "But remember that Prusias was invading sacred soil. Settings can play a powerful part in mystics and it's possible Mina tapped Rowan's magic to strengthen her own. I can't say for certain—sorcerers play by their own rules. But Mina's not here. And our task is not to banish a powerful demon from Rowan but to capture him in his own lair. The circumstances are rather different."

"It has to be the Hound," said Varga, gazing at Max. "He's the only one strong enough."

"Peter," said Hazel impatiently. "If we're to take Prusias alive, Max can't use the *gae bolga*. How then is he supposed to subdue Prusias? By sheer brute force? Forgive me, but that's beyond even Max's capabilities."

Scathach almost laughed. "Do you pretend to know what those are?"

Hazel's eyes flashed, but she said nothing. Folding her arms, she glanced at Cooper. "Are you in charge of this mission?"

"I am."

"What's your position, then? Do you agree with Peter?"

"Perhaps we should ask Max," said Cooper. "He's fought Prusias before. He knows the demon's power better than we do."

The Agent turned to Max. "What do you think, Max? Are you up to this task?"

Max gazed at the floor. The truth was that he had always been afraid of Prusias, and not just a little. On various occasions, the demon had charmed, bullied, and dominated him. When Max had been a captive in Blys, Prusias had ordered him to assassinate a rival. When a terrified Max refused, the demon had exploded in rage—seizing him by the throat and dashing him unconscious. The moment's pain and helplessness were seared into Max's memory. And Prusias had not needed to take his true shape . . .

"I don't know," said Max. "Prusias is very strong. There was a time when he made me feel helpless, but I was younger then. I don't think he fears me, but he does fear this." Max nodded at the Morrígan's blade atop his spear haft. "If we find him, he'll assume we've come to kill him. He doesn't know we intend to take him captive. And Prusias is different from other demons— he's much more human. Maybe that's something we can exploit."

"How so?" asked Hazel.

"I've seen demons commit *ahülmm*," Max reflected. "I watched Mad'raast end his own life rather than risk dishonor. I can't imagine Prusias doing anything like that—he finds life endlessly intriguing. I don't think he'll risk his own destruction if there's an alternative. If we can corner him, bluff him into think- ing I mean to end his existence, he might surrender."

"And if he doesn't?" said Hazel.

"Then I kill him."

"But the Director—" said Hazel, ever mindful of protocol.

"Will have to change his plans," finished Max. "I'm not risk- ing your lives so Prusias can keep his."

Three beeps sounded from the control panel where a light was flashing red. A message scrolled across the display screen, accompanied by a calm, computerized voice speaking German. Varga translated.

"It's an emergency broadcast," he reported. "Workshop's in lockdown. All nonsecurity personnel are ordered to their quarters until further notice. Compliance may result in pardons. Noncompliance may result in arrest and termination."

Hazel raised an eyebrow. "A revolt?"

"Sounds like it," said Cooper. "If the entire Workshop's on lockdown and they're threatening to terminate people, it isn't small."

Madam Petra chewed her lip. "My God," she whispered. "If the Workshop's in revolt, what will Prusias's people do to the hostages?" Rising, she lurched at the acceleration throttle. Cooper intercepted her.

"But my daughter," she gasped. "We have to hurry!"

"Think," said Cooper calmly. "Someone's trying to reassert control, nip a situation before it escalates. For Prusias's henchmen to sacrifice hostages at this stage would only make things worse. Katarina's not in immediate danger. Do you understand?"

Nodding slowly, she stepped back and stared ahead at the tunnel. "How much farther?"

"Ninety-six minutes," said Varga, tapping a map screen.

"Listen," said Cooper, surveying them. "We don't know what'll be waiting for us when we arrive. Riots. Troops. We just don't know. We'll let the passengers off first and see what happens. Once we get off, follow my lead. Until then, try to get some rest."

With that, the Agent proceeded to methodically examine his gear and weapons. Each boot, buckle, strap, and sheath was tested to ensure they didn't fail him at a critical moment. The rest followed his example. As Max knelt to check the dagger strapped to his boot, he felt a hand touch his shoulder.

"Where's your brooch?" Scathach hissed.

Max tapped his right boot. "I put it away before the fighting."

Scathach's brow furrowed. "Let me see it."

He retrieved it, polishing the ivory so the Celtic sun gleamed. When he stood, Scathach plucked it from his hand and began fastening it to his baldric. "You know who made this," she whispered pointedly. "And you know its purpose. Wear it near your heart. Always."

Max didn't argue. Scathach was profoundly superstitious, particularly when it came to anything from the Sidh. She might have been exiled, but she remained touchingly loyal to the realm, its rulers, and its customs. Satisfied that the brooch was back in its proper place, she sat in the cramped compartment's entry. Max sat beside her, closing his eyes and trying to get some sleep. Even thirty minutes would be a godsend. To help him nod off, he focused on the compartment's subtle vibrations, the steady humming of the mechanicals . . .

Cooper's voice jolted him awake.

"We're here."

Opening his eyes, Max rose to see the bewitched engineer was pulling back the throttle as they rounded a curve and headed toward a vast terminal lit by artificial daylight. A dozen trains were sitting idle on its tracks. Two were on fire; Max could make out the small figures of Spindlefingers crawling about the smoking cars. Aside from the busy goblins, the terminal appeared to be empty.

~ 21 ~

DEUS EX MACHINA

Cooper turned to Agent Varga. "Do you see anything, Peter? Any hidden surprises?"

Varga was leaning on his cane, looking out the windshield with a look of immense concentration. He shook his head. "I see nothing."

They watched in silence as the engineer slowed the train to a halt. The smell of burning plastic and fuel filled the car. Hazel leaned close to the engineer.

"Thank you for the ride," she murmured. "When we have gone, you will awake and see to your colleague. Now you will open the doors so the passengers can depart."

The man nodded, reaching absently for a button. There was a buzzing sound and Max saw the first of many passengers hurry off the train, making for large glass doors that were cracked and riddled with bullet holes. No security intercepted them. When the last stragglers disappeared, Cooper looked at Varga.

"Any sense of where Prusias might be?"

"He's here," said Varga quietly. "I'm sure of that. But I can't see where. I'm not getting specific clues to his location."

"We make for the nearest control room," said Cooper, studying a handheld device. "There's one five levels up."

Filing out of the driver's car, the group stepped off the train and onto a platform hazy with smoke. Max could hear the fires now along with the sounds of breaking glass and goblins gleefully looting the burning trains. A hand suddenly seized his arm.

"Come with me," pleaded Madam Petra. "The dormitories. That's where Katarina will be. I know the way!"

Cooper yanked her hand away. "We have other business."

The smuggler glared at him before breaking away, running down the platform and out the terminal. Once she was out of sight, Cooper turned to Toby the finch. "Follow her. She might lead us to Prusias."

"If she does, how will I find you again?" asked the smee.

Rubbing her forefinger and thumb together, Hazel kneeled next to Toby and touched his finch's wing. A faint green thread appeared before fading from view. "This is a pixie tether," she explained. "Only you can see it. You can follow it back to me."

"Can I use it now?" squeaked Toby anxiously.

"Be brave," said Hazel gently. "Today, we must all be heroes."

"Very good," sighed Toby. "But if I don't come back, I expect you to write my memoirs. Tallyho!" Puffing out his chest, the finch became a housefly that buzzed once around their heads before zooming off.

Max and the others pressed on. They walked with swift purpose, stepping through the bullet-riddled doors to find a vast, empty atrium. The room pulsed with red emergency lights. Ahead were several pod tubes. The nearest was half melted and appeared unusable. Several bodies lay at its base, charred beyond recognition. Overhead, a toneless female voice droned from hidden loudspeakers.

"Welcome to the Frankfurt Workshop. Have a productive day."

Reaching up, Max unsheathed the *gae bolga* and attached the scabbard to his baldric. The blade hummed, as though tasting the air and liking what it found. Varga promptly stepped away from it. Ahead, Hazel inspected an undamaged pod tube and waved a hand before its sensor. Moments later, a pod arrived, rising like a silver bubble to hover before them. Once aboard, Cooper entered their destination on the pod's control panel.

"There's a control room on S-Five," he explained. "Its operators might know the location of Prusias's bunker. If they don't, we'll access its surveillance cameras to search the Workshop. One way or another, we'll find him."

They rode the rest of the way in silence. Scathach turned about, studying the pod, the magnetic tube, and the flashing emergency lights at every level. To someone who had lived many centuries earlier, it must have seemed utterly alien. "People really live down here?" she said, amazed. "Humans?"

Varga nodded. "Some have never been to the surface."

The Sidh maiden grimaced. "I couldn't stand it. Give me blue skies. A place where I can feel the wind and hear the sea."

"They probably have those things," said Varga, smiling. "It's just artificial. And you visited the Raszna. Arcanum's deep underground, is it not?"

"It felt nothing like this," said Scathach uneasily. "This feels like a tomb of metal and machinery."

With frictionless ease, the pod slowed and stopped at the desired floor. Stepping out, the group followed Cooper down the dim, red-pulsing corridors. Announcements continued to drone, but Max could also hear faint shouts and the report of automatic weapons. Now and again, the floor shivered with tremors that made the lights flicker.

They were not the first to reach the control room. Its smoldering door stood open. Looking within, Max saw that its operators had been slain. Three bodies were heaped upon the floor; two more were sprawled across broken instrument panels. The room's many monitors had been shattered; computers were a hissing tangle of severed wires and circuit boards.

"I can't believe the engineers would do this to one another," said Hazel, breathing through a handkerchief.

Her husband turned one of the bodies over and shook his head. The man had not been shot, but cleaved from shoulder to sternum. "This was malakhim."

"How can you be sure?" asked Scathach.

Cooper nodded at the door. Near the door's handle, a crude symbol had been traced into the metal as though it were soft clay. It looked like a sword or inverted cross set within a circle. "They left their mark."

The malakhim were Prusias's honor guard, fallen spirits who wore black robes and obsidian masks. The fiends never spoke; their masks betrayed no emotion when carrying out their master's will. They were silent sentinels and killers, indifferent to threats, pleas, or bribery.

"Well," said Varga, "if malakhim are here, then Prusias is, too."

"Why would he send them after these people?" asked Hazel.

"I'm not sure," said Cooper, closing the dead man's eyes.

"Maybe he doesn't want anyone in the control rooms to see what he's doing. Let's get moving. This room's useless."

Hurrying back to the tube, they summoned another pod, which soon had them hurtling up toward another control room Cooper had located on his device. Ten seconds later, Max saw a familiar sight—the soaring, open spaces that housed living redwoods near the Workshop's main gate. As they continued ascending, Max saw that the entire area was swarming with activity as groups of engineers were exchanging fire, using upended tables as barricades while others fled for cover behind the towering trees. Dozens of bodies lay amid the wreckage. A lone figure caught Max's eye—a man fleeing several determined pursuers. He zigzagged through the chaos, stumbling and staggering as his pursuers closed the gap. His pursuers were noticeably smaller, perhaps even children . . .

Max smacked the glass. "Stop! We need to go down there."

"Why?" said Cooper.

Max pointed down. "That's Jesper Rasmussen."

Hazel peered down. "Dear Lord. Are those the haglings?"

Max nodded. "Rasmussen might know where Prusias is. Even if he doesn't, he'll know how to use the Workshop's systems better than we can."

Cooper hit a button. Instantly, they began a swift, smooth descent. *Crack!* A stray bullet struck the surrounding tube, cracking its glass as they set down.

"Hazel, take care of the engineers," said Cooper impatiently. "I don't need another bullet."

"I'll go," said Max, squeezing past Varga.

"No," said Cooper. "We need you for Prusias. No unnecessary risks until we find him."

"But—"

"That's a direct order," said Cooper tersely. As the pod door slid open, he darted out, running with Amplified speed toward the fleeing engineer.

"Solas!" hissed Hazel, spreading her fingers. A blinding flash of light filled the vast hall, triggering shouts of dismay. Furrowing her brow, she extended an arm at the distant combatants, spread her fingers, and then made a tight fist. Weapons flew from their grasp, skittering and tumbling over the floor as though drawn by a powerful magnet.

Meanwhile, Cooper had Dr. Rasmussen slung over his shoulder like a sack of grain as he ran back toward the pod. The engineer was shrieking incoherently, twisting about to keep an eye on his determined assailants. The haglings had not given up the chase. They raced after their quarry, clutching cleavers and hatchets, topknots bobbing as they bellowed haggish invective.

Despite their fury, the haglings' speed was no match for Cooper's. The Agent slipped back within the pod, dumping Rasmussen on the floor. The haglings halted as the pod began to rise, their beady eyes following its ascent. Slamming down her cleaver, Callastrophe Shrope shook her fist as the pod disappeared through a hole in the artificial sky.

Rasmussen gasped for air. "They were waiting for me! Waiting near my door when the order came to return to quarters." His dignity forgotten, the man rolled onto his back and clapped a hand over his eyes. "I've been a nervous wreck ever since that hag disappeared from the museum. I knew those monsters were behind it. I . . . I told my colleagues, but they only laughed at me. And then to discover the creatures lurking—*grinning!*—behind my ficus!" The engineer moaned.

Max nudged him with his boot. "That's the second time we've saved you from the Shropes. You might say thank you."

The thin, totally hairless Dr. Rasmussen paused. Removing his hand, his eyes traveled clockwise about the pod, registering each Rowan face with mounting humiliation. Scrambling to his feet, he straightened his uniform. "What on earth are you doing here?" he demanded.

Cooper jabbed a finger in his chest. "Looking for Prusias. You're going to help us."

"Nonsense," scoffed Rasmussen. "He isn't here! He's defending his city."

Cooper's voice became ominously quiet. "No, mate. He's here. Every snake has its hidey-hole and this is his. Where is it?"

Rasmussen sniffed. "I haven't the faintest idea."

Cooper stopped the pod just before it passed through the roof. "Lie again, and it's back to the hags." His finger hovered over the control pad.

"No!" cried Rasmussen. "Truly, I don't know! I heard whispers of a project, but it was classified and I have less access than I used to. Dr. Tressel was in charge."

"Where's Tressel?"

"In her quarters, most likely," said Rasmussen. "Unless she's joined the insurrectionists. A revolt's under way. Some of our best people have been killed."

"Ours too," said Cooper tightly. "Which is why you're going to come with us to Dr. Tressel's quarters."

"But—"

"*Now.*"

"Level Twenty, Pod Bank C," sighed Rasmussen, nodding at the control panel.

Cooper input the destination and the pod zoomed up the tube, banked sharply, and accelerated sideways until it reached another tube and shot upward. Other pods raced past like passing subway cars, some empty and bullet-riddled, others packed with men and women wearing body armor. They stared at Max and the rest. One woman appeared to shout and raise a fist in a gesture that might have meant solidarity or defiance.

"What is going on?" asked Varga. "Who is in revolt?"

"Dr. Kim's people," replied Rasmussen. "He runs mechanical engineering. Some never wanted to serve Prusias and disapproved of certain projects, particularly those involving genetics. But leadership has been too frightened to say no to anything the king asks of them—it's virtual suicide. When it got out that Rowan had broken through Prusias's gates, Kim's followers saw their chance. They raided the armory and are trying to take over key locations. A surprising number have joined them."

"Where do you stand, Dr. Rasmussen?" asked Hazel pointedly.

The man gave a weary, almost despondent laugh. "Honestly, I don't even know. I sympathize with what Kim's trying to do, but if Prusias stays in power, the consequences to those who took part in the rebellion will be unimaginable. Have you heard about the king's Grand Inquisitor?"

The pod slowed as they reached Level 20. Smoke greeted them as the door opened, a greasy black haze as though oil was burning. With Cooper gripping Rasmussen's wrist, the group followed the scientist down several corridors as shouts and bursts of gunfire sounded in the distance. When they reached a pair of double doors at the end of a hallway, Dr. Rasmussen rang its bell and knocked sharply.

When no one answered, Max sheared through the door's locks with the *gae bolga*. As the doors opened, the group slipped inside to find a large suite with several well-appointed rooms, but no Dr. Tressel. Cooper showed his handheld device to Dr. Rasmussen.

"Any way this can track down her current location?"

The scientist shook his head. "You'd need a control room for that information."

"Where's the nearest?" asked Cooper.

"This floor. By Pod Bank A."

The group hurried out of Dr. Tressel's apartment, plunging through the smoke as Rasmussen and Cooper led them toward a main corridor. They followed it several hundred yards before turning down a side hallway. Cooper paused as gunfire sounded, a short burst from somewhere close. There were shouts, a strangled cry, and the sound of retreating footsteps.

Cooper crept forward, motioning for the others to follow at a distance. Kris in hand, he crouched and sprang upward, clinging to the ceiling like a gangling spider that scuttled swiftly around the corner. Max and the others followed, pressing close to the walls.

Peering around a corner, Max saw three malakhim wearing hooded black robes and obsidian masks. The fiends had no idea Cooper was directly above them. They paid no heed to the engineer dying at their feet. The trio's attention was fixed upon the reinforced door identical to that of the gutted control room they'd seen earlier. From within, Max could hear panicked pleas in German for the malakhim to let them be. While two of the spirits waited with their heavy swords, the third traced their unholy sigil upon the door. Metal groaned as the door began to glow orange and smoke. Within the room, the engineers began to scream.

A shadow slipped past Max. He could barely discern Scathach's lithe form closing upon the malakhim. Above the fiends, Cooper slipped a flask from his belt and silently unscrewed the cap. To Max's surprise, Cooper let the cap fall to the floor. In unison, the malakhim looked down at the rattling cap. When they looked up, Cooper splashed the flask's contents in their faces.

The demons staggered back from the door, clutching their masks as red smoke billowed through the eye and nose slits. Cooper dropped to the ground, ducking as the malakhim swung their swords in wild, lethal arcs. Before they could swing again, Scathach impaled one with her spear just as Cooper thrust his kris through another's mask. The third, which had received the bulk of the flask's contents, dropped its sword and dissolved into a pool of smoldering red liquid.

Max and the others joined them by the door as Scathach shifted out of shadow form. Her lip curled as she gazed at the malakhim she'd slain. Its robes were collapsing, its mask bubbling like melting wax. "Unclean things," she muttered, wiping her spear upon its robes.

Rasmussen stared at the dead engineer and then at Cooper.

"What was in that flask?"

"Blood petals," said Cooper, kicking the cooling door. "Open up. It's safe."

"Who are you?" asked a frightened voice from beyond the door.

Rasmussen tore his eyes away from the body of the dead engineer. "Juergen, it's Jesper Rasmussen. Open the door."

A pause. "Yes . . . yes, we see you on the monitor. Are you part of this revolt?"

Rasmussen looked to be somewhat at a loss. "No, I'm not involved with Kim's people. Open the door, Juergen."

Moments later, an electromagnetic lock released and a thin, stricken-looking man peered out the door at them. His shaking hand held a pistol.

"Put that away," said Cooper, brushing past the man as the rest filed in after him. The room was square, perhaps twenty feet to a side with glowing blue instrument panels and surveillance screens lining three of the walls. Aside from Juergen, there were two other engineers—a thirtyish woman with protruding eyes and her long brown hair in a ponytail and a spare young man with brown skin and a shaved head. They were seated at two of the six available workstations and clutching tranquilizer guns. The woman's was pointed at Rasmussen.

"If this is a trick, Jesper . . ."

Rasmussen almost collapsed into an empty chair. "No trick, Olga. I feel as frightened and helpless as you do."

"What do you want?" asked Juergen.

Cooper rounded on him. "Where's Prusias?"

"I . . . I don't know," said the man, quailing under the Agent's gaze. Over his shoulder, a yellow light started flashing on a control panel.

Cooper's eyes darted to it. "What does that mean?"

"Nothing," said Olga. "A train has arrived in the terminal."

Rasmussen cleared his throat. "Agent Cooper, if I don't know the location of Prusias's bunker, it's unlikely these people will. Dr. Tressel is the person you want."

Juergen looked mortified. "I think she was in the armory when Kim's people revolted. Lots of casualties there."

"Is there a way to know if she's alive?" asked Cooper.

"Her file will have biometric data," said the young male engineer.

"What's your name?" asked Cooper.

"Dr. Rios, sir."

"Pull up her file."

Dr. Rios typed quickly and the face of a woman in her early fifties appeared onscreen, along with a slew of data, such as her rank, sector, serial number, and recent work assignments. Dr. Rios pointed glumly at a flashing indicator.

"Deceased."

Cooper frowned. "Rios, who's the most senior person that reports to Dr. Tressel?"

The man scrolled to another screen. "George Whitner, materials specialist. Dr. Whitner invented the—"

Cooper cut him off. "Is Dr. Whitner alive?"

More keystrokes brought up the image of an intense-looking man with glasses, short gray hair, and piercing blue eyes. "Yes, sir," said Dr. Rios. "Dr. Whitner is alive, has a steady heart rate, and is located on Level Sixteen."

"That's the man I want," said Cooper, squinting at the screen and then inputting some data into his handheld device.

"Where did you get that?" asked an incredulous Juergen.

"Been sneaking 'round here for months," muttered Cooper, now studying a map. "Your toys are right handy." Pocketing the device, he turned to his companions. "I'm going to find this Dr. Whitner and see if I can get the bunker's location from him. You stay here and see what you can find using surveillance cameras. If you come across malakhim or areas where cameras are disabled, they could mean Prusias is close. I'm sure our new friends will be happy to help you."

"How long should we give you?" asked Max.

Cooper looked sharply at him. "An hour. If I'm not back, send Scathach or Peter after me. Not you. Save your energy for Prusias when we find him."

Hazel loudly cleared her throat.

"And not you," said Cooper. "Scathach and Peter are Agents and neither is six months pregnant. Besides, there's no guarantee Dr. Whitner will know where Prusias is. I'd rather you focus on using the resources in here. You might locate him before I do. Lock the door—it looks like malakhim are seeking out control rooms."

Giving his unsmiling spouse a peck on the cheek, Cooper

slipped out the door. When the door's lock sealed, Hazel stood and clasped her hands behind her back. Max almost pitied the engineers.

"You heard him," she said tartly. "Juergen, you and Dr. Rios are going to initiate a systematic scan of the Workshop, starting with the sublevels. Any sign of Prusias, imps, malakhim, or disabled cameras, I want to know. Olga?"

"Dr. Medved," said the woman stiffly.

Hazel inclined her head. "Dr. Medved, I want a report on all personnel assigned to Dr. Tressel in the last six months. If she can't help us, I want to know who else might be able to."

A tremor shook the control room, showering them with bits of rubble and debris. Several instrument lights flashed and one of the screens went dark.

"A blown energy converter," muttered Juergen, pulling up a holographic map of the Workshop pyramid and zooming in on a flashing red dot. "That's bad."

Hazel snapped her fingers. "Then you had better hurry!"

Sheathing the *gae bolga*, Max leaned it against a wall and sat at one of the empty workstations. He felt like he was being shunted to the side until the pivotal moment. He understood the logic of it, but he also found it irritating. His eyes flicked to Dr. Medved, who was glancing frequently in his direction. Max glowered.

"What?"

"I'm sorry," she said. "It's just . . . you're *him*."

She swiveled in her chair to stare at him with unabashed curiosity. There was nothing lurid in her gaze; it was one of remote admiration. Her tone was reverent.

"You're the Original. I almost feel like I know you. You've grown up so much!"

"What are you talking about?" snapped Max.

The scientist beamed. "I worked on your project. My team tried to duplicate your DNA. You gave us more than a few headaches."

"Dr. Medved, that's enough," barked Rasmussen.

"No," said Max. "I want to hear. You worked on the clones?"

"Alpha, mostly," said Dr. Medved proudly. "He was my baby. I nearly cried when we sold him. We all knew Omega had to go—too wild—but I really hoped Alpha would work out. He was magnificent."

Rasmussen squirmed. "This is not the time or place, Dr. Medved. Do you have the reports on Dr. Tressel's subordinates?"

"Just sent them to Juergen," she answered. While Juergen and Dr. Rios were busy scanning surveillance feeds to eliminate or highlight possible bunker locations on the hologram, Dr. Medved's attention remained riveted on Max. "How tall are you?" she asked.

"Six-five."

She gave a satisfied smile. "Just as we predicted. What beautiful genes. Human perfection right in our hands but its deepest mysteries eluded us. How I'd love another go." The woman's tone was wistful.

Scathach's knuckles whitened around her spear. "So you're responsible for those animals."

The scientist almost seemed oblivious to Scathach's tone. "Omega was an animal," she conceded readily. "But that was by design. Not Alpha. Up until the chip, we really thought we'd done it."

"What chip?" asked Max.

Thus far Peter Varga had been sitting quietly, his cane resting across his knees. He now tapped it gently on Max's chair leg. "I think you should leave this for now," he said. "It is upsetting you."

Max glared at him. "These clones work for the Atropos.

Every minute of every day, they're trying to end my life. This woman is going to tell me everything she knows. Isn't that right, Dr. Medved?"

The scientist smiled. "You're the Original. I can do better than tell you. I can show you."

"Max," said Hazel. "We have another task at hand."

"Am I interfering with it?" he replied. "My orders were to sit here."

Pursing her lips, Hazel turned back to study the changing feeds from surveillance cameras. Whenever a screen came up black, Dr. Rios entered the camera's position on a three-dimensional map of the Workshop.

Max pulled his chair next to Dr. Medved as she accessed a different database. The screen went black before three simple words appeared:

Deus ex Machina

"'God from a Machine,'" she translated, before entering a password and placing her thumb on a sensor. "A little joke for the project name. But that was our goal, after all—to create a god in the lab. And we got so close!"

Menus and files appeared on the screen. Dr. Medved selected one and Max found himself staring at three human embryos. The scientist tapped the screen from left to right. "Alpha, Zeta, and Omega."

"The three clones," breathed Max.

"Technically speaking, they're not clones," Dr. Medved corrected. "We could not replicate you, not entirely. Some of your sequences could not be duplicated. Nevertheless, they share over ninety-nine percent of your genetic material. To complete the sequence, we used alternate sources of DNA. Alpha's was synthetic. Zeta's was from superior human stock. Omega's came from more primitive samples. Zeta was the most like you."

"Zeta was Myrmidon," said Max, recalling his final match in Prusias's Arena. He would never forget his feelings of grief and horror when he'd removed his opponent's helmet only to discover a younger version of himself.

"Correct," said Dr. Medved. "Prusias demanded proof of concept and so we accelerated Zeta ahead of the others. Myrmidon performed most admirably in the Arena until he met you. A pity he died, but there are lessons in every failure. We applied them to Alpha and Omega."

She tapped a key and the embryos were replaced with two newborns floating in separate tanks filled with a gelatinous substance. One was noticeably larger and fast asleep. The other was emaciated and shivering, its tiny hands tugging in vain with tubes that protruded from its arms, head, and chest. A sequence of lights flashed from a nearby machine. The sickly child promptly stiffened and began bawling. Immediately, a nurse arrived to stroke and feed its larger neighbor. No one comforted the baby that was screaming; the cameras simply kept recording.

Max felt sick. "Why doesn't someone help him?"

Dr. Medved merely shrugged. "It wasn't part of his protocol."

"But you're feeding the other one."

"Of course," she replied. "Alpha was rewarded whenever his brother suffered. It reinforced his sense of superiority. When Omega was shocked, Alpha was caressed. When Omega was starved, Alpha was fed. One received only negative feedback, the other only positive. The outcomes were remarkable."

With a few clicks, she played many clips on several screens. Max watched in silent horror as the clones were aged in accelerant tanks, subjected to unconscionable experiments, and plugged into combat simulations. They grew before his eyes. Alpha became a larger version of Max, while Omega was neglected and tormented until he was as sly and feral as a jackal.

Scenes from the clones' combat scenarios flickered like pages from a flipbook. Hundreds of scenes, thousands of scenes. Alpha was a juggernaut who dominated his opponents with brute strength and relentless, overpowering offensives. Omega was craftier. He darted in, feinting and retreating, always seeking attacks of opportunity. Whereas Alpha favored sword and spear, Omega preferred knives and teeth.

"Study their patterns," said Scathach, touching Max's shoulder. He nodded. Although the clones were exceedingly skilled and made few mistakes, some tendencies were inevitable. Even Omega betrayed some.

Max watched in morbid fascination as Workshop surgeons injected a pubescent Alpha with nanocompounds to enhance his musculature. When a captive witch carved wards and spells into Omega's flesh, the youth did not flinch or cry out. He merely stared up at the camera, his eyes as dead as a doll's.

What the hell did they do to you? Max had asked this of Omega the first time they'd met. The reply chilled him to this day. *Everything, everything, EVERYTHING!*

Max stared at the floor. *They certainly had.*

He wanted to be angry, to be shocked and outraged by what he'd seen. Instead, he felt a profound and puzzling sorrow. He turned to Dr. Rasmussen, who'd been stealing covert glances throughout Dr. Medved's explanations. "How could you let this happen?" Max asked him quietly. "What was the point?"

Dr. Rasmussen opened his mouth to answer but could not find the words. His colleague spoke up instead.

"We wanted perfection," said Dr. Medved impassively. "But we wanted perfection that we could control. We needed to ensure the clones would obey and that's where we encountered problems."

Rasmussen rubbed his temples. "Please, Olga. Enough."

Max swiveled back to her. "What went wrong?"

The scientist's eyes wandered over his face with an abstracted expression that reminded Max of David. "You did. Your DNA is wildly unstable. All DNA can mutate and cause changes in an organism, but yours does so more radically and spontaneously than anything we've ever seen. This is confined largely to the sequence we couldn't replicate, but the change is dramatic. It's like you become a different order of being. The closest comparison is daemonic *koukerros,* but the triggers of *koukerros* are well known. We could never predict how or when your DNA might change. The clones also have this trait, although it's not as pronounced."

"So the clones . . . mutated?"

Olga nodded grimly. "Simultaneously. Since we'd only observed mutations in the DNA sequence we could not replicate, we did not think the clones were capable of spontaneous change. As it turned out, we were mistaken."

She clicked a file. On the screen, Max saw Alpha and Omega lying on a pair of operating tables while a team of surgeons finished cutting a small, circular hole in their skulls. A number of Workshop officials were in attendance, observing from an elevated gallery. Max saw Dr. Rasmussen among them, grinning at something his colleague whispered, while surgeons implanted what looked like small microchips into the clones' brains. Once these were installed, the surgeons repaired the skulls and sewed their scalps into place.

"As they got older, Alpha and Omega were becoming too willful, too independent," explained Dr. Medved. "Dr. Wagner developed these chips to moderate the functions of their frontal lobes and make them more compliant. However, when we tried to override their brain functions, the clones mutated as some sort of defense mechanism. We lost control entirely."

The recording now showed one of the surgeons, presumably Dr. Wagner, addressing the gallery. When they applauded, he nodded to a technician sitting at a nearby computer. The man pressed a button.

The clones awoke instantly. In a blink, Omega sprang from his table onto the technician, snapping the man's neck and smashing his computer. Meanwhile, Alpha seized hold of Dr. Wagner. The scientist struggled in vain as the muscular clone eased off the table. While his colleagues fled, Dr. Wagner was pinned, kicking and screaming, onto his own operating table. When Omega handed Alpha a trepanning saw, Olga stopped the video.

"You get the idea," she sighed. "We had to secure and gas the room. The sedatives required would have killed ten elephants. The tests we ran revealed a dramatic change in their physiology and capabilities. Alpha was twice as strong as before, Omega twice as quick. We removed the microchips hoping they would somehow revert to their previous state, but they did not and were deemed too dangerous to keep. Given how expensive the program had been, we sought to recoup our losses rather than terminate them."

"So you sold them," Max muttered. "To the Atropos."

The scientist was unapologetic. "Of course. They offered more than anyone else, even the wealthier braymas."

"If you couldn't control them, how do the Atropos?" asked Scathach.

"I can't say precisely," replied the scientist. "We taped the transfer, but the recording was corrupted somehow. Our technicians

believe it was due to some trick or devilry by the guild's representative. Portions are legible, but the audio is useless."

"Let me see it," said Max.

"As you wish," said Dr. Medved, clicking a file.

The footage came from a mounted camera positioned in
the corner of a spartan holding cell. Opposite the cell's reinforced door, Alpha and Omega sat impassively in anchored steel
chairs with computerized restraints about their necks, wrists,
and ankles. As soon as the door opened, the picture scrambled
momentarily and a high-pitched buzzing began. As the image
steadied, Max could just make out a dark figure entering the
room. It wore hooded robes and bowed low to the clones before.

"That's the Atropos buyer?" asked Max.

"Indeed," said Dr. Medved.

The image scrambled once again. "Go back," said Max.

She did as he ordered, pausing the video at a moment of relative clarity. Leaning forward, Max stared hard at the screen.
"Zoom in on him."

The Atropos buyer grew larger until his face filled the
screen. The upper half was largely shadowed and there was intricate skinscrolling, but the smile was unmistakable. It remained
unchanged from when Max had seen it as a Rowan First Year. It
was composed and pitiless, the smirk of one who enjoyed inflict-
ing or witnessing pain.

"You know him," said Scathach, looking closely at Max.

"I think I do," said Max. "His name is—or was—Alex
Muñoz. He used to be a Rowan student. He tortured Connor
Lynch and Ms. Richter when Astaroth conquered Rowan."

Hazel hurried over to peer at the screen, her eyes narrowing
to angry slits. "If Alex serves the Atropos, he's the reason William was possessed and sent hunting after you like a mad dog. I'm
going to wring his neck."

"Get in line behind Connor," said Max grimly. "Alex is why Connor left Rowan for Blys. I'm not surprised he joined the Atropos. The guild's perfect for someone who enjoys frightening others and causing pain. I'll bet Alex entered my name in their Grey Book himself."

"But how could he control the clones?" asked Scathach.

Max had no answer until Dr. Medved continued the video. The remainder was garbled until the very end. Just before the clones were released from their bonds, Alex produced something from his robes and showed it to Alpha and Omega. A closer view revealed a golden object almost like a pocket watch.

"Do you know what that is?" asked Dr. Medved. "We saw it but could not determine why the object would hold any special significance for the clones."

"That's David's compass," said Max heavily. "The Atropos took it from Cooper when he was possessed. Its needle doesn't point north. It always points toward me."

Agent Varga addressed Dr. Medved. "Did the clones already hate Max?"

"Of course," she replied. "He's the Original. When clones learn they're only a copy, it triggers a profound identity crisis that causes most to despise the Original."

"But lots of your people are clones," said Max.

"Yes," said Dr. Medved. "But they're not clones of a superior person who had his own identity and history and deeds. They're simply a combination of desirable traits engineered in a lab. They don't come from any one person."

"So that's why they obey," said Varga quietly. "The Atropos gave them an identity other than trying to be a copy of an Original. In addition, they gave them the tool and even a mandate to destroy the Original they'd come to hate."

Max did not know what to make of Varga's theory. He did

not even know what to make of the clones. He felt more pity than hatred. From the moment of their inception, Alpha and Omega had been slaves, experiments corrupted by twisted science. Someone had taken babies and turned them into monsters.

"Turn it off," said Max disgustedly. "I've seen enough." He turned to Hazel. "How long has Cooper been gone?"

"Twenty-seven minutes."

"Should it be taking this long?" Max asked Rasmussen.

The man considered. "Who can say while things are in such a state? Agent Cooper may have encountered enemies or been forced to go on foot. Perhaps Dr. Whitner fled from him. He's hardly a comforting sight."

"Can we get a visual on Dr. Whitner's quarters?" asked Max.

Hazel shook her head and gestured at the holographic model of the Workshop. It showed a blue three-dimensional pyramid divided into a slew of stories. Throughout the Workshop, substantial sections had been highlighted red where surveillance was disabled. "Dr. Whitner's quarters are here," she said, pointing to a sizable red section. "That entire area is a blackout."

"And no sign of Prusias," said Dr. Rios. "No large congregations of malakhim. And over thirty percent of the surveillance feeds aren't working."

"No," the teacher sighed. "It's hard to pinpoint possible locations when we can't see. Almost a third of the map is dark."

Rasmussen sat up as though a thought had just occurred to him. "That's true," he said. "But we could cross-reference additional data to narrow the possibilities."

"What data?" said Hazel.

"Dr. Tressel's," he replied. "All Workshop personnel wear badges that mark their position relative to broadcast beacons. We could take the last few months of her location data and project it against this map. It would show us where she was spending her time."

"How long will that take?" asked Hazel.

"Five minutes," said Juergen. "Maybe ten. I just have to write a special script."

"Get going," said Hazel. "Meanwhile, let's keep scanning. I want to know where my husband is."

There were over forty working screens in the control room. Each displayed a camera feed for ten seconds before switching to another. The camera's location was indicated by serial numbers at the bottom of the screen. Max scanned the glowing screens, looking for Cooper and any evidence of Prusias and his malakhim. Many screens were black or revealed empty corridors and laboratories. Others showed people running or fighting throughout the Workshop.

"Go back!" blurted Scathach, pointing at a screen along the top row. Dr. Rios hit a button and an empty corridor was replaced by an aerial view of an enormous, high-ceilinged room filled with exhibits. At once, Max recognized it as the Workshop's museum, where they displayed exotic creatures. Some members of the permanent collection were long dead; others (such as Cousin Gertie) had been frozen in a state of suspended animation. Fire was spreading across the museum floor while some of the exhibit cases had been shattered.

"The exhibits," said Dr. Medved uneasily. "Some must be loose!"

"Move the picture left," said Scathach urgently.

The camera panned as Scathach ordered, revealing a dozen people backed into a corner alcove by a creature with a squatty, reptilian body akin to a komodo dragon. But this creature was far larger and boasted six legs and a forked, whiplike tail that swished back and forth. Its serpentine head was adorned with horns whose circular arrangement resembled a crown. The only thing keeping the monster at bay was the long piece of metal one of the people was jabbing and swinging every time the creature advanced.

"I think that's the basilisk," said Dr. Rios.

"Well, I'm positive that's Madam Petra," said Scathach. "Zoom in."

Dr. Medved obeyed. As the image grew larger, Max saw that it was indeed the smuggler. Apparently, she'd succeeded in rescuing her daughter and some ten other children from the dormitories. Now she was all that stood between them and an escaped museum exhibit.

Max's knowledge of basilisks was confined to what he'd read in Rowan compendiums. Their crowns caused some to call them the "king of serpents" but their real notoriety stemmed from a gaze so dreadful it was said to kill anyone who met it. Apparently Madam Petra knew what she faced, for the children looked away while the smuggler studied the basilisk's shadow. Just as it reared back to strike, something small and furry leaped upon its back.

"Is that a *mongoose*?" exclaimed Juergen, frowning.

Rasmussen scoffed. "What would a mongoose be doing in the Exotics wing?"

Hazel cursed softly. "That's not a mongoose. It's a smee we sent to spy on that woman. A silly, heroic smee who's going to get himself killed . . ."

Scathach snatched up her spear. "How do I get there?"

"I'll go with you," said Max, rising.

"No," said Hazel firmly. "William said you're to remain here."

"She's not going alone," said Max.

Scathach almost laughed as she unbolted the door. "I'm not afraid of a basilisk. I slew one on Skye. And I'll not stand by to see Toby or those children hurt—even if it means saving that vile woman."

Rasmussen pointed at a map on his handheld device. "The museum's almost directly beneath us on Eighteen. Go left out the door. A pod tube's no more than sixty meters away."

"What if it's broken?"

"There's an emergency stairwell just past it."

Gripping her spear, Scathach hurried out the door as Juergen opened it. As Rasmussen locked it behind her, an anxious Max turned back to the screens. Toby was no longer a mongoose, but a python coiled about the basilisk's plated neck. The beast paid him little heed, however. Its focus was squarely upon the cornered children as it tried to get around the irksome human in its way. Petra was making a valiant stand, but Max could see that she was tiring. Every swing was a little slower, a little less effectual than the one before it.

Come on, Scathach. Hurry.

"Damn," said Juergen, staring fixedly at his computer.

"What's the matter?" snapped a pacing Hazel.

"There's no location data for Dr. Tressel," he said. "Not for weeks. Whatever she was working on, it was top secret. Data exemptions are rare."

"Which would seemingly reinforce the idea that Tressel's project was, indeed, the creation of Prusias's bunker," said Hazel.

"What about her team?" asked Varga. "If exemptions are rare, perhaps there's data for her subordinates. Overlay their movements on the map. If the bunker was Tressel's project, if many of them are going to one place, it's likely to be the bunker's location. Can you get that information for the people on Dr. Medved's list?"

"Let's see," said Juergen, pulling up a list of names and

entering several commands. Columns of data appeared by each name. "It looks like it's here. I'll need a minute to tweak the script."

The situation in the museum was turning grim. Madam Petra was barely swinging the pole and visibly gasping as she tried to lure the basilisk away from the children. An exhausted Toby was no longer a python but lay curled in his native yamlike shape on the floor just beyond reach of the basilisk's tail, which was swishing back and forth, like a playful cat's. Suddenly, the monster struck. Petra leaped aside, dropping her weapon as the basilisk's jaws snapped inches from her face. Pinning the smuggler with its foreclaw, the basilisk swayed up for the kill.

An explosion of light filled the screen. When the image returned, Max saw Scathach driving the monster back with swift jabs and slashes of her spear. The basilisk recoiled from this new attacker, backpedaling on stubby legs while black blood poured from a wound at its throat. It spilled upon the floor, sending up gouts of smoke as the substance corroded the pale marble. Scathach stepped lightly around it, her attention fixed on the monster's shadow. In one hand she gripped her spear, the other her slender poignard.

When the monster struck, she just leaped beyond its reach while unleashing a vicious counterattack. Scathach's anticipation and footwork were flawless, her counters perfectly aimed and executed. After four or five of these exchanges, the basilisk writhed backward in retreat, leaving a trail of smoking slime upon the tiles.

"She's got him," said Varga. "What a fighter!"

Max grinned. As Scathach positioned herself between the basilisk and the alcove, she pointed Petra and the children toward something, presumably an exit. Struggling to her feet, the smuggler grabbed the hand of a blond girl, perhaps twelve years old.

Katarina hardly resembled the cold and haughty girl he'd met in Piter's Folly; she had grown thinner and she looked frightened and dazed. Holding hands, the two led the other children in the direction Scathach had pointed.

"Scathach probably told them how to come here," reflected Hazel. She turned to Juergen. "How's that script coming?"

"Finished," said Juergen proudly.

Max glanced over to see some twenty blinking dots appear within the Workshop model. Some were stationary, but others were moving slowly in corridors or traveling smoothly in pod tubes. It was like watching a high-tech ant farm.

"Every dot is someone who reported to Dr. Tressel recently," Juergen explained. "This is what they were doing at eight in the morning six weeks ago."

"Can you speed it up?" inquired Hazel impatiently. "I want to see patterns, not watch someone cut their fingernails."

"You didn't ask for time lapse," grumbled Juergen, swiveling back to his terminal. Hazel sighed.

Max returned to Scathach's screen where the unmoving basilisk now lay in a pool of its own blood and venom. Scathach was staring coolly in the direction of the doorway where she had sent Madam Petra and the children. Scores of Workshop people were running past her, fleeing something beyond the camera's view. Hefting her spear, Scathach advanced toward the unseen danger. Max glanced impatiently at nearby screens to see if they gave any indication of what else was happening in the museum.

To his annoyance, one screen still displayed footage from the clones project. In this clip, they were standing beside one another, smiling grimly by a burning archway. Alpha carried his enormous spear while Omega bore a pair of slender knives. Max jabbed a finger at the screen.

"No more recordings. I want to see more of what's happening in the museum."

Behind him, Hazel gave an exultant whoop. Max turned to see the little dots moving much more swiftly about the Workshop hologram. Despite minor variations, the general pattern was unmistakable: the dots were congregating in one of the deepest corners of the pyramid.

"What level is that?" asked Hazel.

"Sublevel Twenty-Two," said Rasmussen, squinting at the map. "Of course. That's the same level and location as—"

"There's your husband," interrupted Dr. Rios, pointing at a screen that showed Cooper running down a smoky corridor with a man slung over his shoulder.

"Thank heavens," Hazel sighed. "Where is he?"

Dr. Rios gestured at the camera's serial number. "Nineteenth level, southwest quadrant. He's on foot, so I'd guess the nearest pods are malfunctioning."

Hazel was visibly relieved. "Well, it doesn't appear that he's hurt. And he has Dr. Whitner. How long until he can reach us?"

"If he has to remain on foot, ten or fifteen minutes," said Rasmussen.

"Well," said Hazel, glancing at the holographic pyramid, "I believe we got the answer first. I'll try not to gloat."

Swiveling back, Max found Dr. Medved glued to Alpha and Omega's screen. The pair walked out from the archway's shadow and disappeared from view. Max waved a hand before her eyes.

"Switch to a live feed from the museum."

The woman blinked as though jolted from a trance. She tapped the screen, her voice ripe with horror. "That *is* a live feed!"

Max's blood turned to ice. He could not move; he could only stare at Scathach's screen as she came to a halt amid the broken glass and dancing firelight. Two long shadows appeared before her, one of which seemed to be carrying a spear. The shadow with a spear stood fast; the other began to circle. Scathach's expression never changed. Inclining her head, she offered the warrior's salute and advanced.

Springing from his chair, Max snatched the *gae bolga* and scrambled to the exit. Based on Rasmussen's earlier directions to Scathach, the museum was just two floors below them, a pod tube just sixty yards down the hall. He didn't wait for the lock but wrenched the door half off its frame as Rasmussen scrambled out of the way. Turning left, Max raced down the hallway. He was scarcely aware of the blaring alarms. He barely registered Madam Petra and the Workshop children as he passed them in the corridor. His mind was fixed on Scathach and those terrible shadows.

The pod bank was in flames, a morass of bubbling glass and plastic. Max made for the emergency stairwell, flinging open the fire door and leaping down the steps.

When Max burst through the doors on Level 18, he could scarcely breathe. His body was numb with panic, the *gae bolga* lifeless and leaden, as it always was when the clones were near. Ahead was a grand archway—the very portal the clones had stood beneath. A great fire was burning just beyond, its brilliance dancing on the corridor wall.

Hurtling through the archway, Max entered the vast museum but saw no sign of Scathach or the clones. Distant shouts and screams echoed in its grand acoustics. Oily fires dotted the entire Exotics wing, as though combustible liquids were seeping through cracks in the floor.

Max looked wildly about, yelling Scathach's name again and again. There was no answer, just the crackle of flames and the dull boom of distant explosions. Trotting forward, he turned in circles, searching frantically for any sign of Scathach or the clones. He yelled her name again, hurrying toward the basilisk when he glimpsed its glinting carcass.

Where was she? Was she even here? Had the clones taken her?

His eyes swept a row of alcoves and galleries. Something was lying there, pressed against the base of an exhibit. Not a thing, but a girl lying in a pool of blood. Max's worst fears had been realized.

He was by her in an instant, kneeling as he took hold of her hand.

"Can you hear me?" he said.

Scathach's eyes met his. Touching her wrist, he felt her life, faint and flickering but life all the same. Gazing up at Max, she tried to speak but only expelled a tiny breath of air, not even enough for a gasp. Glancing down, Max searched for the wound.

It was not hard to find: a spear thrust through the back that stopped just short of piercing the mail corselet above Scathach's heart. She would not suffer long. Pressing her against him, Max trembled with grief and rage. He didn't care if the clones were near. He brushed a thin black braid off her forehead and kissed her clammy, salty skin. He kissed her pale cheeks and graying lips. Scathach was crying, her tears mingled with his and it frightened Max, for he'd never seen her do such a thing. She was far too proud. But gazing down, Max saw that her gray eyes were shining with love, not pain or sorrow. If she could not speak her goodbyes, she would say them another way.

A sudden, wild hope seized him. He ripped the ivory brooch from where Scathach had pinned it to his baldric. "This can save you!" he exclaimed. "This can bring you back to the Sidh!"

Max ignored Scathach's look of dismay. He did not know how the brooch was supposed to work, only that Lugh had made it to ferry him to the Sidh when he died. Pressing the brooch to

Scathach's chest, he spoke in an urgent hiss. "I give its power to her. I don't want it. Bring her back instead!"

Nothing happened. Max repeated his pleas, his voice raw and ragged. His petitions had become mere sobs. Pressing the brooch against her chest, he rocked her gently in his arms.

I love you. I love you. I love you . . .

A moment later, Scathach gave the tiniest shudder imaginable. Pulling back, Max looked into that young, noble face just inches from his own. Its expression was peaceful, the gray eyes sightless.

With a howl, Max slammed Lugh's brooch onto the marble floor. It cracked into pieces, fragile as a sand dollar. "Goddamn you," he seethed. "Goddamn you! Goddamn you!"

At that instant, Max felt something shatter within him. Every bone and muscle, every nerve seemed to split apart, unleashing an inferno burning deep inside. The blaze tore through his being—burning him, choking him, consuming him—until the last scraps of his mortal self had been incinerated. When the firestorm had passed, all that remained was the god.

~ 22 ~

JUGGERNAUT

When Cooper reached Max, he found him kneeling beside Scathach. The lad did not turn as the Agent approached. He seemed oblivious to Cooper's presence, to the encroaching flames, to everything but the young woman leaning against his chest. Cooper surveyed their surroundings but found no sign of the clones. Their absence puzzled him. Their target was here, back exposed, vulnerable. They must be nearby. A second scan revealed nothing.

The Agent's eyes fell upon Scathach. The girl's head was resting on Max's shoulder. One look at her blank, bloodless face told him she was gone.

Damn.

There was not much more to say. Scathach's death was a significant blow for Rowan, the Red Branch, and most importantly for Max McDaniels. There were only two people William Cooper truly loved: his wife and the young man before him. He couldn't begin to imagine the pain he would feel if he lost Hazel. So many that Max held dear had been taken from him: his parents, his Nick, and now Scathach. How would he react to this?

Cooper's wary eyes fell on the *gae bolga,* which lay on the marble floor, its dark blade drinking the firelight rather than reflecting it. Slowly, Max extended a trembling hand over the spear. He made a fist, convulsively clenching and unclenching his fingers as though fighting the urge to seize the awful weapon.

A deep and growing fear welled up in Cooper. It filled his stomach like cold venom, a feeling of imminent danger stronger than anything he'd experienced since he'd encountered the Fomorian many years ago. But this sensation was far worse. And it was building steadily.

"Max," said Cooper.

No response.

Hazel and Agent Varga came hurrying through the archway. His wife stopped to pluck up Toby from where the unconscious smee lay by the shattered exhibit case. Cradling him in her hand, she caught up to Varga, who had slowed to a walk. Upon seeing Scathach's lifeless body, Hazel gave a choking cry. She made a beeline for Max, but Cooper intercepted her.

"Wait."

"William, he needs us!" she gasped.

"Hazel," he said calmly. "Something's wrong."

"Of course something's wrong. Scathach—"

"Not Scathach. Max."

Varga had already stopped short. Shading his eyes, the

prescient was peering at Max as though he perceived something, some energy field or aura that they could not see. He gave a hoarse cry. "Back away from him!"

Cooper obeyed, pulling Hazel with him as they skirted burning pools and broken glass. Twenty yards. Thirty. From somewhere high above came a harsh, rhythmic clanging that sounded like overheating pipes. Cooper kept his eyes fixed on Max until the clanging intensified.

Twisting around, Cooper looked up, following the sound until he spied an observation balcony nestled beneath the roof beams high above. There stood Max's clones, leaning over its railing and gazing down on them. The feral one was striking the balcony with a heavy rod so that its din rang out like mock applause. A second look revealed it was not a rod, but the broken shaft of Scathach's spear.

Meeting Cooper's gaze, the bigger clone—the one that had snapped his arms like kindling—smiled and leaned far out over the railing. His challenge echoed throughout the museum.

"Atropos a-kultir veytahlyss. Morkün i-tolvatha!"

Cooper knew the chilling phrase: *Atropos has cut your life's thread. Die and be damned!*

Varga spun around to locate the speaker. So did Hazel.

Max did not turn, but his fingers closed around the *gae bolga*.

The big clone laughed. "Are you in mourning, brother? Don't shed tears for a coward. She fairly begged for her life."

His head still bowed, Max raised the spear and pointed it at the archway.

Cooper slid sideways, as though pulled by a powerful magnet. So did Hazel. Varga stumbled and spilled onto the floor. An unseen force was sweeping them out of the room. At first, Cooper sought to hold his ground, but it was like struggling against a riptide. Whisked off their feet, the trio was sent sliding and tumbling out of the burning museum. Once they passed beneath the grand archway, they skidded to a stop.

Cooper reached out to Hazel. She was curled up into ball, breathing heavily. One hand still clutched the unconscious smee; the other was pressed to her rounded belly. "Are you all right?" he asked.

"I . . . I think so."

"Stay here," said Cooper, helping her to lean against a nearby wall. Behind them, Varga had already pushed to his feet and was hobbling back to see what was happening. Cooper joined him just beneath the marble archway.

Fifty yards away, Max had risen to his feet. He walked slowly in the direction of the clones, leaning heavily upon the *gae bolga*. His face was downcast, his steps unsteady.

"Is he injured?" Cooper whispered.

"I don't know," said Varga. "I can barely see his flesh. His aura . . ."

He trailed off in bewildered silence. The clones also sensed something was amiss. The huge assassin had ceased his jeering. The wild one peered over the rail like a skeletal gargoyle, his mouth full of jagged teeth. Even at this distance, Cooper could see that Max was shaking violently. When he lifted his head, Varga drew a sharp breath. Cooper merely stared.

Max's eyes were as black as the blade he carried. An expression of cold, contained anger was giving way to one of seething, terrifying rage. Cooper wanted to flee and yet he couldn't move or look away. He was rooted to the spot, an unwilling and powerless witness as the boy craned his neck toward Scathach's killers.

When Max screamed, the exhibit cases shattered. Cooper and Varga were blown back as though a bomb had detonated. Cooper struck the wall in the outside corridor, cracking the marble and falling straight down by his astonished wife.

He lay in a crumpled heap, dimly conscious of a high-pitched buzzing. Someone rolled him gently onto his back. It was Hazel, her anxious face blurry and doubled. She was speaking to him, but her voice was distorted, muffled. When he tried to sit up, his ribs howled in protest. Shifting position, he took Hazel's hand and she pulled him upright.

Standing helped. Varga sat several feet away, his nose shattered. He snapped his fingers by each ear to test if they were working. When he noticed the Coopers, he blinked dazedly and they helped him to his feet. The three turned to look at the museum.

A blinding radiance shone through the archway, so dazzling they could barely look at it. Averting his eyes, Cooper took Hazel's hand and stepped through the archway. Varga followed, his cane scraping on the floor. There was no discussion or debate whether they should go within. Some external force or will was drawing them onward.

The three inched forward, bent and blinded. The air was blisteringly hot and behaving strangely. It felt charged and inconstant, as though agitated particles were darting about like shoals of startled fish. Cooper could feel his skin reddening, burning as though he stood before a blast furnace. Squinting at the marble floor, he tried to follow the pulsing, shimmering rays—rays that originated from a single source.

It was straight ahead. What terrible energies were bombarding them? Bombarding the child in Hazel's womb? But Cooper could not stop or turn back. Stretching forth his hand, Cooper felt his way forward, groping and snatching at the empty air.

Three steps later, he touched something.

Cooper froze as a trembling, unseen hand closed about his own. It exerted very little pressure but conveyed an impression of appalling strength. Cooper felt as though he'd grazed the teeth of an iron trap, one that could snap shut at any moment. But some-how, Cooper could tell this being wanted to communicate, was *trying* to communicate as best it could at this moment. Clearing his throat, he spoke in a calm, cautious voice.

"Max, it's Cooper. Hazel and Peter are with me."

The grip upon his hand tightened to the point of pain. Cooper gave a slow, shuddering exhale. *Carefully, William. Very carefully . . .*

"We're your friends," he said quietly. "Please let us see you."

The grip slackened somewhat. Gradually, the blinding radi-ance began to dim, its heat dissipating. Lights swam before Coo-per's eyes. Blinking them away, he raised his head and gazed at the boy.

Max stood an arm's length away. There was not a speck of white in the boy's eyes. They were black throughout, as dark as the void and rimmed with bloody tears that left red trails down his cheeks. He was breathing heavily, panting like a wounded animal as he clutched Cooper's hand. His other hand gripped the *gae bolga,* which glowed so hot and white it might have been drawn from the sun's core. The spear was utterly silent, and this frightened Cooper far more than when it wailed.

"Are you all right, Max?" said Varga cautiously. "Are you injured?"

No response.

Cooper glanced around the museum. Its fires had been quenched. Everything within it—exhibits, statues, corpses, creatures—was piled high against the walls in smoking, mangled heaps. Somewhere in all that wreckage was Scathach. Were her killers there, too? Looking up, Cooper saw that the balconies had been destroyed. Gaping holes remained where they had been, the edges charred and jagged.

The clones had to be dead. Had to be. But still, he recalled the advice he'd once given Max: *Don't believe it till you've seen the bodies.* The clones were tough beyond reckoning. Just look at where they came from . . .

Hazel inched forward. "Max, are you . . . ?"

She faltered as he turned toward her. It was impossible to tell if Max was really seeing her or simply staring through her. His trembling intensified. When he finally spoke, he managed only one word.

"Prusias."

The word was both a question and statement. Hazel winced, as though frightened the answer might displease him. "The bunker is down on Sublevel Twenty-Two. It's where Bram's Key was hidden."

Cooper groaned inwardly. Of course Prusias would use Bram's Chamber for his bunker. It was tucked deep in the Workshop and had been constructed by the Archmage himself long ago. Only David had been able to decipher and unravel the room's enchantments in their quest for Bram's Key. Was it big enough to house Prusias? Cooper had never actually seen the interior. None of them had. Once they'd opened the door, all hell had broken loose. Only the Workshop knew what was beyond that door. By now they'd have modified it to suit Prusias.

Releasing Cooper's hand, Max dimmed his radiance and brushed past them to make for the archway. They followed at a distance, wary and uncertain. The Workshop appeared eerily empty, its corridors a flashing red haze of smoke and emergency lights. Now and again a tremor shivered through the floor or they heard the report of distant gunfire from an air duct. Apparently, the revolt was still going strong.

Cooper and the others followed this stranger as he walked past laboratories and greenhouses, manufacturing plants, and engine rooms. While Max had dimmed his radiance, it had not disappeared. Flickers of pale fire still danced about his person, illuminating him in the darker hallways and crackling with sudden brilliance and intensity. Now and again, he would stop and lean upon the *gae bolga*, as though gathering himself. It was like watching a newly birthed foal stand and take its first steps.

It would take time to reach Bram's Chamber. If they were on Level 18, it would be forty levels beneath them. Normally William Cooper would pause to work out a strategy, to scout and assess the forces he would face. But with Max in his current state, they were in uncharted waters. The being they followed did not seem interested in precautionary measures.

Instead, he marched stolidly ahead, passing broken pod banks and empty dining halls. Cooper wondered at his objective until they passed through an arch into a sprawling, circular space hundreds of feet across. The arch from which they'd entered was one of six surrounding a cluster of gigantic pipes and bundled tubes that protruded from the floor and soared up until they met the distant ceiling. The biggest pipes were over fifty feet across and made of steel, but the tubes were clear and sheathed translucent cables or glowed with superheated gases. Unattended computer banks were situated along the room's perimeter, but Max ignored these and made for the glass encasement that housed the pipes and tubes. A hand plucked at Cooper's sleeve.

"What's he doing?" hissed Hazel.

"I don't—"

A company of Workshop troops rushed through one of the entrances, a hundred hulking figures encased in full-body armor and assault helmets. Most hefted automatic rifles, but several carried plasma-powered cannons that could melt all but the toughest materials.

"Fade," muttered Cooper.

Hazel and Varga obeyed instantly. As the last soldiers

thundered in, the three spread apart so as not to provide a single target. But Cooper did not think the soldiers had even noticed them. They had either seen Max on some surveillance camera or they had the bad luck to stumble upon the terrifying being now in their midst.

Even so, the group moved slowly as sudden movement would render fading useless. Cooper assumed the soldier's helmets probably had heat-detection capabilities, but under the current circumstances he did not think this would be an issue. Compared to the energy Max was radiating, they would not even register.

As for Max, he did not appear to even notice the soldiers. Instead, he began circling the wall of tinted glass that encased the massive pipeworks.

The troops quickly took up positions, their weapons trained on the intruder. When Max paused at a metal door set within the glass, a soldier issued a command in a harsh, mechanized voice. Cooper could not quite make it out, but didn't need to. Whatever the order was, Max ignored it. Two seconds later, the troops opened fire.

Gun muzzles flashed like strobe lights, discharging thousands of rounds in the space of a sneeze. Instantly Cooper, Hazel, and Varga dropped to the floor. The barrage sounded like hail pounding on a tin roof. Although hundreds of bullets were being fired, they did not strike their target. An invisible barrier repelled them, triggering a spray of sparks as bullets ricocheted to strike the glass wall, metal door, and nearby computer equipment. Some of the soldiers staggered back and fell as though rebounding rounds had struck them.

Cooper was dumbstruck. From his vantage, it did not look like a single bullet had so much as grazed Max.

But they had gotten his attention.

Turning from the door, Max faced his attackers, the *gae bolga* as bright as a thunderbolt in his hand. Upon seeing his face, several of the soldiers dropped their weapons and fled, pushing past the others to disappear down the corridor from which they'd come. But the others maintained their clusters.

Cooper's jaw clenched. *Run, you idiots!*

A moment later, the soldier nearest Max slowly turned and pointed his weapon at his neighbor. The gun was shaking, its laser sight dancing on the target's chest. Other soldiers began to follow suit, turning with rigid, unwilling movements to train their weapons upon one another.

"Stop!"

The voice was Hazel's. She became clearly visible as she rose and broke into a run. Springing up, Cooper raced after her, catching her around the waist and swinging her around to shield her. Max regarded them without emotion, energy shimmering about his form like the sun's corona. His gaze was so remote it might have been starlight from another universe.

Hazel struggled wildly. "You're not a monster!" she cried. "You're Max McDaniels. *Our* Max! And we love you!"

Cooper smiled grimly. Hazel's emotions had blinded her. She insisted on pretending that the being before them was Max McDaniels, the boy she'd taught at Rowan. But she could not have been more mistaken. This was *not* "their Max." Cooper had no idea if it was a god, a devil, or Death itself. But he did know one thing with absolute certainty: this being was about to destroy them.

The realization did not trigger panic, dread, or even sorrow. If they were going to die, Cooper was grateful they were together—he and Hazel and the baby. Love wasn't something he thought he'd ever experience. But he had, and it was probably more than he deserved. He only regretted that he wouldn't get to meet and raise their child. Not in this life, anyway.

These thoughts flashed by as images, impressions, and feel-ings of startling clarity. He never imagined life could be so vivid. An overwhelming sense of peace washed over him. Setting Hazel down, he turned to face Max just as Varga came up beside them.

"I am not afraid," Varga called out to the silent stranger. "I've witnessed this moment many times, Max McDaniels—even before I saw you on that train years ago. And yet I chose to save you that day. And I choose to be here now, even though it may mean my death. Now it is your turn. What will you choose?"

The being lifted his chin defiantly. Cooper felt a glimmer of hope, for it was an unmistakably *human* gesture—a gesture strongly characteristic of the Max he knew.

All at once, the Workshop soldiers laid down their weapons. They did so in perfect unison, as though executing a drill. Max's eyes never left Varga's. Hoisting up their injured comrade, the soldiers retreated swiftly through the archway.

Cooper stared at the guns upon the floor. Why had Max bothered to disarm them? Those weapons couldn't hurt him . . .

They could hurt us.

Was Max protecting them? Whether he had spared their lives and the soldiers out of compassion or merely to defy Peter's visions did not matter. Hazel's instincts had been right; there was still a glimmer of the old Max—*their* Max—within that inhu-man juggernaut.

Turning away from them, Max lifted the *gae bolga* and cut through the steel door set within the glass that encased the pipes and tubes. The blade pierced the material so easily that carv-ing an opening was like drawing an outline with chalk. Pushing the heavy section inward, Max stepped across the threshold and made for one of the largest steel pipes. Cooper and the others followed.

They kept back ten feet or so as Max cut a sizable opening in the pipe's side and kicked it inward. Cold air billowed out, forced from above. Evidently, the pipe was an enormous airshaft. Without the slightest hesitation, Max stepped through the opening and plunged from view.

Cooper glanced at the others. "Can you two levitate?"

Varga nodded. Hazel looked incredulous: *Of course a Promethean Scholar can levitate!*

"Well, then," said Cooper. Without further ado, he took three quick steps and dove through the pitch-dark opening.

He let himself free fall. He felt his body accelerating, the air rushing past as he plummeted in the blackness. As he approached terminal velocity, the sense of movement diminished, replaced by a surreal feeling of weightlessness—as though he were floating and not falling hundreds of feet per second. Far below, he could see Max and the *gae bolga*, two receding lights reflecting on the pipe's interior. The spectacle was strangely beautiful, but Cooper was a pragmatist. The airshaft had no lights or floor markers—no way of gauging where they were. How far had they fallen? Half a mile? More? Would Max know when to stop? Three seconds later, he had his answer.

Clang!

The noise rang from far below, like a sledgehammer striking a spike. It must have been Max, for his radiance was no longer receding but growing larger as Cooper plunged soundlessly toward it. He appeared to be clinging to the pipe's wall as easily as a gecko. Sparks flashed as Max plunged the *gae bolga*'s blade through the pipe wall. A dim beam of light pierced the darkness. It widened as Max cut an opening and slipped through.

Cooper made for the light, now controlling his plunge with subtle applications of mystic energy. The pipe was wide enough that he did not have to expend much, just enough to slow his descent and shape a trajectory that would bring him through the opening. Banking slightly, he twisted like a skydiver, angling his body and adjusting his speed. Catching hold of the opening's rim, he swung himself through and landed nimbly on his feet.

He found himself in a dim cavern of dark, rough-hewn rock. While this room was considerably smaller and less finished than the one they had just left, the basic layout was similar, a central cluster of pipes and tubes surrounded by unattended control terminals. Thirty feet away, an instrument panel was blinking, illuminating veins of quartz and copper in the walls.

Straight ahead, Max was climbing a metal stairway that connected the sunken floor with a walkway leading to a steel fire door set within the rock wall. Above that door, a small surveillance camera was silently panning across the room. A voice hissed behind Cooper.

"Help me through!"

He turned to see Hazel hovering weightlessly inside the airshaft. Reaching within, Cooper took her hand and tugged her inside the cavern as though she were a balloon. She kicked her legs in the empty air until they settled on solid ground. Varga slipped in quietly after her and landed with practiced ease. Cooper was not entirely surprised. Before his injuries, Peter Varga had been a capable field Agent.

Upon the walkway, Max opened the fire door and left the room. The three followed at a distance as the shimmering youth strode down dark, rough passageways hollowed from solid rock. No one at the Workshop actually lived this deep; these areas were reserved for mining and for experiments too disruptive or hazardous for the occupied levels.

Despite its winding ways, Max seemed to know precisely where he was going. As he walked, his aura gleamed on girders and turbines, mine cars and rail tracks. And that aura was growing brighter.

Varga grunted, his cane rapping steadily on the rock. "My soul is close. I can feel it. The demon will not be far."

"And what do we intend to do when we get there?" said Hazel.

Cooper was going to reply when a confused but familiar baritone cried out from Hazel's jacket. "Where the hell am I? Am I dead?"

A tapered, yamlike head peeked out from the jacket's front pocket. Hazel nearly kissed it. "Toby! I'm so relieved to see you conscious. How are you feeling?"

"Groggy," he sniffed. "And out of the loop. Why are you whispering, eh? What's going on? I demand an update!"

Cooper's update was terse. "Scathach is dead, Max has snapped, and we're closing in on Prusias."

The smee sank out of sight.

Cooper turned to the others. "Listen, when we reach—"

"I think we're there," Varga breathed.

They paused on the threshold of a larger cavern served by a pod bank and littered with cargo vehicles and excavation equipment. Across the way, Max stood before a broad ramp that led up to a blast door some fifty feet in diameter. Apparently the Workshop had expanded Bram's Chamber by a considerable margin. Cooper saw its former door mounted above the new entrance like an ornament or trophy, a circular slab of greenish stone inscribed with an image of the Egyptian god Thoth.

"For a secret bunker, it's not exactly subtle," remarked Hazel.

"I think it's safe to say the bunker has been designed to accommodate Prusias's true form," said Varga. "Why else would it need a door that size?"

Cooper had never seen the demon's true form. While he'd been present during the battle at Rowan when the Great Red Dragon rose up from the sea, he'd also been possessed. The only thing he could recall with any certainty was thousands of horrified cries when the demon's heads reared into view from beneath the cliffs. While everyone agreed the monster had seven heads—seven bearded heads with blank, ravenous eyes—people disagreed about the monster's scale. Some swore the demon was a thousand feet long. Others insisted he was even bigger, that his body could circle all of Old College.

And now we've got him cornered. Lucky us.

Just as Max stepped upon the ramp, floodlights in the cavern wall blazed on, spotlighting him with their powerful beams. He stared into their dazzling brilliance as though he wanted the cameras and watchers to see precisely who was at their door.

Crouching low, Cooper and his companions scurried to a more sheltered vantage from behind a rock formation. As they did so, dozens of heavy, gleaming cannons slid forward from recesses around the blast door, their barrels trained on Max.

When he stepped forward, they fired.

The barrage was deafening, a hail of bullets and crackling plasma beams that appeared to obliterate the ramp and nearby vehicles. Billowing plumes of smoke and dust roiled about the cavern floor, obscuring everything but a pale light at their center, a sun half veiled by storm clouds.

The firing stopped, the smoke dissipated, and Cooper saw Max standing atop the rubble of the pulverized ramp. He had barely moved. Staring up at the spotlights, the boy raised the *gae bolga* high.

Lightning erupted from its blade, snaking, forking, seeking, finding. Nothing escaped it; nothing was spared. Every spotlight and camera, cannon and gun exploded or split, warped and melted. When they lay in bubbling ruin, Max advanced toward the gleaming door.

Once he was close enough, he reared back and plunged the

gae bolga three feet deep into the massive door. The *gae bolga* screamed as it pierced the metal, an otherworldly cry that could only have come from the Morrígan herself. Max left the spear anchored there, poised and quivering, as he backed away.

"What's happening?" hissed Hazel.

Cooper had no idea, but Varga was leaning forward, his spectral eye fixed upon the door. "I have never seen anything like this," he breathed. "The door is . . . *dying*."

Even as he said the word, great fissures and cracks appeared in the metal. Its gleaming surface grew dull, darkening until it was the shade of rusted iron.

A blood-chilling moan filled the cavern, greedy and almost sensual.

All at once, the door's material became a dark powder, like charcoal or graphite. It collapsed in a single sheet, the grains streaming about the *gae bolga* as it remained fixed in midair. Walking forward, Max grasped the spear as he passed and strode down what looked to be a lighted tunnel.

An astonished Hazel turned to her companions.

"Do we go after him?"

Cooper's reply was automatic. "Of course. We have a mission."

His wife placed her hand over his and gave him a probing look. "William, do you believe our contributions will make one iota of difference?"

The prospect of abandoning a mission was antithetical to Cooper's code, but Hazel spoke the truth. He questioned very much whether they could tip the scales in the coming conflict. Before he could answer, however, Varga rose.

"I must go on," he said, wiping dried blood from his chin. "Prusias has my soul and countless others in his keeping. It's my duty to recover them." Varga gave an understanding smile. "I do not ask the two of you to join me. This is my mission, not yours. And you have other considerations."

He gestured at Hazel's belly.

She straightened abruptly. "Absolutely not," she said decisively. "You must forgive me, Peter. In all the excitement, I'd quite forgotten about your objective. We may not have much to offer Max, but we can certainly help you."

A groan sounded from her pocket.

From the tunnel's mouth came a rumble like distant thunder. Cooper unsheathed his kris and thumbed its wavy edge. "Come on," he said, rising and setting off across the cavern.

The others followed after him but could not move nearly as quickly. Leaping over the ramp's remains, he dashed inside the tunnel, his boots making little sound as they struck its metal floor. The tunnel went straight for about a hundred yards before arcing left. Ahead, he could see the shadows of running figures approaching. With an Amplified leap, he sprang fifty feet up and clung, upside down, to the tunnel's roof.

The figures soon came into view, a collection of laborers, engineers, and minor demons clutching musical instruments or wearing courtesan's robes. It was a virtual stampede of slaves fleeing the imminent confrontation. Dropping from the ceiling, Cooper ignored their startled cries and continued up the tunnel.

Upon rounding the bend, he saw that Max was walking straight ahead, a solitary figure within a halo of crackling white light. Cooper closed the distance until he'd come within thirty feet. A hundred yards ahead, the tunnel opened onto a dim space where dark, sinuous shapes were gliding through the air.

The tunnel trembled suddenly, as though something enormous was moving about in the chamber ahead. A taunting voice rang out like thunder.

"Come on, you miserable whelp! Come finish what you started!"

Upon hearing the voice, Max broke into a trot and then a run. Cooper tried to keep up, but the boy was pulling swiftly away, sprinting with superhuman speed toward the tunnel mouth. When he reached it, he gave a howl and sprang up out of sight. Willing himself forward, Cooper reached the tunnel's conclusion and gazed up.

High above, a furious midair battle was taking place in a domed chamber the size of an aircraft hangar. At first glance, it looked like huge black moths were swarming about a shimmering white star. But the moths were hundreds of airborne malakhim packed together so tightly that the star's light was being smothered. As more malakhim joined the swarm, it became increasingly dense and spherical. The chamber gradually dimmed as the star was buried in their midst.

Cooper ducked when a black-robed figure glided swiftly past the tunnel entrance. Its obsidian mask portrayed an angelic face whose serene beauty contrasted sharply with its eager rush to join the others. Cooper had never seen malakhim fly or appear in such numbers. Max was trapped within a throng of fiends so densely packed, not even his light could escape anymore. He wouldn't be able to breathe, much less swing a weapon.

Gloating laughter rang out. It echoed from an opening in the opposite wall, an opening so large that it dwarfed Cooper's tunnel. Its impenetrable depths exuded a malevolence that was almost tangible. An honor guard of red-masked malakhim stood before the opening like tiny toy soldiers, their hands clasped atop greatswords.

"Take his blade!" the voice commanded. *"He is nothing without his blade!"*

Above, the grotesque swarming reached greater intensity, like honeybees clustering madly about a queen. Pieces of malakhim fell like rotten fruit—arms and legs, obsidian masks, entire bodies cut in two. But these casualties were few among a tireless press of hundreds. A moment later, the *gae bolga* had been wrenched from its owner's hand and flung out of the living swarm.

The spear's glow faded as it fell, tumbling end over end until its blade impaled the stone floor. And there it stood, upright and quivering, a second Excalibur. A gasp sounded behind Cooper. He turned to see Hazel's bloodless face. Varga crouched beside her, sweating and breathless.

"We have to help him," Hazel panted. "We have to try something!"

Cooper nodded. He was already reaching for his last vial of blood petals. The substance would be useless against Prusias, for the most powerful demons had habituated themselves to its effects. But Cooper had just seen it work very potently against malakhim.

"Inscribe a circle," he muttered. "The strongest you can make."

Varga shook his head. "Those won't work against Prusias unless he's been summoned."

"It's for the malakhim. Quick now!"

Using oil from one of Hazel's flasks, the pair worked swiftly to trace a large circle in a radius around them. While neither had deep experience with summoning, every Rowan graduate learned protections against evil spirits. The most powerful were unique to specific entities, but there were others that, while less potent, had broader applications.

While they were busy, Cooper rummaged through his pack, praying that what he needed was unbroken. His quickly found it wrapped in several shirts—the bottle of scent Hazel had given him as a wedding present. Yanking out the stopper, he dumped its contents and refilled it with the crimson concoction from his flask. Behind him, Hazel gave an indignant grunt.

Rotating the egg-shaped bottle in one hand, Cooper rapped its surface with the blade of his dagger. Tiny cracks appeared in the glass, weakening the bottle without breaking it.

"Bring me the Hound!" roared the hidden speaker. *"I want to taste his flesh, his fire, his soul!"*

The roiling ball of malakhim began drifting toward the dark tunnel. It did not move easily, but listed and dipped as though trying to transport something very heavy. Now and again, the sphere shook with so much violence that slender beams of light managed to escape. Deep within the sphere's core, a furious struggle was still taking place. Five hundred malakhim could barely contain this ball of living, raging fire. Cooper weighed the glass bottle in his hand. Perhaps they could tip the scales . . .

He checked on Hazel and Varga's progress. The two were on their hands and knees, working toward each other as they inscribed sigils just within the circle's border. Hazel was scribbling furiously, whispering incantations.

"Ready?" Cooper asked.

"Not yet," muttered a sweating Varga. "Twenty seconds."

Cooper glanced up. The malakhim had dragged their prisoner within a hundred yards of that yawning crevice. In its shadows, something stirred and thrust smoothly forward so that Cooper could just make out its features.

It was a grinning face the size of a house.

Cooper crossed himself. "Sorry, Varga. Time's up."

Dashing out from the tunnel, Cooper ran across the vast chamber until he came within range of the hellish sphere. Cocking his arm, he hurled the glass grenade with all his might and followed its swift, glittering arc.

The bottle smashed into the sphere's lower quarter, exploding in a cloud of red mist that ignited like flash powder. Its fireball destroyed every malakhim it touched, leaving behind a crater, a weakness the swarm's captive was quick to exploit.

Light burst through, shattering the malakhim's hold with a force that sent them flying like shrapnel. The shock wave also blew Cooper back, tumbling him head over heels while obsidian masks rained down like volcanic debris. As Max landed in a crouch on the chamber floor, Cooper scrambled to his feet and limped for the tunnel. Seconds later, he spied a dozen wraithlike shadows converging swiftly upon his.

Just ahead were Hazel and Varga. They were shouting at him, imploring him to hurry. But Cooper kept his eyes on the closing shadows. They were almost upon him . . . one stretched out a hand to seize him.

With an Amplified burst, Cooper slipped beyond its reach. Taking a running leap, he soared like a long jumper and crashed into Varga. Twisting around, he saw the malakhim skimming low over the ground, racing toward them. Just before they reached the group, the circle burst into bright flames, unveiling ancient wards traced within. The malakhim swerved sharply like a flock of starlings. Circling around, they abandoned this lesser prey and doubled back to assist their master.

"What's happening?" hissed Toby from Hazel's pocket.

A transfixed Varga was staring over Cooper's shoulder. "Nothing," he lied. "Don't look."

Prusias was leaving his shelter.

Cooper had never witnessed anything more nauseating. Seven bearded human heads emerged, each attached by a sinuous neck to a massive serpentine body. The demon slid so smoothly out of the tunnel that his scarlet scales might have been oiled. Coil after rippling coil emerged, each as swollen as a blood-gorged leech. Was Prusias a thousand feet long? Two thousand?

The demon turned slowly about like a battleship circling a harbor. Each of the seven heads resembled Prusias in his human form—darkly handsome faces with plaited black beards—but their mouths were filled with jagged fangs while the eyes betrayed no glimmer of Prusias's laughing, bullying persona. They were hauntingly blank and hungry, the eyes of a rabid animal.

And those eyes were fixed upon Max, who stood weaponless and alone at the chamber's center. Instead of simply attacking, the demon seemed to be gauging his comparatively tiny opponent, assessing him as one might a poisonous wasp. The central head was dripping black blood from ugly wounds upon its face and throat—souvenirs from its first encounter with the *gae bolga*. The head grinned maliciously as the Great Red Dragon reared up and used his inconceivable bulk to drive the *gae bolga* flush as a coffin nail in the stone floor.

"There goes your bite, Hound," the head chuckled. "Care to bark instead?"

Max said nothing. The red-masked honor guard now surrounded him. His radiance was no more than a flicker, but Cooper studied him carefully. The boy's back was straight and that grim, unblinking smile would have given him pause.

But not Prusias. The demon's pride and rage were kindling like wildfire. Blys's king heaved himself up so that his crownless heads nearly scraped the soaring roof.

"What are you smirking about, maggot?" he demanded. "You think your people have conquered me? They've merely taken a city. I'll build a bigger one, raise a stronger army. And when the little Faeregine is slain, I'll return to Rowan. I'll raze its buildings, poison its fields, and devour its people like the sheep they are!"

As these words echoed, the demon's last coil finally slid free of the tunnel. A tiny figure trailed its tapering tip, no larger than a human toddler. It ran across the chamber, waving its arms. The being was an imp—a red-skinned imp in courtier's clothes. Its voice was a squeak in the vast chamber.

"Stop!" he cried. "My king, you must not kill him!"

One of the seven heads whipped about, its voice a simmering growl. "Silence, Mr. Bonn. Go back to my burrow."

But the imp was insistent. "Milord, if you slay him, you will be cheating the Atropos."

"Cheating? I'm doing their job for them."

"Precisely," said the imp. "The boy's name has been written in the Grey Book. It's the Atropos's sacred duty to end his life. If you deprive them of that honor, they may well turn against Your Majesty!"

"Let them!" Prusias snarled. "Let them dare raise a hand against me!"

The imp shook his head in exasperation. "Your Majesty armed them with Set's knife!" he hissed, before softening his tone to one of calm, pleading reason. "Spare the Hound's life and take him captive. David Menlo is his dearest friend. We could use him to negotiate a—"

"I DON'T NEGOTIATE!"

Prusias lashed the far wall with his tail. The shock staggered the malakhim and knocked the imp off his feet. Surging forward, the demon crushed a dozen malakhim in his eagerness to get at the Hound. The central head shot forward, swift as a rattlesnake, its jaws opened wide.

Max sprang to meet it.

Evading the snapping teeth, Max caught hold of a braid in the demon's tangled beard. Swinging under its jaws, he landed on the demon's throat and plunged his arm straight into the festering wound—the very wound the *gae bolga* had made years before.

Cooper had never heard such an anguished howl. The demon's

entire body recoiled, whipping around with such momentum that he crashed to the floor. His minions fled to escape his thrashing coils and heads, which were snarling and snapping blindly at anything they touched.

Clinging to the demon, Max gave an unearthly scream and erupted with light. Prusias went berserk, dashing his head against the floor, trying desperately to shake his attacker off. But his attacker held fast, no longer a being of flesh and blood, but of white shimmering fire whose energies were pouring into the Great Red Dragon.

Prusias began splitting apart, his coils swelling and cracking as the pale fire consumed him from within. The heads were pleading now, bellowing and weeping for mercy from the god that was burning them alive. Even their eyes were ablaze, the sockets vomiting smoke as the seven heads collapsed and writhed on the chamber floor.

The demon's bloated body began to sag and hiss like a punctured zeppelin. As it collapsed, the smoldering hide began to shrivel and contract. Once the last scarlet scraps burned away, the spirit of white fire became flesh again, its form returning to that of the black-eyed god. At his feet, Prusias's human shape sprawled in a heap of purple silk robes. Where the Great Red Dragon's body had lain were thousands of glittering gemstones.

With an exultant cry, Varga started forward, picking his way among the scattered rubies and sapphires, diamonds and emeralds. He made for one in particular, identifying it instantly among the multitude. Cooper and Hazel followed after him, stepping over the jewels as though they were sacred. And indeed they were, for trapped within each was a mortal soul.

To Cooper's surprise, Varga was not the only seeker among the gemstones. The remaining malakhim were also approaching, walking slowly like lost and weary pilgrims. Like Varga, they were drawn to particular stones that they pressed to their breasts as though they'd been reunited with the dearest friend imaginable. And when they did so, their obsidian masks dissolved into a pearly mist, revealing translucent, ghostly faces, both male and female. Each whispered their sin aloud before swallowing their jewel and vanishing.

"I coveted gold . . ."

"I murdered my brother . . ."

"I lusted for knowledge . . ."

"I betrayed my child . . ."

When the malakhim had all disappeared, Varga and Hazel began gathering up the remaining gemstones. The only sound in the vast chamber was Mr. Bonn's quiet sobbing.

The imp came to kneel by his master. Cooper did not know how Prusias remained when the Great Red Dragon had been destroyed, but the demon appeared to be alive and even conscious as he peered up at his conqueror. Gazing down at Prusias with an icy remoteness, Max pointed at the demon's neck.

With a shaking hand, Prusias removed the lymra torque and surrendered it to its true owner. Taking the coppery ring, Max placed it around his neck before extending his hand toward where the *gae bolga* had been buried. The spear rose from the floor, withdrawing smoothly from the rock until it hovered fifty yards away. Once free, it flew straight to its master's hand.

Prusias gave the weapon a baleful stare as Max caught it. Grimacing, he coughed blood into his fist. "I was the Great Red Dragon," he rumbled in a gruff, bewildered voice. "But the Great Red Dragon is no more. How am I alive?"

Max's voice was iron. "You are only Prusias now."

Recalling the Director's orders, Cooper realized the *gae bolga*'s blade was poised perilously close to the demon's throat. Hazel and Varga must have noticed the same thing, for they gathered around him with wary, anxious expressions.

"We need him alive," said Cooper quietly.

Max did not respond, but continued contemplating Prusias and his imp as though weighing a judgment. Several moments passed before he reached down and seized the king by his beard, dragging him up so their faces were inches apart.

"What will it be, Hound?" the demon whispered. "Death or a train ride?"

Releasing Prusias, Max raised the *gae bolga* high. When it struck the floor, they all vanished in a clap of thunder.

~ 23 ~

THE GIANT'S SONG

An instant later, Max appeared in Prusias's throne room, a marble chamber fit for a Roman emperor. Another thunderclap heralded his arrival, its force sufficient to send the room's occupants hurtling back against high walls and massive columns. As its rumble subsided, there were faint groans, the crunch of broken glass, and a heavy, rhythmic thumping somewhere outside the grand chamber. It sounded like a battering ram. Apparently Rowan's forces had won their way into the palace and were trying to force their way within this final sanctum.

Max glanced down at his companions. They lay sprawled about him on the dais that served as a lofty stage for the king's throne. Cooper and Hazel were stunned and Peter Varga was retching. That was hardly unusual—queasiness was a common by-product of teleportation. Prusias was in a ball at Max's feet, his imp clinging to his leg like a frightened child. Max surveyed the rest of the room, his black eyes sliding over hundreds of minor braymas, armored guards, bewildered imps, and semiconscious courtiers lying among broken statues and marble busts. Behind him, Prusias's gruff voice called out.

"What's the meaning of this?"

Max turned to find that the king's massive throne had toppled over, nearly pinning a second, heavily armed Prusias, who was now struggling to his feet. Gripping the golden pommel of his broadsword, this Prusias stabbed an accusing finger at the demon curled at Max's feet.

"Who is this imposter?" he demanded.

Silence.

"I am the king!" roared the body double, substituting volume for conviction. "And I demand you leave my chamber at—"

He never finished the sentence. Under Max's implacable gaze, the double's eyes bulged with helpless horror as his body began to soften and collapse, sinking to the floor as though all of its bones had turned to jelly. There was no distinction between his armor and his person—all were liquefying together, blending into each other as if they were made of the same gooey dough. Within five seconds, an unusually large and terrified smee lay quaking on the inlaid floor.

Silence reigned over the room. Every eye was fixed upon Max. His attention wandered from face to face in the vast hall, registering each. All the demons averted their eyes and bowed their heads. He expected nothing less. Their kind was profoundly hierarchical and almost always deferred to greater strength.

Max pointed the *gae bolga* toward the chamber's gilded doors, now barred with three stout beams. The beams shattered into splinters, and the vast doors swung inward so violently that one was ripped off its hinges. With startled cries, the demons and courtiers scurried away from the opening as the king's enemies poured into the chamber.

In they came, a roaring flood of Raszna war chiefs and Rowan soldiers, brandishing their weapons, faces alight with the prospect of victory. The demons and their servants nearest the doors retreated to alcoves and the area behind the dais.

Max watched Rowan's forces with indifference as they fell into silence and lowered their weapons. They shuffled forward uncertainly as their comrades crowded in behind them. Within seconds, the throne room was nearly filled with enemies and allies all gazing up at the dais where Max stood. A hushed and expectant silence settled over the room.

With just his will and aura, Max could mold this entire throng into whatever he wished—his servants, his soldiers, even his worshippers if he was so inclined. The idea had some appeal. Max had spent years taking orders and completing missions for superiors. Those days had ended.

At his feet, Prusias groaned. Reminded of the demon's presence, Max heaved him up by his thick black hair and displayed the demon to the crowd as one might a hunting trophy. His voice rang out, cold and imperious.

"The war is over. I have ended it."

Cries of *"Sol Invictus!"* and *"Moschiach!"* greeted this pronouncement, but Max did not acknowledge them. To do so might have made him emotional and he was having a hard enough time controlling the monstrous energies coursing through him. They radiated from his core, pulsing and surging, triggering a dangerous impulse to dominate or destroy everything around him. If he was not careful, those thoughts would consume him. He'd be as mindless as Yuga.

Cooper; Hazel; Varga; the Raszna war chiefs Vechna and Titus; Natasha Kiraly of the Red Branch; even Ajax, a refugee who had served under him in the Trench Rats. Max knew their faces and identities, recalled relevant bits of data and history, but that was all. He felt no emotion toward them; he merely sorted them according to their relative power, hostility, and usefulness. Love and affection were intellectualized concepts, not a personal reality. Such feelings had died with Scathach.

But some feelings remained. The strength flowing through Max thrilled and terrified him. He no longer had a truly fixed form but could shift at will between flesh and spirit, matter and energy. Releasing Prusias, he gazed at his hand and watched impassively as it changed from muscle and bone into white-hot fire and back again. No earthly weapon could harm him; nothing on earth could possibly stand against him. He was an immovable object and an irresistible force all in one.

This is why Astaroth wanted to possess me. This is what Bram feared.

Fear. It permeated the entire throne room. Max could sense it any number of ways, but its most obvious manifestation was visual. Auras trembled before him, their contours rippling and buckling. Each told a story. The brayma with the angry red aura would kill him if he could; a trio of kitsune were hiding something— possibly tangible, but most likely a secret allegiance. The imps were universally terrified, but Max could tell they would abandon their masters the instant he commanded their obedience. Reading auras wasn't mind reading, but it was very close. And Max could read hundreds simultaneously. All he needed was a glance.

And while these telltale auras were prevalent among the demons, they were just as common throughout Max's allies.

Among Rowan's coalition, many were not merely afraid or awe-struck by a divine presence; they were not even certain of what they were witnessing. Had a tyrant just been vanquished or usurped?

Once Max beheld the Morrígan, not even he could say.

She moved silently among the crowds, taller than the tallest men with a mane of black tangles that hung about a dusky, age-less face whose hollow eyes flickered with tiny lights like corpse candles. Her broad, almost lipless mouth was so encrusted with blood that she might have been wearing a muzzle. As before, the goddess wore a shroud of raven feathers, but now she had adorned it with garlands of entrails that swayed and dripped with each deliberate step.

Closer and closer she came, weaving her way through the press of Raszna and Rowan soldiers, unseen and unheeded. But those ravening eyes never left Max's. Within his head, he could hear her voice, that chilling whisper brimming with violence.

"Our butterfly has finally spread his wings. And they are bright, and beautiful, and strong. You see now that I spoke the truth. You don't need my blade, Hound. It needs you. And so does the world! For who else is fit to rule?"

The goddess came closer, slipping between the oblivious soldiers.

"Who else is there?" she pressed. *"Not Bram. He's no leader and cares little for the affairs of lesser men. His grandson is clever, but too weak, too corrupted by tainted blood."*

"Mina," replied Max telepathically. *"Mina can rule. She would be just, and she is strong enough."*

The Morrígan stood but ten feet away. Beyond her, no bra-ziers smoked or flickered; no soldiers breathed or blinked. Time had either stopped or slowed to such an extent that its passage was imperceptible. The Morrígan spoke aloud now, her voice ripe with outrage. "Lugh's son would crown a child instead of himself!"

"She's hardly an ordinary child."

The goddess laughed. "Because she banished the Great Red Dragon? You burned the Beast to ashes! Do you imagine the Faeregine could do such a thing? Nonsense! She is but a rose—a rose with thorns—but a rose nonetheless. This world needs a hammer."

The goddess came so close he could smell the blood on her breath. She paced about him, walking through the frozen bodies of Prusias, Cooper, and the rest as though they were vapor.

"A true hunter always eats his kill," she hissed, dragging her nails across his shoulders. "And you *are* a hunter, my prince. You were born to hunt and slay, to rule and master. This is your nature and you can deny it no longer. It must be embraced here and now. In this world, alas, for you have forsaken the Sidh."

Max glowered at her, but the Morrígan jabbed an accusing finger.

"I did not smash that brooch," she hissed. "I did not squander Lugh Lamfhada's gift on a mortal he exiled. Did you expect the High King to claim her dying soul again?" The Morrígan shook her head as though he were pitifully naïve. "Immortality is the greatest honor we can bestow. Such gifts are not given twice."

"Scathach didn't expect any gifts," said Max coldly. "She came to this world without any thought of herself. She came to help me."

"And she has. Her death unraveled the final threads of your cocoon. Her death has given you the world you are destined to rule."

"There is still Astaroth," said Max darkly.

"What of him?" she sneered. "He would never dare stand against you. Not now."

Max considered this a moment. "But the Book of Thoth—"

"Has no authority over you," said Morrígan, stroking the hand that held the *gae bolga*. "Your truename is not in it. But it does hold power over your kingdom. If you destroyed Astaroth and seized the Book for yourself, you would be master of all . . ."

Letting go of his hand, the goddess lifted his chin and stared at him with petrifying intensity—searching, scouring, rending, judging. "But leave Astaroth for tomorrow. Today, all factions must unite under one banner. Today, a god must declare himself king!"

And having said this, she released him and withdrew back into the crowds of speechless, staring soldiers. Time appeared to be flowing once again for braziers were smoking and Max felt Prusias stir weakly at his feet.

Max closed his eyes, shutting out the goddess. Not even the Morrígan would rush him into such a decision. He recalled when he'd seen Elias Bram obliterate Gràvenmuir—the instant Max realized the world had changed forever. That moment had been so poignant, so grand and terrible in its implications. And yet it paled compared to this. This was not destroying an embassy; this was imposing a new age. Max McDaniels was not witnessing history; he would be shaping it for untold generations.

He knew the instant he seized power, many friends would become his enemies. David would view the act as a betrayal. So would Mina. Bram would view it as a confirmation of his misgivings.

And what would the Raszna, his new allies and followers, think? He recalled his conversation with Archon and the immense trust the ancient vye had placed in Max's promise of an equal stake in the new order. All that goodwill would vanish the instant Max declared himself king. His name would be cursed from Arcanum to Silverfalls.

But did any of that matter? These were details, mere bumps that time would smooth or history could rewrite. Max was strongest. This was not a boast or boyish wish; it was a bedrock fact, as certain as sunrise. David would forge elaborate alliances while analyzing countless scenarios. Max could bypass all these complexities and headaches by embracing a simple truth: he was a god among lesser beings.

He would hammer the Four Kingdoms into one empire while bringing all the world's far-flung settlements under his authority. Rowan could continue to exist, as could Arcanum and other schools of magic. They would simply answer to him. And while some would undoubtedly call him a tyrant, they would be mistaken. Tyrants weren't fair and just; they didn't use their immense power to protect the people and improve their lives. But the god-king would do that and more. It could all start today, this very instant . . .

"Max."

A voice interrupted his thoughts, calm and familiar. Max opened his eyes to see David Menlo standing before him, flanked by Miss Awolowo, the Archon Fenwulf, and a dozen Promethean Scholars. The Director's face was grave, but his eyes were full of understanding. There was no fear in David's aura. There was only empathy.

"Max," he repeated gently. "Someone is asking for you."

"Who?"

"The Fomorian," said David delicately. "The giant is badly injured."

The Morrígan's voice seeped into Max's mind, angry and impatient.

"No mortal instruments can slay the Fomorian, young king. The sorcerer is manipulating you, cheating you of your moment. Declare your rule and cast this serpent from your hall!"

Max tore his eyes away from where the goddess stood by the broken door. He would not be manipulated by anyone, including her. The Fomorian was Max's kinsman and had answered Rowan's call. He stepped down from the dais.

"Take me to him."

As he and David left the throne room, three black ravens circled and screeched among the rafters. Their hateful cries followed the pair out the doors. The Morrígan had disappeared.

The two made their way out of the palace, sweeping past smoke-choked hallways and luxuriant halls being looted by Blys's former slaves. Exultant cries were all around them as people celebrated their victory, their freedom, or both together.

Exiting the towering entryway, Max and David descended the palace's many steps amid swirls of cold snow and hot ash. The skies were a dirty red, pressing down upon the world as though they meant to smother it. There was no moon or stars, just the faintest hint of dawn in the light outlining the eastern mountains. Throughout the burning city, horns were sounding—joyful horns trumpeting victory.

An open carriage awaited them, drawn by four of the Raszna's enormous horses. David stood aside to let Max climb aboard. When they were seated, an invisible driver shook the reins and they began the steep descent through the city.

Max was glad for the open carriage, glad for the cold, which helped to clear his mind. The more it emptied, the less he felt like such an alien within his own body. He was changed certainly— changed forever—but he found that his old persona had not been drowned in the flood of Old Magic. The farther he got from Prusias's throne room and the Morrígan, the more he gradually felt like his old self. His fiery form was beginning to seem like a dream. The *gae bolga* was no longer white-hot, but black and merely warm to the touch. Unbuckling its scabbard from its belt, he sheathed the blade and felt its metal go cold.

His mind drifted to the Morrígan. How close had he been to declaring himself king? As sickening as he found the prospect now, Max could not pretend the idea hadn't been wildly seductive. Without David's appearance, Max was almost certain he'd have seized power. He wondered if his friend had any inkling as to the catastrophe they'd just avoided.

The idea was too horrible to contemplate. Looking about, he saw that some mansions in the capital's upper tiers remained undamaged. But most were burning, sending up gouts of flame and smoke to mingle with ashes and snow.

While the city's sights were grim, its streets were packed with soldiers, with half-starved regiments that moved aside and thumped their banners to salute when they swept past. All Max could muster in response was a distant stare.

"Well done on Prusias," said David, glancing over. "Capturing him alive should prove immensely—"

"Scathach is dead," said Max, cutting to it. Rediscovering his humanity was bittersweet. He felt like he was experiencing the pain and loss all over again.

David wilted. "I . . . I'm very sorry," he said heavily. "With all my heart, Max. When I saw she hadn't returned with you . . . Well, I hoped there was another explanation."

Max stared rigidly ahead. "The clones cornered her. I didn't get there in time."

David digested this slowly. "And the clones? Are they still alive?"

Max smiled bitterly. "Of course they're alive. They're my kin, and I'm forbidden to slay them. It's part of my geasa." His whole being was trembling. Max almost laughed at the absurdity—a god afraid to confess a secret!

"You learned your geis, then," said David.

"I have two," said Max indifferently. "Would you like to hear them?"

"No. That is not for others to—"

"The Hound may not refuse a dying wish or knowingly slay his kindred."

David sighed in a manner suggesting he regretted Max's geasa and the fact that he'd heard them. "I see. So slaying the clones would have sealed your own fate. Perhaps that's why the *gae bolga* is reluctant to strike them."

"Probably," said Max. "But I didn't need the *gae bolga* to avenge Scathach. I could have snuffed the clones out like candles. There they were—burning like torches, clinging to a wall like beetles waiting to be squashed. But I held back and let them scuttle away. All because I feared to break my geis."

Max fell silent, consumed by disgust and disbelief. Scathach had sacrificed her home, friends, and immortality for him. And when it had come time to avenge her . . . he'd saved himself. Time might heal many wounds, but not shame. Shame had unique properties. Shame could linger forever.

"You ended this war," said David gently, gesturing at the smoldering devastation around them. "You captured Prusias. That means peace, Max. Peace for years to come."

Max merely gazed ahead as they passed beneath a broken archway.

"Slaying the clones might have satisfied your honor, but at tremendous cost," David reasoned. "By staying your hand you attained something far greater than personal vengeance."

Max laughed bitterly. "You make it sound like I was serving some grand purpose. But that isn't true, David. I thought only of myself."

David spread his hands. "As you wish. I won't pretend to know your motivations. I'll ask only one question."

"What?"

"Would Scathach have wanted you to break your geis?"

Max rubbed his temple. "No. She would have wanted me to complete the mission."

"And you did," said David firmly. "Scathach will be avenged, Max. Now that Prusias has been defeated, others can pursue the clones and dismantle the Atropos. There will be no shortage of volunteers from Rowan or the Raszna."

Max grunted. He might be hamstrung against the clones, but nothing would save the Atropos. The entire organization would be destroyed. He'd see to it personally. Thoughts of that guild led his mind back to the Workshop and the footage he'd seen.

"Did you know Alex Muñoz is a member of the Atropos?"

David twisted about. "How do you know that?"

"I saw a video at the Workshop. He bought the clones for the Atropos."

"You're certain?"

"Positive."

"One moment," David muttered, quickly conjuring a small orb of golden, swirling vapor. "A message from Director Menlo. Baron Lynch of the Raszna is not to harm his prisoner under any circumstances. We need that prisoner for questioning." With a snap of his fingers, David sent the orb zooming back toward the palace.

Max raised his eyebrows. "So Connor finally got Alex. How'd he catch him?"

"Some Raszna found him trying to hide among the palace slaves."

Exhaling, Max watched his breath mist against the reddish sky. The air was biting and tinged with smoke, but it was good to be outside after his journey underground. His adrenaline had dissipated, leaving a yawning void in its wake. Heartbroken as he was, he was slowly appreciating just what they had accomplished: Blys was sacked, Prusias had been captured, and Rowan had made new allies and forged the basis for an ongoing partnership. There was much to celebrate, even if he was in no mood to do it.

"I'm sorry, David," said Max. "With all that's happened, I forgot to congratulate you. I can't imagine there's ever been a finer general."

David waved off the compliment. "I merely coordinated efforts," he said modestly. "You recruited the Raszna. The Coopers sabotaged the gargoyles and unlocked the gates. The troops did the fighting. I paced about a tent."

"With Lilith," said Max, recalling his glimpse of the demoness in David's mirror.

"Ah," said David, taken off guard. "Well, don't be too outraged. She was very helpful when it came to neutralizing the city's more powerful residents. I summoned and Lilith negotiated. The brighter ones understood that our proposal was more attractive than their alternatives."

"Was capturing Prusias alive part of the proposal?" Max asked.

"It helped," said David. "But I wanted him alive anyway . . ."

David trailed off as their carriage finally reached the city's lowest tier, where the outer wall and great gates were located.

It was eerily quiet at this level and difficult to see. The horses whinnied, tossing their heads as they clopped reluctantly forward. Through the reeking haze, Max could make out the suggestions of broken walls, obliterated buildings, and fire-gutted factories. The stench of burning flesh and garbage was everywhere. The carriage swerved as they passed the frozen carcass of a half-charred wyvern. On the roadside, Raszna were laying out the bodies of the dead—allies and enemies alike. The vyes watched the carriage pass with dark, inscrutable eyes. Max looked away. He dreaded seeing a familiar face among the endless rows. Soon enough he would know the names of those who had fallen, but not now. With a hard swallow, he cleared his throat.

"The Fomorian?"

David pointed toward a dark mountain of wreckage.

As the carriage approached, the mountain resolved into distinct shapes and forms. A dreadnought's black tentacles were the first things Max could identify. Each was hundreds of feet long, their undersides riddled with lamprey-like mouths and suckers. They were almost artfully arranged—some draped, some curled, some twisted into agonized poses. The colossal bodies from which they sprouted were barely recognizable, for they had been beaten and bludgeoned to such an extent that it was difficult to make much sense of them. Here and there, Max saw an elephantine leg or a glassy eye, but the general impression was a pile of mangled flesh and machinery that nearly reached the battlements. Among all that carnage, it was difficult to spot the Fomorian. When Max did, he jumped out of the carriage.

The giant was leaning against a cracked gear, huddled like a beggar with his horned head bowed between his knees as though he could not support its weight. His size had diminished to such an extent that he looked tiny against the backdrop of dreadnoughts. While the Fomorian was still much larger than a man—twenty feet at least—his body was but a detail, a speck amid all the destruction he had wrought.

The giant's arms—or what remained of them—hung limp at his sides. He was utterly still, but for the occasional twitch of a ram's ear or a slow exhalation that sent up a cloud of mist.

When Max reached him, he could hardly believe the Fomorian was still living. Hundreds of pinlegs stingers riddled his legs, their stems poking from the giant's blood-matted fur. His left arm and upper torso were almost entirely stripped of their flesh, leaving little more than glistening bone, bits of muscle, and frayed sinew. Each ponderous breath brought a soft wheezing from punctured lungs.

Very carefully, Max reached up and touched one of the horns on the giant's bowed head. It was smoother than Max anticipated and formed a graceful spiral like a nautilus. Even its coloring was more beautiful than Max had supposed—subtle swirls of chestnut and speckled gray with an underside of cream. Stroking the horn, Max leaned close to the torn and bleeding ear that twitched beneath it.

"Can you hear me?" asked Max quietly.

The Fomorian shifted toward him ever so slightly, inclining his head so that its weight pressed against Max's hand. From the giant's throat murmured a deep voice, so hoarse and faint that Max strained to hear it.

"I want to hear the sea."

"I'll take you," said Max. "Would you like David to come? He's here, too."

The giant gave an almost imperceptible nod.

There was a group of Raszna nearby and a large sledge that had been used to transport siege equipment. With the vyes' help, Max hooked a team of horses to the sledge while David levitated the Fomorian off the ground and laid him gently on its pine planks. The giant's weight pressed the sledge's runners deep into muddy snow until David tapped them with the cane and they rested lightly upon the road. Once he'd checked the harnesses, Max came around to sit by the giant's head and stroke the curling horns. Four tawny eyes, some round as an owl's, others more goatlike, stared up from a half-skinned face and watched his breath mingle with the falling snow. When David clambered onto the sledge, he thumped its side and, once again, an invisible driver got them under way. Within minutes, they had left the city, crossed one of the serviceable bridges, and followed the ancient Tiber as it flowed toward the Tyrrhenian Sea.

Max stared at Blys as the city receded. So much smoke poured from the mountain-ringed city that it almost resembled an active volcano. Mortars had wholly destroyed three bridges while another looked ready to topple at any moment. The remnants of Grael's legions littered the icy plains, a glinting feast for countless crows that swarmed like horseflies. The birds' cries carried over the wind, a delighted chorus that followed them over the snow-bound hills.

Despite the furs the Raszna had heaped aboard the sledge, the cold was so intense that Max's hands were numb before they'd gone half a mile. The Fomorian's face was almost blue with cold, but he grunted his displeasure when Max and David tried to lay their furs atop him. Exposed to the elements, the giant merely stared up at the sky and hummed.

Even with an enchanted sledge, it took over two hours to reach the sea. They passed ruins and forests, snow-capped tombs, and lonely towers looking west. What had once been Ostia was now a small port city that Rowan had occupied before the final push toward Blys. The city lay as Rowan left it, largely undamaged since its brayma fled before the invaders had arrived.

Slowly, the Fomorian raised his mangled arm and pointed toward a distant outcropping, away from the city and its empty harbor. Turning the sledge, they made for it, the horses tossing their heads as the runners plowed shallow furrows in the ice-crusted snow.

They reached the outcropping within half an hour, climbing a gentle rise until they reached the summit of a hill crowned with seven cypress trees. Once there, the Fomorian indicated that this was where he wanted to be set down.

David and Max helped him do so, David levitating the giant from the sledge and Max helping him lean his ravaged body against one of the cypress trunks. This time when Max wrapped furs about his body, the giant did not refuse but simply stared out at the choppy waves, his eyes half-lidded as he sniffed the air and hummed in his throat. At last he spoke to his companions.

"Let me see you, kinsman. And you, little Sorcerer."

They did as he asked, walking around and standing before him, Max leaning upon the *gae bolga* and David upon his cane. All four of the Fomorian's remaining eyes fell upon Max, scrutinizing him closely.

"You are changed," he murmured. The eyes wandered from Max to the spear he carried. "Did I work good or evil in mending you?"

"Good, I think. We've defeated Prusias."

"It is not Prusias that frightens me," said the giant significantly. At length, he turned to David. "I would ask a boon."

"Of course," said David.

"Forgiveness," muttered the giant. "You are not a trickster or a serpent. I should not have judged you so."

"You are forgiven," said David. "But surely there is something else we can do. We have excellent healers—"

The Fomorian shook his head decisively. "I am beyond the aid of any that walks this earth. . . ." With a trembling hand, he drew aside a torn flap of skin and revealed a pumpkin-sized hole in his chest. Past the jagged, broken ribs, Max could actually see the Fomorian's gray-blue heart beating within the shadowed cavity. But things were clinging to it, a dozen finger-sized, metallic creatures that were wriggling like hungry grubs. They resembled tiny pinlegs and were almost certainly related in some capacity.

Even as they watched, one bored its way into the Fomorian's heart and disappeared.

The blood drained from David's face. "Will it be over soon?"

"I am of the Old Magic," said the Fomorian, grimacing. "These abominations cannot kill me. But they can torment me. I did not know man could make such things."

The giant said nothing more, as though resigned to this Promethean fate. But his body shivered from the unimaginable horrors taking place within.

"What if we take you to your island?" said Max. "It's where you're strong—"

"I cannot return," interrupted the giant dispassionately. "That was the price of leaving."

Max was aghast. "But it's your home."

Closing his eyes, the Fomorian shifted his weight slightly. "This must be home."

"I didn't know you wouldn't be able to go back," said Max. "I'm so sorry—"

The giant furrowed his brow. "Do not be sorry. Be just. Rowan has won a war, but it must share this world. Even with wild things. Swear this to me, both of you."

Once they did so, David cleared his throat. "I have another oath to fulfill. It is time Elathan's son had a truename."

The Fomorian did not stir. "I saw no Book."

"I do not have the Book of Thoth," said David. "But this cane contains one of its pages. Prusias used most of its power, but I've saved what remains."

At this, the Fomorian gave a shuddering exhale. His bloodied, ramlike features adopted a hopeful, almost childlike expression. "Can you truly do this for me?"

By way of reply, David unscrewed the cane's bejeweled top and drew forth a tissue-thin parchment that was rolled within its interior. Sheltering the page from the wind, David came very close to the giant, almost standing beneath his plaited beard. As David unfurled the yellowed parchment, Max saw that its surface was swimming with silvery words and letters, all truenames. They rose and fell, glided smoothly past, or sank out of sight as though the page had depth. Some of the truenames were written in hieroglyphs, others in runes and alphabets whose origins Max did not recognize. Within several seconds, untold thousands had churned within view. He could not imagine how many a single page must contain. And yet, there was room for only one more.

The words faded at David's command so that the parchment appeared blank. Touching the giant, David whispered something so softly that Max could not catch its syllables. A word appeared on the page, very long and comprised of Ogham runes, which Max had learned in the Sidh. Among the marks and slashes, Max recognized the word for *grandfather* but this was the only portion he understood.

Whatever its full meaning, the name's appearance brought a sudden, sharp intake of breath from the Fomorian. A shiver ran from his curling horns down to his cloven hooves. Hard, tawny eyes cracked open to gaze down at David.

"You kept your promise. I honor that, and you."

As David bowed, the runes sank into the parchment and disappeared. Rolling the page back up, David placed it inside the cane and set it within the giant's hand. Clutching the cane, the Fomorian closed his eyes.

"You may go."

"No," said Max. "I'm not going to leave you here in this agony."

"You can do nothing for me."

"I can end your suffering."

David turned abruptly. *"Max—"*

But Max kept his attention fixed on the Fomorian, whose face betrayed a war of conflicting emotions. Eyes screwed tight, the giant shook his shaggy head and clutched the cane tightly. "Be careful what you ask, kinsman. I will answer true."

Standing on tiptoe, Max embraced the giant's head and felt his warm tears upon his skin. "But I am asking," he whispered. "You have your name at last. There's no need to suffer any longer. Not when I have the means to give you peace."

With a shudder, the broken giant clutched him tight.

"Do you wish it?" Max whispered.

When his kinsman nodded, Max kissed his cheek and withdrew two paces. Head bowed, the giant began a lilting, dirge-like song in a voice so deep that the earth trembled. The words were in a tongue that Max did not know. But their meaning was plain enough. The Fomorian was saying farewell to earth and stone, wind and sky, and the seas that were dearest of all.

And as he sang, a dryad slipped out from one of the cypress trees, a lithe young woman with deep green skin, tangled brown hair, and silvery eyes. Stepping lightly over the snow, she came to kneel near the giant.

Others arrived to hear the giant's song. From the nearest woods came five slender fauns, three goat-legged satyrs, and an ancient centaur wearing a crown of twisted holly. Creeping close to the ring of trees, they bowed their heads and listened in reverent silence. From the sea came water sprites, childlike figures riding wisps of mist whose bodies were all of swirling seawater.

But it was the faeries Max was happiest to see. They came by the dozens, luminous little figures that descended from the skies or skimmed over the snowy countryside to settle atop the giant's shoulders or nestle in his beard and listen. When at last his song was ended, the Fomorian raised his head and gazed with clear eyes at the gray waves.

When Max pierced the Fomorian's heart with the *gae bolga*, the giant did not cry out. He merely gave a great exhale, like an emptying bellows, and leaned heavily against the cypress tree. Withdrawing the spear, Max backed away and came to stand by David.

Blood ran freely from the giant's chest while steam rose off his body, melting the snow and ice about him. Where the snows melted, the earth came to life, sprouting grass and gorse, sea campion and corn marigolds that fluttered in the wind. Extending a hand, the giant touched them, patting them lightly before bowing his head and closing his eyes. The faeries left him then, taking to the air as the Fomorian's body hardened into rough, weathered stone.

Wiping the *gae bolga* clean, Max turned and walked slowly back to the sledge. David remained to gather up the furs, dragging them over the snow and tossing them onto the sledge where Max sat gazing solemnly at the sea.

"Why did you do that?" David asked quietly.

"He was in pain," said Max. "I couldn't let him suffer like that. Not when I could help him."

David's voice was thick with emotion. "But your geis."

"Is broken," said Max indifferently. "It's for the best, David. You don't know what I'm capable of now. I don't either."

"You will grow into your power," David assured him.

"Never invite a god into this world."

Max removed his hand from beneath his mail shirt, where he'd been clutching the wound made by the Atropos knife. He had been clutching it since the giant turned to stone, since he'd felt it tear apart beneath its sash. Gazing down, he saw the hand was red.

Within half an hour, Max was back at Rowan.

The moment he'd seen Max's bloody hand, David had summoned air elementals to transport them—horses and all—in a swift, frigid flight to his command tent. Racing past the bewildered guards, David flung open his battered trunk and levitated a half-conscious Max down its staircase and pulled the lid shut. When they reached the bottom of the stairs, David spoke a password and Max felt a powerful tugging as the wormhole activated.

An instant later, Max lay sprawled atop a bed, staring up at the stars and constellations winking beyond the glass dome in the Observatory, the dormitory room he and David had shared since they were twelve. Nearly a year had passed since Max had been here, and the faint smells of wood smoke and old books were comforting. Less comforting was the fact that something was wriggling beneath him.

"David," Max murmured. "I'm on top of something."

"Of course you are," said David distractedly. He was standing by the bedside table, trying to slide the *gae bolga*'s scabbard over the blade without actually touching the weapon. "Sheets, pillows. Maybe a bolster." Nudging the sheathed spear aside, he pulled up Max's mail shirt to delicately touch the area of his wound. "Does that hurt?"

"No," replied Max dreamily. And it was true. The flesh around the wound was cold, but it did not hurt in the slightest. The problem wasn't pain, but the steady trickling of warm blood down his midsection. Max's extremities were growing numb and he felt increasingly dizzy, like his head was a helium balloon bobbing on a string. The sensation was not unpleasant and might have bordered on euphoric if a cat-sized creature hadn't suddenly writhed out from beneath him with a shrill, insectlike chittering. Max gave a startled cry as a pair of antennae brushed his chin.

"Don't worry," said David. "It's only Chester."

"Get it off me!" Max yelled, pushing feebly against the

pinlegs' segmented forelegs. Issuing an ear-piercing ululation, Chester promptly jumped onto his face, mandibles clicking as it turned about in apparent confusion. Scolding his pet, David tossed the flailing pinlegs aside before pressing a bath towel against Max's stomach.

"Keep pressure on it," said David sternly. "I'm going to get the healers."

"Put Chester in his case," Max pleaded. "Lock him—"

But David was off, dashing around the walkway and out the door. The next five minutes seemed an eternity as Max listened in rapt horror for any hint of the pinlegs' location. At last, David returned with five moomenhovens bringing a stretcher and several medical bags. The matronly, cow-legged healers worked quickly, assessing Max's injury with gentle, probing fingers. They applied several different ointments at its fringes, studied the wound's reaction to them, and exchanged nervous glances.

"Max," said David. "What do you know about the weapon that did this?"

"It was the knife that belonged to Set," said Max, his dizziness returning. "Prusias gave it to the clones. The Fomorian said it's killed a god before."

"Osiris," David muttered gravely. "It must be the blade he used to murder Osiris on the Nile." He turned to the moomenhovens. "Is anything working?"

They shook their heads, shooing David aside. Cutting away the Fomorian's sash, they smeared a pungent ointment into the wound along with three slips of papyrus inked with spells. The papers began to smoke and curl like dying slugs. Frowning, the moomenhovens removed them, making gestures in sign language for David to apply a tourniquet.

"Where are we going?" Max murmured as they slid him onto the stretcher.

"Túr an Ghrian," David said.

Max felt buoyant, as though the canvas stretcher were a magic carpet. David and the moomenhovens trotted beside it, guiding it out the door and down the dormitory corridor past a few stunned or curious faces peering out from their rooms.

By the time they reached the Manse's foyer, Max could stay awake no longer. As they rushed out the double doors, he glimpsed only a starless night before his eyes closed and a wolfhound padded through his dreams.

~ 24 ~

LEVIATHAN STIRS

Max dreamed of a wolfhound but awoke to a dragon.

The eyes staring into Max's were larger than serving platters, the pupils mere pinpricks within the pearly irises. They were set on either side of a horned head whose sleek, elongated planes resembled those of a pike. While the jaws were shut, a number of dagger-sized teeth protruded like a crocodile's. A foreclaw was spread across Max's reclining chest with fully articulated claws and an opposable thumb whose curving talon rested right near his jugular. Max felt like a mouse that had been pinned by a large and watchful cat.

With a sibilant hiss, one of Ember's coils slid past Max's

neck, grazing his bare skin. While the golden scales were smooth as glass, they were as hot as a baking stone. Max recoiled and felt a heavy, unyielding resistance against his legs. He gazed down to see that he was enveloped in a shimmering coil thicker than a tree trunk. With a grunt he tried to free himself, only to find that his arms were pinned helpless to his sides. He could not move, or even see what else was around him; the dragon filled his entire field of vision.

"Let me go," he gasped. The coils about him were so hot it was like being buried in scorching sands. Max struggled vainly against their hold. "Let me go!" he yelled.

Ember's pupils lengthened into vertical slits.

The dragon had been asleep. No longer, however. His eyes focused squarely upon Max while smoke trickled from his nostrils. The massive head eased forward, his jaws parting slightly to saturate the air with a smell like smelting ore and charred flesh. Max turned aside as whiplike tendrils along the dragon's snout flicked and touched his face with surprising delicacy. A sound issued from Ember's throat like the strumming of huge metal harp strings. As the head brushed past Max, he felt the massive coils loosen and ease him down upon a warm stone floor. Once he was free, the dragon slid away like a golden serpent.

Rising slowly to his feet, Max found he was dressed in a simple white robe. His hand strayed to his abdomen, where his wound had been tightly bandaged. It no longer seemed to be bleeding, and his head was considerably clearer than when he had returned to Rowan. Had Ember healed him?

Turning slowly about, he saw that he was in a circular chamber some thirty meters across. Already, the dragon was stretching out and settling its massive body onto a long bed of glowing coals. Seven megaliths were spaced evenly around the room's perimeter, ancient stones crusted with lichen and cracked with age. Max saw the *gae bolga* had been propped against the nearest. He glanced up to the domed ceiling whose frescoes seemed to ripple from the light of an illuminated pool in the room's center.

Max walked toward the pool, stepping over intricate hexagrams, sundials, and moon charts inscribed upon the malachite floor. Like the scrying pool in the Fomorian's caverns, the water's surface was alive with various scenes gliding past and through one another. Central among these was an aerial view of Blys. The city was no longer burning, but illuminated by thousands of tiny torches set along its broken ramparts and avenues. It looked like a crowded, elegant ruin placed within a colossal snow globe.

A deep, lilting voice spoke behind him. "Admiring your handiwork?"

Max turned to find Elias Bram sitting twenty feet away in a niche along the wall. Despite the room's heat, the man wore black robes and a heavy cloak whose hood was pulled up over his tangled gray mane of hair. His eyes gave off a peculiar, almost sinister gleam—like the eyeshine of a wolf in a thicket.

Laying aside a scroll, the Archmage rose and pushed back his hood. He was as tall as, if not taller than, Max and exuded a rawboned physicality that contrasted sharply with his grandson.

"What are you doing here?" asked Max.

Bram spread his hands. "The same as you, Hound. Convalescing."

As the Archmage approached, it was clear he was not only unwell but also not entirely human. The man's eyes *were* like a wolf's, yellow-rimmed and feral, while falcon feathers dotted his temple along his hairline or poked from his steel-gray beard. His hands, Max noticed, were slightly scaled, the fingers ending in talons.

Bram smiled grimly and turned them over. "Magic always has a price. You see what happens from shape-shifting too often.

The body forgets what it is supposed to be. You know of what I speak."

"I'm no shape-shifter."

"Are you not?" said Bram pleasantly. "I've heard tales about a black-eyed god who appeared like a thunderbolt in Prusias's throne room. Did David exaggerate?"

"Where is David?" said Max, ignoring the man's question.

"In Blys. Wars get far more complicated when the fighting stops."

"Where's Mina, then?" said Max, walking away from the Archmage to look out one of the room's many windows. Through the glass, he saw the milky, mist-covered sea a thousand feet below. The water looked almost placid at these heights, but Max soon realized that was because it wasn't moving. The entire shoreline had frozen.

"Mina is at Rose Chapel," answered Bram. "People are learning who has been lost during the siege. She is comforting the mourners."

Max turned to face the Archmage. "Did Ember heal me?"

"The dragon's done what he can," said Bram. "So has Mina. None of us can truly mend that wound. But we have done our best to hold it at bay. My own spells are upon the bandages."

Max almost laughed. "Spells or curses, Archmage?"

A long silence ensued before Bram spoke. "Should I apologize for being wary of you? You frighten me. I daresay you frighten yourself. My grandson told me you willingly broke your geis and took the Fomorian's life. I'd like to know why."

Max turned back to the window. "No one else could end his suffering."

"Very noble. But are you so determined to die?"

"I don't know," said Max truthfully. "I didn't really care what happened. But I don't understand how I'm still alive. My geis is broken."

"Violating a geis doesn't result in instant annihilation," said Bram. "But you'll die within the year. Of that I have no doubt."

"That must please you."

"Please me? No. But I will not mourn when you have departed this world. You did the right thing, Hound. And since you're still capable of service—"

Before Bram finished, one of the floor's sundials slid open to reveal Mina climbing a spiral staircase. Eight months had passed since Max had seen Mina. Her face was leaner, her body more coltish. No more pigtails for Mina; her shining black hair was worn long and loose and framed a face whose preoccupied expression was more knowing and worldly than most ten-year-olds'. Max gave an inward sigh. An Ascendant's responsibilities were considerable and they were chipping Mina's childhood away. Soon it would be gone entirely.

"Max!"

She bounded up the last two steps in a swishing flurry of white robes and a golden, hooded cape. Catching her up, he embraced her and mussed her hair like he used to when she'd follow him around the farmhouse in Blys when he did his chores. She laughed and promptly wriggled free to peer at his bandaged side.

"No blood," she exclaimed. "That's good. Maybe my baby's cured you."

Max glanced at the dozing dragon. "That's quite a baby."

"Everybody's scared of him," said Mina matter-of-factly. "Half the scholars protest whenever Ember crosses Old College to visit the Sanctuary. I keep telling them the crops will fail if he doesn't but—"

"Mina," said Max, embracing her again. "How are you?"

"I'm okay," she said. "David told me how he gave the giant a name and you gave him peace. That was very kind of you. And capturing Prusias! You ended the war!"

"I guess so," said Max, smiling at her. The girl's joy and enthusiasm were contagious. "I need to take a page from your book and see the good in all of this."

"You do," she declared firmly. "I know you're sad, Max. I know you've suffered loss. But you've done a great thing, too."

"Thank you, Mina."

"You've done much, but we need more," said Bram pointedly.

Mina rolled her eyes. "Uncle 'Lias, Max has just come home. He's just—"

"There is no time for reunions or sentimentality," cut in Bram sharply. "Every minute, the danger grows. Did we not see him together?"

Mina sighed and gave a reluctant nod.

"See who?" asked Max.

"Astaroth," said Mina, frowning and pulling Max along to a particularly complex inscription in the floor. "Through there."

Max gazed at the cryptic lines and inscriptions in the swirling green malachite. "What's through there?"

"Nether," said Bram. "This inscription can be used to open a door to that spirit world. Astaroth is somewhere behind this door, Hound. Ever since you and David weakened him on Walpurgisnacht, he has been recovering his strength and watching this world from Nether. He has also been trying to communicate with another universe."

"We don't know that for certain," said Mina stubbornly.

"Come, child," said Bram. "You yourself noticed the peculiarities above Ymir."

"It did look thin," the girl admitted.

Max was utterly mystified. He looked to each of them.

"What are you talking about? Who is Astaroth communicating with? What other universe?"

"I'm sorry," said Mina. "I'll let Uncle 'Lias explain."

"Astaroth's universe," said Bram. "My investigations suggest that long ago Astaroth entered our world from another universe—a dying universe ruled by 'Starving Gods' whom he served and fled. This would confirm what I have always believed, that he is an Outsider who has spent millennia masquerading as a demon."

Max nodded. Although the idea of a dying universe and Starving Gods was new, Bram had previously shared his theory that Astaroth was not a true demon or even native to this world. But Mina's statement remained a mystery. "So what was Mina talking about? What's 'thin'?"

"The boundaries between worlds," Bram explained. "There have always been times or places where these barriers grow thin and even permeable. Spirits visit the earth more freely at certain times of day or days of the year, such as the solstice or equinox. But there are also locations—dimensional crossroads—where crossings are easier and occur more frequently."

"And what does this have to do with Astaroth's former universe?" Max asked.

"You know how I've always been able to see the worlds?" said Mina.

Max nodded, recalling her accounts of worlds grand and tiny, solid or ethereal, whose denizens had been aware of her and eager to make her acquaintance. She seemed to be able to see these other worlds or dimensions whenever she wished, just by letting her eyes relax and focus in a particular way.

"Well," Mina continued, "as Uncle 'Lias said, there are places in any world that are thin. And if you've got enough magic, or try at the proper time, you can cross from one world to another."

"Okay," said Max. "So what's so special about this crossroads above Ymir?"

"It's much thinner than most," answered Mina. "And it exists not just in this world, but in Nether and every other world I've seen. What's more, on certain days these universal crossroads overlap each other. This would make it much easier not just to travel between worlds, but—"

"Between two universes," said Max.

Bram nodded. "Precisely. Even under these ideal conditions, it would require an extraordinary amount of power to open a gateway, but Astaroth is determined."

"So you think Astaroth's trying to open a gateway to another universe?"

"I'm certain of it," said Bram.

"What makes you certain?" asked Max.

"Observation," replied the Archmage bluntly. "For almost a year, Astaroth has been visiting Ymir on these special days and channeling a great deal of energy at the crossroads. He's either trying to rupture the barrier or communicate across it."

Max rubbed his temples. "If you're right and Astaroth fled this dying universe, why would he be trying to contact someone?"

There was a quiet, controlled dread in Bram's voice. "I believe Astaroth is going insane. I believe he intends to sacrifice this world to the Starving Gods he served long ago."

This was too much for Max to digest after all he'd been through. He suddenly felt light-headed, unsteady on his feet. Shuffling to the niche where Bram had been sitting, he eased himself upon a cushion. Mina sat next to him while the Archmage poured each a cup of tea from a pot that had been simmering.

"That doesn't make any sense," said Max quietly. "Every encounter I've had with Astaroth—every conversation—has been about him reshaping the world. Why would he just destroy it?"

"Not destroy it," Bram corrected. "Sacrifice it. The difference is subtle, but important. If Astaroth merely wished to destroy the world, he already has the means. By itself that would gain him very little. But if he surrenders this world to the masters he abandoned, perhaps they will forgive, or even reward, him."

Max set down his tea. "Astaroth has been living here for thousands of years. He's been acquiring power, orchestrating endless schemes, and now he's just going to throw it all away?"

"What has Astaroth always coveted?" asked Bram sharply. "*Why* has he been acquiring all this power over the millennia?"

"He wants to rule," said Max, turning the question over. "No . . . he's never really been interested in ruling. As soon as he got the Book of Thoth, he left ruling to others. Prusias wants to rule; Astaroth wants to create. Every time I've spoken with him, he's said he wants to build a better and more beautiful world. He wants to be God."

"Correct," said Bram emphatically. "And he has learned a painful lesson. In this world, he may be *a* god, but not *the* God. Not even the Book of Thoth can make this so. Astaroth has possessed it now for almost three years. Tell me, how has he used its almost infinite power?"

Max was tempted to say that Astaroth had created a new world, but he hesitated. That wasn't exactly true. Astaroth had not really added much that was new. Instead, he had subtracted—scraped away the modern ideas, technologies, and civilizations that he found objectionable. While magic and mystical creatures had flourished in this new era, Astaroth had not invented them but simply revived them. In retrospect, it seemed that Astaroth had been remarkably restrained.

"He's removed truenames from the Book," Max mused. "But I don't think he's added many. Why is that?"

"Why indeed?" said Bram. "Have you ever seen anything he's created with the Book? Anything wholly new?"

Max searched his memory and recalled the time he'd left Rowan and sailed to Blys alone. He pictured the abominations he'd seen piled atop the rocks or clustering in the sea. "Creatures," he muttered. "Creatures in the sea—like mutated seals or crabs jumbled together. They were braying . . . yelping. They almost sounded in pain."

"I'm sure they were," said Bram. "I'm sure they lived very brief and miserable lives. Do you think they were what Astaroth intended?"

"No," said Max. "He likes order and elegance. Those creatures seemed the opposite of that. Maybe creating is harder than destroying or erasing."

"It always is," said Bram. "But tell me another thing. Did David struggle to use the Book of Thoth? Did he struggle to create?"

It seemed an age ago when Max and David discovered the Book of Thoth beneath Brugh na Boinne in the Sidh. When David had opened its cover, he perceived almost instantly how to use its power. He had even praised the Book's simplicity. Within minutes, David Menlo had created a new species from nothingness—two beautiful birds that had never existed before.

"No," said Max. "It was effortless for David."

"But not for Astaroth," said Bram pointedly. "Despite his power and intellect, Astaroth cannot use the Book as fully or as easily as my grandson. He can erase or modify what exists, but he's unable to create what he wishes. Something gets lost in translation."

"And you think this has driven him insane?" said Max.

"I think it has played a decisive factor," said Bram. "Astaroth has gotten everything he's wanted: He escaped these Starving

Gods, he passed himself off as a demon, he accumulated great power on Earth, and now he even possesses the means to reshape it. And it isn't enough!"

"So he's dangerous," said Max. "Even angry. But that doesn't mean he's going to sacrifice the world."

"Did David tell you what Astaroth said when he restored his hand in Nether?"

"No."

Bram's feral eyes blazed. "'I want you whole when I draw your God out of hiding. I want you whole when your God is devoured!'"

Max said nothing.

"Astaroth *is* going insane," said Bram. "This red winter is but a warning, a symptom of a mind straining not to snap. While Rowan has been warring on Prusias, I have been unraveling all I can of Astaroth's origins to discover a means of defeating him before catastrophe strikes. But my quest is dangerous. Astaroth knows I have been trying to follow him. He knows I've been interrogating spirits—spirits that may know his history. He is hunting me, Max. Rowan is the only place where I am safe."

"What prevents him from destroying you here?" asked Max. "He has the Book."

Bram gestured around at the magnificent chamber. "Rowan was built by Old Magic from another world. The Book of Thoth has no power over it. If Astaroth wished to attack me here, he would have not only Elias Bram to deal with, but also Mina and the first true dragon in centuries. No, it is far easier for Astaroth if he catches me away from Rowan or in the Nether. He is always watching, always lurking. Very rarely can I go about undisguised." The sorcerer gestured absently to the feathers along his throat. "Delving into Astaroth's past has been a demanding and rather dangerous hobby, but the puzzle is almost complete. Only one more piece remains, and I can't get it without you. You must help me."

Max almost laughed. The man's arrogance was boundless. "I *must* help you?"

"I spoke poorly," said Bram. "I am requesting your help, not demanding it. The situation requires—"

"Enough," said Max, holding up a hand for silence. "You know, I've been hearing about the great Elias Bram since I was twelve. But you haven't been too interested in our struggles. No, you started a war and left us to fight it—claimed other priorities while thousands of our people died. Well and good. But Astaroth's your quest, Archmage. You've made that very clear."

Bram's eyes blazed at this rebuke, but he choked back a reply and merely stared at Max. During the long silence that ensued, Mina looked from one to the other and fiddled anxiously with her magechain.

"This won't do," she said at length. "We have to be united."

Bram nodded his agreement and spread his hands in appeal. "I need your help, Hound. Will you at least hear me out?"

Max leaned forward. "You hear me out first. I think you're a coward, Bram. A fraud. You haven't been hunting Astaroth. You've been hiding from him. Hiding in this tower. Hiding behind Ember and Mina. What do you have to say about that?"

"Max!" hissed Mina. "You mustn't say that to the—"

"What? Archmage? Hero? Legend? I don't care about his titles, Mina. He's just a man. And a sorry one at that."

Instead of anger, the Archmage regarded Max with an infuriating blend of empathy and bemusement. After several seconds, he put down his teacup. "Is there anything else you care to say? It would appear you've harbored these feelings for some time."

"I'm not the only one."

"Oh, I'm certain of that," Bram chuckled. "And I'm certain

you're a finer man than I, Hound. You proved as much when you disobeyed the Morrígan."

Max narrowed his eyes. "How do you know about that?"

Rising, the Archmage stretched and reached for a heavy black cloak. "If you feel fit for a walk, I'll explain." The man thumped his chest. "I've been sitting in this heat too long."

"Should I come with you?" inquired Mina anxiously.

Bram cupped the girl's chin, a smile softening his hard features. "No, little one. And no need to worry. This talk is long overdue." He glanced at Max. "Your clothes are on that bench, Hound. You can change behind that screen."

Twenty minutes later, Max and Bram emerged from the great rune-sealed arch that guarded the entrance to Túr an Ghrian. Outside, the weather was bitter cold, with stinging gusts that roared off the sea to bend the coastal pines. But not even the dismal weather could dampen Max's enjoyment of seeing Rowan and Old College once again. Just ahead were Old Tom and Maggie, gray and solid, their windows ablaze with light against the wintry gloom. With a muttered oath, Bram wrapped his cloak about him.

"You'll find the Sanctuary much more comfortable," said the Archmage.

Max fell in stride with him, his boots crunching on the shoveled path as they walked past the academic buildings. Bram squinted ahead at the streetlamps, their lights ghostly in the snow.

"David sensed the Morrígan in Prusias's throne room," he explained. "He even made out snippets of your conversation. The lad is nothing if not perceptive. I'm impressed by your resolve. I'm almost certain I'd have given in. I've given in most of my life."

"I couldn't care less about your sins, Bram."

The Archmage gave him a shrewd look. "You should. We're far more similar than you may care to admit."

Max scoffed. "I'm no sorcerer. David and Mina have more in common with you than I do."

"Not true. Those similarities say little of our core identities. I know David has confided the nature of his father to you. The lad is half demon, a cambion. And Mina is something else entirely. The Faeregine some call her, and it's as good a name as any. But you and I? We are cut from similar cloth. We both descend from gods and humans. The Old Magic in us is stronger than David's and far more volatile than Mina's. The Faeregine is incapable of destruction or evil. But the two of us? We are more than a little capable, are we not?"

Max did not respond.

"I understand you better than you might imagine," Bram continued. "The temptations you face . . . I know how difficult they are. Power is exceedingly dangerous to the one who holds it. I never understood that until I'd been banished from Solas."

Max stopped in his tracks. "You were banished from Solas?"

"Oh yes," said Bram, acknowledging a group of passing scholars. "The historians glossed over it—too embarrassing—but I was stripped of all my titles and banished from Solas when David's mother was a little girl."

"Why?"

"My foolishness nearly ended the Red Branch. The order had been investigating incidents around the world and believed a single entity was orchestrating them. I dismissed their theory, of course. After all, if such grand conspiracies were occurring, wouldn't I have sensed them?"

The sorcerer shook his head at his folly.

"The Red Branch feared the Enemy had detected their activities. They requested my help, but I was busy with experiments I deemed more important. When I ignored them, the Red Branch asked Solas's council to order my compliance. The council did so, but I ignored them, too. Order me? Surely they had forgotten themselves."

"What happened?" asked Max.

"The Red Branch was ambushed," said Bram sadly. "I rescued two, but the other ten were lost. They had been correct, after all. A single being had been orchestrating these events—a being I'd even encountered as a little boy. We know him now as Astaroth."

"And because of this, Solas banished you?"

"They did," said Bram. "And justly. I did not protest the council's decision. Had they not removed me from my post, I would have relinquished it. I was stunned by what had happened. It was the first time I recognized how dangerous power could be. I was not fit to hold it."

"But you returned eventually," Max observed. "You were at Solas when it fell."

"Quite right," said Bram. "But for ten years I lived in the countryside with Brigit and Emer. I'd forsaken magic entirely and tried to forget my past when the council tracked me down. Dark matters were escalating well beyond their ability to contain them. Rumors were circulating that the Enemy was seeking a book that contained all the world's truenames. The council wasn't certain if such a thing existed, but if it did, the potential dangers were enormous. Given this new threat, they asked me to resume my duties as Archmage and recover this fabled book."

Against his wishes, Max found his anger diminishing. People expected perfection from Elias Bram. Perhaps Max had, too. Although he had not participated in the siege, the Archmage had by all accounts saved the fleet when they'd been attacked near the Strait. As the two passed the Manse's frozen fountain, it occurred to Max that much of his life had been shaped by decisions this man had made centuries ago. It was natural to be curious.

"So how did you acquire the Book?" he asked. "I've only heard bits and pieces."

Bram blew on his taloned hands and waited for some Third Years to pass before replying. "It wasn't easy," he admitted. "The first step, of course, was to determine if such a book existed. I scoured Egypt for evidence, but most of the ancient tombs had been ransacked long ago. However, after speaking with spirits in those places, I learned that the Book of Thoth was no myth and that a witch had found it centuries earlier. I traveled on to India and China, where the witches were most numerous and powerful. It was there I learned of the ossuaries and vaults high atop Nepal."

"In the Witchpeaks," said Max, ducking a branch as they walked through the class trees of Rowan's orchard.

"Aye," said Bram. "Living men are not admitted to their holiest places. Normally, I would have been turned away or forced to use trickery. But the witches were unsettled and granted me an audience. As it happened, I was not the first visitor to inquire about the Book of Thoth. In fact, the first petitioner was still present."

"Astaroth?"

The Archmage shook his head. "A blue-skinned imp. As evil as he was courteous."

"Mr. Sikes?"

Bram inclined his head. "Astaroth's servant had offered the clan a vast fortune of gold and jewels, but the witches care little for such treasures and they feared this imp and his master. While they had never fully studied or understood the Book, the witches knew it held great power and were divided as to what they should do. I convinced them it would be disastrous to let Astaroth have it and suicide to keep it now that the Demon knew it was in their possession."

"And they trusted you?"

Bram gave an amused grunt. "Trust the Archmage? Not exactly. There was little love between Solas and the witches. But they trusted me more than Sikes. The imp was too ingratiating, too evasive of their questions. They did not believe his account of the Book's purpose or how his master intended to use it. Ultimately, they relinquished it to me, but only after I'd agreed to their price. They demanded—"

"Three children of the Old Magic," said Max tersely. "I know. I was one of them."

"David too," Bram mused. "And Mina, I suppose. Yes, the witches' price was high, but there was no question of paying it. After all, the Book of Thoth now belonged to me. . . ."

The Archmage sighed. Even now, Max could see him contemplate what might have been.

"In my youth, I'd have used it freely," Bram confessed. "But my mistakes—as Archmage, husband, and father—taught me a great deal. And time away from Solas had been good for me. I'd developed a clearer understanding of who I was, the good and the bad. Until a man knows his flaws, he cannot know himself. I could not keep or study the Book."

"Did you ever look at it?" Max asked.

The sorcerer's mouth twisted into a rueful smile. "Once. Just long enough to give myself a new truename so that the Book could not be used against me. To dare anything more would have been my ruin, perhaps the ruin of everything. I do not possess David's gift for restraint. No, I knew I could not be trusted with it. The Book of Thoth had to be hidden, and quickly, for Astaroth would come for it. Indeed, I'd barely left the Witchpeaks when he overtook me."

The Archmage's eyes darkened at the memory. "I have a long history with Astaroth," he muttered. "History that goes back to my childhood. David can tell you more if you're curious. Despite our long acquaintance, we'd never fought one another—not directly. But we did that day upon the steppes. It was everything I could do to escape, to flee across the world with Astaroth on my heels."

"Where did you go?" asked Max.

Bram looked at Max keenly. "The Isle of Man. I knew Astaroth would hesitate to trespass on the Fomorian's territory. The giant did not welcome me, but he perceived my lineage and was willing to listen. I begged him to take the Book, to keep it safe, but he feared its power as much as I did. Instead, we decided to hide it in another world. Combining our strength, we opened a path to the Sidh, and I crossed over to petition the High King."

"Lugh Lamfhada," said Max.

The Archmage nodded. "Like you, I have walked the road to Rodrubân and heard its warden's challenge. I have crossed the Hero's Bridge and feasted in Summervyne. And I have bowed before your father. As I said, we have much in common."

Max stopped. The man's mention of Rodrubân, of its bridge and warden struck his heart a blow. That warden had been Scathach—*his* Scathach, whose lifeless body was lying deep in the Workshop. His mouth went dry. He found himself staring at the Sanctuary just ahead, at the double doors set within a snow-speckled wall.

"I am sorry," said Bram gently. "David told me of your loss. She was a valiant woman."

Max acknowledged this with a nod, but it took him a moment to compose himself. When he found his voice, it was rough and raw. "Tell me about your audience with my fath—with Lugh."

"He wanted to hear both sides," Bram replied, walking with

Max to the Sanctuary doors. When he tugged one of them open, Max felt warm air that smelled of leaves and soil and growing things. He had almost forgotten such wonderful smells existed.

"What do you mean *both* sides?" he asked, breathing deeply.

Once they passed within, Bram pulled the door shut and removed his heavy cloak. "Astaroth had also found a way to the Sidh," he explained. "The Wanderer has no rival when it comes to traveling between worlds. He followed me there and reached Rodrubân shortly after I did. We were both brought before the High King. I asked Lugh to take the Book, and Astaroth demanded he surrender it."

As they walked through the Sanctuary's tunnel of interlacing trees, Max pictured a radiant Lugh Lamfhada sitting upon his throne while a younger Bram and an ageless Astaroth petitioned the sun god.

"The audience must have gone well," said Max. "Lugh found in your favor."

"He did," said Bram. "But not before shaming me before his court. I am a distant descendant of Nuada Silverhand, who was king even before Lugh. As such, I should have been welcomed in the Sidh. But my betrayal of Marley, my exile from Solas—these actions and many others had tarnished my reputation. Lugh said I was unworthy of my gifts and had brought shame upon my ancestors. I could never visit the Sidh again. Immortality was denied me."

"That's a pretty hard sentence," said Max.

"Hard but fair," said Bram. "At least I was wholly truthful before the High King. Astaroth was not so wise."

Max glanced at the sorcerer. "Astaroth *lied*? I thought he was forbidden to. I thought that was his geis."

"It is," said Bram. "But only since his audience with Lugh. Astaroth's deceits about his identity and the Book's true nature so angered your father that he cast him from Rodrubân and imposed a geis. Astaroth could never lie again."

"Lugh has that kind of power?"

"A great god in his own realm?" said Bram. "Most certainly. From that day forward, Astaroth could not lie without destroying himself. I think that's one reason he has always wished to possess you. Aside from enhancing his power, corrupting Lugh's son would be gratifying."

The pair was reaching the end of the tunnel, where it opened upon the vast enclosure of Rowan's Sanctuary. Ahead, Max could see the expanding township and the Warming Lodge at the edge of a reed-fringed lagoon. The only visible snow was high up in the mountains.

"So, what happened after you left the Book with Lugh?"

Bram shrugged. "I returned to this world, temporarily triumphant. But Astaroth was enraged. He swore to devour me, destroy Solas, and acquire the Book. I suppose I must commend him—he made good on his promises."

The two walked the cobbled lane along the township's edge. Most of the people they saw were refugees too young, old, or infirm to fight in the war. Almost all wore clothes that were stained or muddied from working in the fields. Indeed, as he gazed about, Max saw that the vast plains had been converted for agriculture—a colorful jigsaw of tilled soil and numerous crops. The rest of the world might have frozen, but Mina and Ember's magic had converted the Sanctuary into a colossal greenhouse. Even with this vital food supply, Rowan's forces had nearly starved on their glacial march toward Blys. Breathing deep, Max shaded his eyes and scanned some nearby trees.

"What are you looking for?" asked Bram.

"Nox. I sent her back with Cynthia when the Raszna made

camp with Rowan. I didn't want her hurt in the siege. She wasn't very happy with me."

Bram pointed to some foothills a mile or two away. "YaYa and I saw the lymrills by that outcropping two nights ago."

"How did she look?"

The Archmage chuckled. "Like the largest lymrill that has ever walked the earth. Cuffed her siblings about like kittens."

Max could not help but smile. "Faeries are to blame. They fattened her up."

"Faerie magic would explain it," said Bram. "You must be hungry yourself, for you've been three days in Ember's care. I know a place—middling food, but we'll be able to eat without being disturbed. David is particularly fond of it."

Max nearly winced. "The Hanged Man?"

"You've heard of it, then," said Bram, leading him past charming bakeries and cafes until they left the township entirely and arrived at a shack of pine boards that had been built around the trunk of a sickly ash tree. There was no sign, merely a hanging scarecrow now reduced to a pair of dangling overalls. The shack's greasy windows were dark, its animal pen empty.

"Are you sure it's still open?" asked Max, more than happy to go elsewhere.

"Yes, yes," said Bram. "I was here only yesterday." Finding the door locked, he rapped it sharply.

A moan sounded from within, followed by the scrape of a chair and a heavy *thump* as though someone had walked into a table. Max heard a curse, a fumbling at the locks and then . . .

"Hi, Marta. Nice to see you again."

The Hanged Man's proprietor blinked at Max's greeting. She was a thickset, ginger-haired woman with an undershot jaw and a cringe-inducing scar across her pallid face. Recognition dawned at last.

"I know you," she murmured. "Little Davey's friend. You bought up my bread."

"I did," said Max. "We were hoping to have some now."

"No bread," she sighed. "Got five eggs, some taters, an apple what seen better days, and some butter 'bout to turn. Everything's been goin' to the front, ain't it? Surprised a big boy like you ain't off fighting, but I guess we can't all be heroes." Her piggish eyes drifted to the Archmage, lingering on his taloned hands and feathered beard. "Guess you'll be growing a tail next. Well, come in, you two."

Whistling to herself, Marta led them inside, heaved a dozing cat off a corner table, and wiped it down with a questionable-looking rag.

"S'pose you'll be wantin' tea," she said to Bram. "And you?"

"Coffee," said Max.

"Right," she said, kicking out a chair for each of them. "So what can I get you boys?"

Bram sat. "Five eggs, potatoes, and some privacy."

"What about the apple?" she asked, pointing to a wrinkled spheroid.

"We'll pass."

With a grumble, Marta shuffled away to light the stove and make amends with the sulking cat. Sitting down, Max ran a hand over the table's rough planks. "It's good to be back. Not *here* exactly, but Rowan. I've missed it."

"Savor it while you can," said Bram. "If we do not stop Astaroth, I fear this world will not see another year. It might not see another week. Imbolc is only a few days away."

Max knew the holiday, had attended its festival during his time in the Sidh. It was a day for feasting and celebrating the upcoming spring.

"You think Astaroth's going to try something on Imbolc?"

Bram nodded. "He's visited the skies above Ymir on all the old holy days—when the walls between worlds are thinnest. His next chance will come on Imbolc. We cannot give him that opportunity."

"If he's failed before, why would he succeed this time?"

"He's getting stronger," said Bram simply. "He's had two years to recover from Walpurgisnacht and absorb the strange energies of Nether. Each attempt I've witnessed is more potent than its predecessor. He will break through soon—either to open a way for his Starving Gods or call them to him."

"So, what is it you need from me?" asked Max. "What is this puzzle piece you were talking about?"

Marta brought their drinks, along with milk and lumps of something approximating sugar. Sniffing the milk, Bram pushed it away and spooned some sugar into his tea. Upon sipping it, he promptly heaped more. "Has David shared anything of my investigations? Has he told you of Lord Salisbury or Yaro?"

"No," said Max. "Since I arrived with the Raszna, we haven't had much chance to talk privately. Everything was focused on the war."

"Well, it's time I took you into my confidence," said Bram. "It's time you heard of Yaro, Neheb, and Tartarus."

Over the next hour, Bram shared his discoveries about Astaroth's past and origins. Max learned about Yaro, the imp who had preceded Mr. Sikes—the imp who'd served Astaroth when the Demon was known as Allu and Taluman, Bankou and Phyrael. Max followed along intently, but the most startling revelation concerned Mr. Sikes.

"He was *human*?" Max exclaimed, nearly spilling his coffee.

Bram conceded the last few potatoes. "Yes. And this Neheb was not just any human, but the youngest son of a pharaoh. I've been trying very hard to find Neheb's resting place, but it has been difficult. Astaroth served Neheb's father as a royal magician and took the boy as his pupil. According to spirits I've questioned, the boy soon became withdrawn and spiteful. He chafed that he was youngest—that three older brothers stood between himself and ruling all of Egypt. And so, late one moonless night, he murdered his brothers in their sleep and pretended to have escaped. He accused one of his father's advisers of the crime—a magister who'd never trusted the pharaoh's new magician."

"So, Neheb got away with it?" said Max, hating Mr. Sikes even more.

Bram shook his head. "Justice caught up with him. A cat had witnessed the murders and began following the boy wherever he went. Others joined it. Soon hundreds were gathering outside Neheb's chambers and trailing him wherever he went—arching their backs and hissing. Cats were held sacred in Ancient Egypt and thus many viewed their behavior as divine judgment against the surviving prince.

When the pharaoh questioned his son, the boy confessed, but not before invoking a curse upon his family. If Neheb could not rule as pharaoh, then no son of Egypt should ever rule in his stead. And indeed, the Persians soon overran Egypt and his father was forced to flee. True to Neheb's curse, his father was the last Egyptian pharaoh."

"What happened to Neheb?"

"Crimes against the pharaoh were punished by death," said Bram. "But crimes against one's family were considered crimes against the gods themselves. Since Neheb was guilty of both, his end was particularly unpleasant. While Astaroth rescued the youth's spirit and transformed him into an imp, what remained of Neheb's body was sealed in four urns that were buried in separate, unhallowed tombs. Ancient spells were laid upon these urns. Without all four, I cannot speak with Neheb's shade."

"Do you have them all?" asked Max.

"Three," said Bram. "Only recently have I learned the location of the fourth. Evidently, the witches brought it long ago to their ossuaries. When they tried to commune with Neheb's partial remains, they triggered a powerful curse that destroyed those present. The witches made no more attempts. Neheb's remains were consigned to a vault far below the deepest ossuaries, a vault whose location is known only to the Umadahm."

"Who's Umadahm?" asked Max. "I thought Dame Mako spoke for the witches."

"There are many leaders among the clans, but only one Umadahm," said Bram. "She is groomed from childhood for the position and inherits the title when her predecessor dies. The Umadahm presides over the ossuaries and has final say on spiritual matters. She alone knows the location of this secret vault they call Tartarus."

Max knew his Greek mythology. Tartarus was where the wicked were punished—particularly those who had committed crimes against the gods. "Even if you can raise Neheb's shade, what do you hope to learn from him?"

Bram folded his arms. "Astaroth's truename. If I learn that, I can destroy him. Yaro swore that Neheb knew it."

"But what if he was lying?"

The sorcerer shook his head. "David questioned Yaro with the Seal of Solomon. No spirit can lie to the ring's bearer. Yaro shared what he believed to be the truth. The only way to learn if it *was* the truth is to question Neheb himself."

"So what do you need from me?" asked Max.

"I expect Tartarus to be very dangerous," said Bram darkly. "The witches did not build it themselves. They came upon its doors long ago after digging too deeply in the mountains. No witch has ever gone inside, for they believe only the dead may enter. Whenever they find remains that are accursed, they leave them outside Tartarus's doors. When they return, these offerings are gone. I am asking you to accompany me there."

Max was almost disappointed. "I didn't think Elias Bram needed bodyguards."

"I don't. What I require is a witness. Neheb may be a trap or he may be the key to defeating Astaroth. I intend to find out which and cannot risk that knowledge being lost should something happen to me. I need a companion who is qualified to enter Tartarus and strong enough to escape should things go badly. You are the only person who fits that description."

"You said the witches don't believe the living could pass its doors."

Bram leaned back against his chair and drummed his taloned fingers on the table. "Even if they are correct, you have just broken your geis, your name is in the Grey Book, and you are the son of Lugh Lamfhada."

"What about you, then?"

Bram chuckled. "Astaroth devoured my flesh hundreds of years ago and my orchard apple turned to gold. I highly doubt either of us will register as living mortals."

The Archmage extended his hand. "What say you, Hound? Leviathan is stirring, and I need your help. Will you come with me to Tartarus?"

Max did not take the hand. "One question."

"Of course. What is it?"

"Does David agree with your plan?"

Bram's face darkened with impatience. "My grandson is in Blys accepting the surrender of Prusias's braymas. We don't have time to consult—"

A small sphere of golden light zoomed into the Hanged Man and hovered between the two of them. From its center came

Mina's voice. Though she was trying to sound calm, her distress was plainly evident.

"Astaroth is in Blys."

Without a moment's hesitation, Bram touched the orb and vanished. The teleportation sphere remained, bobbing above the table's wilted centerpiece. Rising from his seat, Max glanced at Marta, who was dozing with the cat.

"We'll settle up later."

The instant he touched the sphere, Max found himself back in Túr an Ghrian where Bram was already standing beside Mina at the scrying pool. Ember had left his coal bed and was circling slowly about the vast chamber, his powerful tail swishing back and forth in agitation.

Max hurried over to the pool, whose surface was fixed upon a disquieting scene.

Astaroth was strolling the streets of Blys.

He was plainly visible in the early twilight, a shimmering figure in white robes, walking barefoot on the icy streets and cradling the heavy Book of Thoth in one slender arm. He might have been a tourist clutching his Baedekker, for now and again he would stop to gaze at a ruined building or the rows of frozen dead as though they were a local attraction before continuing on toward the palace. All around him, hundreds of Rowan and Raszna soldiers converged to form a moving perimeter, as though he were an elephant that had escaped from the circus.

"That's no projection from Nether," muttered Bram. "He's really there."

"What's he doing?" hissed Mina.

The answer was not yet clear, but it was soon evident that Astaroth would not brook any interference. The first soldier who cried out an order to halt—a captain in the Wildwood Knights— was incinerated where he stood. There was no blaze of fire or pyrotechnics. Astaroth simply gestured at the man and he dissolved into ashes.

Shouts and cries sounded from the crowds, which retreated to a safer distance as Astaroth stopped to inspect the captain's remains. Some of the ashes had blown away, but the bulk remained, filling the man's armor and clothing as though they were half-empty sacks. Opening the Book of Thoth, Astaroth extended a hand toward the ashes.

Gray soot and flakes danced up into the air, swirling about to form sinuous, elegant forms. At times, its contours were almost swanlike and burned with a fierce inner fire. But they never held. Time and again they wavered and dissolved, becoming misshapen and even grotesque.

Astaroth's prim, artificial smile disappeared.

Abandoning his creation, Astaroth turned slowly about, gazing upon his ever-growing audience. When they saw his expressionless face, there were shouts and screams, a surging away as people scrambled to get away from this otherness in their midst. As they fled, Astaroth spoke in a silky tenor that rang crystal clear above the din.

"Hell is empty, and all the devils are here," he intoned. "Are we celebrating a victory? Pray tell, what have you won? A bit of land? A few days of imagined freedom?" He shook his head and swept an arm over the ruined city. "A new world, and this is what you've done with it. I had hoped you would be my children—humans and demons, animals and spirits. But you're not my children. I understand that now. You're larvae. An entire planet teeming with larvae that won't do as they're told."

The smile returned.

"The old God punished the wicked with plagues, but I see this winter did not suffice. You require clearer lessons to understand your place. Very well, my little larvae . . . YOU SHALL HAVE THEM!"

Five hundred soldiers dissolved into ash, their armor and clothing falling into heaps as their remains swirled into a roiling gray cloud. To this, Astaroth added the bodies of the dead. Across the city, frozen corpses rose into the air: dead soldiers and wyverns, gargoyles and even dreadnoughts that dissolved into rushing rivers of matter that fed what was rapidly becoming a dark, primordial stew.

And from that stew came monsters.

They burst forth as though a sharp knife had slit a swollen belly. Some sprang, some flew, some hopped or crawled after landing. Some were the size of elephants, others no larger than dragonflies. Many looked crippled or twisted and some were only half formed, so they fell to the earth like gobs of cooling, wriggling tar. The Workshop had never conceived anything so appalling as the profusion of new, malevolent life raining down about the city.

Their creator was gazing skyward, his hand outstretched at the stew's remaining matter as it swirled and coalesced into a single, colossal shape.

Mina gasped. "It's a dragon."

And indeed it was—a dragon with shining, coal-black scales and a hideous head that resembled a skinned goat snapping and frothing as the Book of Thoth called it into existence. The beast looked to be far more massive than Ember, with a bloated body and eight limbs that were so twisted and malformed that only half looked functional as they stretched and clawed the frigid air. It howled as its hide split apart to unleash a pair of folded wings that unfurled to beat the air with frightful force. Fully formed,

it left its creator's control and flew in an ungainly yet powerful flight above the city. Its roar might have been the signal for
Ragnarok.

"He's gone," said Bram quietly.

Tearing his eyes away from the dragon, Max saw that Bram
was correct. Astaroth had disappeared from Blys, leaving an army
of new and hideous creations that were sowing chaos throughout
the city. The Archmage turned to him.

"Do you need more convincing?"

Max shook his head. "No. But those monsters—"

"Are a distraction," said Bram forcefully. "They have nothing
to do with Astaroth's true objective. He intends to sacrifice this
world, Hound. And he will succeed unless we stop him. I am
going to Tartarus. The only question is whether I'm going alone."

Max turned to where the *gae bolga* was propped against the
ancient megalith. With an eager moan, it flew to his outstretched
hand.

~ 25 ~

TARTARUS

Bram walked swiftly to a trunk where he retrieved three Canopic jars inscribed with hieroglyphics. Stowing them in a pack, he pulled on his heavy cloak. "Have you ever been at high altitude?"

"Aboard the *Kestrel*," said Max, for the ship had taken David and him deep into the night sky on their way to the Sidh. "But I don't remember much of that. It was like a dream."

"There is nothing dreamlike about the Witchpeaks," said Bram. "The air is dangerously thin and the cold can freeze flesh in minutes. We will have to climb, for we cannot teleport directly to the witches' temple—Ymir forbids it."

From the trunk he retrieved two pairs of crampons, a stout rope, and an ice ax. Coming over, Max knelt and buckled the crampons around his boots.

"The initial ascent is the most challenging," said Bram, doing likewise. "Once we reach the first ledge, we can join the paths the witches take."

The Archmage glanced at Ember, who was making an angry thrumming in his throat as he circled about the chamber, his attention fixed on the chaotic scene in Blys. Whenever he heard the other dragon roar, Ember bared his teeth.

"Mina," said Bram sharply. "Keep Ember here. Do not let him leave Túr an Ghrian—not even to visit the Sanctuary."

"Why?" asked Mina.

"Astaroth did not create that abomination by accident. The ancient dragons were fiercely territorial. Astaroth is trying to lure Ember away."

Mina looked pale. "He's going to attack Rowan?"

"He certainly intends something. And it seems he'd prefer if Ember weren't here when it happens. Be vigilant."

"I'll sound the alarm," she said.

Bram nodded. "I think that would be wise."

Closing her eyes, Mina clapped her hands together. From far below, Max heard Old Tom's heavy bronze bell begin to toll. Striding over to Mina, the Archmage gave her a paternal pat on the head. "Be safe, child."

Mina nodded and tried to smile. She looked absurdly young in her Ascendant's robes, like a little girl playing dress-up. Coming over to Max, she removed her glittering magechain and held it up. "For luck," she said.

He took it, well aware that Mina was sinfully proud of the many ornaments and charms that hung from its silver links. That

an Ascendant probably didn't need to prove or display her masteries was beside the point. Mina loved collecting trinkets.

"Thank you," said Max, kneeling so she could fasten it about
his neck beneath his torque. "I'll bring it back."

She embraced him fiercely before turning and calling to
Ember. The dragon was crouched by the pool, his golden head
swaying back and forth as smoke poured from his nostrils. When
he did not respond, she repeated her command with an authority
that took Max by surprise. Tearing his attention from the scrying pool, Ember snaked toward them in a soft rustling of scales.

Bram handed Max the coiled rope. "Ember will aid us in our
travels."

Sliding the rope over his shoulder, Max double-checked his
crampons, hefted the *gae bolga,* and nodded that he was ready.
Ember loomed over them, his body as hot as the coals he'd been
lying on. Bram placed his hand on the dragon's chest, just over
where Max imagined the creature's heart would be. There was
a searing hiss, but the Archmage did not wince or flinch as he
beckoned Max to take his other hand. When Bram closed his
eyes, a surge of blazing heat flooded Max's body and everything
went white.

He gasped as they reappeared in a place that was almost pitch
dark and numbingly cold. Releasing Bram's hand, Max reached
blindly about and felt his fingers brush rough stone. A light flared
in the darkness—a green glowsphere that illuminated Bram's
hard face. Looking past the Archmage, Max saw they were in a
small cave with a low, narrow opening. The wind was screaming
in the darkness beyond it, sending snow swirling about them.

Max's breath came in short, rapid gasps. He felt like he was
drowning.

Glancing over, Bram traced a sign with his finger.

The air grew warm, as though Max were sitting beside

a comfortable fire, and oxygen flooded his lungs. He thanked Bram, but the Archmage was already crouched by several crates he'd apparently stowed on previous trips. Fishing through one, he retrieved some dried venison and stuffed the strips in a pocket. There was another ice ax propped against the cave wall, which he handed to Max.

Taking it, Max removed the *gae bolga* from the enchanted spear shaft the dvergar had made for him. Now that it was a short sword, Max buckled the blade to his baldric and shrank the shaft to a baton that he hooked onto his belt.

Bram crouched by the cave entrance. Peering out, he beckoned for the rope. "This is the highest one can travel by magic. From here we must climb, but I know a good path and there's plenty of moonlight to see by. Wind will be the greatest danger. I've seen gusts rip people off the mountain. Stay low." Tying the rope around Max's waist, Bram tethered the two of them together before extinguishing the glowsphere and crawling out the cave entrance.

Max followed, squeezing through the opening onto a shallow ledge half sheltered by an overhang. Far below was a pearly sea of moonlit clouds pierced here and there by jutting, jagged peaks. Mastering an initial sense of vertigo, Max shielded his eyes from blowing ice particles and gazed up to behold countless stars in dazzling clarity. But even at these heights in the dead of night, the sky exuded a red tinge as though the world were infected. Pivoting, Max craned his neck and gazed up at Ymir's summit. Its peak gleamed like a knife beneath the moon.

Hefting his ax, Bram shuffled to the end of the ledge and carved a handhold that he used to swing clear of the overhang. For an older man, the Archmage possessed remarkable strength and athleticism. Every movement was decisive and assured.

He wasted no time or energy, stopping only to check that Max followed.

The two fell into a comfortable rhythm. They moved steadily up the steep face. It was clear Bram knew his way, for he found every little ledge, every natural handhold that might make their passage easier. Max had not done much mountaineering, but he mimicked Bram's techniques and found that they came naturally. He tried not to think about what might be happening in Blys or back at Rowan. Instead, he lost himself in the physical task at hand—anchoring his ax, kicking his crampons into the ice, and ascending another few feet.

Bram did not take them straight up but chose a diagonal route that would bring them to another ledge, which curved up and around the face they were climbing. Squinting through the gusting snow, Max was trying to estimate how far away it was when he heard Bram shout something over the wind.

"What?" Max yelled.

The sorcerer pointed windward where powerful gusts were blowing great plumes of snow off the neighboring peak. Swinging his ax into the ice, Bram turned his face away and flattened himself against the mountain. Max quickly did the same.

Three seconds later the winds slammed into them in a screaming assault of ice that might have torn Max from the mountain if Bram hadn't warned him.

The two did not budge for over an hour, each holding fast with ax and crampons as the windstorm raged around them. When it finally subsided, the two shook the cramps from their hands, flexed their fingers, and resumed their determined ascent. Beneath his bandages, Max's wound had begun to ache and throb. To ignore it, he began counting his ax swings.

The count had passed eight hundred by the time they reached

the ledge. Once atop it, the two sat with their backs against the mountain and took a few minutes to rest.

"The worst is over," Bram muttered, handing Max a strip of venison. The meat was half frozen, but Max chewed it gratefully. Brushing snow from his tangled beard, the Archmage pointed to where the ledge curved out of sight. "This merges with a trail that leads to the great temple. We may encounter others ahead, for this is a holy place and pilgrims come here seeking wisdom or blessings from the witches. Ignore them. They will not trouble us. Are you ready to continue?"

With a grunt, Max rose to one knee and pushed himself up. His stomach wound was burning and he thought several stitches might have torn, but he convinced himself the pain would subside when they got moving again. Clutching his ax, he followed Bram as they hiked along the ledge. While the going was easier, the ledge was narrow and they were far more exposed to the wind. Max did not look down, but watched the nearest peaks for signs of an oncoming gale.

Within half an hour, they crossed the sheer face and rounded the mountain to behold an escarpment up ahead. An enormous stone brazier stood upon it, its flames illuminating a shrine ringed by four great statues and a small stone hut. As they came nearer, Max made out three fur-bundled figures prostrated before the shrine.

Kneeling, Bram removed his crampons. Max did the same, handing them to the Archmage, who stowed them along with the axes. When they arrived at the escarpment, Bram bowed briefly to the fearsome-looking statues before skirting the praying figures and making for a broad stair of rough, stone steps. Within the stone hut, Max saw a young Asiatic woman sitting before a small fire and singing to a little girl who gazed up with blind, unseeing eyes. No doubt, the mother sought a spell or cure from the witches, and they had stopped to seek shelter overnight. The prostrate figures outside the hut were probably relatives.

Bram was ascending the steps, his hood pulled low and his cloak billowing about him. Beneath a snow-capped ridge high above, Max saw two flames burning. The pair trudged on, their boots crunching on the snow-covered steps. The stairs continued for another hundred yards before they ended and the two had to climb the rest of the way over bare ice and snow.

A witch waited for them at the temple's entrance, an archway of carved stone that led down into the mountain. She sat between two braziers, a wizened old thing swathed in furs and chewing betel. Her black eyes flicked warily between Max and Bram. Removing his hood, the Archmage inclined his head.

"Greetings, Dame Hakku. You're looking well."

The doorkeeper scowled. "How do you know my name?"

The Archmage shrugged. "My name is Bram. Did the Umadahm receive my message?"

The old witch spat in her cup. "We do not normally allow men to enter here, but she is expecting you," she said grudgingly. "You and Rowan's Hound may pass, but you must be cleansed before you enter the ossuaries. Umadahm's acolytes await you within."

Bowing low, the Archmage led Max underneath the carved archway and down a flight of curving, torch-lit stairs. They arrived at a circular antechamber whose dark walls were embedded with gleaming bones. It had only one exit, a triangular archway crowned with a human skull.

On each side of the archway stood three barefoot girls in white robes accompanied by a middle-aged witch wearing red robes and a necklace of feathers and finger bones. The acolytes were very young and bore few tattoos or markings upon their faces. They held bowls of polished teak whose steaming contents filled the room with the scent of sage and saffron. Bowing, the older witch introduced herself as Dame Treyva and indicated they must strip to the waist.

Bram did so without question or fuss. Max saw that the man's back was laced with old scars, shiny remnants of self-flagellation. Kneeling before the witches, Bram held out his arms as three of the acolytes anointed his upper body with oil and painted henna runes upon his face.

It took Max longer to remove his layers of clothing and armor. Once Dame Treyva saw his bare torso, she grew pale and hissed something in Nepalese.

Turning, the Archmage stared at Max's blood-soaked bandages. "When did it open?" he asked somberly.

"During the climb. What did she say?"

"That you are cursed."

Max met the witch's frightened gaze. "This curse is my burden, not yours. If Umadahm asks me to leave, I will go."

The witch hesitated, frowning uncertainly, before at last beckoning him forward. When Max knelt, the acolytes smoothed oil on his skin, covering all but his midsection, which they would not touch. Using delicate brushes, the young witches painted intricate symbols upon Max's face, neck, and the tops of his hands. While these dried, two of the acolytes added a dense border of runes around his wound while the others walked around Max and Bram in little circles, chanting quietly in their own language. Once they had finished, Dame Treyva struck a silver chime and invited their guests to dress. Bram glanced over at Max with evident concern.

"Are you fit to continue?"

Max reached for his cloak. "It's just a little blood."

The Archmage gave him a dubious look as Dame Treyva offered Max a cup of tea.

"It will help," she said.

There was compassion in the woman's voice and even a tinge of sadness that surprised Max. Taking the cup, he drained the pungent brew and thanked her. There was nothing magical in the drink, but its warmth was invigorating and the strong flavors cleared his head as they followed Dame Treyva through the arch and began a long descent into the mountain.

Everywhere Max turned, he saw human skulls of various age and condition. They lined ossuary shelves, adorned archways, and peered from illuminated niches set in the wall. The skulls were not displayed as ghoulish trophies. They were simply exhibits in an unusual museum.

Whereas the Archives was a repository of scrolls and books, the ossuaries housed arcana of a different sort—the knowledge possessed by shades and spirits whose mortal remains were housed in thousands of jars and urns, obsidian cases and sarcophagi that lined the shelves and niches of caverns they passed. Within each cavern, black- and red-robed witches were sifting through mounds of dirt and soil, cleaning fragments of bone, or labeling finds with the assistance of tiny homunculi.

When they'd passed a dozen such caverns and several raven rookeries, Dame Treyva took them down a dimly lit passage lined with statues of the many gods the witches held sacred: Hecate and Isis, Artemis and Cybele, Athena and Kali. The passage ended at a pair of large wooden doors carved with leering totems.

"Umadahm is very old and rarely leaves her quarters," said Dame Treyva. "She has convened her council here. They await you within."

Bram did not look pleased. "I must speak with her alone."

"That is for Umadahm to decide," said Dame Treyva, ringing a little chime.

When the doors opened, she ushered Max and Bram into

a low chamber decorated with painted screens, intricate friezes, and shelves lined with ivory carvings and figurines. Through a haze of burning incense, Max saw seven elderly witches sitting in a semicircle around a glowing firepit. Beyond them was a shrunken figure wearing simple sky-blue robes and propped in an enormous bed of carved teak covered in hides and furs.

Max could not begin to guess Umadahm's age. The woman's hair was so white and fine that it fell like braided cobwebs about a wrinkled brown face with large, expressive eyes. As Umadahm squinted at her visitors, her toothless mouth twisted into a broad, girlish grin. Her voice was weak, her accent heavy, but there was no mistaking its warmth and humor.

"Come in," she croaked. "Come where I can see you. I'm almost blind, curse the gods."

Seven pairs of dark, inscrutable eyes followed Max and Bram as Dame Treyva led them around the council to Umadahm's bedside.

"Umadahm, your sister presents the Archmage, Elias Bram, and Max McDaniels, the Hound of Rowan."

Umadahm clucked her tongue. "You meet him at last, Treyva. It is fate, no?"

The younger witch nodded hastily.

"What is fate?" asked Bram pointedly.

Umadahm peered at him. "Our Treyva meeting the Hound. I chose her to be his mother, you see, to raise him when we learned Rowan had children of the Old Magic. For those children were pledged to us, were they not? Pledged by *you*, Archmage, to our ancestors. But Rowan did not honor that promise and much woe has followed."

Max glanced at Dame Treyva, who offered a ghost of a smile before looking away. Now he understood the witch's reaction upon seeing his wound—it had been a look of maternal worry.

Some part of her still regarded Max as hers, as the child she might have raised.

Dame Treyva cleared her throat. "The Hound brings a curse, Umadahm."

The ancient witch raised her eyebrows. "The Hound means to curse us?"

"No," said Dame Treyva. "He bears an evil wound upon his flesh. The mark of Set is upon him."

Frowning, Umadahm beckoned Max closer and took his hand between two that were so delicate they might have been twigs wrapped in tissue paper. Brittle fingers sought out his pulse.

"There *is* evil here," the witch muttered. "But it has no interest in us. It wants the Hound." She gazed up at him. "My beautiful boy, what have you done to yourself?"

Bram cut in. "Umadahm, we must speak with you alone."

The witch released Max's hand and scowled at the Archmage. "Where are your manners? Does Elias Bram give orders here?" She sighed. "No wonder we banished men from our councils. Whatever you wish to say, say before my sisters."

"It involves Tartarus."

Umadahm's smile vanished. She turned to the other witches. "Leave us."

Her sisters looked startled by the sudden order but rose and began to file out the door. As they departed, Umadahm called to one of the acolytes waiting outside, a reedy girl with coarse brown hair and quiet, knowing eyes. "Naomi, you stay here. Treyva, we are not to be disturbed for any reason. Is that understood?"

"Yes, Umadahm."

With a parting glance at Max, Dame Treyva followed the last witch out and closed the door behind her. When Naomi locked it, Umadahm leveled her gaze at Bram. "Where did you hear that name?"

Bram turned from where he'd been admiring a carved tusk. "From one of your predecessors. When I questioned her shade, it mentioned a secret vault beneath the ossuaries, a place that houses the damned."

Umadahm's mouth tightened into a thin, hard line. "If you questioned one of our dead, then you have been trespassing in the ossuaries."

Bram bowed deeply. "Many times, I must confess. I beg your pardon, Umadahm, but I had no alternative. I assure you, I have harmed no one and treated your ancestors with respect. Anything I've borrowed, I've returned to its proper place."

The witch grunted. "A considerate burglar. How comforting." She glanced at Naomi, who had come to stand by her bed. "Beware of sorcerers, my dear. We cannot keep them out and they don't ask for invitations. What is it you want, Archmage?"

"For you to take us to Tartarus."

Again, the witch addressed her protégé. "Another lesson. Sorcerers are moths fluttering around a candle. Boundless curiosity, but little wisdom. Waste no energy fighting them. Sooner or later, they fly into the flame."

If Bram was insulted, he did not show it. "Will you take us there?"

The witch shrugged. "Would it matter if I refused? If you're foolish enough to seek Tartarus, I will take you to its gates. But there I leave you. I will not linger to see them opened or send aid if you do not return. Is that understood?"

"Perfectly."

"Very well," said Umadahm, grunting as she scooted over and dangled her frail legs over the bedside. "Naomi, bring me my slippers and the gray robe. No, the blue. It's warmer."

The slippers Naomi brought were beaded moccasins that looked as old and scuffed as their owner. The girl slid them gently over Umadahm's bony brown feet before helping her up and draping a blue, fur-lined robe over her narrow shoulders. Umadahm tied the robe with slow, precise movements before shuffling past the bed with Naomi.

"Follow me, gentlemen."

The pair walked directly into the firepit's burning coals, plunging from view as though they'd fallen through a trapdoor.

Bram grunted. "I trust you noticed it when we entered. Illusion has never been their strength."

But Max was having a difficult time focusing on mundane details, much less seeing through illusions. His body was growing feverish and his wound was an ever-present agony. Unbuckling the *gae bolga*, he turned it into a spear so he could use it as a walking stick. None of this was lost on Bram, who studied him closely.

"Our efforts to forestall your curse have failed. Perhaps you should stay here."

Max glared at him. "To do what? Rest up for Armageddon?"

"Time is fleeting, Hound. I cannot stop to wait for you."

"You won't have to."

Without another word, the Archmage stepped into the firepit and disappeared. When Max followed, he felt like he'd stepped into a tub of scalding water. There was a sting of pain, a sensation of falling, and then he landed beside Bram. The portal had dropped them into a dim mineshaft that sloped down into blackness. Just ahead, Umadahm clutched a lantern of pale witch-fire while Naomi moved a sturdy handcart to the side. When the way was clear, Umadahm took the girl's arm and they began to descend. Max and Bram fell in step behind them.

As they walked, every noise, even the shuffling of Umadahm's slippers, seemed conspicuously loud. When Bram whispered, his voice almost hummed in the still air.

"How did you discover Tartarus? I understand you did not build it."

"No human built Tartarus," said Umadahm.

"You came upon it entirely by accident?" said the Archmage.

The witch sniffed. "Accident? Some might call it that, but not me. The Old Magic in Ymir doesn't come from the witches, Archmage. It comes from the mountain itself. We pushed, but something else pulled. Perhaps it was pulling all along."

"What were you pushing for?" asked Bram.

"The deeper one goes, the easier it is to converse with shades," replied the witch. "They come more readily and will answer more questions. Because of this, one of the first Umadahms desired deeper caverns for the ossuaries. Goblins were hired to seek the mountain's heart. They found deep places, but Umadahm demanded deeper ones. Eventually, the goblins grew reluctant—some reported hearing strange whispers."

"But you kept going," said Bram.

The witch sighed. "Umadahm did not share the goblins' fears. One day, they broke through the roof of a cavern so vast the torches they dropped would disappear before they struck bottom. Umadahm declared they had found the heart of Ymir and knelt by the opening to pay homage. When she did, the rock gave way and she plunged into the abyss. They say her screams lasted a full minute."

The Archmage grunted. "Why didn't she use magic to save herself?"

Umadahm gave a peculiar smile. "I'm sure she tried, Archmage. Magic is fickle near Tartarus. Perhaps even yours. It is not our realm."

"Whose realm is it?" asked Max.

The ancient witch paused a moment to catch her breath. "I

do not know. And I do not wish to. The only reason we have not sealed this tunnel is because of a pact my sisters made."

"What pact?" asked Bram directly.

Clutching Naomi's arm, the witch resumed her slow progress down the dark tunnel. "You'd have made a very poor witch, Archmage. You have little patience or courtesy."

"I'm sorry to hear that," said Bram, smiling. "Delicacy has never been my strength, and I'm anxious to learn all I can of Tartarus. Please tell me about this pact your sisters made."

The witch patted his arm. "Much better. There's hope for you yet. The pact was made when my sisters recovered the fallen Umadahm. Naturally, her sisters sought to recover her body, but the cavern was so deep it took them months to discover a way to reach the bottom. Magic would not work and no rope was long enough, but our ancestors were resourceful. When they finally reached the cavern floor, they found the Umadahm lying before doors so ancient they could not divine their origins. When they tried to collect her body and flee, they were unable to move it. The body was pinned to the cavern floor by a powerful spell. From beyond the doors, something spoke to them. It said it would release her body if they agreed to bring others as recompense. It wanted the damned, those who had committed terrible crimes against the gods or mankind. If they refused, the voice threatened vengeance."

"And so your ancestors agreed," said Bram darkly.

His sanctimonious tone made Umadahm chuckle. "We don't bring bawling babies to its doorstep, Archmage. We leave remains, and only those that are accursed. In the past, my sisters left common criminals at the door but returned to find the remains untouched. If Tartarus wants you, you've done something bad."

"Have you ever spoken with this voice?" asked Max.

"No," said the Umadahm. "It's been centuries since anyone heard it. But something is down there, something brings the damned inside. I have never seen what that is, spoken with it, or even tried to open the doors. I simply uphold our end of the pact and teach my duties to Naomi so she can carry on when I am gone."

"Are you worried that bringing us will anger Tartarus?" asked Bram.

Umadahm laughed. "Why should Tartarus be upset with me? I am bringing it two potential additions. The poor boy is accursed. And you probably should be."

Bram smiled. "I admire your pragmatism."

She shrugged. "I'm an old lady. We haven't time for anything else."

By now, they had descended far beneath the Umadahm's bedchamber. The air, which had been eerily still, was stirring now. A warm, fluttering breeze blew up from the blackness ahead. The tunnel's grade grew steeper and Umadahm was forced to use a crude handrail anchored to the timber supports.

They continued on for several minutes until they reached some handcarts that had been positioned sideways against a stone slab so their wheels would not roll. Leaving the Umadahm by the carts, Naomi held the lantern aloft as she padded ahead into the darkness.

"Stay here," said Umadahm, addressing Max and Bram. "The rock ahead is unstable and will not bear our weight. The girl will fetch a ferryman. If we are lucky, some will be close."

"What are these ferrymen?" asked Bram.

"Your transportation," said Umadahm cryptically. "Let us hope you're not squeamish."

Up ahead, Naomi had almost reached the tunnel's end. Setting down the lantern, she crawled toward a large opening that must have been the very hole the Umadahm had fallen through. Once the girl reached it, she took up a hardwood staff that was propped against a rock and rapped it gently against the opening.

Tap . . . tap, tap. Tap . . . tap, tap.

The girl tapped the sequence three times before pressing her ear against the rock as though trying to detect some sound or vibrations. When none came, she started from the beginning.

Tap . . . tap, tap. Tap . . . tap, tap.

Naomi had repeated the sequence several times and was in mid-tap when she suddenly backed away and snatched up the lantern.

Behind her, two pale gray spiders the size of garden sheds crept out of the hole. They followed Naomi as she returned to the others, crawling on opposite walls and pausing occasionally to probe the air with a hairy foreleg. Whenever Naomi tapped the staff upon the floor, they scuttled forward to keep pace. While they did have eyes—two rows of cloudy orbs—the creatures behaved as though they were blind.

"Do not be afraid," said Umadahm, holding out a hand as one of the spiders reached out to touch it. "The ferrymen will not harm you. Let them take hold of you."

Her words were less reassuring when a ferryman climbed down from the wall and came within reach. The huge spider loomed over Max, staring blindly ahead, its mandibles clicking. Bristly pedipalps brushed his face before picking him up beneath his arms and turning him about so that his back was to the spider. Clutching the *gae bolga*, Max watched as the other ferryman handled the Archmage in similar fashion.

"Are you coming?" asked Bram, his arms folded tightly over his pack.

Umadahm shook her head. "Forgive me, but I think not. It is a long way down and I am weary. The ferrymen will see you there safely, but take care to make no light and little noise lest you attract attention. Go in peace."

Bowing low, the Umadahm took Naomi's arm and the two began their long trek back to the ossuaries. As the light of their lantern receded, the ferrymen turned and scuttled silently back the way they'd come. At the tunnel's end, Max glimpsed an irregular black hole framed by chipped and fissured rock. When the ferryman slipped inside, he saw nothing but blackness.

The next few seconds were incredibly disorienting as Max was carried upside down while the ferryman crawled along the cavern's roof. Coming to a halt, the spider swung backward and abruptly dropped from the ceiling. They descended in a swift, straight line, suspended by what must have been the spider's thread.

Their progress was so smooth, the cavern so vast and dark, that Max soon lost any sense of time or distance. The ferryman was as silent as death. Now and again, Max heard Bram's muffled cough in the darkness.

The longer they descended, the less Max felt connected to his body. He welcomed this, for it meant a respite from the racking pains that had become a real and present torture. There was no pain, no disquiet. His mind was peaceful, his body numb.

Is this it? Am I dying?

It would not be the worst thing, Max supposed. After all, he was tired of pain. He was tired of grief, of struggle, of resisting the inevitable. There was no sense in fighting. If he wanted to continue living, why had he broken his geis? He tried to convince himself that he'd done the noble thing. He had glimpsed his true power when he'd incinerated the Great Red Dragon in the Workshop and it had terrified him. A dreamless sleep awaited Max—a sleep without wolfhounds or questions. All he had to do was shut his eyes and let it take him.

Let it take him . . .
Let it take him . . .
Let IT take him . . .

Max jolted into alertness, his heart beating like a rabbit's. He stared into the abyss. There was something out there in the darkness. Max could sense it, a brooding malevolence that was following their descent with rising malice. Something below knew that a potential rival was entering its realm—a wounded rival, perhaps a dying rival, but a rival nonetheless.

The farther they descended, the more Max could sense of the entity. It was not demonic, but it radiated evil. And it was old. Not old and alien like Astaroth, but old like the earth, like the molten rock at its core. Strong as it was, Max also sensed uncertainty and this triggered an almost predatory response. The ache in his side diminished, replaced by a surge of adrenaline. It was not unlike Ember's reaction to the other dragon in the scrying pool. Having sensed weakness, a part of Max wanted to find this other being, to conquer it and take its realm. The *gae bolga* grew warm in his hand.

Far below, Max could begin to make out the cavern floor as though it shone with its own soft light. Its surface appeared moonlike, a chalky landscape of cracked and pitted depressions that ended at an immense wall of dark stone. Max soon made out a pair of doors set within the wall. Judging by the coffins scattered on either side, they were no more than twenty feet tall—surprisingly small given the wall and cavern's scale.

Looking over, Max found that Bram was to his right, some thirty feet away. The sorcerer was staring intently at the doors, dangling idly beneath the hideous gray ferryman whose spinnerets released a thick strand of glistening silk. Max wondered if the Archmage also sensed the malevolence around them. As they approached the cavern floor, Max could feel the presence retreating from the doors, withdrawing deeper into Tartarus.

When the ferrymen set them down upon the cavern floor, they flipped over and scuttled up their threads, eating the silk as they went. Within seconds, they were swallowed up by the darkness. Max glanced at a nearby rock and the staff propped against it. He recalled the sequence of Naomi's tapping and wondered how long it would take a ferryman to answer their summons when they left Tartarus.

If they left Tartarus.

Setting down his pack, Bram gazed at the wall some forty feet away. Its doors were made of gilt bronze, green with age, and sculpted with reliefs that had somehow melted into one another. The result was a jumble of twisted, half-formed figures that appeared to be writhing within a pool of shallow metal. Turning from the doors, Bram surveyed the rest of the moonlike cavern and flexed his fingers.

"Solas."

There was no dazzling burst of light, just a dim pulse.

"The Umadahm was right," said Bram. "My magic is dampened here. That is unfortunate." Reaching down, he slipped the pack onto his shoulder. "How do you feel?"

The truth surprised even Max. "Stronger."

This was not the answer Bram expected. He scrutinized Max, searching for signs of his recent weakness. "Remarkable," he said quietly. "And I'd feared you might not survive the descent." He gestured at the inky black sky. "Would you?"

Max flexed his hand. *"Solas."*

There was a flash of brilliant, blinding light. It lasted only an instant, but it brought a smile to Bram's hard and weary face.

"Let's carry on. Neheb awaits."

When they arrived at the doors, Bram peered closely at them before stepping back to appraise the whole.

"What do you make of it?" asked Max.

"The doors are unlocked," he said slowly. "And I detect no magic or spell to keep out the living. Entering Tartarus is less demanding than I had supposed. That is rarely a good sign. The simpler it is to enter, the harder it will be to leave."

"There's something very old and evil in there. It knows we're here."

Bram nodded grimly. "I sensed it, too."

Max unsheathed the *gae bolga*'s blade. The spear moaned as it tasted the cavern's air, hungry and eager.

Opening his pack, Bram tossed aside the ice axes and crampons, some bundled clothing—everything but the three Canopic jars. The discarded items joined the empty coffins and sarcophagi, ancient vestments, weapons, and coins that lay scattered about.

Using his spear butt, Max pushed one of the doors. It gave way like a garden gate, swinging silently inward. A wall of rock ten feet ahead blocked their view so that all one could see of Tartarus from the outside was the suggestion of a diffuse, dusty light. Max heard no sound. He could barely even detect the presence he had felt earlier. Whatever it was, it had retreated far away.

With a glance at Bram, Max crossed the threshold.

The instant he did, the environment changed. It was like entering another world whose torrid, clinging atmosphere was remarkably dense. His first step forward was like wading through invisible sludge. Something burned his skin. Glancing at his hands, Max saw the witch's henna tattoos vanish in a trickle of acrid smoke.

"Look," said Bram, pointing to the threshold they had crossed. Strange markings were appearing in the stone. They were not like any runes or writing that Max had ever seen.

"Do you recognize them?"

The Archmage shook his head and tried to extend his hand across the threshold. It stopped as though it met an invisible barrier. When he tried to pull it back, he found he could not. His palm might have been stuck to invisible flypaper.

"It's draining me," he exclaimed suddenly. "Cut off my hand. Cut it off!"

Max seized Bram's wrist and pulled, grimacing with the effort. There was a sharp crack and Bram stumbled back. The sorcerer bent double at the waist, breathing heavily and clutching a broken wrist. The skin of his palm and fingertips remained on the barrier, a bloody handprint hovering in midair.

"Thank you," he gasped. "I do not think we'll be leaving this way. Let's go on."

Turning from the door, the pair stepped around the barrier to find they were standing on a rock ledge that looked upon a misty land of gray hills and dark lakes. Here and there, shafts of what looked like weak sunlight pierced the gloom to illuminate countless tombs and colossal pillars that vanished in the mist as though they supported the sky. There were no rivers of fire, no devils with pitchforks. In some ways it reminded Max of a quiet, colorless Sanctuary.

On their left, the ledge ended at a perpendicular wall that continued as far as Max could see. On their right, a long stone ramp curved down from the ledge to the ground some hundred feet below.

"Do you know where to find Neheb?" said Max, gazing uneasily at the shrouded landscape. The air's heat and density were already taking a toll. Even the smallest movements met with dull resistance. Just turning one's head was a chore.

"No," said Bram. "But perhaps they do."

The sorcerer pointed to the nearest hills. What Max had first taken for mist were translucent figures moving slowly toward them like sluggish streams of vapor.

Max and Bram descended the long ramp as hundreds of ghostly figures gathered around its base. Sweat coursed down Max's body, stinging his wound. The air was growing so thick it might have been congealing. The two removed their heavy cloaks and left them on the ramp. Whatever jolt of strength Max had experienced earlier was fading rapidly.

All about them, there came a rumble like distant thunder. The ground shook as a tremor rippled across the land. It seemed to agitate Tartarus's inhabitants, for Max could hear them whispering in voices like rustling silk.

"What are these things?" asked Max.

"Shades," replied Bram. "Echoes of departed souls. They have little power or will. It would take vast numbers for them to pose any kind of threat."

While such numbers were approaching, nothing in their appearance or behavior suggested they were hostile or meant to attack. They merely gathered about the ramp as Max and Bram reached its bottom and stepped upon Tartarus's dry, cracked soil. A sea of pearly, insubstantial figures stood before them with faces so faint it was difficult to make out their features. Their eager whispering was even harder to decipher, for they spoke all at once and in hundreds of languages. Max could only catch snippets.

"*. . . living . . .*"

"*. . . trespass . . .*"

"*. . . help . . .*"

"*. . . sorry . . .*"

"Where is the tomb of Neheb, last son of Egypt?" Bram called. His voice seemed to fall upon deaf ears.

He repeated his question in many languages, but to no avail. The shades were like starving beggars clamoring for food.

However, it was not food they wanted but attention, someone to listen to their story. And all the while, Tartarus pressed down upon its visitors, draining their strength, squeezing them slowly in an iron vise.

"Who are you?"

The speaker was a thin, elderly man wearing friar's robes. His question caught Max's attention because it was the first indication that these shades could speak of anything but themselves.

"Who are you?" the shade repeated, pointing at the Archmage. His tone was almost suspicious.

The Archmage spoke in a calm but commanding voice. "I am Elias Bram."

"Bram," the friar hissed, turning to his neighbor. She did the same. Soon thousands were whispering the name.

And then, all at once, the whispering stopped. A hundred yards away, Max saw shades begin moving aside, as though clearing a path for someone to come forward. Bram gasped when the nearest parted to reveal the approaching figure.

The shade was Marley Augur.

Max had not seen him since Astaroth's armies overran Rowan. The two had clashed in the woods, with Max cleaving the revenant's fleshless mouth. Following this humiliation, Augur had been demoted and that was the last Max had heard of him. He had no idea when or how Marley had perished at last. Had the witches brought his remains to Tartarus? Had Astaroth?

Even as a shade, Marley Augur was imposing. He stood a head taller than Max or Bram, a giant of a man in translucent, ghostly mail. Even his form seemed denser, more substantial than that of the other shades. Max could make out his features quite clearly. They were not the rotting, skeletal ruin that Max remembered from their battle in the woods, but those of a handsome, middle-aged man with long, straight hair braided at the temples. The other shades fell back as he came to stand before them.

Bram could barely find his voice. "Is that really you, Marley?"

"Greetings, Elias."

Bram looked and sounded horrified. "What are you doing here? You were a noble man—the best man at Solas. You do not belong with the damned."

"But I do belong here," replied the shade. "I have broken oaths, murdered men, stolen children, and practiced arts so evil, they are not given names. I deserve to be here, Archmage, almost as much as you do."

"What do you want?" asked Bram.

"To watch you die."

Stepping forward, Max leveled the *gae bolga* at Marley Augur's chest. Its point would pierce a spirit just as easily as it pierced flesh. But the shade did not flinch or draw back.

"Not yet, Hound. Soon."

Laying his uninjured hand over Max's, Bram pushed the spear aside. The Archmage was trembling. He stepped between Max and the shade. "This is my fault, Marley. All of it. I wronged you in every way."

Augur remained impassive. "You were my friend, Elias. Brigit loved me and was to be my wife. You stole her and the life we should have had together. You betrayed me out of spite."

The Archmage sank to his knees, clutching his pack to his chest. "I am guilty. Guilty of everything you say. I cannot right my wrong or change the past. I can only beg your forgiveness."

"You only beg forgiveness because you cannot steal it."

"No, Marley. I beg forgiveness because I wronged you. There is no fouler crime than betrayal—it is the most personal." Bram bowed his head, his shoulders shaking. "I am a flawed man who made terrible mistakes. Please let me right them."

Another, more powerful tremor shook Tartarus, but neither Bram nor Augur appeared to notice. The shade gazed down at Bram's bowed head, frowning slightly.

"Augur," said Max.

The shade did not look up. "What is it, Hound?"

"You've waited centuries for this moment. You sacrificed your life, your values, even your soul in the name of vengeance. Was it worth it? Would Brigit be proud?"

Augur's head snapped up. "Do not speak her name!"

"This moment is your opportunity to find peace," continued Max. "Vengeance won't give it to you. Your obsession with vengeance is why you're here. Maybe forgiveness will set you free. Don't waste this chance."

The shade did not reply but returned his attention to Bram. As the Archmage remained kneeling with his head bowed, Max had to lean on the *gae bolga*. He'd been expecting a battle in Tartarus, not this slow suffocation. His strength was ebbing.

"Were you good to Brigit?" the blacksmith asked Bram. "Did you love her?"

"I did my best. And yes, I grew to love Brigit very much."

"And did she grow to love you, Elias?"

Bram nodded. "In her own way and time. But her affection was that of a sister, not a wife. You were her true love to the end."

The blacksmith was silent, but it was clear Bram's words had a powerful effect on him. He gazed at Max momentarily, as though weighing what he had said earlier. Behind him, the shades watched and listened. At last, Augur spoke.

"Look at me, Elias."

The Archmage slowly raised his head.

"You are forgiven."

Tears filled Bram's eyes. "Thank you, Marley. You are the better man. You have always been the better man."

Bram struggled to rise. As Max helped him, he felt the man trembling with weakness. Tartarus appeared to be having a far greater effect on him than it was on Max. Augur noticed this, too, for his face became grave.

"Why have you come here? What is it you seek?"

"A boy named Neheb," Bram gasped. "He was—"

"The last prince of Egypt," said Augur. "All know his tomb, for he has no shade. It is not far, but we must hurry. I feel myself fading. Perhaps the Hound was right and I can leave this place."

Turning, Augur led them through the sea of shades, which parted for them. Bram was staggering now, leaning on Max as he clutched his pack. Max worried whether the Archmage would be strong enough to reach the tomb, much less cast the necessary spells. Hundreds of shades fell in step behind them, their whispers resuming in an endless babble. Ahead loomed gray hills dotted with white tombs beneath the pale, colorless sky. Everything seemed to warp and undulate in the thick, sweltering air.

Max's head was growing light; the *gae bolga* felt heavy and unwieldy as another tremor shivered across the land. He stumbled sideways, clutching Bram, who was barely conscious. Catching himself, Max gazed out at the farthest hills where they disappeared into shadow. The presence he had felt earlier was out there, patiently waiting for its visitors to weaken.

"That is Neheb's tomb."

The voice was Augur's and very faint. As Max turned, he found the blacksmith's shade was barely visible. The shimmer that remained was pointing at a small white tomb by the shores of a nearby lake. It sat alone, surrounded by white, leafless trees. Augur's whisper seemed to revive Bram, who raised his head to look for him.

"Farewell, Elias."

The sorcerer sagged, his legs buckling as Augur vanished

entirely. Taking Bram by the arm, Max heaved him over his shoulder and carried him. The tomb had no door, just a dark opening crowned with an Egyptian symbol like a burning lamp.

Ducking beneath the arch, Max eased Bram upon the stone floor and conjured a small glowsphere. In Tartarus, even this least of spells was more difficult than he cared to admit. The tomb was small, no more than twelve feet to a side with an alabaster sarcophagus at its center. Outside, curious shades were gathering. They did not cross the threshold, but peered through the doorway whispering their sins and secrets.

Max shook Bram by the shoulders. "We're here."

With a wheezing gasp, Bram opened his eyes and blinked several times as he regained his bearings. Sitting up, he reached into his pack and removed the three Canopic jars. One was topped with a carving of a human head, another a baboon, and the third a falcon.

"Open the sarcophagus, Hound. The fourth jar will be within. It will have the head of a jackal."

Going to the sarcophagus, Max slid its heavy cover aside. True to Bram's prediction, he found a Canopic jar that matched the others but for its jackal's head. "It's here."

"Help me up."

Once on his feet, Bram breathed deeply and gathered himself. "Hand me the jars in the order I ask. Hapi first."

"Which?"

"The *baboon*," Bram snapped. "Do they teach you nothing at Rowan?"

Max almost grinned. An impatient sorcerer was a focused sorcerer. Indeed, the man's eyes seemed to blaze as he emptied the three jars into the sarcophagus. Their contents were a fine gray powder that formed a little mound next to the jackal-headed jar. Before Bram opened it, he indicated Max should back away.

"A precaution," he said. "I do not trust my powers here."

Holding the jar in his bloody hand, Bram carefully removed its top. All the while, he spoke softly in Egyptian, as though trying to coax something out. Tipping the jar, he slowly mixed its contents with the rest. When the jar was empty, he set it down and walked clockwise about the sarcophagus with his head bowed, whispering like the shades outside the tomb. Now and again, Max made out the names "Neheb" and "Nectanebo."

Something was happening in the sarcophagus. A swirling of fine dust and gray smoke drifted up in a lazy, pluming cloud that began to take on the shape of someone sitting upright in the sarcophagus. As more dust swirled up, its form solidified into something far more substantial than a shade.

When the last dust settled, Max found himself staring at a slim, adolescent boy with a shaved head and large brown eyes. He wore naught but a white shendyt—a kiltlike wrap—that extended to his knees, which were bent almost to his hairless chin. His skin was brown and smooth except for pale, hideous scars that encircled his neck and upper arms.

Bram glanced at Max. "I trust you don't speak Egyptian?"

Max shook his head.

"I'll translate," said the sorcerer. "You must understand everything that's said." Walking around the sarcophagus, he stood directly before the boy, who gazed at him warily. After each question and answer, Bram translated the Egyptian for Max.

"You are Neheb, son of Nectanebo."

"*I am Neheb,*" said the boy in a soft voice that had not yet broken when he died.

"You have physical substance. Why is this?"

"*I am not a shade.*"

"What are you?"

"*Unique.*"

Max glanced at Bram. What on earth did it mean that Neheb was "unique"?

"Are you bound by the laws of summoning?" asked Bram, frowning.

"If they're properly performed."

"You will answer my questions truthfully, Neheb. If you do not, I will punish you. Did you murder your brothers?"

Neheb hesitated before giving a churlish nod.

"Did you place a curse upon your father's house?"

The boy's smile was chilling.

Bram folded his arms, his eyes boring into the youth. "Did you serve Astaroth?"

"I serve him still."

"As his imp? As Mr. Sikes?"

"Yes."

"How is this possible?"

"My master made Sikes from part of my spirit. Neheb was murdered. Sikes survives."

"Why did he do this?"

"He loves me."

"Astaroth is not capable of love."

"You are wrong."

"Is Sikes aware that I've summoned you?"

"Not yet."

"When will he learn of it?"

"The instant you cease questioning me."

As he translated this, the sorcerer closed his eyes and rubbed them. Max could not decide if it was merely weariness or concern that Astaroth had somehow outmaneuvered him. The boy was not a shade, but something "unique" and unexpected. The sorcerer's questions suggested he was anxious to explore this further, but his strength was dwindling.

Wiping his brow, Max shook the sweat from his hand. The air in the tomb was unbearably hot and still. Outside, the shades' whispering intensified.

"You are tethered to Sikes?" inquired Bram.

"At times."

"Are you now?" asked Bram, peering at the boy.

"No."

"Where does Astaroth come from?" he continued.

"Beyond."

"Beyond what?"

"Anything you choose to name."

"What are the Starving Gods?"

"I see you've spoken with Yaro. He was always foolish."

"Answer my question. What are the Starving Gods?"

"Masters without form, thought, or mercy."

"Why did Astaroth flee from them?"

"They are Masters without form, thought, or mercy."

"What would they do to this world?"

"What they have done to all the others."

"Does Astaroth have a truename?"

The boy squirmed uncomfortably in the sarcophagus.

"Does Astaroth have a truename?" repeated Bram sternly.

"Yes."

"Do you know this truename?"

"Yes."

"Why would he share such knowledge with you?"

"He trusts me."

"Astaroth is not capable of trust."

"My master is a mirror, Archmage. The reflection you see is your own."

"What is Astaroth's truename?"

Leaning back against the sarcophagus, Neheb drummed his

fingers along its sides. He might have been taking a bath. *"I will not say."*

"You must," Bram snarled. "I will force it from you."

"You will have to."

Bram's face darkened. Once again, he walked around the tomb, but this time he gave Neheb a wider berth as if worried the boy posed a physical danger. As the sorcerer began chanting in Latin, Neheb gave a strangled cry and writhed about in the sarcophagus, weeping and cursing his tormentor.

Despite Neheb's crimes, Max found it excruciating to see such a young person suffer.

But the Archmage was unmoved. He continued his incantation, circling slowly and studying the boy's face. Max needed no translation for what Neheb did next. Sobbing, he held up a hand in submission. Bram stopped at once and backed up against the tomb's wall, clutching his injured hand and breathing heavily. It was hard to tell who was under greater strain.

Neheb eyed the Archmage with pure hatred before glancing at Max and then the doorway swimming with shades. Turning back to Bram, he muttered something disdainfully.

"What did he say?" asked Max.

Bram mopped his brow, exhaling slowly. "He will whisper the truename only to me. He refuses to speak within another's hearing."

"Then I'll step outside," said Max. "Don't get close to him."

The Archmage relayed this to Neheb, who sneered as he replied. Bram translated.

"You are mere filth. It is the shades that concern Neheb. If he speaks the truename aloud, they will hear it. He will whisper it only to me."

"He's lying."

"He cannot lie," said Bram. "If Neheb promises to whisper the name, he will. There is no time to debate."

Neheb sat up straighter as Bram took a shaky step forward. He took a second, approaching almost within arm's reach. Outside, the shades' whispering had reached a fevered pitch.

When it was clear the boy would not budge, the Archmage took another unsteady step. Tartarus was winning this war. Bram looked as though he might collapse any instant. Leaning against the sarcophagus, the Archmage bent his ear to listen.

Neheb snarled and seized Bram by the neck, pulling him into the sarcophagus with such speed and violence the man was yanked out of his boots. Max sprang forward to catch hold of something, anything, but he was too late. The sarcophagus's heavy alabaster lid was sliding swiftly over the opening, as though invisible hands were pushing it. Max caught only the briefest glimpse of a helpless Bram, crushed against his captor's chest in a lover's embrace. That captor was grinning, his pale features ecstatic with triumph.

The captor was Astaroth.

The sarcophagus slid shut.

~ 26 ~

STRANGE BEDFELLOWS

Max shoved the heavy cover aside, but the sarcophagus was empty. Within, there was no Archmage, no Astaroth, not even a speck of Neheb's dust. Max was alone in a hot, airless tomb. Outside, the shades were screaming, tittering insanely.

Bram's worst fears were realized: Neheb had been a trap. But Max could not panic or ponder how Astaroth had set this snare. He had to get out, to escape Tartarus, and share what happened with David and Mina. He had no time or energy to do anything else. This was precisely why Bram had brought him—to report what happened in case he didn't make it out of Tartarus. To do that, Max needed to make it out himself.

Staggering out the tomb's door, he waded through the sea of shades. They crowded about him, trying to touch him, embrace him, envelop him. Each icy touch sapped a tiny bit of strength. Max was already weak. Hundreds or thousands of such touches might pose a serious problem.

"Get back," Max snarled, puzzled at their change in behavior. Had the shades been luring them in and planning to attack all along? Had Astaroth's appearance triggered the change? Or were they simply insane?

Despite his warning, they merely crowded closer, whispering, touching, pleading, weeping. Max swung the *gae bolga* about him in a wide arc. Its blade sliced cleanly through a dozen shades, severing them in two. They vanished with no more than a sigh.

This did not have the desired effect.

"The blade can end us!" hissed a shade.

Others realized this, too. Instead of fleeing from Max, thousands of shades were now straining to reach him. Their haunting cries filled the air.

"End me!"

"End me!"

"Give me peace!"

Max pressed on through a gauntlet of shades, slashing left and right in an effort to clear a path before they could touch him. Blistering air seared his lungs. He could manage only a lumbering, uneven trot as he rounded the dark lake and backtracked toward the massive wall. Its door was the only entrance he knew of, and he had no time or energy to seek another. Besides, he had yet to see anything the *gae bolga* could not pierce. If it could not cut through the barrier, nothing could.

Gasping for breath, Max turned when he reached the hilltop. A scorching wind was blowing across Tartarus, rippling the black lakes and rustling the branches of its white, leafless trees.

The wind came from the very hills where Max had sensed that watchful presence. Now that the intruder was weakened and trying to escape, the time had come to pounce.

A dark shadow was moving over the land. The shadow had no visible source, but an unmistakable malevolence radiated from it. Trees bent violently as it passed, as though something huge had skimmed above them at frightful speed. The shadow was coming straight toward Max.

He fled down the hill, holding the *gae bolga* like a bayonet to impale whatever shade was in his path. He staggered as another tremor shook the ground, nearly pitching forward into the dust, before catching himself and running on. The base of the ramp was only a hundred yards away. Max had to escape Tartarus. He had to get out and tell David what had happened. Astaroth had been stronger when Bram was his prisoner. Now that Astaroth had him once again, he might have enough power to open a gate to the Starving Gods. Imbolc was only two days away. . . .

Another tremor. This time Max did fall, tumbling head over heels in the hot, ashy dust. Trailing shades swarmed over him like a crazed mob. Max scrambled to his feet, ignoring their clinging touch, their desperate pleas, as he made for the ramp. The ground now shook with regular, concussive jolts.

Max staggered up the ramp. The doors were just ahead—no more than fifty yards. He would cut his way out, summon a ferryman, and climb out of this hellhole. He'd make his way back to the witches, back to the living!

A shadow fell over him.

Whirling about, Max brought his spear up just as an invisible force bludgeoned him. Even though he'd half parried the blow, he was flattened as if he'd been poleaxed. He lost his grip on the *gae bolga*, which clattered out of reach. Gazing up, a stunned Max lay on his back, seeing nothing but watery shafts of light and the misty sky. But something moved in his peripheral vision. Upon the cavern wall, a winged manlike shadow was rearing back to strike.

Max summoned the *gae bolga* to his outstretched hand. Catching the spear, he brought it up to parry the oncoming blow. This time he was ready and the *gae bolga* repelled its energy with an ear-piercing cry that sent the shades fleeing. His gargantuan foe struck again, pushing down this time with a persistent force as though he wanted to crush Max, break him, grind him into the very earth. The *gae bolga* screamed as it held the force at bay, its metal white-hot as electricity danced and writhed about it.

The weapon was not merely fending off the attack; it was absorbing its power. Energy poured into Max, flooding him like an empty vessel. As he grew stronger, prideful rage replaced his fear and desperation.

Max began to shine.

He noticed it from the corner of his eye, a flickering illumination that surrounded him. But it brightened steadily, growing so intense that it eclipsed even the colossal shadow on the cavern wall. His opponent tried to tug his fist or weapon away, but the *gae bolga* held on as though a magnetic force existed between them. Hissing bolts of blue-white energy ran down the spear's length, flooding Max's body.

As he regained his feet, Max could feel his enemy growing weaker. The being was immensely powerful, but like many powerful beings it did not relish an equal contest. It had expected to dominate a weakened opponent, not one that was fighting back and growing stronger at its expense. Uncertainty was beginning to taint the cold, sadistic pleasure Max had sensed only moments ago.

Another mind, another consciousness made contact with his. It was not unlike the telepathic conversation Max had had with the Morrígan, but this was far more primal, a nonverbal communication of desire and intent. The being no longer wished to fight. It wanted the intruder to leave Tartarus. It would even help him to do so if Max released his hold upon it.

The two reached an understanding.

Max wrenched the reluctant *gae bolga* away, breaking the connection between them. His radiance dimmed and he could once again see the colossal shadow on the cavern wall. The shadow looked to be clutching an injured hand and backing slowly away as its wings folded about it. As it did, Max sensed an unmistakable change in Tartarus. The atmosphere became less dense and even brightened perceptibly, as though a veil had been lifted. That was his cue. Raising the *gae bolga* high, Max struck it upon the ramp and vanished in a clap of thunder.

Max reappeared in the gardens surrounding Túr an Ghrian. Releasing the *gae bolga*, he sank to his hands and knees within a smoking crater. He was utterly spent, drained by the foray into Tartarus and his perilous escape. Closing his eyes, Max breathed deep and tried to regain his bearings. Snow flurries swirled about him, a sharp contrast from the hot, deathlike stillness of Tartarus. Gradually, he became aware that a crowd was gathering about him.

Blinking, Max raised his head to see a ring of astonished refugees, scholars, and several domovoi. One face was familiar and belonged to a trim fortyish man with sandy hair, a soot-stained face, and a look of deep concern. He dropped the box he was carrying and rushed forward.

"Max!" he exclaimed. "Are you all right?"

The man removed his heavy coat and draped it over Max's shoulders, then crouched beside him. "Max, can you hear me? It's Nigel."

Nigel Bristow was the first person from Rowan that Max had ever met, the recruiter who'd administered his Potentials tests. Instead of going off to war, the kind and capable Englishman had stayed behind to help administer in the Director's stead.

Peering anxiously into Max's face, he repeated his question. "Can you hear me?"

Nodding, Max reached for the *gae bolga* and used the spear to push himself up. He almost fell over, but Nigel caught and steadied him. Max heard a sharp intake of breath as Nigel noticed his midsection.

"You're bleeding. We have to get you to the healing ward."

Reaching beneath his shirt, Max felt blood flowing freely. His wound had torn wide open.

"Take me up to Mina. Ember . . ."

"They're not there," said Nigel. "There was an earthquake, Max. A cataclysm. I don't know what else to call it. Fortunately, almost everyone was in the Sanctuary when it struck."

Gazing past the crowd, Max saw that part of Maggie's roof had collapsed. Thick smoke billowed from her broken windows, sending a black haze into the dim red dawn. Right next door, Old Tom was a mess. Rowan's grand old landmark had lost his clock tower, which had toppled over to smash upon the quad. Searchers were climbing atop the mounds of broken stone and tile, prodding with staffs and calling out for any who might be buried within. The scene was utterly surreal. Not twenty-four hours had passed since Max and Bram had set out for Tartarus.

Bram!

The image of Neheb pulling the Archmage into the sarcophagus flashed before him. Max gripped Nigel's shoulder.

"Where's David Menlo?"

"In Blys, I believe. Our forces came under attack. Astaroth appeared and—"

"Nigel, I need David and Mina. There's no time to explain. Do you have a way of contacting them?"

"Yes."

Max craned his neck at Túr an Ghrian. The soaring white spire did not appear to be damaged. This was not entirely surprising. Using Prusias's cane, David had raised it from the Founder's Stone the previous year. The tower had originally crowned Solas and had served as the abode of Ascendants and Archmages alike. As such, Túr an Ghrian was practically saturated with magic.

"I'm going to Mina's chambers. Tell them to drop everything and come there."

"But—"

"*Right now.*"

Leaning on the *gae bolga,* Max made for the steep, broad steps that led up to Túr an Ghrian's entrance. The door was made of rowan wood and inscribed with silver runes that formed a circle around the ancient seal of Solas—a Celtic sun set within a quartered circle. When Max placed his hand upon it, the door allowed him to walk straight through the solid barrier and into a warm, bright vestibule ringed by seven hearths that were always kept burning. Two aged scholars and a domovoi with a forked beard were spread throughout the room, examining windows and walls, presumably checking for damage from the earthquake. They looked up, startled by Max's sudden entry.

"Agent McDaniels," said one of the scholars. "How can we . . . ?"

His eyes fell upon the crimson trail Max was leaving on the inlaid floor.

"Open the door to Mina's chambers," Max panted, making for a tall archway across the room. Droplets of blood fell in a steady patter on the polished stone floor.

"Th-the Ascendant is not here," stammered the other scholar.

"She'll be here soon," said Max. "Take me up there and send for a healer."

The domovoi snapped into action, running ahead of Max to thrust an ornate key into an ancient lock and flinging open the door to reveal a sturdy wooden platform hovering within a vertical shaft. Helping Max onto it, the domovoi closed the door and barked a command in his own harsh language.

The platform began to levitate, accelerating until doorways passed by in a blur. Max closed his eyes and counted to take his mind off the dizzying ascent. Once he'd reached twenty-three, the platform slowed to a smooth and gradual stop. Unlocking the door, the domovoi pushed it open and led Max through a sitting room and into a small library with a spiral staircase at its center. As they climbed its steps, a portion of ceiling slid back to admit them to the summoning chamber at the tower's pinnacle.

Once he'd helped Max up the steps and onto a chaise by the chamber's scrying pool, the kindly domovoi fetched water and asked if he could bring him anything else.

"Just the healer," said Max, easing back. "I'll be all right until then. Thank you."

As the domovoi scampered down the spiral staircase, Max pulled off his mail shirt and peeled off his blood-soaked bandage. A jagged red smile grinned up at him, eight inches across and oozing thick, dark blood. Cursing softly, Max scanned the circular chamber for something he might use as a compress. By one of the windows, he spied a cabinet whose shelves held various hoods and vestments that Ascendants donned for particular ceremonies. Grabbing a long embroidered stole, he wrapped it tightly around his midsection. While he was still trembling from his battle in Tartarus, his energy and adrenaline had receded to leave a fever in their wake. Mopping sweat from his brow, Max closed his eyes and leaned against the window's cool glass. His disquiet went beyond his physical maladies. Max did not just feel wounded and sickly . . . he felt different.

Pushing these thoughts and his dizziness aside, he tried to recollect everything from Bram's conversation with Neheb. The smallest detail might prove critical.

Opening his eyes, Max gazed down at Old College, across the misty canopy that veiled the Sanctuary, to the distant walls and towers that enclosed Rowan's western flank. Túr an Ghrian was so tall that its pinnacle could command a twenty-mile view in every direction. Rowan's outer walls were only five miles away. Even with the morning's snow flurries, Max could see that something was off.

A portable telescope stood by a glass case containing armillary spheres and astronomy charts. Dragging it before the window, Max peered through the eyepiece.

That couldn't be right.

Blinking rapidly, Max wiped the lens and looked again. Beyond the gates, he saw nothing but sea. This would have been fine if he were looking east. But Max was facing due west.

He assumed he'd made a mistake, that his fever and blood loss had left him disoriented. Of course he was facing east! But if that was true, why was he looking down upon Old College's academic quad, the Manse, and even the mist-veiled Sanctuary? These were most certainly *west* of Túr an Ghrian. Beyond the western gates, Max should have seen snowy hills and forests leading into the continent's vast interior. Instead, he saw only sea.

Dragging the telescope before a north-facing window, he swept it past the citadel walls, past the jagged ruin of Hound's Trench, to the outer curtain. Beyond its gates, he glimpsed no farms, forests, or even visible coastline. There was only water.

The same was true to the south.

Growing dizzier, Max staggered back to the chaise where he

sat heavily and tried to process what he was seeing. Rowan had either been wrenched away from the land or the land beyond its gates had fallen into the sea, leaving it to stand alone like a section of Jericho's wall. Whatever the case, the outcome was the same.

Rowan had become an island.

Rapid footsteps were coming up the spiral staircase. Max gazed up wearily as Rowan's Director came into view along with Nigel and two moomenhovens. David took one look at Max before telling him to lie flat on the chaise.

Max pointed weakly toward the window.

"In a minute," said David. "Lie down. We can talk while they see to you. You're as white as a corpse."

Easing onto the floor, Max stared up at the frescoed ceiling while the moomenhovens cleaned and examined his recurring wound. When they applied a balm, it merely bubbled and evaporated. The healers pursed their lips.

"The land," Max croaked, looking from Nigel to David as the two set chairs down beside him. He felt a needle passing through his skin, pulling the edges closed. With a hiss, the wound flared up in protest.

His head was swimming, spinning. He fought fiercely to remain conscious.

"Rowan's not going to fall into the sea," David assured him. "Mina and Ember are stabilizing things. She'll be here soon. What happened, Max? Where's my grandfather?"

"Astaroth has him," Max whispered. "I don't know if he's dead or alive."

David's expression did not change. With no more than a nod, he steepled his fingers and stared out a window with his pale, nearly colorless eyes. After a few seconds, he turned to Nigel. "In my rush to get here, I left my pack in the Observatory. It contains something I need. Would you please get it for me? I'd send someone else, but the material's sensitive."

Nigel took the proffered key. "Of course, Director."

When he'd gone, David turned back to Max, who held his breath as another stitch was pulled tight. Each felt like a hot poker being pressed against his side. David looked anxious. "I'm sorry to ask questions while you're in such pain. What exactly happened with the Archmage?"

His language was telling. The situation no longer involved his "grandfather"; it involved the Archmage. David was distancing himself, separating his personal feelings from the problem at hand.

"I'm not really sure," said Max. "We went down to Tartarus. The Archmage called up Neheb's shade, but it wasn't really a shade at all. Neheb pulled your grandfath—the Archmage—into the sarcophagus. I only caught a glimpse inside before they vanished, but I'm certain I saw Astaroth."

David gave a measured nod. "I see. Mina sent a message that he'd taken you with him to find Neheb, but Blys was under attack from Astaroth. I didn't get the message until after you'd gone. I think it's best if you start from the beginning. When did the Archmage approach you?"

Closing his eyes, Max relayed everything as best he could. As the moomenhovens tried to staunch his wound, Max told David how he'd awoken in Ember's coils to find the Archmage sitting nearby. He shared Bram's fears that Astaroth had gone insane and intended to sacrifice the world by opening a gateway above Ymir. The next attempt would occur on Imbolc.

He tried to sit up. "That's not even two days away."

"Less," said David, urging him to ease back. "Ymir's almost halfway around the world. Imbolc will begin ten hours earlier. We barely have a day."

Breath came in painful gasps. "Then we have to move."

David held up his hand. "Not yet. You need to rest, and I need to think. Strategy's even more important when there's little time—there's no margin for error. If you can, tell me what happened in Tartarus—particularly when the Archmage summoned Neheb. I want to know everything that was said."

Closing his eyes, Max summarized what transpired after passing Tartarus's gates: Bram's injury, the life-sapping atmosphere, encountering Marley Augur among the shades, and finally entering Neheb's tomb. At that point, he recounted every detail he could recall, including Neheb's physical manifestation and his exact responses to the Archmage's questions. David listened closely, interrupting only to clarify certain points.

When Nigel returned with David's bag, the Director thanked him and asked him to take charge of disaster response until Miss Awolowo returned to Rowan. She was expected in several hours. Apparently, Blys had also experienced earthquakes—massive tremors that had riddled the landscape with faults and fissures. Max recalled the tremors he'd felt down in Tartarus. Perhaps they'd been the very earthquakes wreaking havoc above the surface.

The moomenhovens began packing up their instruments and supplies. They had done everything in their power, but the wound was cursed and Max's geis was broken. Medical interventions— even magical ones—were mere stopgaps. They patted Max's hand and offered kind, consoling smiles, but he'd seen that look before in the healing ward. It never boded well.

As they rose to leave, David shook his head. "I'm sorry, but you've heard highly classified information. You'll have to remain here for the time being. Please make yourselves comfortable."

Moomenhovens were mutes, but their displeasure was plainly evident. Using sign language, the matronly, cow-legged healers tried to make David understand that there were other injured people at Rowan.

"Others will have to attend to them. As I said, I'm sorry."

The pair replied with indignant looks before moving to a nearby table. One produced a deck of cards from her apron and began to shuffle.

Turning back to Max, David spread his hands. "Astaroth set an exquisite trap. The Archmage was doomed the instant he set foot in Tartarus. Every step was designed to lure a powerful enemy into a situation that would either destroy him or deliver him—weakened and helpless—into Astaroth's keeping."

"Bram realized Neheb was something different," said Max. "It frightened him."

"It should have. When the time came, I think Neheb was able to call Sikes into his body—and Sikes summoned Astaroth. A chain-summoning, quick as thought."

"But how could Neheb do that if he was under Bram's control?"

"I'm not certain Neheb was under control," David replied thoughtfully. "Or at least not entirely. Recall Neheb's response when the Archmage asked if he obeyed the laws of summoning. 'If they're properly performed,' he said. Remember that Neheb was "unique." The requirements to fully control him—to prevent him from tethering to Sikes—were undoubtedly greater than those needed to raise and question a shade. You say the Archmage could barely stand by the time you reached the tomb. He was so desperate to question Neheb before his strength failed he couldn't take sensible precautions. Once he raised Neheb, it was all over. His neck was in the noose."

While Max admired David's capacity to control his emotions, this detached analysis was bordering on the ghoulish.

"We're talking about your grandfather."

David's cold eyes flicked to Max's. "I'm aware of that. At the moment, I need to think like Astaroth—understand his trap and what it's likely to mean."

Max nodded weakly. He supposed David was right. They had no time for hand-wringing. "How could Astaroth leave so easily? He disappeared the instant the sarcophagus closed. Tartarus's ruler had to lift some kind of barrier before I could teleport out."

"Good question," said David. "I would guess Astaroth and Tartarus's ruler had some prior agreement or truce. He's been wandering this world for a long time. Astaroth probably knew about Tartarus long before the witches stumbled upon it. I'd guess he knew about it even before he planned Neheb's execution."

"You think he was behind that?"

"Oh yes," said David, as though this was perfectly obvious. "Astaroth almost certainly convinced him to murder his brothers. And once that was done, he ensured Neheb would be caught and executed."

"But one of the pharaoh's advisers was executed first. Neheb wasn't even suspected until the cats—"

"Started following him," interrupted David. "Very dramatic, but probably no more than some animals Astaroth bewitched to grand effect. I'd wager he even arranged for a witch to 'discover' the fourth jar and trigger the curse that caused them to take it down to Tartarus."

"Still, what's the point of having Neheb killed and making him an imp?"

"Astaroth prefers elegant solutions," David replied. "He always has. Neheb was extremely devoted to him, highly intelligent, and teachable. In short, a more capable and loyal servant than Yaro. For a mortal to become an imp, they have to commit murder and I suspect Neheb required little convincing. But

Astaroth also saw an opportunity to use his remains as bait—bait for a trap that would destroy any enemy that pried too closely into his origins."

Max wiped his face with a cool cloth. "Neheb died over two thousand years ago. You're saying Astaroth just caught Bram with a trap he built centuries before Bram was even born?"

"Yes," said David. "This trap was set long ago for anyone who got too close. He's probably set others we haven't encountered."

"I don't know how you figure these things out so quickly."

David waved off the compliment. "Educated guesses are easy after the fact."

"So, what do we do?" asked Max, tossing the towel aside. "We don't have Bram, we don't have Astaroth's truename, and we don't have much time."

David peered closely at him. "Do we have you?"

"I'll be fine," Max lied. "Tartarus and teleporting took a lot out of me. Now that the wound is restitched, I just need some food and a little rest."

There was a heavy thud upon the roof. Turning, Max saw golden scales blocking the light as a serpentine body wound around the tower, snaking toward its eastern windows. Central among these was a massive, circular, rose-colored window that gazed out upon the sea. Now it was sliding down into the floor, receding to admit gusts of frigid air and swirling snow.

Ember slid through the opening to spill upon the floor in fluid, eel-like undulations. He used his legs only sporadically, as a crocodile might when skimming over muddy shallows. Flinging their cards in the air, the moomenhovens rolled off their chairs and took refuge under the table. Sitting atop the dragon's back, gripping a pair of spines, was Mina.

Her hair was windswept and her cheeks blue with cold as she slid down Ember's side to land nimbly on the floor. Wriggling out of a fur-lined robe, she tossed it over a chair and ran over to them.

David did not mince words. "Astaroth has the Archmage."

The little girl blinked and then burst into tears. Burying her face in her hands, she sank onto an ottoman, shoulders heaving with despondent sobs.

Max's heart sank. With all that had happened, he'd never stopped to think how this would affect her. Mina had no family. She called Bram "Uncle 'Lias," but the role he played in her life was closer to that of a grandfather. She had lived with him, learned magic from him, and even adopted some ladylike habits at his stern insistence. Her willfulness could drive the Archmage into a rage, but their mutual affection had always been evident.

"I'm sorry, Mina," said David. "We're going to do our best to avenge him. But this is not the time to mourn. How are things outside?"

Sniffling, she wiped her nose with a sleeve. "I . . . I think they're all right. Ember and I circled the entire island. Buildings are damaged, but most people are okay . . ." She paused, fighting a second wave of tears. She looked at Max and her eyes widened in alarm. "You're so pale," she cried, hurrying over and examining his bandages. "Did your wound open?"

Max put on a brave face as he returned the girl's magechain with a soft clinking of its many ornaments. "Not to worry. The moomenhovens stitched it up and every minute away from Tartarus helps. I just need some rest."

With a disbelieving frown, Mina called out to Ember, who slid around so that his head rested next to the chaise. Max found himself looking into a huge pearly eye. When the dragon rested his head against Max's side, he felt a soothing energy seep into him.

Clutching Max's hand, Mina turned to David. "What are we going to do?"

"Max and I were just discussing that," he replied. "It's time I opened this."

From his pack, David produced an envelope sealed with heavy red wax.

"Is that from the Archmage?" asked Mina.

David nodded, touching his finger to the wax, which dissolved into red smoke. Removing a sheet of heavy parchment, he scanned the contents with an impenetrable expression. When he'd finished, he handed it to them and stared up at the ceiling.

Mina held the paper so Max could read it, too.

Dear David,

If you are reading this, then Tartarus was indeed a trap and I am either dead or a prisoner. I pray the Hound escaped. He may have valuable information. If nothing else, he can tell you if I was slain or captured. If the latter, you must act quickly, for Astaroth will use my power to aid him in his quest. All signs point to Ymir and Imbolc.

Without Astaroth's truename, you must overcome him by other means. Few things are capable of destroying him. The Fomorian is no more. Mina is exceedingly powerful, but she is not a weapon of war. Forgive me, David, but you do not possess the strength to overcome Astaroth. The Hound was capable, but he has broken his geis. You may have to look to Ember. The dragon is very young, but he is of the true Old Magic.

If you lack the means to slay Astaroth, all is not lost. Other options exist. Like the Hound, if he violates his geis, Astaroth will be weakened and much more vulnerable. Astaroth is intensely aware of his geis, however. Tricking him into lying or breaking a vow will be almost impossible. Capturing him might be the most realistic option. He has been imprisoned before, and Mina's powers might be helpful in this regard.

Be aware that Astaroth has become much more cautious since your triumph at Walpurgisnacht. If he faces a significant threat, he will not fight—he will vanish. Getting close will be difficult, but if anyone can find a way, it will be you. You are the only person who has ever outwitted him. You can do so again.

I am painfully aware that I leave a great burden on your doorstep, David. This is not the inheritance you deserve, and I am sorry. I'm also sorry that we did not have more time to get to know one another. While I am quick to critique and spare with praise, I am very proud you are my grandson. You are everything I should have been.

Kiss your mother and little Mina for me. I shall miss them.

With love and admiration,
Elias Bram

p.s. Do not underestimate Ymir. The mountain is dangerous.

"When did he give that to you?" asked a teary Mina.

David rubbed his temples. "A few days ago. Right before I returned to Blys."

Taking the letter back from Mina, David slipped it into the envelope. There was no emotion on his face, merely an abstracted gaze Max had seen many times before. He knew his friend was deep in thought, his mind racing through innumerable factors and probabilities. David stood and began pacing by the scrying pool, his hands clasped behind his back.

"Max," he said. "How do you feel? I need a straightforward assessment."

The fever and dizziness were subsiding, but Max still felt pitifully weak. Already, the wound was burning beneath its fresh stitches and bandages. "I'm hurt, David. It isn't good."

"Is Ember helping?"

"A little."

Rowan's acting Director nodded and continued pacing. After a minute or two, he stopped. "With you like this, our chances of destroying Astaroth are almost nonexistent," he concluded. "And I don't think Ember will be able to get close to him. Astaroth did not create that other dragon by chance; he did it with Ember in mind. When he tries to open the gateway, I'd be surprised if that dragon isn't guarding Ymir's summit. We don't have another . . ."

David trailed off, blinking rapidly.

"What?" said Max.

But David did not hear him. He was pacing again, muttering to himself. Max could only make out bits and pieces, such as "risky," "only a theory," "many unknowns." The sorcerer glanced at Mina.

"What is it, David?" she asked. "What's only a theory?"

"Yuga!" he exclaimed.

"What about Yuga?" said Max. He recalled only too well the time he and David had nearly been devoured by the demoness outside Bholevna. She was like entropy itself, a floating, ravening entity the size of a hurricane.

Hurrying back over, David pulled his chair right next to them and sat down. Max hadn't seen him so animated since he'd figured out a way to sabotage the dreadnoughts. His speech was an eager, almost breathless patter.

"Months ago, Queen Lilith brought something interesting to my attention. She wondered why Yuga—supposedly a mindless, insatiable monster—never attacked Blys even though it was relatively close."

David turned to Max. "The reason I asked you to capture Prusias alive is because I suspect he has some means of influencing Yuga. Things have been so busy since we took control of Blys that I haven't had a chance to question him. But it's time Prusias and I spoke. Max, are you all right to walk?"

"I think so."

"Good," said David. "You come, too, Mina. I think having both of you present will make a difference. Prusias isn't afraid of me."

"Where are we going?" asked Max, sitting up slowly.

David helped him up. "The Hollows."

The Hollows were Rowan's original dungeons, a honeycomb of cells hollowed from bare rock deep beneath the Manse. Max had visited them before when he'd freed Ms. Richter, Miss Boon, Bob, and others who had been imprisoned during a coup led by a former commander of the Red Branch. They were a dark, miserable place where prisoners were rendered catatonic by grotesque, batlike creatures called bakas that perched upon their shoulders and plagued them with perpetual nightmares. Max despised the practice even before he'd been subjected to a baka's torments in Prusias's dungeons.

Descending Túr an Ghrian, Max, David, and Mina slipped out its door and crossed Old College. It was midmorning, and the quad was crowded with people clearing rubble, roping off dangerous areas, and trying to come to grips with the fact that Rowan had become an island. The sight of the famous trio making for the Manse brought some cheers but also questions, as people wanted to know what was happening. The three did not stop to answer.

There were broken windows in the Manse and some fallen plaster in its foyer, but Max noticed little other damage as they descended past the dining hall and down a long, dim hallway with a trapdoor at its end. Two guards stepped aside as the three descended a winding staircase of dressed stone that transitioned to rough, dark granite. At the bottom there were more guards, along with Orion, a young shedu that had been the charge of a deceased classmate named Rolf Luger. The shedu sat in a Sphinx-like posture, staring down a row of twenty cells with an unblinking, impassive expression.

Those cells had been updated. There were no more bakas or corroded bars. Gleaming runeglass enclosed the cells now, their sigils glowing a soft blue. The place was eerily quiet.

Max was feeling better after their walk. His limbs still trembled occasionally, but his head had cleared and the pain from his wound had subsided to a throbbing ache. He no longer needed to lean quite so heavily on the *gae bolga* as they walked past the first cells.

"When was Prusias brought here?" he whispered.

"Shortly after you captured him," replied David softly. "Mina had to undo her banishment, but I wanted to get Prusias out of Blys as soon as possible. The situation was too chaotic to look after him properly. I should warn you that Alex Muñoz is also here. Connor gave him up so we can question him about the Atropos."

David walked ahead. Max and Mina followed, passing by cells occupied by some of Prusias's senior braymas—fearsome oni and rakshasa sitting cross-legged by their imps and glowering silently at their captors. Alex Muñoz was asleep in the eighth cell, sprawled on a pallet with an arm flung over his face. He was barely human anymore—Max only recognized him because of the close-ups he'd seen in the archived Workshop footage.

Prusias was in the last cell. The demon lounged with his back against a wall, idly scratching his chest through an opening in his loose blue robe. His black hair was wild, his beard unplaited, his half-lidded eyes burning like two blue coals beneath his heavy brow. In the opposite corner, Mr. Bonn was dutifully washing his master's soiled bandages in a basin of soapy water. Upon seeing their visitors, the startled imp splashed water over the basin's edge. Prusias glanced up, and a piratical grin spread slowly across his face.

"What did I tell you, Mr. Bonn?" he said. "Where there's life, there's hope. Didn't I say it was only a matter of time?"

"You did, my king."

Prusias chuckled. "Oh, I'm not a king, Mr. Bonn. Not anymore. These three have seen to that. But the game isn't over, is it? Evidently, Rowan needs something from us. If they didn't, why would they provide such 'luxurious' accommodations?"

Pushing up from the floor, the demon walked with a slight limp toward the runeglass. There was something vaguely simian about his build—a barrel chest set atop relatively short, bandy legs. Taller even than Max, Prusias stopped just short of the glowing glass and clasped his hands behind his back.

"What can I do for you?"

"You have a means of controlling Yuga," stated David coolly.

Prusias shrugged. "What if I did? I don't anymore, now, do I?"

"What is it, and where is it?"

The demon merely yawned and turned slowly on his heel. "You know, I'm rather tired, Director. I'm not ashamed to say this war was exhausting. Ask me again next week."

"No," said David. "Tell us now, or I can make things extraordinarily uncomfortable for you." He held up his hand so the demon could see the ring he wore.

The demon pivoted back around. "Think twice before you torture demons with the Seal of Solomon. Not even Lilith will approve. And there's no need to get nasty—we haven't even been formally introduced! It's a pleasure to meet you after all these years, Mr. Menlo. I admire your talents as a strategist. How are you at negotiation?"

"I suppose we'll find out."

A delighted Prusias clapped and rubbed his great hands together. "That's what I like to hear. You need something from me; I need something from you. You won't like my demands, of course, but they say a good compromise leaves both parties unhappy."

"What is it you want?" asked David evenly.

Prusias's grin was so unapologetically greedy, it was almost charming. "I want my freedom, Director. And a few creature comforts. Nothing too outlandish."

David shook his head. "Out of the question."

The demon sighed. "That's unfortunate, but I understand things can be touchy after a war. Sleep on it and see if you feel differently tomorrow."

"This can't wait until tomorrow," said David. "What would you accept instead?"

"That's my demand. Let's understand one another, Mr. Menlo. I played an ambitious game and lost. I overreached. I can live with that. But I won't live with captivity. It doesn't agree with me. This world's too interesting to spend one's days in a box. I'd rather perform *ahülmm*."

"That can be arranged."

"Don't make idle threats, Director. If you waste time killing or torturing me, Yuga will remain beyond your control. And I know you need her right away—you just told me as much. And look at the Faeregine. Her eyes are red. She's been crying, poor thing. Something's gone very wrong—something so dire that it's brought the three of you here."

The demon wagged a playful finger at David.

"Here's your first lesson in negotiation: never let the other chap know you're desperate. Do you agree to my terms?"

David's mouth formed a hard, tight line. "If you don't tell me how you controlled Yuga, this 'interesting' world might cease to exist, and you along with it."

Prusias stooped to David's height, their faces inches away from one another. "Then I suppose you'd better give me what I want," he whispered.

"You're too dangerous to be released."

The demon cackled. "Come now. The Hound pulled my fangs. You wouldn't be releasing the Great Red Dragon—just little old Prusias. I know braymas are signing peace treaties with Rowan, Director. I'll sign one, too, if I'm given lands of my own."

David considered a moment. "If you were given lands, you couldn't leave them. And you'd have to let others cross them safely, provided they went with Rowan's blessing and didn't make war upon you."

The demon spread his hands in a convivial gesture. "I've always been a friend to trade. We have an agreement, then?"

"We do," said David. "We'll work the details out later, but you have my word."

The demon gave a gruff laugh. "Your word? No, that won't do, Director. I want the Faeregine's pledge. If she offers those terms, we have an accord."

"Very well," said David impatiently. Turning to Mina, he dictated the detailed terms and conditions in a manner suggesting he'd made many such bargains before. It was almost comical to see Mina—so young and small in her Ascendant's robes—listen so earnestly to legalese. When David had finished, she gazed up at the expectant demon.

"Prusias," she said, "in exchange for telling us everything you know regarding Yuga and the means to control her, you will be freed from imprisonment and granted sovereignty over lands when we sign the peace treaties ending this war. To ensure your good conduct, you must swear an oath not to leave these lands or make war on other peoples or nations. You must also guarantee the safety of any who bear Rowan's mark and wish to trade with you or cross your territory. Do you agree to uphold these terms?"

"I do," said Prusias, bowing his head. Throughout Mina's recitation, he had listened to her with a respectful, almost chastened expression. It was clear the demon regarded an oath made to the Faeregine with something like superstitious awe.

"That's settled, then," said David. "How do we control Yuga?"

When he turned away from Mina, the demon's swagger returned. Glancing at David, he spat a bloody gob on the floor of his cell. "Yuga's too damn powerful to control, but you can communicate with her. There's a green stone the size of an egg set within my throne. If you hold it and concentrate on Yuga, you'll be privy to her thoughts—or what passes for 'thought' in such a monster. She's more like an idiot child having a tantrum. Tantrum or not, she will be aware of you. Suggest she drift this way or that and she usually will. Not right away, but eventually. It's like steering a barge."

David's shoulders sagged. "That's it? That's the extent of the control?"

"That's it," said Prusias. "The stone should still be in Blys, provided your riffraff haven't looted it." The demon's eyes drifted to Max. "Where's the shining god, eh? You're looking sickly, Hound. Rather mortal. Has the clones' scratch started to fester?"

Max gestured at the demon's bandages. "Time to change those."

The demon laughed. "Touché, Hound. Touché. You were always the great wit of the world. When I hear of your death, I'll be sure to raise a glass. Maybe two!"

David tugged at Max's elbow. The three of them left Prusias and walked back down the row of cells. As they approached Alex Muñoz's, Max saw that he had awoken and was leaning against the runeglass to watch them pass. "They'll never stop," he hissed. "Never, Max. And once they get you, it's little Mina's turn. She's in the Grey Book, too."

Max didn't even turn his head to acknowledge Alex's existence. That would have pleased him too much and validated his sense of importance. Instead, Max continued on, looking stoically ahead and swallowing his horror that Mina was also an Atropos target. Alex would not have lied about that; the guild regarded such matters as sacred.

David spoke when they were climbing the stairs. "Put the Atropos out of your mind. If we do stop Astaroth, they'll be next. Our task now is to retrieve this stone."

"What's the point?" asked Max. "Even if Yuga obeys you, she can't reach Ymir in time to help us destroy Astaroth. She's thousands of miles away."

"One problem at a time," David muttered.

As soon as they reached the Manse's main level, David hurried to a side table and rummaged through his pack. Rifling through a folio, he selected two sheets of Florentine spypaper and laid them on the table. Two pens flew up from his pack and began writing as though they were taking silent, rapid dictation.

"Who are you contacting?" asked Max.

"Miss Awolowo and Cynthia," replied David. "We need someone to retrieve the stone and get it to Cynthia. She knows how to use my trunk and can bring it right to us. With any luck, we'll have it within the hour."

Once the messages had soaked entirely into the spypaper, David slipped them back in his folio, grabbed the pens from midair, and tossed them in the pack. "Let's go to the Observatory. Cynthia should be there soon."

Five minutes later, the three were sitting around the table on the Observatory's lower level. Above, golden threads linked stars to form constellations that winked in and out of view in an endless cycle. A fire crackled quietly in the hearth, its light casting a warm glow on the bookshelves and armchairs. The room's quiet, tranquil comforts were a surreal contrast to the crisis they faced.

Kicking off his boots, David shooed away the room's resident pinlegs before it could settle beneath the table. Max watched in silent horror as the hideous creature chittered and scuttled off to bask on the warm hearthstones. He wondered idly if Alex Muñoz would like a cellmate. . . .

"Good," said David, scanning the spypaper as replies appeared. "The Raszna have sent people to the throne room. Cynthia's standing by, and Miss Awolowo says the tremors have stopped and Astaroth's monsters have been killed or driven out of the city—all but that dragon, which flew off on its own."

"So how are you going to use the stone?" asked Mina, examining a jar containing one of David's preserved homunculi.

"I'm not," he replied. "You are."

Mina set down the jar. "You want me to do it?"

"Of course," said David. "If anyone can communicate with her, it will be you."

"But if Yuga's as mindless as Prusias says, how can anyone— even someone like Mina—communicate with her?" asked Max.

"I don't believe she is mindless," said David. "You know about her origins."

Max did indeed. Mr. Bonn had told him the tale of Patient Yuga when Max was a captive in Blys. She had been an imp in long service to a powerful but cruel demon that refused to grant her *koukerros*. Through careful scheming, she managed to bring about the deaths of her master and three other demons to become the floating monstrosity that devoured anything in its path.

"Yuga was clearly brilliant at one time," David continued. "That alone makes me suspect Prusias's view that she's just an 'idiot child having a tantrum.' But even if there's little left of her former intelligence, Mina might still get through to her. She's the most powerful empath I've ever seen. Spirits *want* to talk with her."

Mina looked seriously at David. "What do you want Yuga to do?"

David leaned forward. "To come if she's called. Yuga's much too powerful to summon against her will—even with this." He held up the Seal of Solomon. "She must come willingly."

"To do what exactly?" asked Max, trying to imagine what would happen if Yuga materialized suddenly in the skies above Ymir.

"Oh, any number of things," David replied. "Destroy Astaroth, destroy a gateway . . . Yuga is our last resort if all else fails."

From the second level, there was a dim pulse of light from David's bed. Cynthia Gilley appeared atop the stairs, bundled for cold with cheeks as red as her hair. She was breathing hard, as though she'd run a ways with the milky green stone clutched in her hand. Hurrying down the steps, she gave it to David, who set it on the table.

"What is this thing?" gasped Cynthia, sliding next to him to share his chair. "The Raszna were handling it like it was a bomb. Is it dangerous?"

"No," said David. "If it was, I'd have retrieved it myself."

Cynthia's kind blue eyes glanced from face to face. "What's wrong?" she asked. "Max, what happened to you? You look dreadful."

David sighed. "I wish I could explain, but we don't have time. Every minute counts."

Taking his hand, Cynthia gave David a hard, searching look. "You're scaring me, David. You can take ten seconds to tell me what's going on. I'm your girlfriend."

David sighed. "Fine. Astaroth has kidnapped my grandfather and plans to sacrifice the entire world to 'Starving Gods' from another universe. We've got less than a day to come up with a plan, climb a mountain halfway around the world, and stop him."

"Well, maybe I can help," said Cynthia.

David closed his eyes, as though choosing his words carefully. "Cynthia, do you remember when you told me that I can be patronizing and it's not an attractive quality?"

"I do, and it's not."

"Well," said David delicately, "what I'm about to say might come across as a little patronizing. How can you possibly help us defeat Astaroth?"

Cynthia patted his hand. "For the record, that *was* patronizing. But to answer your question, I can help you because Astaroth can't hurt me."

David rubbed his temples. "What on earth are you talking about?"

Max sat up so abruptly he almost tore a stitch. "She's right! David, remember when we summoned Astaroth as Second Years? He snatched a strand of Cynthia's hair and was going to hurt her when you made him swear—"

"Never to hurt Cynthia or permit her to be hurt by any power under his control."

As David recited these words, his face assumed a look of blank, slack-jawed astonishment. "Oh . . . wow."

"Apology accepted," said Cynthia magnanimously.

David turned to her. "But I couldn't ask you to—"

She cut him off abruptly. "You're not. I'm volunteering, so that's that. If what you say is true, I'm finished anyway if we don't pull this off. Astaroth can't lie or break a vow, right? Well, he either has to break his vow or let me get close to him. If nothing else, I can be a distraction. That's worth something."

"Yes, it is," David muttered. He glanced at Mina. "Are you up for contacting Yuga?"

Picking up the milky green stone, Mina held it between her thumb and forefinger. "Yes," she replied. "But I won't lie to her, David. I won't mislead her in any way about what we'd be asking her to do. Spirits talk with me because they trust me. I won't break that trust."

David looked mildly annoyed by Mina's scruples but gave an acquiescent nod. "Whatever you think is best. We can contact her right here. If it helps, we can use the Observatory to see her."

Mina shook her head. "The scrying pool and Orkney stones in Túr an Ghrian will be better. Plus, Ember's there."

David looked puzzled. "How will Ember help you talk with Yuga?"

The girl scooted off her seat. "He's not for Yuga. He's for Max."

When they climbed the spiral staircase to the summoning chamber, they found Ember dozing on the burning coals and the moomenhovens playing gin. The aggrieved healers sniffed when David asked them to continue their game away from the scrying pool but gathered their things and moved to a table far away from the dragon.

Cynthia had evidently never been atop Túr an Ghrian and went to one of the windows to gaze out. The morning snow flurries had abated, permitting a clear view of a damaged Rowan surrounded by nothing but sea. She gave a startled cry.

"Wh-where did the land go?" she stammered. "Did we just float away? There were earthquakes in Blys, but nothing like this!"

"We haven't floated away," said David. "Thanks to Mina and Ember, we're right where we've always been. Beyond the gates, the land has fallen away. We don't know yet how far."

Meanwhile, Max had raised his shirt to examine his wound. No blood had soaked through the bandages, but his entire midsection ached. Merely brushing the surrounding flesh with his finger was painful. He prayed Ember could help.

Mina was already leading the dragon off the coals. White smoke trickled from the dragon's nostrils as he slid toward Max and the scrying pool. Once alongside, the dragon arranged his coils so that Max could sit on one, lean against another, and still have a view of the images swirling and gliding on the pool's surface. Most were of Blys, where night was already falling. The situation there was far more stable than when Astaroth had loosed a host of monsters. All appeared relatively quiet—a broken city whose battlements and avenues flickered with torches.

While Ember's scales were hot, leaning against them was far more tolerable than being tightly enveloped. Holding the *gae bolga* with both hands, Max closed his eyes and felt the golden dragon's strength flow into him, gathering about his wound as though to wall it off, isolate it from the rest of his body. Max needed this to work; he needed to be strong enough to contribute. He did not regret breaking his geis to end the Fomorian's suffering, but the timing had been unfortunate. Max needed to become the juggernaut once again, the shining god that stormed through the Workshop and slew the Great Red Dragon.

In this moment, that god seemed like ancient history. For several hours, Max had tried to downplay a problem that was becoming harder to ignore. The issue went deeper than his injuries; it went to the core of his identity. Since early childhood, Max has sensed the Old Magic lurking within him. While its presence was sometimes frightening, it had been reassuring, too. It gave him confidence that he could rise to almost any challenge. Max didn't realize what a luxury that had been until the feeling began to fade. It started the moment he'd escaped Tartarus, a growing impression that the Old Magic in him was not momentarily spent but depleted entirely. Max didn't feel like a tired and wounded demigod; he felt like a tired and wounded young man. He felt . . . ordinary.

He did his best to push these thoughts and fears aside as Mina prepared to contact Yuga. David and Cynthia stood nearby, watching in anxious silence as the girl swept her hand to dispel the images in a scattering of light motes. After tucking a black braid behind an ear, she held the green stone as though it were as fragile as a baby bird. Dipping her other hand in the scrying pool, Mina closed her eyes and began to walk slowly in a circle, dragging her fingers through the water as her white robes trailed behind her.

All around them, the Orkney stones began to hum with almost subsonic vibrations. It felt like powerful generators had been turned on. But there was nothing mechanical about the megaliths; they were ancient conductors, antennae that would broadcast Mina's vast powers out into the world.

The edges of the pool began to glow with a golden luminance that spread gradually toward the center. As it intensified, it lit

Mina's placid face from beneath and sent rippling, watery reflections dancing on the ceiling and nearest columns. Mina smiled briefly, as though she'd heard or felt something that pleased her. But her smile soon faded.

When the pool suddenly turned black, Mina screamed.

David darted forward to grab her, but she held up a hand to stop him. Mina's scream was subsiding, trailing away into an eerie silence. Within the pool, black tendrils appeared to be writhing and thrashing just below the water's surface. They snapped and flailed, merging and combining, flickering now and again as though there was a hidden core of burning, blazing energy at its center.

The image within the scrying pool was Yuga.

The water began bubbling, but Mina did not remove her hand or cease her circling, not even when steam started whipping off the pool. Her face was screwed into a seething, straining grimace as though she was experiencing intense pain and doing everything in her power not to cry out again. Tears streamed down her face. Her pace slowed. She was shaking now, sobbing and gasping for breath. Sinking to her knees, Mina rested her head on the pool's shallow rim, her hand still immersed in the pool, which boiled like a witch's cauldron. With an ear-piercing wail, she suddenly dropped the stone and fell backward as David hurried forward to catch her.

Yuga vanished. The pool's surface became like glass. It barely rippled as Mina lifted her blistered hand from the water and clutched it against her chest. She was weeping in racking sobs of misery and grief. They continued until the subtle humming of the Orkney stones finally lapsed into silence.

With a slow, shuddering exhale, Mina pushed to her feet and wiped her face with a sleeve. "It's done," she said, but there was no gladness or triumph in her voice. "Yuga will come if I call her—she'll let herself be summoned. She *wants* to die. I don't blame her. The only things she feels—the only things she can even remember feeling—are pain and fear and hunger. I think when Yuga tricked her master, she underwent *koukerros* so quickly and so many times that something spun out of control. The poor thing doesn't even understand what she is!"

"Thank you, Mina," said David quietly. "I know that was difficult, but I can't tell you how important that was. Yuga changes the game."

Mina nodded and rubbed her small hands together. The angry red blisters faded. "Just tell me you have a plan."

"I believe I do."

~ 27 ~

YMIR

The four discussed and debated David's plan until early evening when they shared a supper of hot soup and bread from the kitchens' meager supplies. The moomenhovens, rather shaky after appearances by both Ember and Yuga, eagerly accepted David's offer to spend their sequestration in the quiet comfort of Mina's quarters below. And thus it was just Max, David, Mina, and Cynthia sitting in Ember's shadow as they parsed the plan's details and reviewed their roles and responsibilities.

Despite hours of contact with Ember, Max did not sense the Old Magic returning. While he certainly felt stronger and more energetic than before, the improvement was purely physical.

There was no sense waiting any longer for a sudden or miraculous change.

"There's something I have to tell you," he said, wiping his mouth. "I lost something in Tartarus, something I've been hoping Ember could restore. But it hasn't happened, not even a little bit."

"What did you lose?" asked Cynthia.

"My powers are gone," he replied soberly. "I don't think they're coming back."

"Do you want to stay behind?" asked David frankly.

Max shook his head. "No, but my condition might alter the plan."

"Mina," said David. "Can you see Max's aura right now?"

"Of course," she said, chewing a piece of bread. "I'm looking right at him."

"Is it different?"

Mina almost sounded apologetic. "It's like a regular person's."

David turned back to Max. "Can you still use the *gae bolga*?"

Max closed his hand around the powerful weapon where it lay propped against a table. The spear felt warm to the touch. It did not cry out or writhe out of his grasp as it would if anyone else tried to claim it.

David reached for another piece of bread. "The plan stays as is. Your condition complicates things, but it may also help in some way. You'll be harder to detect once you're on your own. Speaking of which, it's probably time to ask if she'll help us. Do you want us to go with you?"

"No," said Max. "We're old comrades in arms. I doubt she'll need much convincing. Anyway, I also want to see if I can find Nox."

"Make sure you get some sleep," said David. "We leave at four in the morning."

"I'll be here."

When Max left Túr an Ghrian, Old College was dark but for the Manse's lights and a few bonfires burning about the quad. The earlier gusts and gales had died away, leaving a cold, still evening with a gibbous moon.

His boots crunched through crusted snow by the old refugee camp. The buildings were largely uninhabited, as most were away with Rowan's army. Those who remained had moved to warmer quarters in the Sanctuary. A fox was prowling by the edge of the forest. It stopped to peer at Max and sniff the air, then continued casually on its way. All over the world, life was carrying on, he thought, oblivious to the possibility that everything could be coming to an end. If they did not succeed, no one would ever see that beautiful moon wax full.

Scathach's caravan lay past the camp. It had been her home when she came to Rowan disguised as Umbra, to protect Max from the Atropos. The brutal winter had not been kind to it, for the caravan faced the sea, with nothing to shield it from the elements. Nestled against a backdrop of pines, it was half buried in a snowdrift. Sweeping its little steps clear, Max opened the door and ducked within.

It was like stepping back in time. Many months had passed since Scathach lived here, but it still smelled like her hair and clothes, even her skin. Almost instinctively, Max flicked his fingers to conjure a glowsphere. But no light came, not even a spark. It was like he'd forgotten how to walk. His only option was to light a kerosene lamp, using flint and tinder like a non-magical person. Hanging its chain from the ceiling hook, he gazed about the snug space with its little bed and locker, tiny table, and chair. There were mouse droppings on the floor and small bits of stuffing chewed from the mattress, but the place was otherwise just as Scathach left it.

A linen shirt hung by the bed. Taking it in his hands, Max

sat on the chair to stare at the faded tarot signs upon the wall. The Hierophant, the Moon, the Lovers . . . Max stared at this last one. The artist's dubious talents had given Adam a look of cross-eyed astonishment that had never failed to make them laugh. He and Scathach had laughed a lot in here, particularly in the weeks before departing on *Ormenheid*. Big dreams could be born in small spaces. And they'd shared many in this little caravan, dreams of a life together after the world regained its sanity.

But those dreams died in the Workshop. Max's gaze drifted to the image of Justice, to the expressionless king holding a sword and scales. When he had pierced Umbra's disguise and guessed her true identity, Scathach had become mortal once again. The proof was the return of Scathach's shadow, which Lugh had taken when granting her immortality. When she noticed its reappearance on the caravan wall, Justice had been staring her in the face. Max wondered if she had realized this at the time. He certainly hadn't, but he did so now. And it made him angry.

The faded tarot might have been Lugh Lamfhada sitting in judgment on his throne in Rodrubân; Lugh ignoring Scathach's anguish and Max's pleas to spirit her back to the Sidh. Scathach had served Lugh for centuries, had been made Warden of Rodrubân. But the moment she acted against his wishes—even for a noble and selfless purpose—he'd turned his back upon her. Lugh wasn't just; he was petty.

Taking his boot knife, Max cut a strip of the shirt's hem and knotted it around his torque. He needed Scathach with him tomorrow, even just her echo. Folding the shirt, he laid it on the bed and blew out the lamp.

He left the caravan, walking west through the woods and slipping into the graveyard outside Rose Chapel. Lighted candles shone in its windows and its pews were filled to capacity. Within, Max could hear a clergyman telling the assembled to be strong, to love one another, and trust in their Creator. He spoke of Job and how he'd kept his faith despite many trials that would have broken lesser men. Max envied the people inside, those faithful souls who had no idea what Astaroth was planning atop Ymir.

Turning away from the chapel, Max crouched by Scott McDaniels's tombstone and brushed the snow away. He was sorry his mother wasn't buried here, too; they'd set Bryn McDaniels's body adrift in a little skiff when she'd died. Her resting place was somewhere in the cold depths beyond Brigit's Vigil. One farewell would have to do for both. Kissing his fingers, Max touched them to the name etched in granite and left the cemetery.

When he entered the Sanctuary, he was glad to find YaYa dozing on the Warming Lodge porch. The ki-rin's black, leonine body rose and fell, its contours shimmering as though dusted with moonlight. She stirred and raised her massive head as he stepped on the porch's creaking floorboards.

Since Rowan's founding, the school had had many Directors. But in almost four centuries, there'd been only one Great Matriarch; one being who spoke for the Sanctuary's strange and diverse denizens. She was now looking at Max, her broken horn glinting in the dim lamplight. Max bowed, as one always did when meeting YaYa. When she spoke, her tone was tranquil, its gravitas befitting a creature born over eight hundred years ago.

She returned the bow. "Greetings, Max. I understand you won a great victory over Prusias. But I see something troubles you. What has happened?"

At the ki-rin's invitation, Max leaned the *gae bolga* against the porch railing and sat down beside her. It was comforting being so close to YaYa. With Bram's blessing, she had served as Max's steed when Prusias attacked last spring. Together they had shown the Enemy just how formidable even an aged, half-blind ki-rin could be.

As the moon rose, Max told YaYa how Bram had been captured in Tartarus and of Astaroth's intent to open a portal to the Starving Gods.

"I'm sorry about your steward," he added, uncertain what else to say. In many ways, YaYa knew Elias Bram better than anyone. She'd been his charge since he'd first arrived at Solas, had seen him grow from boy to Archmage.

"Do not feel sorry for my master," said YaYa calmly. "He met his grandchild, made peace with Marley, and continued his life's work. We will help him finish it."

"I was hoping you would say that," said Max. "I came here to ask for your help."

"And you shall have it. I have my own score with Astaroth." Tilting her head, the ki-rin showed Max the jagged foot of ivory that protruded from her forehead. It was all that remained of the horn she had broken against Astaroth's side when Solas fell.

Something black bounded over the railing as nimbly as a cat but landed like a pig of lead. As it wheeled to face them, Max saw two golden eyes, an arsenal of curling claws, and a limp rabbit clutched between powerful jaws. Nox looked less like a lymrill than a young black panther with a row of needle-sharp quills down her back. Dropping the rabbit, she inched forward, nostrils quivering as they scented the evening and the steward who'd sent her away. It was not lost on Max that her quills were half bristling.

It was one thing when her father had been upset. Nick had been a normal-sized lymrill. His tantrums or grudges resulted in little more than shredded sweaters and punctured shoes. But a swipe from Nox's paw might take off Max's boot and everything inside it. Given the way she was staring at him, Max was grateful for YaYa's presence. No animal—not even a freakishly large and indignant lymrill—would misbehave in front of YaYa.

"Nox," said Max soothingly. "Don't be angry. I couldn't keep you in Blys for the battle. I sent you here for your own good."

Unlike Nick, whose alert, otterlike eyes had been expressive, Nox's were like molten gold and much harder to read. She padded toward him, the quills of her foxlike tail rattling softly. Inches away, she nosed at the wound beneath his clothes and bandages before peering into his face with a hint of her old affection.

The quills flattened as over two hundred pounds of compact, impossibly dense lymrill sprawled across Max's lap in an unmistakable attitude of possession. Her servant had erred, he was very sorry, and she—being a superior being—had deigned to forgive him.

Stroking Nox's quills, Max sat on the porch and told YaYa of David's plan. When asked if she felt up to climbing Ymir, the Great Matriarch merely looked at him. Ki-rins could gallop over any surface—land, air, or sea—as Max had experienced firsthand during the Battle of Rowan. Despite her age, YaYa was not overly concerned.

Nox had fallen asleep. Max felt his own weariness settling in and asked if it would be all right if he stayed here and slept on the Warming Lodge porch. YaYa lay down so he could settle comfortably against her. Max did so with a feeling of quiet contentment. This could well be his last night on earth. What better way to spend it than under the stars with these two?

"I know what Nolan was," he said drowsily.

"I thought you might," she replied softly. "Även was a great believer in you, Max McDaniels. I am, too."

It was shortly after three in the morning when Max awoke and slid his legs out from beneath Nox. He'd gotten almost five hours of sleep, which was more than he'd managed in weeks. Slipping inside the Warming Lodge, he found YaYa's saddle—an immense assemblage of leather, wood, and horn—and dragged it out onto the porch where she had arisen. Stepping over Nox, the ki-rin stood still so Max could position the saddle behind her withers before cinching the straps and adjusting the stirrups.

Nox stirred, spreading her claws as she yawned and rolled onto her back, scratching her quills against the planks. A golden eye cracked open, accompanied by an inquisitive mewl that reminded Max sharply of her daddy. He crouched over her, rubbing the lymrill's warm belly as she hooked a forepaw into his jerkin.

"I have to go, Nox. You stay here and sleep."

If Max thought these words would have any sort of effect, he was sadly mistaken. Nox had no intention of misplacing her steward again. Unhooking her claw, she rolled nimbly onto her feet and scored ten deep lines in the wood as she stretched.

Max didn't put up a fight. He wanted to spend as much time with Nox as possible, and there was no harm in letting her accompany them to Túr an Ghrian. Besides, she would simply ignore any command to stay put.

Climbing into YaYa's saddle was no trivial feat. The ki-rin stood eight feet at the shoulder and was far larger than any destrier. Jumping up, Max grabbed the pommel and swung his body over the leather seat. He strained his stitches but fortunately his wound had numbed considerably from his time spent with Ember. Leaning over, he grabbed the *gae bolga* from against the railing, and the three made for the Sanctuary tunnel.

Beyond the tunnel, it was snowing dry little flakes that coated the campus with a fine white powder. Other than the guard stations and sentries, all of Old College seemed to be sleeping. All but Túr an Ghrian, whose pinnacle blazed like a beacon against the dark red sky.

Nox would not be left behind when Max dismounted to

lead YaYa within the tower. And she mewled ferociously when the scholar suggested she might remain in the entry chamber. Instead, she scrabbled in after YaYa as the ki-rin ducked and squeezed her way onto the levitating platform. Sitting back on her haunches, the lymrill nipped Max's hand and fluttered her tail excitedly. Max hoped there was food up top; that was the only thing that could possibly placate her once she learned she would not be joining the mission.

Fortunately, there was food in the summoning chamber—scrambled eggs and bacon, a pot of coffee, toast, and strawberry jam. Given the endless winter, this was a veritable feast.

"A last supper, I see," said Max, nodding hello to David, Mina, and Cynthia, who had already dressed and were seated around a table.

"Just breakfast," said David. He was peering closely at one of four rings that lay upon a jeweler's cloth. "A typical breakfast on a typical day," he added dryly. "I left you some coffee. Cynthia can't believe it."

Cynthia glanced up, offered an obligatory smile, and resumed staring at her untouched toast. Max had seen that face many times before, a detached, almost sickly expression so common among soldiers before their first battle. This was not Cynthia's first battle, of course—she'd served with distinction as a Mystic in Max's battalion—but Astaroth was a far cry from Stygian crows and ogres.

"You should eat something," said David.

Max nodded, heaping some eggs and bacon on a plate. Not too much, just enough for a foundation. He skipped the coffee entirely. Having greeted YaYa and Nox, Mina returned to the table and plucked up a silver circlet.

"What is that?" asked Max.

"It's for YaYa," she replied. Walking to the ki-rin, she asked

YaYa to lie down so Mina could slide the circlet over her broken horn. Squinting, Mina resized the metal circlet as easily as one might cinch a knot. "I'm sorry, YaYa, but you'll stand out against the snow and we don't want you seen. This should help."

As she fit the circlet snugly on the base of YaYa's horn, the shaggy black ki-rin turned pale ivory. Everything, including her nose, tongue, gums, and even the saddle, was a shade of white. Against a backdrop of snow, YaYa would be virtually invisible to the naked eye. Her aura would not be, but if all went well, Astaroth's attention would be elsewhere.

"Do I get one of those?" asked Max.

David shook his head. "We want as little magic on you as possible. You'll have to do with conventional camouflage." He pointed to a table where there was an assortment of white winter clothes, boots, and furs in Max's size. There was even a white covering for the *gae bolga*.

"However," said David, plucking up one of the four rings, "you do get one of these. It will keep you warm and help you breathe near Ymir's summit. Don't lose it."

Max took the ring and grabbed an armful of the white garments to change behind one of the Orkney stones. Nox came along and proceeded to chew on his boot as he checked his bandages. There were two small spots of blood, but nothing that caused immediate alarm. Once he'd pulled on his mail shirt, he slipped into a white jerkin, a hooded fur coat, and insulated breeches, gloves, and boots. There was also a white woolen head covering with openings for his eyes and mouth, but he would put that on just before they left.

When he stepped out, he found David, Cynthia, and Mina donning outer clothes of oiled hides and sealskin. Unlike Max and YaYa, they would not be camouflaged. In any case, he imagined Ember would be a conspicuous sight charging up the mountainside. It was hard to hide a dragon.

Mina was busy at the scrying pool. She perched upon its rim and peered into its depths, plucking lightly at the air with her fingers as though trying to catch invisible threads. As it had when she'd contacted Yuga, the pool began to glow with a golden luminance. A picture was forming within its center, a rippling image of three wooden shrines ringed by stone idols on an icy promontory. Flags whipped in violent gusts. Far below the promontory, Max could see a hamlet half shrouded by blowing snow. The ledge looked like it might be a base camp on the pilgrim's trail to Ymir.

"Is Astaroth at the summit?" asked Max.

David nodded. "I've been in contact with the Umadahm. Astaroth ascended the mountain late last night. The dragon is with him and nearly melted the entrance to the ossuaries. The witches are trapped inside, but that's not a bad thing at the moment. They're waiting things out in the deeper vaults."

"It's ready," said Mina, climbing down from the scrying pool.

David put on his ring. "Final check. Is everyone clear on what they need to do? Any questions?"

There were none.

"Just do your jobs," David continued. "Max, you have everything you need?"

Max pointed to a canvas backpack holding crampons, rope, a flare, and a pair of ice axes.

"And, Mina, you have . . . ?"

The girl produced the green stone from the pocket of her parka.

"All right," said David, downing the last of the coffee. "This is it. We have a long way to the summit. No use wasting your energy before we get there. Max, wait fifteen minutes before following us."

Max went around to give each of them a fierce embrace. "I'll see you at the top," he said to Cynthia. "You'll do great. *Sol Invictus.*"

"*Sol Invictus,*" she murmured, pecking him on the cheek.

Ember eased up from his bed of coals, steam rising off his scales. Max saw that a special saddle had been fitted to his back with rings and leg straps to accommodate up to eight riders. Mina climbed into the first position, followed by Cynthia, and then David. They looked tiny—mere mice astride a python. As the dragon circled the chamber, smoke began pouring from his mouth as though fires were kindling within him. Sliding sinuously forward, he reared up and dove into the swirling scrying pool.

There was no splash, not even a spilled drop of water as Ember disappeared with a final lash of his whiplike tail. Rushing to the pool's edge, Max spied the wingless dragon rippling like a golden streamer as he flew toward the icy promontory. The moment he landed, Ember snaked around the shrines and began a swift sidewinding ascent up the mountain. Seconds later, Max's friends vanished from view.

With a puzzled whine, Nox jumped onto the pool's rim and peered into the portal like a bear waiting for a salmon to leap. Max barked at her to get down. She did, albeit reluctantly, waddling away to nose about by the breakfast table.

Max went to YaYa and stroked her ruff. "You know what to do?"

The ki-rin nodded.

Satisfied, Max double-checked his equipment and shrank the *gae bolga*'s spear shaft so that the weapon resembled a long-handled short sword. Buckling it to his side, he put on his ring and pulled on his gloves before ringing a silver chime.

Seconds later, a blue-robed domovoi arrived from Mina's chambers below. He bowed.

"Please take Nox back down," said Max. "Once she's outside, she'll find her way back to the Sanctuary."

With an anxious glance at the lymrill, the domovoi said he'd return with a few extra hands. As he departed, Max came to kneel by her. Once again, the animal peered into his face with an expression that said she knew he was leaving. Once again, she hooked a claw into his clothes, this time piercing his sleeve.

Max stroked her whiskered jowls. "I'm sorry, Nox. I don't know what else to say. I have to go. But if I come back, we won't ever be parted again. That's a promise."

With a surly mewl, the lymrill unhooked her claw to waddle off and investigate the remaining bacon. Max checked the hourglass David had left by a leather folio with documents intended for Miss Awolowo in case Rowan survived but he did not. Almost fifteen minutes had elapsed. He'd give it another two or three before they followed Ember. Much of David's plan relied on misdirection and disguise. He wanted Astaroth's attention far away from the portal when Max and YaYa bolted through it.

Reaching up, Max swung into the saddle again. He glimpsed his and YaYa's reflections in the nearest window—a white rider on a white ki-rin. On a snowy mountain, they would be very difficult to see.

Four domovoi came up the steps bearing bacon, cheese, and a silver spoon that should have brought Nox running. But the lymrill merely flicked her ears and ignored them. When they tried to corral her, she slipped easily out of reach. Max glanced at the hourglass. The portal would close in less than two minutes. He did not have time to dismount and collar Nox. She'd go willingly once he had gone. Pulling down his mask, Max nudged YaYa forward.

The powerful ki-rin lurched into motion, trotting around the summoning chamber in a rocking gait that would smooth out at full gallop. The domovoi backed away, but Nox mewled in an unmistakable cheer as YaYa rounded an Orkney stone and accelerated toward the scrying pool. With a bounding leap, the ki-rin dove through the portal and into the blizzards of Ymir.

Max held on tightly as YaYa galloped on the air, curving down toward the promontory. She was descending rapidly, with sudden plunges that seemed as though the mountain were pulling her down, grounding flight of any kind. Still, YaYa managed to land with no more than a mild jolt. Rounding the promontory, she gathered speed for a leap up to a ledge.

Max was scanning the mountain for a sign of Ember when he saw something dark plummet from the sky. Steering YaYa hard to the right, Max turned about just in time to see Nox land like a meteor in a snowdrift.

His heart froze. The lymrill must have dived right after them, plunging some three or four hundred feet. She must have broken every bone in her body. The drift wasn't that deep—the ledge was too windy. She—

What she did was burrow out of the drift, give an irritated grunt, and shake the snow from her coat as a dog might dry itself. Nox didn't even limp but hurried toward an astonished Max and YaYa as though this was all part of the fun.

Max glared down at her. "Stay here!"

But as soon as YaYa began trotting along the ledge, the lymrill followed, bounding next to them like a hound alongside a horseman. Max cursed at her. Not only was Nox putting herself in danger, but she was also putting the entire mission at risk. A great deal depended on Max and YaYa not being seen. Their camouflage was pointless if a jet-black lymrill was climbing the mountain with them. Max felt like an idiot for letting her come up into Túr an Ghrian. Of course she'd leap through the portal!

Spurring YaYa forward, he bent low and held tight as she traced the cliff face, rounding the mountain and leaping up onto another ledge some twenty feet above. Such a feat was well beyond Nox's capabilities. Glancing back, Max saw the lymrill stop, her indignant mewl lost in the howling wind.

Crouching low, Max held on to YaYa as she continued racing sideways, putting considerable distance between themselves and Ember. While Ymir required its visitors to ascend on foot, this did not deter YaYa. The ki-rin's muscles worked like a machine, strong and steady, never flagging as she navigated the steep terrain with ease. Despite her prodigious weight, her great paws barely left a print.

With a deep chuff, YaYa leaped fifty feet to a ledge that would shield them from the sun, whose rays would create conspicuous shadows on the snow. The dragon might not be Astaroth's only sentry on the mountain. At the very least, Mr. Sikes might be keeping a lookout while his master made whatever preparations were necessary before Imbolc. Clinging to YaYa, Max tried to glimpse the summit, but it was completely obscured by a wreath of clouds. As high as the ossuaries were, Ymir's peak was still a good ways beyond.

A jolt of pain lanced through his side.

YaYa had made another great leap to a shelf of exposed rock. Her landing was soft, but Max had to catch himself as the momentum pitched him forward. The sudden movement tore some stitches. Cursing silently, he hung on tightly as YaYa began a steep, zigzagging climb.

Aside from hanging on, Max's main objective throughout the ascent was to conserve as much energy as possible. He tried to relax, to trust in YaYa's strength, and let her do the work. David had estimated the climb would take eight or nine hours. Given this, Max let himself slip into a meditative state, a trick Scathach had taught him during his time at Rodrubân. There was only this moment, this second, this heartbeat. Past and future were mere concepts; there was no sense expending any thought or energy on them. All that existed was this moment . . . this second . . . this heartbeat. . . .

Twilight had settled when Max heard the dragon.

It came from high above, an earth-shaking roar that echoed across the Witchpeaks.

YaYa leaped aside as an avalanche hurtled down the chute they were climbing. Landing on a ledge, she nearly lost her footing as the mountain shook from some other impact. He heard a distant scream. Was that Cynthia? An instant later, there was another roar—different timbre, but no less furious.

From the ridge above them, there were fierce snarls and growls as though wild animals were tearing each other apart. Light flashed in the darkening sky, a pluming burst of yellow-green fire. The mountain shook. More trees were snapping. The sounds of conflict grew louder. Chuffing suddenly, YaYa leaped to a ledge beneath an outcropping just as Ember came tumbling over the side.

The dragon writhed like a serpent as he fell, fire and smoke billowing from his snapping jaws. Max's heart skipped a beat. Ember was tumbling too quickly; he couldn't see if David, Mina, or Cynthia were still on his back. If they were . . .

Max ducked as a shadow fell over them. Something huge landed on the outcropping above them, triggering a hail of stone and rocks. More stone cracked as a black dragon leaped off in pursuit. It passed right over them; a grotesque creature of appalling size. Its wings flapped heavily as it took flight, creating violent updrafts, before it dove and banked toward the ledge where Ember had landed.

Whereas Ember was sleek, this dragon was a tank. There was nothing elegant about its shape or symmetrical about its wings and goatish head. Its flight was ungainly, but also powerful. More yellow-green fire crackled from its open mouth, dancing around fangs six feet long. Ember was trying to recover from his fall but was struggling to right himself on the cracked and crumbling shelf. Mina's dragon was clearly injured and utterly exposed.

From above, lightning flashed, a brilliant bolt that forked before striking both of the black dragon's wings. It gave an ear-splitting roar as the leathery membranes tore and burned. Careening wildly, the dragon crashed against the mountainside beneath Ember's ledge. Ember seized the opportunity and scrambled over the side to attack his opponent in a frenzy of flying snow and sputtering green flames. Another roar was cut short as Ember's jaws closed on the black dragon's throat. Desperate to break free, the black dragon heaved itself back in a shower of blood. Wheeling, it made an awkward, lunging dive down to a ridge several hundred feet below. Ember snaked after in determined pursuit, his body wreathed in a nimbus of flickering red flames.

Tearing his attention from the dueling dragons, Max tried to locate the source of the lightning. He assumed it was David—Cynthia wasn't nearly powerful enough to unleash such a bolt, and Mina did not practice destructive magic. If David or the others were up there, they would need help reaching the summit.

Just do your job.

David had emphasized this point several times during their discussions of the plan. No one was to deviate from the plan at this stage—not for *any* reason. David's strategy had two separate initiatives. While they would be most effective if they worked in tandem, they could also succeed independent of one another. This all went out the window, however, if people started improvising.

Just do your job.

Max's job was to reach the summit. He could see it now, a jagged peak framed against the moonlit clouds by a peculiar halo—as though some disturbance or force was keeping them at bay. He and YaYa were well above the tree line, but there was still another seven or eight thousand feet to climb. They only had a few hours until midnight, until Imbolc would officially begin. Praying the others were safe and could reach the summit, Max urged YaYa on.

The ki-rin climbed tirelessly, giving a wide berth to where the dragons had been fighting. Another hour passed. Something unusual was happening high above. The cloud halo remained and appeared to be rotating slowly, as gusts whipped and howled across the mountains. Max thought he could hear a voice carrying faintly upon the wind.

Twenty minutes later all doubt vanished. There *was* a voice coming from above. Its presence was unmistakable whenever the wind settled—a thin, high voice chanting things that Max could not make out but that often ended in pleading cries. Within the halo, the sky was starting to shimmer in buckling waves, like a faint red aurora.

YaYa redoubled her efforts, chuffing and panting, ascending at breakneck speed. It was everything Max could do to hold on.

With David's ring, Max could stay warm and breathe comfortably, but it could not counteract muscle fatigue. As the summit grew closer, Max realized dully he'd been riding at a gallop for over eight hours. That would be a challenging stretch over flatlands, but upon a mountain it was excruciating. His arms throbbed; his hands had long since cramped into stiff, painful claws. And the journey wasn't over—he'd have to climb the final leg by himself.

"Aaaaaaahhhhh!"

The sound was unlike any of the cries Max had heard before. This was a scream of pain, and its tone was deeper than the earlier, beseeching cries.

This voice belonged to Elias Bram.

YaYa shivered with rage at hearing him in such agony. Max prayed she could keep her focus. Their objective was not to rescue Bram. According to David, any attempt would be futile and compromise the core mission. If YaYa stormed the summit now in an effort to save her steward, Astaroth would simply vanish. David had been adamant that they could not act prematurely, that they must wait until Astaroth began opening the portal. Once he did that, he would be utterly spent and unable to flee.

Faint chanting resumed, followed almost immediately by another scream. But YaYa kept on course, pushing farther west toward a small ledge a few hundred feet below the peak. As they approached it, the ki-rin slowed so Max could dismount without forcing her to stop and potentially draw attention to her powerful aura. As she passed the ledge, Max stepped off as if she were a moving trolley car. YaYa did not break stride but continued on as Max crouched on the ledge and pressed his back flat against the mountain. In five swift bounds, she disappeared around an outcropping.

Max shook out his hands and slid his backpack off his shoulders to access his equipment. He worked quickly, affixing the crampons and laying out the ice axes with the rope. Craning his neck, he saw that YaYa had picked the perfect spot to leave him. From here, his climb was not too steep and there were no significant overhangs or protrusions.

An aurora was shimmering in the sky above, but it bore little resemblance to the splendor and beauty of the northern lights. This was a dull red, a color of fevers and boils, sickness and burns. It looked like the sky was being brought to a simmer.

There were also lights on the mountain. Now and again, Max spied incandescent flashes and billows of superheated smoke that carried away on the wind. Assuming they originated near Astaroth, he couldn't be more than twenty or thirty yards from the spot where Max would emerge.

Max gathered himself for the final stage. His eyes swept the moonlit mountain below, looking for any sign of his friends. He saw no living things below, not even—

He blinked. There *was* something moving. It had just emerged into view, a dark four-legged creature traversing a moonlit ridge.

Was that Nox?

He was thrilled she was alive but horrified to see that she'd followed him this far. The lymrill was still far below him—a mile at least—but the animal was moving steadily, nose to the snow as though tracking a scent.

Taking up the axes, Max began to climb. He stopped when there were lulls in the chanting, but with the wind howling atop the peak, he doubted anyone would hear the soft crunch of his crampons. When he finally reached the top, Max scooted against a rock and peered over the edge. What he saw nearly made him sick.

Astaroth was devouring Elias Bram.

Not in a conventional sense—there was no biting or chewing—but there was no other word for what was occurring. The Archmage was bound upon a flat stone that served as an altar. He was evidently still alive, for although he no longer had the capacity to scream, he was moving his legs, kicking weakly as Astaroth circled slowly around him. One hand held the Book of Thoth, the other a slender black rod shaped like a viper. On a finger, Astaroth bore the Founder's Ring—a Rowan artifact he'd taken from Ms. Richter when his forces overran the school.

Bram's head was missing, along with much of his shoulders, arms, and torso. The man's body was unraveling into glowing strings of light that snaked into his captor's chest. Astaroth's pale face was hideously blank. His mouth moved mechanically, voicing the incantations to absorb his ancient enemy.

The two were just thirty yards away, at the center of a rocky shelf just beneath Ymir's peak. Something flitted down to the stone on which Bram was bound, a blue-skinned imp no taller than a candlestick with silver hair and glowing yellow eyes. Mr. Sikes . . . Neheb . . . Max wasn't certain what to call him. He could only say that the imp looked delighted as he walked over Bram's body to survey his ever-dwindling form.

Ducking out of sight, Max unbuckled the *gae bolga* from his belt and extended the handle so that it became a long-bladed infantry spear. He would remove the sheath only when he was ready to strike—he could not trust the weapon not to wail or scream.

Peering back at the scene, Max saw that Bram had nearly disappeared. Astaroth was shining as he had when Max had seen him on Walpurgisnacht almost two years ago. From afar, it must have looked like a tiny star had settled atop Ymir. Mr. Sikes gave a sardonic bow to the Archmage's final scraps as they dissolved into motes of light that streamed into his master. Despite his triumph, Astaroth remained expressionless, his face as smooth and dead as a doll's. Cradling the Book of Thoth, he simply turned and gazed up at the flickering red aurora, studying the stars as though they would tell him precisely when Imbolc had begun.

A distant dragon's roar cut through the wind. A startled Mr. Sikes turned instantly in its direction, but Astaroth remained motionless. Hopping down from the altar, the imp walked nearly to the summit's edge and gazed out at the peaks and valleys below. As he did, Max noticed a slight movement just beneath the shelf, a glint of eyeshine as something flattened itself against the mountain. At first Max thought it must be Nox, but these eyes appeared to be more feline and they were almost certainly looking at him. Sikes did not notice the creature almost underfoot; he was busy staring at a distant valley where a forest was now ablaze with yellow-green flames. He turned toward Astaroth.

"N'aagha sylvastruh istarh."

But Astaroth did not seem to care that N'aagha was burning any forest so long as it did not disturb him. The imp's master appeared to be in some sort of trance. Frowning slightly, Mr. Sikes left the ledge and returned to his perch upon the altar. As he did so, Max saw the creature beneath the ledge turn about and crawl stealthily away. A tail flashed briefly in the moonlight, pale and spotted. It certainly wasn't Nox. A small snow leopard perhaps, but Max had no idea why one would be prowling such barren heights in the middle of the night.

Unless that snow leopard was David or Mina . . .

A cry sounded, high and unearthly. Astaroth had spread his arms wide, gazing up at the stars as though to greet Imbolc, to greet this day when the boundaries between two worlds—and even universes—might grow thin. Shining brightly, he opened the Book of Thoth and found the page he wished.

Again Astaroth began to chant in a language reminiscent of the Fomorian's strange, winding songs. As he did, the shimmering red auroras began to connect to one another and rotate opposite the clouds. Max ducked as a powerful gust whipped across the summit.

Astaroth's chanting continued, its pace and pitch increasing until it assumed a crazed, almost hysterical quality. With a bloodcurdling cry, he stabbed the viper rod at the sky, releasing dazzling bolts of energy that fed into the swirling auroras. Mr. Sikes watched in awestruck fascination as they began to glow a dull orange. An eerie stillness fell over Ymir as the wind died away.

More energy poured into the auroras, which swirled ever faster, blazed ever brighter. The strain on Astaroth was plain. He was shaking violently, smoke rising off his body as his face twisted into a silent scream.

Max glanced around the summit's ledges. How much longer did they have to wait? Above Ymir, the sky was starting to burn and smoke. Within the auroras, Max no longer saw just the stars—he saw hints of other worlds, other stars, as though he were looking at overlapping transparencies.

Taking up the *gae bolga*, Max exhaled and prepared to spring over the ledge.

And then he saw Cynthia.

She stepped out from behind an outcropping some fifty feet to Max's right, almost rigid with terror. Mina was behind her, holding the older girl's hand and urging her forward. As they walked into the light, a startled Mr. Sikes nearly fell off the altar. Shrieking at Astaroth, he whipped out a thin blade no longer than a finger and vanished in a puff of smoke. In a blink he reappeared right by Cynthia's ear, his blade poised to slash her jugular.

"NO!"

The imp flew backward, jerked away from Cynthia as though snagged by an invisible hook. He fell at his master's feet as Astaroth, breathing heavily, mastered his obvious rage. Slowly, mechanically, the pale face assumed its characteristic smile. But its eyes were hollow black slits, utterly alien. When Astaroth spoke, his voice was not the urbane tenor that Max associated with him. Its pitch, timbre, and even accent were inconstant, as though Astaroth was too spent or distracted to maintain all aspects of his disguise.

"Mr. Sikes," he said coldly. "This is Cynthia Gilley. I swore not to harm her or permit her to be harmed by any power within my control. You nearly made me break that promise."

"I beg pardon, my lord," said the imp, regaining his feet.

Astaroth gazed at Cynthia. "Poor little puppet. Do you think you are the first to try and trick me into breaking my geis?" He tutted before turning his attention to Mina. "The Faeregine as a human? What a strange notion. Come out and let me have a look at you."

But Mina would not move. She remained firmly behind Cynthia with one hand in her pocket, undoubtedly clutching the green stone that would summon Yuga.

"And where is your puppet master?" said Astaroth. "Surely David Menlo is here. If he does not show himself, there will be consequences." He thumped the Book of Thoth.

A snow leopard bounded over the ledge by the girls and transformed into David. Like Mina, David stood behind the untouchable Cynthia. Astaroth's dead-eyed grin stretched wider.

"Not very chivalrous, but I'm happy you're here, David. I wanted you to witness this moment. Shall we draw the Creator out of hiding? Shall we see if God exists?"

"Master," said Mr. Sikes nervously. "There could be others lurking. The Hound—"

"He is not here," Astaroth interrupted. "I would have sensed his presence a mile off. I doubt he even escaped Tartarus. The only other one to fear is Bram, and we know where he is."

Mr. Sikes tittered.

Astaroth gazed up at the swirling auroras and skies that still shifted and shimmered within their borders. "Your grandfather has made me stronger, David, but the gate is stubborn. You and the Faeregine will help me open it."

David shook his head. "I can guarantee that will not happen."

Astaroth did not respond immediately. Instead, he remained focused on the heavens while Mr. Sikes watched Max's friends. Had he been just a little closer, Max might have attacked. His former self could have closed the distance in a heartbeat. But Max was not his former self. The instant Astaroth realized he was present, Max would be slain out of hand. He had to wait for a better opportunity.

"And why wouldn't that happen?" said a distracted Astaroth to David.

"We will summon Yuga."

This got Astaroth's attention. He turned away from the skies and focused on David. "Impossible," he scoffed. "Yuga cannot be summoned."

"She can," said David matter-of-factly. "And when she is, we will all be destroyed."

Astaroth walked slowly toward them. "Mutually assured destruction? How twentieth century."

David backed away with Cynthia and Mina. "That's right. No gateway. Just Yuga. Are you strong enough to withstand her? I know you're not strong enough to flee—you've spent too much energy. If we call Yuga, everyone dies. Unless you accept our terms."

"What would those be?" said Astaroth.

David and Mina continued backing away, keeping Cynthia between them and Astaroth, who followed them like a shark casually trailing bait. David was leading their enemy toward Max's hiding place.

"Surrender the Book of Thoth and promise to leave this

world forever," said David. "Reinvent yourself someplace else. You're better at that than trying to play God."

"And who will play God in my stead, David Menlo?" asked Astaroth. "You? The Faeregine? Good luck. I have watched mankind go from caves to space stations, but they have remained savages throughout. The beauty and rarity of this world are wasted on them. My masters and I will make better use of its matter."

Releasing Cynthia's hand, Mina pulled back her hood so that Astaroth could see her clearly. Ymir's summit was so still, not even a breeze fluttered her long black hair. "You're like Yuga," she said. "In pain. Misunderstood. I don't think you even know what you are. Please let us help you."

Astaroth's smile became dangerous. "Do you remember your past incarnations, Faeregine?

"No," said Mina. "Each is new. Instinct tells me what my purpose must be."

"What a luxury to be born knowing such things," said Astaroth. "I've had to create my own identities and purpose. There have been many. . . ."

Reaching up with one hand, Astaroth calmly tore off his face. Cynthia screamed as it dangled in his hand, a bloody mask of skin, revealing a mass of writhing, ropy black tendrils beneath. Even as he dropped the mask on the icy rock, a new face emerged from the teeming matter—that of a bearded Mongolian. This melted away to reveal an elderly African woman, which was momentarily replaced by more faces of every age, race, and gender.

Human faces were replaced by demonic visages, some bestial and others beautiful. "Who would you like to meet?" he asked. "Phyrael? Baphomet? Woland? Allu?"

When he spoke this last name, Astaroth's face became a misshapen lump of pale, scarred flesh. Its only visible feature was an enormous oval mouth filled with sharklike teeth. As he advanced, David and the others backed farther away. Max was ready. Another twenty feet would bring Astaroth within striking distance.

But then he stopped. Allu's hideous visage became Astaroth again. But there was no smile, no expression, only a blank hollowness. "God should not have to wear disguises."

"You're not God," said David.

A chilling smile crept across Astaroth's pale, masklike visage. "Not yet. But soon."

"The Book of Thoth cannot make you God," said David. "You are simply insane."

"An interesting word," mused Astaroth. "Einstein said that insanity was doing the same thing over and over again and expecting different results. In ten thousand years, I have learned the ways of this world, conquered its inhabitants, and acquired the Book of Thoth to shape it. But that is as far as I can go. As you have pointed out, David, I did not make this universe and can never be its true Creator. And the Book of Thoth will not allow me—an outsider—to use its powers fully. If I were insane, I would continue playing a game I couldn't win. A rational mind would end the game and start a new one."

"What new game?" asked David. "Your masters will destroy everything and you'll be punished for abandoning them."

Astaroth nearly laughed. "Punished? My masters have consumed almost all of the matter and energy in my universe. They created me to find more, and I have. My gift will sustain them for eons. And while my masters feed, I will take the matter that is my due and create a new little universe hidden away from them. And there, I will not be an outsider. I *will* be God!"

The instant he said this, David attacked. Reaching past Cynthia, the sorcerer released a bolt of coursing energy that Astaroth merely absorbed into the viper rod.

"So crude, David Menlo. Didn't your grandfather teach you how to shape it?"

Astaroth released the bolt back at them. It forked viciously around Cynthia and would have obliterated David but it struck an invisible barrier and was channeled harmlessly into the rock. Astaroth laughed.

"Faeregine, was that you? Well, you've tasted Menlo's magic. Now try mi—"

Mr. Sikes cried out as YaYa leaped over the summit's opposite ledge. She was a blur of white as she raced at Astaroth. He barely had time to turn as the ki-rin roared and impaled his chest with her jagged horn. There was an explosion of fiery light and YaYa was flung backward, striking the pinnacle's base with a hideous crack.

But Astaroth was hurt. He staggered sideways, still clutching the Book but dropping the viper rod as light and smoke gushed from the wound.

David attacked again. This time Astaroth did not have the viper rod and was forced to absorb the spell with his hand. A connection formed between him and the sorcerer, a hissing, buckling rope of raw energy. David gasped and clutched Mina's shoulder as though channeling some of her power. Even so, he could not sustain this much longer.

He would not have to.

Max was over the ledge and running. Astaroth had his back to him. He was only thirty feet away . . . ten feet . . .

The *gae bolga* screamed.

Astaroth whipped about, his expression one of utter shock as the spear impaled him through the heart. Staggering, Astaroth did not cry out but stared at Max as though trying to understand how he could possibly be here. As he did, torrents of energy shot into Max. Just as Astaroth had devoured Bram, the *gae bolga* was devouring him. And as it did, the Old Magic rekindled in Max like spent coals blazing back to life.

But Astaroth was recovering from his initial shock. Gasping, he dropped the Book of Thoth and wrapped both hands around the spear shaft. Instead of pushing the weapon out, he pulled it deeper, grinning like a madman as he staggered toward Max.

"Joined at last," he hissed. "Let's call them together!"

The viper rod flew to Astaroth's hand. Stabbing it skyward, he screamed and sent a crackling bolt of energy into the aurora's midst. It pierced the many worlds like a lance of white light, ripping a hole in the universe with a sound like shattering glass and bursting metal.

Max wrenched the *gae bolga* out of Astaroth, who sagged to his knees.

"My masters will revive me!" he laughed. "You've won nothing!"

Raising his arms, he cried out to the gateway in an alien tongue. His flesh was burning away to reveal a faceless, shapeless core of wriggling black tendrils.

Max speared it again, shuddering as its hideous energies flowed into him. He glimpsed Mr. Sikes as the imp darted over the ledge and fled down the mountain. Max paid him no attention. If the portal was open, if the Starving Gods were coming, he needed as much of Astaroth's and Bram's energy as possible.

He knew he was shining, that David and the others were retreating from him just as others had in the Workshop. Turning, Max saw YaYa crumpled against the base of Ymir's peak. The ki-rin was dead, her neck broken. Already, she was combusting from within, burning away like a disintegrating phoenix.

David was not merely shouting; he was screaming. The ringing in Max's ears muffled the sound, but there was no mistaking David's desperation. The sorcerer had snatched the Book of

Thoth and was rifling through its pages. Mina stood beside him, clutching the green stone. Her face was turned toward the sky.

The sky!

Max gazed up.

Within the auroras, the sky looked to be a flat, pale gray. And this struck Max with a peculiar horror. He was looking at a universe without light or dark, just endless gray, as though whatever scant energies remaining had settled into a strange, featureless equilibrium. He was looking at a cosmic corpse.

But every corpse had its scavengers. Like distant black stars, several dark pinpricks had appeared in the gray monotony. They were approaching the gateway, converging at unimaginable speeds. Already the tiny black stars had grown into what resembled little spiders. A final surge of energy flowed into Max. Glancing down, he saw what looked like a burning black starfish covered in wriggling cilia. Astaroth's true form resembled his masters. He was a tiny replica—a cosmic spore sent out to seek prey.

Removing the *gae bolga* from the melting mess, Max turned to see David kneeling and flipping through the Book of Thoth at a frantic pace. He paused occasionally, scanning a few lines, before hurrying on to the next. Max knew he was looking for the proper spell or truename to close the gate. He had to find it and quickly. A few feet away, Cynthia had collapsed onto the snowy summit and was staring up at the skies in mute horror. Mina crouched beside her, watching the gateway and holding the green stone tightly in her hand.

Gazing up, Max saw that one of the stars had grown much larger than the rest. It was so close that he could clearly see its wriggling, flailing contours. It was blotting out the others, nearly filling the entire opening. A few more seconds and it would be here.

Max heard Mina cry out.

A flash of sickly green light filled the skies. The aurora disappeared. So did the moon, stars, and everything else. For an instant, Max thought the black star had burst through the opening. But he was mistaken. It was not a Starving God that was trying to devour them.

It was Yuga.

The demon Mina had summoned filled the heavens, covering the landscape for hundreds of miles. A hollow moaning shook the mountain as lightning flashed from deep within Yuga's depths. As it did, countless funnel clouds formed, trailing down like a jellyfish's tendrils. Perhaps Yuga could destroy the portal. Perhaps she could block it and buy them time until David found the spell he needed. Regardless, they still had to protect themselves from the tendril descending toward them with a sound like a cyclone.

Max raised the *gae bolga* to meet it. Electricity sparked between them. The tendril recoiled momentarily before seeking to reach them from another angle.

The second time the *gae bolga* stabbed into the swirling black vortex, the tendril tried to recoil but was held fast. Unfathomable energies poured into Max. He tried to release the *gae bolga* but could not. His hands were fused to the weapon, which was burning white-hot.

Max was burning, too, shining like the sun. Too much power was coursing through him. He was but a lesser god—a mere demigod—and this far exceeded his capacities. He was already brimming with energies leeched from Astaroth and Bram. He could not absorb any more.

With a scream, Max channeled everything he could back into Yuga.

The tendril burst into brilliant blue flame that raced up its length, consuming the swirling funnel as it went. When the fire reached Yuga's core, the demon ignited like a pool of gasoline. A moaning shriek filled the air as the flames spread, radiating outward like a shock wave. All around them, Yuga's tendrils were withdrawing, retracting swiftly into her burning body. She was no longer moaning but shrieking as though in unimaginable pain. But Max sensed that something else was happening to the demon—something that had nothing to do with Max's fire.

Gazing about, Max saw that the roiling black storm appeared to be shrinking, contracting toward its center. The sight was so odd it took a moment for Max to understand what was happening. And then it hit him.

Yuga was being dragged into the other universe.

And it was happening quickly. As Yuga was pulled farther into the gateway, her burning tendrils vanished. For all her awesome size, Yuga was disappearing at an astonishing rate.

Max glanced at his friends. Cynthia's eyes were open, but she looked to be in a state of shock. She slumped on her side next to David, who had apparently found the page he needed. The Book of Thoth lay open on his lap, and he was reciting the page's dense contents as quickly as he could. Mina knelt beside him, looking exhausted and terrified. The little girl held his hand so tightly her nails had drawn blood.

As Yuga was sucked through the portal, the skies began to clear as though a great storm was departing. Distant mountains now shone with moonlight. The demon was no longer moaning. The lightning in her depths flickered with far less frequency, as though she were a brain whose neurons were failing to fire. Yuga was almost gone—the shadow surrounding Ymir could not be more than twenty miles across. Max turned to David.

"You have to hurry."

David did not look up from the Book but beckoned furiously

for Max to take his other hand. Max did so, and felt an immediate mingling of energies between himself, David, and Mina. He knew what they wanted to do, as if they'd shouted it. Gazing up, he pointed the *gae bolga* at the gateway. Yuga's last extremities were disappearing like dregs down a drain.

"*—asch nühl mitravael!*"

The instant David finished the incantation, a bolt of energy erupted from the *gae bolga*. It shot into the night sky like a comet, striking the gateway's center. There was a flash of light and the portal filled with an orange incandescence that looked like molten glass. Its glow intensified to a searing heat they could feel from miles away. And then the portal vanished, collapsing upon itself like an imploding star. There was no dying universe, no Starving Gods—only a tranquil view of the Pleiades.

Releasing Max's hand, David pushed the Book off his lap and collapsed into a gasping heap. Mina was trembling with exhaustion, her chin puckering as the tears came in a steady flow. Poor Cynthia hadn't moved at all. She lay on her side like a discarded doll, breathing slowly and staring ahead with sightless eyes.

But there was nothing broken about Max. Indeed, he was shining even brighter than he had in the Workshop. Reaching down, he picked up the Book of Thoth. He had handled it before, but only to keep it safe or to surrender it to Astaroth when Rowan had been conquered. He glanced at Astaroth's black, oily remains.

How times have changed.

Max liked the Book's weight, substantial and reassuring. He liked its heavy golden cover and the image of old Thoth himself etched with expert care. Raising that cover, his eyes fell upon the very first sheet of papyrus—upon its ancient symbols and ciphers. And these he liked best of all. For Max now understood them.

He comprehended them immediately. No intermediate steps,

no translation or interpretation. Max simply knew what they meant. The Book's first pages contained truenames of basic elements and forces, the building blocks of everything that would come after. He turned several pages, stopping at one containing incantations of terrible power, recitations whose formulae combined particular truenames to great effect. There were thousands of them.

When Max turned another page, he saw it: the very spell Astaroth had used to create this red winter that had plagued the world since June. It was astonishingly simple—no more than a dozen truenames combined in precise sequence. Max could fix that easily. In fact, he could fix many things—*any* things—that struck his fancy. Max could restore what he wished, even make them better if he chose. The possibilities were infinite. . . .

Max lost himself in the Book of Thoth until a light caught his eye. He glanced up from a page, irritated by the interruption. To his surprise, he saw that the sun was rising. Its orange rim peeked above the distant horizon, painting the eastern sky with golden light. Max hardly believed it possible. How long had he been standing here?

He turned to find David watching him carefully. The sorcerer stood some twenty feet away, his arms folded as he scrutinized his friend with an attentive frown. Max might have been an alchemical experiment, a potion distilling in a retort. Their eyes met. David said nothing, but he did not need to.

Closing his eyes, Max could hear Scathach's voice.

"You are the child of Lugh Lamfhada. You are the sun and the storm and the master of all the feats I have to teach. You are these things because you must be."

Those words had been his battle hymn, an incantation that called the Old Magic forth. But at this moment, they struck him as having a fundamentally different meaning and purpose. The child of Lugh Lamfhada had a responsibility to be whatever he must be—and no more.

Closing the Book of Thoth's golden cover, Max walked forward and delivered it into his friend's safekeeping—a friend whose wisdom and judgment he trusted far more than his own. When David accepted the Book, Max felt like an immense burden had been lifted.

"We did it, David."

David's eyes filled with tears. "I guess we did."

"Where are Mina and Cynthia?"

David pointed over Max's shoulder. Turning, Max saw them sitting with their backs against a rock face, not far from where YaYa had died. Mina was holding Cynthia's hand and speaking softly to her. To Max's immense relief, Cynthia no longer looked catatonic, but dreamy, as though she was under hypnosis.

"I'm cautiously optimistic," said David. "If Mina's successful, Cynthia won't remember anything from last night. I'll just tell her she conked her head doing something heroic. Not many people could witness what she did and not lose their minds. And then there are others who seem completely unaffected."

David pointed to a glossy black rock near Mina. Evidently aware that it was being discussed, the rock raised its head and revealed herself to be Nox chewing contentedly on what looked to be a badly savaged rat. As a delighted Max hurried toward it, the lymrill gave a companionable mewl.

From her jaws fell Mr. Sikes.

~ 28 ~

THE RED WINTER TREATY

The wolfhound loomed over Max, no less terrifying for being so familiar.

"What are you about? Answer quick or I'll gobble you up!"

Max did not have a chance to answer, for an urgent knocking interrupted the dream. As Max awoke, the monster withdrew into his subconscious where it would lurk until the next time he shut his eyes. He no longer dreaded these visits. Since Ymir, they came so often he'd grown accustomed to them. Few nights passed when he didn't dream of the wolfhound.

And few nights passed when he wasn't awoken by urgent knocks. But that was the price of having Rowan's Director as your roommate. David's reaction to these frequent intrusions on his sleep had become routine. From across the Observatory, Max heard the inevitable groan as David slipped on his robe and shuffled reluctantly to the door.

The instant the door was opened, someone burst in and began chastising David in a strong Scottish brogue. "I've been knocking for three minutes, Director. Three! The longest Gabrielle Richter—God rest her soul—ever required to answer a door was forty-two seconds. And that was when she had the flu."

"Good morning, Tweedy," David yawned. "Happy Midsummer."

"Don't you 'Happy Midsummer' me. This island's bursting with visitors for the treaty signing and you're content to act like it's any old . . ." Tweedy trailed off into a stupefied silence. Max hardly needed to open his eyes to know the Highlands hare was now gazing about their room.

"Y-you haven't packed?" Tweedy sputtered.

David sighed. "I know. I'm sorry. I've just been a little busy—"

"Ha!" roared the hare. "I don't want to hear it! Room Three-Eighteen needs to be reconfigured. We need it for the new class, not to mention that the recently-confirmed-and-no-longer-temporary Director of Rowan cannot live in the dormitories."

"That's a lot of hyphens," observed David.

"This is not the time for one of your smart replies," Tweedy snapped. "Do you know what smart replies got sassy kits in the Burrfoot clan? A red bottom! There are countless things to do, Director, and I hadn't planned for your gross negligence when it came to packing your personal effects."

"Well," said David, "I suppose I knew you'd do a better job."

"Hmph," said Tweedy. "And where's McDaniels? Sleeping, I have no doubt. Has *he* packed?"

"No!" Max called out from beneath his pillow.

A second later, his bed curtain was ripped aside and his pillow was yanked away as Tweedy harangued him on the importance of respect for one's elders, rising early, and keeping a tidy room. Rolling out of bed, a bleary Max agreed that Tweedy was right, and he should indeed be ashamed, and that rising late was a sure sign of moral decay.

"It's already half past eight, McDaniels. I've been up since three making certain everything will run just so. And what have—Dear God! What happened? Are you all right, my boy?"

The hare was staring at the injury whose dressings Max had begun to change. Over four months had passed since Imbolc and Max's wound had worsened from a raw red gash to an area of blackened, necrotic flesh that covered most of his midsection. Anyone with a lesser constitution would have died months ago. Hours spent in Ember's coils could cause the infection to retreat but these interventions were becoming less effective. Disheartening as this was, there was a bright side: dead tissue didn't hurt nearly as much as living tissue.

"I'm fine, Tweedy," said Max, rubbing the area with an ointment that was medically useless but marvelous at masking the smell of rotting flesh. "Hand me one of those, will you?"

The hare brought over a fresh bandage from the stack upon a chair. "This is a perfect example of what I'm talking about, McDaniels. Any lad gritty enough to put up with such an injury can manage to rise at a decent hour and make himself presentable."

"I am making myself presentable," said Max, finishing the bandage and reaching for a shirt. "Can you hand me those pants?"

Tweedy eyed the pair in question on the floor. "Those are *trousers*," he sniffed. "Canvas trousers of a type favored by transients, gadabouts, and pirates."

"They're *pants*," said Max, slipping them on. "Very comfortable pants."

"Comfort has no place in the wardrobe of a young gentleman."

This was stated with the authority and conviction of a commandment. With a sigh, Max buckled the *gae bolga* about his waist. It was a shame they could not simply enjoy a moment's peace after years of struggle, but Max could not ignore reality. They may have defeated Astaroth and conquered Prusias, but the Atropos remained a threat. Mina did not go anywhere without Ember or considerable security.

"Tweedy, we're going to get some breakfast," said Max. "Have you eaten?"

The hare was picking up stray clothes. "I had a modest meal at five before taking a brisk constitutional. Others might learn from my example . . ."

"And others will," said Max, pulling on his shoes.

"Yes, yes," said Tweedy. "You two go on. I'm going to whip this calamity into shape."

Bidding the hare farewell, Max and David slipped out of the Observatory and into the hallway where four members of the Bloodstone Circle stood at attention. Max hated the idea of bodyguards and absolutely refused to let them follow him unless he was with David, in which case he had no choice—Rowan's Director was required to have security. As he closed the door, David paused to polish its brass number.

"Room Three-Eighteen," he said quietly. "I'm going to miss it."

"Life goes on," said Max. "I wonder what it'll be next."

David grunted. "A yurt."

From within, they heard Chester's high-pitched chittering followed by a scream that might have reached the Burrfoot clan. Max and David hurried away with the four Agents in tow.

Their friends were waiting in the Manse's foyer—Sarah, Lucia, Connor Lynch, and a fully recovered Cynthia. The girls did not have to be in their scarlet Seventh Year robes until later and wore casual clothes. Baron Lynch, however, was here in a diplomatic capacity and dressed accordingly. He'd arrived two days ago with a sizable Raszna contingent that included scholars, soldiers, and students. Thus far, Connor had only assumed his human form. Max suspected this had nothing to do with diplomacy and everything to do with making a favorable impression on Lucia's protective father.

"There they are," Connor exclaimed, hoisting Kettlemouth as though the comatose bullfrog might actually greet them. "We almost thought you weren't coming."

"Sorry," said David, smoothing his navy robes and adjusting the recovered Founder's Ring. His office had rigid standards of attire, a fact he bitterly resented. "Are they still serving breakfast?"

"You're the bleeding Director, David," said Connor. "You can get breakfast whenever you want. We just have to slip into the kitchens quietly."

"What do you mean?" said Max as they headed down a flight of steps. Once he heard the voice holding court in the dining hall, no explanation was required.

No one was eating in the dining hall. Instead, Max saw twenty young Raszna wearing Rowan First Year robes and standing at attention. The vyes were arranged in a line, shortest to tallest, their eyes fixed on the same pillar. Among them, Max spied Lupo, the talkative page who had been his guide at Arcanum. Miss Awolowo and a Raszna professor stood off to the side looking rather uneasy as a hag addressed the young vyes. While the clasped hands and measured pacing suggested the hag was a person of some consequence, she chose to remove any doubt.

"You will never meet anyone more important at Rowan," she

declared, pivoting suddenly to see if a young Raszna was eyeballing her. He was not. "I control not only your food supply but also your access to reasonably priced soaps and personal care items. If you offend me, ignore me, or laugh at the ogre's jokes, you will face my wrath. Is that understood?"

"Mum!" cried Miss Awolowo. "Get on with it!"

The hag made a hideous face that Miss Awolowo failed to catch, as she was now apologizing to her Raszna counterpart. Mum turned back to her audience.

"Pay no attention to that interruption," said the hag breezily. "Now, if you'll pull back your sleeves, we're going to play a little game where I give each of your arms a teensy sniff."

"Why do you do that?" asked a Raszna girl.

"So I know not to eat you, dear."

"I heard you once tried to eat the Director," said Lupo.

"THAT WAS A LONG TIME AGO!"

The hag's outburst and subsequent tirade presented a perfect opportunity for Max and the others to slip inconspicuously into the kitchen. There, they found Bob hunched upon a stool and spooning dough onto baking sheets. "Is Mum frightening the guests?" he muttered, glancing at David's bodyguards.

"She's doing her best," said Sarah, standing on tiptoe to kiss the ogre's cheek.

Setting down his spoon, the ogre appraised them with grandfatherly affection. "My little ones are all grown up," he sighed.

"And hungry," said Sarah. "Did you save us anything?"

The ogre nodded toward a chafing dish beside a stack of plates and silverware. A cloud of steam rose as Sarah raised the cover.

"Ooh!" said Connor, reaching past her to grab a sausage. "I almost forgot about these. My chef tried to make them but they just don't taste the same."

The ogre shrugged. "Bob has gift."

"You're a baron!" Lucia hissed at Connor. "Use a knife and fork like a human being."

"But I'm not a human being," said Connor, taking Cynthia's fork. "Not entirely anyway."

Lucia groaned. "Don't remind me. If my father knew you were Raszna, he'd never let me sail with you."

"Where does Lucia go?" inquired Bob.

The Italian beauty lifted her head proudly. "Arcanum. I was chosen to lead a Mystics course as part of the academic exchange."

"Lead?" said Connor, his mouth full of ham. "I thought you were a teaching assistant. Like one of five." He froze when he noticed Lucia's expression. "What? Did I get that wrong?"

"Anyway," said Cynthia quickly. "We're very proud of Lucia. Lots of students volunteered and only a few got picked. It's an honor."

"It is," said Bob decisively. "I know you stay put, Cynthia, but what about Miss Amankwe? Is she leaving us, too?"

"No," said Sarah, heaping a plate with fresh fruit. "You're stuck with me for at least another year. But once I graduate, I plan on joining the Vanguard."

"Not Red Branch?" asked Bob. "I thought Red Branch was best."

Sarah laughed. "Not even Cooper made the Red Branch right out of school. But give me a few years, and who knows?"

"Well," said Connor, "I know someone who's going to be mighty disappointed to hear you're not coming back with us." While in Blys, Sarah had struck up a romance with a young captain in Baron Lynch's trading fleet.

"Markus can write me," said Sarah primly. "And now that trade's resumed, I think his boss could send him to Rowan now and again, don't you?"

"That could be arranged," said Connor, inspecting some sweet rolls.

The ogre turned to Max. "And what of you, *malyenki*? What will you do now that the . . . troubles . . . have passed?"

"I don't know," said Max, happy to pretend that they had. "The first thing I have to figure out is where to live. David and I are being evicted."

Connor stared. "From the Observatory? But that's your room!"

"It's a Manse dormitory room," David corrected. "We need it for students. With the Raszna and a new class starting in the fall, space is tight."

Baron Lynch did not approve. "You should make the Observatory a museum," he said. "Someday, people are going to want to see where Max McDaniels and David Menlo lived. It's got historical significance."

"Listen to you," said Cynthia. "So cultured!"

Connor wiped his hands on a dishtowel. "I know about these things. My people in Enlyll have been saving every little thing from the médim. Heck, someone tracked down the carriage that Max and Scath . . ." He trailed off, looking anxious.

Few people spoke Scathach's name in front of Max. Avoiding it had almost become an art among those closest to him. Another taboo topic was Max himself. Connor, Sarah, and Lucia never mentioned the time Max unveiled his true nature while addressing the Raszna in Amber Hall. They treated Max as they always had. And for that, he was very grateful.

"Well," said Max, trying to put Connor at ease, "I hope the carriage fetched a decent price. It was expensive."

"It fetched a bloody fortune," said Connor.

"So, where will *malyenki* live?" Bob persisted.

"There's a caravan I might use," Max replied. "At least until I figure something else out."

"Mmm," said the ogre, eyeing him shrewdly. But he said no more.

When Old Tom began chiming, David quickly downed his coffee.

"Where are you off to?" asked Cynthia.

"Meeting with Archon," he replied. "We're touring possible sites for the 'Bram Institute of Advanced Magical Research.' What do you think of the name?"

Cynthia wrinkled her nose. "It sounds very technical."

"Good," said David. "That's exactly what it's going to be. Do you want to come? We're thinking about putting it near Southgate."

"Can't," said Cynthia. "I promised Lucia I'd help her pack."

"Well, I'm off, too," said Sarah, setting her plate in the sink. "I'm demonstrating Euclidean soccer to the Raszna students. You should come, Max. It's been ages since we've had a game."

Max smiled, but demurred. He'd tried kicking a soccer ball a month ago and nearly torn his wound wide open. "That's okay," he said. "I'm meeting the Coopers in the Sanctuary."

"Don't be late for the treaty signing," said David. "You're center stage."

"Ah," said Max, snagging a last sausage. "But unlike you, I don't have to say a word. I can just stand there looking serious. Thanks for breakfast, Bob."

Max headed through the inner kitchen before slipping out a service door. With all the visitors and activity at Rowan these days, he rarely used main entrances or pathways. He was the Hound of Rowan, Bragha Rùn, the Raszna's *moschiach*, the shining hero who'd conquered Prusias and slain Astaroth. Not even Mina's renown approached his.

And this was not a good thing. Max could barely walk through Old College without being mobbed. While he refused to have a security detail, he appreciated David posting Agents to restrict access to their hallway. This was not merely a precaution against the Atropos but to prevent people from pestering him at all hours. Max could not even eat at the Hanged Man without people seeking autographs or interviews.

To protect his privacy as best he could, Max varied his routine and attire and sometimes employed illusion. He was getting so good at changing his appearance he'd even fooled Cooper once or twice. At the moment, however, his disguise consisted solely of an old cotton jacket whose length hid the *gae bolga* and whose hood hid Max's hair and the torque around his neck. Still, with his eyes downcast and his hands thrust in his pockets, he might have been any tall, introverted teenager. Rowan had plenty of those.

The path he took through the orchard was nearly empty. While this was certainly welcome, Max had come this way to visit a certain class tree. It took him a few minutes to find the apple he sought, a particularly large one that had turned to gold the instant Gabrielle Richter died aboard the flagship. David deserved every bit of credit and acclaim he'd received for leading Rowan to victory. But in people's eagerness to praise him, they often overlooked his predecessor. Max did not.

Touching the sacred apples was forbidden, but Max paused to pay his respects before continuing on. For some reason, he felt closer to Ms. Richter here than by the memorial they'd erected for her by Northgate. There were so many graves there. There had been many white tombstones and memorials following the Battle of Rowan, but the number was growing quickly as ships returned from Blys with the remains of the fallen. Even those without remains to bury were given their own marker, their name and unit chiseled in the stone. The graves were all past North-gate, many thousands of them on either side of the Hound's Trench, that dead black chasm Max had made with the *gae bolga*. Max hated to look at it. He rarely ventured past Northgate.

The Sanctuary was where he spent most of his time these days. Not because it was warmer than anyplace else—David had ended the red winter as soon as they obtained the Book—but because he felt most comfortable there. Ever since Rowan had become an island, it felt small to Max. Strange as it seemed, the Sanctuary was much more spacious than the entire island that housed it. There was room to roam, and the wild things that lived in the foothills and mountains did not particularly care who he was, so long as he left them alone.

The Sanctuary gate was open and Max received more than several curious stares as he passed people in the leafy green tunnel. Many were Rowan students or faculty, but there were out-siders, too—Raszna scholars, witch envoys, representatives from distant human settlements, even a proud-looking brayma who had fought against Prusias in the war. Thousands had sailed to Rowan to partake in today's history-making events, and almost all wished to see its famous Sanctuary for themselves.

Skirting the busy township, Max made for the lagoon by the Warming Lodge. The Coopers and Bristows had already arrived and had set up blankets and baskets for a picnic. Nigel, ever immaculate in a pressed blue shirt and tan slacks, saw Max coming and picked up his daughter Emma in the hope she might wave hello. But the toddler wriggled out his arms to resume play-ing with Lucy, a robust pink piglet that was rolling in the nearby grass.

While the Bristows had always been the picture of domestic bliss, the Coopers were a different story. Marriage might have changed William Cooper, but fatherhood triggered complete metamorphosis. The man lay on his back upon the blanket, holding up a tiny bundle in his wiry arms. He was cooing to it, his scarred face twisting into grins of idiot delight whenever the baby so much as gurgled. This was an unprecedented sight, as was the image of him barefoot, bareheaded, and wearing summer clothes. A green linen shirt? If not for the Red Branch tattoo and the sheathed kris lying casually on the blanket, Max would not have believed it was Cooper.

"William," said Hazel, perusing the morning *Tattler*. "I think we should put her under the parasol. She's getting too much sun. Frankly, so are you. Do not—do *not* put her by Grendel!"

Max only now noticed the Cheshirewulf lying in the grass by the blanket. With each slow breath, the beast's powerful, gray-striped body faded entirely from view.

"C'mon, love," said Cooper, now cycling the baby's legs. "Grendel's gentle as a lamb with her."

"Just watch he doesn't roll," said Hazel, adjusting her sun hat. "Max!" she exclaimed, catching sight of him as he walked up. "So nice you could make it. Have a muffin. I made them myself. Who would have guessed I have a talent for baking?"

Max peered at the blackened lumps lovingly arranged in a tin. "They look great, but I just ate with Bob in the kitchens."

"Was Mum there?" asked Nigel, pouring Max a juice.

"She was."

"And was she behaving?" Nigel inquired hopefully.

"Of course not," said Max. "She was terrorizing the Raszna students."

"You need to have a talk with her, dear," said Emily Bristow, brushing grass from Emma's dress. There was little mistaking mother and daughter; both had strawberry-blond hair, fair skin, and light freckles. "She won't take you seriously otherwise."

"I know," said Nigel, frowning. "But Gabrielle's the only one Mum ever really listened to. She barely behaves with Ndidi."

Cooper plucked up the baby and rose to join them. "Maybe *this* Gabrielle should set that hag straight." He kissed the infant's tummy as she blinked and gazed about like a sleepy puppy. Cooper handed her to Max. "Here you go. You share a birthday, after all."

This was true. Gabrielle Cooper had been born on March 15, the very day Max turned nineteen. Max was not terribly familiar with babies. He'd spent a little time with Emma Bristow and there had been Gianna, Isabella's daughter at the Blys farmhouse. But he still regarded them as mysterious beings. Hefting Gabrielle like a loaf, he peered at her, smiled with kindly intent, and watched her round little face curdle with disapproval. This person was not familiar to her, was not even practiced in the art of holding babies. She must be returned to her father—immediately. Her crying ceased the instant she was handed back.

Cooper was visibly pleased by her loyalty. "She just needs to get used to you. A bit of babysitting and you'll be old friends."

"Ha!" boomed a familiar baritone. "Max McDaniels a babysitter? Don't be absurd, man."

Max turned, gazing about until he spied a small yellow towel on which Toby was lounging in his native form. He had mistaken Toby for a pair of shoes, for there was a second smee right next to him. The other specimen was somewhat larger and paler, but rapidly turning an angry red in the bright sun.

"Toby," said Max. "I didn't see you. When did you get back? Who's your friend?"

"Don't pretend you don't know me, sir," said the other smee. "It demeans us both."

"I'm sorry," said Max, coming over. "Do I—"

"Reginald was Prusias's body double," Toby explained. "We go way back. Had a few adventures in Monte Carlo back in '74."

"Seventy-three," corrected Reginald.

"Right you are," said Toby agreeably. "Well, it's been ages since I've bumped into this scoundrel. Didn't even recognize ol' Reggie when you popped him out of his disguise. No offense, chum, but you've put on a few."

The other smee raised his apparent head to peer at his midsection.

"Anyhoo," continued Toby. "When I finally recognized him, I told William they couldn't clap ol' Reggie in irons—he was just an actor hired to play a part. Once they let him go, we've been catching up and seeing a bit of the world. Had to get back for tonight, though. Peace always brings out the ladies. Ladies in high spirits. Ladies with a new zest for life . . ."

"Dear Lord," sighed Hazel. "Toby, you are disgusting."

"Ha!" laughed the smee, flipping over. "You're just sorry you're out of the game, my dear. When I've got a tan, it's not even fair."

"How am I looking, Toby?" inquired the other smee.

"Crispy, Reggie. Crispy."

"Is that good?"

"It's fantastic."

Max left the smees to their chortling, rather optimistic predictions for the evening and sat on a blanket to talk with the others. After thirty minutes of perfectly pleasant chitchat and several unsuccessful baby holdings, Cooper nudged him.

"Could I get a private word?"

"No shop talk, William," said Hazel, changing Gabrielle. "Not until noon. You promised."

"It'll just take a minute," said Cooper, leading Max a little ways around the lagoon where the selkies Frigga and Helga were turning lazing circles in the water.

"What's up?" said Max.

"I know you keep turning down security, but I don't think you should be walking around alone," said Cooper. "Not in the Manse. Not in Old College—certainly not through the Sanctuary tunnel. If I'd known you were going to do that, I'd have come to get you."

"You're worried I can't look after myself?" said Max.

"Let's have a look at that stomach, and I'll tell ya."

"I'm fine."

Cooper folded his arms. "There's over five hundred ships anchored off Rowan. This whole island's crawling with visitors—braymas, witches, Workshop, you name it. Treaty or not, there's plenty that'd like to see you dead."

Max said nothing.

"Alex Muñoz didn't have poison on him when he was put in the Hollows," continued Cooper. He waved pleasantly to Hazel, who looked like she might come to Max's rescue. "Someone slipped it to him so he could take his life before he was questioned. You think that was a coincidence?"

"No," said Max. "But if the Atropos are here, you think a few bodyguards are going to make a difference? I'd just get them killed. Anyway, I'm sharper when someone *isn't* watching my back."

Cooper frowned. "Without security, you're practically inviting an attack."

"That's a risk I'm willing to take," said Max with a polite firmness suggesting he was done discussing the matter. "Anything else?"

"Yeah, actually. The Red Branch needs a new member. Since Scathach can't designate her replacement, it's my duty to name one. There's plenty of candidates, but I wanted your opinion first. Anyone leap out at you? Can't guarantee I'll pick them, but they'll get first look."

Max considered a moment before answering. "Lady Nico."

"But she's Raszna," said Cooper pointedly.

Max only shrugged. "So what? She's well qualified, and the Raszna are our closest allies. It'd send a strong message if we asked one of them to join. And I think Scathach would approve. She had a lot of respect for Lady Nico."

"I'll think about it," said Cooper, swatting a mosquito. "No promises, but it's an interesting idea."

"There you are!" cried a shrill voice behind them.

The two turned to see Hannah, a plump white goose, waddling swiftly across the grass followed by a dozen downy goslings. They gathered around, pecking everything in sight while their mother caught her breath.

"I heard you were here," said Hannah, fixing Max with her beady black eyes. "Listen, it's a busy day, so I'll cut right to the chase. I want your endorsement."

Max glanced at Cooper, who looked as confused as he was. "Endorse what?"

"My candidacy," she said pointedly. "I'm running for Great Matriarch."

"What?"

"That's right," she said, buffeting Honk, who was now pecking his siblings. "We all loved YaYa, but she's not here anymore and we need a new Great Matriarch. I'm throwing my hat in the ring."

"I . . . didn't know it was an elected office," said Max hesitantly. "I thought it was more of an honorary title."

With a sniff, Hannah examined her wingtips. "Things change, Max. I miss YaYa, but I'm a practical goose and this place needs another Great Matriarch. Who's going to preside over matchings? Who's going to spank lazy stewards who blow off their duties? The satyrs are *this close* to starting trouble with the fauns. How do I know? Because I know everything that goes on around this place, that's why."

"Do you have any other qualifications?" Cooper deadpanned.

She thrust out her chest. "I'm a single parent raising twelve goslings that never grow up. That's as matriarchal as it gets!" Turning back to Max, the goose's voice became pure honey. "So, what do you say, dear? Can I tell people I've got your vote?"

Max offered a firm yes.

The moment he did, Hannah turned toward the selkies and cupped a wing to her beak. "Did ya hear that, girls?" she hollered. "He endorsed me! So get off the fence, already!"

Frigga and Helga submerged.

Max left the Sanctuary soon after, returning to the Manse with Cooper, who insisted on accompanying him all the way to the Observatory. Bidding the Agent farewell, Max went inside to find that Tweedy's stubbornness had overcome his shock at encountering Chester. The pinlegs had been stuffed back in his glass case, antennae undulating, while Max's and David's possessions had been organized and placed by moving crates. The hare had even gone so far as to lay out what Max was to wear for the treaty signing.

Removing his shirt, Max sat on the edge of his bed and carefully peeled off his bandage. It was damp with sweat and blood, while the blackened area had grown since this morning. When he prodded it, the impression from his finger remained, as if everything beneath was rotten. Exhaling, he reached for the balm and began cleaning and bandaging it anew. The process was unpleasant and tedious, but he would not have to do it for much longer. Once he'd finished, Max eased back against his pillow to watch the Observatory's twinkling constellations. It was far more soothing than the balm.

The Red Winter Treaty was to be signed at sunset in the gardens of Túr an Ghrian. Max started getting ready well in advance, aware that Tweedy would combust if he looked anything less than perfect. It was, as he had been informed many times, a *historic* occasion. Everything would be saved and documented for posterity. David had even promised to shower.

When Max emerged from Room 318, he was dressed in a corselet of silver mail, the simple black tunic of the Red Branch, a white cloak, and black boots and breeches. Tweedy had pressed and polished everything that could be pressed or polished. Max carried the *gae bolga* as a spear, not a sword, for this was how his enemies had seen him on the battlefield. Given that some would be in attendance, David had thought a reminder would be useful.

Agents from the Bloodstone Circle were waiting outside to accompany him. As they walked through the Manse, Max reflected on how hard David had worked to bring so many disparate parties together. The signing itself would largely be a formality, a ritual to sanctify terms and provisions already agreed upon. Most of the negotiating had taken place in the weeks and months leading up to this evening. With two notable exceptions, Max did not expect any drama.

By the time Max and his escort arrived, many people had already congregated in the fragrant gardens surrounding Túr an Ghrian. This gathering was not nearly so large as the celebrations that would take place later to commemorate the treaty's signing. Only a few hundred people would attend this meeting—the signatories themselves, key dignitaries, and the various entourages. Most were glancing uneasily at the dragon.

Ember was twined about the tower's base with smoke trickling from his nostrils. They had not seen Ember for several weeks following his encounter with N'aagha. When he reappeared at Rowan, he was shockingly knocked about, with one eye gone and great gouges in his sides. But Ember's powers of recovery were remarkable. Looking at him now, one would be hard-pressed to find the merest scratch. Even the dragon's eye had regenerated. N'aagha's fate and whereabouts remained a mystery.

A large round table was center stage, its chairs reserved for those who would sign for their respective factions. Seated around it were the main players: David Menlo; the Archon Fenwulf from the Raszna; Queen Lilith of the allied braymas; Dame Mako of the witch clans; and Dr. Kim, who had led the Workshop revolt. Others were seated, too—envoys from regions that had remained neutral, a rakshasa speaking for lesser braymas in the former Americas. In all, twelve figures sat around the table with the purpose of dividing up the world and agreeing to some basic principles to keep the peace.

Max took his place, standing behind David's right shoulder while Mina stood behind his left. The symbolism was clear: Rowan's political leadership flanked by embodiments of its armed might and magical heritage. The other signatories had their own people beside them. Lady Nico and the towering war chief Vechna stood by Fenwulf. A pair of elegant kitsune stood behind Queen Lilith. Situated on either side of Dame Mako were a very young acolyte and the ancient Umadahm. One of Dr. Kim's attendants was a pleasant surprise—Max had not seen Jason Barrett for almost five years.

Of course, many other Rowan people were in attendance— Miss Awolowo, Nigel Bristow, most of the Red Branch and Bloodstone Circle, all the Promethean Scholars, and a slew of senior faculty. While the Agents were positioned here and there to provide security, the others sat in chairs waiting patiently for the proceedings to begin.

The Director's opening remarks were courteous, brief, and delivered with a composure that almost brought a smile to Max's face. David's audience could have no inkling how nervous he had been in the weeks leading up to this moment. Max had heard many versions of this address and even more fits of cursing as David strived to hit the right notes.

Having done so, he moved briskly into the key provisions and agreements. The largest and most controversial involved Queen Lilith and those braymas who had joined Rowan in the war against Prusias. In exchange for her support, Rowan and the other factions granted the Queen additional lands. As a result, she would control much more territory than her realm of Zenuvia, but considerably less than that which comprised the Four Kingdoms. In addition, David handed over the hated Seal of Solomon as a pledge of good faith between Rowan and Lilith's people. For her part, Lilith pledged that demons would remain within these lands and not make war upon their neighbors unless their boundaries were violated.

Of course, there were many other provisions to this agreement—endless clauses detailing rights and responsibilities, the settling of disputes, and so on—but Max knew it was the main point that ruffled so many feathers at Rowan. The "Puritans" (as David called them) were offended by the very idea of an accord with "evil spirits," while the "Jingoists" (another David label) questioned whether these allies had made significant contributions. In their minds, Rowan had won the war all by itself and Lilith's rewards were far too great for her minor role.

David laughed off most of these criticisms, privately sharing with Max that Lilith had convinced dozens of braymas to abandon Prusias or remain neutral in exchange for her promise to share her expanded territory. David believed strongly that a mutually beneficial agreement with daemona was the only way to achieve a lasting peace. As Lilith was highly rational and not nearly so bloodthirsty as her counterparts, David viewed her as a valuable partner.

The treaty's next sections were far less controversial. Rowan's Director and the Raszna's Archon formalized their ongoing alliance and partnership. The witches and Rowan officially made peace and promised future cooperation. In exchange for various pledges made to the Faeregine (whose person and word were regarded as sacred), the independent braymas were granted lands in places where they could thrive but were unlikely to come into conflict with human beings. These lands were typically located at extreme elevations and latitudes.

David addressed the Workshop last since their situation was unique. Their cooperation with Prusias had played a key role in the devastation he wrought around the world. They supplied him with hideous engines of war, and many of their researches and technologies violated laws of nature. While many at the Workshop claimed they'd been forced to comply with Prusias's demands, David believed the Workshop's activities had posed a significant threat well before the war.

"Astaroth and I disagreed about many things," said David, addressing Dr. Kim, "but not everything. I believe certain technologies create problems that far exceed their benefits and that things designed with good intentions can be used to horrific effect. For the Workshop to exist going forward, it must agree to the conditions I've stipulated. They are not negotiable."

Copies of David's stipulations were provided to all the signatories. With the exception of Dr. Kim, everyone nodded their approval. The engineer looked like he might be sick.

"B-but this is almost everything we do," he stammered before reading a portion of the list aloud. "Artificial intelligence, cloning, genetic engineering, synthetic compounds, automated weaponry, nanotechnologies . . ." He looked in appeal to David. "Director, I realize the previous leadership acted irresponsibly, but—"

"You agree to these stipulations or we will destroy everything in the Workshop."

"What about our people?" asked a stunned Dr. Kim. "You're threatening genocide."

David shook his head. "Nothing of the sort. Your people would be relocated and given new memories. They'll have a chance to start over."

"Why must this be negotiated?" asked Lilith. "You have the Book. Do what you wish."

David looked around the table. "The Book of Thoth is no longer accessible," he said simply. "Once I dispelled Astaroth's winter, I used the Book's power to put it beyond reach . . . forever. It will continue to function, but it can never again be found."

This astonished almost everyone present, including some of the Rowan attendees. Max and Mina already knew, of course; David had done it before they left Ymir.

"I don't understand," said a man representing the human settlement of Piter's Folly. "You could have fixed things. You could have made the world like it was before Astaroth!"

"No," said David firmly. "I could not. That's the great danger of the Book. No one can foresee the consequences of using it—not even Astaroth. The world is changed. Our task now is to move forward. The only question at present is whether the Workshop will be moving with us."

Dr. Kim fidgeted with his pen. "I'm not sure I can sign this on my own authority."

"That's precisely what we're here to do," said David. "If you're not empowered to speak for the Workshop, there's little point in having you at this table."

"I *am* empowered," said Dr. Kim defensively. "I just . . . well, this isn't fair."

Rowan's Director fixed him with a withering stare. "I'm not remotely interested in what you think is fair. My interest is laying a foundation for peace, not indulging your hobbies."

"But advancements—" pleaded Dr. Kim.

"Are *not* advancements if they can destroy the planet," said David sharply. "I can't put it more plainly than that. If the Workshop refuses to content itself with a smaller playground, it won't have a playground at all."

"Hear, hear!" said Dame Mako.

Rubbing his temples, the scientist stared miserably at the agreement.

"We have other business to attend to," said David impatiently.

Max thought Dr. Kim might whimper as he signed the papers with a golden pen that would be stored in a museum with the treaties and everything else associated with this day. Once Dr. Kim had signed, David thanked him and authorized Dr. Barrett to oversee compliance before moving to the final item on the agenda. As they reached it, Max heard an undertone of anxious whispers. Even the signatories looked nervous.

David turned to William Cooper. "Bring him here, please."

Cooper and five other members of the Red Branch entered Túr an Ghrian. They returned several minutes later with a shackled but delighted Prusias.

"My, my," he chuckled to the imp on his shoulder. "It looks like we've crashed a party, Mr. Bonn. Look at that big round table with all these fine folk about it. Nice touch, Director. Very Arthurian."

David ignored the demon's cheek. "Just over there," he said, directing the Agents to position the demon by some flowers. Prusias leaned over to sniff them.

"Never liked hydrangeas," he remarked. "They're the bourgeoisie of flowers."

"Let's get this over with," David sighed. "Prusias, the only reason you are here, the only reason you can see this beautiful sunset and smell that grasping, middle-class hydrangea is because we made a deal several months ago. Do you remember?"

"I most certainly do," said the demon, grinning.

"In exchange for some useful information, we agreed to grant you your freedom—with certain conditions. Please share what those were."

"With pleasure," said Prusias. "In exchange for that information, I'm to be granted my freedom and lands of my own."

David held up a finger. "Provided?"

The demon looked bored. "Provided I don't leave them, make war, or interfere with anyone who has Rowan's leave to cross my lands. Did you hear that, Lilith? Even you can slink across if the Faeregine says so."

The Queen of Zenuvia looked coolly at her former rival.

"Very good," said David, handing Cooper a ribbon-tied scroll and several documents for the demon's inspection. "Here are your lands. Thousands of square miles, which is more than you deserve."

Prusias ripped off the ribbon, his eyes devouring the deed's particulars. "Where are they?" asked greedily.

"A map is in the documents," said David.

Rifling through the pages, the demon found the coordinates, gazed at the map, and glared at the Director. "These are at the bottom of the bloody ocean!"

"I never said your lands wouldn't be covered by water," said David. "You can rule those deeps, Prusias. You can even bring your braymas, provided they take the same pledge you have—any ship bearing Rowan's seal is free to pass without harm or interference."

Prusias looked like he might explode. "I reject this!" he snarled. "I reject this, you smug little twit! I do not accept!"

"Those are the terms," said David calmly. "Mina offered them to you, and you agreed to them. Are you reneging on a pledge you made to the Faeregine? I can't speak to those consequences, but I can assure you that refusing this deal means you will spend eternity in a cell that I will design personally. You will never escape, and no one will ever find you."

Max had never met a finer poker player than David Menlo. He suspected Prusias hadn't either, for the demon was now studying David's impassive face. And it was clear he was beginning to realize how badly he'd underestimated Rowan's new Director in the Hollows. Not only had David fooled him into thinking he'd been the winner in their negotiations, but he also did not look like the sort who issued idle threats. He might even enjoy making good on them.

Prusias blinked. "No," he muttered. "No, I'm not refusing the deal. You think I'm finished? I'm going to build something down there—something far grander than Blys. There will come a day when my kingdom is the greatest on Earth!"

"We look forward to it," said David. "When you sign that document, this war ends, and a ship will take you to your new lands."

Prusias practically snatched the golden pen from Cooper's hand. He signed with a dramatic flourish, his signature covering half the page. "There! Now, I demand these ridiculous shackles be removed and our ship made ready. I'm not staying here one second longer than necessary."

As Cooper unlocked the demon's shackles, Mr. Bonn gave a small cough. "Director, may I speak?"

David silenced Prusias's protest. "Of course you may speak, Mr. Bonn."

"Well," said the imp, "my master promised to grant me *koukerros* once the war was over. If I understand correctly, that is now the case. I would like him to make good on his promise—here before the Faeregine."

"This is preposterous," Prusias growled. "You're my imp!"

"Did you make this promise?" asked Mina, at David's left shoulder.

The demon's whole being seemed to writhe with discomfort as he looked at this young girl in her white robes and open, expectant face. It was clear he could not bring himself to lie to her. "I did," he confessed. "But it was said in passing. A little joke to placate—"

Mina's voice had an icy authority. "You will grant him *koukerros* right now."

Prusias almost wilted. He glanced at Mr. Bonn with an expression of mingled anger and anguish. "So you're abandoning me, eh? Right when I need you."

Mr. Bonn's smile was almost compassionate. "It's time for a new chapter, master. One for you, and one for me. We've had many good years."

Prusias gave a grudging nod, his savage features oddly introspective. "Aye, Mr. Bonn. That we have. Very well, then."

The demon took hold of Mr. Bonn's little hand and closed his eyes. A ball of green fire erupted around their clasped hands, growing brighter and brighter. As Prusias shuddered, Mr. Bonn gave a gasp of pain. The imp's body burned away like tissue paper, leaving behind a lithe little spirit of shimmering air. Springing from Prusias's shoulder, it gave an exultant cry and soared off into the twilight. Max watched it longest.

Later that evening, Max left the Observatory. He'd ditched the ceremonial garb from earlier, opting instead for his worn and comfortable travel clothes. Stopping at the threshold, he gazed back at the room's beloved dome, constellations, and sleigh beds before locking the door behind him. The movers were coming early the next morning. Tweedy would make certain the important things ended up where they needed to go.

Old College was crowded with merrymakers celebrating the treaty signing. So was the Sanctuary. Max had never seen the township more packed—its square and avenues, shops and restaurants were teeming with revelers. Stopping briefly to buy a bag of toffees (Max could never resist toffee), he bumped into Aurvangr and Ginnarr, the dvergar smiths who had made the *gae bolga*'s spear shaft. Max greeted them pleasantly.

"It's the Boy!" said Aurvangr, elbowing his brother. They always called him "the Boy" as though he were the only one in existence.

"You're the one who's always grousing about it," sniffed Ginnarr. "You ask him."

"Ask me what?" said Max, holding out the bag of candy.

A grateful Ginnarr took a toffee, but Aurvangr twiddled his fingers anxiously. "I hate to bring this up," he said. "But when we lent you *Ormenheid,* it was for three years. She's six months overdue. We didn't want to say anything with the war and all the troubles, but now that the treaty's signed, we want her back. She's very special."

Max popped a toffee in his mouth. "Yes, she is. What other ship can sail itself against weather, wind, and tide? She could probably fly if you asked her to."

"Very special," Ginnarr repeated proudly. "You understand we're not trying to be greedy. *Ormenheid* is an heirloom of our people."

"I know," said Max. "I'm truly sorry to have kept her so long. Would it be okay if I gave her back in a few days?"

"The Boy wants to have a little fun," chuckled a relieved Aurvangr to his brother. "I understand. Who wouldn't like to take a pretty girl sailing in this weather? You keep her another week, okay? Then we get her back."

"Deal," said Max, shaking hands.

Nox was waiting by the Warming Lodge, chewing casually on an iron ingot. She rose at Max's approach, padding toward him and fluttering her tail in greeting. Crouching, Max stroked her quills and gazed about at the Sanctuary's foothills and forests, its ring of mountains, and the distant dunes.

"C'mon," he said, scratching Nox's ears. "It's getting late."

The two walked through the Sanctuary tunnel into Old College. With Nox at his side, it was silly to pretend he wasn't Max McDaniels, so he didn't bother with his hood. In any case, it was a warm night and he wanted to feel the breeze.

To his surprise and delight, Max ran into David as he and Nox passed by the Manse's fountain. The visibly bored Director was listening to an urgent plea by a Raszna student who wanted to switch roommates. Catching sight of Max, David held up a finger for him and Nox to wait.

"I have nothing to do with roommate assignments," said David, not unkindly. "You'll have to take that up with Tweedy."

Evidently this was unacceptable. Before stalking off, the indignant vye declared that Tweedy was "horrible," that Rowan "smelled funny," and that he wished to return to Arcanum. With a sigh, David came over to Max and ventured a cautious pat of Nox's head.

"Any interest in being Director?" he asked.

"Nope," said Max. "I'm glad I ran into you, though. Nice job at the signing. You were kind of a badass."

"I try. What's with the bag?"

Max thumped his pack. "Thought I might camp out in the caravan. I don't need Tweedy's movers waking me up at six in the morning. Do you get to take a break now?"

The question earned an incredulous look. "A break? I'm going to my fourth dinner. Apparently, if you don't host a fancy dinner tonight, you don't really count in the new scheme of things. This one's with the witches. But let's talk about your camping out at the caravan. I assume you'll refuse for the thousandth time when I insist you take some Agents with you?"

Max grinned. "You assume correctly, Director. And you'll get no sympathy from me for having to attend all these dinners. That's what you get for creating your little 'Pax Rowana.'"

David blinked. He looked startled, even amazed by the expression. "That's really clever."

Max gave a nonchalant shrug. "I've been told I'm the great wit of the world."

"The very peak of the bell curve," said David, a curious twinkle in his eye.

Feeling rather pleased, Max said good night and set off across Old College. He hadn't made it twenty yards before David's voice called after him.

"Tweedy made that up, didn't he?"

Cursing David's intuition, Max shouldered his pack and carried on.

It took Max nearly an hour to walk from the Manse to Scathach's caravan. It was only two miles, but Nox liked to dart into the woods, clamber up trees, and generally make her presence known to whatever poor creatures were trying to sleep.

Max was content to take his time and let her stretch her legs. Midnight was still a few hours away and it was a beautiful evening with a sky so clear he might have been standing atop the Witchpeaks. As he walked along the cliffs, he listened to the summer breeze, the crashing surf, and the distant ring of Old Tom chiming ten.

The caravan looked very pretty in the moonlight. There were flowers around it now, some of Scathach's favorites planted among the vines that snaked through its wheels.

After Ymir, Max had recovered her remains from the Workshop and buried them here with some driftwood as a headstone. For a girl who'd lived in two worlds, he thought that was fitting. Besides, Scathach wouldn't have wanted anything fancy—just a little plot by the sea. And that was what she had.

He looked around for Nox, but she had not returned from her latest detour. Setting down his pack, Max knelt by the grave. After all the noise and activity on campus, he was grateful for a bit of quiet. He knelt in silence for a few moments before touching his fingers to the headstone.

"You and no other."

As he expected, two shadows slipped silently from the woods. Rising to face them, Max drew the *gae bolga* and offered the warrior's salute.

It was not even six when a loud knocking woke David. What surprised him was not the knock, but the fact that he found Bob standing outside the Observatory's door. David had never seen the ogre look so grim.

"You must come, Director. Something bad has happened."

"What?" said David, his pulse quickening.

"Bob does not know exactly. Perhaps you will. We go outside."

David asked no more questions. Pulling a Director's robe over his head, he slipped on some shoes and scurried after the ogre, who was taking long, rapid strides down the hallway. A pair of guards followed as they hurried out the Manse's front door and into the golden dawn.

"I go early to docks to buy crab," Bob explained. "A fisherman showed me. I told him stay quiet and came right to you."

"What is it?"

"Bob not sure. It might be our Max."

David broke into a run.

By the time they descended the cliff steps and clambered far up the rocky beach, David could scarcely breathe. But he did not stop until they'd almost reached the spot that Bob indicated, a little cove past a dune crowned with sea grass. Coming to a wheezing halt, David told the guards to remain and went ahead with Bob.

Two bodies were lying ten feet from the water's edge, arranged side by side and covered with stones. The hasty burial had done little to dissuade the seagulls, which had arrived in great numbers and took reluctant, screaming flight at the ogre's approach.

David was almost numb when he removed the first few stones from the larger mound. Although it was bruised and bloodied, the face was all too familiar. It was only when he spied burn scars about the jaw that he exhaled. Max had only one facial scar—a thin white line that ran from cheek to chin. This person did not.

It was far easier to identify the other body. The smaller, emaciated clone stared up at the peach-colored sky with glassy eyes and an open mouth full of broken teeth.

"What make those?" asked Bob, pointing at some gruesome claw marks.

David closed the clone's eyes. "A lymrill. He finally met an animal wilder than him."

Bob looked around anxiously. "You think Max okay?"

Rising, David noted the piles of loose rocks and boulders that looked like they'd recently tumbled down the cliffs. One of the largest bore a bloody handprint. More blood had soaked into the sand, little droplets scattered about the many footprints whose number and patterns suggested a prolonged and furious struggle. Two sets of footprints stood out from the rest, however. One set had been made by a pair of boots, the other by heavy paws that had walked side by side away from the burial mounds. They ended at the water's edge.

"I think Max is okay," said David thoughtfully. "But I don't think we'll see him or Nox again. I think they've left us for good."

A sad, deep rumble sounded in the ogre's chest. "Bob will miss his little Max. But he thought *malyenki* might be leaving."

David looked up at him. "How did you know?"

A grunt. "Before Bob was cook, Bob was ogre. Where you think he go?"

David gazed out at the ocean's swells and then up at the sky where the last stars of evening were fading. "I don't know, Bob. But yesterday was Midsummer. With a ship like *Ormenheid*, Max could have sailed just about anywhere. I think that was the idea."

David returned to the Observatory physically and emotionally exhausted. What he wanted was sleep; what he found was Tweedy and a work crew packing up everything he owned. David glanced longingly at his sleigh bed, the lone piece of furniture that would be moved to his new accommodations.

"Tweedy, can I please get an hour of sleep?"

"Not a chance, Director. Busy day, you know."

Nodding dazedly, David sat on his bed and gazed up at the Observatory dome. Orion gazed back.

"Oh," said Tweedy, hopping over. "Some incompetent left something for you on McDaniels's bed."

The hare handed over a bundle wrapped in a plain brown bag with David's name scrawled on it. Reaching within, David pulled out a mail shirt whose links were so fine, so tiny, it could be folded like cloth. Antonio de Lorca had bequeathed the armor to Max years ago when there was a city called Salamanca. Max was returning it to the Red Branch.

The bag also contained a letter. Setting aside the shirt, David opened the letter and read in silence. In true Max fashion, it was not particularly long or well written, but it brought a smile to David's face.

"Tweedy," he said, holding up the shirt. "This needs to go to the Red Branch vault."

"Very good," said the hare, noting it on a clipboard. "And the letter? Should it be filed?"

"No," said David. "It's not an official document. More of a personal invitation."

"You can toss it in the fire, then. You're booked solid for the next six months. When's the event?"

David folded the letter. "If I'm lucky, not for a very long time."

For once, Tweedy was speechless.

Epilogue

Twilight was settling when Max climbed down from *Ormen-heid* and spoke the words that would send her sailing back to Rowan. While Nox explored the empty beach, Max watched the longship rise and fall on the gray waves until she disappeared in the mist.

The lymrill bounded over as Max removed the bandages from his midsection. The linen was clotted with dark blood and the scented balm. But the skin underneath was whole, the flesh firm and strong. When Max washed the area with seawater, he could find no trace of the awful wound. Catching sight of his wrist, he noticed that his Red Branch tattoo had also disappeared.

Curious, Max touched his cheekbone and felt a thin raised slash that ran all the way to his chin. For whatever reason, that scar remained.

Attaching the spear shaft to the *gae bolga,* Max used the weapon as a walking stick as he and Nox journeyed up from the beach to a quiet countryside. Crossing a field, they came upon a dirt lane that led to a road of worn white cobbles washed clean by recent rain. Max walked down the road's center as it wound through a country of old forests and weathered hills. Here and there moonflowers rose from the hedges, their white blossoms opening to greet the evening. Nox padded beside him, snorting at the occasional hare but generally content to sniff the breeze and enjoy a stroll with her steward.

A chorus of crickets and churring nightjars accompanied them as they walked. From far off, Max heard the sound of a child's laughter and the hint of a fiddle. But there were no other people on the road. For the moment, it belonged solely to them.

They did not see anyone until they crossed a stone footbridge that spanned a quiet brook. The girls were twins, no more than six, and they stood barefoot beneath a willow tree clutching lanterns that illuminated dusky, knowing faces. They must have been awaiting Max, for as he approached, they bowed to him and Nox and fell in step behind them.

Max soon saw other people. They approached over fields or stood beside the hedges and flowers that lined the road: farmers and weavers, shepherds and smiths, woodcutters and reddlemen dusty with chalk. Some leaned on scythes or spades; others cradled infants or quieted little ones who stood on tiptoe to glimpse the newcomer. None spoke, but all bowed or removed their hats as he passed.

As Max continued, the spectators increased. Among the candles and lanterns, Max recognized faces he had known once upon a time: a stablehand from Rodrubân, a faun that sang in Summervyne, a faerie from the Fomorian's cave, a man who helped with the standing stone. Each bowed as Max passed and then followed silently behind the girls.

It was not long before Max saw six figures in gleaming mail. The shield maidens stood at attention, composed and stoic but for Ula, whose tears shone plain on her ruddy cheeks. As Max passed, they also bowed and joined the slow procession.

The strange parade continued on through the twilight, following the road as it crossed an ancient forest and fed into an open stretch of shallow hills and well-tilled fields. In the distance stood Rodrubân, its ivory towers impossibly beautiful against the deepening sky.

A farmhouse stood upon the nearest hill, its windows spilling light upon its porch and gardens. From within, Max heard the clink of dishes and a man's laughter. He wanted very much to go inside, to leave the road and walk up the gravel path toward its door. When he did so, Nox and the twin girls followed, but the others remained behind—hundreds of silent figures watching from the roadside.

As Max climbed the hill, he saw that his way was blocked. Something was sprawled across the path—a dark shape that watched him with glittering, implacable eyes. Clutching the *gae bolga,* Max walked toward it.

The wolfhound stood as he approached, growling low and baring its fearsome teeth as it ground its paws into the gravel. Max met its impenetrable stare as the beast padded toward him. When it rose and placed its massive paws upon his shoulders, Max did not resist. He merely let the *gae bolga* slip from his grasp.

The wolfhound's weight nearly staggered him. Pressing its broad head against his, the animal panted and growled, its breath hot as a furnace. From its throat came a familiar question.

"What are you about? Answer quick, or I'll gobble you up!"

This time Max did not run. He did not attack or let the monster devour him, as he had in so many dreams. Placing his hands atop its paws, he gazed into the wolfhound's face as though it were an old and trusted friend.

"I'm Max McDaniels. And I've come home."

As he spoke these words, the monster's features melted away and he beheld the Morrígan. The goddess was clad in dark mail and wore a cloak of raven feathers about her shoulders. Her aspect was still fearsome, but there was no hatred or anger upon her face. Picking up the *gae bolga,* she placed the spear back in Max's hand.

"The Sidh shall have its prince at last," she intoned. "A prince strong and wise, tested and tempered. A prince worthy of the people he will rule. Soon you will come to Rodrubân, where Lugh Lamfhada awaits you. But for now, your place is here. Three gifts await you inside. Two are from your father. One is from me."

Stepping back, the Morrígan bowed to her future king and stood aside so that he could complete his long journey.

The porch creaked as Max stepped upon its planks. The farmhouse was old but finely built of red oak, and its beams and trellises hung with flowers. Its windows were curtained but for a small round pane in which a single lamp was burning. Leaning the *gae bolga* against the wall, Max took hold of a worn brass ring and knocked.

When the door opened, Max went numb.

Scathach looked just as she had when he first saw her atop Rodrubân—strong and proud, fierce and beautiful. The sight was so unexpected, so overwhelming that Max was speechless. Taking his hand, Scathach tugged him inside.

"I'm dreaming," he murmured. "This can't be real."

But as Scathach embraced him, Max could feel her warmth,

her life, the beating of her strong heart. Holding him close, she whispered the oath he'd spoken at her grave.

"Those were fine words, my love. Did you mean them?"

Max kissed her. "I did. I do."

Wiping away her tears, Scathach almost laughed. "A poor guest I am. If I keep you all to myself, they'll never have me back!"

Max was puzzled. "Whose house is this?"

Scathach didn't answer directly but led him through a sitting room to a snug kitchen of wood and brick. Within, Bryn and Scott McDaniels were setting dishes on a table, looking just as they had when he'd been a boy. When they beheld their son, there were no joyous cries or exclamations, just a silent embrace that lasted until Nox gave an impatient snort. After all, supper was ready, the candles were lit, and a place had been set for Max.

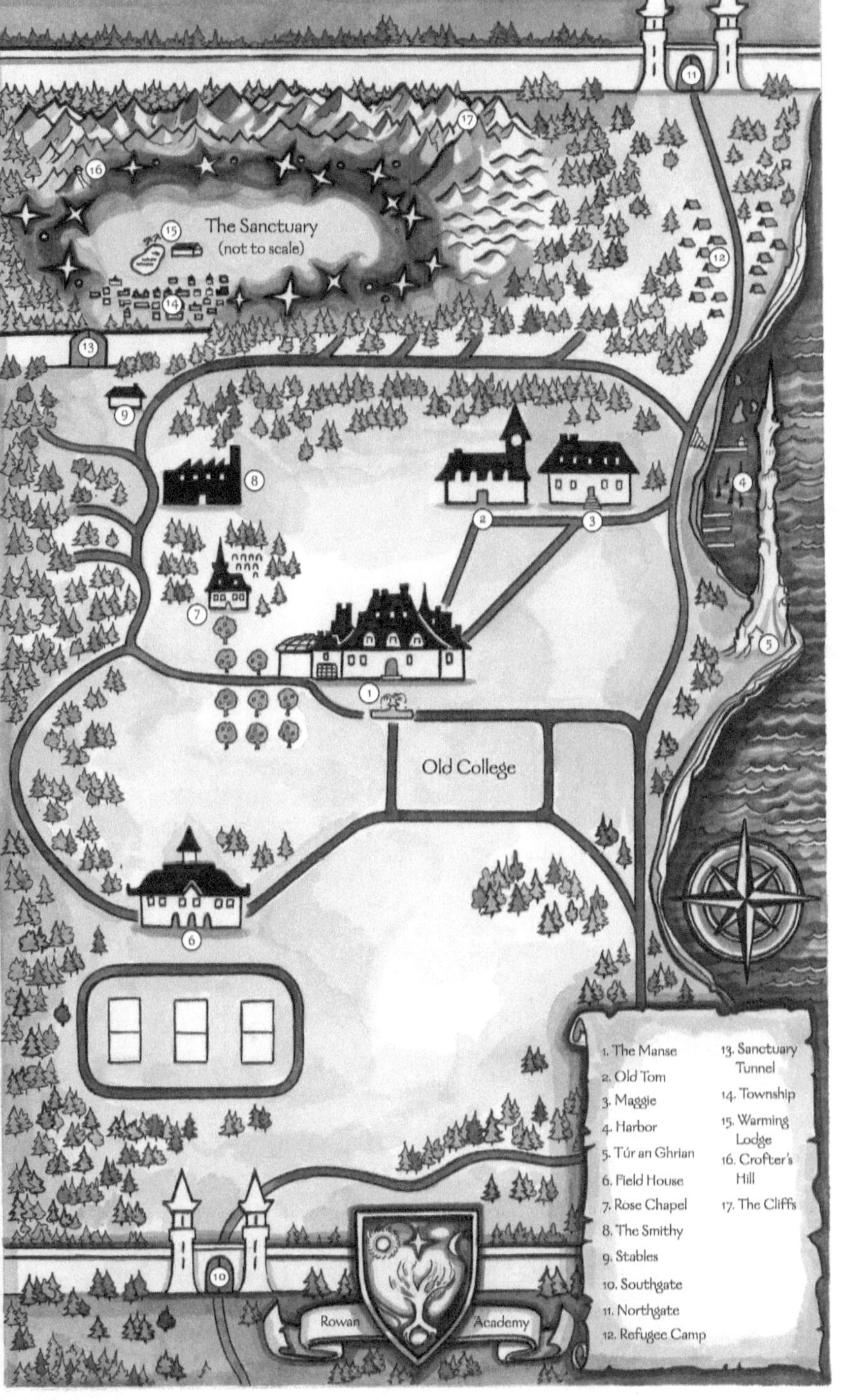

The Sanctuary
(not to scale)
Old College
Rowan
Academy
1. The Manse
2. Old Tom
3. Maggie
4. Harbor
5. Túr an Ghrian
6. Field House
7. Rose Chapel
8. The Smithy
9. Stables
10. Southgate
11. Northgate
12. Refugee Camp
13. Sanctuary Tunnel
14. Township
15. Warming Lodge
16. Crofter's Hill
17. The Cliffs

Pronunciation Guide/Glossary

This guide is to help readers pronounce some of the more challenging names and terms found in the Tapestry. Many of the words are of Irish origin, while others are simply the author's own creations. Some nuances have been sacrificed in the name of simplicity, and this should not be interpreted as a scholarly work on Irish pronunciation.

Name/Term (Pronunciation) Definition

Archon (AR-kon) A title designating the Raszna leader; archons are always male

Atropos (AH-truh-pos) Among the three Greek Fates, Atropos cut the thread of life; the name was adopted by an assassin guild known for its ruthlessness and fanaticism

Bragha Rùn (BRAH-gah ROON) "The Red Death"; Max McDaniels's alias in Prusias's Arena

Brugh na Boinne (BROO nah BOYNE) "On the Boyne"; a river in Ireland

cambion (CAM-bee-un) The offspring of a demon and a mortal woman

Cúchulain (KOO-hull-in) The Hound of Ulster; an Irish hero who was the son of the deity Lugh and a mortal woman

daemona (DAY-moan-uh) The demons' preferred term for their kind; one that classifies their spiritual essence without automatic association with evil

Elohir (ELL-oh-heer) Scattered, nomadic elder vyes who do not congregate with others

Emer (AY-verr) The wife of Cúchulain; also the name of Elias Bram's daughter

Faeregine (FAIR-uh-geen) A legendary being that appears in different forms and in different ages to protect those in danger; all spirits hold the Faeregine sacred

gae bolga (GAY BULL-gah) Cúchulain's spear, which was forged anew by Max McDaniels and the Fomorian. Its strike is almost always fatal; its wounds never heal.

grylmhoch (GRILLM-hoke) A massive, amorphous creature of unknown origins that Max encounters in Prusias's Arena

koukerros (koo-KERR-os) The transformation that occurs when a demon has consumed enough souls to become a higher order of spirit

Lugh (LOO) A sun deity; High King of the Tuatha Dé Danaan, who slew Balor of the Fomorians. Lugh is the father of both Cúchulain and Max McDaniels.

Magyarün (MY-ah-roon) Elder vyes that prey upon mankind and often serve Astaroth, Prusias, or other demons

malakhim (MAL-ah-keem) Fallen spirits that wear obsidian masks and serve the demon Prusias

médim (MAY-deem) Ritualized contests that mark important demonic gatherings; the contests include alennya (arts of beauty), amann (arts of blood), and ahülmm (arts of soul)

Morrígan (MOH-ree-gan) A Celtic war goddess whose willful and terrifying essence comprises the *gae bolga*

rakshasa (rock-SHAH-sah) An ancient and powerful type of demon

Raszna (ROZ-nah) A tribe of elder vyes that live underground and have developed sophisticated schools of magic, such as Arcanum and Silverfalls

Rodrubân (ROD-roo-vaan) Lugh's castle and lands within the Sidh

Scathach (SKAW-thah) A warrior maiden originally from Scotland (Isle of Skye) who has trained many heroes, including Cúchulain and Max McDaniels

Sidh (SHEE) A hidden realm home to the Tuatha Dé Danaan and other magical beings

Solas (SUH-las) Mankind's greatest school of magic; destroyed by Astaroth in 1649

Tuatha Dé Danaan (TOO-ha DAY DAN-ahn) The Children of Danu; a race of divine beings that conquered the Fomorians and ruled Ireland before departing for the Sidh

Túr an Ghrian (THOOR un GREE-un) The highest tower at Solas, where the Gwydion Chair of Mystics resided

Umadahm (OOH-mah-dahm) A title designating the high priestess among the witches

ACKNOWLEDGMENTS

"What are you about? Answer quick, or I'll gobble you up!"

At long last, Max has answered the question and his journey has reached its end. Whew! It's been quite a ride for both our hero and me. While Max had to battle vyes and demons, his creator wrestled with deadlines, a growing family, and the challenges inherent to a big undertaking. Although it's bittersweet to say goodbye to Max and company, it's also the proper time to say farewell. A victory's been won, a new age looms, and our hero has departed for a new life and new adventures. What will the future hold? That's between you and your imagination.

This journey would not have been possible without the support and expertise of many people. On the professional end of the spectrum, my sincere thanks to *The Red Winter*'s editor, Jim Thomas. Jim is the Tapestry's third editor and stepped into the breach without missing a beat. Every writer should be so lucky to collaborate with someone like Jim. His keen intelligence, attention to detail, and unflagging enthusiasm made all the difference on such an ambitious manuscript.

I would also like to thank Mallory Loehr and Random House for giving me an opportunity; Nicole de las Heras, whose art direction led to stunning design; Jenna Lettice for pulling the components together; and Cory Godbey, who provided such beautiful covers. My agent, Josh Adams, has been a steady voice of reason and support from the beginning.

As writers—particularly those with looming deadlines— tend to retreat and cocoon, I'm very fortunate that my friends and loved ones have stuck by me, forgiven stretches of radio silence, and offered encouragement along the way. Special thanks to Terry Zimmerman, Victoria Polak, John Neff, Gerald Zimmerman, John Neff Sr., Margaret Norfleet Neff, Salem Neff, Kathleen and John Stanley, Diane and Jim Raymond, Christopher Casgar, Orestes Tarajano, Brian Payne, Scott Kemper, Matt Markovich, Mike Markovich, Gordon Rubenstein, Krista Ramonas, Travis Nelson, Ed McDermott, Dan Kanka, James and Katherine Rothschild, Jacqueline Duncan, Sean Carroll, Kevin Wong, Josh Richards, Greg Medow, Mike Buckley, Anne Schafer, Michael and Catherine Farello, Scott and Loretta Dahnke, Marilyn Mawn, David Linn, Sergio Lagunes, Diane Reidy, Curtis Kroeker, Andi and Christopher Shurley, Sarah and Doug Reed, and Professor Larry Moore, an invaluable mentor since my days as an undergraduate.

I'm also happy to say that I've made some new friends in the last few years, namely those readers whose dedication to Max & Co. is nothing short of spectacular. Special thanks to Tristen, Suree, Rebecca, Valerie, Kenny, James, Sharon, Oscar, Ryan, Jake, William, Colette, Eugenia, Maura, Dorsa, Maddie, Sarah, Shannon, Amadi, Tyler, Tessa, Emily, Kimberly, animegirl, the students of PS 321, the faculty and students of the Schools of the Sacred Heart in San Francisco, and many other Tapestry fans who have embraced the story and its characters, and have stuck with Max through some pretty tough scrapes. I wish I had a lymrill for each of you.

Finally, my deepest thanks go to my wife, Danielle, and our

sons, Charlie and James. Their love, joy, and understanding made all the difference and kept me moving forward. To say they are a source of strength and inspiration is wholly inadequate. I am a very fortunate and grateful fellow. Thank you. I love you.

About the Author

Henry H. Neff is a former consultant and history teacher from the Chicago area. Today he lives in Montclair, New Jersey, with his wife and young sons. You can visit Henry at henryhneff.com.